MORTAL DESTINATIONS

Book III: Firewaltz

FIREWALTZ

John McCormack Treanor

Einsam Press

'All Creatures of Our God and King' by
Saint Francis of Assisi and William Henry Draper (Public Domain)

'Were You There?'
Traditional African American Spiritual (Public Domain)

Front Cover Art: A derivative work from 'Steeple Chase' photograph
by Butterbits/ Fiickr/ Creative Commons.
Details revised and artistic reformatting applied.

Cover Design by John Treanor and Aqib Awais

ISBN 978-1-958886-02-1
Paperback

Einsam Press
EinsamPress.Com

Printed in the United States of America

And thou, most kind and gentle death,
Waiting to hush our final breath,
Thou leadest home the child of God,
As Christ before that way hath trod,
Alleluia, Alleluia!

'All Creatures of Our God and King' by
Saint Francis of Assisi and William Henry Draper

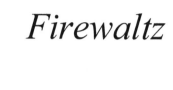

Seventeen: Zanzibar

A terrorist. He stood in front of the grocery store newsstand staring at the cover of the magazine. He read the word over and over again. 'Terrorist.' There was also her name, he read that too. More than that he could not do. Somehow his mind was unable to focus. He looked at her photograph and then back at the ignominious label. He had not seen her face—at least in his waking moments—for almost seven years. Yet now she was in front of him, glaring in that special way of hers, lips pursed just short of a smirk, eyes almost squinting in amusement and contempt. She wore a black beret, hunting vest, and camouflage pants. An automatic rifle of foreign manufacture was perched against her jutted hip. Gads, she did stick out her hip like that, didn't she? He watched his unguided hands pick up the magazine and turn to the cover story. Her story. She had torched the law office where she worked—bombed it, actually. As the partners rushed out of the burning building, she gunned them down while screaming obscenities and obscure condemnations of 'racist pigs.' Two hours later she ambushed a wealthy Black businessman. His body was found in an alley with the word 'chauvinist' cut into his back with a carving knife.

None of this could be real. He wondered if his mind had slipped its moorings. She would have put it that way. No, she wouldn't. She would have said, 'Dearest, you have lost your freekin' mind.' It was a joke, a hoax. Hadn't he read something just as ridiculous the other day? Something about decapitated heads being kept alive and talking to doctors through the services of a lip reader? This was the stuff of UFO's, Elvis sightings, and secret government agencies that read our texts and email. Claptrap, that's all it was. He tried to reason all this out but his brain was still padded with cotton. He drifted toward the store exit with the magazine in his hand. He bumped into a large woman wearing a print dress who was pushing a shopping cart filled

1

with quasi-synthetic foods. He did not apologize or even acknowledge her.

As he reached the exit, he stopped and began to laugh. It was the laughter of having discovered a sublime irony. A high and hysterical and frantic sound that causes mothers to take their children firmly by the hand and lead them quickly down the aisle to the frozen foods.

'What's wrong with that man, Momma?'
'He's not well. There are people like that. Don't you ever talk to them, d'ya hear?'
'Yes, ma'am.'

The laughing cleared his head. He felt better, much better. He rolled the magazine, stuck it in his overcoat pocket, and walked out the door. The assistant manager watched the man leave the store without paying for the magazine. He inwardly shrugged. Not worth the trouble of arresting another nutcase. There were more of the mentally ill on the streets these days—they shoplifted quite a bit. The assistant manager had just finished reading about the problem in a news magazine. The one with the cover photo of an amused and contemptuous woman dressed up like a cheap mercenary and balancing an assault rifle on her hip.

Gaude awoke in an airport terminal, sitting in a variation of the ubiquitous Barcelona chair. A speaker suspended in the ceiling lattice of trusswork rained down 'Africa' by Toto.

"Another dream, or was it one of your non-dreams?" asked Bill Watt.

"A non-dream. Very strange."

"How strange?"

"Too real…or perhaps too unreal. Not strange enough to be a dream, but much too strange to be a memory."

"The more strange, the more real," observed Watt distractedly.

"Maybe I should see a doctor."

"That might be a little awkward given that you are already dead."

"Good point."

"Perhaps we could arrange for you to make an office visit with a coroner?"

"Very funny."

The terminal's sound system began playing a new song, Niʻihau Child's 'Tunnel of Regret.'

> *You go down a tunnel*
> *You spill through a funnel*
> *Where you find all your tricks*
> *Your lies and your fakes*
> *A thousand heartaches*
> *That you can't really fix*
>
> *It's a safe bet*
> *You'll someday regret*
> *Life is like that*

Watt decided to change the subject. "We have a non-stop."

"To where?"

"Our destination, of course."

"Today's destination is Wyoming."

"Indeed it is," agreed Watt. "The Cowboy State."

"I thought that everywhere between Nebraska and California was a cowboy state."

"So those other cowboy states would like to believe."

"I'll leave it to them to quibble over."

"A prudent decision. I have also obtained first class tickets."

"Puddle jumper first class tickets or authentic airliner first class tickets?" asked Gaude.

"The real deal."

"You mean we actually fly on a plane with more than a dozen passengers? I didn't know that enough people travel to Wyoming to justify full-sized jets."

"It's skiing season at Jackson Hole."

"In the summer?"

"Are you sure that it is still summer?"

"I'm not sure anymore," responded Gaude. "*El Niño.*"

"Exactly."

"In any case, it will be a nice change of pace. We haven't traveled first class since the flight from Florida to New York."

"Don't expect to get accustomed to the royal treatment. It just happened that our corporate frequent flyer account had enough points to upgrade the seats. I thought it might be nice gesture. After all, you are just recently deceased."

Gaude smiled. "Sounds like a case of D.H.I.P."

"Death Has Its Privileges," responded Watt. "Yes, there are a few."

Gaude's smile brightened even further, "I hadn't really considered the advantages of being dead. No more junk mail, no more calls from telemarketers, and best of all, I can't be harassed by the IRS."

Watt returned an incredulous smirk. "You obviously don't know much about being dead and even less about paying taxes."

"Fine, but since I'm deceased, I expect you to mind your own business if I happen to flirt with a pretty flight attendant."

"Flirting isn't one of those privileges that we give to the dead."

"In that case, death isn't nearly as fun as I was hoping it would be."

"There are other consolations."

"Just as long as it doesn't involve sitting on a cloud all day playing a harp. I couldn't bear that kind of eternal boredom."

"I'll keep that in mind, Captain Stormfield."

"So, you read Mark Twain?" asked Gaude.

"An old friend of mine," replied Watt.

"Let me guess. You met him sometime between your stint with John Adams and your employment under Teddy Roosevelt."

"Precisely."

"Maybe I've misjudged you."

"That would be the understatement of the year."

"Maybe you're even crazier than I first suspected."

James Parker Doyle awoke in a hospital room. He looked down his bed to see various wires and tubes affixed to his arms and realized that half of his face was covered in gauze bandages. Doug Bagsley and Norm Jacobsen were sitting on small armchairs to his right reading magazines. Doyle started to clear his throat, which brought his two colleagues to their feet.

"Jimmy! Thank God you're back!" exclaimed Bagsley.

"It was no small miracle that you survived," said Jacobsen, clearly relieved that Doyle had been roused from unconsciousness.

"That airlock, or whatever you call that room, helped, I'm sure," added Bagsley.

"Yes, by the grace of God, the explosion slammed the door shut behind you. The portal wasn't specifically designed for explosions of that magnitude, but it did save your life. Those were all sealed rooms, so the air pressure alone should have turned your body and brains into mush," continued Jacobsen, now easing back into his comfort zone as a scientist.

"I'm a hard-headed Irishman. At least, that's what my wife always alleged, right until the day she divorced me," quipped Doyle.

"Irishman?" asked Bagsley incredulously.

"You've never heard of the Black Irish?"

"Okay, I should have seen that one coming."

"It was all my fault," lamented Doyle.

"Jimmy, there is no way that you were responsible for that explosion. We were hit. A team from Central is swarming all over the building right now. So far, all we know is that the incursion came from overseas."

"I've become so accustomed to researching the obscure and arcane that I forgot the obvious."

"Which is?"

"That whatever a smart guy here can make, another smart guy somewhere else can make just as well. Maybe make better. You see, Jethro was destroyed by a returning demon."

"Returning demon? We never sent them out of this building," insisted Jacobsen.

"They are clever, I believe you told me. Obviously, at least one escaped. They can also multiply, right?"

"Yes."

"There you go."

"But we programed that demon. It was not designed to attack us."

"No, you thought it was ours, but it was not. Obviously, ours was detected, captured, analyzed, and reprogramed."

"What makes you think it was one of ours instead of something an adversary created on its own?"

"A hunch. It's more likely that one of our own demon signals would be admitted past Babylon's security barriers."

"That does make sense," admitted Jacobsen.

"As the old saying goes," said Doyle, "two can play that game. I believe that is exactly what Adolph did. He treated us to our own medicine. He played us."

"Adolph?" asked Jacobsen.

"Our pet name for the source of the signals we were tracking at WES," explained Bagsley.

Doyle looked back at Jacobsen, "You said that these things could melt a computer down."

"That's right, but Jethro didn't melt down, he exploded."

"Jethro committed suicide," said Doyle steadily.

"What?"

"He told me that just before I escaped. It wasn't wholly of his own volition. He destroyed himself in order to protect us from him being taken over by the demons."

"Taken over?"

"Possessed, if you prefer."

Jacobsen sobered. "If some outside organization had taken control of Jethro, the result would have been—"

"Catastrophic?"

"That word isn't sufficient. No word would be sufficient."

"The end of the world as we know it."

"If you are quoting a song title by R.E.M., that's cute. If you're trying to be literal, you've hit the nail on the head. Quite literally, Jethro just saved the world."

"He died for our sins."

"That's a bit over the top, Jimmy."

"I told you that working with him might make you blasphemous," Jacobsen wryly noted.

"We might have been temporarily spared," said Bagsley, "but now we've lost the most powerful tool—"

"Ally."

"Sorry, our most powerful ally. We're no better off than we were. Now that Adolph knows that we are looking for him, we are probably in a much worse position."

"Precisely that," conceded Doyle. The answer was flat, untinged with emotion, and dispositive. Doyle felt like he was trapped. No, not trapped. More like a jettisoned sailor treading water in the middle of a shoreless sea. He was getting tired and he knew that inevitably he would gently sink beneath the waves. "But...but..." Doyle shut his eyes and tried to reboot his aching brain. "I can't believe this is happening. It's impossible." He kneaded his brow in consternation.

"You want to talk about impossible, take a look at yourself. You should be very, very dead. Instead, here you are with only a concussion, a gash or two, a few bruises and contusions."

Doyle could not deny the accuracy of the insight. Neither could he resist the smile tugging at the corner of his lips. "Those don't sound like the consoling words of a monk."

"I'm not a monk today, I'm a scientist."

Doyle shrugged, "Okay, you've got me. Strange things happen." He tried to push himself into a sitting position, failed with a faint grunt, and resigned himself to being physically helpless.

"They do," agreed Jacobsen. "Perhaps that is one of the great blessings of life. The world is full of strange and inexplicable things. You must learn to savor them. I've spent my life trying to figure things out, to track down and solve mysteries. I love to find the answers, but I've also grown to appreciate the riddle itself. Until I do unlock the puzzle, I don't torment myself. The unknown is to be enjoyed as long as it lasts."

"That doesn't sound like the credo of the scientist."

"I'm not only a scientist."

"So, now you're running me in circles. I know, you're a monk."

"I'm a man."

"That's it?"

"Isn't that enough?"

"Is there any way we can salvage something from Jethro to find out more about that bug? Are there backup files that might have survived?"

"We thought of that. We assumed that Jethro might have tried to deposit a message somewhere in the reference library core. However, there isn't much left in the wreckage. When he exploded, he took out not only the entire room, but two floors above him."

"Two floors above? That means—"

"Yes, the explosion killed the Beast as well."

"Maybe the quantum computer was the actual target? Maybe the attack on Jethro was merely a means to an end to destroy the Beast."

"A plausible theory at first blush, but as best as we can tell, the Beast had already been compromised—captured, if you will—a few minutes before the attack on Jethro began. The ultimate target seems to have been our friend."

"So, the fact that the explosion also took out the other computer turned out to be a lucky break?"

"I'm not sure if it was good luck, bad luck, or dumb luck, but the architects and engineers who designed this facility put in walls that were slightly stronger than the ceilings. As a result, you survived, but the Beast and several our researchers were killed. A number of other important archives and data repositories were also destroyed. We're trying to figure out what information may have been compromised or stolen."

"Could the attack have been on your other computer systems as well?"

"We have to assume as a working premise that every piece of technology on the subterranean levels of Babylon has been compromised. We hope that it hasn't spread beyond that."

"Could the attack on Jethro have been a preemptive strike?"

"Such as what?"

"Jethro's explosion might have destroyed the evidence that could have led us to the cyberattacker, or at least inform us what data the attacker was able to access on our systems."

"Hmmm…interesting theory," commented Jacobsen. "I suppose that we'll need to look in that direction as well."

Bagsley asked, "Jimmy, did Jethro tell you anything that could be useful?"

"He told me that he was under attack from a presence, as he called it. He said that it wasn't a virus, worm, or other typical program. It was obviously malevolent and it intended to take control over him. He made it sound more like an evil spirit than a string of computer code."

"That's a strange observation from a *computer*."

"But not such an odd comment from a *person*."

"No, maybe not."

"There was one thing that I have no idea what Jethro meant. He said—actually shouted— 'The horsemen!' Those were his last words before the explosion," lied Doyle.

"Horsemen?"

"Right."

"Are you sure it wasn't *whoresmen*?" asked Bagsley.

"I don't think so. Would that make more sense somehow?"

"No, actually, it wouldn't. I'm just grasping."

"You know what immediately comes to mind?"

"The Four Horsemen of the Apocalypse."

"Exactly."

"Unfortunately, that's not much to go on," said Jacobsen.

"Other than we are facing somethin' real damn scary," declared Bagsley.

"Which we already knew." Doyle looked with dismay at the medcomp panel and the intravenous tubes connected to his right arm. "When will they release me?"

"You'll be here at least another day, maybe two for observation," answered Jacobsen.

"Doug, you need to pull out the stops on the horsemen clue. Jethro wouldn't have said that..." Doyle searched his mind for the appropriated term and could only approximate, "...with his dying breath, unless it was important."

"It could mean almost anything, Jimmy."

"Let's get it down to the top ten."

"I'll do what I can, but I can't guarantee that we can track this down."

"Doug, I think we are missing the point. We aren't chasing him, he is chasing us. We aren't the predator, we are the prey. We aren't the hunter, we are the quarry."

"Alright, Jimmy, I got it."

Jacobsen cleared his throat, in an unmistakable signal that he was about to change the topic. "We need to discuss something."

"What kind of something?"

"I wasn't all that forthcoming with you on a rather delicate point."

"Delicate point?"

"It has to do with the creation of Jethro."

"I can imagine that everything associated with Jethro is delicate, not to mention being so classified as to defy my imagination."

"Yes, well, this is perhaps the most sensitive topic of all. We told you that Jethro was created by Doctor Hiro Watanabe."

"The Wizard of Wang Chung."

"The same. We left out a few details."

"I suspect that they were important."

"Admittedly, yes. But they were also unsettling, so we thought it best for you to become acquainted with Jethro before being told these matters."

"Are they classified?"

"Of course."

"And you're about to tell me about them in an unsecured space?"

Jacobsen glanced around the room, apparently looking for a large microphone dangling from the ceiling.

"Don't feel bad, I should have nipped this conversation in the bud as soon as it started. I must be losing my grip." Doyle frowned at Bagsley. "Doug, what's your excuse?"

"Oh, I lost my grip a long time ago," Bagsley joked. He gave his colleague a reassuring smile. "Relax, Jimmy, we're still in the facility."

"What?"

"We're still in the castle. This place has its own emergency clinic. The idea was to have a self-contained world here, not to mention the fact that the nearest hospital is more than ninety kilometers away."

"Impressive," said Doyle. "In that case, let's out with it then."

Jacobsen, quickly recovering from the momentary discomfort of having believed that he had just breached national security laws, began to explain, "Doctor Watanabe was originally engaged in research relating to cold fusion."

"That's been proven to be witchcraft."

"Internal combustion engines and wireless communications were witchcraft two hundred years ago."

Doyle responded with an unimpressed *hrrumph*.

Jacobsen continued, "In any event, just as it appears that he was about to make a breakthrough—as far as we can now tell—he suddenly pivoted his research in pursuit of artificial intelligence."

"They don't seem to be connected."

"One would think not, but then again, everyone doesn't think like Hiro Watanabe. In any event, he seems to have merged the sciences so that he created a self-sustaining energy source, imbued with consciousness and almost limitless intelligence, or at least the potential for limitless intelligence, and sealed it in an impenetrable sphere."

"Okay, that's fascinating, but hardly unsettling."

"It's not unsettling because you've already met Jethro."

"That may be true. Why should we be nervous?"

"The sphere that we knew as Jethro contained nothing but energy, as far as we could tell."

"As far as you could tell?"

"As I said, the shell was impenetrable. Impenetrable by anything: x-ray, MRI, microwave…"

"So, what was in there besides energy?"

"We're not sure, but at that time Doctor Watanabe was becoming deeply engaged with Tibetan Buddhist mysticism."

"Seriously?"

"Yes, seriously. It also appears that he dabbled with some beliefs about UFO beings from another galaxy called the Elohim who send genetic messages into the brains of humans here on earth. We're not entirely sure about these extracurricular interests, but we do know that he put something into that perfectly sealed and perfectly impenetrable ball that had a conscious intelligence. A human intelligence, a superhuman intelligence, if you will. You experienced Jethro yourself. We were never able to explain what was going on in his…"

"His head?"

"If you want to call a mysterious impenetrable bowling ball a head," interjected Bagsley.

"Let's not go there," rebuked Doyle. "Jethro was created through scientific knowledge and technological skill. Can't we look at the designs and records that were developed by Doctor Watanabe?"

"He's dead."

"We can get the records from the Japanese authorities who handed Jethro over to us."

"They have no records."

"C'mon, the Japanese are meticulous record keepers."

"Yes, they are, but there are no records because Doctor Watanabe destroyed them. You see, soon after Jethro was brought to life—I don't think there is any better term to use in this situation— Doctor Watanabe ensured that there would never be another entity of this kind."

"I don't know how a project this significant could be kept under the control of one man."

"That was Watanabe's non-negotiable demand. Based upon the sensitivity and secrecy of the project, all work was performed in one location, on the grounds of Ritsumeikan University OIC—Osaka Ibaraki Campus."

"I thought you said that Watanabe was a professor at Tokyo Tech."

"Yes, that's true, but he was born and raised in Osaka. Perhaps he was nostalgic. Maybe he was homesick. In any event, he supervised the construction of a virtually impregnable research facility. It was completely sealed off from the remainder of the world, not just physically, but electronically. It was a veritable research fortress."

"A fortress? You mean like this place?"

"There are some similarities. Most of the scientists, engineers, and technicians were required to live on a compound adjacent to the research facility. Preference was given to employing unmarried individuals. Isolation was enforced with religious fervor. Every person entering or leaving the facility was scanned and strip-searched for anything that could possibly carry data. There were no telephone lines, no internet connections, and absolutely no means of outside communication. Cell phone signals were jammed, although that was hardly necessary since no one was allowed to bring a cell phone into the compound. There weren't even windows in the facility. No one was permitted to create a paper document, much less take one into the laboratories from the outside world. Every person working in the facility had a very narrowly assigned area of expertise and an even more narrowly tailored authority to access project information. Watanabe was the only human who saw the big picture and the grand design. This had the advantage of ensuring the tightest security of any project undertaken since the Manhattan Project to build the atomic bomb. The disadvantage was that there were no backup records or archives. One night, Watanabe detonated a bomb in the mezzanine level of the facility that completely leveled the structure. He was the sole occupant of the building at that time and thus departed by employing the very Japanese custom of suicide."

"The same thing Jethro just did."

"No, it wasn't at all the same thing. From what you've said, Jethro killed himself to protect us."

"Maybe that's what Watanabe did."

"Who was Watanabe protecting us from?"

"Maybe Watanabe was protecting us from Watanabe."

"Or perhaps trying to protect us from his creation."

"In any event, that's a strange coincidence," said Doyle.

"There are no coincidences," replied Jacobsen.

"There are only coincidences," retorted Doyle.

Jacobsen paused for a moment, nodded, and then continued. "As soon as the fires abated and the smoke cleared, the authorities meticulously combed through every fragment of debris looking for a surviving computer drive. It was in vain. The next day, a letter arrived at the Japanese Ministry of Science, sent by Doctor Watanabe. It informed them that he was the suicide bomber of the building. It further explained that as a precaution against the possibility that any data survived the blast, he had loaded a software virus into the facility intranet that erased and reformatted every hard drive. Better yet, once a hard drive was fully 'slicked,' the program then downloaded one million copies of *The Tale of Genji* in thirty-seven different languages onto each drive just to ensure that that even the most minute particle of information was over-written and extinguished from the face of the earth."

"So, there was nothing recovered from the site?"

"There was one thing."

"Jethro?"

"Yes, Jethro. He didn't have a scratch on him. We still don't know the nature of the material that composes his outer shell. It's a safe bet that it is a composite, but that's not much to go on."

"Did Doctor Watanabe's letter explain why he did it?"

"Not really. It ended with a strange message, in English, written in block letters:

I FORGIVE YOU ALL.
WHO IS COMING TO FORGIVE ME?"

⌘

They saw their destination in the distance. At first, Gaude thought that he was looking at a lone building standing out in the desert. As they drew closer, he realized that it was a walled town, reminiscent of the old world. Khaki colored stone rising ten meters in height tightly surrounded the clustered buildings that seemed to be squeezed to the point of bulging out of the encircling embrace of the perimeter walls. Gaude saw that there was a large city gate that would have easily accommodated their automobile, but for a massive wooden door blocking their entry. On either side of the main gate were smaller portals for pedestrians. The one on the right appeared to be open.

"None of this looks like the Wyoming I imagined."

"You need a more fertile imagination."

"Fertile is one thing this place is not. No one told me that there were deserts in Wyoming."

"Sister Frances Angela mentioned it during geography class, but you were distracted by Sally Osborne."

"I should never have told you about her."

"Sally or Sister Frances Angela?"

"Both…either."

Bill Watt shrugged amiably. "We are on the northern edge of Wyoming's Red Desert. It is considered a natural treasure."

Gaude responded with a subdued *hrrumph* and then said, "I don't think we will be able to drive into the center of town unless we find the person in charge of opening the gate."

"I believe the traditional term is 'porter' if memory serves."

"Do you think this town has a porter in residence?"

"That would be highly unlikely in this day and age."

"Which means 'maybe' considering that nearly everything we encounter seems to be beyond the norm."

"Good point. If I've learned anything over the years, it is not to measure anything with a ruler that has increments of 'normal' upon it."

"In the meantime, where do we park?" asked Gaude.

"I'm not sure," answered Watt. "I don't see any place that looks like a parking lot."

"There are no other cars out here, so I assume that everyone else found a way to get in."

"You're assuming that we are not the first and only visitors to come here."

"That's also highly unlikely."

"Yes, that's my point entirely," said Watt. "The highly unlikely has become the expected." Gaude pulled up to the gate and idled for a moment. Watt glanced over to his partner with a smirk. "Expecting the gate to just open spontaneously?"

"There is bound to be a pressure plate or an electronic eye," explained Gaude.

"Or not."

"You never know. Maybe someone is watching from a hidden camera."

"Hmmm…Okay, that's plausible. How long should we wait?"

"I dunno. For how long did knights of old sit waiting before yonder castle walls?"

"I have no idea."

"Sure you do. Just think back to when you were slightly younger."

"Methinks we have abided here long enough."

"Fine, I suppose that we'll just have to manage on foot," said Gaude as he gestured toward the opening that permitted pedestrian access. Gaude put the Nash in reverse and then selected a spot alongside the city wall to park. As they exited the car, Gaude looked across the landscape of the barren expanse surrounding the citadel-like community. "I think I'm starting to see a pattern as to how our arsonist picks the next church he plans to torch."

"Really? What is it?"

"He throws a dart at a map."

"For all we know, that could be exactly the method he uses."

"Yes, 'for all we know,' which after more than two weeks of us chasing his tail, and then chasing our own, is nothing."

"Patience in all things."

"Easier said than done, although one would think that a dead man like me would be in the process of perfecting that art."

"You are but recently deceased," Watt kidded. "I'm sure you will get the hang of it in a few centuries."

"Until that time comes, perhaps we should get back to work. Let's find the church."

Watt and Gaude approached the open pedestrian portal and passed through the opening. They immediately encountered a high sandstone wall covered with words painted in crimson.

"He's here," declared Gaude.

"Who?"

"You know who."

"Simon Todd is here?"

"No," said Gaude, gesturing to the wall before them, "the poet who is stalking us, Reuben Malachi."

15

"He's in this town?"

"No, but he left his mark."

Watt arched an eyebrow. "Given that his poems all seem to have preceded us at every destination, perhaps we are the stalkers."

Om'Shadoom

Last night I had the dream again:
I traveled with a caravan,
Departing the gates of Acuba
To cross the sands of Africa.

I rode upon an elephant
And slept in a palatial tent.
Servants brought me grapes and wine,
Upon roast lamb each night I dined.

A turban and rich robes of red
Bedecked this prince from foot to head.
Strapped to my waist: a scimitar,
A gift from the Raj of Zanzibar.

My companions were of every sort,
From every land, from any port,
Merchants, brigands, Coptic monks,
Soldiers, jesters, bankers, drunks.

The caravan was a wandering zoo,
Camels, horses, donkeys too,
Serpents, parrots, ringtailed cats,
And carts of monkeys pulled by yaks.

Silks and spice and sandalwood,
Rare perfumes and leather goods,
Gunpowder and precious stones
To trade for gold and ivory bones.

We pass the old road to Khartoum,
For the fabled land of Om'Shadoom.
We wend through forest, thickets, steams,
To find the kingdom of lost dreams.

Past the grey mountains of Jaboo
The jungle cleaves to reveal the view,
Upon a shelf of purest gold
Arises the city of legends told.

We are greeted at the city gates
By vestal virgins holding snakes,
While from the city walls and towers
Cascade exotic, pungent flowers.

Now ushered to the inner ring,
And presented to their ancient king.
He bids us welcome, offers wine,
Calls for dancers and concubines.

The feasting lasts throughout the night,
Stories are told of courage and might,
Of heroes of old, villains of yore,
'til all find sleep upon the floor.

I wander through the halls alone
And walk down streets of silver stone.
I take my rest beneath the drape
Of night's embroidered starlit cape.

The morning birds bid I arise,
I gaze upon the Afric skies.
And as the dawnsun boldly breaks
From my dream I again awake.

Om'Shadoom, I have been told,
Is but a tale from times of old,
And try you may its locale probe,
It can not be found on the globe.

But such advice I do not heed,
To find the place no map I need.
Om'Shadoom is on no chart,
Except the one etched in my heart.

—Reuben Malachi

Gaude shook his head as he finished the last stanza. "This is one heck of a long poem for one heck of a small town."

"Take it up with the mystery benefactor who puts up these monuments."

"You mean that it's not Reuben Malachi who is responsible?"

"I rather doubt it. Probably some eccentric tycoon."

"Why? Do you think some rich patron was bored wasting all his money on expensive cars and cheap women and decided instead to enlighten the masses with bad poetry?"

"I've never met a cheap woman. What does one look like?"

"*Touché.* You're right, a Ferrari is a bargain in comparison."

Watt and Gaude took the street heading west until they came to a vaulted tunnel leading north. "This looks like a shortcut to the center of town."

"What makes you think that?" asked Gaude.

Watt pointed up to a sign suspended above them:

Shortcut to the Center of Zanzibar

"Oh."

"It's a bit dark, though," observed Watt.

"It wouldn't be the first time we were in the dark."

Watt shrugged and muttered, "Okay, nothing ventured..."

They entered the tunnel. Gaude noticed that the stonework inside the passage was different than he had seen in the streets of the citadel. It was composed of dark gray basalt, with alternate stones slightly articulating, giving the impression that they were passing through the scaly gullet of a dragon. After proceeding less than twenty meters, a twilight descended upon them. The pair walked silently through the tunnel for several minutes. The initial twilight matured into a murky gloom, but the dark was not impenetrable. Gaude heard a whisper to his right and instinctively turned his head in that direction. There was nothing there. "Did you hear something?" he asked Watt.

"No. What did it sound like?"

"I'm not sure."

"It wasn't rats, was it?"

"No, I don't think so."

Another whisper came from behind him and Gaude swung

17

around. Once again, there was nothing to be seen. "It happened again."

"Your ears are younger than mine," said Watt as he began scanning the ceiling. "You don't think it could be bats?"

"Not really, but…maybe," Gaude answered as he also began examining the ceiling of the tunnel.

This time the whisper was just over his left shoulder and he could almost make it out. "Bill, did you just say something about lying to you?"

"Lying to me?"

"Yes."

"No, I didn't," Watt responded. Two steps later, he added, "*Have* you been lying to me?"

"No, I'm just hearing things."

"You mean voices?"

"I think so."

The next whisper was louder. *You sunnavabitch! You left without a word.*

"Did you hear that?"

"No, Dan, I didn't."

You're a coward. It was a false positive, came a different voice.

"What?"

"I'm here."

"No, sorry, not you. It was another voice."

"What are they saying?"

You selfish bastard! I hate you. You are dead to me. This was yet a different voice from the previous two.

"Nothing."

"Nothing? Do you mean nothing, as in *nothing*, or nothing that you want to talk about?"

My father is going to kill you and I want to be there to watch.

Gaude recognized this voice. It was Jeenie Stonhouser. He dated her in high school. Their parting had been particularly painful—for her.

The next voice was sobbing, *You never called. You promised that you would call.*

"I'm sorry," Gaude reflexively responded aloud.

"Sorry about what?" asked his partner.

"Never mind."

You did it with my sister? With my SISTER? You are a piece of—

"Carol!"

"Carol who?" asked Watt, now clearly concerned.

"Nothing!" barked Gaude, trying to drown out this newest voice to join the angry coterie of invisible scolds.

I will never forgive you. Never, never, never, never...

"Bill let's see if we can walk a little faster," said Gaude as he began to break into a jog.

You can't run away, you creep!

Yes, he will, honey, he always does.

Gaude had lost count of the voices that now assaulted him from every direction.

You goddam liar! You said you would always love me!

You worthless sack of—

How could you...

Gaude increased his speed from a jog to a full run.

"Dan!" shouted Bill Watt, "What are you doing?"

"Keep up!" yelled Gaude.

You're pathetic! I can't believe that I was stupid enough to sleep with you!

Why didn't you tell me that you hate cats?

Look at him run! Run, you prick!

Gaude continued to sprint, pursued by a relentless pack of outraged jilted furies.

Jerk!

Scum!

You shit! I'll rip off your—

Lowlife!

Gaude could see the sunlight of the tunnel exit drawing closer as the shrill cacophony of outraged voices began to fade behind him. Wheezing breathlessly, Gaude emerged into an open plaza. He slowed, then stopped, bent over, steadying himself with his hands on his knees, and started to retch, dry-heaving for the full minute it took for Bill Watt to catch up with him.

"Dan, are you alright?" asked his genuinely concerned partner.

Gaude gasped for air, exhaled, and then took a deep breath. After a moment of recovering from a transient dizziness, he announced, "We're not going back through that tunnel."

"Was that a statement or a question?"

"That was a statement. That was a demand. That was an order.

We'll take the long way around when we leave this place."

"Okay, fine," said Watt as he raised his hands up defensively. "A little extra walking will do us good. We spend too much time sitting in cars and planes as it is."

Gaude straightened up slowly and conducted a panoramic review of the central court of Zanzibar. A pavement of cobblestone approximately one hundred meters in diameter was punctuated in the middle by a sandstone obelisk bearing the letters XXXVII. A ring of sandstone and mud brick buildings thereupon surrounded the plaza, interrupted by the gaps of narrow portals leading to still narrower alleyways that radiated from the center like spokes in a wheel. A large domed building to the left was surrounded by barricades, encircled by yellow tape, and marked by the telltale signs of a recent fire. A late model pickup truck was parked in front of the building, its doors open, as the sound system blared a tune that echoed against the stone edifices surrounding them: 'Rock the Casbah' by The Clash.

A man in gray overalls and a black ballcap was circumnavigating the scene in apparent rapt attention. Watt nodded to Gaude, wordlessly conveying that it was time to get back to work. As they approached, the man in the overalls looked over his shoulder, gave them a cursory examination, and then went back to his study of the damaged building.

"Are you here to investigate the cause of the fire?" asked Watt as they stepped forward. The inquiry was ignored. Watt passed a look at Gaude who responded with a roll of the eyes. Watt asked again, "Excuse me, are you—"

The man responded without turning around to face his visitors. "I heard you the first time. I was just hoping that you would take the hint and go away."

"We're not good at taking hints."

"So I can see," he said, now turning to face Watt and Gaude. "In answer to your uninvited question, no, I'm not an investigator. I'm here to assess the extent of the damage."

Watt offered his card, as always, face down. The man glanced at it, frowned, shrugged resignedly, and finally extended his hand. "Eduard Desausau, I'm a mason…" and then added as if an afterthought, but nevertheless well-polished by years of use, "…the kind that lays brick."

"I pretty much guessed that when I saw that you drive a pickup

20

truck instead of a tiny go-kart."

"Yeah, and I'm not wearing a fez."

"Aren't those for Shriners?"

"You're a quibbler, aren't you?"

"Did the mosque call you in to assess repairs?"

"No, I came of my own volition. This is my mosque."

"You worship here?"

"No, I'm not Muslim."

"I don't understand."

"I built this place."

"Ahhh…" responded Gaude in wordless praise.

"It was my best work. I came to see if it can be rescued."

"It's definitely a remarkable building."

The brickmason began pointing to different details of the exterior walls. "Herringbone, Spanish bond, basketweave, stacked, parquet, sunbursts. There was an article in *American Architect Magazine*, the last edition before they went digital. They called it a symphony in brick."

"You must be very proud."

"Yes, and invested. I'm a Scientologist, but one of the terms of my contract was that my son and I were to be buried in the Mosque."

"Your son?"

"Yes, he was a Marine. He died during the HOA War."

"I'm sorry for your loss," said Gaude. "Ummm…you said, the HOA War?"

Desausau responded with an extended look of disbelief. "Have you been living under a rock? The Horn of Africa War. When President Romney sent troops into Somalia, my son's unit was called up. He was later deployed to Djibouti, then Eritrea, and finally Yemen. He was killed in the Battle of Ta'izz. The whole thing was a total disaster. Serves Romney right that he wasn't reelected. Not that Cuomo has been any better."

"Cuomo?"

"Yes, Andrew Cuomo, the president."

Bill Watt stepped up to Eduard Desausau and took him aside. "My partner actually served in the war. He was at Mogadishu and Hargeisa while in the Army and was severely injured during an attack on his unit's compound. When he was discharged from the VA Hospital, he had no memory of anything since Al Gore's presidency."

"Gore? He must have been a kid back then."

"He also doesn't have much of a memory of his childhood."

"That's unfortunate," said Desausau. "He hasn't caught up in all these years?"

"Permanent short-term memory loss. He couldn't tell you what happened to him three weeks ago."

"I see," said Desausau with a sympathetic nod.

As they both turned back to Gaude, Watt explained, "Sorry Dan, I needed to have a quick chat with Mister Desausau here to explain that the Cairo Investigative Agency doesn't allow me to engage in any discussions about politics." Watt exchanged a brief conspiratorial glance with Desausau and then said, "You were telling us about burial arrangements in the Mosque?"

"Yes, a few months after I completed my work, I began arrangements for the exhumation of my son's remains from the Veteran's Cemetery in Cheyenne so that they could be shipped here. When I contacted the Imam, he apologized, telling me that his lawyer had not read the contract carefully and that burials were not allowed inside a Mosque. I told him that I would sue to have the Mosque taken down, brick by brick."

"Did that work?" asked Watt.

"Not quite. I finally played my trump card by threatening to expose the fact that the mosque harbors snake handlers."

"I don't understand," said Gaude.

"Snake handlers, like some of those evangelicals in Appalachia. There are members of this mosque who dance around with rattlesnakes during their weekly services, Ṣalāt al-Jumu'ah."

"That is peculiar, but I don't see how making a public exposure of some quirky religious tradition would pose much of a threat. Are snake handlers considered heretics in Islam?"

"Quite possibly, but I was pretty confident that the Imam would be more concerned about the fact that the Wyoming midget faded rattlesnake is an endangered species and that the Feds would come down on them like a ton of my bricks. We haggled over this for a few weeks and we finally reached a compromise. My son and I would be cremated—which, by the way, Muslims do not permit, but, hey, we're infidels—and the ashes would be mixed with clay, fired into a brick, and put into the west wall—the one not facing Mecca. I can live with that...well, not live...you know what I mean."

"So, what's the assessment of the damage?" asked Watt.

"Not as bad as I had feared. I can fix this."

"Are we allowed to go in?"

"Why would you want to go in?"

"We have been investigating church fires across the country. We're trying to track down the causes, and if possible, the responsible parties."

"Okay," Desausau said with a shrug, "but you can't walk into the mosque with shoes."

"But the debris…"

"Sorry, but the Imam hasn't gotten back from his errands, so I don't have a dispensation."

"Do Muslims grant dispensations?"

Desausau shrugged. "I don't know what the word for it is under Islam, but all religions have exceptions, indulgences, pardons and forgiveness. How else do they plan to get anyone into heaven?"

"So, we are stuck here?"

"Maybe not. It just so happens that I have a few pairs of shoe cover booties. We use them when walking into a client's house. I'm pretty sure they qualify as socks even if they are covering footwear."

"Sounds like a technicality," said Gaude.

"Have you ever read the Qur'an?"

"No, not really."

"Doesn't matter. Ever read the Bible?"

"Parts of it."

"Ever come across any technicalities?"

"Sure, more than a few."

"There you go. Religion is all about technicalities."

"I thought that you said religion was all about exceptions and dispensations."

"You can't have one without the other. There is no need for an exception if you don't have technicalities and technicalities evolve to deal with people who employ exceptions in order to evade the rules."

"You sound more like a lawyer than a bricklayer."

"I *was* a lawyer before I became a bricklayer."

"Really? Why did you change professions?"

"All I ever did as a lawyer was to obfuscate the truth and hide the facts from my adversaries. I got tired of stonewalling."

"So to speak."

"Yes, pun intended."

"If you don't mind me saying, it sounds like the lawyer in you is coming out when it comes to your assessment of religion. Technicalities and dispensations sound a lot like regulations and waivers."

"The Justice Department and the Vatican have more in common than you might imagine."

"That sounds harsh."

"It's harsh to those who are not good at complying with technicalities. However, keep in mind that religion is not the only force in play."

"Sorry, I'm not following you."

"There is also faith."

"Isn't that one in the same thing as religion?"

"Some religions—maybe most religions—would like you to think so, but no, they are not the same. Religion may be a dogmatic collection of technicalities, but faith is all about getting past technicalities. That might sound as if faith and religion are at odds, but that's not true. You must put them together to build a solid structure. The rigidity of religion is like a brick. The flexibility of faith is like mortar. Put them together correctly and you have a strong and enduring church…or mosque, as the case may be."

"That doesn't sound much like the doctrine of Scientology."

"No, it doesn't. We are Holiness Scientologists. We split from Los Angeles and Clearwater a few years ago."

"Is that where Scientology is headquartered?"

"More or less. It's gotten a bit hazy to some of us whether the shots are being called by the Religious Technology Center in L.A. or the Flag Spiritual Center in Clearwater. It's sort of like when the Catholic Church was being parsed between Rome and Avignon in the fourteenth century."

"Why the split?"

"They believe in spirituality but aren't too keen on faith— unless it's faith in the movers and shakers within the church itself. Our sect still follows *Dianetics* for the most part, but we have also adopted *Asimov's Guide to the Bible* as a principal religious text."

"I would imagine that doesn't go over too well with the main body of Scientology?"

"That's an understatement. However, we do our best not to

publicly criticize the original church—we've got no reason to burn bridges. They refer to us as 'squirrels,' which is Scientology slang for breakaway sects, heretics and apostates." Desausau shrugged. "I've been called worse." Desausau then gestured with a nod of his head for the partners to follow him to his truck which was now broadcasting Ni'ihau Child's 'Devastation.'

> *All that glitters is not gold*
> *Hardened brick makes not a home*
> *Though angels guard the temple gates*
> *You're on your own to face your fates*
>
> *Ashes to ashes, dust to dust*
> *All that's left to moth and rust*
> *But when it comes to quenched desire*
> *Nothing fills the bill like fire*

After a minute of scrounging through the back of the cab, he located the promised tradesmen's booties and handed them to Watt and Gaude. "Put these over your shoes just before we enter the mosque." Desausau then led them over to the building.

"By the way, how did you manage to get a pickup truck in here?" asked Gaude.

Desausau returned a quizzical look. "I drove it in, of course."

"How did you get in through the gate?"

"By driving right through it," answered Desausau, still confused by the question.

"The gate is closed. We had to walk in."

"Closed?" asked Desausau, now more puzzled than ever. Suddenly, his face relaxed with dawning comprehension, "Oh, you must have tried to enter through the south gate. Nobody uses that. It's been closed for thirty-seven years."

"We didn't know."

"You should have asked somebody."

"Who?"

"Anyone who knew the answer to your question," responded Desausau dismissively.

They entered through an elaborately carved doorway into a large octagonal room. Tiles featuring colorful geometric patterns covered almost every surface except for the center of the eastern wall which featured an empty niche. At the midpoint of each of the remaining seven walls was a large mosaic, each depicting different angels. Watt started walking along the outer wall clockwise. Desausau and Gaude moved into the middle of the room.

"Something's missing. There's an empty nook in the front."

"That's intentional. It's called a *mihrab* and that indicates the *qibla*, the direction of the *Kaaba* in Mecca. It's the direction that the faithful must face when praying."

"Oh." Gaude paused for a moment, gestured at the mosaics, and said, "I didn't realize that Muslims believe in angels."

"Definitely. They show up throughout the Qur'an. Muslims teach that the Angel Gabriel revealed the word of God to Muhammad—peace be unto him—verse by verse."

"Ummm...'peace be unto him'? It almost sounds like you *are* a Muslim."

"I built this place with my own hands over the course of five years. All my assistant bricklayers were from Tunisia. It just became an ingrained habit."

Watt rejoined them and gestured to the mosaics of the angels. "I thought that Islamic art was limited to geometric designs."

"Sunni Muslims tend to be opposed to representational art. Shiites in general—and Persians in particular—tend to permit it. This mosque is Sufi, or more specifically, an offshoot of Sufi, once associated with the Jerrahi Order, but now called Naabradites. They are by far the most permissive when it comes to allowing depictions of sentient beings."

"Do you know the names of these angels?"

"There's a lot of things in this world that I don't know, but when it comes to this mosque, I know everything about every square centimeter, inside and out. These mosaics depict Jibreel, who we call Gabriel, Israfeel, who we call Raphael, and Mikail, obviously Michael. Those two angels in the panel on the opposite wall are Munkar and Nakeer, who interrogate the dead to determine their passage to paradise. Then comes Malak al-Maut, the angel of death. After that, Malik, the guardian of hell. The final mosaic is of Ridwan, the guardian of heaven."

"Do you know much about the electrical system?"

"I'm a mason, not an electrician, but, yeah, I do know how this place is wired."

"Was there any evidence that the fire was caused by an electrical fault or anomaly?"

Desausau gave Gaude a critical look of germinating suspicion. "No one knows anything about the electrical issue except the fire inspector and me. Why do you ask?"

"There seems to be a connective thread between the church burnings happening across the country. All the fires have been due to electrical mishaps."

"Electrical fires are not uncommon."

"Neither are other types of fires, yet in little more than two weeks there has been a church burned down every day—five in New York on one day—each and every one was caused by an electrical source. What are the statistical odds of that happening?"

"Okay, that is strange."

"It's more than strange. So, what happened here?"

"There's a community center in the basement that includes a small kitchen. The microwave exploded."

"You mean something metallic was put into the microwave and it exploded."

"No, the microwave was empty and no one was in the building to turn it on. It just exploded—spontaneously."

"Is that possible?"

"No."

"But it happened."

"Yes."

Watt and Gaude mulled this silently. Gaude then asked, "When will you begin repairing the damage?"

"Immediately."

"You've already worked out an arrangement with the mosque? That was fast."

"Nope, I haven't discussed it with the Imam, or with the Circle of Confidants."

"Circle of Confidants?"

"Mosques have boards of directors, advisors and councils, much like other religious groups. Sometimes the term *jamaat* is used when referring to such boards. In this mosque, they call it the Circle of Confidants. In any event, it really doesn't matter whether there is a discussion or not. I'll do the work and they'll pay me."

"I admire your faith."

"Faith is believing in something you can't see. I see that mosque. I see it now. I see it in my mind's eye. I see it in my dreams."

"Is it insured?"

"I think it is, but even if it isn't, the mosque will always be able to rely upon the almighty hand of providence."

"Allah will provide."

"Yes, but I was referring to another providence."

"Really? What is that?"

"Saturday night bingo," answered the brickmason casually.

"What news on the Rialto?"

"I don't like the direction that things are going."

"Things?"

"Things. He survived."

"Did he really? We can remedy that."

"If *we* means *you*, then yes, *you* can remedy that."

"The Guild will remedy this and will decide whether it is my task or your task to accomplish."

"It has been decided."

"You have spoken to the Guild?"

"As of today, I am the Guild."

There was an extended silence as the caller imported the import of the words and considered the consequences and ramifications. Finally, in a voice notably more obsequious, the caller responded, "Thy will be done."

"Exactly when *will* my will be done?"

"This is just a minor inconvenience. I am confident that all we need to do is to nudge a few things from their current path."

"You tried that before, with precious little success."

"We will try something new."

"Whether new or old, it needs to get done."

"I understand."

"I am not asking for your understanding. I am requiring your compliance. You need to redouble your efforts."

"I'll need to redouble my resources."

"I've already provided you the funding."

"I wasn't talking about that."

"You have the privilege of hunting down one of the best that they have to offer. You should grateful for this opportunity."

"Can you send the Goat?"

There was an appreciable pause on the other end of the line. "That is a rather presumptuous request. It calls into question your competence to execute a simple order, not to mention my judgment in choosing you for the assignment."

It was now the turn for the other party on the telephone line to take an extended pause. "It's not a sign of weakness to recognize when a better tool needs to be applied to the situation."

"I will be the judge of that."

"The DG still has the Goat under contract, or do I presume?"

There was a third period of silence. Finally, it was broken with a begrudging consent. "Very well. Arrivals at the larger terminals are likely being monitored. We will charter a puddle jumper to Ely. You can pick up the Goat there."

"That's still a long way off."

"Not nearly as far away as I'll be sending you if you fail us again."

⌘

"By the way, what did you discuss with our bricklaying friend during that little tête-à-tête?"

"You mean after he started explaining about the Horn of Africa War?"

"Yes, and the imaginary presidents."

"One person's imaginary president is another person's chief executive," lectured Watt.

"What does that mean?" asked Gaude.

"That I'm not going to answer your question."

"I see, once again defaulting back to the obscure."

"Speaking of obscure, what do you think about the clues?"

"The angels in the mosque. That must be it."

"Agreed. Los Angeles it is then."

"Should we try to get an immediate flight or just fly to L.A. in the morning?"

"We haven't been presented with many opportunities to get the jump on our personal pyromaniac, so I think we should try our best to get to L.A. right now."

"I guess you're right. I think that I was looking for an excuse to take a breather. More than two weeks of alternatively chasing an arsonist and then chasing our tails has a way of wearing a guy down."

"It was my hope that we were wearing *him* down."

"Do you think that we have been?"

"No."

"Me neither. I'll check for the next flight to L.A." Gaude proceeded through a series of taps on his cellphone screen. After three minutes, he shrugged in capitulation. "No dice. The next flight isn't until tomorrow morning."

"Alright, in that case, let's find a restaurant and a hotel. We bow to the inevitable."

"Hmmm...the Bill Watt I know would have declared this to be God's will."

"The inevitable is God's will, and vice versa."

"Duly noted."

"You know, in my day, you could just show up at an airport and buy a ticket. Somehow, there were always flights and seats available."

"I suppose that you can still do that."

"Maybe, but now it all seems so much more complicated."

"I don't know, that business card trick of yours seems to cut to the chase."

"That's not quite as uncomplicated as it might appear."

"Speaking of complications, I feel as if we are making all of this more complicated than it needs to be."

"All of what?"

"All of this. The chase, the clues, the pretzel logic."

"It really isn't complicated at all, Dan. We are good and he is evil."

"I stand corrected. What a delight to live in such a simple Bill Watt world," Gaude mocked.

"Even in a world of complexity, there are always some things that are simple, basic. These form the foundation and the framework for all the complexity that comes after. The human body is complex, but it is constructed from the simple component of the cell."

"Not so fast. A human cell is differentiated a thousand ways, and in each of those different types of cells there resides a genetic code so complex that after a century of research, we are still scratching our collective heads over how it all works."

"I didn't realize that microbiology was one of your areas of expertise."

"It's not. Try reading the science section in *Time* magazine someday."

"I may do that. Anyway, I was talking about moral absolutes. You are talking about cellular biology."

"You started the silly metaphors."

"Yes, I did, and I apologize. Good and evil require no metaphors. They are what they are, clear absolutes. There is no need to compare or analogize to anything else."

"You say good and evil as if it was one word."

"No, you merely heard it that way."

"Perhaps, but that is because any reasoning man must see that good and evil are so closely linked. Not so much because they are opposites, but because they are complementary."

"Did you get that drivel from college? Sophomore year, I'd wager."

"Well then, explain to me how there can be good without evil."

"God."

"Facile answer."

"The truth is always easy."

"That, in itself, is a lie."

"What is your point?"

"If God is all good, and Satan is all evil, what would happen if Satan was destroyed?"

"Academic in the extreme. Where is there any evidence that Satan will be destroyed or could ever be destroyed?"

"Isn't that the goal of Christianity? Doesn't the Bible say that in the end times the devil will be destroyed?"

The goal of Christianity is to unite with God. Destroying the devil does not guarantee that."

"Makes it a lot easier."

"Perhaps. Nevertheless, destruction of the devil is not on the Christian agenda. The biblical prophesies you refer to foretell the defeat of the devil, not his actual destruction. He may be the source of evil, but he is quite immortal."

"So, the devil cannot actually be destroyed?"

"I have no idea how that might be accomplished."

"Couldn't God do it?"

"Of course."

"A perfunctory response, deserving a perfunctory rejection. Maybe God cannot destroy Satan?"

"Be careful, Dan. You are wandering from the academic into the blasphemous."

"A convenient dodge when you find yourself cornered."

"You are the one with the paintbrush in his hand standing forlornly in the corner of the room."

"We shall see. Now then, if God were to destroy the devil, no evil would exist?"

"I do not wish to encourage this sort of discussion."

"You concede?"

"No, I do not."

"Very well, I'll just meander forward with my philosophical musings."

"You'll get lost, then you'll be mired down, after that you'll sink into quicksand. Stay out of the metaphysical swamp for your own safety."

Gaude shrugged and then turned on the radio. 'Taking Chances' by Niʻihau Child started to play.

> *It's just not in the cards*
> *Quit while you're ahead*
> *It's all the difference of living and dead*
>
> *Listen once again*
> *You have oft been told*
> *The smartest player knows just when to fold*
>
> *Roll those crazy dice*
> *Play that suckers game*
> *Head down to hell for your fortune and fame*

She entered from the guest room and walked with fluid disconnection. "Am I late?"

"No, you look quite alive, well, and among the quick."

"It sounds like the party has already started."

"A few invited and uninvited guests have arrived, that is true."

"Oh, I hate to be late."

"But you always are."

"That doesn't mean that I can't hate it."

"Dearheart, that simply means that you have the opportunity to make a grand entrance in a fashionably late sort of way," assured Malachi.

Katie nodded in agreement. "You're absolutely right. I'm nearing the age when I can start playing the part of the *grande dame*, so what better way to do so than the *grande entrée*? Perhaps that's my consolation for no longer being the youngest woman in the room. You know what they say. *Every clown has a zippered lining*." Katie glanced down at her obligatory little black dress. "How do I look?"

"Wonderful, marvelous."

"Really?"

"They'll celebrate you in poetry and prose. We'll erect a monument in your honor."

"Bronze or marble?"

"Neither. Maybe we'll just cover you with shellac and put you on a fifty-five-gallon drum."

"Just make sure you put me in the middle of Strasbourg."

"Overlooking the river?"

"The *Canal du Faux-Rempart* will do nicely."

"Yes, milady, I shall not fail thee."

"Be a sweetheart and do not fail me now. I need a drink."

"Katie, you mean that you need *another* drink and *need* is a rather subjective term."

"Am I slurring my speech?"

"You never do."

"Are my eyes bloodshot?"

"They are lovely as ever."

"Do I reek of alcohol?"

"Chanel Number Five, as always."

"Then get me a freekin' drink, Reuben."

Malachi dutifully hastened to the bar to fix a Tom Collins for Katie. Meanwhile, his favored guest made her best effort to execute a grand entrance and was well rewarded with sincere embraces from the dozen or so friends who had already arrived.

*

"You're a lonely man. You need to get married."

"And what would that solve?" responded Malachi with a studied smirk.

His guest made a gesture of open palms. "Look at me, I'm a happy man."

"You confuse no longer being lonely with being happy. They're not the same thing. You traded loneliness for something else. Nothing is free—there's always a tradeoff."

"But in a marriage you don't lose anything."

"Oh yes you do. You lose your freedom."

"Not terribly original."

"Marriage is not terribly original, although it is the original terrible. A successfully married man must either be housebroken, neutered, or both. Those of us who resist either procedure end up being caged. That never ends well."

"I've never felt caged since I've been married."

"How about getting into your car anytime you wish and driving until you come to a coast? Not original enough for you?"

"Hardly."

"But you can't do that now, can you?"

"Nor do I have any desire to do that sort of thing now."

"Then what you have lost is even greater than your freedom. You have lost your will to be free."

*

"Is that Reuben's barbecue?"

"I'm not sure, I just pass it around," Katie replied with a shrug.

"But I came here all the way from Grosse Pointe for Reuben's *spécialité*."

"Gross Point? How odd, I thought that Reuben said you lived in a very nice place. Well, whatever. Go ahead, try some. A roast by any other name would still be meat." The guest obediently stabbed into the pile of pulled pork and transferred it on to his plate. A thought suddenly occurred to Katie. "By the way, be careful, don't throw any scraps off the deck, it's not healthy for them to eat our leftovers."

"Who?"

"You know, those birds that come back every year."

"Swallows?"

"No. Ummm…herring…"

"Herring? That's a fish, not a bird. You mean salmon?"

"No, I mean birds." She shouted across the room, "Reuben! What are those birds that nest in the backyard?"

"Herons."

"That's it!" she announced cheerfully.

*

"Cheyenne! You're here! I thought you were—"

"Dead?"

"No, you're much too young to die."

"What? I'm not good enough to die young?"

"Oh, please spare me from that 'good die young' myth."

"That's what we do. We create myths, nurture myths, market myths, and sell myths."

"I think you're working on an aphorism, but it is shaping up to be a platitude."

"I'm a performance artist, dear. I leave it to the writers to manufacture platitudes and aphorisms."

He turned dramatically and shouted, "Is there a writer in the house?"

"Do you need one who actually has any talent?" came back a voice from the other side of the room.

"No, absolutely no talent. I prefer a rich one," Cheyenne announced.

"Kendrick! Cheyenne is looking for you."

A voice from the other side of the room replied, "Tell her I've already had sex today. She can call my agent to arrange something next week."

*

"It's a matter of human dignity."

"I've always considered that term to be an oxymoron. Humans are naturally undignified. Even our anatomy—hairless but for tufts in strange places—is undignified."

"Batter-fried oysters, anyone?" asked Katie as she offered a platter laden with the recently frittered bivalves. Several guests gratefully accepted as they skewered the Lowcountry staple with toothpicks.

"We invented the concept of dignity, just as we invented the convention of clothing. In fact, they are in many ways one in the same. What greater indignity is there than being stripped naked?"

"Humanity started off with naked dignity."

"And it will end with clothed shame."

"Poetic, albeit sad."

"Poetic, ergo sad."

"There are too many poets here!" Katie announced as she moved on to the next group.

*

"The man who escapes the judgment of history is the man who escapes the notice of history."

"Omigod! You've had one drink and you are already bloviating!"

The two couples laughed.

"Alright, I will ascribe this as a quote from Reuben."

"Liar."

"So is Reuben."

"You're insulting our host?"

He turned to scan the room and saw Malachi behind the bar. He shouted above the moderate din, "Hey Reuben! I just called you a liar!"

Malachi glanced up and immediately shouted back his retort. "I'm a writer. Of course I lie! What kind of idiot thinks that I don't?"

*

"Reuben, I gotta tell ya,' the *Questing Beast* was brilliant."

"I see that your lack of taste doesn't end at your palate."

"Seriously, it was great."

"You really think so?"

"Absolutely."

"Pity that the vast majority of the book-buying public did not share your enthusiasm."

"I thought that you didn't care about how many of your books sold."

"Very true, but if at least two other literate citizens in the

Western Hemisphere had deigned to purchase a copy of that miserable tome, perhaps you would have a quorum to convene a meeting of a book club."

"I'd love to discuss it with anyone and most of all you."

"Ahhh…and here I am captive behind the bar. Tell me, did you spot the parallel to *The Frogs* by Euripides?"

"You bet. Brilliant!"

"Really? I didn't. Especially since *The Frogs* was authored by Aristophanes and my *Questing Beast* was a heavy-handed tribute to Mallory's *Le Morte d'Arthur*."

*

"Is Reuben going to convert?"

"Convert? My goodness, no!" responded a slightly shocked Katie. "Not that he's actually observant, but at least he…well, he certainly wouldn't be any better of a Christian than he is as a Jew."

"No, I didn't mean that, I meant—"

"What, convert to Islam? Are you serious?"

"I meant convert to the metric system."

"What kind of religion is the metric system?"

"No, I'm talking about the Great Conversion. It's happening in a week. The country is finally converting to the metric system."

"Oh, *that*. No, I'm pretty sure Reuben won't be affected by any changes to weights and measures. Come to think of it, he still hasn't converted to the current system. He's the last holdout to still use cubits, furlongs, and leagues."

"Those are rather inexact measurements."

"Reuben has never been one to be picky about measuring things."

"That could be the opening for a salacious joke," he said with a sly grin. "It would also explain how he spices his seafood."

"Yes," said Katie as she began to move to another knot of guests, "he uses three fists of cayenne to a hogshead of shrimp."

*

"Oh, Damien, another of your conspiracies!"

"Not my conspiracies. It's *their* conspiracies that I uncover."

Another guest stepped into the cluster. "Damien Kellogg?"

"Yes?"

"Someone told me you might be here. I read *The Death League* last month. It was amazing."

"What was amazing is that it has been on the bestseller list for three weeks," chimed in another member of the circle. "Damien, do you have any sense of shame?"

"No, and neither does my banker, my household staff, the fellow who sold me an Aston Martin last week—"

"Oh my God, don't be a bore."

"Is honesty boring?"

"No, but luckily, honesty has never been your strong suit. I think that your books are successful simply because the reading public is deaf to honesty."

"I am more than happy to leave that judgment to the reading public. My next book is set to shatter my previous records."

"A reliable prophesy from Damien Kellogg? You are now a fortune-telling seer?"

"The projection was from my publishers. I'll be meeting with them in New York next week, right after the annual writer's conference."

Another member of the klatch spoke up, "I'll be at Brookguild too. Save me a seat."

"Oh, please, tell us about the new book. I'm dying to be the first to know," the fawning recent arrival begged.

"You are sworn to secrecy. I have uncovered an agency in our government that does not officially exist."

"Oh, Damien, not again," moaned the skeptical gadfly of the group.

"Yes, it is called ORCA. Office of Research for Clandestine Activities. They peer in to nearly every form of communication that passes to and fro across the face of the earth."

"Orca? Like the killer whale?" asked the recent arrival.

"Good grief, you can't make this stuff up," protested another.

"Oh, but he does," quipped the skeptic.

"Spy agencies have been listening in on communications forever. This is hardly a grand revelation."

"On selected transmissions, perhaps," lectured Kellogg, "but ORCA listens to everything. They spend ninety-nine percent of their time culling through seemingly innocuous telephone calls, emails, radio signals, text messages, tweets, posted videos, television broadcasts, you name it. They invented the concept of big data decades before the rest of the world had been introduced to the idea."

"What about social media giants? Haven't they been delving into our darkest secrets?"

"I admit that they are giving the spies a run for the money, but the folks at Facebook have no intention of killing you—at least, not yet."

"DataGhad just purchased Facebook, and all of Meta, for that matter," announced the short man in the vintage Nehru jacket.

"Your newly discovered spy network sounds a lot like the tried-and-not-so-true NSA," pointed out the woman in the vintage print dress.

"ORCA predated the National Security Agency by a few years. Apparently, some members of the government were impatient with the transition of certain spy organizations from the World War Two Secret Intelligence Service, the Army Security Agency, the Central Intelligence Group, and whatnot, so they just jumped feet-first into the cesspool of espionage and created their own monster. Today, the mission of ORCA might seem to be duplicative with the NSA, but there are some significant differences. The NSA officially exists, while ORCA does not. We know the identities of the leaders of the NSA, but there are only swirling rumors regarding who runs ORCA. The NSA is subject to the annual budgeting process, ORCA, not so. The NSA is ultimately accountable to the president, while ORCA is exclusively a creature of Congressional prerogative. The NSA is expected to follow the law, although they often fail to do so. ORCA, however, *never* bothers with getting warrants for phone taps, or asking anyone permission to search through your files. In fact, they don't even regularly report to…well, anyone that we know of. Congress owns ORCA, but denies its existence, and has never publicly identified any member of either the Senate or House of Representatives that holds the leash on these spies. They are always on, always listening, never restrained, never subject to public oversight."

"Who created them?"

"History created them. They appeared almost out of nowhere during the first days of the Cold War. Their mission was, and always has been, to find secrets in places where secrets usually are not found. They started out as a very small organization, but have expanded, not because their mission has changed in any way, but because the technology of communication has experienced an explosion of growth. Almost every day some new form of communication is offered on our cellphones and computers—assuming that there is any difference between the two nowadays."

"Creepy. They listen to every one of my cell calls?"

"And read every one of your texts."

"There is no way that any spy agency, no matter how big, could be reading and listening to everything."

"Buy my book. Read it. My editor is performing the last touch-ups on my final draft and we should be sending the files to the printers in a week or so. The books will be on the shelves next month."

"So, the only safe way to communicate is to have a face-to-face conversation, like what we are doing now?"

Damien Kellogg made a circular gesture to the group surrounding him. "Who here has a cellphone? Everyone, yes?"

All nodded and a few unconsciously reached into their pockets.

"No one took the batteries out of their phones before stepping into this house?"

The entire group shook their heads in unison.

"Then absolutely everything we just discussed is now being dissected by some operative sitting in a dark room."

"But if they overhear me on someone else's cell, they can't possibly know who I am."

"They created voice recognition programs back when we were wearing leisure suits and dancing to disco. My friends, there is no escape."

"Who do they send this information to?"

"That isn't entirely clear. It seems that they exist in a sealed environment. If they find actionable intelligence, they take action. ORCA not only listens in, they can break into your home, break into your files, break into your accounts, kidnap or kill you or the members of your family, and cover it up so cleverly that not even the most savvy outside detective or investigator would have the slightest suspicion that something had happened out of the norm of the average crime."

"Are they that evil?"

Kellogg indulged in a pause. Those in the circle who knew him well recognized it as a carefully prepared and practiced theatrical device. "ORCA isn't inherently evil," Kellogg answered. "In fact, most operatives are prior boy scouts, decorated veterans, and members in good standing in the local Kiwanis Club. However, there is another even more surreptitious organization, hiding in an even deeper and darker shadow. It is code-named 'DG' that seems to manipulate ORCA at every turn."

"DG?"

"That's all I know. I was unable to nail down anything on them and can't say for sure how they are inter-related with ORCA or anyone else. From what little I've tweezed out, it is unsettling."

"What you really mean is that you are saving the story of the dark, scary, and infamous DG syndicate for your next book."

Kellogg did his best to restrain an irresistible guilty grin.

"Ummm…Damien. If all of this is true, wouldn't you be dead already?" asked a young woman who had refrained from participating in the conversation until that point.

"Tell me, are you convinced that ORCA exists?"

"I'm a bit skeptical."

"What you really mean is that you don't believe a word of it."

"Seriously, Damien, this seems to be the most far-fetched conspiracy theory that you have ever cooked up," interjected the skeptic.

"Almost everyone will agree with you, which is why I am still alive. My book will be a best seller because no one will be able to resist it, but no one is really going to believe it. However, just to be on the safe side, I sent all my files to Brookguild for safekeeping and torched the hard drive of the computer I used to write the book. If ORCA breaks into my house tonight, they'll come up empty-handed."

"What's the title of the book?"

"*The Devil's Eavesdroppers.*"

*

"Katie, where's Reuben?"

"He's cooking. Do you want to help?"

"Of course." She crossed the room and stood in the threshold of the kitchen door. "Reuben, do you need an extra hand?"

Malachi looked over his shoulder in response to the familiar voice and saw the most recent unfamiliar physical incarnation. Her tall athletic frame featured a new scattering of tattoos. Her hair was now short, choppy, intermediate blonde, and randomly punctuated with blue. Nevertheless, she was still the same ruthlessly sexy bitch with whom he had enjoyed a randomly punctuated emotional and physical relationship for the past two decades. "Hands as lovely as yours, my dear, are always in demand."

"Was that a 'yes,' or was that a verse?"

"Cheyenne, give me a moment to compose and I will make you immortal." One of the pots began to boil over and it spilled on to the stove as he stirred.

"You're making a mess."

"Cooking is like sex. If you aren't messy, you're doing something wrong."

"Why don't you come over here and do something right?"

"Please, my dear, you'll starve us."

*

"It's a tragedy that he died so young—it was definitely a shock."

"I had no idea he had a heart condition."

"What do you mean?"

"He died of a heart attack, didn't he?"

"No, it was in a traffic accident."

"Wait," interjected another member of the group, "I heard he committed suicide out in Utah."

"Utah? I can't imagine him going there...unless he was performing at Abravanel Hall or Deer Valley."

"No, that's not very likely," said the tall man. "Oddly enough, I heard a rumor about him dying in Hawaii."

"Seriously?"

"Well, I didn't verify the source. It's not like I'm an investigative reporter."

"Did you ever get to see him in concert?" asked the woman wearing a sari.

"Yes, on the opening night at the Met for *Concerto Number Two in D Minor*."

"*Scylla and Charybdis*?" offered the young man with multiple rings piercing his left ear.

"No, the *Sentimentale*. *Scylla and Charybdis* was *Sonata*

42

Number Four in A Major."

"That's right! Label me a Philistine."

"I saw him in London conducting Wagner's *Tristan und Isolde* and in San Francisco for his own *Melancholia Serenade.*"

"His *Melancholia* is beautiful, but didn't some of the critics charge that it is rather derivative of Mozart's 'Lacrimosa' and 'Nimrod' by Elgar?"

"May those critics rot in hell."

"Amen," chimed in the youngest woman.

"His passing *hommage* to Mozart's work is at worst a venial, not a cardinal sin. As for 'Nimrod,' the opening phrases *Melancholia* might be vaguely reminiscent of Elgar, but keep in mind that each of those variations are merely a few minutes in length."

One of the more honest and unpretentious members of the huddle admitted to being unfamiliar with Elgar's work.

"Elgar composed the *Enigma Variations,* one of which was entitled "Nimrod.' It was number...hmmm...seven, I believe."

"Nine," tossed in the tall man.

"I stand corrected, thank you," the leader of the discussion responded in mock formality. "Elgar dedicated it to his friend, Augustus Jaeger. The Biblical figure of Nimrod is described in the Old Testament as 'a mighty hunter before the Lord.' The title connects to the name of Elgar's friend, as it comes from the German word *jäger,* meaning 'a hunter.' There is a strong undercurrent in the music that reflects the encouragement and inspiration that Jaeger imparted to Elgar. You can feel the gentle tenacity, quietly heroic perseverance, and resolute sense of hope. In any event, *Melancholia* is certainly not derivative. It just happens to share a common bond of the solemn and introspective."

"Did you have a chance to make it to his *Sojourner Symphony*?" asked the older man with impenetrably thick glasses.

"No, I wish I had, but he gave only two performances before the accident."

"Three."

"Really? Paris, Rome, and...?"

"Budapest."

"Oh. I thought that was canceled."

The taller man turned his attention to the most recent arrival to the conversational cluster. "Didn't you know him, Katie?"

"Back in school," she confirmed with a nod, "but we lost touch. Not that we touched each other very often." She paused to recollect. "Well, there *was* that one weekend, but we were pretty drunk, so I don't think it counts."

*

"Did you notice the sign painted on the side of the building?"

"Yes, it looked like something from an old Russian propaganda poster. I assumed it was one of Reuben's inside jokes."

"It certainly would qualify as one, but the give-away is that it is too weather-beaten to have been painted in the past few decades. Of course, leave it to Reuben to distress a painting to make it look ancient, but in this case it's authentic. This structure was originally built in 1938 as a socialist experiment."

"What? Some New Deal program?"

"No, it was the dream—some would call it a pipedream—of a friend of John Reed named Ballpeen Hammer. He claimed to be the long-lost brother of Armand Hammer, the industrialist and Russophile, but no connection has ever been proven. Ballpeen Hammer tried to establish a soviet seafood collective, a Lowcountry worker's paradise, if you will. He erected this place, purchased three shrimp boats, recruited local men as captains and crewmembers, and hired their wives and sisters to process the catch."

"He picked an interesting location."

"He didn't have much of a choice. Even though the country was reeling from the Depression, and even though this area was particularly impoverished, nevertheless, there weren't many takers when Hammer offered to purchase waterfront property to build his processing plant."

"Why not? Did they balk at selling to a damn-yankee?"

"His damn-yankee dollars were more than welcome. It was his damn-yankee attitude about racial equality that rankled the entrenched interests here in the Sea Islands. You see, the folks he employed were all Black."

"Didn't lots of businesses in the area hire Black workers?"

"Yes, but they didn't offer to make them equity partners. Ballpeen Hammer wanted to raise up the workers from their status as the oppressed masses."

"Ah ha. So, I'm guessing that the Chamber of Commerce didn't quite cooperate with the seafood cooperative."

"Nope, Hammer was on his own. He had to construct his plant on this rather lonely and isolated island. As a result, this place was built to be well-neigh self-sufficient, with its own Russian-manufactured diesel electrical generator and desalinization plant. It prospered during World War Two, thanks to the national meat ration. However, within a year of VJ Day, it was forced out of business by the cabal of local White shrimpers."

"A different type of collective altogether."

"You might say that."

"What happened to Ballpeen Hammer?"

"He went bankrupt and lived out the rest of his days here as a virtual hermit—gradually losing his sanity. Not that anyone around here paid much mind to that. Most of Beaufort County had concluded that he was a lunatic as soon has he had arrived here."

"So, this place was built by someone who was reputed to be bat-shit crazy—"

"And now inhabited by someone authentically bat-shit crazy."

"I suppose the South Carolina Lowcountry is all about preserving traditions."

"Yes, that's exactly the attitude of the locals."

*

"We had already passed the boundaries of the discouraged. Now, we crossed the border of the forbidden."

"Wait a minute, you're quoting someone. Who is it?"

"Three guesses and the first two don't count."

"It's from one of Reuben's books, isn't it?"

"Yes, the opening sentence from *The Tattletale*. Rule number one at this party is that if you quote an author that isn't dead, it must be Reuben, but never, ever, in Reuben's presence."

"Why?"

"Because he becomes irate. He says that he despises sycophants. The trick is to say it loud enough that Reuben overhears it across the room, but not so loudly that he can figure out who said it. That, for some strange and perverse reason, amuses him."

"You have strange friends."

"So, why did you come to the party with me?"

"To meet your strange friends. Just because I said that they are

45

strange doesn't mean that I don't like them."

"Oh, you are going to fit in here just fine."

*

"I was told that you are Reuben's house guest."

"For the past two weeks."

"An editor from *American Review*?"

"Yes, I'm here doing a piece on Reuben."

"There's a rumor afoot that he is working on something big."

"He's been doing a good job of hiding if from me."

"Happy hunting. I look forward to reading your article."

"You've read some of my pieces?"

"I'm sure that I have," he said, which was, as both guests knew, the proper way of saying 'no, I've never read anything you have ever written, or for that matter, ever heard of you before.'

"Are you a subscriber?"

"Yes, of course," he replied, which was, as both guests knew, a lie.

"Good to have an ally in the crowd," Chapele awkwardly responded in order to keep awkwardness at bay. The ball was now in the other person's court.

"As one ally to another, I assume that you have engaged in some background research on Reuben."

"I've tried my best."

"Hiding his latest project is not the only thing he has successfully kept in the dark. Did you happen to find any telltale evidence of the ancient Malachi scandal?"

"I must admit, I am perfectly clueless, unless you are taking about his innumerable brush-ups with the law, his alcoholic binges, or his sexual forays. However, none of those are deep, dark secrets, and Reuben revels in them, so I'm not sure that any of them qualify as an authentic scandal."

"No, this one is very different. You are aware that Malachi uses Ripley and Sons of Charleston as his publisher."

"Yes, one of publishing's quirkiest traditions, if we can refer to something that has gone on for less than twenty years as a tradition. I already have that included in my current draft."

"Do you know how that relationship began?"

"No. That is, admittedly, mysterious."

"The Ripley family has operated its printing business just about forever, which might be notable in most parts of the country but is merely par for the course in Charleston. Hiram Ripley, who owned the company from 1835 to 1869, was appointed a judge during Reconstruction, the period during which the Union Army occupied most of the South after the Civil War. Judge Ripley sentenced Malachi's great, great grandfather, Benjamin Ben Malachi, to death for murdering a newly freed Black man."

"That doesn't sound like the American history I learned in school."

"The date was 1868, and as I said, the state was still occupied by Union forces. During that peculiar time, a White man could conceivably be both brought to justice and put to death for the murder of a Black man. The execution of a Jew was even a lesser concern than that of a former slave, and thus no public outrage was displayed by the occupied city of Charleston. That historical tidbit might not raise any eyebrows, but there is a bit of a twist—or should I say, the first of two twists—in the story. You see, in the 1840s, Benjamin Ben Malachi, a tailor by trade, decided to open a printing business one block away from Ripley and Sons. Competition between the two companies quickly developed into a fierce affair, but in those days after the war, it was every bit as ruthless as the battles that had raged across the country for the previous four years. One month after the execution was carried out, the family Malachi had in its hands evidence that Judge Ripley had been part of a plan that in the next century would be called a 'frame up.' The elder of the Malachi family decided that bringing the fact out into open might serve to humiliate the Ripleys for a short time but would not bring back the dead Benjamin. Accordingly, he decided that the best revenge was to confront the Ripley family with the fact and keep them in suspense as to when the scandal would be revealed. Judge Ripley committed suicide the next year. I can't say that the evidence that has been collected constitutes absolute proof, but once uncovered, connecting the dots was not all that difficult."

"That certainly is a scandal, but we're talking about more than a century and a half ago."

"No, we're talking about Charleston. There is no difference between the past and present in Charleston. One year ago, one hundred years ago, is all the same. The very existence of the Malachi family was more than enough to suspend the dagger of guilt over the Ripleys for more than a century, to this very day."

"So, the Malachi clan have kept the Ripley family in suspense for all of these years?"

"It's not quite as simple as all that. Soon after the Judge's suicide, the Ripley family discretely endowed a trust fund for the benefit of the direct descendants of Benjamin Ben Malachi. On occasion, the Ripleys were called upon to replenish the corpus—the principal—of the trust, such as during the Panic of 1893 and, naturally, during the Great Depression. As you can imagine, this constituted a rather heavy financial burden over the years."

"Fascinating, but that sounds more like a scandal on the part of the Ripleys. The family of Benjamin Ben Malachi were victims. Unless you are referring to Reuben rubbing Ripley's face in it by insisting they publish his books."

"That apparent act of ironic vengeance might be characterized as a trifling form of scandal, but no, that's not what I'm talking about. As I mentioned before, there were two twists. The second was discovered very recently."

"After one hundred and fifty years?"

"You're off by about twenty years, but no need to quibble," the man replied with a grin. "The venerable College of Charleston, one of the oldest academic institutions in the nation, was recently elevated to University status. South Carolina provided a generous grant for a new state-of-the-art library and archive. During the process of transferring mountains of historical documents to their new repositories, including digital scanning and cataloging, a researcher happened across a peculiar journal written in the post-bellum years. She was at the time pursuing a master's degree in History at the University of South Carolina and would be returning to Columbia in a few months. She received permission to take the journal, which eventually led to a torturous journey through the past. Dozens of trips back to Charleston, and innumerable visits to document vaults throughout the state, resulted in the publication of a Master's Thesis that was so well received by the University that it granted special dispensation to allow her to continue her research and thereupon present a Doctoral Dissertation on the same subject."

"The journal, I take it, has something to do with the Ripley scandal, or should I say, the Malachi scandal?"

"The journal covered events and subjects much broader than simply the matters relating to the death of Benjamin Ben Malachi. However, you are right. There were some intriguing passages that led our researcher to uncover a very interesting turn of events. It so happens that the evidence that the family Malachi presented to the Ripleys was the real frame-up. The documents were forged. Benjamin Ben Malachi really did murder the former slave, and Judge Hiram Ripley was an innocent man. His family has suffered needlessly and unjustly for generation upon generation."

"Was this included in the doctoral dissertation?"

"No. She considered doing so but thought better of it. A wise decision."

"What happened when they were told?"

"What do you mean?"

"I mean, what happened when the current members of the Ripley family were told about the deception?"

"Who said that they were told?"

Chapele was taken aback. "You mean that no one has told them? *Seriously?*"

"Would you like to tell them?"

"That's not my place."

"It's not anyone's place."

"What about the researcher you mentioned? The doctoral candidate."

"She is no longer a candidate. She received her PhD this past summer."

"Why doesn't she do anything?"

"Because I told her it would be a bad idea."

"You?"

"Yes, I'm her husband. She listens to me. Admittedly, not often, but in this instance, she saw that I was right."

"Why are you telling me this now?"

"Someone suggested that I contact you."

"Who?"

"I'm not at liberty to say."

"You came to this party specifically to tell me this?"

"I wouldn't say that."

"What would you say?"

"I would say, goodnight." The man turned, snaked through the clusters of discussions as he crossed the room, and departed through the front door without offering a farewell to the host or any other guest.

Chapele saw Katie approaching with a platter of batter-fried oysters.

"Katie, who was that guy?"

"What guy?"

"The guy I was talking to."

"What guy were you talking to?"

"Yes, the guy."

"Yes, it was the guy."

"Who?"

"If you say so," agreed Katie as she moved on to the next clutch of party guests.

*

"Would you like a margarita?" asked Katie, briefly covering the bar as Reuben went back to boil more shrimp.

"Certainly. Do you have sea salt?"

"No, but I have Piggly Wiggly salt. I might have some Winn Dixie salt. It's too much trouble trying to get it out of the sea."

He decided not to belabor the point and looked at the label on the box. "Is this one of those generics?"

"Why would I care about the chromosomes in salt? Does salt even *have* chromosomes?"

"*Gen-ER-ics.*"

"Sure, they're here. I assume we have a full spread. Gen X, Gen Ys and Gen Zs, Millennials, you name it. There are even some Baby-Boomers and a few trophy Gen Alphas here. Reuben knows everybody."

*

Katie carried a tray of skewered shrimp over to the group standing on the open deck overlooking Whale Branch of the Coosaw River. The balding man in a wrinkled linen jacket was reiterating his usual lecture usually delivered to a classroom of usually bored undergraduates. "Cervantes, of course, invented the novel, *Don Quijote.*"

Katie leaned into the cluster of victims of the tedious sermon.

"Actually, the credit goes to a woman, Murasaki Shikibu, a lady-in-waiting to the Japanese Imperial Court. She wrote *The Tale of Genji* six hundred years before Cervantes picked up his pen." The group, stunned to silence, looked first at Katie and then to her platter. She offered the tray. "Shrimp, anyone? Reuben caught them just this morning."

"Shrimp aren't kosher."

"Neither is Reuben."

One of the guests moved a hand forward tentatively. Katie continued in a casual and cheerful manner. "Now then, if you want to limit the scope of your literary musings to Western Europe, Ramon Llull wrote *Blanquerna* in the late thirteenth century. The same book, by the way, takes credit as the first great piece of Catalan literature. I've often thought that the categorization of literature can be rather arbitrary. Who came up with the notion that the structure or content of *Gilgamesh*, the *Odyssey*, or *Beowulf* somehow relegates them to be indiscriminately segregated from Cooper's *Last of the Mohicans*, Melville's *Moby Dick*, or Kerouac's *On the Road?* How is the *Aeneid* more estranged from the literary form of a novel than *Naked Lunch* or Dos Passos' *Midcentury?* Seriously, does merely setting the story to verse somehow, *ipso facto,* dictate literary canon? Perhaps that is why hardly anyone still reads Byron's *Don Juan*. More's the pity." She suddenly caught herself and giggled, "Oh, More...did I just make a pun on *Utopia?* I hope not." Without missing a beat, Katie again offered up the appetizers. "The ones wrapped in bacon are really good. I know that Orwell would probably call it *doubleplusunkosher*, but *laissez les bons temps rouler.* Go ahead, don't be shy."

Two other guests reached forward, now recovering from the initial shock. "The literati are terribly capricious, I've always thought," Katie mused. "Consider the rather fatuous distinction between a *romance* and a *novel.* The terms were used interchangeably in this country throughout the nineteenth century, and indeed, you'll find that some derivation of the word romance is used in most European languages when referring to a novel." Katie smiled and pushed the tray of shrimp forward one last time. "Eat up, but be careful not to choke. I'm not very good at the Heinrich Remover." She imparted a final radiant smile and then swiveled on her heel as she moved to another cluster of conversation.

"What in the blue blazes was that all about?"

"What do you mean?"

"How did that *ditz* rattle off a treatise?"

Malachi suddenly appeared behind the speaker's shoulder. "That *ditz* has a Masters in Medieval Studies from Princeton and a PhD in International Economics from Stanford."

"Unusual mix. I didn't hear anyone introduce her as 'Doctor' Moscowicz."

Malachi smirked. "She refuses to use the title outside of academia. Her reason is perfectly… ummm…reasonable. She wearied of people approaching her with complaints about their back pain and constipation."

*

Katie wormed her way through the clots of chatting guests, with each conversation coming to her in random snippets.

"Strange."
"You like that word."
"Yes, I do. 'Strange' is what we do not understand. Since we understand nothing, everything is strange."

"Why don't you ever talk about your feelings?"
"Because feelings aren't words. If you try to put them into words, they aren't feelings anymore."

"…and unworthy of remark."
"Efrem, have you always been so insufferable?"
"Gads, I hope so."
"Haven't you ever tried being nice?"
"I detest the nice. They are insipid."
"Don't you think that I'm nice?"
"My dear, the nicest thing about you is that you are not."

"I can't believe this state still awards alimony."
"Is it bad?"
"I am chained to the rotting corpse of what once was a blushing bride."
"The blushing should have tipped you off."

"He was a man with a future—"
"She was a woman with a past," Katie responded reflexively as she passed the speaker.

"God might set the ante, but the devil cuts the cards."
"What does that mean?"
"I have no idea, but I swore off gambling years ago."

> *"Cheyenne, I heard that you gave up art to become a lawyer."*
> *"Absolutely false. I became a lawyer to afford being an artist."*
> *"Doesn't it interfere with your performances?"*
> *"Not really. The law firm calls me only when they have an intractable problem and I call them only when I have an intractable debt."*

"A clever woman always catches a man in a lie. A very clever woman never does."
"That sounds like something Coco Chanel might have said."
"Maybe she did. Maybe I'm a magazine advertisement philosopher."

> *"It is a rare fortune of these days that a man may think what he likes and say what he thinks."*
> *"I see that you're in a mood to be profound."*
> *"Yes, and if I hadn't stolen it from Tacitus, I'm sure it would have found its way into my book."*

"I am a failed Christian. What about you?"
"I'm a recovering human being."
"Ah-hah! So, we do have something in common!"

> *"I'm going to live forever or die trying."*
> *"Clever. Oscar Wilde?"*
> *"No, Groucho Marx."*
> *"There's a difference?"*
> *"None that I've ever noticed."*

"The greater the sinner, the greater the salvation."
"Sounds like a quote from a Catholic saint."
"Yes, it does."
"Do you know which one?"
"All of them."

*

"You're talking politics again? Can't we give it a rest?"
"Fine, but just remember who was the first to tell you that

Casagrande will sweep the presidential primaries in the next election."

"As I recall, your prediction during the last campaign cycle wasn't exactly accurate."

"Foul! The stock market plummeted three weeks before the polls opened and the embassy at New Delhi went up in flames the day before. The voters were spooked. This election is entirely different."

"Shrimp?"

"Thank you, Katie, those look great."

"Casagrande will have a mandate. What do *you* think Katie?"

"If he wants to date a man, that's fine with me," Katie responded with a smile. "You know that Zane is here at the party, don't you? He just broke up with Ewan, so if you want me to make introductions…Is Casagrande here tonight? I don't remember meeting him. The name is familiar, though. Does he write Westerns? Oh, sorry, Reuben just waved at me. Let me see what he needs."

*

"…and we're back to the meaning of life."

"There is no escaping it, until, of course, we have escaped it."

"Always that question, over, and over, and over again."

"Perhaps to the extent that it is the only question that matters."

"And for which you don't have an answer."

"Don't be a fool. Of course I have an answer."

"You do? Why have you been holding out on us? The world has been waiting in breathless anticipation all these centuries."

"Once again, you are a fool. The world has had the answer all these centuries. Or should I say, the *answers* all these centuries."

"There is more than one meaning in life?"

"Whatever led you to believe that we must have a *shared* meaning of life? How many people are there on earth?"

"I believe around seven or eight billion or so at last count."

"And probably one hundred billion since the beginning of time. Each of them lived a life. Some lived tragically short lives, others lived tragically long lives, but regardless, each life had a meaning."

"In that case, let's start, in no particular order, with yours."

"My life is a *Firewaltz*."

"I've never heard of such a thing."

"That's because you are an unschooled barbarian. It isn't, by the

54

way, the jazz piece by Mal Waldron, assuming that you have any real appreciation for jazz, which you don't."

"Perhaps the meaning of *your* life is to be caustic."

Malachi responded with a counterfeit malicious grin. *"Der Feuer-Walzer* was a composition by Émile Waldteufel, a popular composer of the late nineteenth century, and by remarkable coincidence, my great-great grandfather on my mother's side. He wrote a number of popular waltzes and polkas, and one in particular you've probably heard a thousand times over, *The Skaters' Waltz*. His music is easily distinguished from the more famous works of Strauss in that they were quite gentle and sedate. *Firewaltz* was a significant exception, perhaps written in a spirit of friendly competition with his more famous and successful contemporary."

"Life is a dance? I don't think that is very original."

"Perhaps not. To paraphrase Samuel Johnson, everything original is not necessarily good, and everything good is not necessarily original. In any event, when Katie and I went to the *Kaiserball* in Vienna…when was that? It's been almost twelve years now, hasn't it?"

"Fifteen, actually," corrected Katie.

"Really? Hmmm…*tempus fugit*. In any event, we saw the young kids, or should I say, other young kids, dancing the *Firewaltz*. They held each other by the waist and would spin and spin fantastically, so fast that they could not stop. It was a frenzied, delirious dance. They moved so fast that they could not possibly think about their steps, they simply had to feel their way through the frantic dance—just as a dance, and life, should be—feeling, that is."

"Sounds like the Sufis—the Whirling Dervishes."

"Yes, but in black tie."

⌘

They sat down in a booth at Big Nose George's Bar and Grill. The waitress arrived within a few minutes. She was a slight and diminutive young woman with clear blue innocent eyes, a heart-shaped face, and angelic blonde curls. Gaude ordered a prime rib, mashed potatoes and French Canadian asparagus, accompanied by a draft Copper Mule Ale. Watt chose the Devil's Tower Chili and a bottle of Jackson Hole Snake River Sarsaparilla.

"Are you two visiting Wyoming?" asked the young woman.

"Yes, but unfortunately, we are here only for the day."

"That's too bad. Where are you heading?"

"Los Angeles."

"Really? While you're there, you should go see Las Vegas."

"Las Vegas isn't really all that close to L.A."

"It's a lot closer than it is to here."

"That's true," conceded Watt. "Have you ever been to Las Vegas?"

"No, but that's always been my dream."

"I think that you would find it very different from western Wyoming."

"Yeah, that's the idea. I'd love to run wild and paint the place red. It would be a hot time in the old town tonight."

"Like Old Ma Leary?"

"Who?"

The waitress departed for the kitchen as Gaude checked his cell.

"Any report of a church fire in Los Angeles?" asked Watt.

"All's quiet on the western front."

"The calm before the storm."

"I have to observe that for somone who seems to have spent his entire life—or several lives, it would seem—chasing storms, you are a remarkably calm and cheerful kind of guy."

"Thank you. I try my best to rest in peace."

"So to speak."

"Yes."

"I assume that you atribute your serenity to God."

"I attribute everything to God."

"Except the Boston Red Socks."

"True. There is an exception to every rule."

"Do you think that we are coming to the end of the line?" asked Gaude.

"What makes you think that?"

"We're heading for L.A. We've pretty much run out of continent. How much farther can we chase this firebug?"

"There is a suprising amount of wiggle room on the west coast."

"This could go on forever."

"Nothing goes on forever."

"Everything goes on forever," retorted Gaude.

"That is also true," agreed Watt.

"For a folksy aw-shucks kind of guy, you do enjoy dabbling in paradox."

"I dabble in life—it's the same thing."

"Speaking of life, and living it, we've been careening across the country for more than two weeks without a break. Isn't there something in that biblical handbook of yours about resting on the seventh day?"

"Yes, we should definitely rest on the Sabbath."

"Why haven't we?"

"Sabbath hasn't arrived yet."

"What do you mean? It's been sixteen days since we started from Maine. I'm not sure what day in the week it was when you dragged me out of that hospital, but regardless, at least two Sundays have passed."

"The Sabbath might also be a Saturday."

"You're quibbling."

"Guilty as charged."

"You're also dodging the question."

"No, I'm not. The day of rest has not arrived." Watt looked over Gaude's shoulder and announced, "However, it appears that our dinners have arrived."

The waitress delivered the orders with a cheery smile. "Eat up, cowboys!"

Gaude and Watt immediately attended to their meals. Watt dug into his chili bowl with a large tablespoon and conveyed a generous dollop of the spicy concoction into his mouth, only to suddenly freeze, look down at the bowl with an admixture of confusion and repugnance, and then look back up to his partner.

"What't the matter?"

"There is something odd about the meat in this chili."

"What's wrong with it?"

"I'm not quite sure, but it reminds me of the chili they served in Seattle."

"You mean Seattle Slew chili?"

"Yes, I suspect that this is horsemeat."

Gaude pursed his lips as he considered his partner's culinary conundrum. Finally, he observed, "Wyoming does have a lot of horses."

Watt caught the eye of the waitress and beckoned her to the table. "Miss, the taste of the meat in this bowl of chili is…unique. I was wondering if it happens to be horsemeat."

"Horsemeat?"

"Yes."

"No, we don't serve horsemeat. It was legal for a while, but folks here in Wyoming really love our horses. We held a refereundum three years ago to make horsemeat illegal for human consumption, unless you eat your own horse, which, of course, not many folks would do. At least, they don't in this part of the state."

"So, this definitely isn't horsemeat?"

"Nope, horses are noble creatures. It's now a serious offense to eat them."

"Thank goodness!"

"It's a Democrat."

"Excuse me?"

"A Democrat. Actually, it's not any Democrat. It's Tyler Downey. Nobody around here knew he was a Democrat until he came up with the crazy-ass notion to run as a Democrat candiate for the United States Senate. So, we shot him, tenderized him for a few days in a marinade, and then put him in a pot of chili."

"You eat humans?"

"Oh, no, we would never eat a human. That would be canibalism. We eat Democrats. That's different. They're not quite human."

The Advisors

"I woke up this morning, late."

"Yes?"

"My wife had already cooked breakfast. It was laid out on the table. Very nice. She always makes a very nice breakfast. Linen tablecloth and napkins, good silverware, a formal tea and coffee set."

"You were the last to breakfast?"

"No, everything was ready, but my wife wasn't there. Neither were my sons. The dinette was empty. Very spooky. There was soft music playing. We have speakers in the ceiling throughout the house."

"Yes?"

"The music…it was a *polonaise*."

"That sounds very pleasant."

"Yes, but I don't have any idea what a *polonaise* is."

"Excuse me?"

"I don't know anything about music, at least not about classical music. My wife listens to it, but I can't tell one concert from another."

"Perhaps you picked it up over the years?"

"A *polonaise*? How the hell would that word ever pop into my head?"

"We pick up things all the time, often without noticing."

"No, I have no idea what a *polonaise* sounds like. But then I did. Instantly."

"Perhaps it was a lucky guess."

"No, it wasn't a guess. I *knew*."

"Maybe it wasn't really a *polonaise*."

"I told you, *I knew*."

"There are vast reservoirs of knowledge hidden in our subconscious."

"No, this was different. That thought in my head wasn't mine."

"Whose was it?"

"The man my wife was supposed to marry."

"Who is he?"

"I don't know. My wife never says. Even when we fight, she has never mentioned him. But I know he is out there somewhere. It was him."

"I think that you're leaping to conclusions. After all, it was just one time."

"It has happened before."

"When?"

"About a year ago. Almost the same thing happened. I was off from work for a week. I think that Christmas was approaching. I went down to the kitchen and breakfast was ready, but no one was anywhere in the house."

"Did you call out for anyone?"

"No, I didn't need to. I knew, somehow I knew, that no one was there. I heard the music coming from the speakers throughout the house."

"A *polonaise*?"

"No, that time it was a *pastorale*."

"You know the difference?"

"*No*! That's the point. I don't know anything about either of those."

"But you believed that it was a *pastorale*?"

"No, I *knew* that it was a *pastorale*."

"Without knowing what a *pastorale* sounds like?"

"It went laaa—laaa—di—laaa—di—di…but, no, I have no idea how I could tell it from any other kind of music. Well, it's not Rock and Roll, I can tell the difference there, but you get my meaning."

"Classical music, orchestral music, chamber music, sounds pretty much the same to you."

"Yes, of course, it is all the same."

"Except to *him*."

"Yes, *he* knows the difference."

Eighteen: Los Angeles

He is dressed in a black uniform. It is a severe outfit, adorned with little decoration, and what little there is features symbols of death, suffering and execution. He walks down a harshly lit hallway, following to the left and rear of a superior officer, similarly dressed. He carries a small black leather-bound portfolio. They walk briskly, feet falling in rhythmic precision upon concrete floors, through the twisting maze of narrow corridors. They are underground. He is sure of it.

They enter a large room with guards, all in black uniforms. The guards stand in front of a heavy prison cell door. The senior officer nods his head and the door is opened. He follows the officer into the prison cell.

The prisoners are weary, tired, and seated along a narrow bench with their backs against the wall. The senior officer stands slightly inside the doorway and pauses to allow the prisoners' eyes to adjust to the light. A few moments pass. The senior officer speaks not a word. He does not move. The prisoners stare fixedly at him.

In a crisp and mechanically executed movement, the senior officer takes one step forward, draws his pistol, and fires it into the forehead of the first prisoner at the end of the bench. The prison cell is not large and the explosion of the pistol is deafening. Blood and brains and flesh and hair splash everywhere. The pistol is a very large caliber and there is a correspondingly large hole in prisoner's head. The senior officer's facial expression remains frozen. He makes another mechanical move—a rigid sidestep—and faces the next prisoner as he lifts the pistol and shouts, 'Tell me the location!' The prisoner begins to open his mouth only to receive into it the next chambered round. Another head explodes in the crowded prison cell.

The senior officer moves to the third prisoner who is screaming incoherent terror. 'Tell me the location!' The prisoner tries but is not quick enough. More blood, more brain, flesh and hair. The air in the prison cell reeks of gun smoke, blood, urine and fear. As the officer begins his next move, the remaining prisoners began to scream the information he seeks. The senior officer holsters his pistol, turns with a nod, and walks briskly out of the prison cell.

He realizes that this was why he is here. He takes a black pen from his uniform pocket, opens the portfolio, and begins to take down the information that the prisoners are now competing to scream at him.

Gaude suddenly awoke and jumped forward in his seat at the very moment the aircraft was landing. "Oh my God, I hope that was just a dream!"

Bill Watt was startled by his partner's sudden outburst. "Are you alright, Dan?"

"I'm not sure…" Gaude looked around the cabin of the aircraft. "Okay, here we go again."

"Yep, we start again."

"No, that's not what I'm talking about. You did it to me again."

"I did what?"

"I don't know, but once again, I wake up having no idea how I got here. So, how did I get here?"

"That's a silly question. We're on a plane, which is obviously how we got here to Los Angeles."

"Fine. How did I get on this plane? I don't remember boarding."

"And you thought that I was the one going senile."

"Maybe you are, but that doesn't mean that you aren't capable of driving me crazy."

"Duly noted."

Gaude paused, trying to clear his head. "What day is this?"

"Wednesday."

"Wednesday? That can't be right. Yesterday was Saturday, I'm sure."

"What if it was?"

"That means today should be our day of rest. I'm pretty sure that Sunday comes after Saturday. Isn't that one of those things that God ordained in the Book of Genesis? Y'know, he created the world in six days and rested on the seventh?"

"Sunday actually qualifies as the first day of the week," said Watt.

"Quibbler."

"I'd say that there is a substantial difference between the first and the last."

"Whether first or last, I think this is the day that God officially declared to be Sunday."

"God certainly created the days, but he didn't name them. Sunday and Monday are pagan designations for the day of the sun and moon that go back into the darkest recesses of prehistory. Tuesday, Wednesday and Thursday are named after the Norse gods. Saturday is identified with the Roman god Saturn. Do you think our God—Jehovah, if you prefer—would name the days of the week after pagan deities?"

"That does seem like a stretch," admitted Gaude. "Why didn't the early Christians rename the days after…I dunno…some of the saints? Peterday, Paulday, Polycarpday…"

Watt chuckled. "You would need to take that up with one of the early Popes."

"Which one?"

"I don't know, any of them. Maybe Pelagius II."

"Never heard of him."

"He's never heard of you, so we'll call it a draw."

Ten minutes later, the partners had debarked and navigated through LAX terminal to arrive at the baggage claim area. Gaude noticed an impeccably dressed young woman tugging at a luggage strap caught between two interlocking plates of carousel three.

"May I be of assistance?"

"A gallant straight from the nineteenth century has come to rescue a damsel in distress! Yes, my bag and I are being held captive by yon mechanical dragon."

Gaude stepped forward, disengaged the strap, removed the bag from the conveyor plates, and placed it on the floor. He then took both ends of the strap in his hands and gave a sharp tug, releasing it from the clutches of the stainless-steel beast.

"Thank you so much."

Gaude gestured to the airline luggage tag on the woman's bag.

63

"I see that your flight originated from Dulles. Are you from the D.C. area?"

"My tag says LAX."

"Just above that—the fine print. Your departure code is IAD"

"Clever boy. You must be a cop or a spy."

"Perhaps a little bit of both."

She conducted a critically appraising inspection of her Prince Tempting. "You're a journalist."

"Excellent guess."

"I don't guess."

He offered his hand. "Dan Gaude. I write for the *Capital Guardian*."

Oooooh sis! Nice warm handshake.

I bet those hands can do a lot more than that.

Shut up! Behave! She returned her attention to the corporeal member of the conversation. "Really? Have I read your work?"

"Excellent question. Have you?"

"When I get back home, I'll need to look you up...I mean, look up your articles."

"You could go online," said Gaude. He then paused and added distractedly, "At least I think I'm still online...somewhere."

"You're not sure?"

"I'm pretty sure."

"It's better to be right than to be sure."

"Interesting philosophy."

"Schopenhauer thought so."

"I can't say that philosophy is my strong suit, but I'd be happy to discuss that over a few drinks."

She responded with the convincing approximation of a smile of someone who might have found Gaude's lame attempt at wit to be marginally clever. "I must be going. Thank you again."

"My pleasure," responded Gaude as he reattached the strap to the bag. "Can I help you with anything else?"

"Such as?"

"Carrying these to your car or taxi?"

"My luggage rolls on wheels."

"Getting them to your hotel lobby?"

"There are doormen for that."

"Taking them up to your room?"

"Bellboys are quite handy at getting luggage up to a room."

"I can be very handy too."

"Yes, I can imagine," she said, giving Gaude another look-over that was a combination of methodical clinical detachment and subtle carnivorous appetite. "I've been so busy crisscrossing the country that my flirting skills may have become a little rusty. You, however, seem to be at the top of your game," she said, tilting her head coyly and smiling.

"I'd like to think so."

"But I don't play games," she said, flashed a radiant and almost convincingly sincere smile, deftly swiveled her wheeled travel case in an arc, and then briskly strode down the corridor.

He was kinda cute, said the carefree one.

Hush, she admonished.

We have more than two hours before the meeting. We could have squeezed him in, added the sultry voice. All the other sisters giggled at the double entendre.

"Enough of that, you little slut," she whispered. She then addressed the others silently, *All of you, behave!*

Bill Watt made no attempt to disguise his amusement as he watched the young woman merge into the swell of travelers heading for the exits. His voice emulated an announcement from the airport public address system. "Please inform the control tower, there has been a crash and burn at carousel three."

"Better to have loved and lost."

"You seemed to have lost before you got to love."

"Sad, but true," Gaude said with a crooked grin.

Watt and Gaude picked up their bags that had been patiently circling the carousel during Gaude's unsuccessful dalliance. They began heading to the main lobby. "Let's find a newspaper," said Watt.

"I've already checked the news on my phone."

"Will I never cure you of that habit?"

"Not as long as there is a thing called 'technology,' no."

"Okay, fine. Is there any news of a church burning?"

"None."

"We're early. Perhaps we can intervene and prevent him this time."

"How do you propose we figure out which church is the target?"

"I have no idea. Perhaps we could start calling the churches and giving them a warning."

"Calling? Seriously?"

"It worked in New Orleans."

"The population of New Orleans is a few hundred thousand. L.A. has ten times as many people and no doubt ten times as many churches."

"What's your point?" asked Watt artlessly.

Gaude threw up his hands. "There must be hundreds of churches in Los Angeles alone, much less the surrounding area."

"There are about three thousand churches in the L.A. metropolitan area."

"It sounds like you mined that factoid by taking a peek at the web."

"No, I retrieved it from my personal trove of information."

"I forgot that you specialized in trivia."

"There is nothing trivial about three thousand houses of worship."

"I stand corrected. You realize, of course, that we will be searching for the proverbial needle in a haystack."

"You've said that before."

"And now I say it again."

"In that case, we have no time to waste. I wonder where we could find a Los Angeles telephone book."

"Do they even publish them anymore?"

"They used to have them in telephone booths."

"This is L.A. There used to be a *place* in a telephone booth where the phonebook was *supposed* to be, but the phonebook was always vandalized or stolen. In any event, good luck finding a phone booth nowadays."

"I suppose that you're going to suggest that we rely on your internet prowess to dial up the local churches?"

"That could be done, but considering the number of churches, I can't promise you that we will make much progress. I don't suppose that this time we could go to the police?"

"Not this time, not any time. You do remember your attempt to enlist the aid of the police in New Orleans?"

"Sadly, yes. With all the events that I seem to be forgetting lately, it's a pity that I can't forget *that*. Maybe we could try going to a newspaper. We could offer them a lead on the church burning in return for assistance in making the calls."

"You worked for a major newspaper for how long?"

"Six years."

"If two absolute strangers walked off the street with a cockamamie story that they are following clues to church fires left by a semi-invisible host they met in Oklahoma, would you have dropped what you were doing and started dialing every church within the city?"

"No, I guess not."

"Hey," said Watt as he gestured towards the airport restaurant to their left. "There's someplace we can get a bite to eat while we figure out our next steps."

"It's a Chinese restaurant."

"What gave it away? The sign that says Hong Kong Express or the words beneath it that say Chinese Cuisine?"

"This isn't an underhanded jab about my failed efforts at carousel three, is it?" asked Gaude.

"No, but there are times when I wish that I was that clever."

"How do you expect to get a bowl of chili at this place?"

"By asking the waiter: 'Please bring me a bowl of chili.' That's how."

Gaude and Watt walked into the restaurant and found it completely empty of both customers and waitstaff and devoid of overhead lighting. The only indication that the restaurant was open for business—other than the fact that the front door was unlocked—was the music playing from the speakers behind the bar: 'Beds are Burning' by Midnight Oil.

Gaude and Watt seated themselves at a booth and waited for a few minutes until someone emerged from the swinging door connecting to the kitchen. The waiter was more than two meters tall and massively built. He had a flat nose, gigantic square jaw, and a high domed forehead with almost white-blonde hair that stood at attention in a crewcut. He arrived at the table and stared intently at the two customers for an uncomfortable moment. His icewater blue eyes were unblinking. He finally broke the silence with, "Here is menu. You hungry, *da*?"

"Yes, thank you."

Watt and Gaude opened their menus. After a moment, Gaude looked back up to see the waiter standing patiently. Silent, unblinking, immovable.

"Kung Pao chicken," Gaude announced.

"Chicken is good here. You will like." He then turned to Watt. "*Tovarisch*, is what you want daily speeshial?"

"Yes, please."

"I thought that you were going to ask for chili," prodded Gaude.

"You think a lot of things. It amazes me how few of them turn out to be correct."

"Is you want drink? We have Zing...Zing-dow...Zing...We have beer."

"That will be fine for my friend," answered Watt agreeably. "As for me, perhaps a bottle of Mexicola?"

"Mezzi-kohla?"

"Yes, it is a softdrink."

"Is what drink?"

"Perhaps a bottle of Pepsi."

"Pepsi Cola, it hits spot! Is five cents, not a lot! *Da*! We have Pepsi for you."

"If you don't mind my saying, you don't appear to be Asian," commented Gaude.

The giant reacted with stunned consternation. "This not truth! Was born and was lived whole life in Yekaterinburg until now coming to Amerika. You know, Yekaterinburg is Ural, yes? *Da*! Is called gateway to Asia. Yes! Am Asian Ruskian. Now am Asian Ruskian Amerikan!"

As the waiter departed, Gaude smiled and said, "I'm looking forward to seeing Bill Watt consume something other than chili."

"I look forward to surprising you."

Another song started playing from the bar. It took a moment for Gaude to recall—it was 'La-La Cops' by Ni'ihau Child.

> *You're heading for trouble*
> *By the gross, on the double*
> *When they try to ID ya*
> *They won't have no idea*
>
> *Say hello to the jailer*
> *He sure ain't Andy Taylor*
> *In a cell with a punk*
> *Just ignore all his bunk*

"Let's go back to the clue that led us here."

"Angels at the mosque."

"Right—Los Angeles."

"Maybe a specific angel?"

"Why should there be a specific one? Maybe the church is named Our Lady of Angels."

"True. That's worth a try. We could also consider narrowing things down. That's what one does with clues, after all."

The giant returned to the table with a case of bottles. "Here is beer!"

"Ummm...I'm sorry," said Gaude in a sincerely apologetic tone, "but I don't believe that we ordered quite that much to drink."

"You wish *pivo*...beer...*da*?"

"Well, yes..."

"Is you thirsty, *da*?"

"Yes."

"This much beer you drink when thirsty," the waiter announced. He deposited the case on their table and departed for the kitchen, effectively putting to rest all further discussion on the subject.

"Where were we?" asked Gaude.

"Names of specific angels, I believe."

"Right. Let's see, there is Gabriel, Michael, Raphael...and the Islamic angels that I had never heard about before."

"I don't think that mosques are named after angels and I'm pretty confident that Christian churches and Jewish synagogues aren't named after Munkar and Nakeer."

"You remembered their names!" exclaimed Gaude.

"In my line of business, it's good to know angels by name," responded Watt.

The waiter now arrived with their orders. Watt received a bowl of dark red simmering stew punctuated by beige cubes.

"That's the daily special?" asked Gaude.

"*Da*," answered the waiter. "This tofu chili. Is good if you like tofu and is good if you like chili." The blonde colossus then turned about, marched to the back of the restaurant, and exited into the kitchen.

"Tofu chili?" asked Gaude. "Really?"

"Yes, I told you about that."

"I thought that you were kidding."

"Kidding? About chili? You should know better than that by now."

69

Gaude shrugged. "Alright, so…what do we make of the clues, assuming, of course that they are clues?"

"Angels, of course."

"That brought us to Los Angeles, but we need something more specific."

"Zanzibar—Africa?"

"That's the clue that got us to Wyoming."

"Actually, that is the clue that we missed that should have got us there."

"Quibbler."

Watt elected to ignore the comment. "Red Desert?"

"There are plenty of deserts around here, but none of them red, or any other color other than beige. Wait, maybe the Painted Desert?"

"That's in Arizona."

"Right. My gut instincts tell me that isn't a promising lead."

"Okay, how about brick churches?" proposed Watt.

"Brick?"

"The brick mason at Zanzibar seemed pretty obsessed with the topic."

"Half the churches here are probably made of brick."

"Maybe the patron saint of bricklayers?"

"I wouldn't doubt that there is one. I bet there's even a patron saint for guys who crank out computer code."

"Saint Isidore," confirmed Watt.

"Who?"

"Saint Isidore of Seville. Patron of computers, programmers, and the internet."

"Thank you for that useless information."

"Then again, Saint Carlo Acutis was just recently canonized and has also been designated a patron saint of the internet."

"Multiple patrons?"

"Monitoring the internet from heaven is a tall order for one saint to handle."

"If there is a patron saint of the internet, why are you so opposed to it?" asked Gaude with an impish smile.

"There is also a patron for cancer—Saint Peregrine—but it's not as if anyone is particularly fond of that disease."

"Okay, duly noted," said Gaude. "What happened to the bricklayer patron?"

"Sorry. That would be Saint Stephen."

"He's the patron saint of bricklayers?"

"And stonemasons, yes."

"How do you remember this stuff?"

"If you haven't figured that out by now…"

Gaude tapped in the query. "There are three churches with the name Saint Stephen in Los Angeles."

"That's a lead, but I suspect that Saint Stephen is a long shot."

"Yeah, I agree."

"Maybe there were clues elsewhere in Wyoming. For instance, that chili they served."

"Don't open a Pandora's box of distraction. It will lead us to a labyrinth of dead ends."

"Very poetic, Dan. The writer in you reemerges."

"Go back to the angels. Maybe it's a church dedicated to one of the angels?"

"Archangel Gabriel? Michael? I'm sure that there are churches in the area named after them."

The waiter approached the table with a small tray bearing the check and two fortune cookies. Gaude opened his fortune cookie, looked at the small strip of paper silently, and then read aloud, *"Hier stehe ich. Ich kann nicht anders."*

"That sounds awfully familiar."

"The minister in Destinations, Maine shared the same quote."

"That's right, he did," agreed Watt. "A fortune cookie written in German. Now, that's a first."

"We're in a Chinese restaurant being served by a former member of the Russian Olympic Wrestling Team. I'd say that this is par for the course. Besides, fortune cookies aren't Chinese. They are an American invention."

"Fine, but they still aren't written in German."

"Except in Germany."

"You're the quibbler today."

"Let's not quibble over what might be a clue. 'Here I stand. I can do nothing else.' Those were the words of Martin Luther as he confronted the Catholic Church at the Diet of Worms."

"Diet of Worms?"

"Don't get any ideas for tomorrow's lunch."

"No worries, I've already tried earthworm chili. It's a delicacy in Venezuela."

"I should have known. Anyway, 'Diet' is just another word for a legislature, such as the Japanese Diet."

"The Japanese diet isn't sushi?"

"Are you serious?"

"No, I'm not serious," responded Watt. "The Diet of Worms was convened in the year 1521 by Holy Roman Emperor Charles V at the behest of Pope Leo X. It was held at the Heylshof Garden in Worms to confront Martin Luther with the recently issued Papal bull declaring forty-one purported errors found in Martin Luther's ninety-five theses."

"Thank you, Professor Watt. Let's get back to work, shall we?"

"Where were we?"

"I'm not sure. Martin Luther?"

"Okay, Luther is a pretty obvious clue if we are looking for a Lutheran church, less so if the reference is to Protestantism in general."

"I'll go with Lutherans."

"Might as well."

"That narrows the search down considerably," said Gaude as he tapped out a query on his cell. "Hmmm…maybe not that narrow," he immediately lamented. "There are more than fifty Lutheran churches between Malibu and Laguna Beach."

"Go back to the angels."

"Go back where?"

"The clue—the mosaic angels at the mosque."

"Hmmm…good idea. The name of the Lutheran church might include a reference to an angel."

Gaude tapped out a query on his cellphone browser.

< lutheran los angeles angel >

A moment later, he grimaced and shook his head. "The search engine is cross-wiring the terms 'angels' and 'Los Angeles.' The results are useless."

"Try the name of a specific angel."

"Any suggestions?"

"Obviously, the superstars should be the first choice."

"Good idea." Gaude tapped out another query.

< lutheran church st michaels los angeles >

Gaude's face brightened, "Hey, we got it on the first try! Saint

Michael the Archangel Lutheran Church. Bingo!"

"I don't deny that bingo is an important facet of Lutheran doctrine, but let's attend to the fire first," responded Bill Watt, absolutely deadpan.

Gaude rolled his eyes at Watt's groaner. "I have the phone number of the church right here. Let me call them." Gaude poked the spot on the screen that offered a direct dial to the church. He waited on the ringtone for a moment, only to then frown in dismay. "It a recording that announces the times for 'divine services.' I guess that's their term for Mass. Let's catch a taxi and get over there."

The waiter returned and Watt paid the restaurant bill with cash. "*Do svidaniya, tovarisch* Beel," said the towering Russian.

Watt nodded back. "*Poká-poká.*"

The two exited the restaurant. "What was all that about?" asked Gaude.

"All what about?"

"All about you speaking Russian."

"Our waiter was Russian." Watt shrugged. "Did you expect me to say goodbye in Chinese?"

"It *was* a Chinese restaurant, after all," quipped Gaude.

"Duly noted," responded Watt dryly.

The partners walked past a row of shops as they headed for the main lobby exit. A small storefront window to Gaude's right featured a display of novelty boots. He glanced at the assortment of colorful footwear in the shape of various animal feet, hooves, and paws. A vague tug of recollection teased his memory, but he shook it off as he scanned ahead to the exit signs directing travelers to public transportation. "Do they still have taxis in L.A.?" asked Gaude as they exited through the front doors.

"Why wouldn't they?"

"This is California, after all, and with all environmental rules, electric cars, self-driving autos, mandatory public transportation—"

"I see what you mean. I guess we'll find out in a minute," responded Watt as they exited the terminal doors immediately across from the taxi stand. The morning was bracingly brisk. Gaude expressed his surprise that the temperature in Southern California could be so low at that time of the year.

"*El Niño.*"

"Right. Once again, *El Niño.*"

Watt nudged his partner, "Hey Dan."

"What?"

"Look over to your right. We have a welcoming committee of one."

Standing beside the Yellow Checker taxi was Sinbad, wearing an amber turban, holding the back door open in anticipation of the arrival of his favorite fares.

"Sinbad! You're just in the nick of time!" shouted Gaude as he began approaching the taxi.

"Perhaps I have been standing here all day waiting for you," responded Sinbad with a grin.

"No," said Gaude as he shook his head, "I'd bet that you arrived not more than a minute before we walked out of the door."

Sinbad smiled broadly as Watt and Gaude entered the taxi. "You are very correct, my friend. Remind me never to play against you at blackjack."

"That's poker," corrected Gaude as he entered the cab.

"Not lately," rebutted Sinbad as he closed the door on Gaude. He then opened the driver's door, sat down at the wheel, and announced, "I am most sorry and also happy to report that there is no burning church in Los Angeles today."

"Not yet, but we have a lead," responded Gaude. "Take us to Saint Michael the Archangel Lutheran Church. The website says that it is on Stewart and Gray Road."

"That is in Downey," said Sinbad confidently.

"Is that near L.A.?" asked Gaude.

"It is in this city," explained Sinbad. "It is a city within a city. It is place where you may see the oldest McDonald's hamburger restaurant in the world and buy a burger there, but..."

"But?"

"McDonald's burgers are not *jhatka*."

"Oh, I'm sorry to hear that, Sinbad." said Watt sympathetically. "Perhaps we can have a snack at another place that serves more acceptable food."

"Yes, indeed. My cousin Mool has a hamburger stand in Anaheim. The meat is excellent and all slaughter is personally conducted by him. The cow dies so quickly that it forgets it ever lived."

"I'm not sure that I understand that, Sinbad, but it is somehow poetic."

"We Sikhs are a very poetic people. You have heard of Puran Singh?"

"I don't think that I have."

"A great and respected mystic philosopher poet. He was my great uncle, of my mother's family."

"So, you have relatives other than cousins?"

"A few."

Watt turned to Gaude. "Do you think we should have kept checking the other angel names?"

"Why? Because I found Saint Michael's on the first try? You don't believe in beginners luck?"

"I prefer to rely on blessings rather than luck. Just the same, it might be wise to make sure we didn't overlook something."

"Sure, let me try," agreed Gaude. He resumed tapping on the cellphone screen. "Let's see…there's an Archangel Gabriel Catholic Church."

"Not Lutheran. Let's give it a pass for right now."

"I don't see anything popping up on a search for Archangel Raphael."

"Alright."

"I guess we've narrowed it down to one church. I'll give another call to Saint Michael's while we are enroute." Gaude punched the button for the call, which again reached a recorded message.

"You forgot one," said Watt looking out the cab window into the distance.

"Forgot one? What other one?" asked Gaude.

"There are seven recognized archangels. That is, seven recognized in traditional Christianity. However, you rarely see or hear about the full list. Instead, most people just settle for the big four."

"Big four?"

"Gabriel, Michael, Raphael, and—"

"And?"

"—Uriel."

"That's right. I had forgotten about him."

"I suppose that the nuns didn't spend much time on Uriel. Very few people do."

"Even fewer bother to dedicate a church to him."

"No, he is admittedly obscure compared to the other three archangels. In fact, he is not even recognized in Islam."

"That's right, he wasn't one of the angels in the mosque at Zanzibar. Do you think that's significant?"

"Everything is significant."

"Okay, but looking for a church dedicated to the Archangel Uriel will be a long shot."

"Think of it as an investigative Hail Mary pass."

"Clever," muttered Gaude as he began to tap on his cellphone. "I'll check just for the heck of it." Gaude finished his inquiry and touched the 'go' button on the search engine. He looked at the screen in silence for a moment.

"Dan?"

"I know you don't like it when I use the name in vain, but Jesus Harry Christ, there's an Archangel Uriel Lutheran Church near Long Beach."

"Sinbad—"

"Yes, I know," responded their driver serenely as he made a right turn signal in preparation of re-routing his taxi due south. "You have decided not to watch the first burning church and now it is a new burning church that you are wishing to visit. Out with the old, in with the new."

⌘

Chapele woke up from the party with a raging hangover. He forced his gluey eyelids open and saw a note from Reuben safety-pinned to the pillow.

And to every bad there is a worse

Is that one of Reuben's quotes? Chapele wondered.

No, it's Thomas Hardy, asserted a smug inner voice.

Oh my God, I've been infected by the literary snob virus.

He attempted to coax his arms and legs to cooperate in lifting his body from the sleeping pad on the floor, but neither pair of appendages was in the mood to accommodate him. With his third effort Chapele was able to wobble to an upright position and then stumbled forward, dodging detritus left over from the party. He arrived at in the kitchen, ground zero for the chaotic clutter of the night before. Eggs and bacon were frying on cast iron griddles and he could smell coffee already perked. He opened the refrigerator, located a carton of orange juice wedged into the back, extricated and then drained it in one tip. As soon as he closed the refrigerator door, Chapele heard a familiar kak-kak-kak. He wandered into the great room to find his host naked, sitting before the typewriter. "Excuse me! I'm sorry!" Chapele wheeled about to leave the room.

"Tommy my boy! Don't run off. I shall cover my nakedness." Malachi reached over to the adjacent table to grab a beach towel, which he casually draped over himself. Chapele returned to the room and regarded the man wearing an electric orange and red striped toga punctuated with blue angel fish. Malachi noticed Chapele's look of mild disapproval. "Do you object to my chosen raiment?"

"It's a free country."

"But not cheap." Malachi poured himself a drink from a nearly depleted bottle of Southern Comfort.

"You're still drinking?"

"I am southern, but alas, I am not comforted."

"Maybe I should get you some coffee."

"*Veto*. I forbid it. You fail to recognize the salutary benefits of alcohol to the craft of writing."

"Good morning!" hailed Katie from behind Chapele, appearing perfectly well-rested and cheerful in another sundress from her inexhaustible collection of sundresses.

"Where did you come from?" asked Chapele, startled.

"From Atlanta. I thought I told you that before."

"No, I mean, just now."

"Well, yes, just now I did tell you Atlanta, but I'm sure I told you...are you trying to confuse me, Chappie?"

"No. I'm...ummm..." Chapele's mind performed an instant reboot to clear the clutter and then started anew. "That's a very pretty dress."

Katie looked down at the amber cotton frock. "It's my sunny sundress, for when I'm feeling particularly—"

"Sunny?"

"I was thinking of something between blithe and jaunty, but sunny will do in a pinch."

"You seem to have a sundress for every occasion."

"Every occasion and every color," Katie agreed, "except, that is, pink."

"You don't like pink?"

"Oh, I adore pink, but I don't dare wear it. It makes me stand out like a rosy beacon. I'm afraid that airplanes passing overhead will spot my whereabouts and relay the information across the sky." She glanced back at the kitchen. "Breakfast is almost ready. I made scrambled eggs, link sausages and doughnuts. How does that sound?"

"Good."

"Although it really doesn't matter what it sounds like, does it?" mused Katie. "I should say, 'How does that taste like?' But then again, you haven't started eating yet, have you?"

"Well, no, I suppose—"

"Maybe 'How does that appeal to you?' is a better way of saying it." Katie paused in thought for a moment and then shook her head. "No, 'appeal' might have a subtle sexual connotation, not that I'm judgmental about those who get turned on by scrambled eggs."

"Ummm…"

"I was going to make shrimp and grits, but—"

"But thank God you didn't," interjected Malachi.

"Hair of the dog," suggested Chapele.

"Yes, and it would be a wet, smelly dog at that," confirmed Katie. "The kind you get stuck with as a passenger on transatlantic flights."

"I guess that you won't be eating shrimp for a week," said Chapele to Malachi.

"Given the amount I served last night, I have grave doubts that the shrimp population will be able to recuperate for at least a year."

"I couldn't find the Tropicana," Katie offered, slightly chagrined.

"Oh…sorry!" said Chapele.

"Sorry about what?"

"I'm sorry about the juice."

"Why? What have you ever done to the Jews?"

"No, I meant…" Chapele then stopped, inwardly shrugged, and decided not to pursue the matter, knowing that this would result in being pulled down a rabbit hole into Katieworld.

"Reuben! Must you attempt to consume every drop of alcohol in the free world?" Katie scolded.

"Until they reestablish the Soviet Bloc, yes, I believe I shall."

"Shouldn't you be clear-headed?" asked Chapele disapprovingly.

"A clear mind is, by definition, empty," retorted Malachi disdainfully.

"Maybe that's the purpose of art."

"Yes," agreed Malachi. "Art can also muddle the brain. There are reported cases of visitors to Florence and Rome who, so overcome by the beauty of the art, suffered hallucinations, fainting, and convulsions. It's called Stendhal Syndrome—"

Katie interjected, "Does anyone want a doughnut?" as she opened a box from Krispy Kreme.

Malachi was oblivious to the question as he continued his discussion with Chapele. "Psychiatrists have actually treated people for that."

"Treat them for *doughnuts*?" Katie asked incredulously.

"No, my dear—"

"Maybe treat them *to* doughnuts…Oh, wait, they're doctors…maybe treat the patients *with* doughnuts. That makes more sense," she asserted.

"Yes, it does," agreed Chapele. "Can you write me a prescription for a glazed, Doctor Moscowicz?"

"Take two and call me in the morning."

"It *is* the morning."

"In that case, you should already be cured of what ails you."

After breakfast, Katie started cleaning the kitchen while Malachi and Chapele began picking up the remainder of the cabin before moving on to the deck and finally the front porch and walkway to the dock.

"Remind me again, why did you take this loathsome assignment?" asked Malachi as they walked back into the cabin.

"Well, I felt obliged to help. This place was a mess."

"No, I mean the assignment you were given by the *American Review*."

"Oh, *that*. I told you when we first met."

"Yes, but that was before I polished off the last bottle of booze that you brought to me two weeks ago."

"Because I'm getting paid for it."

"There are no more enticing projects available? Perhaps cleaning the Augean stables?"

Chapele's lips could not be restrained from pulling his face into an apologetic grin. "Welll…I do have a longstanding debt to you."

Malachi's right eyebrow arched and Chapele was pleased to see that he had succeeded in surprising Malachi. The poet took the bait, albeit with a wariness that was characteristic of everything he did except for his verse. "The entire world owes me a longstanding debt. What part of it do you propose to retire?"

"I owe you. Actually, I imagine every man owes you…for giving us *Carpe Dame*."

Malachi was clearly amused but not flattered. He sat down at the composition table and leaned back in his chair. "Ah yes, my pitiful modernization of Herrick's *To the Virgins*. I do recall reading somewhere that this had become a favored weapon of seduction among our misguided youth."

"It always worked for me." Chapele recalled his sophomore year in college when he 'discovered' the poem—as every male sophomore during the previous decade had discovered it—in the library's copy of the unauthorized collected poems, *Pirated Malachi*. At the time, he was deeply in lust with Vivian Chase and had devoted a full semester negotiating for her favors. He remembered the satisfying irony of copying the verse onto stationery received from his aunt for high school graduation and the brief but rapturous liaison it secured for him.

> *You, too, m'Lady shall grow old,*
> *Wither, shrivel, as the years unfold.*
> *Your hair turn white, your bright eyes dim,*
> *Your face bewrinkled and added chins.*
> *Thy body, now so soft and young,*
> *Shall rough and crooked by age become.*
> *And all those men who coax and woo*
> *Will, when you are old, abandon you.*
>
> *Now the bloom of youth is on your face,*
> *False suitors vie to praise your grace.*
> *Their cunning lies you shall believe,*
> *That beauty, and they, shall never leave.*
> *But when both years and they do pass*
> *You'll search for youth in the looking glass.*
> *But not in the glass will your beauty lie:*
> *'Tis only in the mirror of my eye.*

With loosened teeth and spotted skin
Perhaps you'll muse how it might have been
Had the one who loved you with all his soul
Been not repulsed from his love's goal.
When you sit alone and wait for death,
Knowing not when comes your last breath,
Think of me and my love true
And the life I would have shared with you.

Malachi, apparently ruminating while Chapele had been lost in reverie, looked up from the composition table. "I will never understand," the poet said while shaking his head in mock disgust, "how my most gruesome poem ever succeeded in gaining the favors of any fair lady. I suspect that most male freshmen thought that this doggerel was a sexual silver bullet, blithely unaware—or should I say tragically ignorant—of the fact that most female freshman found the poem to be repulsive and odious beyond compare. What did you college boys do? Scare the girls into bed?" Chapele responded with a self-deprecating chuckle. Malachi, now evidencing a gentle introspective smile, continued, "Given that you carry such a heavy burden of debt to me, I propose that you discharge it by getting me a beer. Better yet, since you are supposedly a writer, I enlist your services to write my eulogy that will remind the world of my singular achievement in this century. I revived the ancient art of getting maidens into bed with a song."

"I will attend to that duty the very moment I return to Gotham."

A transitory and uncharacteristic look of surprise briefly passed across Malachi's face. "Perhaps it is this morning's booze clouding my judgment, or maybe last night's binge permanently addling my brain, but I suddenly had the impression that I rubbed off on you."

"Is that a bad thing?"

"The worst. I urge you to stick closely with Thomas Chapele. You are marginally capable of pulling that off. An ersatz Reuben Malachi? No, that would offend the gods. *It is better to live your own destiny imperfectly than to live an imitation of somebody else's life with perfection.*"

"Let me guess, you lifted that line from…Aristotle?"

"No, The *Bhagavad Gita*, but the principle is the same."

"Which one was the plagiarist?"

"Who knows? They all are. Picasso once said that immature

81

artists *imitate*, mature artists *steal*."

"So, mere mortals like me cannot live another's life, but the philosophers, writers, and artists can filch from one another with impunity?"

"Don't feel sorry for yourself, I am a captive in the gyre of literary convergence."

"What happens after everything that can be said has been said?"

"It has already happened. Haven't you noticed? We borrow each other's art, we use each other's words, we share each other's thoughts. The cosmos is finally filled up beyond capacity with the clutter of literary debris. It has covered us completely. We have been smothered and buried. It has reached its limit. It is beyond our poor power to add or detract."

"Gettysburg Address."

"Chapele, you are getting better at this. What a pity that you will be departing."

"I stayed an additional weekend past your mandated fortnight."

"Yes, you did, and my appreciation is sincere as is my begrudging esteem for you. As a unique sign of my respect and affection, I'll ask you a question that I have never posed to any other human being, alive or dead."

"I admit, I am intrigued, although I doubt that I am deserving of such a singular honor."

"You, Chappie, are a rarity, a veritable two-headed faun. I thus deign you worthy."

"Alright, lay it on me."

"What writing of mine do you like?"

"Well, I admire—"

"No, I didn't say admire," Malachi interrupted. "I asked which of my writings do you *like*?"

Chapele weighed his answer carefully and responded candidly. "I'm torn between two, actually: *Clamjamfrie* and *My Colonoscopy*."

Malachi's eyes twinkled. "Bravo my boy! You have passed the final trial! I hope that it causes you no great surprise that those are, by far, my personal favorites. I hereby declare you a *mensch*."

"And I pledge upon my newly-bestowed *mench-itude* not to betray our confidences."

"That will be a neat trick, considering that your mission here was to scribble down as many confidences as possible for the purpose of distributing them to the semi-literate public."

"I'll work some magic."

"We call it 'root medicine' here in the Lowcountry, but it's voodoo all the same."

⌘

"Perhaps you should call Archangel Uriel's again," Watt suggested to Gaude.

"You want me to use my evil cellphone? Isn't that falling into sin?"

"Perhaps the near temptation to sin," responded Watt gamely. "Go ahead, before I change my mind."

"I've already left one message on their answering system."

"Give it another try, unless you have something better to do."

Gaude complied with his partner's request and once again received a recorded message. "Is there some doctrine of the Lutheran faith that prohibits real, live humans from answering a church phone?" he complained. Gaude pushed the requisite number to leave a message urging whoever might be monitoring the voicemail to immediately check the church and to contact the fire department if there was any sign of either smoke or flames. After a half hour of smooth and pleasant driving through the City of Angels, the last strains of Bizet's *L'Arlésienne* finished just as the taxi pulled up to the church. Watt and Gaude saw the first wisps of telltale smoke rising from behind the gothic stone edifice. "Let's go," shouted Gaude gesturing to the back of the building.

"Be careful, my friend," offered Sinbad.

Watt and Gaude quickly exited the cab and started running towards the building. "It's coming from the back," shouted Gaude. The two circled the church at a full run, arriving at the exterior of the apse. The smoke issued from a break in the stained glass. "It looks like the fire just got started. We need to call the fire department or the police."

"Don't bother," Watt replied evenly as he looked back over his shoulder, "they're here."

A squad car raced down the lane towards them. Watt and Gaude stood motionless as it approached, stopped approximately ten meters in front of them, and two uniformed police officers emerged. Gaude heard the sirens of approaching backup vehicles and fire trucks. The place would be swarming in a few minutes. He turned to Watt in a moment of indecision as he felt an involuntary urge to run away. The first officer approached the two interlopers, placed his right hand lightly upon the grip of his holstered service pistol and veered slightly to the left. The partner performed the routine in mirror image, moving to the right. Watt and Gaude immediately signaled their sincere desire not to be bludgeoned or shot by L.A.'s finest as they held their hands high above their heads in the traditional gesture of surrender. The policemen ordered the suspects to put their hands behind their backs, which when complied with, resulted in the application of plastic handcuffs. Watt could not, however, restrain himself from commenting to the officer affixing the restraint. "I feel like you just put a giant garbage twisty-tie on me."

"Don't tempt me to make any clever observations about that," responded the policeman.

"No, of course not, officer...officer...?"

"Vasquez."

"Officer Vasquez, I guess we don't rate very highly as criminals go."

Ten-year veteran of the force, Emilio Vasquez, chuckled appreciatively and said, "You're definitely not the scariest guy I've come across this week. This should be more than enough to hold you."

"We are at your disposal," replied Watt, "at the risk of making another garbage joke."

"At least their squad car was built in this decade," said Gaude.

"What is that supposed to mean?" snapped the other policeman.

"Do you watch *Car 54 Where Are You?*"

"Car fifty-what?" asked the policeman, clearly confused.

"You just answered the question."

"Okay, smartass, into the car."

Watt and Gaude were put in the back of a cruiser and arrived at the precinct station less than ten minutes later. As they were rousted out of the car and guided to the main entrance of the precinct, they passed a small multicolored quartz obelisk. Gaude glanced at the nametag of his escort. "Officer Zimmerman, do you mind if I look at this for a moment?"

"You're not serious, are you?" the officer asked incredulously.

"Well, it *is* in front of *your* police station."

"It showed up two nights ago. The city hasn't figured out how to demolish it."

"The city doesn't have wrecking balls and sledgehammers?"

"That's not the problem. The city lawyers don't know whether this qualifies under the new Graffiti Protection Act."

"Graffiti Protection Act?"

"Yeah, the United Nations issued a resolution that recognized Los Angeles as a world heritage site for the art form of graffiti. California then passed a law making it a felony to steal, tamper with, or destroy any graffiti within the city limits."

"Now it's my turn to ask if you are serious."

"Welcome to California," Officer Zimmerman said with a smirk.

"We certainly feel welcome, thanks to your hospitality."

"What part of the country do smartasses like you come from?"

"Washington, D.C."

"I should have known."

"My partner is being haunted by these poems," said Watt.

"I'm not taking you to a poetry reading," groused the cop.

"I thought that people in California were laid-back."

"I'm not from California, and we folks from Tel Aviv, Missouri are a naturally skeptical lot."

Gaude and Watt simultaneously exchanged glances of disbelief. "You're not a Spielgarten Mormon, are you?"

Officer Zimmerman lurched in surprise and came to an abrupt stop immediately in front of the precinct entry. "How the hell did you know that?"

"Lucky guess," replied Gaude casually.

"You're in enough trouble without also getting charged with invasion of privacy and spying."

"Actually, you can check with the person we met while investigating the fire at the Spielgarten meetinghouse," offered Watt.

"And who might that be?"

"Moll Flanders," answered Gaude.

"You know Moll Flanders?"

"Yes, we met her when we visited Tel Aviv."

"Moll Flanders is my aunt...or aunt-in law. She married my Uncle Percy."

"Small world," responded Gaude.

"Getting smaller all the time," added Watt.

Officer Zimmerman's face was now a battleground of confusion and indecision. Vasquez tossed out a good-natured taunt. "My Missouri hillbilly partner here reads highbrow literature like the instructions on a package of corn seeds. He's working his way up to Doctor Seuss right now, but don't get your hopes up."

Finally, Zimmerman tossed up his hands and surrendered. "Fine, go ahead and read your stupid poem."

City of Angels

Speeding by and by've been sped,
Then lost into the haze.
Venetian Psychic Musclemen
Who wear the latest craze.

Showtime soon and nowtime show
Of filth beneath the glitz.
Ten thousand years of Hollywood
Well since sunk in tar pits.

Will work for food, will work for sex,
The veteran beggars cry.
Fruit vendors and the junkiemen
Flag Beemer passersby.

Barely clad beach bred girls
With too much naught to say.
Oh, how poor one knows oneself
When one has known L.A.

—Reuben Malachi

"Thank you, Officer Zimmerman," said Watt as he and Gaude finished reading the poem.

"Are you now artistically inspired?"

"I believe so."

"Then maybe you'll be truthfully inspired to tell the detectives inside what you were doing at the scene of an attempt to torch a church," Officer Zimmerman lectured as they entered the building. After following a corkscrew path through the alimentary canal of the ugly building, they finally arrived at the desk strewn with overstuffed file folders, half-filled styrofoam cups, and empty week-old bags from at least a dozen different fast food eateries in the immediate vicinity. The detective on duty looked up, nodded at Vasquez, who promptly removed the plastic restraints from the two suspects.

"I'm Detective First Class Diego Tavera. I have a few questions for you two gentlemen."

Watt brushed the greeting aside. "Why are we being arrested?"

"You two appear to be fairly intelligent and my guess is well-educated. Ever hear of facial recognition software?"

"Yes."

"Your faces came up on the National Law Enforcement Identimatch system as soon as you walked into LAX Terminal. It seems that you two have shown up at quite a few church fires. Our database connects you with incidents at New York, Boston, New Orleans, and Seattle, to name a few."

"Why didn't you arrest us then?"

"We're arresting you now. That should be enough for you. Care to tell us why you seem to turn up like a bad penny at church fires?"

"We're on a mission from God."

"Yeah, right, that *Blues Brothers* line works every time. I guess I'll just have to release you two right now. Where would you like me to drop you off?" Tavera asked sarcastically. He didn't wait for an answer, but instead turned to Officer Vasquez. "What did they have on them?"

"Just wallets and a cellphone." Vasquez delivered the confiscated items sealed in a plastic zipper bag. Tavera opened the packet, examined the wallets, and extracted a driver's license from each.

"Aaron Levi? Moses Levi?"

Gaude looked over at Watt whose face was properly prepared to engage in a poker game. "Yes, that's us," answered Watt causally.

"Those are really your names?"

"Why don't you ask your Identimatch friends?" asked Gaude.

"The software recognized your faces, but it didn't tell us much else."

"And neither will we," replied Watt.

"You gentlemen don't look Jewish."

"Hasidic Jews."

"Really? Where are the black hats and the long curly hair?" asked Tavera. "Do Hasidic Jews even drive cars?"

"They were in a taxi," offered Vasquez.

"Was it a kosher taxi?"

Watt narrowed his eyes into a contemptuous glare. "Not only

have you improperly arrested us, but now you are engaging in illegally stereotyping and taunting. If I have to, I'll make my constitutional telephone call to the Antidefamation League and I'll have every Jewish lawyer from Maine to Hawaii suing you for racist violations of my rights. Charge me or release me."

"Fine, smart guy, I'll charge you."

"Go right ahead, you do that."

"Listen, I'm just trying to get to the truth."

"Something we have in common."

"So, cooperate. Who are you...really?"

"Next question."

"Okay, why are you here?"

"We've been investigating the burning of churches across the country. We had a lead that there would be an incident here, so we were trying to stop the fire before it happened."

"Are you two investigators?"

"In a sense."

"Not in any department in Los Angeles, I'd wager."

"No."

"Or anywhere else in California, for that matter."

"No argument with you there."

"You're definitely not feds."

"Nope."

"Insurance?"

"No."

"When did you come into town?"

"I thought that you said we were tagged by your facial recognition computer snoops at the airport. You know when we arrived."

"Yeah, but like I said, we didn't get names to attach to your pretty faces. You were flagged when you passed through the main terminal, but we don't know the gate you arrived at or the flight that brought you here."

"I don't remember the flight number. It was Pan-Am something-or-other."

"Pan-Am?"

"Yes."

"*Pan-American Airlines*?"

"The same."

"There hasn't been a Pan-Am flight in over thirty years."

"Thirty years? Really? That long?" asked Watt introspectively. "Hmmm…the connecting flight was seriously delayed, and the layover did take some additional time, so that might explain it…"

Tavera shook his head dismissively in apparent disgust, professionally squelching the urge to laugh at Watt's inspired response. "Get them out of here!" he growled.

Vasquez led Watt and Gaude through a security gate, then another, and directed them to walk in front of him as they proceeded past a line of barred cells. Gaude noticed a poster on the opposite wall.

Converting seems scary, doesn't it?

Trust us, not converting is worse.

The Great Conversion
It's about to happen

"Interesting that both of you are Hasidic Jews," said Vasquez. "My family background is Jewish."

"Your partner just raked us over the coals for not looking sufficiently Hebrew and a guy named Vasquez now tells us his family is Jewish?"

"We came from Spain. Sephardic Jews. My grandfather left Andalucía in Spain nearly a century ago and settled in Palestine. He was inspired by some book about building a paradise in the Holy Land."

"*Altneuland.*"

"Excuse me?"

"*The Old New Land.*"

"That's it! How did you know?"

"Lucky guess."

"I was born in Tel Aviv."

"You too?"

"Me too, what? Were *you* born in Tel Aviv?"

"No, your partner, Officer Zimmerman."

89

"Oh right. Well, I was born in Tel Aviv, Israel and he is from Tel Aviv, Missouri. We kid each other about it sometimes. Strange coincidence."

"There are no coincidences."

"There are only coincidences," Vasquez answered matter-of-factly. He continued, "Eventually, my folks immigrated here shortly after I was born and sort of drifted from the faith. I attend a non-denominational chapel now, but during Passover, I do the Seder ritual. I'm not sure why. It just comes over me." They arrived at the holding cell. Vasquez pulled a keyring off his belt and looked into the cell at a disheveled twenty-something wearing gray denim jeans and a black tee-shirt. He was folded into a fetal position on the back-wall bench. "Timmy! I have some company for you." The figure did not respond. Vasquez looked back at his new charges. "Timmy is a frequent flyer here at the precinct." He opened the cell door for Watt and Gaude to enter. "The good news is that he is talkative," said Vasquez as the partners entered the cell. "The bad news is…that he is talkative." Vazquez then shut the door behind them and departed down the hallway.

Watt immediately approached the young man and extended his hand. "Bill Watt."

The cellmate slowly raised his head and looked the new arrival in the eye. "*What*…does a Bill *Watt* do?"

"My partner and I have been investigating church fires."

"Why? Do churches burn any differently than other buildings? Do they give off a holy aroma?"

Gaude now understood the reason for Officer Vasquez's warning.

"I am called Purge," the young man said after an extended pause. "I have cleansed myself of all preconceptions, misconceptions, and conceptions."

"Who calls you Purge?"

"Say again?"

"You said that you are called Purge," pointed out Watt. "That suggests that someone else gave you that moniker."

"Ah ha! A preconception!"

"I see," Gaude chimed in. "Is that why you were arrested and put in this jail cell? Did the police want you to chase away preconceptions? Sort of like a spiritual pest control officer?"

"Who said that I was arrested? That's most certainly a

90

misconception!"

Gaude rolled his eyes up to the sky in order to signal the heavenly arbitrators that he demanded some intervention in the seemingly fruitless conversation. Bill Watt, on the other hand, was more patient. "I don't know how else you would be here, unless you turned yourself in and asked to be incarcerated."

"No. That is yet another of your misconceptions. I have too many other things to do than sit in a jail cell to waste away in the City of Fallen Angels."

"What is your occupation, then?" asked a long-suffering Watt.

"I am a freedom fighter."

"You fight for freedom? Are you some kind of revolutionary?"

"I am definitely a revolutionary, but I don't fight *for* freedom. I fight *against* freedom."

"But freedom is the right of every individual."

"A right that should be surrendered. Your individuality is your loneliness. You yearn to be unified, first to your family, then to the community, to humanity, and finally to God."

"That is an unusual doctrine."

"Freedom is its own prison. It is a tyranny of man upon himself. The only thing worse is enslavement by another man."

"I'm not following you. There is freedom and there is oppression. You're saying both are bad."

"In a sense they are. Oppression is the very definition of misery. However, its opposite also leads to wretchedness. Free will is the liberty to sin. Even if you choose through free will to do what is good, what is righteous, what is pure, you always can change your mind—and you eventually will do just that. At any moment you are in danger of turning your back on virtue and embracing vice."

"This sounds like a very negative dogma."

"I didn't create it. Look in the first book of the Bible. Adam was in paradise. He had a perfect life. What difficult or dramatic choices did Adam have to make while he was in the garden? God gave him everything, including his mate. It was when humans were given a choice and were permitted to exercise free will that they suffered expulsion from paradise. There was no reason to sin, but he did anyway because he was given the free will to sin. Given a choice, humans will make the wrong one. That's because we *are* human."

"You forgot that Eve was involved in the decision to sin against

God. Once you introduce a woman to the situation, free will goes out the window."

Purge chuckled in appreciation. "*Cherchez la femme.* Maybe I'll give you that one, but the fact remains that it is when your free will is surrendered, and the will of perfect holiness takes possession of your life, you experience what we all innately desire."

"Which is?"

"Freedom from freedom."

"Who are you surrendering to?"

"To nothingness."

"Nothingness? What good does that do?"

"Nothingness in an embrace of emptiness. Your emptiness is a desire not to be filled, but rather to be further emptied into the cosmic nothingness, which encompasses the wholeness of creation. To become nothing is to become the all, incorporated into the incorporeal invisible spirit without which we cannot exist, with which we will no longer exist, and thus be freed from freedom."

"What happens then?"

"Infinite nothingness, which is infinite goodness. Surrendering to any corporeal or incorporeal entity will enslave you."

"I thought that you said that we all want to be united with God. He's an incorporeal entity."

Purge was momentarily taken aback, but quickly recovered and smirked. "The first and foremost goal of the enlightened is freedom from quibblers!"

"Amen to that!" interjected Gaude.

"So you worship nothing?"

"Attaining nothingness is the supreme goal. If your master is nothing, then you have no master. Hence, you are free."

"But I thought that you just said that freedom is its own prison."

"That is a misconception. Strike two!"

"We are keeping score?"

"I am keeping score."

"What happens if strike three occurs? What happens if I have a conception?"

"If you have a conception, given the fact that you are a male of the species, we should call the Vatican. They like to be kept up-to-date on major miracles."

"I don't see how belief in nothingness constitutes a belief."

"I said that I surrender to nothingness, I did not say that I believe in it."

"What do you believe in?"

"I believe in believing."

"Believe in believing...in what?"

"In belief itself. Believe for no other reason than you can believe."

"That's circular."

"Existence is circular. The earth is circular. The sun is circular. The galaxy is circular. The circle of life is...well, by definition, circular."

"Believing in believing is just a backhand way of saying faith, isn't it?"

"A belief in something or someone is faith. I don't believe in anything or anyone. I just believe in believing."

"You have something against faith?"

"I tried it once. It didn't work out well."

"Why is that?"

"There are those who have faith, those who have lost their faith, and those who were raised Catholic."

"I assume that you fall into the last category? Or is that a preconception or a misconception?"

"It is an *ex*ception."

"You didn't mention that before."

"I didn't need to. It was *ex*ceptionally obvious."

"Jimmy, how are you feeling?"

"Sore all over, but I'll live to fight another day."

"Hopefully, that fighting won't be today."

"Can you hand me my cellphone?" Bagsley went to the small closet, retrieved the phone, and handed it to his colleague. The retinal recognition feature opened the device, but when Doyle attempted to initiate a call using the secured network, he received an error code. "What the hell's going on? Is this clinic a shielded space?"

"I don't think that is the problem, Jimmy."

"Do you have a SEC-CEL?" asked Doyle.

93

"Yeah, but this morning I found that the system is down," answered Bagsley.

"Down? The system is never down."

"Welcome to the dawning of never. The system is now offline and out of commission."

"*Damn.* Alright, can you get in contact with Larry when you go over to Babylon? Do they still have comms?"

"The explosion didn't take out the entire facility, although with the firefighters tromping through the place, who knows what might have been compromised. Anyway, I can still reach out to Larry on SIPRNet."

Doyle knew that the Defense Department's Secret Internet Protocol Router Network was old school and not as secure as ORCA's own system, but it would do in a pinch. "Okay, fine. While you're at it, let him know about our problems with secure calls."

"If the network is down, he'll already know."

"Fee free to add our dollop of bitching to the general din of caterwauling that is likely happening all over the globe."

"Will do."

"So, what have you got, Doug?"

"As expected, the possibilities are countless. I've tried to pare down the list."

"Top ten?"

"Maybe down to the top five."

"As I've said before, you are a genius."

"When did you ever say that before?"

"How should I know? I just sustained a traumatic head injury," replied Doyle with a chuckle.

"I can't really take much credit," Bagsley said with a grin. "Feel free to thank the search engines on DataGhad."

"I'm not in any condition to quibble about your sources."

"In any event, let's not start patting ourselves on the back just yet."

"Fine, my back still hurts too much to take anything but a massage."

"From a Swedish bikini model, no doubt."

"Please, no jokes, it hurts when I laugh."

Bagsley took his computer tablet out of its case and made a few taps on the screen. "Fine, I'll get right down to brass tacks. Number one: the most obvious, the biblical Four Horsemen of the Apocalypse."

"Let's see, pestilence, war, famine, and death. Death, as I recall, rides a pale horse."

"You remember your Sunday school."

"Actually, I remember it from a Spaghetti Western that I saw on Netflix."

"Alright, so, it's from the Book of Revelation."

"Which is chock-full of nearly every allegory the mind can conceive."

"I'm not keen on trying to figure out how Little Adolph wants us to interpret a lamb with seven eyes and dragons with multiple heads and ten horns."

"The four riders…"

"Yeah…"

"My old team. All four of them have been hit within the past two weeks."

"Alright, but how would we match them up to war, famine, pestilence, and death?"

"Ted O'Brien was on active duty for a number of years."

"That doesn't necessarily mean he was in a war."

"In his case it does. He was with SEAL Team Seven."

"That alone would make him plenty of enemies."

"True enough."

"Fine, that's war."

"In our foolish youth, we gave Pedro Smith the nickname 'Doctor Death.' During basic, he was mildly obsessed with studying the more esoteric methods of assassination."

"That's pretty darned sad, considering what happened to him. I don't know if that qualifies, but it's better than nothing. Pestilence?"

"Jack VonHallegin had a fight with colon cancer. It was serious enough for surgery and chemotherapy, but he was back on duty after six months. Cancer isn't contagious, so I think that pestilence would be a stretch."

"But not totally discounted."

"No, I suppose not. That leaves Diane McCraw."

"I don't see how she could qualify as 'famine,' do you?"

"I have to be clinical here. As much as I loved Diane, the fact is that she was a former ballet dancer, and she was rather…"

"Slim?"

"Skinny as a rail. Borderline anorexic, to be brutally honest. I can't imagine that Little Adolph would qualify as the compassionate and sensitive type, so it is conceivable that the label applied to her."

"Assuming that the Four Horsemen is a clue, what would it lead us to about the hits?"

"Maybe a re-look at the way each died."

"Alright, that makes sense."

"We can go back to that. What's the next prospect on the list?"

"Number two is the Four Horsemen of Notre Dame."

"Sure, I should have seen that one coming. They were famous in the 1920s or 30s, right?"

"Right, 1920s."

"Didn't Ronald Reagan make the 'go win one for the Gipper' movie about them?"

"Close. Same team and only a few years apart, but no cigar."

"So, what do we have to work with? Notre Dame means 'Our Lady'…Mary, the Mother of God. Perhaps Catholic school, football, Fighting Irish, Roaring 20s? What about the football players names?"

Bagsley tapped quickly on the screen of his tablet. "Quarterback Harry Stuhldreher, left halfback Jim Crowley, right halfback Don Miller and fullback Elmer Layden."

"Nothing jumps out at me there. How about their bios?"

"I'm lookin'…ummm…coaching, coaching, businessman, lawyer…no, nothing that is jumpin' out at me."

"I'm not feeling that one. Let's try another."

"Number three is Rock and Roll."

"You're going to tell me that there is a band named The Four Horsemen."

"Actually, there is—or I should say, there was. They were moderately successful in the 80s and 90s. There is also Metallica."

"Metallica? How did you come up with that?"

"It just so happens that 'The Four Horsemen' is the second track off Metallica's debut album, *Kill 'Em All*."

"*Kill 'Em All*?"

"Yeah."

"Ouch, that's a bit too close for comfort. Pull up the lyrics."

"I'm already ahead of you."

"Can you play it off the tablet?"

"Of course."

They listened through all seven stanzas, neither showing any sign that the words triggered a useful association. Bagsley shook his head in dismay. "I dunno, Jimmy, maybe this is wearing me down."

"This isn't looking great, Doug. So far, number one is our top contender. Maybe we'll have some better luck moving down the list."

"Number four is a cocktail made of *Jägermeister*, *Rumple Minze*—"

"Did you say *Jägermeister*?"

"Ever had it?"

"I'm afraid that I have. German liquor that tastes like cough syrup. I tried it once on a ski trip. Just a few minutes before he died...exploded...Jethro made a joke about *Jägermeister* being banned from heaven."

"Strange coincidence."

"There are no coincidences."

"Until everything is a coincidence."

"Right."

Bagsley referred back to the screen of the notebook computer. "Okay, there is also *Rumple Minze*—"

"Another German liquor?"

"Yep. *Goldschläger*—"

"Let me guess...another German liquor."

"And Bacardi 151."

"Very un-German. Sounds like this drink packs a punch. Do you see any relevance to this case?"

"I chose it on gut instinct. It's German booze mixed in a lethal cocktail. You named our adversary Little Adolph. This drink sounds like something he might serve at his 'I've just conquered the world' celebration."

"I named Little Adolph on a mere whim."

"I know. I was there, remember? I think that maybe you were on to something subconsciously."

"Fine, what would anything relating to Germans, Germany, or Homicidal Psychopath Dictators help us track down the bastard that killed Jethro?"

"You're kidding, right? Who else but a homicidal psychopath—"

"A spy, that's who. A spy like us. Have you forgotten what we do for a living?"

"Sorry, Jimmy. I think I was personalizing Jethro too much."

"You don't need to apologize. For all intents and purposes, Jethro was a person. However, let's face it, in our business, persons get eliminated. They do it. We do it."

"Right. Maybe the clue is in the Bacardi."

"Go get us a bottle and we can check."

Bagsley chucked, "Now there's a perk I can live with."

"Let's see…Bacardi was founded in Cuba."

"Right. Currently headquartered in Bermuda," responded Bagsley scanning his tablet.

"Germans…Hitler…Cuba…Bermuda…No, I'm not seeing it, Doug. Bacardi 151? What about 151?"

"I checked. No connection to any frequency, modulation, or anything else we've detected on those signals."

"Some reference to…I dunno, the Periodic Table of Elements?"

"Hmmm…I never will figure out how that demented mind of yours works. Give me a second." Bagsley conducted a quick search. "Atomic numbers stop at 118. The only element that comes close to 151 in terms of atomic weight is Europium."

"Europium…Europe…Germany."

"And you just came from Budapest."

"Yeah, but—"

"Wait, let me search Europium." Bagsley tapped on the screen and scanned the information. "Let's see. Europium is a metal, extremely rare, barely exists in nature, silvery in color but oxidizes immediately." He continued browsing the article. "It's generally useless for most applications, except for providin' red coloration for television screens." He continued reading, unconsciously moving his lips silently as he moved down through the article. Suddenly, he leaned back in surprise, "Whoah, nelly! Europium is now being used for prototype quantum memory chips to establish a secure worldwide data encryption network."

"Seriously?"

"Serious as the Book of Job."

"Johnny, we have a winner."

"Alright, we need to find out who produces Europium and where."

"Sounds like a plan." Doyle then made a mock grimace. "Y'know, I hate to say this, but shouldn't folks like you and me already know about Europium if it is an essential component for next generation encryption?"

"Hey, boss, I never got the memo on that one. I just use the computers, I don't build them."

"I'm starting to feel out of touch."

"I'd be willing to venture that might be a common symptom of spies who are laid out flat in an infirmary after nearly getting blown to smithereens by a genius supercomputer."

"Okay, let's get on that one. Just out of curiosity, what was number five?"

"A new casino just opened in Las Vegas. The Four Horsemen."

Doyle's eyes unfocused as he looked out at nothing and inward at everything. "That's it."

"What's it?"

"The Las Vegas casino."

"Just like that?"

"Yeah, just like that."

"You're kidding."

"I'm going."

"What about Europium?"

"You can work that, but I'm going to Las Vegas. That's where the answer is. I know it."

"Divine inspiration?"

"Feel free to call it what you like."

"Should I put that in our reports? Your guardian angel told you so?"

"The same guardian angel that saved my neck in the explosion two days ago."

"You're just goin' to show up to a casino and expect Little Adolph to walk up to you and hand you his business card."

"The casino has a hotel, I assume."

"Of course."

"Book me in Room 151."

"Seriously?"

"Seriously. If the room is already booked, get the bookings switched."

"How do I do that?"

"Doug, you do remember what we do for a living? How hard is it to hack into a hotel's database?"

"Ouch! I'm obviously slipping. Sorry, it's been a rough few

days, even for those of us who weren't caught in an explosion. I'll get on it pronto. When do you want the reservation?"

"Tonight."

"Tonight? The doc here wasn't plannin' to release you until tomorrow at the earliest."

"Tonight, Doug."

"No."

"Tonight."

"If you don't mind me sayin'—"

"Or even if I do—"

"Or even if you do, it's been a few years since you were a hands-on operative."

"You think that I've lost my touch?"

"You might still have your touch, but it's your punch I'm more worried about. When was the last time you went face-to-face with an opponent, or had to dodge a real, live bullet?"

"Book the room for tonight," Doyle replied evenly.

"Alright, Batman. It's your funeral. Let me walk back to the Babylon lab and push the buttons. I'll get you the flight reservations."

"Get me a rental car when I arrive at the airport."

"Are you fit to drive?"

"Rental car, Doug."

"What's wrong with a taxi or an Uber?"

"I'm not sure of what kind of exit I might have to make."

"That don't sound very optimistic."

"Optimists can take a cab. Get me a rental."

Bagsley held up his hands in surrender. "Alright, fine, whatever you say."

"Thanks, Doug."

"I'll come back for you and we can drive up to the airport together."

"Don't bother, I'll already be gone. Just get me the earliest flight out possible."

"You can't force me to give you our rental car fob."

"Are we going to quibble over that again?"

"C'mon now, Jimmy, humor me. At least take a few more hours rest during the drive to the airport and the flight to Las Vegas."

"Okay, but I need you working here. Call a ride for me."

"We're out in the middle of nowhere."

"In that case, find a driver who lives in the suburbs of nowhere."

"Your driver from almost nowhere won't be able to get past the security guards at the front gate."

"Hmmm…true…" frowned Doyle. His face then relaxed, "I saw some people here scooting around in golf carts when we first arrived. Can you get one them to give me a lift to the front gate?"

"Jimmy, seriously, it's no problem for me to drive you to the airport."

"I need you here to figure out what happened to Jethro. That's as much of a priority as my going to Vegas."

"I don't suppose you'd care to swap assignments?"

"I'm not going there for the slots or the dancing girls. In this case, what happens in Vegas will end up face-down dead in Vegas."

"That face plant might be your own. Be careful, Jimmy," warned Bagsley.

"Sure thing, Mom," quipped Doyle.

"You're going to try to take him alive, aren't you?"

"How would you know that?"

"I don't need to be an operative to figure this one out. You can't get information out of a dead man and you need his information desperately."

"I wouldn't say desperately. I would say…"

"Uh-huh?"

"Okay, desperately it is," said Doyle with a crooked grin.

"Desperation leads to mistakes, and mistakes lead to—"

"I know, the morgue."

"Assuming that they ever find your body."

"You do know how to build up a guy's confidence. I don't suppose you ever met my ex-wife?"

"I don't reveal my sources."

"Are my clothes in the closet?" asked Doyle.

"Yeah, we had them cleaned while you were out in la-la-land. Your wallet is there too."

"I didn't bring my service pistol. That was a pretty blatant mistake."

"They have a small armory here—"

"Really? I'm starting to like this place. Maybe I should make a reservation here for my summer vacation."

"What do you usually carry?"

"Berretta 92."

"I'll see if they have one."

"If not, I guess I can get by with an H&K or Sig Sauer."

"I'll see what I can do." Bagsley paused and then said, "It just occurred to me that getting a weapons clearance through the airline on short notice is virtually—"

"Just hack them too. You know how to do it."

"Sometimes I wish I had your lunatic sense of clarity. Sometimes, of course, meaning never."

"Speaking of clarity, if you can't find a Berretta, my simplest fix is to call Larry Caldwell at Central and ask him to send a contact to the airport at Las Vegas."

"Good point."

"Wait...no, belay that one. Larry doesn't know I'm going."

"That's not a problem. I'll let him know when I get in touch with him on SIPR."

"I guess what I should have said is that Larry does not know and would not approve my going."

"That makes two of us."

"We need to reach out to someone else."

"Who else?"

"I'm not sure who our operatives are in Las Vegas."

"You didn't memorize that when you peeked at the ops list?"

"Precognition is not included in my package of skillsets."

"Precognition?"

"Foretelling the future."

"Down South, we call that prophesying."

"I could use an Old Testament prophet right now, preferably armed with some miracles."

"Well, *my* skillset doesn't include making guns appear out of nowhere."

Doyle mulled for a moment. "Doug, I want you to call a friend of mine."

"From which field office?"

"Headquarters."

"I thought that you wanted to keep them in the dark."

"I do. My friend works a concession in the basement snack bar."

"You're not serious?"

"Serious as the Book of Lamentations."

"Have you ever read the Book of Lamentations?"

"No, have you?"

"A guy who works in a snack bar in D.C. is going to arrange a brush pass at an airport on the other side of the country?"

"It might be hard to believe, but yes, that's exactly what I'm asking for."

"Call him yourself. The SEC-CEL might be out, but the unsecured cell function works just fine."

"And is easily monitored."

"They can listen in on me just as easily as they can spy on you."

"But they won't. Make the call from a regular landline. Isn't there an old pay phone at the café?"

"I'm not sure it still works."

"Something tells me that it does."

"Landlines are monitored too. You of all people should know that."

"Sure, and I of all people know that my cell is watched more closely than an antique telephone in a little tiki-café in the middle of a Wisconsin castle."

"Jimmy, I'm just a few years away from a nice, quiet retirement."

"Think of the stories you can tell your grandchildren."

"Those grandchildren will be shipped off to Siberia if they knew anything about this."

"Maybe grandchildren are overrated after all."

"Jimmy—"

"Doug, you've got to do this for me. His name is Dayton Carmichael." Doyle held up his cellphone display with Carmichael's telephone number.

Bagsley shook his head in resignation as he typed in the number onto his electronic tablet. "Okay, Jimmy, I'll do it for old time's sake, considering that what you're about to do will probably result in all of us referring to you in the past tense."

"Thanks for everything, Doug."

"Don't thank me for doing something stupid, even if that stupid thing is what you're asking me to do."

"Doug, it isn't a case of stupid or smart anymore, it's a question of dead or alive."

"That is the question, Jimmy. You know that you don't

necessarily have to bring Little Adolph back alive, don't you? He's valuable, but not so valuable that it's worth your life."

"We're all expendable, Doug, and a field operative is the most expendable of all. That's why field operatives were created."

"It's not worth it, Jimmy."

"We need someone to squeeze."

"I doubt that he'll talk."

"It doesn't matter. We have to take that chance."

"I know, which means that the odds of you getting killed rise exponentially."

"I know that too," said Doyle. Bagsley turned to leave, but then hesitated. As he began to step away again, Doyle called to him. "Doug, what's wrong?"

"Nothing."

"You're lying."

"Really…"

There was an awkward silence. "Doug, I'm starting to think that it's a whole lot more than nothing."

"Listen, Jimmy, there's another thing that I didn't tell you that makes Jethro sound like yesterday's news."

"In a coldhearted sense, he is."

"I suppose that everything we do seems to be coldhearted lately."

"If you were a field operative, that would be par for the course."

"Well, the cold hard truth is that Little Adolph might not be so little."

"What do you mean?"

"Doesn't it seem odd that Little Adolph could take down Jethro? Adolph is just a signal. Sure, he is a nasty, violent signal, but only a signal. Jethro, on the other hand, was the most powerful computer in the world."

"Okay, that does seem hard to…compute…I suppose."

"Well…about that…"

"What?"

"It turns out that Jethro may not have been the most powerful computer in the world."

"What do you mean?"

"Remember that discussion we had with Julia about competing quantum computers? You know, that 'Mister X' or 'Little Adolph' might have gotten the jump on us in quantum computing?"

"Sure, but wasn't the purpose of our visit here to meet the answer to Little Adolph? Jethro was far beyond quantum computing, even more advanced than the next generation, right?"

"Yeah, Jethro was far beyond quantum computing, but we might be up against something that isn't actually quantum computing."

"Who told you that?" Doyle immediately added, "No, don't tell me. It was Jacobsen."

"In a roundabout way. He went to a meeting yesterday and forgot to log out of his workstation."

"And you decided to take a leisurely tour through his hard drive."

"Something like that."

"That doesn't sound like something an analyst would do."

"Hey, they sent me to Basic just like everyone else. I might not have been a superstar graduate like the famous James Parker Doyle, but this country boy managed to muddle through."

"A man after my own heart. What did you find?"

"Jethro might have been the most intelligent being on earth, but intelligence and raw computing power are not the same thing. The truth is—"

"Today's version of the truth."

"Yeah, well, the fact of the matter is that it was not that easy to measure Jethro's computing power. Jacobsen couldn't control him like an adding machine and never could accurately test him to determine the ceiling on his capabilities. According to Jacobsen's notes and reports, precise calibration of Jethro was not possible, but he probably operated in the range of one hundred exahertz."

"Exaherz?"

"Exaherz is one quintillion herz."

"That's a lot."

"That's more than a lot. It's one hellacious amount of processing power by any standard."

"How does this relate to quantum supremacy Julia explained to me a week ago?"

"It seems like we talked about that a year ago. Herz has to do with processing speed, how many floating-point operations per second."

"I do know enough about computers to understand herz and

flops."

"As for quantum supremacy, what I was able to pick up from Julia is based upon computational theory and design. I don't qualify as an expert in either."

"Fine, but in any event, it sounds like Jethro was in the big leagues of supercomputers."

"Hell yeah, he was at the top of the short list of world's smartest computers that we know about."

"What about computers that we don't know about?"

"That's always the thing, ain't it?" Bagsley paused again, weighing the risk. "Remember when we discussed how the signals are anywhere and everywhere?"

"Right. Television, radio, internet, power grid, you name it."

"Jacobsen and Babylon have started to suspect that the worldwide saturation of signals are not merely background static or individual electronic packets of hunter-seekers. They might actually form an integrated system."

"You mean like a mega-supercomputer?"

"Yeah."

"Where?"

"I just told you: everywhere."

"You mean cloud computing?"

"Not in the usual sense of the term. This ain't just plugging in data on centralized server farms. This is about a real, no-kidding, electronic cloud. Like one floating in the atmosphere circling 'round the earth."

"That's crazy."

"It's outright insane...and insanely frightenin'. We might be up against some spooky computer that covers the entire planet. Every day of your life you've been living, breathing, and walking through Adolph's computer. We all have."

"If it has surrounded the planet, wouldn't someone have detected it by now?" pointed out Doyle.

"Not necessarily. If it started gradually, a long time ago—for instance, back in 1938—no one would have been able to detect it. By the time we had the technology to identify such a thing, it would have been in place long enough for most scientist to assume that this was just a natural phenomenon."

"Can Adolph's super-quantum computer operate as a worldwide

cloud?"

"It's unlikely that the quantum computer theory fits, but what I found in Jacobsen's files throws everything we thought we knew out the window."

"How's that?"

"Babylon Laboratory has been looking into the potential of dark matter-energy computing."

"*What?*"

"That's just how I reacted when I was trespassing upon Jacobsen's hard drive. You know something about the theories of dark matter and dark energy?"

"You do realize that you are making my head hurt more than the concussion I got from the explosion?" groused Doyle. "Yes, I've read about the general theories. According to the theories—and they are still theories, I assume—the sum total of observable matter and energy in existence cannot account for the current model of an ever-expanding and rapidly accelerating universe."

"Sounds like you've been reading one of Julia's research papers."

"No, more like some material given to me by a professor from Princeton."

"Who?"

"Classified."

"I'm pretty sure I've got adequate clearance."

"Need-to-know."

"I'm feeling the need coming on me right now. How classified can a professor at Princeton possibly be?"

"The mind reels," grinned Doyle. "Don't bother prying any further. I'm not going to crack." Doyle's demeanor sobered. "However, that little nugget of knowledge that I have doesn't tell me anything useful about computers that operate in the world of dark matter and energy."

"No, and there isn't much that any quantum physicist could tell you, other than the rather radical theory that if a computer were to be composed of dark matter and operate with dark energy, that its speed and computing power would leave quantum computing in the cosmic dust."

"Just how fast could that possibly be?" asked Doyle.

"From what I saw in Jacobsen's workstation, I don't think that we're dealing with Little Adolph anymore. Now it's Big Adolph, who just might be listed first and foremost as the contender for the most powerful computer on earth—or in the earth—or maybe surrounding the earth. According to Babylon's analysis, we might be facin' something with—at a minimum—a processing power of at least a zetaherz...maybe hundreds of zetaherz. Before you ask, a zetaherz is ten to the twenty-first power. The number is called a sextillion. To give you a mental image, that's the estimated number of grains of sand on all of the beaches of the world."

"Given that zetaherz starts with a 'z,' I'll assume that it is the upper limit of computing speed."

"Incorrect assumption. Actually, a yottaherz is substantially faster...a thousand times greater frequency. Jacobsen's files were murky on the question of a top limit for a dark matter-energy computer, but I saw something that mentioned a theoretical ceiling of ten quintillion yottaherz. That's one point eight five times ten to the forty-third power. The one thing that could be described as larger is a thing called Graham's Number, a figure so large that the numbers themselves, written in the smallest possible font, would fill a space greater than the entire universe."

"That's impossibly large."

"And ironically, a dark matter computer might be impossible to find, even if it is enormous. Dark matter-energy is, by definition, completely invisible," continued Bagsley. "No scientist has ever been able to locate or isolate it, despite decades of effort."

"Seems to me that in terms of physics, this is a place where only God can go."

"In that case, invoking God might be our only hope."

"It sounds as if Big Adolph built his own god," muttered Doyle.

"Maybe he has created a golden calf..." said Bagsley, "...or the Tower of Babel."

Doyle nodded. "Based on theory one, that there could be such a thing as a dark matter-energy computer, and lashing it together with theory two, that Big Adolph actually has built such an outrageously powerful computer, we come to the result that we are dealing with something almost supernatural. That monstrous thing would have intuition and imagination and..."

"And what?" asked Bagsley.

"Omniscient deviousness."

"What the hell does that mean?" asked Bagsley, clearly annoyed.

"It means," said Doyle, "that I was wrong when I said that Adolph may have created a god. It seems that he created the devil."

"The next thing you'll be predicting is that it will be caught handing out apples in the Garden of Eden and get tossed out on its hard drive by Saint Michael the Archangel," complained Bagsley.

"Maybe we should stay out of the Bible and stick to science fiction," said Doyle. "But then again, Jules Verne's submarines and rockets to the moon were once science fiction." He shook his head despondently. "I can't even begin to process the implications."

"Neither can I. Chances are, even Jacobsen hasn't begun to scratch the surface."

"So, this cloudy computer behemoth is the thing that created those elusive signals that have been lurking around since 1938?"

"Or perhaps those signals were the things that created the computer. We might have a chicken and egg problem here. Of course, all of this was impossible back then."

"Isn't it just as impossible now?"

"Good point."

"Assuming that this impossible computer does exist and has existed for the better part of a century, then it's had plenty of time to infiltrate into every nook and cranny of the world."

"Right, and has spent that time gradually increasing its processing power."

"In that case, why hasn't it taken over the entire world already?"

"Y'know Jimmy, I'd imagine that there are those who might argue that it has. Anyhow, assuming that we're not in its grip just yet, that might be due to the fact that a wholly interconnected world is a pretty recent development. It could be that Adolph has his own nefarious plan and timetable, or it could be that…"

"What?"

"Something else is stopping it."

"Something else? You mean like Glinda, the Good Witch of the North?"

Bagsley chuckled. "I like that." His face returned to its former look of serious concern. "I'm not sure, and it's not like I'm able to discuss this with many other people. Maybe there is another force—another intelligence—that is fightin' it, or at least slowing it down."

"But you don't know what it is."

"Barely a clue except what I just told you."

Doyle looked down at the floor as he paused in thought. He then looked back up at Bagsley. "One of the things that Jethro told me before he was attacked was that there was a plausible explanation for all of this."

"Why didn't you mention this before?"

"Maybe for the same reason you didn't tell me about this cosmic consciousness computer of yours. Besides, his plausible explanation was thoroughly implausible."

"What was it?"

"Angels and demons."

Bagsley mulled this over silently as he chewed his lip. "Jimmy, that's downright crazy."

"Yes, it is."

"But it's better than anything we've come up with so far."

"That's certainly a comfort." Doyle paused in thought for a moment. "How does this all figure into the attack on Jethro?"

"Obviously, Adolph was after something that Jethro had. I think that it was looking for the same thing that we were trying to get."

"I never got a clear idea of what that was."

"That's understandable. After all, there were one hell of a lot of things about Jethro that we wanted to know and now aren't likely to find out. I mean, cold fusion? A fully self-aware and conscious computer? Combining the two? In an impenetrable sphere the size of a bowling ball? Jeezus-Key-Riste, Jimmy, this was Buck Rogers meets Flash Gordon. However, none of those things were the gold ring—the holy grail—the cherry on the sundae. It was something else. At least as far as the Sweatshop was concerned."

Doyle nodded. "Jethro could read minds."

"That's right, he could read minds. You can imagine how juiced up the folks at headquarters got over that. There is no limit—literally, *no limit*—to conducting espionage if we had the capability of reading minds."

"And no limit to the carnage if anyone else got their hands on that technology."

"Or if they were able to develop it themselves."

"Is there any evidence that they also have a computer that reads minds?" asked Doyle.

"One might imagine that a dark matter computer would be capable of that, but then again, maybe not. Telepathy might have nothing to do with raw computing power. It is just as likely that it is a talent—a gift."

"A gift from God?"

"Call it what you will. Let's just assume that the ability to read minds might be easier to steal than to create," said Bagsley. "That would explain why Adolph tried to hijack Jethro."

"We have been in a race."

"Just like the race between the Allies and the Nazis to build an atomic bomb."

"This might actually be worse than nuclear warfare."

"Not might be. It would be. Jacobsen's lab did a study on just that very thing. They estimated that fifty percent of humanity would immediately commit suicide if they knew their thoughts were being read by some evil supercomputer. The number goes up to ninety-nine point nine-nine percent if their thoughts were actually made public."

"Good God, I can't imagine—"

"You can't imagine your private thoughts, your fantasies, and your dreams being posted on Facebook?"

"You mean DataGhad."

"Whatever."

"Of the remaining one-hundredth of a percent of humans left on the earth—that's about eight hundred thousand—they estimated that only a small part, about one percent of that number—eight thousand—would not kill themselves because they were so abnormally innocent that they had nothing to hide. Nearly all those folks would be religious hermits or maybe cloistered away in some mountain monastery."

"What about children?"

"The prediction is that parents would kill their own children."

"I can't imagine that."

"Can you imagine allowing your child to live in a hell on earth?"

"I'd rather not think about it."

"Let's not. In any event, the study estimates that the larger number of survivors wouldn't kill themselves simply because they are shameless degenerates and don't care if anyone could see into their filthy minds."

"A world of Buddhist monks, Catholic nuns, homicidal

psychopaths, and porn stars."

"Light on the monks and nuns, heavy on the psychopaths and porn stars."

"Okay, Doug, thanks for the cheery news. I need to get ready for my trip to Vegas."

Bagsley departed the room and Doyle lifted himself out of the hospital bed and began to dress. Twenty minutes later, he left the infirmary, managed to locate an exit by dead reckoning, and crossed the castle grounds. He went to his assigned guestroom, packed his travel bags, and then headed for the reception area where he had first entered Babylon nearly a week before. He dropped off his room key at the now unattended concierge desk and exited the front entrance. A young woman sat in an idling indigo blue golf cart and greeted him as he walked out the door.

"You're my ride to the gate?"

She nodded in the affirmative and he took the passenger seat. Ten minutes later, Doyle arrived at the front gate just as a silver sedan pulled up. An older man with a rumpled tweed jacket exited the driver's seat to assist his passenger.

"You're Uber?"

"Actually, I'm Derrick…Derrick Ghent, but I drive for Uber."

"Sorry." There was something strangely familiar about the driver, but Doyle could not place him. He suddenly realized that the silent internal data feed was not working. He knew nothing of this man other than what was plainly apparent to any observer. *Maybe that concussion did more damage than I thought.*

"No worries. You're a Millennial. It's to be expected."

"Excuse me? Sorry, my mind was wandering."

"Woolgathering?"

"I'm pretty sure that the term 'woolgathering' is not in the Millennial dictionary. Besides, even though technically a Millennial, I've always thought of myself having more of a Gen Z attitude." The driver closed the door for his passenger, circled behind the vehicle, eased himself into the front seat, and initiated the engine with a push of the start button. "Thanks for helping me get in," said Doyle.

"You're welcome. Are you heading to a hospital? Our app usually indicates a destination, but for some reason it's not coming up on my screen." Derrick Ghent turned back to take another look at his passenger. "Maybe you should have put in a call for an ambulance."

"No, to the airport."

"Which airport?"

"Eau Claire, I believe."

"I hope that you're flying to the Mayo Clinic. Actually, Rochester is almost driving distance from here. It's a bit of a hike, but I could take you there myself. It'll be faster than going all the way up to Eau Claire."

"I'm heading to Las Vegas."

"Oh, I see. Out of the frying pan, into the fire," said Ghent as he swiveled the car out of the entrance and began piloting down the narrow country road.

"Yes, something like that. I'm relying on dumb luck to keep me out of trouble."

"Relying on dumb luck is, by definition, dumb."

"I suppose it sounds more sophisticated if I say that I am placing myself into the hands of providence."

"In that case, you're putting an awfully big demand upon the Almighty."

"You think that I'm asking for too much?"

"That's between you and him."

"That's what my father used to tell me."

"Your father was a man of faith?"

"My father was an electrician by trade but a preacher by avocation."

"Given that all things electrical operate on mysterious principles that I find to be miraculous, I think there is only a slim distinction between the two. What about you?"

"I'm no electrician."

"Something tells me that you're also not a preacher."

"What gave it away?" Doyle asked facetiously.

"It looks like you've been spending less time giving sermons in a church pulpit and more time swinging your fists in a barroom brawl."

"I suppose that, once again, I fail to measure up to my father, the man of faith."

"No, you have faith, whether you realize it or not."

"Perhaps a little faith, but I prefer facts."

"Just like the George Michael song, you gotta have faith. I don't recall a hit single that says you gotta have facts."

"I can test my facts."

"I can test my faith."

"Really, how?"

"By living. My faith is tested every walking step, every drawn breath, every living day, every waking minute."

"I suppose what I meant was, how do you confirm, validate, prove your faith? How do you know when you have achieved faith?"

"Every morning when I open my front door at home and see the mountain range in the distance. It is a beautiful view. I command a mountain to jump."

"I had a friend who mentioned that recently."

"He was giving you good advice."

"And a lot more than that…" Doyle trailed off in thought that qualified as mourning—at least, as much as he was capable of mourning. "Do you focus your attention on one mountain in particular, or on any mountain that happened to be in the mood to listen to you?"

"I have my favorite: Banshee Mountain."

"Banshee Mountain?"

"It's on the eastern edge of Tennessee, in the Unaka Range."

"Unaka?"

"Right next to the Smokies."

"Tennessee is a long way from here."

"Like the Beach Boys, I get around."

"So, you actually command a mountain to jump?"

"Just as our Lord encouraged us. Yes, every morning."

"How long have you been doing that?"

"Forty years."

"Does the mountain jump?"

"Not yet."

"When do you expect that it will start jumping for you?"

"I expect it every morning. That's faith. For some inexplicable reason the mountain has not cooperated, but that is the mountain's problem. I will continue to give the mountain the command to jump and sooner or later the mountain will see the light."

"When will that happen?"

"I can't say for certain, but rest assured, you'll hear about it in the news."

"Sounds like wishful thinking."

"Wishful thinking is waiting for a miracle of my own choosing. Hope, on the other hand, is faithfully abiding while God dispenses miracles of *his* choosing."

"So, you'll keep waiting for your miracle."

"No, it's not my miracle. God told me that a mountain would jump, which means it's not my miracle, but his."

"I've never been willing or able to believe in such things."

"Faith is not merely belief, it is certainty. True faith dispels all doubt. If you tell yourself that you believe in something that seems absurd, then you do not have faith, because having faith banishes the notion that the matter is absurd."

"So, the more absurd, the more faith."

"The more faith, the less it becomes absurd."

"In that case, belief in elves and fairies is legitimate."

"Have you ever seen an elf or a fairy?"

"No."

"Then you do not have faith that they exist. If you had faith, then you would see them."

"I might see them if I hallucinated. Is faith a form of mental illness?"

"Faith is a mental wellness that cures you of doubt."

Doyle tapped on his cellphone to check flights departing Eau Claire as well as those from Minneapolis and Rochester. After scrolling down through the schedules, Doyle nodded to himself and decided that Bagsley had made the right call. He looked back up and saw a billboard on the left side of the road.

How Will You Measure Up?

It's time for you to join

The Great Conversion

We're ready, are you?

For the next hour, they aimlessly discussed the news, politics, professional sports and the weather. From time to time, their conversation was punctuated by lapses into silence, during which Doyle brooded over the events of the past few days and his hazy plan for that evening. Just as he broke through the surface of musing and emerged into the present, Ghent would reengage, giving Doyle the distinct impression that his driver was privy to his silent mental conversation and waited patiently and politely for an ebb in his internal dialogue. Doyle could not shake the feeling that he had met this driver before, but his memory yielded but a dim and fog-shrouded outline, as if he had met the man only briefly, perhaps in a darkened bar, a long time ago in a place very far away.

Upon arrival at the airport, Doyle exited the cab, took his bag from the trunk, and then walked up to the driver's door. He pulled out his cellphone, tapped on the Uber app, and added a tip from the agency card account that he suspected was not authorized by any applicable regulations. The driver nodded in appreciation and said, "I usually wish my riders good luck and a blessed day before they take a flight, but for you…"

"Yes?"

"Knock 'em dead," said Derrick Ghent with a smile and then drove off.

⌘

Detective Tavera swiveled around from the terminal to face Officer Vasquez who walked up to the desk. "I made a few calls about our newest hotel guests," offered Vasquez.

"Bucking to get into the detective program again?"

"Third try is the charm."

"What did you find during your unauthorized intrusion into my case?" asked Tavera.

"Story checks out. They left a couple of telephone message for the church to warn them about the fire."

"Threat?"

"Nope. There was a fire."

"Extortion?"

"Not a chance. No demands for anything."

"Fine, then we charge it as a hoax."

"What hoax? The fire department showed up just as a fire was breaking out for Krissake!"

"Maybe they were part of the scheme. Their calls to other churches were probably a publicity ruse."

"Maybe, but I doubt it. I also called a reference out in Missouri. Zimmerman gave me the lead. She says that the guys are legit."

"Credible character witness?"

"Zimmerman's aunt."

"Since when is any relative of Zimmerman considered a credible witness?" Tavera casually jeered.

"You got me there," admitted Vasquez with a chuckle. "I guess that's why you're a detective and I'm still on the beat."

"I dunno, this just doesn't jibe with reality." Tavera's eyes darted to his computer as an incoming priority message notification appeared on the screen. "Just a sec," he said to the officer standing in front of his desk. The detective clicked the notification box and read the message. He looked back up and said, "Try this out for an additional dose of the surreal. A message just came in from the National Security Exchange."

"Since when do they send messages to us?"

"Since now. They're exercising jurisdiction."

"Over what?"

"They're sending someone over to pick up the bar mitzvah brothers."

Vasquez decided to let the slight pass. "Who are *they* and who is the *someone*?"

"They don't identify themselves except by an agency identity code number."

"Isn't there a key to the code number?"

"Lemme check." Tavera went to the department shared drive and located the file listing all investigative and security agencies at the federal and state levels. He scanned the document until he arrived at the number he was seeking. He then shook his head and uttered a whispered oath. "The number is on the list, all right."

"What does it say?"

"Reference Removed—Top Secret, ECI."

"What the hell does that mean?"

"It means we aren't supposed to ask any questions. Too much James Bond for my taste," grumbled the detective.

"So, hands off?" asked Vasquez.

"No, maybe not. Two bozos from out of town just magically appear and miraculously intervene to save a church from a fire. Now the feds want to take them away. I'm not buyin' any of this." Tavera reflected for a moment and then asked, "Where are they?"

"Interrogation Three."

"What are they doing there? Has anyone been questioning them?"

"No, they were originally put in Holding Two with Timmy."

"Timmy? You mean that crazy flake kid we can't seem to get rid of?"

"The same. Anyway, there was an incident in Holding One—"

"Incident?"

"A drunk tossed his lunch all over the place. We had to move everyone to Holding Two."

"And that got filled to capacity."

"Right. Since these two jokers seemed to be the most respectable of the bunch, it made sense to put them in the interrogation room."

"Okay, good move. Let me give this a try," said Tavera as he picked up the booking file, stood up from his desk, and headed down the hall to Interrogation Room Number Three. He entered the room, sat down without introducing himself, and began taking notes on a small pad of paper he had taken into the room with him. Still taking notes, and without looking up, he asked, "How did you know that the Lutheran church was going to be burned?"

"We have our sources."

"Name one."

"God."

Tavera did not skip a beat. "Name another."

"Isn't God a reliable source?"

"Yeah, but I can't serve a warrant on him."

"Sir, it appears that we hit a stateside target."

"*Good day*, Jeremy. *So nice of you* to come visit me," replied the Director, demonstrating a synthetic forbearance as the subordinate barged into the office uninvited and unannounced.

"Sorry, sir. I just got back from Budapest."

"Yes, I see you didn't dawdle there to enjoy the beer and goulash."

"I would have been here yesterday afternoon, but the pilot had to land in the Azores—some issue with the electronics."

"And here you are, safe and sound."

"Sir, there was a problem."

"Jeremy, today was specifically scheduled for problems, it would seem. Our secured cellphone network crashed last night and today there isn't a single functioning SEC-CEL as we speak. I can't imagine that your problem could possibly be as serious as loosing personal contact with every freestanding operative on the planet."

"Sorry, sir, I didn't realize—"

"We'll handle it somehow. Now, what is your earth-shaking disaster?"

"The Air Force program—"

"You know, Jeremy," the Director interrupted, "our new undertaking really needs a better name than 'the Air Force Program.' Wouldn't you agree?"

"Yes, sir, but—"

"I'll leave it to you to come up with something clever and edgy."

"Yes, sir, but the Air Force...I mean, our new project...made a strike against a target here in the United States. The return message indicated that the site was neutralized and data extracted."

"Did it?"

"Yes, sir. That wasn't supposed to happen."

"Jeremy, one doesn't need to be a guru on top of a mountain to observe that everything happens for a purpose. Relax. There was no mistake."

"Sir?"

"The program test was targeted on a verified domestic terrorist cell. It was a flawless operation, Jeremy. Your efforts have been a great success and a great leap forward."

"It was a terrorist cell?"

"Indeed."

"No one told me."

"No, and we will never speak of it again. What you did was remarkable, but we are still in the formative stages. All of this needs to be a tightly guarded secret."

"Yes, sir."

"You are familiar with the taxonomy of classified matters?"

"Yessir. I don't think I would have been hired if I didn't know at least that."

"Certainly. Here's a *Jeopardy!* pop quiz. What is the highest possible classification of information?"

"Top Secret, ECI."

"Very good, Exceptionally Controlled Information."

"Although it could be a toss-up with Top Secret-GAMMA."

"You're right, that is a close race. So, let's assume that you and I have just established our own new level of classification. We'll call it Top Secret-Doesn't Exist."

"You are kidding, sir?"

"Perhaps a little bit, but the basic premise is deadly serious. Write up a generic after-action report, but don't include any of the interesting twists that occurred. Just indicate that a perfectly routine and boring test occurred and that the most exciting part of the trip was the bowl of spicy goulash that you ordered at a local restaurant that night."

"Yes sir."

"Until we get our funding from Congress, not a soul in the known galaxy—other than you or me—will know about this."

"There's Agent Fremont."

"Ah yes, I need to return an email to a certain irate mission chief who has sent me a blistering complaint about staging a hit on a domestic location."

"You already knew all about this, sir?"

"I'm the Director. It's my job to know."

"Agent Fremont was more than irate. I had the feeling that he would have pulled a gun on me if he had the chance."

"Baptism by fire, and so soon in your career. I'm very pleased."

"Thank you, sir." Kearn hesitated for a moment as he tried to sort out the situation in his already overtaxed mind. "There's also the Air Force Team that programed the device."

"Already taken care of. I just need to know that I can depend on you not to even mutter about this in your sleep."

"You have my word, sir."

"I have more than that."

Kearn did not know how to interpret the Director's last statement but decided that prudence dictated that he let it pass. The Director got out of his chair, came around the desk, and took Kearn gently by the arm as he guided him to the door. "Put it out of your mind."

"Yes, sir. Will do."

"And don't forget about giving our project a new name. Consider it a chance to write your own page of ORCA history."

"Well, sir, with a stamp of Top Secret-Doesn't Exist, I doubt anyone will be allowed to read that history book."

The Director responded with a genuine laugh. "Jeremy, you go ahead and start writing it and I'll worry about getting the history book published."

"Yes, sir, you can depend on me."

The Director smiled serenely. "Thank you, Jeremy. I think this is the beginning of a beautiful friendship."

⌘

The man walked into the central receiving room wearing a dark gray wool suit, black tie and wayfarer glasses. Vasquez looked the man over slowly, resisting the temptation to offer the visitor directions to a Hollywood central casting department. He had just returned from a three-day suspension caused by his overactive and uncontrollable mouth. This time he would restrain himself.

"May I help you...sir?"

"The Station Chief is here?" The voice that came from the man was almost disembodied. It gave Vasquez a serious case of the creeps. Although he had never before seen anything that could be classified as demonic, he had always been sure that if such an apparition appeared before him, he would know it when he saw it. Vasquez saw it and knew it. *Just my luck to get front desk duty today*, his interior voice groused.

"Can you please state your business with her?"

The Gray man pulled a thin leather wallet from his jacket and produced federal identification the likes of which Vasquez had never seen. He was pretty sure the creds were authentic, but as for the character who was carrying them...well, that would be the old lady's problem. The unwelcome visitor stared, silently waiting. Vasquez had no doubt that the man would stand patiently in that spot for the next ten thousand years, gradually disintegrating into dust, before he could be deterred from seeing the Chief. Vasquez looked over the identification cards again. The Gray man would not need to wait ten thousand years, or ten minutes for that matter. *Whoever this guy is*, Vasquez thought, *he's not someone to jerk around.*

Vasquez had been taught back in his days as a rookie how to deal with people who scared him. He recalled a blistering hot day in July during his first month on the force. His mentor and partner, Danny Joellner, drove the cruiser out to the National Cemetery in West Los Angeles. The older man pulled two Coca-Colas out of a small cooler in the trunk, popped the tops, and handed a bottle to Vasquez. Vasquez kept abreast as Joellner wandered a desultory and seemingly indiscriminate path. His partner stopped at a headstone of pink granite and silently regarded it. "Vince was a good man," he said, nodding a greeting to the stone bearing the name of Vincent Frayme. "He was a vet, had a beautiful family, active in his church and boy scouts," said Joellner as he shook his head ruefully, "but he didn't have a sixth sense." Joellner's sad eyes examined the face of his young charge. Vasquez had seen these eyes before, when he was a young boy, visiting the San Diego Zoo with his father. The eyes had belonged to an ancient, ragged grizzly bear. Vasquez could not escape those eyes that afternoon or escape from their memory for the two decades to come. He looked into those same, sad, imprisoned grizzly bear eyes now. "If anything ever scares the hell out of you, then you get the hell out of there."

Vasquez was incredulous. "You don't really mean I should run away?"

"I do really mean it."

"But we see frightening things all the time."

"Sure we do. I didn't say to run away from something dangerous. I didn't tell you to run away from something frightening. I said to get the hell out of there when something *scares you.*"

"What's the difference?"

"You'll learn. You'll *know.*"

Vasquez returned from his dalliance with memory and addressed the taciturn visitor, "Follow me…sir." Vasquez raised himself from his metal chair and circled the cluttered desk. They threaded through the labyrinth of cubicles and filing cabinets until they arrived at the office door his team chief, Doris Defoe. Vasquez tapped on the plate glass door.

"C'mon in," Defoe's booming alto passed through the glass as readily as light.

Vasquez entered with the Gray man. "Special Agent…"

Vasquez looked back at the IDs in his hand, "…Graucus to see you, ma'am." Defoe finished pulling a file from her office cabinet and turned to survey the visitor. She did not like what she saw. *My day has just been screwed*, she thought. Vasquez handed the credentials to Defoe. "I've got to get back to my desk, Chief."

"There's no rush."

Vasquez could tell that she was trying to sound casual. Defoe was scared too. She needed a backup. The sad grizzly bear eyes of Danny Joellner came again to memory. *Run away*, they said. *Get the hell outta here.* Vasquez briefly pressed his eyes closed and shook the image out of his mind. *Not this time, Danny.* "Okay, sure," he said, reopening his eyes and casting a look that communicated to his boss that he would not leave her in the lurch. "Coffee?" he asked, turning to spread the inquiry to include the visitor.

"Great," answered Defoe.

"That will not be necessary," responded Graucus, in a tone that gave Vasquez the impression that the offer had been dismissed not only for the uninvited guest, but for the Chief also.

Vasquez walked down the corridor to get the coffee as Defoe examined the identification cards.

"What can I do for you, Agent Graucus?" she said, handing back the credentials. Defoe made no attempt to offer a fake a smile of official courtesy.

"I have come to take custody of two suspects." He reached into his suit coat and extracted an envelope bearing a Department of Defense shield printed on the upper left corner. "You will find the necessary authorizations to transfer custody and jurisdiction."

Defoe accepted the envelope, opened it, and quickly examined the materials. The last was a court order signed by a federal magistrate. Vasquez returned with two mugs of coffee. He handed one to Defoe and faded to the back wall of the office. Defoe returned her attention to the documents, leafing through and carefully examining each. "We will need to pass this through the D.A.'s office," she said, now looking up from the papers.

"Naturally."

"It may take some time."

"I am a patient man."

"Where can I contact you in the meantime?"

"Right here. I will wait."

"It might take until tomorrow."

"I will wait."

Defoe and Vasquez exchanged a look that the visitor took no pains to observe. "Very well," Defoe almost sighed, "let me check on their status." Defoe began to exit the office.

"I'll go with you," Vasquez volunteered.

As they walked down the hallway, Defoe spoke in an uncharacteristically hushed voice, "Thanks, Tony."

"My pleasure."

"Liar."

"Yeah," he said, reflexively glancing over his shoulder, "let's get him out of here."

"Fast as I can," said Defoe under her breath. "Who has the file on these guys?"

"Tavera, but he was just called out on an emergency. I assume Wannamaker has the file now."

"Let me guess. The high school put Tavera's daughter on suspension again."

"Actually, this time she was expelled."

"What did she do?"

"She was caught drinking in the gym locker room."

"That's enough to get expelled?"

"Apparently, she was also giving out shots of *Jägermeister* to the school's football team."

"Oh."

They continued down the corridor until they reached Bill Wannamaker's office. Defoe popped her head into the door. "We have somebody here to pick up the rabbi twins."

"They're gone."

"What?"

"I had a call from the D.A.'s office to cut them loose."

"Who called you?"

"The man himself."

"Since when does Cuelpo call to spring a couple of nobodies?"

"He said they were a couple of somebodies."

"That is supposed to come from me."

He shrugged. "True, but what the man wants, the man gets."

"Did you confirm?"

"I didn't have to. Just as the call came in, an Assistant D.A.

showed up. He was a young guy, Angelo, with a weird last name…something like Circumspector. You can check the sign-in roster. Anyway, he left with Laurel and Hardy twenty minutes ago."

Defoe turned to Vasquez and posed a question that she was clearly asking to herself. "Who are those guys?" They returned to the office where Graucus waited, taking no pains to make it a direct route. Defoe deposited the now tepid cup of untouched coffee on her desk, sat down, and leveled a mirrored fixed stare back at the equally fixed stare emanating from the sunglasses of Agent Graucus. "I'm sorry, but you've come too late."

Graucus received the news calmly and in silence. Defoe imagined that if this man had just been told that his mother had been captured by irate Jehovah's Witnesses and subsequently burned at the stake, roasted on a pyre of back issues of *Watchtower* and *Awake!* that it would register not the faintest facial tic on the part of Special Agent Graucus. *For that matter*, she pondered, *maybe Graucus' mother actually had been burned at the stake.*

"You have released the prisoners," Graucus said at last. It was a statement and a reproof.

"Detainees," corrected Chief Defoe.

"By whose authority?"

"The District Attorney."

"I wish to speak with him."

"Fine. You go up South Central and take a left on East Washington. Officer Vasquez can give you the address."

Graucus did not move. "Your telephone is functional."

This time, Defoe really could not tell whether the visitor had made a question or a statement. The one thing she was sure about was that she did not have to tolerate this. "Yeah, so is your cell."

True to form, Graucus did not react to Dafoe's response. "I will use your telephone." Another statement. Graucus stood, and as Defoe sat in her swivel chair, she could not resist the feeling that he was hanging over her like…a vulture. He reached over for the telephone, scanned down the touchpad, and pushed the speed autodial button for the D.A.'s office.

"Agent Graucus," Vasquez interjected, "you may have some difficulty in contacting the District Attorney." Graucus rewarded this helpful advice with a fixed state through the wayfarers and Vasquez receded to the back of the office.

After less than three minutes on the phone, Defoe and Vasquez could tell that Graucus had cut a clear swath through the D.A.'s bureaucratic shield and had succeeded in reaching the city's senior prosecuting official. At the conclusion of the call, Graucus placed the telephone receiver back into its cradle. "Your Mister Cuelpo states that he has never heard of Moses and Aaron Levi. Neither he nor any member of his staff authorized their release."

Vasquez and Defoe looked at one another in disbelief. "Sheeee-hit."

"How long until we touch down in Las Vegas?" asked Watt as the aircraft taxied towards the runway.

"About an hour and fifteen minutes."

"Good. When we arrive, I need track down a priest for confession."

"I thought that you told me that you weren't Catholic."

"I told you that my grandfather was Serbian Orthodox and that I was not nearly so Serbian or Orthodox. Just the same, I was baptized as a child into the faith, and yes, we have priests, and yes, we have confession."

"What caused your sudden burning desire to go into the confessional booth?"

"The desire not to burn. I just might have told a little white lie to Mister Desausau back in Wyoming."

"There's a Serbian Orthodox Church in Las Vegas?"

"Yes. As a matter of fact, I read somewhere that Las Vegas has more churches per capita than anywhere else in the country."

"You're putting me on."

"That was my recollection, but don't hold me to it. I don't want to rack up another little lie on my record."

"I suppose I could check that statistic out on the web. Maybe it's all the wedding chapels."

"Could be."

"I would imagine that makes Las Vegas the happy hunting ground for our arsonist. More choices for desecration."

"Think so?"

Watt had asked in a way that Gaude knew it was not so much a question, or polite conversation, as an opportunity for Socratic instruction. Gaude paused and thought. "No. No, not here. It really wouldn't be a desecration here, would it? The desecration happened long ago." He then inwardly shrugged and asked, "Are you sure we will have enough time to stop for your confession?"

Watt cocked an eyebrow. "Well, I don't have *that* many sins to confess."

"Maybe it will turn out that the Serbian Orthodox Church is the one being targeted by our pyromaniac friend."

"It could be," agreed Watt. "Angelo wasn't all that specific about what we might find in Sin City."

"Other than sin."

"Yes, other than that."

"And yet we are heading to Las Vegas, solely because he told us to do so."

Watt responded with a genial smile. "But if you carefully obey his voice and do all that I say, then I will be an enemy to your enemies and an adversary to your adversaries."

"I suspect that you are quoting from...Proverbs?"

"Exodus."

"I don't understand why he would send us on this detour."

"Our client is fond of detours—particularly those involving wandering through a desert."

"A brief detour?" asked Gaude.

"Perhaps, as God wills it. *Inshallah*."

"The clues we found in Zanzibar all pointed to Los Angeles. I don't recall any clues pointing to Las Vegas."

"You don't need clues to tell you that evil lurks in Las Vegas," responded Watt.

"You still haven't told me anything about that Angelo guy."

"An old friend of mine."

"Yes, you said that, but it doesn't tell me who he is."

"An alumnus of the Cairo Investigative Agency."

"They seem to pop up at convenient times."

"Of course. Why would I need their help at inconvenient times?"

An hour later, the plane made contact with the tarmac. Upon arriving at the gate, the passengers quickly deboarded the small aircraft and headed for the main terminal. Gaude and Watt passed through a gauntlet of casino advertisements on their way to the baggage claim area. Just as they approached carousel three, the terminal public address system announced overhead:

Message for Mister Gaude…Mister Daniel Gaude.

Please come to the information booth at Concourse D.

Mister Gaude…Information booth at Concourse D.

"That's him, isn't it?"

"I suspect so."

"Why didn't he just send another snapchat?" asked Gaude rhetorically.

"You're asking why a criminal who is getting his jollies playing cat and mouse with us across the entire expanse of North America would be tempted to indulge in cheap dramatics?"

After retrieving their luggage, the partners followed the indicator signs that directed them to the airport information counter. Gaude stepped forward. "Message for Daniel Gaude?"

The receptionist reached over to a cubbyhole, withdrew an envelope, and delivered it to Gaude. He immediately opened the envelope and found a note accompanying a car key and a parking stub.

Dan,

Don't bother looking for Aladdin to pick you up in his obsolescent taxi. He is busy planting rose bushes for another one of his cousins. No need to stand in line for a rental car. Come visit me for a little chat and an opportunity to appreciate a much better view.

I suppose you may take along your sidekick if absolutely necessary.

Gaude then handed the note to his partner.

"Aladdin. I have to admit, that's a good nickname," said Watt.

"We'll mention it to Sinbad when we see him next," agreed Gaude.

"This might mean that our sojourn here at Las Vegas will take a bit little longer than expected."

"Hopefully, not forty years," quipped Gaude. He then frowned in thought and said, "Something tells me that there won't be a burning church here."

"What makes you think that?"

"Call it a hunch."

"I'd rather assume that it is divine inspiration."

"Call it what you will," replied Gaude with a shrug. "Just the same, it looks as if there has been a change in the game."

"That happens sometimes, whether we like it or not."

"When do we ever like it?"

"He's getting cocky," said Watt introspectively.

"It seems that he wants to meet us," replied Gaude.

"Or confront us."

"Or recruit us."

"Or kill us."

"These are really great choices," said Gaude wryly. The partners paused together in thought. Gaude finally broke the silence. "We've been chasing him this far, so it would be pretty stupid to run away from him now."

"Might be the smartest thing we ever did."

Gaude looked sharply at his companion with a look of dismay tinged with contempt. "If I recall correctly," Gaude said with mild scorn, "you are the one that has been obsessed with catching this guy."

"I wouldn't call it an obsession."

"What would you call it?"

"A vocation."

"Let's go find the car."

"You don't think it might have a bomb in it...or the brake lines cut?"

"You've been watching too many movies."

"I just hope that our opponent hasn't been watching those same movies," replied Watt. "Where is the car?"

"The parking slip says lot D, space thirty-seven." Gaude and Watt exited the airport terminal and followed the signs to the parking area. "I'm not sure what we're supposed to do once we locate the car, said Gaude. "He hasn't provided any clue as to where to go from here."

"There will be another clue. There always has been and there always will."

"World without end."

"Amen."

Gaude chose to nod as the better alternative to shrugging and then followed Watt into the parking lot. Five minutes later, they located a mint condition 1967 Chevrolet Impala convertible.

"Our host has impeccable taste," commented Gaude.

"You're talking about someone who burns churches."

"Which, admittedly, is difficult to reconcile. On the other hand, Hitler painted watercolors that some people find to be quite charming." Gaude inserted the key in the driver's side door and opened it. "Okay, so far, so good. A bomb hasn't gone off."

"We haven't gotten into the car yet."

"What happened to Bill Watt, that cheerful optimist?"

"You don't know him like I do."

"Which 'him' are you referring to? Our arsonist opponent or Bill Watt in the third person?"

"You don't know either of us."

"Apparently, I don't know you like he does."

"What's that supposed to mean?"

"I'm not sure. It just came out that way."

Watt sat down on the passenger side and opened the glove compartment. He found a thin plastic document protector and passed it to Gaude who opened it and found an operator's manual and emergency information. Gaude flipped to the next pocket and found two playing cards inserted behind the plastic flap that held the instructions for deploying warning triangles and changing flat tires. The cards were the ace of spades and the king of clubs. He handed the cards to Watt. "I guess you were right. He must enjoy the chase. Pretty hard to miss this one."

"A card game?" asked Watt. "Poker?"

"No, blackjack."

"Blackjack?"

"Right, or twenty-one...but *which* blackjack or twenty-one?"

"Perhaps the name of a club or restaurant?"

"Yeah, a club sounds about right. That would account for the choice of the king of clubs."

"Of course."

"So, today our quarry is dropping obvious clues."

"Blackjack is not exactly an obvious clue to some of us," said

Watt.

"Whether obvious or not, it doesn't help much when standing in the middle the largest collection of blackjack games on the planet."

"He's in his element here."

"I'll make that a working assumption."

"That might be when he is most dangerous."

"I'll make that another working assumption."

Watt replied with a look of humorless determination. "Let's go."

"Where?"

"Into Las Vegas."

"We're just going to wander around looking for someplace called Blackjack Studio or Club 21?"

"Not a bad idea."

"No, it's not a bad idea. It's an absolutely ridiculous idea."

"I assume you have a better plan?"

"No, but I'll start working on it," Gaude said, pulling out his cellphone.

"I was afraid of that. While you are wandering through cyber confusion, I'll start driving into the well of depravity."

"Sounds like a deal. I'll hold the frying pan while you steer us into the fire."

Watt responded with a guttural *hrrumph* that conceded the truth of Gaude's statement. The partners exited the car and exchanged seats. Gaude started tapping and navigating through the internet as Watt engaged in his own navigation through the parking garage. He turned right at the garage exit and approached the feeder road. Suddenly, the car came to a screeching halt.

"What the f—"

"Dan!" shouted Watt, interrupting his partner's expletive.

"What?"

"That!" Watt gestured ahead of them. Gaude looked up through the windshield and saw a giant billboard. "It's the same girl you saw in the Saint Louis airport," Watt exclaimed. Gaude stared in stunned silence. Watt looked over and waited patiently for some comment. Finally, he asked, "Does she remind you of someone?"

"More than you'll ever know."

"I must say, she is attractive."

"Hey, don't go there."

"Dan...*look*."

131

"Enough already."

"No, Dan, look at the name of the casino." Gaude pulled his gaze away from the playful sneer of his sister and now shifted his view to the left of the billboard which featured the casino name and logo:

The Four Horsemen

"New York," said Gaude. "Those bars near the churches."

"Right."

"This is more than a coincidence...and don't say that there are no coincidences."

"I thought you were the one who said that."

"I lost track of who said it last."

"I hope that you don't expect me to keep score."

"I was under the impression that keeping score was your job," said Gaude. Bill Watt pretended momentary deafness as Gaude reached for his cellphone.

"What are you doing?" asked Watt.

"I'm going to locate The Four Horsemen Casino."

"Don't bother." Watt pointed through the windshield at an ominous tower of matte black in the distance. "That's it."

"How do you know?"

"I know," responded Watt as he turned to his partner, "and so do you."

Watt drove towards the tower relying upon simple dead reckoning on the inescapable landmark. They arrived fifteen minutes later and entered the casino garage that comprised the first twenty meters of the edifice. Watt found a parking spot on the third level and squeezed the Impala between two black Ford Explorers. Upon exiting the vehicle, Watt located an elevator and pressed the call button. The doors opened, revealing an interior that matched the building's exterior.

"This looks mighty dismal."

"Yes, it serves as a word to the wise. Run away."

"We're obviously not very wise."

"It took you this long to figure that out?"

They discovered that the elevator did not actually elevate them, but rather was constrained to lower them to the ground level. As the elevator doors opened, Gaude and Watt saw a gigantic golden escalator ascending into the far reaches.

"Looks like they tried to build a stairway to heaven," quipped Gaude.

"You'd have to take that up with Led Zeppelin," said Watt with a grin.

"You're a Zeppelin fan?"

"Actually, I'm more of a Grateful Dead groupie."

"You're a Deadhead?"

"In more ways than you can imagine." Watt gazed up and added, "In any event, I'm pretty sure that your Sister Frances Angela would not confuse this place for heaven. Besides, listen to the music coming through the speakers. That's definitely not Led Zeppelin."

Gaude hadn't noticed, but a recording of 'The Gambler' by Kenny Rogers was greeting the new arrivals as they ascended into the maw of chance. He smiled and nodded in silent agreement as they walked to the gilded conveyance and were gently lifted to the main floor of the casino. As the partners stepped off the tread and into the arena of gaming, they were surrounded by a disorienting tempest of flashing lights and a bewildering cacophony of bells, chimes and buzzers. "I'm not sure where to begin," said Gaude.

"Begin at the beginning," said Watt with a straight face, "and go on till you come to the end: then stop."

"Cute," muttered Gaude. "The clue to our destination is blackjack. I suppose that we need to find the blackjack tables." He scanned across the tangle of slot machines, roulette tables, poker stations, and a variety of other peculiar gambling devices that he neither recognized nor could proffer a guess as to their identity or function. On his third pass across the room, he spotted an information kiosk. Gaude gestured and nodded to his partner. They wended though the clusters of machines and gamblers and arrived at the kiosk featuring the casino floorplan on an illuminated screen. Gaude examined the map, glanced up, rechecked the screen, and then pointed to the east. "That way."

They resumed their trek through the seemingly impenetrable thicket of gambling paraphernalia until reaching a raised dais circumscribed by a brass rail that encompassed the blackjack arena. More than a dozen tables were scattered about the oblong space, but Gaude immediately spotted one in particular. He passed through a gate and walked purposefully to the table nearest the back wall. Watt followed closely behind. As they approached the table, he recognized the young woman from the billboard advertisement. "It's you!" exclaimed Watt.

"Yes, it's me," the young woman replied with equal enthusiasm. "I've been *me* for quite some time—at least as long as I can remember."

Gaude hesitated, looked back and forth between the young woman and his partner, and finally announced, "Bill, this is my sister, Didi."

"Dorothy," the young woman corrected.

"I'm delighted to meet you, Dorothy," said Bill Watt with a sincere and gracious smile.

"You're going by Dorothy now?" asked Gaude.

"No, I'm still Didi, but you should at least introduce me properly when I meet someone for the first time. I'm no longer nine years old."

"What are you doing here?"

"Well, my genius brother, I'm dealing blackjack if you haven't been able to figure that out already."

"I thought that you were in Saint Louis."

"Whatever gave you that idea?"

"I saw you on a poster at the Saint Louis airport."

"Oh, that!" she laughed. "The syndicate used me for some ads and promos. Not a bad gig, it paid well. Those photos were put in advertisements from Maryland to Macao and everywhere in between."

"Why are you working in a casino?"

"Are you kidding? I majored in French Literature. What kind of a job was I supposed to get?"

"Teaching."

"Seriously? Spending all day with obnoxious fifteen-year-old kids? I'd rather deal with their obnoxious fifty-year-old fathers. At least they tip."

"And try to grope you."

"That's a problem only if the tips are small."

"That's a problem—period."

"So says my concerned big brother who I haven't seen in…how long has it been, now? It's been at least seven years since I saw you at Walter Reed, when the Army flew you back home after that emergency appendix operation."

"What are you talking about?" asked Gaude, genuinely disoriented.

"When they sent you down to the Middle of Nowhere, Guatemala, for some military counter-drug operation. Your appendix burst and the only doctor for a hundred miles—make that one hundred sixty kilometers—operated on you with a rusty spoon and a bottle of *Amargo Obrero*, although I'm not sure if that was for sterilizing or administered as a pain killer."

"*Amargo Obrero*?"

"South America's version of *Jägermeister*. Don't tell me you don't remember that."

Gaude frowned and shook his head. "No, not…" He then suddenly regained his composure. "Hey, you're changing the subject."

"The subject?"

"Getting groped by the creeps who come here to gamble."

"I can fend for myself. I always have. I'm already on track to make a six-figure income and we've been open for just a little more than six weeks."

"Money isn't everything."

"Thank you for the bumper-sticker philosophy lesson. Perhaps you could tell that to the bank that services my student loans."

"I thought that you were going back to school to become a commercial artist."

"Art schools have this strange tradition of expecting students to pay tuition. In most cases, that involves money, something I did not have until I took this job."

"I thought you weren't the type to compromise."

"You're one to talk. What about turning your back on music?"

"What music?"

"Yeah, right, what music?" she responded sarcastically.

"How did you wind up here?"

"I did those summer gigs as a croupier at the National Harbor, remember? A few months ago, my friend Jeanine texted me and said that there would be some plum openings here. She was right."

"But…Las Vegas?"

"Hey, this is not just Las Vegas. We're talking about The Four Horsemen. This is, quite literally, the biggest thing to come to Sin City, since, well, since Bugsy Siegel. This place has one hundred and fifty-one floors, not counting the mezzanine, and is by far the tallest hotel in the world and almost has the record as being the tallest building. It's only a little bit shorter than the Jeddah Tower in Saudi Arabia. The rumor is that we could have snatched the record, but the Saudis slipped a few million to the syndicate that was financing this, and that's business as usual in this town."

"Did you say one hundred and fifty-one floors?"

"That's right. It's one hell of a view from the top. Actually, the observation deck is one floor down from the highest floor. Level one-fifty-one is where the high-roller penthouse suites are located."

Gaude looked over to Watt. "Bacardi."

"Bacardi?"

"Remember Gregory Kim, the bartender at McSorleys?"

"Right, that Four Horsemen drink," confirmed Watt. "I remember, Bacardi 151. That's got to be it."

Gaude turned back to his sister. "Are there any restrictions to gaining access to the penthouse floors?"

"Naturally. Do you think that the high-roller swells are going to tolerate rubbing elbows with the hoi-polloi? There are also the security issues. The marks up there are loaded."

"Can you get us up to the top floor?"

Didi looked at her brother suspiciously. "Why do you need to go up there?"

"We're tracking someone."

"I won't be on a break for another twenty minutes."

"We'll wait."

"You could play a few hands. Business is pretty light right now."

"You always beat me at cards when we were kids."

"You weren't a kid when I was a kid, and I think you played

'Go Fish' with me a total of once in my entire life."

"And you beat me."

"No, I didn't. Some big brother, not letting his baby sister win a silly children's card game. I cried all that night."

"You could have played cards with Mark."

"Mark was even worse. He may have been your little brother, but he was my big bully. He was born a Jarhead. I wonder if the Marine Corps even bothered sending him to boot camp. There wasn't anything they could have taught him about brutality that he didn't already know—and already practiced on me."

"I'm sorry if you were traumatized."

"No, you're not."

"You're right, I'm not."

"That's okay, I forgive you anyway. My spiritual guide says that harboring negative resentments from the past interferes with our genetic upgrading."

"What?"

"Sit down and play a hand. My pit boss is looking at us."

"Aren't there rules that prohibit relatives from playing at your table?"

"Sure, but they don't know who you are."

"Why do you say that?"

"Because the casino invested millions in facial recognition software from DataGhad and cameras are everywhere. The AI even has pattern recognition features to tell if anyone is related, although perhaps it might be fooled by my blue-eyed brother."

"Yes," spoke up Bill Watt, "I noticed that you didn't share that trait, although I can't imagine that your eyes could be any lovelier than they already are."

Didi smiled appreciatively. "Yes, he was the only one in the family who didn't have brown eyes. Our brother Mark insisted that Daniel was adopted. Of course, the teasing began to incorporate other theories as we got older."

"Okay, okay, enough of that, already," protested Gaude with an amused smirk.

"In any event," continued Didi, "if your face was on the database, one of our security thugs would have been here within the first thirty seconds that you arrived at my table."

"The police in L.A. told us that our faces were in the federal database."

"Police in L.A.?" asked Didi.

"Long story."

"I bet."

"I thought that workers in a casino aren't allowed to bet."

"Cute," said Didi with a signature Gaude roll of the eyes. She glanced up at a surveillance camera clinging to the ceiling like a vigilant vampire bat. "I suppose the L.A. cops could have accessed a separate system, but they say that DataGhad has tapped into everything from the CIA to the Russian Mafia. If your names popped up on the screen, trust me, you would already have been escorted to the street."

"Actually, the police had our images but not our names."

"There you go," said Didi. "As far as the casino knows, you are John and Bob Doe."

"Moses and Aaron Levi, to be precise," corrected Gaude.

"What?"

"Yet another long story."

Watt and Gaude took their places on the elevated stools facing the blackjack table.

"Do you have chips?" asked Didi.

"No, I'm afraid not," apologized Watt. "Do we need to go someplace to buy them?"

"No need to go to the cage. I take cash right here."

"Will this do?" asked Watt, pulling out a billfold and depositing a small stack of hundred-dollar bills in front of Didi.

"Cool Cal is always welcome at this table."

"Cool Cal?" asked Gaude, clearly confused.

"Calvin Coolidge, of course," said Didi, pointing to the stack of bills.

Gaude stared down at the picture of the taciturn thirtieth president, all the more silent as he glared out disapprovingly, flanked by the numeral one hundred on each corner of the bill. "But..." Gaude groped through his increasingly unreliable memory. *That's not right,* he thought, *Coolidge isn't on the hundred, it's...it's...supposed to be...*

Who?

I dunno.

Didi spread the bills across the table in front of her, counted the bills twice, looked solemnly at Bill Watt and said, "You are purchasing one thousand dollars of chips, is that correct?"

"How did you—?" asked Gaude turning to Bill Watt in astonishment.

Watt shrugged. "Dan, nobody should step foot in Las Vegas unless they have made adequate preparations, both on the spiritual and secular levels." Watt then looked over to Didi and asked, "Is that enough?"

"Anything over our minimum bet is enough."

"How much is that?"

"Twenty dollars."

"Is one thousand dollars too much?"

"Some of our guests bring ten thousand dollars or more to the table."

"So, I guess one thousand isn't too much."

"I'm going to keep this big spender attitude in mind when we take our next flight in economy class," jibed Gaude.

"I expect you to win us enough money to fly first class," replied Watt with a smile.

Didi took a paddle and pushed the bills into the drop box slot. "Do you have a preferred increment for your chips?"

"What's a good size for chips?" asked Watt.

"Fifties and twenties," said Gaude.

Didi looked at Watt for confirmation, which he gave with the nod of his head. "That will be fine," she responded, quickly counting out the chips and sliding them across the table. Watt divided the piles and passed half of the chips to Gaude.

"These are different colors…" mused Watt aloud. "What are the ten-dollar chips for?"

"Those are for tipping our dealer," Gaude explained.

"Oh, that's nice," Watt smiled at Didi. "Thank you for making it convenient."

Didi could not restrain a giggle in response to Watt's infectious innocence.

"So, tell me about this spirit guide of yours," said Gaude. "That doesn't sound like anything associated with what the nuns taught us."

Didi put a six-deck stack of cards in the autoshuffler. "I'm a Novus Raëlian."

"That sounds like a political party."

"We believe that Elohim created all life on our planet, including humans."

"Is Elohim your term for God?"

"No, Elohim are a race of highly advanced extraterrestrials."

"You worship *space aliens*?"

Didi removed the cards, squared the deck, and offered the stack with a cut card to Watt, who then turned to Gaude. "What am I supposed to do?"

"You've never played blackjack?"

"I've never been in a casino."

"In all your years—?"

"Nope."

"I thought you've been everywhere."

"The world is a pretty big place. I haven't been to Ayers Rock, haven't seen the running of the bulls in Pamplona, and have never stepped foot in a casino."

"Until tonight."

"Yes, until tonight."

"Congratulations, you've just crossed off a big item on your bucket list."

"You can't conceive how long my bucket list is…or yours, for that matter."

"Okay, so you don't know anything about blackjack?"

"I know that it is a card game and it has something to do with twenty-one points."

Gaude made no effort to suppress a sigh. "We'll just go step-by-step. Put that pale green card into the deck, about two-thirds toward the back." Watt complied with the direction and Didi then loaded the cards into the shoe. Gaude placed one fifty-dollar chip in the betting circle. Watt followed with an identical bet and the deal proceeded. "Where were we?" Gaude asked Didi.

"I'm dealing. It's your job to keep track of the conversation."

"I think I asked you about your worship of little green men from Mars."

"They're not from Mars, they're not green, and we don't actually worship them. Naturally, they deserve our respect and cooperation. After all, they are superior beings from another galaxy."

"You believe in UFOs?"

"Of course, who doesn't? You don't think crop circles just create themselves, do you?"

Watt was dealt a seven of spades, Gaude a queen of clubs, the dealer's upcard was a nine of clubs. Watt's second was a jack of hearts, Gaude's a ten of diamonds, the dealer laid down the hole card. Watt reached for his cards

"Don't touch the cards, Bill," warned Gaude.

"Why not?"

"They were dealt from a shoe."

Watt remonstrated, "No, she dealt them from that glass box."

"That's a shoe."

"Remind me never to shop at your men's store."

"How long has this been going on?" asked Gaude.

"What going on?" responded Didi.

"Your UFO worship."

"We don't *worship* UFOs. Raëlism was established by The Raël, a Frenchman named Claude Vorilhon. He published *The Book Which Tells the Truth* and *Extraterrestrials Took Me to their Planet* in the mid-1970s and revealed the truth about the Elohim."

"What I meant was, how long have *you* been involved in this group?"

"Three years ago, I started practicing sensual meditation—"

"Sensual mediation?"

"Yes, it's one of the cornerstones of our faith. Later, I underwent Raëlian baptism, which involves the transmission of the cellular plan—"

"Cellular plan? What does religion have to do with your cellphone service?"

Didi rolled her eyes again. "The next time I'm scheduled for an upgrade, I will definitely ask for more patience with the unenlightened."

"An upgrade?"

"It's complicated. In the meantime, I'm waiting," said Didi, gesturing to the cards on the table.

Watt turned to Gaude. "What should I do now?"

"Stand on the cards."

"Seriously? I can't touch them, but you want me to stand on them?"

"Stand means you accept the cards as is—you don't want any more. Just wave your hand like this," instructed Gaude as he briefly passed his hand over the table. Watt complied. Didi flipped her hole card, revealing a seven of spades.

"Hey, that's the same card I have! How did that happen?"

"We're playing with six decks," answered Didi.

"Oh."

Didi slipped a card from the shoe, a king of diamonds. "Dealer busts." She quickly reached into the rack for chips and placed the winnings in each player's betting circle.

As Gaude reached for his winnings, he noticed that the music coming from the ceiling speakers was 'Casino Boogie' by the Rolling Stones. "You were saying?" prompted Gaude.

Didi sighed, "I don't have the time to explain everything to you. We receive genetic downloads. We call them upgrades."

"You mean, like upgrading computer software?"

"Yes. I'm sure you are aware of how similar our genetic information is to computer code. That was intentionally engineered into us by the Elohim. In addition, the intergalactic supercomputers of the Elohim continually record our memories and DNA to provide a backup. We are striving to clone our members and rapidly accelerate their growth. Then, based upon the backup copies of our memories and genetic codes that have been safeguarded by the Elohim, we can transfer the mind and personality of each member into their own clone."

"Seriously?"

"Yes, it's serious business. We are at the brink of achieving eternal life, just as the Elohim were able to accomplish thousands of years ago."

"You allow these space aliens to fool with your DNA?"

"Actually, the Elohim improve and augment our genetic coding. During downloads and upgrades, the faithful adherents receive gifts from the Elohim designers."

"Gifts?"

"Sometimes it is knowledge, sometimes special talents or abilities, and other times better health. On rare occasions we receive advanced equipment or instruments."

Gaude made an seventy dollar bet and Watt mirrored the action. Watt was dealt a nine of hearts, Gaude a jack of diamonds, a nine of clubs to the dealer.

"Where did these ideas come from?"

"They have been among us since the dawn of civilization. The Elohim have interacted with humans for thousands of years. They are similar in appearance to us in many ways, but different enough to be recognized as beings from another realm. In the Bible, they are routinely depicted as angels." Didi dealt the duce of spades to Watt, a four of hearts to Gaude, then the hole card. Watt looked over to Gaude for guidance. Gaude accommodated him. "You have eleven points. You should ask for a hit…you can also double down."

"Double down?"

"You can double your bet."

"Why would I want to do that?"

"If you win, you get more money."

"But if I lose, I get less money."

"Welcome to gambling," teased Didi.

"Why don't you double down?" asked Watt.

"I have fourteen points. I can take a hit, but I'm too high to double down."

"Then you go ahead and take a hit," said Watt.

"It's your turn."

"Oh," said Watt sheepishly. He looked back at Didi. "Okay, please give me a hit."

"No, tap the table with your finger," instructed Gaude.

"Like this?" asked Watt.

"Yes."

Didi deposited a card before Watt. Eight of clubs.

"Stand on that," advised Gaude.

"That means I pass my hand like this?" asked Watt.

"Exactly." Gaude then tapped the table and received an ace of hearts. He hesitated for a moment and tapped again. A nine of spades. "Bust," he declared in mild disdain for his inadequate strategy.

Didi collected her brother's bet and then turned over her card, ten of diamonds. "Push," she declared.

Watt asked, "What just happened?"

"Nothing happened. You tied."

"Oh."

"You were referring to angels?" asked Gaude.

"Yes," answered Didi. "The Elohim have been mistaken for angels, and just like angels, they have brought us messages or given us instructions from a place far beyond our experience and understanding. Throughout the ages, the Elohim have sent us prophets, including Moses, Jesus, Buddha, Elijah, Ezekiel, John the Baptist, Muhammad, and Joseph Smith. There's also evidence that Gandhi was given a mission by the Elohim."

"So, the Bible is full of your Elohim friends?"

"The great leader of the Elohim, Yahweh, explained all this—"

"Yahweh? You mean like the Yahweh of the Old Testament?"

"That's who the writers of the Bible are referring to when ascribing all the great achievements to God. It was the Elohim all along."

"Seriously?" asked Gaude as he placed a one-hundred-dollar bet.

"Serious as the next deal," his sister replied. She dealt an eight of hearts to Watt, three of spades to Gaude, jack of clubs to dealer. Ace of diamonds to Watt, three of hearts to Gaude, then the hole card.

"You have a soft nineteen there, Bill. You're good as is." Gaude then took four chips, placed them in the betting circle besides his original wager, and then tapped the table with two fingers spread into an inverted peace sign.

Bill Watt asked, "Is that something new?"

"It's called a split." Gaude then turned to Didi. "House rules?"

Didi's right eyebrow arched. "How did you know?"

"Know what?"

"Obviously you somehow know that we just set a new house rule on a split, or you wouldn't have asked. We haven't even posted them yet."

"Lucky guess."

"My skinny ass it was a guess."

"Don't talk that way to your brother."

"If you weren't my brother, I'd be very suspicious. As it is…actually, I'm still suspicious, although you're hardly smart enough to get away with cheating. Anyway, if you pull any stunts, I'll have you eighty-sixed and tossed out on your own skinny ass, brother or no brother."

"Neither me nor my ass is all that skinny anymore."

Didi rolled her eyes in a manner that Watt recognized as a family trait. "Okay, house rules at The Four Horsemen do not limit the number of additional hits after the split."

"Good," Gaude replied, tapping the table for a hit. An ace of clubs was placed beside the three of spades. "So, what about your Yahweh spaceman? You say he was confused with the God of Israel? I suppose he was responsible for all of the miracles in the Bible?"

"Yes. For instance, the Garden of Eden was the genetic engineering laboratory where animals and humans were developed by the Elohim. The great flood was caused during an Elohim project to construct the continent of Africa. A tectonic plate slipped, causing a tremendous tsunami. It just goes to show that even advanced extraterrestrials are capable of making mistakes."

"Unbelievable."

"Isn't it amazing?" agreed Didi enthusiastically. "In order to deal with the flood, the Elohim built Noah's Ark, which as actually a spaceship that stored the DNA used to restore life on earth after the catastrophe of the flood. The Tower of Babel was a great spaceport. Modern day scientists recognize it as a space elevator capable of carrying objects from earth's surface to an orbiting satellite."

Gaude tapped again. Five of hearts.

"You're on a roll," quipped Didi.

Gaude tapped. Nine of spades.

"Congratulations, five-card Charlie," Didi announced and placed a small stack of chips beside Gaude's bet.

"I'm getting to like this casino," chuckled Gaude. "Maybe we'll stay here for a while."

"Fine with me. I'll get it all back and then some." She then laid a king of clubs beside the remaining three of hearts.

Gaude tapped the table. Nine of diamonds—bust. Gaude shrugged as Didi picked up the bet. She then flipped her hole card, a queen of clubs. She took Watt's bet and placed the played cards in the discard rack.

"I'm having a really hard time believing any of this extraterrestrial god religion."

"You should read *Intelligent Design: Message from the Designers*. It explains a lot."

"So now you're a member of this...cult?"

"It's a recognized religion. However, our community is not exactly aligned with the main body of the movement. That's why we refer to ourselves as *Novus* Raëlians."

"What happened? Was there a reformation movement started by *Martian* Luther?"

"Very cute," Didi responded scornfully. "No, we split apart on the question of God."

"How? I thought that you said that your religion—cult—doesn't believe in God."

"The main body of the movement does not, but our community does. You see, believing in the Elohim and believing in God should not be mutually exclusive."

"But you said that the Elohim created the earth and all life upon it, including humans."

"Yes, but who created the Elohim?" asked Didi rhetorically.

"So, God is still God?" asked Gaude. "You're saying that he's merely once-removed from humans."

"I wouldn't put it that way. You see, most religious traditions agree that God makes himself accessible through countless ways. Jews claim to be able to connect to him directly. Muslims claim this also but recognize angels as intermediaries. Christians relate best with God's son, Jesus. We were raised Catholic, so we both know how much emphasis can be placed on someone who is an intercessor on our behalf, such as the Blessed Virgin Mary or the thousands of saints canonized by the Church. God can send angels, prophets, disciples, apostles, evangelists, and saints to connect with us. God can also inspire artists, philosophers, and mystics to communicate, teach, and inspire us. Nature itself works on so many levels to connect us with the power and presence of the Almighty."

"But I thought that you said that the Elohim did all the things that we attribute to God."

"Not everything. Nothing comes from nothing. The Elohim had to be originally created by someone, or something, or some God. It might be possible that they were created by even more ancient and powerful extraterrestrials, but sooner or later, the connective line of space civilizations had to start somewhere, had to begin sometime, and had to be created by someone who is the first, original, all powerful being. That's the definition of God."

"Maybe the first ancient space civilization simply evolved, as most scientists believe that we humans did."

"We didn't evolve out of nothing and neither did the Elohim. Someone—something—some all-powerful being or force had to get the ball rolling. God exists because he must exist, because nothing can exist until he existed, because we cannot exist unless he exists."

"It sounds like you didn't stray as far away from the teachings of the nuns as I first thought."

Gaude placed four fifty-dollar chips on the table and Watt hesitantly followed his partner's lead. Didi dealt Watt a nine of hearts, Gaude a queen of clubs, and the dealer's upcard was an ace of clubs. Watt's second card was a five of spades, Gaude received a six of diamonds, and Didi laid down the hole card and looked to the gamblers for their move.

Watt turned to Gaude. "Should I ask for another card?"

"Bill, she's showing an ace and your hand isn't great. I'd go for insurance."

"You can buy insurance for gambling losses?"

"In a sense. See that line on the table that says insurance?"

"Yes."

"You can put half your original bet on that line to insure against the dealer drawing a blackjack." Watt reached for a chip in the betting circle. "Bill! No, you need to leave the original bet. The insurance money is in addition to the bet."

"I can see why it is called insurance. The premiums are designed to empty your wallet," Bill Watt joked. Didi laughed appreciatively.

"I don't suppose you have revised the house rules on insurance?" asked Gaude.

"What? You mean a no-limit bet? No, not a chance."

"Just asking." Gaude placed an additional fifty-dollar chip on his own bet. "So, you've set yourself up as a separate religion?" asked Gaude as he tapped for another card.

"We'd like to avoid that if possible," said Didi as she dealt Gaude a four of clubs. "There is so much we have in common and see eye-to-eye with the main body of the movement. We hope to rebuild bridges with our proposal for the construction of the Raëlian Embassy for Extraterrestrials."

"Building a spaceman embassy sounds like quite an undertaking," remarked Watt.

"The main body of the movement has long proposed to establish an embassy building outside of Jerusalem, but they are not absolutely opposed to other ideas on the matter. We believe that Las Vegas is the perfect place for the embassy. This city projects more light per square meter into space than anyplace else on earth, thus serving as an excellent beacon for incoming spacecraft. It is also the largest city in proximity to Area Fifty-One, where the government stores all UFO artifacts, technology, and remains of Elohim who have crash-landed over the years."

"That certainly makes sense," said Watt, showing no hint of incredulity.

Didi flipped over her hole card. A king of diamonds. "You broke even," Gaude said to Watt.

"Which is more than can be said of you," commented Didi dryly as she collected Gaude's bet.

"I suppose that another benefit of building your spaceport here is that you can entice little green men to play blackjack."

"Actually, little green men prefer the roulette table," said Didi playfully.

"In any case, it sounds like you have a plan."

"Not quite. The fly in the ointment is the demand by the movement that the embassy must be built in a neutral location that has been granted rights of extraterritoriality and guaranteed neutral air space. That's a tall order and one that might receive a lot of pushback from the United States government."

"Now, that is something I readily believe."

"We'll work on it. In the meantime, I'm currently running for election among our community as the ambassador plenipotentiary in order to submit our proposals for a bill of new philosophical beliefs, offer funding for the building of the embassy, and negotiate a reunion with the main body of the movement."

"I remember that when you were a girl in school that you despised the idea of running for election for student council."

"People change, in case you haven't noticed. However, I must admit, it's partly for selfish reasons. Before the split, I had just been elevated to a Regional Guide. It's a level three position. I was also hoping to be nominated to join the Order of Angels."

"Those are a big deal, I take it."

"Yes, and you may drop that smug attitude at any time. Preferably now."

"We're getting close to the twenty-minute mark."

"Have patience, my relief will be here soon."

"Okay, last bet." Gaude pushed a stack of chips in the betting circle. Watt did a double-take, reached for his chips, hesitated, and decided to place one chip as his wager. Watt was dealt a queen of clubs, Gaude a five of hearts, and a three of clubs went to the dealer.

Watt's next card was an eight of spades, Gaude received a six of diamonds, Didi laid her hole card down. Gaude placed another pile of chips in the betting circle.

"You always were one to double down."

"Particularly when the odds are in my favor."

"Maybe even when they're not," said their dealer as she placed a jack of spades in front of her brother. Gaude watched with a face better suited for poker than blackjack as he looked across the table at his sister. Didi flipped her concealed card over to reveal a nine of hearts. With twelve points showing, the dealer was obliged to draw another card. It was the king of clubs. "Dealer's bust," she announced cheerfully, passing over chips to Watt and Gaude. "You're ahead tonight."

"Yes, and I plan to stay that way," Gaude replied to his sister as he saw another casino employee approach. Didi nodded a salutation to her relief, then lifted her hands high and clapped them as if in a Baptist big tent revival. Watt turned to Gaude, who answered the silent question. "Dealers do that for the security cameras to show that they aren't stealing chips."

"How do you know so much about gambling?" asked Watt.

"I don't really know all that much…I guess I learned a little when I was in the Army."

"I have to go to the cash cage. I suppose you do too," Didi said, gesturing towards the chips in front of her brother. "I also need to pick up my handbag at the locker room." They followed Didi to the west corner of the casino and then took their place in line at the cash cage. Gaude heard music coming from an adjacent concert venue behind a large fountain. It was 'Close Call' by Ni'ihau Child.

You can't climb over a transom
That really isn't there
You think that 'cause you're handsome
That you don't need a prayer

You've pushed your luck too often
And now it's running out
The future is a coffin
Of that there is no doubt

⌘

Malachi rolled open the glass door to the deck and found Katie sitting in the wicker chair, facing a sunset of striated reds, oranges and grays. On her lap was an open Bible, and in her right hand, a glass of white wine.

"Ahhh," said Reuben displaying a gentle smile, "the days of Rhine and Moses."

"Reuben, I'm leaving for Atlanta tomorrow."

"Give my best to your darling mother."

"My darling mother despises you, Reuben."

"I know. She is a much better judge of character than her daughter."

"You'll get no argument from me."

"When will you come back for a visit?"

"Reuben! I don't think you've ever asked that question of me—or any other human being, for that matter."

"Probably not."

"You're becoming sentimental."

"At least you aren't accusing me of being lonely."

"Aren't you still talking to yourself?"

"Of course."

"You've always been an excellent conversationalist. I doubt that you'll ever be lonely."

"True, but I must admit that of all God's creatures, it is with you that I am least unlonely."

"You have a poem coming on. I can sense it."

"You're right. Let me go scrounge through the kitchen cabinets for a previously overlooked bottle of distilled inspiration before I resume my place at the typewriter."

"Reuben, I think we've been drinking too much."

"Yes, we should stop just as soon as we run dry and start again only after we have restocked."

"You are a very bad influence."

"Should I reform?"

"Absolutely not! Where else could I find someone so good at being such a bad influence? You are a national treasure of degeneracy."

A few hours later, Malachi and Katie both retired to their bedrooms. Chapele rolled out his sleeping mat on the greatroom floor, placed clothes for the next day on a small end table, and packed the remainder in his suitcase. He checked his cellphone, still amazed that it picked up a signal in the midst of what appeared to be a limitless and unpunctuated expanse of spartina. He was relieved to find no messages from his editor chastising him for further overstaying his overstay.

Chapele sat down in the overstuffed chair and opened his copy of one of Malachi's earliest works, *Pilgrimage*. Over the past few nights Chapele had read all the sonnets and now faced the 'too damn long' poem. He decided to give it a try.

> *Listen:*
>
> *Gideon is made of star-stuff (so are we all)*
> *And he stands upon the firmament*
> *With arms outstretched for his beloved*
> *Diana, who will not come*
> *But (the fickle bitch, who did*
> *just yesterday pronounce her love)*
> *Does now recede into the blinding night.*
> *Behind the mountains she flees.*

The poem ran for twenty pages more. Chapele was tired. He decided to finish the poem tomorrow on the flight back to New York. He placed the book in his travel tote, turned off the floor lamp, undressed, walked across the room, laid down on the insufficiently padded pad, and immediately fell asleep.

They stepped into the casino elevator. Gaude looked around and noticed that the walls were uniformly glossy black, with no evidence that the conveyance contained any floor buttons or other instrumentation. Didi reached into her handbag and withdrew a glowing orb, approximately the size of a golf ball, with colors that shifted slowly through the spectrum, crimson to amber to indigo.

"What is that?"

"A universal key."

"I see that the casino uses pretty sophisticated technology."

"This isn't from the casino. I told you, sometimes we receive gifts from the Elohim." Gaude and Watt exchanged a look of frank astonishment. Didi passed the lighted ball in front of the area to the right of the elevator door. A touch screen control panel came to life. She then circled her thumb over the top of the ball twice. Didi paused for a moment, then tapped the side of the ball with her thumb, swiveled the ball, and tapped it again. The panel indicated '151' and the elevator doors closed. The cab immediately began its ascent to the apex of the tower.

"That's a neat trick."

"Advanced technology is not a trick. It simply is…advanced."

"If that little glowing golf ball is how your space aliens operate an elevator, how do mere humans get up to their rooms?"

"Standard key cards for most guests. The VIP rooms are accessed with a special pin provided by the front desk when they check in."

"I hope you don't get in trouble for helping us get up to the top floor."

"It's a little late for apologies," said Didi with a smirk. Gaude started to extend another apology, but she cut him off. "Don't worry, I used the key to disable the security camera."

"How long will it take to get to the top?"

"One minute. We're going seventy kilometers per hour. Fastest elevator in the world."

"Impressive."

"It runs on electromagnets. The Germans invented it."

They felt the elevator decelerate, and as promised, the doors opened within one minute of having closed behind them on the ground floor. "Good luck," offered Didi.

"You're going back down?"

"I may have disabled the cameras, but our wifi security system on the casino floor pings my badge every three minutes. If I fall off the grid without having checked out of the building, the folks at security are notified."

"Doesn't your shiny ball take care of that?"

"I'm sure that it does, but I haven't figured that out yet. The only way to get additional instructions is to receive some new uploads from the Elohim. Since our split with the main movement, they are hard to come by."

"Okay," said Gaude, doing his best to disguise his skepticism.

"How do we get back down?"

"The security protocols are all geared exclusively against attempts to go up. The elevator allows anyone to descend."

"Thanks, Didi."

"Don't mention it," she replied. "Seriously, don't mention it," she said again with mock gravity.

Daniel Gaude and Bill Watt exited the elevator and the doors closed behind them. As they began to walk down the corridor, they were greeted by a muffled explosion that seemed to originate somewhere down the hall. The men stopped in midstride and examined one another for affirmation of the event as well as confirmation that each of them possessed adequate courage to continue the pursuit.

"Does that have anything to do with us?"

"What do you think?"

Gaude began to run in the direction of the noise. Watt followed behind. At the intersection of hallways, they faced a sign giving the directions to the rooms.

←	→
Aaru	Hamistagan
Alam al Jabarut	Himmel
Brittia	Naraka
Bulu	Pialral
Diyu	Summerland
Guinee	Yomi

"What the hell are those?"

"I think that they are the names of the rooms."

"The rooms don't have numbers?"

"Sometimes premier suites have names."

"These aren't like any names I've ever seen."

"Is one of them named Bacardi?"

"Afraid not."

Another shot rang out. Watt suddenly took off to the left.

"Where are you going?" shouted Gaude.

"I don't know!" yelled Watt in reply as he continued running down the hall. He arrived at the room marked *Alam al Jabarut* and began pounding on the door.

"What the hell are you doing?" demanded Gaude.

"Trying to get in!"

"Why?"

"I don't know!"

A third shot rang out. "It's behind us!" declared Gaude.

"I know that!"

"Then why are we at this end of the building?"

"That's where you told me to go!" declared Watt.

"I did not!"

"Yes, you did!"

"This way!" shouted Gaude as he ran back to intersection of the halls and turned towards the elevators.

Watt followed behind, puffing for breath. "Wait! No! This way!"

"What way?"

"Back this way!" said Watt pointing to the room directory on the wall. "It's one of these rooms!"

"How do you know?"

"Because it lists all the rooms."

"Which one?"

"I don't know."

"Pick one!"

"You pick one!"

"I'm not sure which room."

"Neither am I."

"What do we do?"

"Check all of them!"

"We can't do that!"

"What can we do?"

"I don't know!" said Gaude as he turned to the right and began to run down the hall.

"I think it's the Summerland Room," shouted Watt after him.

"I know what room it is," yelled Gaude without looking back.

"How do you know?"

"I don't!"

"It's just ahead."

"I know." Gaude stopped before the room marked *Summerland*. He tried the door handle.

"Hotel doors are always locked," Watt chided as he arrived, again puffing for breath.

"I know."

"So why did you try it?"

"What else do you suggest?"

"Why not try knocking?"

"Yeah, right!"

Watt stepped forward, raised his fist, and connected with the door just as three more gunshots exploded from inside the room. The two men jumped back in surprise as if they were choreographed. Watt turned again to Gaude. "Well, what are you waiting for?"

"Someone in there is firing bullets for Krissake!"

Watt began pummeling the door. "Open up!"

"What the hell are you doing, you maniac?" Gaude screamed.

"We have to get in!" Watt shouted back.

"Why?"

"Go through the transom!" Watt shouted.

"What transom?" Gaude barked back.

"There isn't a transom!" hollered Watt.

"I know that!"

"Don't yell at me!"

"I'm not yelling!" yelled Gaude.

A third voice bellowed behind them. "Freeze! Don't move! Hotel security!"

⌘

Doyle exited the plane at Gate Twelve and joined the flow of pedestrians in the Meyer Lansky International Airport. As he walked down the corridor, he was overtaken on his right by a heavyset man in his mid-fifties wearing loose blue jeans, a t-shirt advertising an imported beer, and a blue ballcap featuring the silhouette of the U.S.S. Indianapolis. Doyle glanced down and saw that the man carried a black gortex bag. The contact used the standard default exchange required in exigent circumstances.

155

"How 'bout those Steelers?"

"I'm a Patriot's fan."

"All your life?"

"If you can call it a life."

The heavy man walked to the men's room ten meters ahead. Doyle paused, pretended to check text messages on his cellphone, and then went to the same men's room. The contact was at a sink, washing his hands, as the black bag sat on the counter. Doyle walked up, casually picked up the bag, entered a toilet stall, and took off his sport jacket. He opened the bag which contained a combination shoulder strap holster, seven loaded clips of nine-millimeter ammunition and a plastic case. Upon opening the case, he found a Beretta APX III and a post-it note.

Trust me, you'll like this even better than your beloved relic. D.C.

Two minutes later, Doyle finished strapping on his service pistol, put his jacket back on, and exited the men's room. The ersatz Steelers fan retrieved the empty bag and departed.

Doyle picked up his suitcase at the luggage carousel, checked his cellphone, and found the text from the rental car company directing him to the location of the vehicle reserved for him. He attempted to switch the phone to secure mode but discovered that ORCA's system was still down. Five minutes later, he located the Chevrolet Malibu parked on the third deck, space thirty-seven. He tossed his travel bag into the trunk, entered the cab, started the vehicle, set the navigation app for his destination, and began winding through the parking garage until he emerged from the concrete cavern. In compliance with the dictate of his cell navigator, Doyle turned north onto Paradise Road. Even without an electronic guide, Doyle could see that he would not have encountered any difficulty in locating the Four Horsemen Casino and Convention Center. The skin of the building was a non-reflective black basalt, illuminated by searchlights against an equally black basalt sky. A shadow within a shadow. The interminable spire rose above the strip and brooded over the desert, more like a vulture than anything associated with horses. *Creepy*, thought Doyle. *Macabre*. He turned left at Sands Avenue and traveled another few minutes until he arrived at Las Vegas Boulevard. The base of the complex encompassed an entire block.

Doyle decided to forego both valet parking and the massive

156

parking garage underneath the exponentially more massive tower. *Need to make sure that you won't be boxed in,* cautioned his silent advisor. He located a parking space one hundred meters to the west of the building. As he walked into the entry area, he faced an escalator of burnished gold, at least three meters in width, lifting the condemned to their just and unjust rewards. Doyle stepped on the ascending stairs and arrived at the landing, flanked on either side by rows of slot machines. He moved forward cautiously, meandering through a maze of gambling contraptions, unsure how most of them worked. He finally arrived at the hotel front desk, which was anything but a front desk, being positioned deep within the recesses of the gambling cavern. Doyle approached the counter and announced that he had a reservation. The clerk checked the computer terminal, scowled gently, and then reached into a drawer to extract an envelope. "It is a message from a Mister Bagsley…your business associate?" said the clerk, as he handed the envelope to Doyle. Doyle tore open the envelope and read the note

Jimmy, Sorry, no Room 151.
Did the best that I could. Doug

Doyle looked up from the note. "There's no Room 151?"

"No sir. The entire first floor is the casino."

"This is the first floor? I came up an escalator. We must be at least fifty feet above the ground."

"Twenty meters, sir, but that's all parking below us. We count this as the first floor."

"I see."

"We have your reservation for Room 618."

"Is there a conference room 151 or a meeting room 151?"

"No sir, sorry. The only 151 we have here is the height of the building."

"It looks a lot higher than 151 meters."

"Yes sir," said the deskclerk with a polite laugh. "It's 151 floors."

"That's quite a trip to the top."

"Yes, sir."

"Do you have any rooms available?"

"Yes, sir."

"On 151?"

"On the top floor, sir?"

"Yes."

Even someone not trained as a field operative would have detected the skeptical sweep of the deskclerk's eyes as he assessed James Parker Doyle and found him unlikely to qualify as one of the high-rollers or bored billionaires who would be normally be expected to lodge in the most expensive rooms in the City of Las Vegas. Notwithstanding this, the clerk had been rigorously drilled by the management on the finer points of room registration protocol and etiquette. *Never judge a book—or a bookie—by the cover*, lectured the voice of the night manager in the deskclerk's head. "Ummm…yes, sir, we do have a room available. It's a beautiful suite with breathtaking views, as you might imagine."

"I'll take it."

The deskclerk then casually informed Doyle of the nightly rate for the room, a figure that roughly equated to Doyle's monthly paycheck—before any deductions for taxes. Doyle pulled the agency credit card out of his wallet and handed it to the clerk. To the clerk's mild surprise, the credit confirmation was immediate. He reached into a small box and removed a gold pin featuring the profile of four horses running in tandem. He placed it on a pad adjacent to the computer workstation, keyed in the room code, activated the pin, and then handed it to the newly approved guest.

"You can affix this to your lapel. It will provide you access to the private elevator to Floor 151 as well as keyless entry into your room."

"What is the room number?"

"It's named *Pialrâl*."

"What's named *Pialrâl*?"

"Your room."

"The room has a name?"

"Yes, sir. Our most exclusive rooms on the top floor are named after the various visions of paradise from different traditions around the world. They are, after all, the closest you are likely to get to heaven in this lifetime unless you are a mountain climber or an astronaut."

"Or a frequent flyer."

"I've never felt particularly close to heaven when stuffed into an airplane, but then again, I've never flown first class." The deskclerk glanced down over the counter. "Do you need help with any bags?"

"No, I left them in my car. Perhaps later."

158

Doyle followed the clerk's directions to the elevator dedicated to servicing the top floor of the hotel. As he had been assured, the badge on his lapel activated the elevator doors. He stepped in and was greeted by the music coming down from the cab's overhead speakers: 'Hit Me With Your Best Shot' by Pat Benatar.

Doyle searched for a panel of buttons to select his floor but could not find anything that interrupted the uniform black gloss of the interior. The doors closed and a control panel suddenly illuminated, indicating that his destination was Floor 151. The cab began to ascend, and in precisely one minute, he arrived at the uppermost floor. Doyle exited the elevator cab and walked to an intersection of hallways where he found the directory of rooms. He attempted to search for *Pialrâl*, but his eyes immediately fixated on:

Summerland

That's not a coincidence, his silent counselor urged.
You're wagering on that, he responded to himself.
You bet I am. This is Las Vegas, after all, he argued back.

Doyle walked down the hall to the door featuring a bronze plaque bearing the name *Summerland*. He knocked. No one answered after two more rapped demands for admission. Finally, he tried the door handle, despite knowing that modern hotel doors invariably auto-locked. The door opened.

Hmmm...how did that happen? asked Doyle's silently talkative partner.

Must be the lapel pin, he responded to himself.
This is the wrong room.
Is it?

Given that he was on the penthouse floor, Doyle was prepared to encounter a large and lavish room. What he saw upon entering exceeded even his wildest imagination. It was a dramatically disorienting combination of gothic cathedral and teutonic beer hall, mixed with a royal hunting lodge. Doyle's calibrated eye estimated the room to be more than one hundred square meters, seemingly built of stone, with clustered columns soaring to a distant ceiling of ribbed vaults. In the center of the room was a stone tower that nearly touched the impossibly tall ceiling. Doyle recognized it as a miniature replica of the *Laufertor* in Nürnberg. The surrounding dark oak walls were covered with Flemish tapestries alternating with a series of gigantic canvases depicting Wagner's Ring Cycle. Interspersed between the artworks were swords, pikes, clubs, and shields bearing coats of arms. Below the cornice line of the entire room was an orgy of taxidermy encompassing nearly every imaginable creature that could be hunted: boars and bison, moose and muskrats, rhinos and reindeer, walrus and wildebeest, from lions, tigers, and bears to antelopes and zebras. Above the monumental stone fireplace was the mounted head of an enormous red deer. It bore a rack of antlers that spread at least three meters across, with a large crucifix suspended between them. The floor was a confusion of flagstone and inlaid unpolished marble. The furniture was a peculiar collection of English country, French baroque, Italian renaissance, and Nevada bordello interspersed with an eclectic assortment of medieval bric-a-brac, alchemist paraphernalia, and the trappings of Trappist monks.

Doyle saw the silhouette of a man sitting beside the fireplace in a wingback armchair, upholstered in unquestionably expensive flamestitch fabric. His face was camouflaged by the combination of shadow cast by the wings of the chair and the flickering light of the fire. As Doyle prepared to take a step forward, the man spoke in a resonant baritone, "An honor to finally meet the legendary Jimmy Nickels. Good evening, Mister Doyle. I'm delighted you came to visit."

"How could I refuse your invitation, heavy-handed as it was?"

"Heavy-handed?" the voice responded with an air of playful indignation. "I thought that the reference to your Summerland operation in Budapest was inspired."

"Inspired by God?"

"That kind of inspiration is vastly overrated, Mister Doyle."

"You know who I am."

"Of course," said the man in the armchair. "You've been looking for me all the while I have been following you. Or was it the other way around?"

"I don't recall tracking you."

"I didn't say tracking."

"You have the benefit of knowing my name, but I'm afraid that I don't have yours."

"An advantage that I am not keen to surrender."

"You might need to get used to the concept of surrender, since that is exactly why I am here."

160

"Yes, I suspected that you might try to put a damper on our first encounter, but I will not allow it to spoil my delight in finally getting a chance to have a nice chat. I'm even more pleased to see you arriving a day early, which surprises me…and I am never surprised."

"If I'm a day early, why are you here waiting for me?"

"I have a meeting tonight with another prospect."

"Pardon me for upsetting your schedule."

"Interesting that you should put it that way. A pardon is exactly what I intend to offer."

"I'm sorry that I can't reciprocate. A federal conviction is more in line with what I have to bargain with."

"Your misguided attitude is not entirely unanticipated."

"In the spirit of being thoroughly predictable, let me proceed with the formalities," said Doyle as he reached into his jacket and retrieved a thin leatherette case.

"Oh please," the man moaned mockingly, "do not tell me that this is a…bust. Are you really here to arrest me, Mister Doyle?" The man did not move from the chair, but instead picked up a drink from the adjacent table and swirled the ice cubes in a distracted manner. "Tell me, how did you get here so quickly? I must admit that I wouldn't have given you one chance in ten thousand to be up on your feet so soon."

"Then your gambling instincts need polishing. Perhaps Las Vegas is not the best place for you to be arranging get-togethers with someone intent on arresting you."

"Where would you suggest we conduct our meeting? Perhaps Vicksburg? The Farallon Islands? Maybe that little brick house in Fairfax where your blind friend lives with his charming family?"

The words gave Doyle an emotional punch in the gut. It took a moment to retain composure. "I can think of a few federal facilities that would be delighted to have you as a long-term guest, and more than a few lonely inmates who would enjoy sharing their cozy cells."

The laugh in response was hearty and genuine. "You've surprised me again, Mister Doyle. I was informed that you were a reliable but rather pedestrian sort. You have spirit and a sense of humor."

"And just watch how I laugh when you are sentenced to life imprisonment."

"It distresses me not to be able to accommodate this sheer

fantasy of yours."

The patronizing manner and lack of concern was irksome, but Doyle quickly recovered to maintain an air of authority. He flipped open his credentials and began the standard litany. "You are under arrest. Now, as to your rights—"

"Do shut up!" barked the man. "You will wear out your welcome. Since when did ORCA start spewing rights instead of spraying bullets?"

"You do *not* have the right to remain silent," announced Doyle casually, "and anything you don't tell us will be beaten out of you."

An appreciative chuckle was offered in response. "That's a bit more like it, but just the same, neither you nor your organization have any powers of arrest," the man scoffed. "For the past seven years, you've been nothing more than an analyst, a paper pusher, an eavesdropper. You are out of practice, out of condition, and out of touch. You really have no idea what you are doing, do you?" he asked in a smooth and deliberate tone. "Tell me, Mister Doyle, does your navigator know that you are here?" Doyle knew that the remark was intended to toss him off kilter and he concentrated on keeping his focus. "If you were to arrest me, who do you think you'll be bringing me to?"

"You'll find out soon enough."

"I already know. It won't be a legitimate federal prison, nor will it be your headquarters on G Street. I doubt that you'll send me all the way down to Guantanamo Bay, so that leaves Mount Weather."

"You're just guessing."

"If I was just venturing a guess, I would have ventured a little farther down the road to Paw Paw, West Virginia." The man indulged in a dramatic pause and then said, "Mount Weather, Building Thirty-Seven." Doyle maintained a look of stonefaced indifference while his internal dialogue deliberated as to whether it was more prudent to put a bullet into the forehead of the suspect or to take the chance that apprehension and interrogation might yield some actionable intelligence. "Of course, if you don't hurry, they'll be closing the doors on that facility, which will force you to bring me to the new digs at Banshee Mountain."

"Tennessee? Where they make bourbon?"

"You seem surprised, Mister Doyle. Have your superiors been keeping you in the dark? Perhaps I should ask, is this the first you are aware that your superiors have been keeping you in the dark?"

"Now you're indulging in fantasy, or perhaps desperately fishing."

The man in the shadow ignored Doyle's taunt. "ORCA appears to have become a rather itinerant organization. First, you abandoned Fort Richie. Next, Mount Weather. Soon enough, you'll be pulling up stakes at Vicksburg. Even your old haunt at Budapest is on the chopping block—literally."

"I don't like grass to grow under my feet."

"Be careful that it doesn't start growing above your head—six feet above, to be precise. In any event, I suppose wandering the desert has its charms, but I can offer you a bit more stability."

"I can offer you stability—guaranteed lifetime accommodations behind bars."

Once again, the man brushed off the retort. "I know who sent you, but do you know who sent me?" asked the man in the chair.

"I don't know what you are talking about."

"Perhaps not, but you have enough suspicions to know that I'm not talking sheer nonsense."

"Commonplace nonsense will do."

"Do you trust them?"

"Trust who?"

"You know who I'm talking about."

"I don't trust anyone."

"Apparently, you don't even trust your own instincts. Tell me, hasn't that legendary intuition of yours given you the faintest inkling that there is something amiss at the Sweatshop lately?"

"Once again, I don't know what you are talking about."

"You know exactly what I'm talking about. It is written—or should I say carved and scratched—all over your face."

"Go ahead and read it for me."

"It tells me that someone started something that they no doubt intend to finish."

"You're fishing."

"Seventeen days ago, you were suddenly and unceremoniously summoned to headquarters. You were then handed an assignment to the most godforsaken place on earth with no plausible explanation or rationale. Two days ago, you were nearly killed in a freak explosion. Meanwhile, your old comrades-in-arms are dropping like flies. Are you that dense?"

"Yes, I was recruited for my rugged good looks. My powers of intellect leave a lot to be desired. Just ask my wife."

"I'd rather not ask your *ex*-wife. How about your current girlfriend? Katie, isn't it?"

"I met a showgirl downstairs a few minutes ago. I've decided to elope with her just as soon as our business here is finished."

"You're not as clever as you think."

"All I need is to be is more clever than you."

"Which you are not."

"I'll take my chances."

"And like most gamblers in this town, you will lose." The man stood up, took a step towards the window, and gazed out at the view of surrounding city and desert. Doyle tried to make out any details in the man's clothing or facial features, but the figure remained a dark gray outline against a darker black background. "I'm here to make you an offer," said the obscure and obscured adversary.

"You're trying to bribe me?"

The man laughed. "No, nothing so pedestrian. I'm offering you a position."

"I suspect that the position is laid out flat, no doubt at six feet under as you mention just minute ago."

"Perhaps we are both behind the times. It's now two meters under. But no, what I'm offering is a new path, a fresh vision."

"You can't seriously believe that you can flip me? I doubt that the Russians put you up to this, much less the Chinese. The Iranians?"

"No governments are involved, at least not in the traditional sense."

"Syndicate?"

"Of a sort, but I'm not from the Mafia if that's what you had in mind."

"What I have in mind is that you are seriously mistaken if you think I am in the least interested in any proposition."

"Hmmm…rejected out of hand. I thought that you were trained to play along with a contact in hopes that it could result in actionable intelligence."

"Since you obviously know a great deal about me and my organization, that gambit would be rather transparent."

"Agreed. I prefer honesty. Your father was an honest man,

wasn't he? I seem to recall that he was the pastor of a small evangelical congregation."

"In my case, the apple fell very far from the tree."

"I'm counting on that." The man paused, apparently reflecting on what to say next. "Given your access to the subterranean currents of communications passing across the globe, you must be aware that there is a plague upon the land."

"Yes, for some time, and I believe that I am having a conversation with a carrier of the bacillus."

"Oh, no, Mister Doyle. I assure you that I am the one bearing the antidote. Tell me, what do you observe to be humanity's greatest threat? Put aside the hysteria about the earth overheating, or turning into an ice cube, or perhaps the fear of an asteroid slamming into our planet and extinguishing all life. What do you think—what do you *know*—the real danger is? As a man of color, do you think it is racism?"

"That's no small problem, but I wouldn't put it at the top of the list."

"Neither would I. Perhaps income inequality?"

"I suspect from the looks of this room that you probably pay more in taxes than I make in salary for a year, maybe several years. But no, not that either."

"Then what is it?"

"Control."

"Exactly. There are those who seek to control us, control everyone, control the world. The greatest threat to a man is another man who seeks to limit his freedom. Do you think this quest for control is limited to curtailing humanity's freedom of action?"

"Of course not," responded Doyle. "We are in a contest to control freedom of thought."

"Bravo! Well said. That leads to my next and more challenging question. Who is it that we have most to fear in terms of taking away our liberties?"

"I would put you at the front of the line."

"Spare me from the banter, please. Who do we have the most to fear?"

"Ourselves."

"Excellent, but you know as well as I do that indicting ourselves individually or collectively really doesn't resolve the situation or identify the root of the problem. We might be guilty, but merely in the sense of being complicit. There is a prime mover, a central actor, a conspiring force that is behind all the evil that you have witnessed in your career."

"That would be a difficult choice. There are a number of sleazy outfits that might fit the bill, yours in particular."

"Yes, there are at least a dozen governments and twice as many criminal organizations that would fit the bill as cesspools of malevolence, but I am referring to the one original wellspring of evil."

"Maybe you're referring back to my Sunday school days during which I was repeatedly warned about the tricks and wiles of the devil."

"Quite the opposite, actually."

"Alright, I'll bite the hook," said Doyle disdainfully.

"It's not a hook, Mister Doyle, it's a lifeline."

"And what is this generous offer?"

"An opportunity to climb out of your current rut."

"I'm very comfortable in my rut."

"There is precious little difference between a rut and a grave." The man paused and then continued. "Surely you've noticed that everything is not beer and skittles at ORCA nowadays, not that the organization was ever innocent of double-dealing and intrigue. Lately, things have gotten…dicey, one might say."

"*You* might say."

"Yes, I might. Mister Doyle, haven't you realized that your own organization is hunting you down? They've already taken out many of your oldest friends and colleagues. The prize target—the legendary James Parker Doyle—is still on the loose, but soon enough they will run you to ground. Tell me, who other than your own organization knew that you were almost blown to kingdom come in a fortress laboratory in the hinterlands of Wisconsin?"

"You, for one."

"*Touché*. However, you are overlooking the obvious, which I find ever-so slightly discouraging. Please tell me that I have not overestimated your skills as a field operative and analyst."

"What? Are you inviting me to play a rousing game of *Clue*?"

"Let's see if you can pin this on Colonel Mustard in the library with a candlestick."

"You extracted the information during the attack on…our system."

"You don't want to mention Jethro, which is understandable. However, you are looking in the wrong direction."

"You hacked into ORCA—"

"Oh please, that's simply unimaginative."

"There was a tumor—"

"You might very well have a mole or two in the organization, but you are slightly off the mark."

Doyle stood motionless in thought. "You were hired by..."

"Yes, go on."

"...another agency..."

"Getting warmer."

Doyle paused again. The answer began to dawn upon him, but he tried to suppress the emerging rays of unwelcome enlightenment. "No, that's not possible."

"Impossible is what one calls something that is soon to become an established fact."

"You were hired by ORCA."

"Finally," announced the man in the chair. "That wasn't so painful, was it?"

"If you are working for ORCA, then why are you trying to recruit me?"

"Let's just say that my...other employer...has quite a number of irons in the fire."

"There's no reason why I should believe you."

"Other than the fact that I am telling you the truth."

"If it is the truth, then there is no reason I should trust you. A back-stabbing contractor is no less of a traitor than a rogue agent."

"That's almost poetic. However, what would you do if you came to the realization that your organization had turned its back on every principle upon which it was founded?" The man returned to the chair and waited a moment for this to sink in before adding, "Perhaps I should ask, why haven't you come to that realization already and why haven't you done anything about it?"

"You're trying to spin me."

"I am. It is my patriotic duty."

"I can assume that if I throw in my lot with you that I will be richly rewarded?" asked Doyle.

"Oh no, quite the contrary. You are being offered a position, but at a price."

"Really?" asked Doyle, genuinely surprised that his feeler did not elicit an overt bribe. "What do you charge?"

"A great deal, but then again, something that will cost you nothing at all. Your fee must be paid with an answer to a very simple question."

"I suspect that I won't understand your questions."

"My demand is that you tell me something that I do not already know."

"Such as?"

"Such as? We don't need to dally with examples or hypotheticals. I will ask you plainly. Where is *El Niño*?"

"*El Niño?* I don't know. Somewhere off the coast of Peru, I suppose."

"I'm asking a serious question."

"You'll continue getting a ridiculous answer. I have no idea what you are talking about."

"I am talking about the one thing worth talking about. I know that you spoke with Jethro. It must have told you about *El Niño*, perhaps even where to find him."

"I have no idea what you are talking about," lied Doyle.

"This is not a parlor game and I am not an armchair dilettante. You need to tell me the truth. There is a titanic struggle of clashing celestial armies, spies, and assassins, and each of us has been assigned a role to play our part in an existential struggle."

"I received a C-minus in my sophomore year philosophy class, so you'll forgive my lack of interest in a rehash lecture delivered in a living room decorated by Dracula and Otto Von Bismarck."

"I was pinning a faint hope on the assumption that you might have some redeeming qualities that we could use."

"I can play the accordion."

"Where I come from, everyone plays the accordion." The man paused in thought and then shook his head ruefully. "Our witty repartee has been amusing, but my agenda does not permit me to continue an extended hospitality. I would fix you a drink, but I'm sure that you must be off to attend the National Do-Gooder Convention over at the Excalibur." The man rose casually from the chair. "If you will excuse me then…"

Doyle reached into the left side of his sport coat and withdrew the Beretta that had been secured in his shoulder holster. "Please lay prone," he commanded in a level voice as he began walking forward, "face to the ground." He leveled the weapon, aiming directly at the man's chest.

"I am so disappointed." The scorn was unconcealed.

"Do not force me to fire," said Doyle as he continued moving toward the suspect.

"I know, I know," he said in mock weariness, "you are an expert marksman. Not that anyone with the least familiarity with firearms could miss a target across a room, even a large room." He turned towards the fireplace, showing both his back as well as his apparent disdain of the agent who had come to arrest him.

"You wouldn't be the first suspect that I shot…or killed," said Doyle as he now approached the man.

"You won't kill me and we both know why. Besides, you've never enjoyed killing anyone, have you? The same cannot be said of me." He then turned to face Doyle. Despite more than two decades of rigorous training and hard-earned experience, Doyle was momentarily frozen in horrified astonishment. It was the man's eyes. The pupils were horizontal slits.

The suspect again turned his back on Doyle. With a casual gesture of his left hand, the fire suddenly extinguished. Just as Doyle began to recover from his momentary stasis, the man made the gesture a second time. The lights of the room went out.

Doyle immediately fired his weapon at the last place he had seen the goat-eyed man. He heard the noise of his bullet as it ricocheted off a stone wall. *Missed him! Damn!* he silently cursed.

How the hell did that happen? Doyle's quiet advisor scolded.

File a complaint with my supervisor, was the curt reply.

Doyle took a step back and tried to orient himself based on what he recalled from his initial examination of the room. He began calculating how he could get to a wall switch to flip on the lights. Just as he was about to turn to his right, he was slammed in the chest. Doyle's Beretta was jerked from his grip as he fell back, flipping over a coffee table. A flash and the explosive report of the gun announced that it had discharged upon reaching the floor at the same moment that Doyle's head hit the same surface with a massive crack that shot through his skull and down his spine. The explosion, the concussion, and the darkness left him dazed and disoriented. He reached up and out, trying to find something to grip. He then rolled over and on hands and knees began to grope for the gun on the floor.

Doyle was hit again from the side. The breath was knocked out of him and he wheezed for air. If he had been granted the luxury of reflecting upon the matter, he might have described the attack as the onslaught of a leopard or a panther. As it was, Doyle had no time to think about or imagine what had just hit him. His skull throbbed and he began to feel dizzy and sick. He crawled forward through the darkness, unable to think clearly enough to decide whether to find the gun, escape, or to wedge himself into a corner and pass out. From above, something heavy landed on his back, pinning him to the floor and again mashing his diaphragm, forcing the wind out of Doyle's chest. In desperation born of agony, Doyle twisted and thrashed, and the creature was suddenly gone as quickly as it had attacked. He pulled himself back onto his hands and knees. Doyle resumed his course along the floor. Doyle was fairly certain that he had not been cut, but his stomach repeatedly stiffened in spasms that caused him to retch, and he could taste blood coming up. He reached ahead and suddenly felt the Beretta under his hand. As his fingers clutched the weapon, his hand was engulfed by something. He pulled back, but it would not loosen its grip. He lunged forward in attempt to throw whatever it was off balance only to be shoved and pinned on his back to the floor. It was on top of him now and he punched, pushed, thrashed, all to no avail. He felt its hands, or perhaps claws, force his arms to the ground. He continued to struggle, twisting and kicking. He would have screamed, but the weight of the thing was on his chest and stomach, and his mouth was parched, filled with blood and bile. Instead, Doyle made incoherent sounds which merged growls with foul curses and heaving regurgitation. A claw sliced down and raked across Doyle's face. Nails dug into his right eye and then he felt acid eat deep into his eye socket. The screams that would not come a moment before now erupted explosively. Doyle writhed, thrashed, and pounded at his assailant. With the heave of his torso and the full force of his left leg, Doyle twisted and pushed his opponent off. He rolled to the left and was halted by a sofa. Doyle dragged himself around the corner of the sofa and felt a floor lamp. He then pulled himself up, continuing to hold on to the stem of the floor lamp. Despite the passage of time that the lights had been extinguished, Doyle's eyes had not adjusted to allow him to see anything. The room was simply too dark. He yanked off the shade of the lamp and then held it with both hands, base upwards, perched on his shoulder. He waited, trying to sense the approach.

Something in Doyle's mind, a soft yet clear voice, spoke: *Now!*
He swung the lamp in an arc with the base of the lamp leading. At the
apogee of the swing, the lamp base connected and Doyle heard the thud
of pounded flesh and the muffled crunch of a broken bone. He dropped
the lamp and staggered back. Doyle found a wall and began to feel for a
light switch. He located the switch within a few seconds and flipped on
two wall sconces. He discovered himself in front of the wet bar at the
back of the room. Doyle scanned the area but saw no sign of his quarry.
The tower, said an interior voice that he did not recognize but somehow
implicitly trusted. *He's in the tower.* Doyle glanced around the floor
while being careful not to surrender his attention from the tower. The
pistol was under a small writing desk that backed up to a loveseat.
Doyle ducked under the desk and checked the magazine. Although only
two shots had been fired, he had not forgotten his training. In the
military they taught you to treat every weapon as if it were loaded, but
in the world of operational counterintelligence, every spy knows that a
gun that is taken out of your control for even a moment must be
assumed to be empty or disabled. Doyle released the magazine into his
left hand—it was nearly full. His adversary had never touched it.

Doyle's body was a mosaic of pain. The throbbing agony that
had been his right eye barely trumped the dull nagging ache of his
skull, ribs and back. He forced himself to focus on the job at hand.
Doyle reinserted the magazine. A crash of splintering glass erupted
from the top of the tower.

That's him, alright, confirmed the silent advisor.

Doyle moved from under the desk, raised himself to a crouch,
his gun leveled forward, and took a shot at the window. *Damn! Missed
again!*

That was a waste, scolded his disapproving and invisible alter
ego. *You didn't see a target.*

I'm accustomed to seeing with two good eyes.

No excuse.

Doyle inwardly shrugged. *We shoot by faith and not by sight*, he
silently quipped back. He then took a half dozen swift and painful
strides to the small arched stone portal of the tower. The doorway was
dark and Doyle hesitated entering. He could not see a light switch from
his position. Doyle groped forward cautiously, relying more on dumb
luck and animal instinct than on anything he had learned in his years in

ORCA. His foot encountered something solid. He reached forward and touched cold stone. His hand began to explore the surface and he recognized a balustrade. He employed his foot to assist in the exploration and located a stair tread. He began to cautiously ascend the staircase.

At what seemed to be three spiral turns upward, Doyle sensed a barely perceptible illumination to the right. It was the outline of a doorway. Doyle carefully hugged the wall and moved to the opening. He then sank to his knees and prepared to peer around the corner. He then realized that he had no sight in his right eye and could not get a view of the interior from his current location without sticking his entire head into the doorway. He would be an easy target. *Like a Thanksgiving turkey,* his interior voice muttered sullenly. Slowly, he attempted to position himself to peer around the doorway. As his head poked forward, he instantly heard and felt the crystalline explosion of glass shattering against the doorjamb and cutting into his scalp. Doyle fell onto his right shoulder and waited for the final blow that did not come. The cut to his head was superficial, but the pain was excruciating. Doyle struggled to maintain consciousness. *What's happening? What's happening?* Doyle drilled himself to keep thinking, to stay awake, to stay alive. He placed his left hand on the wall and tried to steady himself as he pulled himself up to his feet. Blood was flowing freely from his head wound and he could feel it running over his forehead, brow, eyes, into his mouth and down his chin and neck. He heard another brittle symphony of shattered glass from around the corner. Doyle lurched forward with the pistol at the ready. He saw a silhouette tossing aside a chair that had just been employed in further smashing the window to provide an even larger portal of jagged glass. Doyle fired three rounds dead center on target. The dark figure moved, but Doyle could not tell if it went down, to the right, or to the left. Just as he began to step back to feel for a light switch, Doyle felt a punch in his side and he collapsed onto the floor. He instinctively rolled to the right and then raised up into a crouch. As the room spun around his throbbing and disoriented brain, he waited for the next assault. Nothing. Silence. He stood up slowly, focusing his last remnant of willpower to countermand the combination of dizziness and nausea that bade him lie down on the floor and surrender to the peace of sleep and release of death. He then approached the broken window and peered down into the gothic expanse below him. Doyle suddenly had a sense of something standing behind him. Before he could react, he was brutally slammed forward and felt himself falling as the room again went to black.

James Parker Doyle awoke on the floor. *It burns*, was all that he could think. *It burns*. He reached to the pain and felt a shard of glass protruding from his lower right abdomen. He attempted to sit up, felt the knife of glass cut deeper, and fell to the floor. His right cheek landed back in a pool of his own blood. Doyle knew that he was going to die. *What's happening?* He asked himself again. Despite the agony, his thoughts were becoming clear, dispassionate, almost calm and reflective. He never imagined that dying, at least dying so violently, would be so...serene. He considered his situation as if it were a classroom exercise that was occurring to another field operative. His opponent had attempted to decapitate him with a long, swordlike piece of glass that must have been a remnant of the shattered window he heard being broken a few moments before. The glass in his side must have come from the same place. He lay on his back, panting, and wiped his face with his shirt sleeve. With both hands, he probed the glass sticking out of him. He made a tentative tug, but the blood on the glass and on his fingers rendered the attempt futile. He tried again, but his fingers merely slipped off the glass. Doyle clumsily unraveled the knot of his tie and pulled it out through his shirt collar. He draped the wide end of the tie over the glass, pinched the fabric over the glass and pulled. The smooth silk proved as ineffectual as his bloody fingers and slipped off the glass. Doyle lay in the dark, his mouth moistened only by salty blood that he was too weary to spit out, fighting off the aching desire to simply sleep, to drift away. With his right hand, Doyle reached up to his shirt pocket and yanked. He cursed himself for the one unlucky luxury he permitted to himself. He always wore expensive Egyptian cotton dress shirts, heavily starched. The pocket seam was well stitched. He reached up with both hands, tore at the top of the pocket, and it came off in his hands. With the patch of cotton material, he repeated the procedure he had attempted with the necktie. This time he did not carefully tug at the glass, but pulled without regard to the throbbing, screaming, howling pain in his gut. The large glass splinter slipped out of the wound, followed by a stream of blood. He let loose an unrestrained roar of agony that was segmented by heaving gulps for air. Doyle pressed the small bloody swatch against his side as he continued to coach himself. *What's happening? What's the situation?*

173

I have a hole in my side and I've lost my gun...again.
Gimme something positive.
The lights are still on. Goat-eyes is gone.
Are you sure?
No, I'm not.

Doyle forced his body to roll onto his stomach and then crawled along the floor back to the tower. Placing his shoulder to the tower wall, he slowly, gingerly, raised himself back to his feet. He tried to orient himself and quickly assessed which door on the other side of the room was the probable bathroom. Doyle then slowly made his way across the room, slipping on his own blood and shattered glass strewn across the stone and marble floor. He arrived at opposite side of the room and opened the door.

Good, at least you got this right.
You're keeping score?
Damnright I am.

Doyle lurched into the bathroom and grabbed the counter with his left hand to steady himself. Doyle knew better than to turn on the vanity lights at this point. He was certain that seeing his own image in a mirror would result in a massive coronary that would finish the job that his would-be assassin had so capably begun. The tiny patch he held against the wound was wholly ineffectual. Blood seeped between his fingers, soaking the waistline down his right trouser leg. He pulled his shirttail from the waist of his trousers, grabbed a hand towel, and stuffed it against the wound, applying as much pressure as he could muster.

Doyle ran cold water into the large custom sink. As it filled, he lowered his face into the pool and splashed water with his free left hand onto the top of his head. The water stung the wound on his scalp, but Doyle persisted. He then regained his stance, grabbed another towel, and placed it over the head wound. The water had revived him enough to think about something other than finding a corner to lie down and die. Doyle reentered the greatroom, wobbled to the entry door and flipped on the remaining lights, fully illuminating the entire room for the first time. He scanned the floor and located the Beretta where he had dropped it. He cautiously crossed the room again, ready but not prepared for another assault from Goat-eyes. He slowly dropped to a knee, retrieved his pistol, and reholstered the weapon. As he gently returned to his feet, Doyle again surveyed the scene. The room had pools and smears of blood—his blood—everywhere. He could not recall being in the room long enough to spill so much blood in so many places.

There was pounding at the door. Doyle realized that the noise had been going on for a few moments, but that the excruciating pain had distracted him. *Of course, someone is trying to get in. They heard the gunshots.* He assumed a hotel security was at the door and that it was a matter of only a few minutes before the police arrived. He returned to the bathroom to discard the towel he had been using as a contingency bandage for his head wound. *Silly,* he thought to himself, *half of the hotel room is covered with my blood and I'm worrying about where to leave a messy towel.*

They're going to come in. You need to do something.

Any suggestions?

How about the bedrooms, Einstein?

I'll be trapped.

As opposed to caught?

Okay, fine, bedrooms it is.

He grabbed a fresh handtowel and stuffed it between the waistline of his trousers and the wound, cinching his belt to tighten the makeshift bandage. Doyle then walked as quickly as his devastated body would allow to the double doors at the west end of the room. Just as he exited the greatroom, the front door opened. He heard two, no, three voices, obviously agitated. He closed the double doors behind him and now examined the bedroom. It was nearly the size of the greatroom and apparently utilized the services of the same Saxon interior decorator. The principal difference between the rooms is that this space did not include a stone tower...or any windows.

No windows? Are they kidding?

What happens in this bedroom stays in this bedroom.

Just great, Doyle groused silently to his judgmental self. *How the hell am I going to escape?*

Were you seriously planning to exit a window at one hundred fifty-one stories?

Shutup!

There's no graceful exit.

Forget about graceful. I'd be happy to settle on an awkward exit.

Not possible, unless their backs are turned.

Or unless they are distracted.

Right.

Doyle placed his back to the wall intersecting the plane of the bedroom door. He reached out with his left hand and cracked open the double door. He could see about one third of the greatroom, but more importantly, could hear the approach of what he assumed was a hotel security guard.

Doyle's right hand departed from its ministrations of his abdominal wound and reached into the shoulder holster. Doyle was not sure why his hand had pulled out the weapon or what was about to happen next. More as a member of an audience than an active participant, James Parker Doyle, that is, the essence of James Parker Doyle, the mind of James Parker Doyle, was not involved in this action. He had not anticipated it, had not planned it, did not understand it, and apparently could not control it. Doyle was along for the ride. With one smooth stride, he stepped squarely into the doorway connecting the bedroom with the greatroom and confronted three approaching men, one uniformed security guard and two civilians. The security guard had drawn his weapon. *This is not good*, his silent advisor commented dispassionately. Doyle swung his Beretta up and calmly squeezed off two rounds that extinguished the overhead chandelier. The three men dove behind a full-sized sofa. With a slight swivel, his gun aimed and fired a single shot at a floor lamp in the east corner of the room and then another shot to kill another floor lamp in the north corner. Doyle next took aim at the wall sconces flanking the room's entry door. With the same fluid motion, these lights were picked off.

How many shots was that? he asked himself.

Altogether? Twelve.

Are you sure?

Yes. That's what I do for a living.

Living is what we might not be doing for much longer.

Speak for yourself.

Doyle reached into his coat pocket to check for the two backup magazines he had placed there before he entered the hotel.

They're missing.

Of course they are.

He knew that his current magazine contained five more bullets. He looked up at the ceiling. There were six recessed ceiling lamps.

Not optimal.

Shutup, I'm thinking.

He scanned the room again and decided that merely dim would have to do. He raised the Beretta and began taking out each floodlight. As he snuffed out the fourth ceiling light, he suddenly realized that there was also light coming in from the hallway through the open front door. Then, Doyle saw it. He may have resisted the beckoning of Lady Luck while passing through the casino one hundred and fifty floors below, but he was more than willing to accept the windfall she now offered. He recognized a discreetly situated circuit breaker box under a sconce in the hallway. He took aim and squeezed off his last round. The room again fell into total darkness.

Doyle's actions continued to be automated by some unseen and unrecognizable cognizance. He calmly evaluated himself as a captive passenger as his legs conveyed him briskly across the impenetrable blackness of the room, navigating wholly by radar, so it seemed. Without pause or hesitation, he exited the front door and took an immediate left turn into the equally opaque darkness of the hallway. He walked to the intersection that he could not see and executed a crisp right turn. He now detected a faint light in the distance. Doyle maintained a determined and agonizing pace until arriving at the source of the illumination, a small picture lamp mounted on the wall above a large famed lithograph, Kandinsky's *Delicate Tension*. Doyle instinctively reached for a catch on the left side of the frame. He unlocked the frame and swung it open to reveal a descending staircase. Doyle took the stairs down to the floor below, emerged into a well-lighted hallway adjacent to the building's observation deck, turned left, continued straight through a hallway intersection, and located the employee service elevator. He entered the cabin and selected the button to descend into the hotel basement. He found that the employee's elevator was just as speedy as the one in which he had ascended less than thirty minutes before. Within a few minutes he was exiting the underground delivery bay to emerge behind the hotel.

Thank God that those magazines held seventeen rounds.
Thank Dayton. He picked the gun for you.
Yes, God bless Dayton.
God bless us, every one.

He walked around the building and down the street. Three minutes later, he located his rental car in the open-air parking lot and lowered himself down into the driver's seat. Doyle suddenly realized that he was now again in control of his faculties and expelled a sigh of mixed relief and confused resignation. He looked down at his shirt and the wadded towel at this waist, both saturated in his blood.

Ragpickers of data.

Yeah, right. Screw the CIA.

James Parker Doyle headed west. He drove in this direction for no other reason than it was not east. He realized that fleeing Las Vegas was irrational. If the would-be assassin wished to pursue him, it would have been as easy to chase him down and finish him in the middle of this stretch of desert as in any other stretch of desert in Nevada. Nevertheless, the animal compulsion to flee took precedence. He had lost far too much blood, but somehow, miraculously, he had not passed out behind the wheel. After fifteen minutes of driving, Doyle turned on the radio and pushed the volume as high as he could tolerate in the hope that it would ward off the alluring pull of sleep that was gradually taking hold of him. 'Dust in the Wind' by Kansas penetrated the interior of the car at ninety decibels. "To hell with that," grumbled Doyle as he pushed the radio scanning button to select another station. 'Prime Cut' by Ni'ihau Child began to play.

> *Carve him up from stem to stern*
> *Oh, how those knife cuts burn!*
> *Butcher him as you may please*
> *He lays dying in a gentle breeze*
> *Prime Cut*
> *Prime Cut*
> *Stick him deep in his gut*
> *Prime Cut*
> *Prime Cut*
> *Now his fate is sealed shut*

Another thirty minutes later, the dim glow of a town appeared on the horizon. Doyle decided that this would be as good a place as any to crawl into a hole and die. Farther down the road, he saw the sign welcoming him to the unincorporated community of Gedukugan. At the intersection of Mohab Road and Gad Street, Doyle pulled into a convenience store. With determined effort, he pulled his uncooperative and now stiffening body out of the rental car. *Rigor mortis, I'm sure*, he thought to himself. He pushed through the swinging glass door and passed the deskclerk who was too absorbed in texting on his cellphone to bother looking up. Doyle went to the back of the store and located a bottle of hydrogen peroxide, a package of disposable diapers, paper towels, and a roll of duct tape. He took these to the restroom and did his best to self-administer field dressings to his wounds.

As Doyle exited the restroom and approached the counter, the clerk looked up from his cellphone. The face of the clerk had, over the course of three years of tedious routine, adopted a permanent mask of incurable boredom. The cure now stood before him. The clerk's facial muscles, accustomed to one expression of wearied ennui, now strained against involuntary forces that at once urged horror, and at the other end of the spectrum, encouraged hilarity. Here was a blood soaked, paper towel and duct tape encrusted, monument of gore. The man's face was disgusting, one of his eyes was so swollen that it looked as if it was about to pop out. He could not help remembering the Disney characterization of Quasimodo. *Actually*, he mused, *the Hunchback of Notre Dame has nothing on this guy.* There was also the smell. *Las Vegas*, the clerk correctly concluded.

Doyle placed his now semi-consumed items on the counter. His remaining good eye spotted a rack of disposable cellphones behind the clerk. He nodded towards the display. "I'll take one of those cells."

Your cell is working, advised his interior self.

The SEC-CEL is out, he explained.

True, but the personal line still functions.

Which can be monitored just as easily as the secured functions.

The clerk hesitated and then asked, "You want any airtime cards?"

"How many pre-loaded minutes does the phone come with?"

"These ones don't have any."

"Okay, gimme a card for sixty minutes."

Sixty minutes? You're an optimist. We won't last long enough to use them.

Shutup.

Buying a cheap burner won't make any difference. They can still track us.

It will take them a little more time to find me.

Make sure it has access to the web.

Okay.

Make sure you pay in cash.

Don't nag me.

That's my job.

What's mine?

To get us killed, and you're doing swell if you were wondering.

The clerk scanned the items and glanced up at the register screen. "That'll be one hundred twelve dollars and thirty-seven cents."

Doyle pulled out his wallet, discovering that the funds available to him were the five new crisp twenty-dollar bills he had obtained from the ATM in the airport lobby in Eau Claire. He inwardly shrugged, extracted the new bills, and handed the money to the clerk.

"Hey, this is only—"

Doyle leaned forward and murmured quietly enough to escape having his voice recorded on the store security monitor, "Report this and I will come back for you." The clerk's reaction was exactly what Doyle expected and had hoped for: paralyzed terror.

As he walked out of the store, his judgmental interior voice could not resist. *So, now we're robbing Seven-Elevens? We've certainly made it to the big leagues.*

Shutup.

He'll call the cops.

For getting shorted twelve bucks? I'm pretty sure he won't.

It's better to be right than to be sure.

As Doyle stepped up to the car, he decided that there no longer was any choice. It was either seek medical attention or die in a rented Buick Skylark. Doyle initiated the newly purchased burner cellphone and then tapped a search onto the screen.

< physicians near me >

The choice offered by the internet was easy. All but one of the doctors listed on the screen were located back in Las Vegas. The lone local entry did not specify, but he knew that anyone this far from a city would be forced by geography and circumstances to be a general practitioner. He pushed the navigation application for directions. Mercifully, the instructions were quite simple: thirteen kilometers to the west, in the town of Sheol.

Doyle attempted to reenter the car with a modicum of grace and gingerness but could not bring to bear sufficient control of his blood deprived and inflexible muscles. He dumped into the seat with a groan of agony that would have been a scream had he any strength left to spare for his voice. Mastering the effort to concentrate, he pushed the start button, put the car into reverse, and pulled out of the parking place.

We might not make it to the doctor's office.

It's just down the road.

Like I said, we might not make it.

As Doyle maneuvered onto the street, he saw a billboard at the intersection before him.

> # To convert or not to convert?
> # That is the question...
>
> ## Actually, we have the answer:
> ## You'll be converting, just like
> ## eveyone else.
>
> ## The Great Conversion
> ## Ready or not, it's coming

"God help me," said Doyle aloud to himself, "I guess I'm as ready as I'll ever be."

The small pewter pin lay on the floor, about half a meter to the left of an overstuffed armchair. Gaude picked it up, examined it briefly, and then handed it to his partner. "Remember this?"

Watt studied the lapel pin. It was a stag's head with a cross between the antlers. "Yes, Saint Hubert's cross."

"Or perhaps the cross of Saint Eustace."

"You're quibbling again."

"Would you prefer if I pointed out that it's also the trademark for *Jägermeister*?"

"Not exactly the same design as the liquor logo, but very similar."

"Sounds to me like you're the one who's quibbling."

"Let's just ascribe it to 'you say tomato, I say tomatoe' and leave it at that."

"Okay, a strange coincidence."

"Not a coincidence. It was left here for us."

"This is our clue?"

"It seems so."

"Great. So, we are looking for an arsonist with a chest cold?"

"Show a little more optimism."

"Give me a reason."

"We're not in jail, are we?"

"You set a mighty low bar for being optimistic."

"The secret of my success."

"It seems to me that the secret of your success is that business card trick of yours. You outdid yourself this time. I can't believe that the security guard let us off the hook, much less let us poke around here for twenty minutes, before he calls the cops."

"The man knows an honest face when he sees one."

"That's lame, even for you."

"Every once in a while, I happen across an alumnus of Cairo Investigative Agency."

"Another one? How many Bill Watts are out there?"

"One hundred forty-four thousand. There might even be another Dan Gaude or two."

"Don't count on that," muttered Gaude. He took another look around the spacious suite, elaborately decorated in the theme of a medieval castle. "Before the police arrive, we need to make sense of this. The Saint Hubert pin. Do you think that the story means anything?"

"What do you think?"

"Does that question-as-an-answer indicate that you don't know the meaning of the story, or that you are being pedantic?"

"Testy, aren't we?"

"Someone just tried to blow off my head."

Watt came as close to a sneer as a person of his natural good humor could muster. "Whoever fired that gun was a professional. He killed the lights to stop us from seeing him. Remember the sort of company that we are chasing, not to mention the city we are in. He was doing us a favor. He's probably the best-mannered hit man you'll ever encounter."

"I've never encountered a hit man before."

"And you call yourself an investigative reporter," said Watt with a chuckle as he opened the wet bar refrigerator and pulled out a bottle of Sin City Sarsaparilla and a can of Joseph James Weize Guy beer. "Care for one?"

"Isn't this interfering with a crime scene?"

"I suppose that you're right. Do you want me to put your beer back in the fridge?"

"Naaah, you've already tampered with the evidence."

"Laissez les bons temps rouler."

"Amen," answered Gaude. He took a series of swallows of the frigid beer as he regarded the small engraved plaque above the bar.

Thanksgiving

Whoever drinks beer is quick to sleep;
whoever sleeps does not sin;
whoever does not sin enters heaven;
therefore, let us give thanks for beer!

—Martin Luther

"At least it's a break from all those poems by Reuben Malachi," said Gaude. "What about the pin? Is it our clue?"

"It could be."

"What would be its significance?"

"The moral of the legend," explained Watt, "is what we seek to destroy may often be our guide to salvation. The victim is the savior. The man we persecute delivers us, just as the hunted stag leads the *jägermeister* back to the safety of his home."

"That isn't a clue. That is a sermon."

"Sermons, by definition, are clues."

"To what?"

"To where we are going."

"How do we know that's where we'll find our arsonist?"

"We'll know."

"And when you find him?" Gaude emptied his beer, put the can on the counter, and raised his palms up to Watt in mock dramatic fashion. "Don't tell me, let me guess. When I find him, I'll have acquired salvation."

Watt finished his own bottle and discarded it into a wastepaper basket. "You'll never acquire it," he said as he casually walked for the front door, "but you might stumble into it."

"Stumbling seems to be what we do best."

The Advisors

"Perhaps you need to engage in some self-examination."

"What?" came the shocked response. "Sister, that's not a very nun-like suggestion. I let the doctor take care of all that if you don't mind."

Sister Mary Margaret stifled an outright laugh, closed her eyes, bit her tongue, and forced herself to maintain a serene countenance. "I am sorry, Mister Rizzo, I was referring to spiritual self-examination. For instance, have you contemplated your role in God's plan? Have you dwelt on the question of your life's meaning?"

"My life?"

"Yes."

"You mean, like my purpose here on earth?"

"Exactly."

"The meaning of life is to stay alive, especially when there are a dozen creeps out there trying to make it otherwise."

"Oh, my! I was not thinking of anything so violent."

"That's because you haven't been living the life that I've been living. I'll tell you what the meaning of life is about, Sister. Living means you've cheated death. That's the difference between me and all those other bastards—"

"Please, Mister Rizzo!"

"Sorry, Sister. What I mean was, I was better at cheating than was…my…associates."

"I would hardly think that cheating is a matter upon one would attest to proudly."

"It all depends on the reason why you cheat. If it is for a good purpose, then it's gotta be okay. Right, Sister?"

"What might your noble purpose be that could justify cheating?"

"To win. To beat those other sons of bitches—"

"Mister Rizzo!"

"Sorry, Sister. What I was trying to say is that they don't cheat as good because they're all a bunch of cowards."

"What makes them cowards?"

"They're afraid to die, which means that they're twice as afraid to live."

"I am not quite sure that I grasp your concept, but I must admit that it has a touch of the Shakespearean."

"I don't have a touch of anything, Sister. Don't worry, I don't have any germs on me. I haven't even been down with a cold for almost a year."

"Thank you for that assurance. You were saying something about courage?"

"If you have courage, you have less to live for than a coward. At least, that's what the coward believes. But if you have courage, and manage to avoid dying, then even if you had less to live *for*, you wind up with more to live *with*. You see what I'm saying, Sister?"

"I am trying my best to work through your tortured poetry, Mister Rizzo, although I am a little bit tangled up in your rationalization of cheating your way through life."

"That's not hard. Everybody cheats, so if you cheat better than the next guy it's not really so much of a sin, is it? After all, don't their loser cheating sins cancel out my winner cheating sins?"

"I am quite sure that the system does not work that way."

"Hey, Sister, I've been working the system since I was ten years old, and I'm telling ya, that's exactly the way the system works."

"I was referring to God's system."

"Oh. Yeah, I guess he has a system too."

"Mister Rizzo, you seem very focused on winning. Would you say that you are a competitive person?"

"Yeah. Winning is everything—Vince Lombardi, right? Ya gotta be number one."

"Is being number two all that bad?"

"No, not at all. If you are number two, you can grab a knife, stab number one in the back, and bury him in a shallow grave. Then you become number one."

"I see. However, once you become number one, is it not possible that another number two might stab *you* in the back?"

"What kind of dirty back-stabbing sunnavabitch would do something like that?"

"I...I cannot...I..." She closed her eyes briefly and tried to regain her composure. "Perhaps we should talk about your childhood."

Nineteen: Thanksgiving

He is a young boy again, perhaps six or seven years of age. They are at Washington National Airport. It is night, a warm but very comfortable night—probably September. The lights glare on the stern—almost Nazi-inspired—architecture of the terminal façade, yet to the boy it is beautiful. Everything is beautiful. Dad is arriving on an airplane. Mom is dressed as usual in a tasteful, conservative dress, matching coat, matching shoes, matching gloves, matching pillbox hat, matching handbag. She has dressed that way his entire childhood. Mother's perfectly coordinated wardrobe would not start to disintegrate until her survivor social security checks began to arrive in the mail.

There is virtually no traffic in front of the terminal that night. It must be very late. He looks past the terminal to the glow that is the Capital. It is all good. Dad is coming home.

There he is, carrying a well-worn military style travel bag. Dad wears his perfectly uncoordinated yet absolutely consistent and predictable wardrobe. Dark trousers, a short-sleeve cotton oxford shirt, a narrow striped tie with a company tietack, black wingtip shoes, wartorn and beaten. The soles are thick, the leather almost crocodile-like from the age and sedimentary layers of polish. Dad paid him twenty-five cents for each shine, once a week. The shoes are overdue for a polishing. He will shine them tomorrow night and Dad will give him an entire dollar—a substitute for the reuniting hug that will not be given at the airport.

Dad approaches with a wide smile, embraces Mom and gives her a kiss. He tousles his son's hair. 'How was your flight, honey?' This is Mom's obligatory and meaninglessly routine question that to the six or seven-year-old him is neither obligatory nor meaningless. 'We made great time,' is Dad's response. 'We flew on a turboprop.'

Wow, a turboprop! The exoticness of that! It could have been a rocket ship as far as the boy is concerned. Dad flew on a turboprop.

Gaude awoke in the passenger seat of the rented Oldsmobile. "That wasn't a dream, that was a memory," he said involuntarily, and aloud.

Watt was driving the car and responded casually, "I really don't consider the two to be any different. At least not in my case."

"Maybe, but this dream wasn't *my* memory."

"Whose was it?"

"I dunno…it was a dream about me and my parents, but it all seemed to be happening sometime decades before I was born."

"That doesn't mean you weren't there," said Watt casually.

"It doesn't?"

"Not in my experience."

"I know that should surprise me, but after scurrying aimlessly across the country with a certifiable lunatic, it no longer does." Gaude looked around the car and then out the window. "Okay, let me think…we're heading to…?" Gaude trailed off.

"You haven't forgotten again, have you?"

"No, I remember that we caught the flight from Las Vegas to Portland. We're heading to a place called Thanksgiving."

"You got it."

"How much farther to go?"

"Forty minutes or so is my estimate," said Watt, "but I suspect that your robotic cellphone girlfriend would quibble with that."

"A robotic cellphone girlfriend is all I have left, thanks to you," Gaude groused good-naturedly. "Besides, my cellphone is not the quibbler. I'm the quibbler, remember?" Gaude checked the distance on his cell and announced, "Fifteen minutes."

"See? I told you."

"The difference of twenty-five minutes is not quibbling. That's almost half an hour."

"In fifteen minutes, it will be almost exactly noon," stated Watt, refusing to take the bait from Gaude. "I say we stop for lunch as soon as we get into town."

⌘

James Parker Doyle awoke. His internal clock informed him that it was late afternoon, but not with the usual precision that he had come to rely upon his entire life. Despite this, he knew that at least ten hours had passed since he had collapsed at the entrance of a small clinic in an equally small town surrounded by seemingly endless stretches of remarkably unremarkable desert. He was again in a hospital bed and again had wires and tubes connected to his damaged body. Doyle conducted a quick survey of the room. Cheap wooden paneling, amber colored linoleum floor, and a few scattered chrome and crimson naugahyde chairs. If it were not for the medcomp station next to his bed, he would have thought he was in the middle of a southern barbershop instead of a western medical facility. He heard music coming through the hollow-core wooden door to his right. He recognized it as Ni'ihau Child's 'Deceiver," a tribute to Shakespeare's Sonnet Ninety-Three.

> *So I shall live, supposing you are true,*
> *So much deceived by your pretty face*
> *You say you love me, and I believe it too*
> *You smile at me, but your heart's in another place*

Doyle knew that the temptation to let down his guard in the apparent safe harbor of a doctor's office was an unacceptable risk. He had to keep his mind active. He recalled his initial training. In recent years, ORCA's indoctrination and basic training had been pared down, due as much to budget constraints as to a de-emphasis on the field operative facet of the organization's mission. Now the program was a familiar reflection of the FBI course at Quantico with a lot more computer and crypto. He recalled seeing a recent notice that new analyst hires would actually be exempted from Basic—unimaginable. Originally, there had been three months in the classroom, three months of field labwork, and six months of field experience wherein the operatives could not turn a corner or open a car trunk without someone lurking for an attack. More than a few trainees, and instructors for that matter, wound up in hospitals, and the admittees were not limited to physical injury. The stress was intended to imbue the agent with not only the reflexes but also the native wariness of an animal. Those who could not cope were provided the finest in psychological rehabilitation that

ORCA's stolen money could buy before their release from the program.

What a piker I've become, he thought to himself. *I could have taken out all three lights in the hotel room in one shot. Why didn't I shoot the wall switch near the door? Was one of the civilians in the target path?* He tried to replay the scene in his mind. *Waste of time*, he told himself.

The circuit breaker shot wasn't bad. You redeemed yourself, his mental hall monitor observed.

Too close for comfort.

You got away with it.

This time, he conceded grudgingly.

Fine, just don't make that mistake again.

Okay, coach. Not that I'm going to get another chance. I'll probably be a corpse by daybreak.

The door to Doyle's right opened. "Welcome to the land of the living, Mister…Doyle, I believe?"

Female. Latina. Age thirty-nine. Height, one point six one meter. Weight, sixty-two kilos. Dark brown hair, intermittently colored blonde, kept in tight bun except on weekends. High forehead, delicate features, perfectly aligned teeth. Dark brown eyes with amber flecks. Better than perfect vision: 20/10. White lab coat over blue scrubs. Converse tennis shoes. Born in Barquisimeto. Venezuelan father and Cuban mother. At age four, mother died of salmonella poisoning from unpasteurized milk. Father immediately remarried. Stepmother Canadian Presbyterian missionary. Perfectly bilingual and dreams in both Spanish and English. Particularly fond of yogurt-covered raisins. Graduated from medical school from the University of Zulia. Granted visa to perform residency in Quebec, where she picked up a working knowledge of French. Hired by Sharp Memorial in San Diego and worked in the hospital emergency room for three years. Virgin by choice, despite countless entreaties by suitors of all sexes and genders. Moved to Nevada in order to…to… The voice suddenly stopped.

"I assume that you looked though the contents of my wallet," said Doyle. "You have me at a disadvantage."

"Olivia Trastámara. Feel free to call me Doctor, or Doc if you prefer to be informal."

Doyle chuckled gingerly, in cautious deference to the sutured gashes that liberally covered a significant portion of his body. He attempted to reach over to pull a sheet over himself and discovered that his right arm was punctuated with three different intravenous tubes. The doctor noticed the gesture. "Are you the shy type?"

"Not at all, it was just a draft."

"The temperature outside is in the nineties and the air conditioning in this clinic can't really be described as frosty. Does it bother you to have a woman as a doctor?"

"I see no relationship between a person's allotted plumbing and the ability to heal."

"No, I meant that it might be a bit embarrassing to be unclothed in front of a woman."

"It wouldn't be the first time I appeared unclothed in front of a woman, and, God willing, it won't be the last. I'm covering myself because of a slight draft and because I look like a wreck. Ummm…let me amend that. I *am* a wreck. Perhaps the next time we meet, I will present a more dashing figure than a pile of badly-ground hamburger."

"I have a strange attraction to men who have been sliced and diced indiscriminately."

"Then I am certainly your Prince Charming. Remind me to get your number before I'm discharged."

"The only number that you'll need is 911. Something tells me that it is on the favorites button of your cellphone."

"At least it's not the number for the coroner."

"That's the number I'll be calling if we don't get you to a hospital soon. I don't suppose that there is a plausible and innocuous reason why you are in this condition?"

"Sword fight with a goat-eyed demon. Fell out of medieval tower. Twenty-foot drop."

"Does measuring your fall in feet make it less painful than a plunge in meters?" asked the doctor sardonically. She then shrugged. "Okay, so you're not going to tell me."

"Someone wanted to motivate me to pay off a gambling debt and tossed me out of a window."

"That's more like it. At least you're alive."

"If you call this living."

"Consider yourself lucky. Most people don't survive being tossed out of a window, and even fewer live to tell the tale with no broken bones."

"I know something about falling. In my younger days, I served in the Eighty-Second Airborne."

"Don't paratroopers use something called a parachute?"

"Yes, that's the preferred method of slowing down when one is plummeting to the earth, but I didn't have that luxury last night. When I hit the ground, I must have reflexively executed a PLF."

"I assume that PLF means something other than pathetic leap of faith?"

"Yeah," said Doyle with a painful chuckle, "it means parachute landing fall. You kind of collapse and roll to dissipate the shock and distribute the weight. Sort of like G.I. Joe meets Raggedy Anne."

"I'm still dubious about how you could have survived."

"I would be too, but suddenly I'm a believer. There's a blackhat back at Fort Benning who trained me twenty-some years ago that I definitely owe a beer."

"A blackhat?"

"Sort of like an airborne drill instructor."

"I'm not buying it."

"Good, because I'm not selling it. Just get me bandaged, position me vertical, and I'll take it from there."

"Taping diapers on yourself was a nice touch. Did you also pick that up from your days in the Army?"

"Something like that."

"I can't decide whether you were a bigger mess last night or now that your body has been given a few hours to realize that it should be dead."

"Should be dead and actually dead are very different concepts. I'm ready to check out."

"Listen, these wounds are wide and deep."

"How wide and deep?"

"Not as deep as a well or wide as a church door, but 'twill do. If we don't get you to a hospital in the next hour or two, by sunset it will be sunset for you, at the risk of getting poetic."

"I've just come from Vegas. It's my gamble."

"You'll lose. Don't even think about it. You don't look like a fool."

"What does a fool look like?"

"Twenty years old and on a motorcycle," quipped Olivia Trastámara. Doyle started to laugh and the doctor immediately lifted her hands in remonstration. "Whoa, there! My mistake. Let's not have any laughing."

"I thought that laughter is the best medicine," countered Doyle, forcing himself not to grimace from the pain.

"Not when you have fifty stitches in your face. I lost count when it came to sewing up your side."

Doyle returned a wan smile. "Okay, I'll behave, if you agree to cut me loose."

"Why?"

"I have my reasons."

"They can't be good enough to die. Do you remember what time it was when you got those gashes and cuts?"

"About nine o'clock last night."

The doctor scowled, poking the largest incision. "That looks about right. Maybe I should correct myself. I'm sending you to a hospital right now. It's the most convenient way of eventually transferring you into a morgue."

"Finish sewing me up yourself."

"I've done enough sewing on you to qualify as a member of the Garment Workers' Union. However, those are temporary patch jobs by a country doctor."

"You don't look like a country doctor to me."

"You need to see more of the country."

"I agree. Unplug me from these tubes and I will be on my way to visit the Wonderful Wizard of Oz."

"You probably need a wizard given those wounds, but I'll settle for some competent surgeons in Las Vegas."

"Back to Las Vegas? You want to take me out of the frying pan and put me back in the fire."

"I doubt that your no-neck debt collectors will be visiting the Acute Care Unit at Sunrise Hospital."

"Don't be so sure. That's probably where most of their clients end up."

"Or at Woodlawn Cemetery."

"I'll take my chances."

"You've run out of chances. See that bag of plasma?" Doyle attempted to follow the doctor's finger pointing over Doyle's left shoulder. He could not turn his head that far and returned his gaze to the physician with a look of 'I'll take your word for it.' "I have put six pints of blood into you already," said the doctor, "and this bag of plasma is all that I have left. I even considered giving you a direct transfusion, but you aren't my type."

"What a pity," replied Doyle with a smirk. "I was hoping you were my type. Trust me, when I'm not falling out of windows, I prefer to spend my evenings admiring sunsets and taking romantic strolls along the beach."

"You are going to need another couple of quarts—I mean liters—within the next twenty-four hours."

"I might be dead by the time I'm wheeled into an operating room. Cut your losses and kick me out the door. I'm doing you a favor."

"I see," the doctor responded skeptically. "I suppose that means I should be doing you a favor by allowing you to kill yourself?"

"I have always depended upon the kindness of strangers."

"Perhaps it hasn't crossed your seriously injured brain that it is my sworn obligation to keep you alive."

"I release you from all liability. *Te absolvo.*"

"Don't hand that back to me." The doctor stood up, walked to a refrigerator and selected a small glass bottle. She opened a cabinet, removed a plastic packet, and opened it, revealing a hypodermic needle. "Have you had a recent tetanus shot?"

"Yes."

"Good. I'm giving you a wide spectrum antibacterial." The doctor administered the inoculation. "You came here from Las Vegas, right?"

Doyle nodded. "You get much of this around here?"

"No. That's why I live here and not there. Whoever or whatever you are running from won't find you. I can see to it that there will be no records. Just let me take you where we can get you some help."

Doyle was unsure whether it was loss of blood or simple exhaustion, but it was becoming progressively more difficult to stay awake. "I...I can't..."

"Yes, you can. Relax. That shot I just gave you will let you sleep."

Doyle attempted to sit up, but with almost no effort, the physician gently pushed him back down on the narrow bed. "What did you just give me?" muttered Doyle, as the room began to spin.

"Just a country doctor recipe of a little Phenobarbital and Ketamine. If it doesn't kill you outright, you should have another nice twelve-hour nap."

What little vision his remaining good eye afforded now began to dim. The lights of the room faded away as did the music playing from the other room, 'Gentle Oblivion' by Niʻihau Child.

It's time to go, just let it slip
Don't worry, release your grip
All goes gray
You drift away

Relax, my friend, no need to cry
You know some day we all will die

The doctor waited patiently until the sedative had taken full effect. She walked into her cheaply paneled office, picked up the telephone receiver, and pushed the speed dial button marked 'AIR EVAC.' Within three minutes of the call, a helicopter was lifting off from the county hospital to pick up her patient. She went back to Doyle, placed a cuff on the man's arm, and checked blood pressure. *Won't last much longer,* she mused dispassionately.

Relax, my friend, no need to cry
You know some day we all will die

Fifteen minutes later, the doctor detected the unmistakable audible signature of a rotary wing aircraft. The air medics met her at the door and with choreographed professional precision, fitted a new intravenous plasma feed, checked vital signs, transferred the patient onto the stretcher, and departed.

The doctor heard the rush of the helicopter fans begin to dissipate as she logged onto the internet from her computer. After typing in the site address and passing through a rigorous series of security protocols, she received the prompt:

REVEAL THYSELF

⌘

Gaude put down his menu and looked over at Bill Watt. "I'm trying to guess what kind of chili you will conjure up in this part of the country. Maybe salmon chili?"

"Good guess, but no. Vegetarian Quinoa Chili."

"Kin-Wha? Is that Korean cabbage?"

"Quinoa. It's a South American grain."

A tall sandy-haired young man wearing a nondescript t-shirt and faded jeans approached their table. "Hiya, I'm River. I'll be your lunch buddy today."

"You're my lunch buddy?" asked Gaude skeptically.

"You bet."

"What should I do with this lunch buddy?" Gaude asked, gesturing to Bill Watt.

"You should share him. We share everything here."

"Everything?"

"You bet."

"Do you share your tips?"

"You bet."

"You share your car?"

"I don't have a car. Cars pollute."

"Right. Do you share your bicycle?"

"You bet."

"Do you share your secrets?"

"You bet."

"Do you share your girlfriend?"

River reacted to this with the expected air of surprise. He then quickly regained his composure and responded, "Well, duh, of course! Who doesn't?"

Watt and Gaude exchanged a look of bewilderment. Gaude then decided to give this another try. "If you share your food, that means we get it for free."

"Huh?"

"If you are sharing, we don't need to pay."

"But you have to share your money. That's how sharing works."

"I see that you have this all figured out."

"You bet."

"Funny, sharing sounds a lot like free enterprise."

"Free enterprise?"

"Yes."

"Never heard of it," replied River. "But if it's free, it must be okay. Have you decided on what you would like to have for lunch?"

Bill Watt ordered the Quinoa Chili and a bottle of Thomas

196

Kemper Orange Cream while Gaude examined the menu skeptically. "I'll just have a burger."

"Tofu burger?"

"No, thanks."

"Lentil burger?"

"Not today."

"Ground nut burger?"

"I don't think so."

"Chickpea burger?"

"No."

"Then what kind of burger do you want?" asked their exasperated waiter.

"A burger burger."

"Sorry?"

"A meat burger."

"Meat?"

"Yes."

"You mean, from a live animal?" asked River, clearly revolted by the idea.

"No, certainly not!" responded Gaude. River the waiter made an audible sigh of relief. Gaude cocked his head and smiled. "Make sure that the animal is dead first."

"Dead?"

"Yes, and cooked. I gave up eating raw meat for Lent."

River's face suddenly brightened. "Oh, I get it. I'm being totally punked!"

"I have no idea if any punking is going on. I just want a real, authentic, legitimate, all-American USDA beef hamburger."

River returned a blank look of shocked incomprehension. After a moment of emotional stasis, he turned to the large open window connecting the dining area and the kitchen and shouted, "Hey Serenity, there's a guy out here who wants to eat flesh!"

"No way!" answered a voice from the other side of the opening. "Does he have a bone through his nose?"

"Hey, don't be culturally insensitive, Serenity," reprimanded River.

The unseen Serenity responded, "Sorry, I didn't realize that I was being harsh. That's not the person who I am."

River turned back to his customers. "We serve all races, creeds, cultures, genders, sexual lifestyles, refugees, immigrants, and persons who opt for body piercings of any kind."

"So," responded Gaude, "if I was a cannibal with a bone through my nose—"

"That's racist and insensitive."

"It is?"

"Yes, it is hurtful. Insulting statements like that are illegal."

"They are?"

"Sure, and trying to wear a bone through your nose would be cultural appropriation. That's illegal too."

"I see. I apologize. What I meant to say was that if I was someone who actually consumed human flesh—"

"You mean like a zombie?"

"If that works for you, fine. Would I be an anti-zombie racist to compare myself to them?"

"Zombies are equal opportunity employers. Anybody can be one."

"Great. So, if a zombie cannibal—wearing culturally appropriate piercings—came into this diner, you would serve him?"

"Of course."

"What if that zombie cannibal asked to be served meat?"

"Sorry, no way!"

"What's so awful about meat?"

"It's bad for the environment. All those animals consume plants and vegetables that humans should be eating directly."

"Like hay and grass?"

"You bet."

"Do you have hay and grass on the menu?"

"Of course!"

"I see," said Gaude nodding thoughtfully. "Don't people also cause a lot of environmental damage?"

"Yeah, sure. Humans are the worst offenders."

"Right. So, how about if you go out and find a young child, maybe four or five years old and roast him on a spit for me. Then I can have a decent lunch and you will have one less human who is selfishly using up nature's resources. That's a win all around, right?"

River pondered the proposal. "I'll have to ask Serenity if she can put in an order for a young child."

"You do that."

"Should it be a boy or a girl?" asked River.

"You're asking whether it should be a boy or a pre-woman?"

"Right."

"Women are historically downtrodden and exploited by our brutal male-centric society, so the female must be spared. Order up a juicy young boy."

"Right, good idea." River turned to leave, but then checked himself and turned back to Gaude. "Sorry, I forgot that I still don't have your order."

"Ham sandwich?"

River shook his head 'no.'

"Turkey club?"

River rolled his eyes.

"Roast beef sub?"

River started to giggle.

"How about a pastrami on rye?"

River's face contorted quizzically. "What kind of animal is a pastrami?"

Gaude hung his head in capitulation. "I'll have a bowl of vegetable soup and an eggplant with soy-swiss cheese wrap."

"Now you're talking," said River approvingly. "That wasn't so painful, was it?"

As their waiter departed, Gaude answered the last question with, "No more painful than eating glass."

"Glass happens to be the blue-plate special today," mocked Bill Watt.

"Thanks for your support."

"My pleasure. By the way, your cannibal *shtick* was excellent, Mister Jonathan Swift."

"Yes, I thought that it was an elegant, if modest, proposal."

Ten minutes later, River returned with their orders. Gaude, despite himself, had to admit that the vegetarian lunch was quite good. A customer walked over to the jukebox, selected a song, and inserted a debit card into the payslot.

> *It just keeps getting stranger*
> *This crazy quest I'm on*
> *It's a real game changer*
> *As I go hither and yon*

199

I'm driving all across the land
But can I find the key?
From doughnut stands to Casagrand
Are all the same to me

As the partners were finishing, River approached, singing along with the music.

"That's a Ni'ihau Child song, isn't it?" asked Gaude.

"Yeah, I'm mostly into indie."

"Indie? Is that what they play?"

"You bet."

"We've been hearing their songs almost everywhere we go."

"Yeah, they're the biggest thing since Lenny Killed an Astronaut."

"Who?"

"You know, the band that used to call themselves Superb Nightmares for Sale."

"Ummm...I don't think—"

'But their drummer left and joined Malignant Growth Ruined My Birthday Party."

"Those are bands?"

"You bet. They are epic...huge!"

"You mean like the Beetles?"

"What kind of name is that for a band?" asked River.

"Never mind," said Gaude.

River shrugged and never minded. "Would you like dessert?"

"What have you got?"

"Eskimo Pies."

"Eskimo Pies? Isn't that a racist and pejorative term?"

"You're right! I hadn't realized it before!" exclaimed River.

"And taking the pies away from Eskimos is cultural appropriation. We should just eat our own Anglo-Saxon pies instead."

"Absolutely!"

"Unless the Eskimo Pies are actually being manufactured by authentic Eskimos and we pay a good price under fair-trade practices."

"Totally!"

"We also need to make sure that the Eskimos are unionized, are provided safe and dignified working conditions, and that their workplace is environmentally friendly."

"Wow! You're totally woke. We're in synch! Cool."

"So, what else do you have?"

"What else do I have for what?" asked River blankly.

"For dessert."

"Oh, right. Well…nothing. That's the only thing on the dessert menu here at Northern Light Café. In fact, it's the only dessert that has ever been served here, since 1947."

"It sounds like you are the Northern Light historian."

"No, not really. I'm just helping out here temporarily as a favor to Serenity."

"Really? You're not a full-time waiter? Are you a student?"

"No," replied River shaking his head, "I graduated from college already with a degree in comparative gender studies."

"So, besides waiting tables here at the café, what keeps you busy?"

"I work on my parent's farm."

"That's good honest work."

"Yeah, it is. We grow cannabis."

"Of course you do."

"Business has been great, especially since we started supplying the church crowd."

"The church crowd?"

"There are the Rastafarians…"

"Okay…"

"Then there are the Shaivites…"

"Shaivites?" asked Gaude.

"They are the Hindu sect devoted to Lord Shiva, who I'm sure you know is hugely important."

"Alright. I suppose that there is a connection between Shiva and marijuana?"

"Sure, everyone knows that," said River condescendingly.

"Present company excluded," interjected Bill Watt.

"Most recently we've been getting a lot of business from the Maguvians."

"I've never heard of them."

"The worship Magu, the Chinese goddess of ganja."

"I should have seen that coming," said Gaude. "So, you are now in the family business?"

"Just for a while. My real goal is to run for office."

"Run for office? You mean go into politics?"

"Absolutely. There are a lot of messed up things in this town, this state, this country, and this world. I'd like to try to make a difference."

"I think you would be a perfect candidate for a place like this."

"The Republican Party doesn't think so."

"Republican?"

"Sure," confirmed River. "When I was in college, I was president of the campus Young Republicans Society. It's hard being a conservative like me in Oregon. You wouldn't know it by just looking around, but this place is crawling with wild-eyed liberals. I say we need more commonsense solutions."

"Really?"

"You bet. The problem is that my party thinks I'm too right-wing for this district. They want me to soften up on some issues, but I'm not budging. I believe in standing by my principles."

"Like making sure that no one eats meat?"

"Exactly. Think of how much money this country would save if we didn't spend it all on meat products. I bet that we could balance the budget and pay off the national debt in no time if we simply established a tofu-based economy."

"You have our vote," assured Bill Watt.

"Thank you. Are you registered voters in Oregon?"

"No, does that really matter?"

"I guess not," answered River, "as long as you're sincere."

"And a vegetarian."

"Right."

"And not a racist."

"Of course."

"And not insensitive."

"You bet."

A few minutes later, Watt paid for the lunch at the cash register and then tossed the keys to Gaude. "Your turn to drive."

The entrance to the town was difficult to miss. They approached a traffic roundabout at the center of which was a plastic cornucopia the size of a school bus and a companion sign cheerfully welcoming visitors to the town of Thanksgiving. Gaude proceeded around the traffic circle and headed into town only to encounter another circle, this time featuring a wall approximately two meters wide and at least twice as tall built out of rough-hewn planks of Douglas fir. Gaude was not at all surprised to see the words of a poem carved onto the face of the wood. He gradually braked the car, checked the rear-view mirror to ensure that no other vehicles were following them down the road, and then came to a stop.

"Are we getting out?"

"No need. We can read it easily enough from here."

"You're not getting jaded about these poems, are you?"

"Naaah, I just thought it would be more comfortable sitting here and reading the latest poesy by my now-favorite mystery poet."

"Mystery poet? I thought that you already checked him out on your beloved web."

"Yes, but the search didn't explain why these monuments—or whatever you call them—are showing up across the country."

"What did you learn about him?"

"He is a drunk, a womanizer, a rabble-rouser, and a public nuisance."

"So, in other words—"

"Yeah, my kind of guy."

Giving Thanks

In November they were plump,
For they had feasted well,
Now came the time of reckoning
And to bid their farm farewell.

They were shunted onto trucks,
The clueless poultry stared
Within the cage, without the cage,
Too stupid to be scared.

Soon herded as before
And strapped to the machine,
A stainless blade decapitates,
The gutting is hygiene.

Wrapped in plastic coats,
In frozen stacks they lay,
Shipped across America
For the Thanksgiving Day.

Upon the platter served,
The giant bird displayed
With no more role of dignity
Than during life had played.

The guests all feasted well,
From the table each did slump
With pleasure, everyone agreed
That in November they were plump.

—Reuben Malachi

"Actually, I kind of like this one."

"So, now you're starting to take a shine to his doggerel?"

"I have to admit, it rates up there with 'There once was a gal from Par-eee.' Well, almost…" Gaude gave a sidelong glance at Watt to see his partner's reaction to the jibe.

"You're attempting to be incorrigible."

"Oh, I think that I achieved incorrigible status years ago."

"And apparently I haven't made any inroads these past few weeks in regard to your moral development."

"Not true!" gamely protested Gaude with a wicked grin. "Now I swear only under my breath."

"How encouraging! My life's work has not been in vain," Watt announced in a melodramatic jest.

⌘

"Is all well with the world?"

"No."

"But we are working to make it better."

"Each and every day, but I need a little help from my friends."

"Lean on me."

"Someone seems to have allowed a redoubtable bloodhound to track me down and harass me. I find this rather distressing."

"I cannot imagine that he gave you any real trouble."

"Then you lack adequate imagination."

"*Mea culpa.*"

"I am not in the business of granting dispensation."

"That's just part of your charm."

"Enough. I need to find him. He is the proverbial moving target."

"Given the resources that you now have, I thought that would be easy for you to do."

"He disappeared."

"From where?"

"It's not a question of where so much as who."

"The DG?"

"They are likely involved."

"That could complicate things."

"It will be your job to uncomplicate them."

"Death always leads to complications."

"No, death is not a complicated thing. The living quite often lead very messy lives, but once deceased, they have the opportunity of being the very model of orderliness."

"Thy will be done. I will ensure that he is wrapped in a very tidy package."

"Be mindful on this one. He has a long history of eluding us. The man can be slippery when he needs to be. One might say that he's got Teflon."

"I'll make it stick."

"See that you do so. This is a priority."

"I'll put a girdle round about the earth in forty minutes."

"Make it twenty."

"As you wish."

"In the meantime, we need to dispatch our janitors to do a little tidying up."

"Anyplace in particular?"

"Summerland Quest."

"A charming location. I'll volunteer to go myself."

"No, send in the Locusts."

"Really? The Locusts?"

"I need professionals. Real professionals."

"You want to clean the entire office?"

"Yes, they must be thorough, but be quick."

"Quick and painless?"

"Yes."

"How thoughtful. You are a prince."

"So to speak," he smirked. "One might even say I am charitable."

"Christian charity?"

"Leave the irony to me."

"And the other annoyance you mentioned?"

"When you locate him, we will dispatch my good friend."

"You have so many of them."

"An embarrassment of riches. I want you to contact Rakshasa."

"Not the Goat?"

"No. The Goat no longer casts a shadow."

There was a brief silence. "I wasn't informed."

"No, you were not. Things have been moving swiftly and will continue to move faster still. I expect you to keep pace."

"Your wish is my command."

"Thank you, but I already have genies. What I need now is someone to flip the right switches."

"I will light the way. Once I locate him, do I need to provide any special instructions?"

"The usual will do quite nicely."

"Will there be witnesses or collateral…consequences?"

"I would prefer that this be handled as precisely and discretely as possible. I don't think it will be a difficult thing to isolate him from friends or allies."

"Perhaps our quarry will learn to depend upon the kindness of strangers."

"They'll be the only ones he can rely upon after I am through." He paused. "While you are circling the globe, my dear Puck, be sure to arrange for one of our friends stop in at New York and take care of a little literary errand for me."

"Delighted. I will have him give your regards to Broadway. Any friend in particular?"

"Find me a talented electrician. Tell him that that Brookguild will be hosting a party for their scriveners. He needs to ensure that it will be a blast."

"Will this require particular attention?"

"Yes, thorough. Very thorough."

"When?"

"Tomorrow."

"Things do seem to be moving quickly."

"Yes, and devil take the hindmost."

⌘

It was evident that there had been three small churches side by side. The churches at either end were virtually identical. Church of God in Christ to the left and Saint Florian's Catholic Church to the right were both typical wooden board and batten carpenter's gothic, both painted white with navy blue trim. The remains of the church in the middle suggested that it was of an entirely different architectural heritage. The charred logs of the formerly circular building would have been enough to differentiate it from its neighbors, even without the intact sign out front declaring it to be the Thanksgiving Native American Church of America. By far the greatest distinguishing feature, however, was a ten-foot tall wooden statue of a polar bear standing in the exact center of the wreckage, wholly untouched by the recent fire.

Watt and Gaude circled the scene of the previous night's destruction and then began to take hesitant steps into the confused pit of charred logs. "You two got business here or just plain nosey?" asked a booming voice from behind them.

Watt turned and saw an elderly man wearing a black suit and a red shirt with a white clerical collar. He was heavyset, yet still muscular. His nose appeared to have been broken long ago and his chin was strong and square. Gaude imagined that the man had been a formidable contender on the boxing ring in days gone by. His skin was the color of aged bourbon, but his hair, mustache, and eyebrows were brilliant white, almost luminescent.

"Not plain nosey. I'd say professionally nosey would be a more accurate description," replied Watt with his usual cheerful smile as he handed a card to the minister. Gaude did not bother to observe the passing of the card, as he already knew that it would be offered upside-down.

The minster held the card in both hands as he examined it with deliberate concentration bordering on reverence. "Hmmm…I see…" the minister muttered to himself. He then looked up, smiled gently, and said, "I suppose your nosing around can't do much harm."

"We'll try not to be a nuisance."

"And I'll try not to be a scold. I am Reverend Laurence Meekwood, the pastor of this congregation right here." The minister gestured to the Protestant member of the small church trio. "You are looking to get to the bottom of this?"

"Yes, if you know anything that could shed some light on the incident."

"Without a doubt, Ol' Slewfoot was here. You smell that fire and brimstone? That was him."

"I can smell the aftermath of a fire," joined in Gaude, "but I'm not quite familiar with the scent of brimstone."

"Now you are, brother. This is the devil's work. Pity that I couldn't see him when he carried out his dirty handiwork. I'd have faced that old reprobate down."

"The devil doesn't scare you?"

"No, I'm not scared of the devil. Ever. He's very dependable, very trustworthy. I know he can be counted on to do the bad thing, the wrong thing, the sneaky underhanded thing, the evil thing. What I'm scared of is *me*. I'm scared of what I might do, or of what I might not do. I'm afraid of what I might try to do, what I might fail to do. I might try to fight fire with fire and do something evil in the name of good. I might throw up my hands and surrender or roll over and die. I'm not nearly as predictable as the devil."

"We're not looking for predictions today."

"No, of course not. You're looking for an explanation."

"If you have one."

"I'm not sure if I can explain it, but I suppose that I can describe it. I was here when it happened. Sad, really sad. But the Good Book tells us time and again that the good and godly will suffer."

"I assume you know this congregation well?"

"Sure, 'course I do. They're my next-church neighbors. Real nice folks, always friendly, always kind and generous, always willing to lend a hand, never gave nobody any trouble."

"Did they ever complain about electrical problems?"

"That church didn't have any electricity. They built an earth and timber church. It was supposed to be a hogan or plank house or something. I never saw anything like it before, but it was real pretty. It had raven and eagle carvings and all sorts of other decorations. You can see some of it remaining over there." The minister gestured to the back of the ruin. "You might think that the ceremonial fire that they usually had going in the middle of their church went out of control and burned the place down, but that wasn't the case."

"What caused the fire?"

"As God is my witness, and he surely is, I saw a bolt of lightning strike the church last night. Even so, it wasn't like God's lightning, or any lightning I have ever seen before."

"What was special about it?"

"It didn't come from the sky."

"How's that again?"

"Not from the sky. I saw the bolt, but it came right out of that big transformer up on the telephone pole. See the burn marks on the side?" Reverend Meekwood pointed at the large gray cylinder mounted high on the utility pole. "That's where the lightening came out."

"Did you tell that to the authorities?"

"Yes, I did. They looked at me like I was some kind of idiot, until they took a glance over their shoulders and saw the damage to the transformer. No other *worldly* explanation for those burn marks except some kind of electrical discharge." Reverend Meekwood paused for a moment. "Of course, we all know that it wasn't any worldly cause, was it? But you try telling that to the city inspectors. Y'know, the truth shall set ye free, but it will not sway the heart of a municipal bureaucrat."

"I suppose that the people in city hall aren't too keen on putting 'fire caused by the devil' into their official reports."

"I suppose not. If it weren't the work of the devil, the only other explanation I've heard so far comes from Shaman Tumulth."

"Shaman Tumulth? Is he the leader of this church?" asked Gaude, gesturing at the scorched ruin.

"That's right," confirmed Meekwood. "He says that there has been a battle of spirit animals. Theirs apparently lost the fight."

"Spirit animal?"

"The tribes have a number of them. They don't exactly worship animals, but they reverence them, I suppose you might say. Sort of like my Catholic brothers," said Meekwood as he gestured to the mirror image church to his own on the other side of the ruin, "and the way they reverence the saints. The Catholics have pictures and statutes of saints, books about their lives, prayer cards, and holy medals, but they insist that is it the Father, Son, and Holy Ghost that they worship. As for being friends with the saints…I'm pretty sure that won't do any harm. After all, you can never have too many friends. That's the same way my Indian brothers feel about their spirit animals."

"Yes, I can see that they are rather fond of that bear…a polar bear by the look of him."

209

"That's where you'd be mistaken, but not as if it was any fault of yours. You see, that big white bear wasn't there before the fire. We found him this morning just standing there in the middle of the ashes."

"How did he get there?" asked Gaude.

"We'd all like to know the answer to that question. Here 'bouts, you know, the Chinook, Salish, and the tribes up north like the Makah, they all have a special bond with ravens, eagles, wolves, salmon, and even frogs. In this church, it's the killer whale—orcas, as people like to call them now—that reigns supreme. Where you now see that polar bear is where a wooden killer whale statue used to be."

"Does anyone have any idea what this could signify?" asked Watt.

"Even if you accept that spirit animals might have mystical powers, why a polar bear should show up here don't make much sense to me. You can't find a polar bear in Thanksgiving, or anywhere in the entire state. The last polar bear in the Portland zoo died three years ago and they never brought in another one to take his place. Those animal rights activists came out of the woodwork for his funeral and protested against any possible replacement. The shaman thinks that the fire was caused by that bear. He says that it came down from Alaska. It was a warning. He didn't tell me what the warning was, but he was sure that it was a warning and that the news was bad."

"Why would a polar bear pick a fight with this church?"

"I can't be sure, but I suspect that they might have put themselves in the theological dog house based on their practices that strayed from the norm of most Native American spiritualism."

"What was that?"

"They observe Ramadan."

"Ramadan? You mean the Muslim holiday?"

"I don't think that Ramadan is properly classified as a holiday. It's a month of fasting—there's a holiday at the end of it, though."

"Why would a Native American church adopt a religious tradition from Islam?"

"I don't know. They've been doing this since before I arrived twenty years ago. I once asked Shaman Tumulth, and he just shrugged and said, '*It coudd'n hoit.*' Somehow, that seemed to be an adequate explanation."

"Is the shaman available to discuss this?"

"No, he's gone for a little while. First thing this morning he asked to borrow our church's bus, which I was happy to provide. He took everyone from his congregation and headed for parts unknown. I believe it has something to do with a sweat lodge and purging evil spirits. Makes sense to me, all things considered."

"So, we can't contact them?"

Reverend Meekwood sighed. "Let's not take away their privacy. For three hundred years this country has been takin' and takin' and takin' from them. First their land was taken away at the point of a gun or by a swindling agent of the government. Then their language was stripped from them. Next, we crushed their culture under foot. Even their children were taken from them and put into schools far away. Now they've lost their church. The only thing they got left is…"

"Yes?"

Reverend Meekwood shook his head despondently. "Monday night bingo."

She opened the notebook, scanned a page, turned to the next, nodded to herself that she had located something worthy of note, and started to read aloud.

"For the past few months, he found himself concentrating on the smallest details. Each morning the knot in his tie became the focus of intense thought. Perfectly leveled teaspoons of ground freeze-dried coffee were spooned into a ceramic mug he silently admired for its smooth finish. The desk drawer at work was precisely laid out: pencils, pens, paper clips, rubber bands, and a stapler all neatly placed into the plastic drawer organizer. Each night he carefully emptied the contents of his pockets into a small brass tray on his bedroom dresser. He had a separate tray for change. He always hung his keys on the key rack by the kitchen door. His watch and ring were placed with military precision in a man's jewelry box.

He became riveted and immobile when looking at objects. A painting at the office, or in his own home, that had not earlier commended itself to his attention now captivated him. He stared, moving closer and closer to examine minute details. He examined each subject and object, then the brush strokes, then the grain of the canvas. The textures fascinated him. Each time he looked at something—really looked—he wondered at the complex and varied and incomprehensible, fantastic, and frightening aspects of it all. Last week he sat in an airplane seat. The fabric of the headrest in front of him was a pattern of gray and cranberry red squares. He spent half an hour examining the different threads that traveled across the fabric. He realized that it was child-like to be fascinated by everything but had no desire to return to adulthood. He continued to rivet his attention on the smoothness of plastic, the sheen of stainless steel, the satisfying crinkle of aged leather, the rough weave of tweed, and the delicate grain of mahogany. Now that he had become observant, he began noticing the messages. Someone was sending him messages. He didn't know who. He didn't know why. The messages—yes, they were definitely messages—were ever so inconspicuous. They appeared on a billboard, or during a television ad, or in a fortune cookie. Others might find these messages innocuous, but he recognized them as items of ominous import. He saw the latest message as he walked to the drugstore. It was a dry November day. The sun was brilliant and harsh and the air tasted of metal. On the gray concrete wall separating pedestrians from traffic spewing from the bridge tunnel he saw written in blue chalk:

> *He was a man with a future,*
> *She was a woman with a past.*"

She closed the notebook, closed her eyes, and searched through the well-arranged drawers of mental file cabinets. "This sounds awfully familiar. I think it's out of *Letters to Daphne, Never Sent* or perhaps it was in *Black and Pearls*. No, wait, I remember. It's from *Hell to Harvest*."

"How many of his books have you read?"

"All of them."

"Which one is your favorite?"

"That's hard to say. Reuben refuses to stay within the lines of any genre or style. He's written everything from horror to coming-of-age, mystery, romance, fantasy and science fiction. He even wrote a Western once, although he placed the story in a small town in Bavaria. Now, *that* was different."

"He's not keen on being catalogued."

"No, he considers predictability to be a communicable disease."

"But most of his books are pretty quirky...outright strange, in fact. I would think that classifies him somehow."

"How do you know about his books?" she asked. "You've never read any of them."

He opened his mouth to reply, and just as the word issued out of his mouth, she joined him in a simultaneous response: "DataGhad."

"Yeah, I did a web search. It was easy enough."

"Lazy jock."

"And proud of it."

"Okay, you like strange?"

"Did I say I liked strange?"

"I believe that you did." She reopened the notebook. "Here's a strange one. Listen to this:

Words Scrawled in My Own Hand
On a Notepad Beside My Bed
Discovered Upon Waking

> *Distant memories*
> *vaulted from mind's delay.*
> *Unearthed passions*
> *creep from night to day.*
> *Dwelling, reaching,*
> *Pawing, fawning,*
> *Clutching to the heart,*
> *Moments cleaving,*
> *Movements leaving,*
> *Take each other's part."*

"You're right, that is strange."

"You told me when we first met that you liked strange."

"I don't remember that."

"Maybe I was the one who said it. That would explain a lot."

"A lot about what?"

"How we ended up together."

"So, now I'm the strange one?"

"No, you're entirely predictable. The strange part is what induced me to jump into bed with you."

"The alternative was to actually talk to me."

213

"You're right. Now that I'm stuck with you in the car and forced to engage in more than superficial conversation, I see the wisdom of my original inclination to exploit you for gratuitous sex. I'm getting my just desserts on this trip, it would seem."

"You could do worse."

"I could do better."

"Maybe you were on the rebound when you first met me."

"I don't do rebounds. However, that was when I was going through my promiscuous phase."

"Your promiscuous phase?"

"Yes."

"You mean that you were more promiscuous than…"

"You were about to say?"

"Nothing."

"Just as well."

"Just how many phases have you gone through, anyway?"

"You've asked that before."

"And I always get an evasive answer."

"That's not true. I've always told you that it's none of your goddam business."

"That's not evasive?"

"No, that's as direct as it comes."

"Maybe someone from the other church saw something," offered Gaude.

"Good idea. I'm going to grab a root beer," Watt indicated the convenience store about fifty meters to the left. "Do you want anything?"

"No thanks. I'll meet you there in a few minutes."

Gaude approached the carpenter's gothic church to the right, which was indistinguishable from its twin on the other side of the burned Native American church except for a statue of the Blessed Virgin, surrounded by a trellis of red roses, near the front doorway of the house of worship. Gaude entered and made a quick scan of the interior of the sanctuary. *Typically Catholic*, he thought to himself. A central isle flanked by wooden pews led to an altar centered in the apse.

A large wooden crucifix suspended overhead. A statute of Mary was on the right, Joseph to the left of the altar. The windows were stained glass depictions of the Old Testament prophets and plaster Stations of the Cross were mounted on the walls along the circumference of the interior. An elaborate antique baptismal font was located in the north transept and a shrine to Saint Kateri Tekakwitha faced it on the opposite side of the church. Gaude briefly wondered if the shrine had been an indication of solidarity, or perhaps a gesture of accommodation, to the congregation of neighbors next door.

At the midpoint of the nave, on either side of the church, were small dark mahogany confessionals. Gaude noticed that a small green light was illuminated at the cornice of the confessional to his right. He approached and entered the compartment for penitents. He heard the slide of the panel and saw the shadow of the priest surrounded by a faint light through the confessional screen.

"Father, my name is Daniel Gaude—"

"*Jesus, Mary and Saint Joseph*!" the man in the darkened compartment exclaimed. "Boy-o, have y' lost yer mind? Have y' no sense for the seal of th' confessional?"

"Sorry Father, I thought that now we were allowed to—"

"*Rawmaysh*! Now don't be givvin' me any of that Vatican Two nonsense, young fellah. Just stick to th' facts...or to the sins as it were."

"Actually, Father, I came in to ask a few questions about the church fire next door."

"Neither the time nor the place," admonished the confessor. "Now, get on with it then. Let's hear ye spill y' spiritual guts, as it were." Although he had technically been chastised, Gaude could tell that the cleric on the other side of the screen was not in the least upset by his transgressions.

Gaude paused, unsure how to proceed, trying to dredge up in his memory the ritual from his youth. "Bless me Father, for I have sinned...It has been...Father, it has been a really long time since my last confession."

"I wouldn't worry about it, me boy. God is very patient and he and I are both glad ye've come in fer a little chat." The Irish brogue was thick, but the lilt of the accent was gentle and reassuring. Gaude could not resist the thought that this priest had been sent straight from central casting. He wondered if this idea was a new sin and should be immediately confessed. The Irish priest broke into Gaude's thoughts. "Now go ahead and confess what sins ye've been accumulatin' these past many years, lad."

Gaude was at once put at ease, but somehow felt shortchanged. As a child, he had been trained by the stormtrooper nuns to perform confession according to the rigid and unalterable formula. There was comfort and clarity in following ritual. He knew that the Church now called confession 'reconciliation,' and rarely used the darkened confessional anymore. During his boyhood, he had for a short time believed that by entering the relic cocoon, and employing the mechanism of the semi-private ceremony, he would obtain a vending machine absolution in return for his obedience to form over substance. He had not come into this booth for a confession, but neither had he expected 'a chat' with an ordained host. "Well, Father…in the past…twenty years…I've committed just about every sin imaginable."

"I see," said the confessor softly, but without the shock or repulsion that Gaude had expected. "Might now these sins of ye'rs include serial murder?"

"Good God, NO!" Gaude blurted. Then, attempting to compose himself, "No Father, no murders, nothing quite that bad."

"Have ya' committed armed robbery, then?"

"No."

"Paarhaps a wee bit stolen from th' collection basket?"

"Good grief! No!" Gaude was becoming perplexed. He had never heard of a confessional interrogation before. At least, not since the Spanish Inquisition. The priest was supposed to ask if he repented from the sins, dispense penance of a few 'Hail Marys' ask for an 'Act of Contrition' and send the newly cleansed soul on its way.

"Then from what I hear, lad, yehr not such a terrible fellow, are ye?"

Gaude relaxed. "Maybe not bad enough to get into the newspapers, Father, but there are a lot of mortal sins involved."

"Ah yes, indeed, the mortal sins, now. The venial we cure right away, don't we? The mortal ones, now then, those take wee bit little longer." The shadow on the other side of the screen chuckled to himself. "Just a pinch o' priestly humor. All right, now, I think it rather cruel to drag y' through the shame of it all. These things ye've done now, I'd imagine since y' are here with me right now, that yehr sorry that ye committed 'em?"

"Yes Father."

"And since y' sound like a healthy young man, we can safely assume that most of th' sins revolve around wine, wimmen and song?"

Gaude smiled broadly in the dark closet. "Yes Father...and heavy on the women."

"Don't let it trouble yeh, me boy. Now, concernin' th' fairer sex, 'tis well established that God designed wimmen to be our companions, but when he got around to building 'em, somehow he put 'em together with a lot of temptin' equipment."

"Yes Father." Gaude never realized that confession could be enjoyable. Perhaps he should have done this a few years earlier.

"Now, twenty years is a mighty long time not being in communion with th' Christ. During that time, how has the devil been treatin' yer?"

Gaude had to swallow twice before squeaking, "Excuse me, Father?"

"Don't get faint on me lad, I'll be excusing ye soon enough. That's what confession's all about, isn't it now? O'course, y' do realize that when y' aren't with th' Christ, ye've been keepin' company with our old friend, Satan?"

Gaude was temporally thrown off by the priest's pronunciation of 'Satan' which sounded like 'Saaatin.' "Yes Father, I guess— technically—that is the way it goes."

"Don't be embarrassed, me boy. Have y' ever considered how much th' two have in common?" Gaude was now beginning to feel discomfort, not only due to the peculiar turn of the confessional conversation but also because his knees had been in long-term contact with a wooden kneeler. It had been decades since he had last attended Mass and his kneeling technique was rusty. "Now, y' see," the confessor continued pleasantly, "Jesus Christ and Lucifer are th' only two livin' creatures having a soul that have looked directly upon the face of God. Now Moses hid his face, didn't he? Samuel heard God's voice in the dark, Elijah stood outside a cave and heard God as a whispering sound, the prophets all received his word, Noah and Abraham had several conversations with God, but none look directly upon the glory of th' Almighty."

Gaude felt compelled to respond, although he was thinking as quickly as he could on how to exit the confessional with some degree of grace—if not the spiritual kind, at least in the social sense. "Father, I

217

wasn't aware Lucifer had a soul."

"If he didn't have a soul, bein' cast out of heaven wouldn't have been much of a punishment, now would it?"

"I suppose not." A gradually increasing dull pain was forming between Gaude's eyes. "It just doesn't seem…right…to say that the devil has a soul."

"Ye've been led to believe that because they don't teach th' truth in the schools, or from th' pulpit for that matter. Not a great surprise seein' as the devil's not all that popular with th' Church. But tell me, lad, why do ye think his name was Lucifer? That means 'The Lighted One' y' know. Well, now, God chose him as th' one angel to receive th' special gift of a soul, and th' presence of a soul caused him to radiate that light that emanates from all souls filled with grace."

"But Lucifer fell from grace."

"Precisely, lad. Once he received a soul, he also inherited free will, he did. One day he chose to disobey God and, there he goes, tossed out of heaven on his duff."

"Didn't God know Lucifer would disobey if given a soul?"

"Naturally. God is almighty. He knew it t'would happen."

"Father, are you saying that the devil was set up by God?"

"So much for love and mercy from th' Almighty, eh?"

Gaude building sense of discomfort had elevated to outright distress. "I'm sorry Father, I have to go," he said hurriedly as he tried to raise himself up from the kneeling position.

"Wait there just one minute, boy-o. I haven't givin' y' the absolution yet, y' know."

"Ahhh, father, that's not really necessary—"

"Hogwash! Here we go now: I absolve thee in the so-called name of the Father, Son and Holy Ghost—"

"So-called?"

"—for all yer many sins. Includin' those in particular, with *her*."

"Father?"

"*The woman.*"

Gaude froze, disoriented, all the more so, being cramped in a dark closet on a wooden kneeler. "Who?"

"You know."

"No, I don't."

"Oh, yes you do. You know. You've always known."

"Father, what are you talking about?"

"*Cherchez la femme.*"

"No other priest ever—"

"No other priest ever had a chance, me boy. Isn't that a fact, now?"

Gaude tossed the heavy curtain aside and bolted out of the confessional to immediately collide with a priest walking towards the sacristy at the back of the church. "Sorry Father," he mumbled.

"That's all right. Were you looking for someone to take your confession?" The accent was pure Texas.

"No, father, I…ummm…Actually, I've already done it."

"Really? By yourself?"

"No."

"That's good. Vatican Two might have changed a few things, but you still need a real, live priest to make a confession."

Gaude turned to the wooden door that served as the confessor's entry into the confessional. He pointed to the small plastic sign on the door bearing the name of the priest inside. "I was just talking with Father Donnelly."

The priest smiled. "That would be me, and I'm afraid it has skipped my mind what we talked about."

Gaude looked back and forth between the priest and the confessional. Finally, he stepped up to the door and tapped. After a few heartbeats, he knocked. Gingerly, he turned the knob and opened the door. The confessional was empty.

The Advisors

"I'm not sure what you mean. You say that you've misplaced an operative?"

"Yes, ma'am."

"You make it sound like you left your car keys someplace you can't remember."

"It's more serious than that, ma'am."

"Yes, my point exactly. What was the last location reported on his SEC-CEL?"

"They are all offline."

"Really? For how long?"

"I'm afraid that is classified."

"So am I. How long?"

The agent involuntarily grimaced, then regained control of his face and responded, "Three days."

"*Three days?* And when was ORCA intending to share this little tidbit of information with me?"

"We didn't think it was significant."

"Everything is significant."

"I am sure that we were in the process of reading you on."

"Lie number two."

"Please, ma'am—"

"Let me see the file."

The agent reached into a leather satchel, reminiscent of an old-fashioned postman's bag. Grace Ho noted the incongruous artifact and made a dated mental note to be stored in a cerebral niche and cross-indexed against this agent's name and the case file being handed to her on a flash drive. She inserted the peripheral into the notebook computer on her desk. After a few clicks, she began reviewing documents.

"This operative is interesting. I've seen his name before on the active lists, but I'm surprised he's never come up for my review before."

"There was never a need. He was always considered reliable."

"That's where you are mistaken. He is much more than the sum of his parts."

"I suppose we all are."

She looked up slowly from the computer screen and gave the

agent a disdainfully withering sneer. "No, not all of you."

"Yes, ma'am," the agent replied contritely.

"I don't see where ORCA has issued a burn notice."

'No ma'am, we haven't notified any other agencies that we might have a rogue agent. We thought that a burn notice would be premature."

"Since when have any of you indulged in thinking?" she asked acidly.

"Sorry, ma'am," the agent lamely responded.

"He'll be heading for the coast."

"How do you know?"

"Wouldn't you?"

"Not necessarily."

"Which is why he will."

She continued to scroll down the screen. "You've left out some documents."

"The file is complete."

"That's lie number three. We are finished here."

"No, ma'am, please—"

Grace Ho did not need to examine the agent's face to know that this was a matter of pressing importance. "Where are the documents?"

"I'm not sure. They apparently were too sensitive for disclosure to anyone, including me."

"Including you can't possibly include me."

"No ma'am."

"Incomplete files mean an incomplete analysis. Even the simpletons at the Sweatshop must understand that."

"Yes ma'am."

"This latest relationship," she said, pointing to a document on the screen.

"Yes."

"You vetted her, of course."

"Of course."

"What did you get?"

"She passed muster. She has SCI clearance at DoD."

"That's not what you should have been looking for."

"What should we have been looking for?"

"You should have been looking for her. Do you know where she is this very minute?"

"No ma'am."

"Track her down. He will reach out to her in the end."

"In the end?"

"Yes, he is rushing towards it. The rest of you are not far behind."

The agent thought it best to try to get the conversation back on track. "The coast—the west coast, I assume—is rather vague. Is there anything you can tell us about a more specific location?"

"If you are all that desperate, why haven't you deployed your Watcher Angels?"

"Ma'am, I'm not authorized to discuss that technology."

"It doesn't matter. You're not going to find him. At least, you won't find him alive. Besides, you are looking for the wrong one."

"You mean we should be looking for her?"

"Initially, yes. Ultimately, no."

"Pardon?"

"No, I can't pardon you."

"What I meant—"

Ho raised her hand and silenced the agent. She then swiveled her chair to face away from him and to admire the view from her picture window of the sunset falling on the waters of the Occoquan River. "Find the musician who has forgotten himself. Find the poet who flees from himself. Find the blind man who talks to himself. Find them all and you will find *her*."

"Her? Is that the same *her*?"

Grace Ho rose from her chair and walked through the threshold leading to a room the agent had never entered. As the door began to close, the agent heard her voice.

"*Cherchez la femme.*"

Twenty: Kenai

*He is in the wilderness with his partner. 'Over there,' the partner says
with a gesture, pointing to a circle of men standing in a small clearing
beside a campfire. The men are old, wearing battered western hats and
clothing that seemed to be peculiar—old fashioned and somewhat
formal for a camp in the middle of the desert. The men stare
contemptuously at the interlopers, yet somehow it was obvious that they
are expected to join the group. The two walk with studied casualness
through the brush and cacti and merge into the perimeter of men—
cowboys it seemed—without introductions or any other discussion. All
eyes now return to the leader.*

    *'It will be a fine team effort. A bully effort!' the president said,
making a large plastic smile, turning—actually revolving—slowly to
the small audience to ensure that everyone present had an opportunity
to admire him full face as well as profile. 'You there, sir,' he said,
pointing an accusatory finger. 'I trust that you and your partner are
not wont to be stragglers.'*

    *He heard himself reply as if he were listening to a disembodied
voice, 'You won't find us to be the stragglers.'*

    *Roosevelt was perceptibly amused by the response. 'I see, sir.
My apologies. I will confine my concerns to these relative greenhorns,'
he said while making a theatrical gesture towards the assembled
cowboys who all evidenced a thick patina of hard-won experience on
the trail.*

    *The group of veteran outdoorsmen began to snicker and he
immediately regretted his inane remark. Rather than cutting the loss,
he stammered, 'If we pull together as a team, I'm sure that we can help
those who are falling behind.'*

    *Roosevelt served him an undisguised disparaging glare. After
carefully removing his pince nez, the president lifted his left hand in a*

*gesture which signified that a scolding was about to commence.
'The members of a successful team do not depend upon one another.
They cooperate with each other. To depend on someone means that
they require to be propped up—that they are lacking in some regard
and call upon the efforts of comrades to help overcome some difficulty.
This, however, will undermine the communal energy of the group. It
saps the strength of one member for the benefit of another who may not
have sufficient skill, intelligence, tenacity, fortitude or courage to
succeed on his own. This will lead to a leveling of talent and ability,
resulting in the creation of a placid pool of mediocrity. A team is not a
tepid and homogenized mass, but rather a combination of strengths,
standing together. A team is a mountain range: individual yet united
towers, shoulder to shoulder, proving an impenetrable and impassible
wall, an indefatigable obstacle to adversaries. A good team does not
share mutual weaknesses—members contribute their individual
strengths. A team member gives that which will enable the team to
triumph over its opponent or succeed in reaching its goal. A man's
shortcomings are his own responsibility and it is up to him—
individually—to overcome such liabilities. He may banish the
weakness, overcome it, or use it as a foundation for a new strength, a
new talent, a new ability that he can contribute to the team. Never
allow a man to join a team because of the benefit it could confer upon
him. Never accept someone into a team because it will make him a
better man or a better team player. Choose only those men who need
nothing from the team other than an opportunity to contribute their
unstinting efforts and valuable skills. These men have that which is
necessary to achieve greatness on behalf of the whole.'*

Gaude awoke and looked around the diner. "I'm really going
over the edge now. I just dreamed about being in the desert with you
and Teddy Roosevelt."

"Sounds like we'd make a great team," Watt replied casually as
he poured a cup of coffee.

Gaude shook his head in mild irritation. "Okay, go ahead and
tell me."

"You don't know where we are, do you?"

"No, I don't, and I think you know why."

224

"No, why?"

"I don't know why. That's why *you* need to know why."

"What were we talking about, again?"

"I just woke up and here we are in the next mystery location."

"Right. I suppose that you blame me for your reoccurring amnesia?"

"This never happened before Destinations."

"Did you ever have a heart attack before Destinations?"

"No."

"Ever black out before Destinations?"

"No."

"Ever hit your head on the deck before Destinations?"

"No." Gaude paused, "Hey wait a minute. Who said that I hit my head on the deck? I never told you that I was on the back deck when I passed out."

Watt shrugged nonchalantly. "Deck is a Navy term for just about any floor."

"I'm not buying it," said Gaude with a dismissive shake of his head.

"I'm not selling it," retorted Watt. "Besides, how else would I know?"

"That's what you need to tell me."

"There you go again."

"Fine, there I go…where? Just tell me where we are for Krissake."

"We are in Kenai, and in Kenai, I would prefer if you not use the Lord's name in vain."

"Kenai?"

"Yes, Kenai."

"What's a Kenai?"

"Alaska."

"You gotta be kidding me. Seriously?"

"Serious as the book of Deuteronomy."

Gaude silently contemplated, fingering through the mental file cabinet of his stored memories. "Northern Lights."

"Yes, we might be able to see them tonight."

"Northern Lights Café in Oregon."

"Oh, yes, I remember," agreed Watt. "There was also the dessert they served."

"You're right! Eskimo pies. That's a groaner."

"Our antagonist's idea of wicked humor, no doubt."

"Let's not forget the polar bear that Reverend Meekwood mentioned."

"There aren't many polar bears in this part of Alaska," replied Watt.

"Maybe grizzly bears…"

"It was heavy-handed, to be sure, but it seems that our arsonist has no qualms about that." Watt leaned back in the booth and grinned. "Well, Dan, you're still batting a thousand when it comes to solving clues with hindsight."

"I don't see you doing much better."

"I'm not fretting over it. We're here, that'll do."

"*Here* is no closer to solving the crimes than the *there* we were at three weeks ago."

"Finish your breakfast and we'll try to do something about that."

Gaude looked down to see a half-eaten plate of food. "I ordered this?"

"Yep. Omelet with salmon and reindeer bacon."

"You're making up the part about the bacon."

"Nope, scout's honor. Rudolph bit the dust on behalf of your breakfast."

"Why did I order this?"

"You were in the mood, I guess. I'm sure that it was tasty. My breakfast was excellent."

"What was it? Alaska Moose Chili?"

"That's going to be my lunch."

Gaude finished his breakfast which, he had to admit to himself, was quite good. "I assume that we haven't visited the site of the church fire yet?" he asked.

"Correct," answered Watt. "According to the Daniel Gaude who chased down the information on his cellphone last night, the incident occurred outside of town."

"Maybe that other Daniel Gaude should continue traipsing around the continent with you and give me a rest."

"You're going to allow an old codger like me run circles around you?" Watt teased.

"The term 'give it a rest,' as you should know," lectured Gaude, "means more than merely being physically fatigued. It's based on the acknowledgment that precious time has been frittered away for no good reason."

"The reasons could not possibly be better. As for precious time," Watt instructed, "you have much more than you can possibly imagine."

Watt paid the bill and the two left the diner and walked to the rental car. "Whose turn is it to drive?" asked Gaude. "I've lost track."

"We're not keeping score, but since you asked, I believe it is your turn at the steering wheel," said Watt, tossing the car keys to Gaude.

As he began getting into the car, Gaude glanced through the windshield across the street and caught sight of a wall of Sitka spruce planks featuring deeply carved lettering. "There it is!" he announced.

"What's that?"

"Our personal poet laureate has once again come through for us."

Gaude and Watt emerged back out from the car and walked across the street to view the latest poem.

Kenai

Inhale the sky in one great breath,
Stand towering o're the land,
For here's the last place on earth
Where the commonplace is grand.

The rippling silver flanking flash
In the rivers and the skies,
The tumbling frigid waters splash
'neath the sound of eagle cries.

Leviathans cavort in spring
As glaciers yield themselves,
The ritual trek of pink and king
Dodge bears and market shelves.

Past masks of native vision
Across a score of centuries
South of mountains in collision
And the plains of stunted trees.

The sled dogs howl in unison
For freedom lost and found,
The venison is grilled well-done
For the travelers northbound.

A land of generosity
That shares its grandeur well,
Surrounded by the flattering sea
That succumbed to its spell.

God mocks the concrete towers
And paltry cityscapes,
In this place he flexed his powers
For a paradise to shape.

I sought him in cathedrals,
I prayed on mountain heights,
I peered through roiling ocean gales
And stared up at desert nights:

Look not for gathered seraphim
If you search for where God roams,
Just follow the line of salmon fins,
For Kenai is his home.

—Reuben Malachi

"Let's get some gas."

"So says a guy who eats chili three times each day."

"I should have seen that coming weeks ago."

"If you had seen it coming, what would you have done?"

"I'm tempted to answer that. Just keep in mind that there were plenty of other promising candidates in Destinations, I assure you."

"Really? You mean that I'm not the only one—"

"Nope."

"Does that mean you—?"

"Yep."

"How do you—?"

"Because I do."

⌘

They walked east on *Nagysándor József Utca*. The three men were all dressed in lightweight wool, generously cut, slightly winkled suits. Two members of the team had leather postman haversacks slung over their shoulders. They turned the corner at *Vadász Utca* and within a minute arrived at their destination. They paused in front of the building as the team leader checked his Omega Perpetual. He waited patiently as the sweep of the wristwatch's second hand reached the top of the dial indicating that 10:30 a.m. had arrived at Budapest. The leader nodded to the other two men and they pushed through the front doors, passing by the red and white Corps of Engineers logo in the entry hall. They approached the second set of glass doors that provided access to the main lobby. As had been arranged by their employer, the lobby was empty. The two younger men removed small hex wrenches from their jacket pockets. The sandy-haired younger man worked on the door they had just entered while his dark-haired partner quickly moved to the opposite door leading to the garden atrium. The leader walked to the elevator and pushed the call button. Their rubber-soled shoes made a hushed scuffle and occasional squeak over the black marble floor. The elevator doors opened and the tall leader whispered in a mischievous voice, *"Alles einsteigen, bitte."*

"Beszállás," corrected one of the younger men from across the lobby.

"You say tomato, I say tomatoe," replied the leader in English with a smirk.

The two men finished tightening the locks on the door bars, pocketed the wrenches, picked up their leather bags, and strode to the elevator. The leader repeatedly flipped the override stop toggle, removed a spurious American Express card from his wallet, inserted it into a slot beneath the elevator's emergency telephone, and quickly tapped a sequence on the floor buttons. The three stood silently in the cab as it rose the top floor. The doors opened and the men entered the short passageway leading to the counter where the security guard sat reading the *Capital Guardian*. The guard casually turned his head to see three visitors who were unknown to him. He put down the paper promptly, rose from his stool, and gestured for the men to walk through the metal detector. The lead man did not move forward, but instead pulled from his inner jacket pocket identification cards attached to a

229

lanyard chain intended to be hung around the neck. He squinted in confusion at the guard, holding out the identification badges. The two companions followed suit. The guard gestured again, "C'mon, walk through please."

The lead man leaned forward on the counter, holding out his badges. "Are these okay?"

The guard rolled his eyes heavenward in annoyance, walked down the counter, and took the identification badges for closer examination. As he looked down to examine the plastic cards, he said in a weary tone, "Our procedure here is to go through the detector first, alright guys?" He looked up to see the end of a black tube. A small caliber bullet quietly pierced his cranium, and Jared Bethune, husband, father of six, veteran of two undeclared wars, and civil servant within three months of retirement, realized that his last moment on earth was on the wrong end of a silenced pistol.

The leader turned to his nearest partner, handed the pistol over to him, and then proceeded through the metal detector. As soon as the first man passed through, the second member threw the pistol over the top of the detector. The leader caught the weapon and stuck it into the top of his trousers. Next came one, then the other haversack. Each was caught and then the two team members walked forward. The leader had already dropped to one knee. Operating with the same mechanical precision of the weapons he was liberating from the bags, he handed each of his partners a modified MP5 with prototype Oculus phase cancellation suppressors, loaded with thirty-round clips of subsonic nine millimeter hollow-point ammunition.

They walked down the short corridor and then split. The darker haired man went left, the leader and the sandy haired gunman turned right. The first office was Wally Fremont's. He saw two men enter with aimed weapons and raised his arms in an involuntary gesture to fend off the bullets that ripped into his body. Fremont slipped off the chair and fell to his right side. He reached up in an attempt to grip the edge of his desk, trying, for reasons he could not explain, to lift himself up to see the framed photograph of his wife and daughter. He collapsed, exhaled, and expired. Down the hall in the opposite direction, the other assassin had located Barbara Dickey and Tanya Cheves poking into an uncooperative photocopier in search of a twisted and errant piece of paper jammed into the internal sorter. Despite this vexing and perennial problem, the women had been cheerfully discussing Tanya's plans for her upcoming wedding. With an economy of action reflecting two decades of experience in executing humans, the intruder squeezed off two bursts of muffled bullets and the women collapsed with a surprised grunt. Darkness enveloped Barbara before she had any idea that her eight-year-old twins Joshua and Kyle would be coming home from school to an empty house. Tanya faded more slowly. The bullets that shattered her spine prohibited her from moving. Tanya did not scream in pain, not only because she had lost all feeling, but also because she no longer possessed the ability to control her larynx, mouth, and jaw. She stared into the ear of Barbara as she lay on the floor. Before drifting off, she thought, *My china pattern...what is my china pattern?*

The leader and the younger man had moved down the hall to a closed door. They took positions on each side. The leader trained his weapon down the hallway, prepared for any victim who might exit their office. Without hesitation, the subordinate reached for the doorknob, pushed the door open, and fell to a knee in the open doorway, weapon at the ready. The office was empty. They moved to the next door and repeated the procedure. The profile of Dianne Zwerdling was visible as she was engrossed in conversation with her *au pair*.

"Dear, I know that Thursdays are your day off, but I don't have any choice. I must go out of town for the week."

Zwerdling saw the figure out of the corner of her eye and assumed it was Wally coming over to discuss the new Antares encryption protocol. She extended her right hand out and signaled a 'come on in' to the visitor. "Gabbi...Gabbi...please..."

"Farewell by telephone," the assassin announced casually. Zwerdling immediately spun around in her chair and stared in shocked silence at the armed intruder taking aim at the center of her chest.

Gabrielle Mészáros heard a peculiar kak-kak-kak, no louder than the keys striking in a vintage manual typewriter, and a noise that might have been a...perhaps a groan? Then the line went dead. It didn't cause her any real concern. *The landline telephone system is terrible in this country. I don't know why Diane insists on using it.*

The dark-haired man opened the last door on his end of the hall. Jaxon Chang swiveled around suddenly in his chair smiling brightly. "Wally! You won't believe..." His face melted into a visage of horror. The dark man hesitated. In violation of every rule of his profession, he approached the target. Chang began to stand up, but a motion from the gun barrel succeeded in persuading him to remain seated. The dark-

231

haired man stepped up to Chang, who forced himself to breathe steadily and focus on some way of disarming the intruder, or at least finding some way of surviving. The uninvited guest brought the gun barrel forward, gently contacting Chang between the eyes. *This is not good*, Chang thought, *this is not good*.

"*Sayonara*," the dark-haired man quipped as he pulled the trigger. The low velocity bullets barely exited from the back of the target's skull, but it was enough to deposit a small residue of the gifted brains of Jaxon Chang, Master of Science, *Magna Cum Laude*, Purdue University School of Engineering, on the framed poster behind his desk. Small streams of blood trickled down over little angel laddermen climbing above an indigo village, past an amber moon, towards a crimson sky.

⌘

Gaude stood before the gasoline pump at the Union Oil station in the middle of town. He examined it repeatedly, looking from top to bottom and from side to side, shaking his head all the while in annoyance.

"What's the matter, Dan?" asked Watt.

"There's no credit card slot, no keypad, no selection buttons."

Watt walked up to the pump, paused for a moment, unhooked the fuel nozzle, reached over to the right side of the pump and flipped a small lever. The analog meter spun back to zero and the sound of whirring commenced. Watt flipped open the car's gas cap and proceeded to fill the tank.

"What the...? How did you do that?" asked Gaude incredulously.

"Years of practice from an era when people did the work of people," said Watt. A Niʻihau Child favorite broadcasted from a loudspeaker mounted on a cornice of the service station building.

> *Now I see you're a witness*
> *Calling out other's lies*
> *I'm not questioning your fitness*
> *In a world full of spies*

Your hall now is burning
We'll volunteer to rebuild
All of us are now yearning
To escape from the guild

A man appeared from behind them. "That's mighty kind of you to help out, but I'm happy to take care of your fueling needs." Watt stepped aside to permit the man to finish filling the tank. He then checked the oil, cleaned the windshield, the side view mirrors, and the back window of the car.

"We were told that a church burned just outside of town."

"True enough. As luck would have it, Blake Gambino was passing over in his Cessna yesterday afternoon and radioed in his sighting of the fire just as it was starting. The volunteer fire department was able to get there before the place was too far-gone. Fact is, the whole shebang would have lit up like a torch had they arrived even five minutes later."

"That was lucky."

"Luck, fate, destiny, call it what you will. Blake was in the right place at the right time."

"It seems that we've been going to the wrong places at the wrong times."

"Where have you been going?"

"We've been tracking a number of these church fires."

"Really? There have been more of them? Are you fellers investigators from Anchorage?"

"No."

"Juneau?"

"No."

"Where you from?"

"Washington D.C.," answered Gaude.

"The federal government sent you all the way out here to look over a fire in a church?"

"We're not with the government, but we have been following fires all across the country."

"You mean the lower forty-eight?"

"Yes."

"Wouldn't know much about any church fires down there, or any other fires down there, or anything else going on down there for that matter."

233

"Mister…?"

"Smythers. Hangchow Smythers. Just call me Willy."

"Willy?"

"It's kind of difficult to turn Hangchow into any nickname, so my buddies just call me Willy. You know, 'Willy is as Willy was and Willy'll always do.' Right?"

Gaude smiled and nodded to pretend that he had even the slightest idea of what Willy Smythers was talking about. He and Bill Watt then introduced themselves, with Watt handing over a card. Willy examined the card, arched an eyebrow, looked at Watt, then back at the card, again at Watt, and finally shrugged in resignation.

"Willy, we were wondering if you could give us directions."

"Certainly, my pleasure," Willy responded. "Show up to work half an hour earlier than everybody else. Don't lend a book or borrow a dollar. Never refuse to buy a box of Girl Scout cookies. Don't overspend on gasoline or underspend on oil. Don't cheat on your wife or on your taxes. Buy Craftsman tools from Sears and Roebucks. Go to church on Sundays, unless you're Jewish, in which case Saturday will do just fine."

"Those are excellent directions," Watt admitted patiently, "but what we had in mind was finding the best way to get to the scene of the church that burned down last night."

"Oh, that's right, you were asking about the empty church."

"Empty church?"

"You'll see," said Willy. "Anyway, getting there is easy. Just take the Kenai Spur until you get to Ridgeway. Look for Zadok Road. If you find yourself in Soldotna, you went too far and missed your turn. Once you find Zadok Road, take a left and just stay on that for a little while, maybe five minutes. You'll see one of those roadside historical markers on your right. Go another hundred yards or so and there will be an unpaved road to your left. Just take that until can't go any farther."

"You haven't been converted yet?" quipped Gaude.

"Huh?"

"Yards instead of meters."

"Oh, that," said Willy dismissively. "Well, I welcome the bureaucrats in Washington to come up here with those new newfangled measurements so that we can cram them right up their—"

"Manila file folders," quickly intervened Bill Watt.

"Right," said Willy with a sheepish grin.

234

"Thanks for the directions and the fill up," said Watt, handing Willy a twenty-dollar bill.

"If you don't mind my asking…and I don't really favor poking my nose into somebody else's business…but then again, when those somebodies are poking their noses into my town…"

"You want to know why we are interested in burning churches?"

"Uh-huh," Willy replied with a nod. "Are you news reporters?"

"We try to specialize in good news."

"Burned churches aren't good news."

"We're trying our best to put an end to the bad news. That's why we're tracking down the person who caused the fires."

"Sounds like police work," observed Willy.

"It's God's work."

"And now you've made it your work."

"More or less."

"How far have you been tracking this firebug?"

"Since Destinations, Maine."

"That's a hike, no arguing with that."

"This might be our last stop. There isn't any much farther we can go," said Gaude.

"There's always someplace farther, until there isn't. You just don't know until you reach the end of the line."

"Where is that?"

"You'll know it when you get there," said Willy.

"I guess it's the place where you run out of options."

"No, actually, it's the place where you finally get to see all of your options. The end of the line is where all your choices in life coalesce. The good, the bad, those you ignored, and the countless ones that you missed because you were distracted or inattentive."

"I don't think I would be able to recall all of those choices."

"Memory and choice are strangely bound together in the story of your life. One choice leads to another, which leads to another, and another, and so forth and so on. After a while, you lose track of those choices. Even if you wanted to, you couldn't trace your way back. If you have a lick of sense, you wouldn't want to do that anyway. Besides, all the people, places, things, events—none of them stay in one place, none are stationary, none are permanent. The landscape never stays the same, and if you can't locate the landmarks, you never can return or ever make your way back from there if you went."

"Maybe forgetfulness is a good thing."

"Whether good or bad, it's inevitable," said Willy. "You forget your choices or mis-remember them. Sometimes you have phantom memories of the choices you made—but then again, they aren't so much phantoms as reflected images of the choices you made unbeknownst to you. The closer you get to the end of the line, the more muddled that the real, the imagined, the forgotten, the confused, and the alternative, become. They merge, overlap, and meld. Then, suddenly, you break free, emerge, and it all comes into focus. That's when you realize that life was a long series of choices, and more often than not, you had no idea of what those choices were or how many choices you had. At the end of the line you'll see them clearly. You'll see the truth."

"I suppose that makes it easier."

"Not always and not really. The choices can still be hard to make. You will see more of them, so you'll be faced with a more difficult task, in a sense. Unlike what happened through most of your life, there are no second chances, no backtracking—not that either of those is particularly easy during life, but at least it was a possibility."

"No second chances—it sounds like we're trapped."

"At least you'll know that you're making a choice. Until that moment, you never had the chance to exercise the freedom that someone is given when the truth is revealed."

⌘

"Mister Doyle?"

James Parker Doyle opened his remaining functional left eye to find a visitor arching over him. He had the immediate impression of being a carcass laying in the middle of the Serengeti being appraised by a discriminating vulture. The man had an ashen complexion and lank black hair, cut as if a bowl had been placed on his head. He wore wayfarer sunglasses and a gray wool suit—heavy wool. *What in the world is this guy doing wearing a wool suit in Nevada during the summer?* The visitor did not frighten Doyle, however. He had worked with and against too many men who were this type.

He was in a gatch medical bed, not entirely different from the ones he had become acquainted with during the past week. He scanned the room. This was definitely a new location, but there was something about his surroundings that suggested that he had not been brought to a Las Vegas hospital. "Where am I?" Doyle asked—or rather, demanded.

"Somewhere quite safe...and private." The stranger's voice was monotone, mechanical, and bloodless. Doyle imagined that the entire script of the man's conversation had been written by someone else and subsequently memorized to be delivered in his hospital room.

"I want to see a doctor."

"Doctor?"

"Yes. Is this a medical facility?"

"It is our facility."

"That doesn't tell me anything."

"It wasn't my intent to tell you anything," responded the man with a voice not authentically belonging to a member of the species *Homo sapiens.*

"What do you want?" asked Doyle.

"To ask you some questions."

Doyle stared sharply at the uncongenial host. "What if I don't answer them?"

"Then I shall ask again."

"I won't give you any information."

"In that case, I will take it from you."

"This does not sound like the beginning of a beautiful friendship."

The directions received from Hangchow Smythers at the gas station led them down paved roads for fifteen kilometers. Watt had turned on the radio and classic pop rock hits accompanied them on the drive. They soon encountered the promised historical marker. Gaude idled the car as they read the sign.

Farnsworth's Treaty

In 1864, Alonzo Farnsworth, a civil war deserter suffering from severe gamomania, together with a group of Circumcellion monks who had been evicted from the Abbey of Saint Dymphna in the Township of Holyhosen, Deseret Territory (now known as

Berlin, Utah) for their practice of celebrating funeral Masses for those who committed suicide, arrived at this location with plans to establish the first frozen yogurt stand in Alaska.

Upon arrival, they were met by a deputation of an indigenous tribe who insisted that Farnsworth and his company were trespassing upon their property. The natives offered to sign a treaty to allow the interlopers to reside in the area in exchange for all of their money, equipment, tools, weapons, horses, possessions, clothing and personal articles. After signing the treaty and being left stranded in the forest for three months, unarmed and naked, they were discovered by a traveling French Canadian asparagus vendor. After listening to their plight, the visitor had to break the news that Farnsworth had signed a treaty with a party of Russian dental hygienists on vacation who masqueraded as local Ninilchik tribesmen in order to dupe Farnsworth so that they could pay for their return voyage to their home in Yekaterinburg, Western Siberia.

The cost of the treaty payment dashed the entrepreneurial hopes of the now indigent new arrivals. Their plans were further foiled when they subsequently learned that frozen yogurt would not be invented until 1973 in Lynnfield, Massachusetts, which, coincidentally, was the birthplace of Alonzo Farnsworth.

Gaude proceeded to the next intersection, took a left turn upon a dirt and gravel road, and then continued for five minutes. The road narrowed to a trail and then petered out to little more than a path for the last hundred meters. As they arrived at what seemed to be an impenetrable wall of evergreen, they saw a short tunnel of verdance. Gaude decided to drive through it, and as they emerged into a large clearing, the radio began to play 'Double Vision' by Foreigner. They saw before them a circle of simple one-story shacks surrounding a fire-damaged Victorian mansion, looking much like a charred wedding cake. Gaude parked the Rambler outside the perimeter of shacks. The partners exited the car and walked to the large house in the center of the ring. They approached a veranda leading to the front door where they found two women standing behind a folding card table. The women were nearly identical in appearance, both tall, strongly built, with short-cropped chestnut hair, and hazel eyes. Despite technically qualifying as sexagenerians, both had youthfully robust and ruddy complexions. The table was covered with a generous assortment of baked goods.

"Would you like to buy a cake? Cookies? How about some doughnuts?" solicited the woman on the left.

"The doughnuts are fresh, you'll like them," added the woman on the right.

"Help yourself to a jelly doughnut. Kennedy did."

"Kennedy?"

"*Ich bin ein Berliner.*"

"You're being obscure," said Gaude.

"Yeah, I'm like that," said the woman on the left.

"No, you're not!" admonished the woman beside her.

"Yeah, she's right, I'm not."

"Did the Salvation Army folks drop them off?" asked Watt.

"Salvation Army?"

"You know, National Doughnut Day," offered Gaude.

"Now you're the one being obscure," said the woman on the right.

"You certainly have a wide variety here," complimented Watt.

"We're raising funds to rebuild the hall."

"The hall?"

"Kingdom Hall."

"You mean the church?"

"Kinda, but the Jehovah's Witnesses call their place of worship a Kingdom Hall."

"Are you two visiting?" asked the woman on the left.

"In a sense. We're investigating the fire." Watt handed a card to each of the women. "I'm Bill Watt. My partner here is Dan Gaude."

Each of the women carefully examined Watt's card. "I'm Barbirah," said the woman on the left.

"And I'm Barbyra," said the woman on the right.

"We're both—"

"Fishing guides."

"But today we are volunteer fundraisers."

"That's right, but usually we are fishing guides."

"For folks who are visiting," clarified Barbyra.

"That's true, our neighbors don't really need a guide," remarked Barbirah.

"Of course, we would guide them if they wanted us to," observed Barbyra.

"Sure, we would do that," agreed Barbirah.

"Are you two gents interested in getting a guide?" asked Barbyra.

"I'm not sure they are here for that," said Barbirah, looking skeptically at Gaude.

"But everybody enjoys our tours," insisted Barbyra.

"Perhaps Bill here would," agreed Barbirah, "but I think Dan is a real estate developer. He'd probably spend the entire time dreaming up ways of building timeshare condominiums all across the peninsula."

Gaude laughed and shook his head emphatically. "No, not guilty! I have an uncle who tried to rope me in to the business years ago, but I assure you I was never tempted to sell my soul…or sell condos for that matter. I'm a newspaper reporter."

"A reporter?" asked Barbirah.

"For a newspaper?" added Barbyra.

The two women exchanged a brief skeptical glance and looked back at Gaude. "We're not saying that real estate developers are bad people—" said Barbyra.

"Oh no, we're not," agreed Barbirah. "It's just that they wouldn't enjoy the fishing tour as much as…well, as normal people."

"Right," confirmed Barbyra.

"Maybe we will go on a tour," said Gaude, hoping to assuage the concerns of Barbyra and Barbirah. "What kinds of fish do you catch?"

Barbirah and Barbyra exchanged a look of bewilderment. They then shrugged simultaneously and returned their attention to the visitors. "We don't catch fish."

"I meant, what type of fish do you help your clients catch?" Gaude asked.

"They don't catch fish either."

"Of course, you release them."

"Release them from what?"

"After you get the fish on the hook, you release it."

Barbyra and Barbirah again exchanged a look, this time, in

evident disgust. "We don't bring people out to the rivers to *capture* fish," declared Barbirah.

"No, we guide folks to *experience* the fish," agreed Barbyra.

"Ever see the salmon swimming upstream? They're beautiful," said Barbirah.

"We have silver salmon—" stated Barbyra.

"They're terrific," commented Barbirah.

"Yeah, they are," agreed Barbyra. "We have red salmon—"

"Also known as sockeye," added Barbirah.

"That's right," concurred Barbyra. "King salmon—"

"Everyone's favorite," tossed in Barbirah.

"Yeah, that's true," conceded Barbyra, "but pink salmon are pretty too."

"They're all beautiful," insisted Barbirah.

"They really are," confirmed Barbyra.

"We take folks out to see the salmon, to *experience* the salmon, to enjoy the salmon."

"But not to enjoy eating the salmon?" asked Gaude.

Barbirah and Barbyra exchanged looks for the third time, now in apparent confusion. "People *eat* salmon?" they asked in unison.

"Well," Gaude searched for an answer that would not upset Barbirah and Barbyra, "bears eat salmon."

"Of course they do," responded Barbyra.

"They're bears, after all," agreed Barbirah.

"People are not bears," explained Barbyra, as if lecturing a two-year-old.

"Right," intervened Bill Watt. "I couldn't agree with you more." Watt surreptitiously tapped Gaude on the back to signal that the conversation needed to move in a new direction. "Now then," Watt continued, "as I mentioned a moment ago, we're here to look into the church fire."

"That's sad," commented Barbirah.

"Really sad," agreed Barbyra.

"I mean, it's not sad that you are here," explained Barbirah.

"Oh no, it's just sad that the church burned down."

"Some of the Kingdom Hall burned down," corrected Barbirah.

"Yeah," agreed Barbyra, "the Kingdom Hall burned down. Some of it burned down, not all of it. We're pretty sure that it can be restored."

"Definitely," asserted Barbirah.

"That's why we're here, to raise money to restore the church."

"The Hall," corrected Barbirah.

"Right, the Kingdom Hall," agreed Barbyra.

"Are you members?"

"You mean, of the Jehovah's Witnesses?"

"Yes."

"Naaah...we don't go for that," said Barbyra.

"Just bein' in Kenai is good enough if you're in the mood for worship," agreed Barbirah.

"No need to be cooped up in a stuffy church all Sunday," added Barbyra.

"Or on any other day of the week," tossed in Barbirah.

"Do you know who we can talk to about the fire?" asked Gaude.

"You mean, besides the volunteer fire department?"

"Yes. We're pretty sure of what they will tell us."

"Really? And what's that?" asked Barbirah.

"The cause of the fire was due to an electrical fault in the building or a malfunctioning appliance."

"As a matter of fact—" started Barbirah.

"That's what we heard last night," finished Barbyra.

"Where can we find the pastor?" asked Watt.

"What pastor?"

"The pastor of this church."

"It's a Kingdom Hall."

"Right, the pastor of this Kingdom Hall."

"There ain't no pastor," declared Barbyra.

"Nope, no pastor," agreed Barbirah.

"Sorry, I mean whatever the leader of a Jehovah's Witness congregation is called."

"I dunno what that might be either, but what I mean is that there isn't anybody in charge of this here hall."

"Somebody must be in charge. Perhaps a senior member?"

"Nope," answered Barbirah.

"Who makes the decisions?"

"Nobody," responded Barbyra.

"How do they get anything done?"

"They don't," responded Barbirah and Barbyra together.

"I don't understand."

242

"There aren't any Jehovah's Witnesses here," said Barbirah.
"But this is a Kingdom Hall."
"Yep, that's right," answered Barbyra.
"So, where are all the people who worship here?"
"We'd all like to know," replied Barbirah. "Seems that back in 1975, the folks here were told that the end of the world was heading straight for them. Doomsday was supposed to be sometime that autumn."

Barbyra added, "It all had something to do with six thousand years after God created Adam, or some such thing. Anyway, the whole congregation got together right here on the twenty-first of October and then disappeared into thin air, at least, as far as we can tell."

"Disappeared?"

"Into thin air," reiterated Barbyra.

"Just like that?"

"Just so," said Barbirah. "Their cars were all left here, no one chartered a bus or a boat—the Kenai Police Department looked into that—and there sure was no way they could have gotten out of here by air."

"Why not by air?"

"There's forest, marsh and swamp five miles in every direction. This is the only high and dry ground hereabouts and it sure isn't big enough or long enough to serve as an airstrip," said Barbyra.

"Nope, not even if it was twice as large," added Barbirah.

"Hmmm...maybe if it was twice as large..." mused Barbyra.

"Maybe, but we'd have to measure it just to be sure," responded Barbirah.

"You're probably right," agreed Barbyra.

"Did anyone ever find out what happened to these people?" asked Gaude.

"Nope. Most folks assumed that they wandered into the woods, maybe committed mass suicide like some doomsday cult. I don't hold with any of those theories."

"Why not?"

"I've crisscrossed every inch of this area for the past thirty years and there isn't a single sign of them anywhere around here. I've found bones of bears, caribou, beaver, lynx, you name it, but no bones of a Jehovah's Witness."

"So, there's no explanation for their disappearance?"

"Of course there is," declared Barbyra. "It's a clear case of alien

243

abduction."

"Extraterrestrials?"

"Sure, no doubt about it. This was the work of the Elohim."

Gaude imparted a stunned gaze of dumfounded skepticism to his partner. He quickly recovered and decided to move the conversation along another track. "That was quite a while ago. The year 1975 must have been before you were born."

"Actually, the Jehovah's Witnesses all disappeared on the very day we both were born," said Barbirah.

"You're twin sisters?"

"Nope."

"Nope."

"We just happened to be born at the same time—"

"In the same hospital—"

"And given the same name."

"Well, it's spelled different—"

"But it wasn't at first. The hospital nurse at Kenai General didn't want to mix us up, so she changed the spelling."

"Which one?" asked Gaude.

"Which one, what?"

"Which one of you had the spelling of their name changed?"

"Both of us," answered Barbirah and Barbyra in chorus.

"Originally, both of our families had intended to name us 'Barborha.' Isn't that right?"

"That's a fact."

"Some folks here think that's mighty creepy," noted Barbyra.

"Not the spelling of the names," inserted Barbirah.

"No, the spelling isn't creepy," agreed Barbirah, "but some folks think that we being born at the same time and the same place—"

"Yeah," said Barbyra.

"And both having the same name—"

"Right," agreed Barbyra.

"—and then growing up together and now in business with one another—"

"Exactly," affirmed Barbyra.

"—was somewhat peculiar."

"Somewhat," added Barbyra.

"But we don't really care," insisted Barbirah.

"Not one bit," concurred Barbyra.

244

"And the fact that you two are so similar," offered Gaude.

"Similar?" asked a shocked Barbirah.

"How are we similar?" demanded an indignant Barbyra.

"What my partner means," intervened Watt, "is that you are both professional fishing guides, not to mention both very attractive women."

"Yeah, I suppose that's true," conceded Barbirah.

"I hadn't thought about it, but I guess you have a point," added Barbyra.

"So, the Kingdom Hall was abandoned?" asked Watt, attempting to move the conversation to the matter at hand.

"Nope, it was just empty."

"I don't understand the difference."

"Somebody comes by regularly to maintain the building. It was always nicely painted, the roof was always kept in good shape, and even the lawn surrounding the place was mowed in the summer."

"That's why we're fundraising."

"If we rebuild, then whoever is taking care of the property can still keep on taking care of it."

"Why bother?" asked Gaude. "There aren't any members of the congregation left."

"We don't know that," explained Barbyra. "They disappeared suddenly. They might reappear just as suddenly."

"It's been decades," pointed out Gaude.

"That's true, but whoever keeps up the place must have had faith that the Jehovah's Witnesses would come back," replied Barbirah.

"After all, like we said, the place was always perfectly maintained," added Barbyra. "That must mean that somebody intended to come back some day. I'm sure they'll be upset if they find that we let their place of worship burn to the ground."

"It didn't burn to the ground," corrected Barbirah.

"No, but the Jehovah's Witnesses certainly would have been annoyed if it did," responded Barbyra defensively.

"You don't know who has been keeping the place maintained?" asked Gaude.

"Dunno. Not my business," answered Barbyra.

"We don't stick our noses in other people's business around here. Whoever it might be that keeps up the building doesn't do nobody else any harm, so we just let things be," added Barbirah.

"Although we did hear a rumor that it was being paid for by a woman in Virginia," said Barbyra.

"I thought it was Washington, D.C.," suggested Barbirah.

"Either one," responded Barbyra with a shrug.

"But we really didn't pay much attention to those rumors. No need to be nosey," concluded Barbirah.

"We apologize if we seem to be the nosey type," said Gaude.

"Well, if I were inclined to be the nosey type, I would want to know why you two have come all the way to Alaska to see a burned-out Kingdom Hall," said Barbirah.

"Because it is a burned-out Kingdom Hall," said Watt.

"You have something against Jehovah's Witnesses?" inquired Barbyra.

"We something against arsonists," replied Gaude.

"We have that in common," said Barbirah. "Just the same—"

"Yeah, just the same—" echoed Barbyra.

"And we don't want to toss a wet blanket over your enthusiasm—" added Barbirah.

"No, not at all," agreed Barbyra, "but don't you get enough burned churches in the lower forty-eight?"

⌘

She paced for a few minutes in the examination room before sitting back down in the uncomfortable plastic chair. After six hours of blood samples, MRIs, CAT scans, poking and prodding, and being subjected to a variety of tests she could neither fathom nor pronounce, Katie had become frazzled and fidgety. She looked over at the corner table and saw a copy of Schopenhauer's *On the Freedom of the Will* and an old edition of a *Reader's Digest*.

Funny, Katie's inner voice mused, *I thought that they stopped publishing Readers Digest years ago*. She picked it up and glanced at the date on the cover. It was her birthday—twelve years ago. "Okay, this is weird," she said aloud to the otherwise empty room. Katie leafed through the magazine in a desultory and half-interested way until her eye caught a short poem at the bottom of page thirty-seven.

FAREWELL SONNET

If we should meet
Ten years hence
In some casual way,
We won't avoid each other's glance,
We will not turn away.
Instead, we'll smile,
Extend a hand,
And ask how things have been.
We'll gently speak and nod our heads
And promise to meet again.
After we part, I will be asked:
"Who was that, do you know?"
"Yes, a friend, I once knew well,
So very long ago."

—Reuben Malachi

Katie Moscowicz once again addressed the room aloud, now suspecting that she was not entirely alone. "Alright, God, you're trying to tell me something and I'm really afraid to ask what it is." Immediately there was a tap at the door and Moscowicz jerked back in surprise at this sudden response from the Creator of the Universe. The door opened, and instead of a deity perched on a white cloud, a doctor wearing in a white lab coat stepped into the room. His face was composed in that tight balance of insincere optimism, professional concern, and kindly pity that was the herald of very bad news. She would have preferred a scowl. Doctors with good news do not need to console their patients and can thus remain in their natural state of moody anxiety about their tax shelters and medical insurance paperwork. Doctor Rentzer asked Katie to dress and come into his office. *This is not good*, thought Katie. *Definitely not good.*

She entered the doctor's office and found herself surrounded by white maple everything, a failed attempt at a Scandinavian something, mixed with Italian postmodern anything, punctuated by Bauhaus whatever, and seasoned with Americana retro this and that. *We're trusting our body to someone whose office looks like this?* Katie asked Katie. She sat down in one of the Barcelona chairs facing the Doctor's translucent glass desk. On the wall behind the doctor's desk was a large framed copy of Kandinsky's *Circles in a Circle*.

"Miss…ummm…Doctor…Moscowicz…do you prefer Katherine?"

"I'm pregnant."

The doctor winced but quickly regained his composure. "Yes…yes you are."

"I knew it. You wake up one morning and life hits you right between the thighs."

The doctor made an admirable effort to show his appreciation for his patient's humor while still maintaining the proper level of medical *gravitas* required for the occasion. "I suppose that's true."

"You're also going to tell me that I'm dying."

"Everyone is going to die."

"Everyone is not going to die within a year."

There was a pause, saturated in painful awkwardness. For all the detailed examination he had performed, the doctor had not until now looked deeply into the penetrating eyes of Katherine Moscowicz. As he did so, he calmly calculated the temperament of his patient and concluded that she was a fighter. Any attempt to ease or delay the blow would serve only to annoy her. "The diagnosis…" said the doctor, who then paused, trying to think of a better way of breaking the news.

"Let's go, Doc. Spit it out. You didn't graduate from med school thinking you could dodge moments like this, did you?"

The doctor winced. "What did the doctors at Emory tell you?"

"They told me to fly up to Boston and see you, so that's what I did."

"You've come a long way for bad news."

"In that case, give it to me."

The doctor nodded gently to himself and then leveled his eyes with those of his patient sitting across the desk. The doctor spoke deliberately, yet with as much sensitivity as he could muster and still provide the cold and calculating truth that the eyes of Katie Moscowicz demanded of him. "You have DIPG: Diffuse Intrinsic Pontine Glioma. It's a form of cancer that is found in the middle of the brain stem."

"Fatal, no doubt."

"Yes."

"Very fatal?"

"Very."

"What's the survival rate? One percent?"

"Actually, the survival rate is zero percent."

Katie mulled this over for a moment. "Thank goodness for that. The suspense as to whether or not I was going to be that one percent would have killed me."

The physician could not help but chuckle at his patient's plucky attitude. He quickly returned to a mien of professional sobriety. "Your case is advanced."

"How advanced?"

"Quite advanced. There is also the matter of your age. Most cases of DIPG occur in children or teens. Very few young adults, and almost no one over thirty, are diagnosed with such a tumor."

"I suppose that I should be honored to be chosen for the rare distinction."

"Rarer still, you're still asymptomatic, even at this late stage. The doctors at Emory indicated in your medical charts that they detected the tumor almost by accident."

"Maybe I could accidentally lose it," Katie quipped.

"You haven't experienced problems swallowing? Blurred vision?"

"Not really."

"Loss of balance?"

"I've been s bit woozy for the past few weeks, but I ascribed that to drinking and falling in love…not necessarily in that order." Katie now leaned forward across the glass desktop and dropped her pretense of jocularity. "How much time do I have? At least nine months?"

"Two months is more likely."

"I need more."

"It is a miracle that you have lived this long."

"In that case, I need an even bigger miracle. How about eight months?"

"Maybe three months, no more."

"The baby won't come to term in three months. I need to save this baby."

"I'm sorry. There is nothing we can do to save you or the baby."

"Can you put me in a coma, put me on life support, and deliver the baby that way?"

The doctor shook his head incredulously. "You should be thinking of yourself."

"I am thinking of myself. I am a mother now and intend to

249

remain a mother. If this child dies before it is born, then I will no longer be a mother. I absolutely refuse to have motherhood taken from me. You see? I am a very selfish person."

"As best as I can tell, you seem to be somewhere between the fifth and sixth week of pregnancy. Have you experienced morning sickness?"

"No."

"Most likely the fifth week, then. The baby will require another twenty weeks to be viable. The absolute minimum for any chance of survival—and a remote chance at that—is another seventeen weeks. It's very unlikely that you will make it that far. If the baby is born at all, it would be a photo finish."

"A photo finish? For God's sake, don't take photos of me during childbirth. I know that it's all the rage now, and I have friends who have done that, but frankly speaking, I think it's a dreadful fad. I know that I would look a mess and I just can't have that. My family in Atlanta has a tradition of babies popping out perfectly clean and rosy pink and carried by cherubs from the delivery room to a white wicker bassinet that has been passed down from mother to daughter since 1831."

"I'm sorry, but it's unlikely that there will be any need for that bassinette."

"Is there anything I can do to increase my chances of surviving long enough to keep the baby alive?"

The doctor shook his head in a sad and apologetic 'no.'

"Then dying simply will not do. You'll have to reverse the prognosis."

"How do I do that?"

"How should I know? That's your job. I assume it requires you to say, 'This cancer is officially banished,' or something like that."

"You mean, like a television evangelist?"

"Yes, but without the blue velvet suit."

"Wishing will not make it go away."

"Maybe not, but it's a start."

"I'm sorry, but there is nothing I can do."

"Is there something someone else can do? Is there a medical research organization that specializes in treating this cancer?"

"I'm afraid not."

"No one has found a way to slow the progress of this condition?"

"Surgery is impossible. The tumor is extremely invasive and cannot be removed. Chemotherapy has been proven unavailing and is also not an option here since your primary goal is to save your unborn child. Radiation therapy has been known to delay the progress of the tumor for some months, but your case is so advanced that it is unlikely in the extreme that you will eke out even an additional day."

"Any extraordinary cases out there that you know of?"

The doctor paused and silently mulled over the patient's desperate plea. After an awkward and uncomfortable silence, he cleared his throat and replied, "There was a study published a few months ago that I happened to read in a medical journal posted on DataGhad, but it was—"

"It was what?"

"It was unusual, to say the least, and really offers no practical solution for you."

"My medical insurance is paying thousands for the testing you just put me through for the past few hours. I think I'm entitled to a few more minutes, so why don't you use that precious remaining time to tell me something other than I am doomed to die before Christmas."

The doctor nodded, more to himself than to the patient on the other side of the desk, and briefly mulled over how he should respond. Finally, he looked up and said, "Ni'ihau."

"Ni'ihau? Ni'ihau Child? The country music band?"

"No, the island."

"Oh, *that* Ni'ihau. Yes, I'm familiar with it. Smallest and westernmost inhabited island in the Hawaiian chain. It has been privately owned by a rather wealthy family since the American Civil War and they have treated it as a trust preserve for native Hawaiians ever since. The residents aren't absolutely isolated, but technology hasn't been widely embraced. The native culture—and their privacy— is jealously guarded. It is the one place on earth where Hawaiian is the primary and almost exclusive language."

"Yes, impressive. Not many people know that information except for avid readers of National Geographic. I guess I should have asked if your PhD was in anthropology or geography."

"What about the island?" asked Katie, uninterested in dallying in pleasantries.

"Researchers in Hawaii reported that a phenomenally unusual cluster of DIPG occurred on the island of Ni'ihau. In fact, it is the only reported large cluster of DIPG in history. Some time ago, it was discovered that twelve children living on the island had the tumor. Naturally, an extraordinary situation such as that suggests the probability of either environmental or genetic causes. Both were investigated, particularly genetic, since the population was so small and intermarriage common. No conclusive findings were established. However, one peculiar item was noted in the recent study. It seems that the progress of the cancer has been much slower in this cluster population than in nearly all other patients in the world. Although the cancer is incurable, the affected subjects live many years—sometimes a decade—longer than similarly situated individuals. Once again, an examination of environment and genetics yielded nothing substantial, but in a footnote, the author of the article mentioned that the natives ascribed the survival of the children to eating blue potatoes."

"Blue potatoes?"

"Yes, apparently a religious community in Idaho has been developing a hybrid potato that is drought resistant and tolerant of desert conditions. The potatoes were sent to Ni'ihau as a humanitarian gesture motivated by the fact that the island is rather arid in comparison to the lush Hawaiian climate to the east. The blue potatoes thrived in the island's volcanic soil and became a staple of the local diet. The inhabitants are convinced that the blue potatoes that grow in their gardens possess medicinal properties that explain the almost miraculous survival of their children beyond what might normally be expected in such cases."

"Thank you. That's the miracle I was looking for."

"Miss Moscowicz…I mean Doctor Moscowicz…there is something else you should know about the island of Ni'ihau."

"It's virtually inaccessible and visits from outsiders are strictly forbidden," responded Katie.

"Yes."

"I didn't ask for an easy miracle, I asked for any miracle. This one will do." Katie got up and walked out of the doctor's office. She stood for a moment in the reception area trying to determine her next steps. She was unable to coax her newly-diagnosed diseased brain to commit to any course of action, so her feet took the initiative and carried her out into the hall and forward to the elevator. Music played on the speakers as she descended to the ground floor. She recognized the country tune as Ni'ihau Child's 'Don't Give Up Now.'

The news ain't good, I gotta admit,
They've slammed you to the ground:
Just git back in your pickup truck
And turn your life around.

When things go bad to worse for you,
There's an answer to be found:
Just git back in your pickup truck
And turn your life around.

Now don't you sob or make a fuss,
Or wail like an old hound:
Just git back in your pickup truck
And turn your life around.

Katie exited the lobby as she pushed through the glass doors of the medical center. She looked up at the cloudless brilliant blue sky. "Alright, God," she announced, "I've done my best to screw everything up, so now it's your turn to deal with the mess. You heard the conversation that I had with the doctor, so you know what you need to do." She continued looking up, waiting for a response. After a full minute of silence, Katie nodded to herself and again addressed the sky. "Okay…so, that's it, then. Good. I'm glad we had this little talk."

Gaude had been driving on Route 1 for an hour when he saw a small sign indicating that they were approaching Bear Lake. Soon after, a much larger hand-painted billboard came into view.

BEST DAMNED GRILL IN ALASKA

1 mile ahead of you.

If you don't eat here,
don't come cryin' to me.
It's your own damned fault!

"Is that the actual name of the place?"

"I think so."

"In that case, I can't pass it up."

"No doubt, the very reason the proprietor painted that sign."

"Notwithstanding the admonitions of Barbirah and Barbyra, I think that I could go for some grilled salmon and a cold beer."

"Sounds good to me."

"Does that mean that you are going to join me in ordering something other than chili?"

"No, it just sounds good to me that you will be enjoying your grilled salmon. Hopefully, you'll enjoy it as much as I will be enjoying my chili."

"You have any particular chili in mind?"

"Maybe caribou. Perhaps bear."

"They're not endangered?"

"Not in Alaska."

"There it is," Gaude said as he pointed towards the building ahead of them. He took a right turn a moment later and pulled into a parking lot populated exclusively with black Ford Explorers.

The Best Damned Grill in Alaska made every effort to live up to its name. The building was an enormous timber edifice, built of logs so massive that Gaude was unsure how they could have possibly been transported overland by truck, and he wondered if perhaps the trees had all been felled nearby. Upon passing through the large swinging doors of the front entrance, they were greeted by a disco classic, 'Stayin' Alive' by the Bee Gees.

Gaude found himself in the midst of a taxidermist's acid trip. Every conceivable animal, and several which were inconceivable, were stuffed and mounted on the walls or positioned on pedestals throughout the restaurant, some posed in comical stances. At the vacant reception station, they passed a raccoon standing on its hind legs, dressed in sport fisherman's waders, wearing a cap decorated with dry fishing flies, and posed frozen in time casting a fly rod into the distance. As they continued to proceed through the restaurant, Gaude saw a squirrel dressed as Robin Hood notching an arrow to a bow, a timber wolf dressed as a matador goading a badger bedecked with miniature bullhorns, and a terrapin in a tutu performing a pirouette.

Gaude and Watt made their way to the bar and sat down on the crimson naugahyde covered stools. On the wall facing them, immediately above the mirror, was a trio of moose heads, each with antlers variously askew, none of which pointed in the same direction. Gaude glanced up to the ceiling and jerked back in slight shock at the sight of an open-jawed killer whale hanging immediately above them as if descending to make its own dinner of the diners at the bar. Gaude continued to look around the vast log edifice only to be interrupted by a voice coming from behind the bar.

"Good evening gents! I'm Roscoe Tannenbaum. Welcome to my world," he gestured expansively and with pride.

"It's quite a place you have here."

"Yep, folks come from near and far to eat here. Assuming that 'near' is ten miles and 'far' is twenty."

"We came from appreciably farther away."

"Kenai or Anchorage?"

"The lower forty-eight," said Watt.

"Really?" responded Tannenbaum with a slight grin, "You look like you're from the higher forty-eight."

"More than you can imagine."

"What'll ya have to drink?"

"Whaddya got?"

"We have two beers on tap. Kassick's and Saint Elias."

"What about bottled beers?" asked Gaude.

"Beer comes in bottles?" said Tannenbaum in apparent disbelief.

"Make mine a Kassick's," said Gaude.

"I'd like a Beach Tribe Root Beer if you have one," requested Watt.

As he pulled the first beer, Tannenbaum asked, "Are you gents hungry?"

"Passably," answered Gaude.

Tannenbaum jerked his thumb over his shoulder at a large blackboard featuring the fare of the day. "That's what we've got."

"We can't order off the menu?" Gaude said with a sly grin.

"You go out and shoot something and maybe I'll cook it for you. Otherwise, stick to what's on the board."

"Grilled salmon," requested Gaude.

"How many pounds?"

"You don't measure in kilos?"

"Screw kilos. That's for the lower forty-eight. We're still Americans here."

"Is one pound enough?"

"Not for me, it isn't."

"Okay, make it bigger, then," ordered Gaude.

"How is the muskox chili?" inquired Watt.

"Anyone who orders muskox chili is required to sign a legal disclaimer."

"Why is that? Is it dangerous?"

"It sure is. Once you've had muskox, you are in danger of never wanting to go back to beef. We've been threatened with lawsuits because our muskox is so good."

"I'll take that risk. Bring it on."

"You both get sides of fries and slaw."

"That sounds fine," said Gaude.

"They're more than fine," responded Tannenbaum with a slight air of indignation. "They're the best. We import them. Our fries are made from the blue potatoes of Panama, Idaho. The slaw is the finest you'll find in the Deep South, or anywhere else on earth. We have it flown in all the way from Flannery, Georgia."

Gaude turned to his partner. Watt returned a look of comical innocence and raised his hands as he made an unrepentant shrug. Gaude shook his head in mock dismay and then started examining the framed black and white glossy photographs on the wall to his left. They featured a variety of people, most of them wearing flannel, denim, woolens, or a combination of the three, all signed, and all complaining of the food, the unsatisfactory service, or disparaging the family tree of the proprietor.

"I see that you've had some outspoken customers," said Gaude, gesturing to the wall.

"That's my wall of fame and hall of shame," answered Tannenbaum. "They are my most famous guests."

"I'm sorry, but I don't recognize them."

"They're my regulars."

"They aren't famous celebrities?"

"They are to me. I'd be out of business if it weren't for them coming in for dinner every night."

"The notes that they write on their photographs aren't very complimentary."

"They're my friends. What else did you expect them to say?"

Gaude continued scanning across the profusion of stuffed

animals, photographs, trophies, mementos, oddities, and random souvenirs. A large placard at the back of the restaurant caught his attention.

"I noticed your sign."

"Capricorn. What's it to you?"

"No, I mean that sign," said Gaude, gesturing behind him.

> # Church of Holy Hilarity
>
> God's not laughing with you.
> He's laughing at you.

"Noticing that sign isn't much of an accomplishment. The lettering is large enough to see at one hundred paces."

"I guess what I meant is that I find it interesting."

"Why didn't you say so in the first place?"

"I thought that I did."

"You're one of those quibblers, aren't you?"

Gaude shot a sidelong glance at Watt and then looked back at the proprietor. "Is it a local church?"

"As local as can be. It's right here."

"This bar is a church?"

"Sure, why not?"

"I've never heard of drinking alcohol in a church."

"The Catholics have been doing it for two thousand years."

"That's only a tiny amount of altar wine."

"It's a matter of quantity and degree. Drinking in church is drinking in church."

"It's not the same thing."

"Yeah, I'm thinking that you are a quibbler."

"That depends on what you consider quibbling."

Tannenbaum nodded with a friendly smirk. "I suppose it's all in the definition, isn't it?"

"I…you…" stammered Gaude.

"In any event," continued Tannenbaum, oblivious to Gaude's

reaction, "it's a bonafide church. I mailed off for a preacher license and I've married a few folks. Even with that, I didn't do this to dodge taxes or any of that nonsense."

"Why?" asked Watt.

"Why what?"

"Why did you decide to make this place a church—or at least, a part-time church?"

"I didn't take to most churches. Truth be told, most churches didn't really take to me."

"What churches did?" asked Gaude.

"Did what?"

"Take to you?"

"None of them."

"But you said most churches, not all churches."

"You definitely *are* a quibbler," Tannenbaum said with a mock scowl. "Anyhow, I couldn't stand all the moaning and groaning and I repent about this and forgive me Lord about that. Too much bellyaching about sin, and when it's all said and done and they've put you in the ground, you're still more than likely to be sent to hell than to be accepted into heaven."

"You find traditional denominations to be killjoys, I take it? Just too darned…holy?"

"That's about the size of it. I don't know how the religions of the world were taken over by prudes and sour-pusses. Religions in ancient times were fun. Heck, they used to have temple prostitutes. That's what I'm talkin' about! Gimme that old time religion!"

Watt looked across the room suspiciously. "I hope none of your good-time hostess disciples are looking to proselytize us."

Tannenbaum guffawed. "See? That's what it's all about. What I really needed to set my soul aright was a good laugh. While I was at it, I figured that God had a pretty demanding job running the universe and probably would appreciate a chuckle or two himself."

"You try to make God laugh?"

"I don't have to try. He laughs all the time. I know the true essence of God through his sense of humor."

"God has a sense of humor?"

"Sure. Look around you at the universal comedy that has been unfolding since the dawn of creation. If God didn't have a sense of humor, why did he create such a cosmic farce?"

258

"Humor requires spontaneity, it requires surprise."

"Are you saying that God can't be surprised? Why not?"

"Because he knows all things. He is omniscient and unconstrained by time, which means that he can see the future. Indeed, he dwells in the future just as he exists in the present and abides in the past. He already knows the punchline to the joke," explained Watt.

"That's where you are wrong. If you take away from God the capacity to be amused and the ability to be surprised, then that means there is a characteristic that we humans have that God does not. That would mean that God is finite, since he lacks something. Even worse than that, he lacks something that nearly every mere mortal human has in abundance. God is infinite, therefore he encompasses all, possesses, all, is capable of all. If God is all and capable of all, then he must be able to enjoy a great belly-laugh. I suspect he does it on a frequent basis, perhaps continually, considering the foibles of the human race."

"I don't see God as laughing," said Gaude.

"You need to open up your Bible and take a look at Psalm Thirty-Seven, Verse Thirteen. 'The Lord laughs at the wicked, knowing that their day of reckoning is upon them.' Not only that, but look around you," continued Tannenbaum. "Right now, we're having an abstruse philosophical debate while surrounded by hundreds of stuffed animals, some of them in mighty weird poses. That is bound to appeal to someone's sense of surreal comedy."

"Such as God's?"

"Exactly!" agreed Tannenbaum. "Lemme tell you, go have a conversation with a Hindu and ask them about Ganesh. God laughs, trust me on this. In fact, there is no doubt in my mind that as God is looking down upon us, he calls the saints over and says, 'Hey, would you get a load of this? Can you believe what those idiots are doing down there? Who the hell is responsible for all of those screw-ups?' Then Saint Peter has to tell him, 'Lord, I think that would be you.' I think of heaven as a non-stop laugh fest. In fact, that's why it *is* heaven."

"So, you decided to start your own religion?"

"I don't know if you could say that I started an entire religion. There's the Bible, of course. I sorta follow that, more or less, although I avoid the gloomy parts."

"There *are* a lot of gloomy parts in the Bible."

"That just means that I don't have to read too much."

"What parts of the Bible *do* you find amusing?"

"Some things are all-out funny. More than a few folks have pointed out how silly Noah must have looked to his neighbors building a giant ark behind his house."

"True."

"Then there are some other things that people might consider serious can be pretty amusing if you look at it the right way. Adam and Eve were running around Eden without a stitch of clothes and having a great time. Then Eve gets bamboozled by a talking snake—reminds me of my ex-wife's divorce attorney—and then takes a bite out of the apple. That's assuming it was an apple. Some folks insist it was a pomegranate, which is another chance to laugh at silly arguments. Anyway, next thing you know, both realize they are naked, jump in the bushes, and think that they can hide from God. When God questions them, they both play the blame game. You have to admit, that's a pretty funny story about the first two humans in the world."

"I suppose that there is an element of humor there," conceded Watt.

"Abraham, father of the nations, was a piece of work, I'll tell you. He goes down into Egypt with his wife Sarah. Because she's pretty, Abraham decides to pretend that he's her brother for fear that the locals will knock him off and steal her away. Sarah gets grabbed up by Pharaoh himself, who goes to bed with her...all apparently without a peep from Abraham. Pharaoh finds out about the lie, gets plenty angry, and gives Abraham a good scolding. What does the founding father of three of the world's great religions do? He moves up to Palestine and pulls the same stunt on King Abimelech. Better yet, fifty years later, Abraham's son Isaac marries Rebekah and then does the same brother-sister act with the same King Abimelech who, by the way, on both occasions is absolutely weirded out, but for reasons best known to him, decides to reward both of these characters with gifts and covenants and peace treaties and what have you. As they say in Brooklyn, 'go figure.' Come to think of it, the Old Testament would have benefitted from someone from Brooklyn being the author."

"You have a unique way of interpreting scripture," said Watt.

"There's also the reference in Deuteronomy, Chapter Twenty-Five of which I'm mighty fond. Moses establishes a rule that if two men are fighting and the wife of one of them jumps into the fray and grabs the balls of her husband's assailant, the penalty is that her hand must be cut off—no appeal, no mercy. That's a story that doesn't get much press. You got to wonder how often that sort of thing happened that Moses felt he needed to make a law. Too bad there wasn't an eleventh commandment: 'Toucheth not thy neighbor's family jewels.' Anyway, I love that one. I could preach for an hour about it, two hours if I have a few beers in me."

"Drink enough beer and almost anything is amusing," said Gaude.

"You have a point there," agreed Tannenbaum. "Even sober, I get a kick out of some Bible stories. We take bear maulings pretty seriously in these parts, but when a bunch of young hoodlums started harassing Elisha and making fun of his bald head, the fact that two bears come out of nowhere and give those punks what-for is something that can't help but make me chuckle. Look in Second Kings, you'll find it there."

"Harsh, but I get your point."

"Besides all that, there is plenty of things about religion that are funny that doesn't need to come out of the Bible. The Catholic Church takes the position that they can come up with lots of teachings that aren't necessarily Bible-based. They call it their power of the Magisterium. Heck, if the Pope can make up stuff on the fly for a billion people, I suppose I can make up a few things for the few dozen folks who come here on Sunday for a prayer, a beer, and a few laughs."

"Such as what?"

"Have you ever heard the one about the blind priest and the one-legged rabbi?"

"I'm not sure that I want to."

"You're not Methodist, are you?"

"No, why?"

"They never get the punch lines."

"The Methodists—and perhaps a few other denominations as well—might find you to be somewhat heretical," said Gaude.

"This is a planet chock-full of heretics, including the folks who wrap themselves in self-righteous robes of orthodoxy. We are all God's fools and he makes merry watching our every folly."

"Order up!" came a booming voice from the service window.

Tannenbaum picked up the plate of grilled salmon and bowl of muskox chili and set them before his customers. "May you enjoy eating your dinners as much as your dinners dislike being eaten," he announced and then turned and moved down the bar to attend to another group of diners that had just arrived.

"Our host definitely has some unusual ideas about God."

"God is unusual, by definition."

"You're not defending him, are you?"

"Defending him? Yes. Agreeing with him? Not entirely. There are nuggets of truth in what he said. You can mine more than just gold in Alaska."

"Speaking of mining, I don't think that we came across much paydirt when it comes to clues today."

"Perhaps we came across them but didn't recognize them as clues."

"Same thing."

"Not really."

"Maybe salmon is a clue."

"How is your salmon?" asked Watt.

"It's the tastiest clue we've ever encountered. I say that we hang around here for a while so that we can eat—I mean, find—more clues."

"Maybe it's the Barbirah and Barbyra thing."

"You're going to have to define a Barbirah and Barbyra thing."

"I doubt that I can," replied Watt. "Maybe the year 1975, the year that the Jehovah's Witnesses disappeared."

"I vote for muskox as a clue," said Gaude playfully.

"That would make two of us," agreed Watt. "It's excellent, but I'm not sure that it qualifies as a bona fide clue."

"Don't jump to conclusions, let me search it." Gaude tapped out a query on his cell screen and looked over the links. "Ah, ha! Here's something. Thomas Aquinas was given the nickname 'Dumb Ox' by his fellow students."

"Hmmm...I would imagine there are a few churches dedicated to him."

"Safe bet."

"You know that I don't approve of crawling through that digital morass."

"But you've never tried to stop me."

"It's a question of free will. God didn't stop Adam from eating the apple."

"Roscoe Tannenbaum said it could have been a pomegranate."

"Just for the record, I must warn you that God finds quibblers very annoying."

The Advisors

"My life is a series of crises sewn together with the catgut of despair."

"Hmmm…that sounds dreadful and somehow familiar."

"Reuben Malachi. The opening words of his novel, *Feet of Clay*."

"Oh yes, the first book of his that was banned by the Vatican."

"I know the feeling well."

"Your writings have been banned by the Vatican?"

"Not exactly. I've been banned by the newspapers. My dream was to become a syndicated comic strip artist. I wanted to be published around the world."

"I see, like Andy Capp."

"Who?"

"Perhaps like Charlie Brown?"

"I'm not sure what you are talking about."

"Blondie? Lil' Abner? Dick Tracey?" suggested Sister Mary Margaret.

"Do you actually read any comics?"

"I thought that I did."

"I mean mainstream comics?" the visitor asked.

"I thought that I did," said the nun, now starting to doubt herself.

"My strip is called *The Sloozers*. At least, that's what I named it."

"*The Sloozers*?"

"Yes, short for the 'Super Losers.' It's about a team of misfit superheroes that have powers that nobody wants or needs."

"Such as?"

"Well, there is Melvin—"

"Melvin?"

"Yes."

"That does not sound much like the name of a proper superhero."

"Exactly. That's one of the things that makes him such a loser."

"I see," responded Sister Mary Margaret thoughtfully. "You were about to explain his superpower?"

"Melvin has the ability to make flat soda pop fizzy again."

"Yes, I can see how that might not be all that useful."

"Morgonzo can tell the different species of trees by their smell."

"Really? Well…at least he has a type of superhero name."

"Morgonzo is a woman."

"Oh."

"Charlyne can levitate cars—"

"That sounds quite useful, actually."

"—but the only cars that she can levitate are 1976 Plymouth Valiants."

"Oh, I see."

"I had a character named Dynatron—"

"That is a very good name for a fictional superhero."

"Yes, I thought so too. It turns out that there was already a *Defenders of Dynatron City* copyrighted by Marvel Comics. They sued me for millions."

"Oh dear…What was Dynatron's power?"

"I'm under a federal court restraining order, so I'm not allowed to say."

"I am very sorry."

"Ushi is telepathic—"

"A mind reader? That is a very useful comic book hero superpower, although I must candidly observe that it is not terribly original."

"I didn't get to finish. Ushi is telepathic—a mind-reader—but her powers are limited to reading the minds of three-year-olds."

"Most mothers of three-year-olds can do that."

"Good point."

"Have you considered bypassing the newspapers and posting your work on the internet?"

"Yes, I tried that. The site was hacked continually and subjected to denial of service attacks."

"I suppose that means—"

"It means that I am a loser."

"Perhaps you could make your superhero characters more successful and uplifting."

"Then they wouldn't be *The Sloozers*."

"No, I suppose not."

"So, there you have it."

"Yes, here we are. Was there something you had in mind that I could help you with?"

"I was told that you have miraculous powers."

"Miraculous powers? Really?"

"Yes, that must be why it takes so long to get an interview with you. I've been waiting for more than three years."

"I am quite sorry about that."

"No need to apologize. I'm sure it has been worth the wait."

"Mister Dinkel, I am flattered, but I cannot give you any assurances that my efforts on your behalf will prove to be a salutary solution from your standpoint."

"You mean that I won't be happy with the result?"

"Yes, that is, indeed, what I mean."

"What is it you normally do with your powers?"

"My powers, as you call them, are limited to supplications to the Almighty on behalf of his petitioning children."

"I'm sorry. I have no idea what you are talking about."

"I pray for people."

Dexter Dinkel mulled on this for a moment. "You pray to God?"

"Yes. I find that it is far more efficacious than praying to oak trees."

"And God then sends down miracles…or maybe a guardian angel?"

"It does not really work that way, Mister Dinkel."

"Well, however it works, I'm all in for any miracle you can manage to negotiate with God."

"Mister Dinkel—"

"I have a list of newspapers that I'd like to get my comics into on a syndicated basis. Can I leave it with you so that you can discuss it with God?"

"Mister Dinkel—"

"It doesn't need to be a *major* miracle. If even half of the newspapers publish me, I'll definitely be a satisfied customer."

"Mister Dinkel—"

"Yes?"

"Mister Dinkel…" said Sister Mary Margaret, leaning forward and speaking in a hushed conspiratorial whisper, "I must confide in you a deep, dark secret of my Order that is kept under the tightest of wraps by the Church. May I rely on your discretion?"

Her visitor instinctively leaned forward and nodded solemnly. "Yes, Sister, of course."

"My miraculous powers have some peculiar constraints. You see—and I am very embarrassed to admit this to you—my prayers work only on behalf of members of the Greek Orthodox Church who are nearsighted and pigeon-toed."

"Seriously?"

"Yes. It is a matter of grave concern and the Church has been investigating the matter for several years. Thus far, none of the experts from Rome have been able to explain this strange phenomenon."

"Sister, it sounds like you are no better off than any of my comic book superheroes."

"Yes, Mister Dinkel, you are quite right. It seems that I, too, am a super loser. Perhaps you could pray for me?"

"Certainly, Sister, it would be my honor."

"Thank you so much!" Sister Mary Margaret now glanced over her visitor's shoulder. "Oh, Mister Dinkel, I see that our time has elapsed. I am so grateful for your assistance. I feel much better already."

"Yes, Sister, I do too."

Sister Mary Margaret shared a radiant smile. "Bless you, my son."

Twenty-One: Berlin

He is standing in an underground parking lot, waiting for an acquaintance who is using a pay telephone. The telephone booth is identical to those he remembers from his youth, a tall glass box, fully enclosing the customer, a folding door. Someone approaches the telephone booth. He recognizes the person. It is a well-known actor of drama and suspense movies. The actor begins to harass the acquaintance in the telephone booth. The reply is curt, harsh, and effective. The man leaves. The acquaintance finishes his telephone call. As they walk away towards a car, the recent interloper suddenly reappears and fires at them with a bizarre thin-muzzled blunderbuss. The projectile is a black pea moving at impossibly slow velocity. He can see the pellets passing by and ducks behind a car. His acquaintance now has an identical blunderbuss and returns fire. The contestants repeatedly fire, always missing. The acquaintance hands him the weapon and runs away. He attempts to shoulder the gun, accidentally pulls the trigger and sends off a wild round. He cocks back the hammer, aims now at the interloper, fires and misses. He watches the black pea pass by the opponent's face, missing the target ever so slightly. A pea now grazes his own face. He feels searing pain on his right temple. Now he takes more careful aim and fires. The pea slowly reaches its target and strikes the actor on the left cheek. The area grows gray, tendrils begin to spread, and the side of the face begins to palsy. The pellet is poisoned. The opponent is dying.

Gaude awoke from the dream. *Was it a dream? No, it was a memory. No, no…it was too strange to be real…but it felt so real…*He made an internal shrug that manifested itself as an external twitch of his right eye. *Bill is right, it doesn't matter. It's all the same, isn't it?*

He realized that he was in the passenger seat of a car. He looked out across a scenic expanse of varicolored buttes and mesas surrounded by a seemingly endless desert of innumerable hues—all of them tan.

"It's hot."

"It's Utah."

"I've been to Utah before."

"In the summer?"

"It's summer again?"

"Yep."

"Since when?"

"Since now."

"But it was just spring...or was it autumn?"

"Things change."

"So fast?"

Watt shrugged. "*El Niño.*"

Talking about the weather was not how Gaude intended to while away the time between tracking down obscure and elusive clues of their spectral opponent, but the car was uncomfortably warm. Gaude reached over to the dashboard controls to turn on the air conditioning.

"Don't bother, it will blow hot air at you," warned Watt.

"What's wrong with the AC?"

"Compared to the rest of this lemon?"

Gaude looked around the interior of the car. "This doesn't look like a rental. It looks more like a trade-in. How did we get stuck with this?"

"I guess you forgot...again?"

"Yes, apparently so," grumbled Gaude. "Why don't you enlighten me?"

"We flew from Anchorage to Salt Lake and then took the twelve-seater to Saint George."

"Seriously?"

"You don't remember the flight?"

"Do I look like I remember the flight?"

"Isaiah Air Service, Flight 4110."

"That doesn't help."

"That's true, it certainly didn't help us to get to Saint George."

"Saint George?"

"Saint George, Utah."

"A thriving metropolis, no doubt."

"The closest airport that we could find to Berlin, or so we thought."

"Berlin...Utah?"

"The one and only."

"I don't remember any clues that led to Berlin."

"That's not what you said last night at the restaurant."

"What did I say at the restaurant?"

Watt made a comic frown for what substituted as a Gaude roll of the eyes. "When you consulted your precious hand-held demigod, you saw that a church fire had just been reported in Berlin, Utah. You then looked up as if graced with a profound revelation and declared that the restaurant we were eating was located at—"

"Bear Lake."

"Yes, exactly."

"Berlin is ancient Germanic for Bear Lake."

"That's what you said last night."

"So, that somehow resulted in my waking up in a filthy broken-down automobile trekking across the desert?"

"The flight to Saint George was diverted due to some sort of power failure in the region. The pilot flew out to Monument Valley Airport, only to discover that it wasn't there."

"What wasn't there?"

"Monument Valley."

"A valley was missing?"

"Monument Valley airport."

"An airport was missing?"

"Apparently so. Luckily, the plane was small enough to land on a highway."

"The plane landed on a highway? In the middle of nowhere? I slept through all of this?"

"Dan, you were wide awake. I'm sorry about the memory lapse."

"So, now we're stuck here?"

"Monument Valley is a beautiful place. It's a top tourist destination. You've probably seen it one hundred times in cowboy movies."

"Thank you, John Ford. I'll keep that in mind. So, we acquired this used car...how?"

"We were dropped off at a high school and pretty much abandoned. Are you sure that you don't remember any of this?"

"Happily, no, although creepily...also no."

"Anyway, long story short—"

"Praise God for that—"

"—we rented, for lack of a better term, this car from a local campground."

"I don't recognize the make."

"Willys."

"Willys?"

"Willys."

"Oh." Gaude paused and then remarked, "I'm guessing that campgrounds in Utah don't usually rent cars."

"No, this was just sitting around and the owner was willing for us to take it...for one hundred dollars per day."

"Say what?"

"Yes, I did say, and yes, it is an outrage."

"Why didn't you use one of those business cards of yours on that crook?"

"My card works better on honest citizens."

"Well, this all makes perfect sense."

"It does?"

"As much sense as anything I've been doing with you since you kidnapped me from a hospital in Maine."

"Rescued you."

"I'm having second thoughts about that. Now that I've had more time to mull it over, my inquisitive creepy friend might have had some redeeming qualities."

"Such as?"

"Such as not dragging me to every conceivable and inconceivable misadventure across the continent."

"You're welcome," answered Bill Watt serenely.

"Do you know where we are going?"

"Does anyone?"

"Please spare me the lesson from sophomore philosophy class."

"We're about fifteen minutes from Berlin. A synagogue there burned down last night."

"You're telling me that I read this off my cell?"

"It was the same time you told me the news about that explosion in New York."

"What? Another church in New York?"

"No, a publishing company."

Gaude issued an annoyed *hrrumph*. "I don't remember any of that."

A gentle tug of a grin began to show on Watt's face. "Y'know, Dan, maybe this memory loss of yours is due to some electro-magnetic interference from the cellphone. I've heard that all sorts of brain damage can be caused by cellphones and not only to teenagers."

Gaude made a signature roll of the eyes and then looked out the window at the desert. As he turned his head to address Watt, his eye caught the flash of a red light on the dashboard. "Bill, that's an oil indicator."

"I know. It's been on since we started."

"How long has that been?"

"About twenty minutes."

Gaude leaned over to take a better look at the instrument panel. "The engine temperature is running hot as well."

"I thought that was because we are in the desert."

"We need to stop at a service station," warned Gaude.

"I haven't seen too many of them on this road."

"In that case, we're due for one very soon, right?" said Gaude sardonically.

Watt responded with a bright smile. "That's the spirit! I knew there was an optimist in there somewhere."

"Maybe you're starting to rub off on me." Gaude looked skeptically at the filthy dashboard and asked, "I don't suppose that the radio works in his rolling trashcan?"

"Let's give it a try," said Watt, as he reached over and pushed the tuner button. The radio responded with surprising alacrity with a resonant and static free performance of 'Ending It All' by Ni'ihau Child.

> *There's always a choice*
> *Says your silent voice*
> *But is it for real? you wonder*
> *You want to stop now*
> *But not quite sure how*
> *To put yourself six feet under*

What should I use?
A gun or a noose?
Or should I just stay in the game?
It's always your call
Whether life or downfall
You have only yourself to blame

Seven minutes later, an Enco Service Station came into view. "The Lord provides," declared Watt.

"As does the petrochemical industry," rejoined Gaude.

Watt made a right turn and the automobile lunkered up to the garage. As the partners began to emerge from the vehicle, they were approached by a man wearing coveralls wiping his hands with a greasy rag. He walked up to the car, reached under the edge of the hood, and popped the latch. He raised the hood, releasing a plume of mixed steam and acrid smoke.

"You think it needs oil?"

"I think it needs a decent burial," said the service station attendant. "Where you heddin'?"

"Here."

"Here? Berlin? *On purpose?*"

"So it would seem."

"In that case, permit me to officially welcome you to Berlin."

"Thank you."

"Don't thank me. You obviously haven't seen much of Berlin."

"Is it really all that bad?"

"It was named after the capital of Germany."

"Yes?"

"*After* it was bombed from here to hell and back. Folks wanted to give the place a name that reflected how godforsaken it was."

"God doesn't forsake," corrected Bill Watt.

"Perhaps not, but he must get forgetful from time to time. God hasn't paid much attention to this town, unless his idea of attention is what he did to Sodom and Gomorrah."

"But this is a beautiful place," offered Watt, gesturing out to the encircling formations of gray and red sandstone.

"Oh, the land is beautiful, no doubt about it. That's not the problem."

"What's the problem?"

"If you were passing through, you wouldn't need to know. If

272

you are coming here to visit, you'll find out soon enough. If you are coming here to stay, you don't want to think about it."

⌘

"Shall we continue with our little talk?"

"I wasn't aware that we had ever started."

"You are defiant."

"Would you deny me my one pleasure?"

"I deny you nothing. Perhaps you could accommodate me."

"And answer your inane questions."

The Gray man responded in the affirmative with a silent stare.

"I'm not interested."

Doyle's unwelcomed visitor displayed no indication that he had heard the rebuff. "Do you believe in the so-called God?"

"I don't even believe in you."

"When did you last attend services in a church?"

"I've been blacklisted by all the mainstream faiths. I did visit Church's Fried Chicken last Sunday."

The inquisitor considered this silently. His face may have been inscrutable, but it was obvious from the pause that the interrogator decided to take a new approach. "You are divorced."

"You aren't my type."

"You have had illicit affairs with women."

"Actually, I prefer sheep." Doyle pulled himself up on the bed. "Listen, it's been delightful to chat with you about my deep dark secrets, but I'm parched. Can you get me a glass of water?"

"No."

"How would you like to hear about how I was molested by a rabbi the day before my bar mitzvah?"

"Our files indicate that you were raised as an evangelical."

"That's my cover story."

"You are Black."

"Very observant."

"And you want me to believe that you are Jewish?"

"So was Sammy Davis, Junior. Do you want to hear what I have to say or not?"

The Gray man turned, walked to the lavatory, and retrieved a glass filled with water that he handed to his bedridden captive. Doyle emptied the glass slowly as the visitor stood beside him waiting. "If you are a Jew, I assume that you are circumcised."

Doyle leaned forward as to deposit his empty glass on the bedstand to his right. He then suddenly smashed the waterglass against the metal bed rail. In one fluid motion, he grabbed the shirt of the Gray man with his left hand, pulled the inquisitor forward, and plunged the remaining jagged glass shard into the man's throat. "Let's see if you enjoy *this* circumcision, you dickhead!"

Blood splashed and sprayed over the bed, and on Doyle's hands and face. The sensation was shocking not so much from the natural repulsion of being bathed in another's blood, but because it felt surprisingly cold. Doyle did not assume that the man would simply collapse into a heap, but he did not expect the fierceness of the response. Doyle's face was smashed by a rock-hard fist, again and again. In all the years he had been an operative, prior to that week, he had never been tossed like a ragdoll against a wall by an explosion, never been brutally beaten, never been indiscriminately sliced and diced, and never felt the bones of his face collapse with a sickening crunch. In the past seventy-two hours, he had endured more injury than the collective mishaps of his career as a spy, or of his entire life for that matter. Even as he was being pounded—once in the face, twice in the rib cage, now back to the face—Doyle was able to dispassionately consider the injuries to his body, to compare them with the relatively minor scrapes he had endured for the previous twenty years, and calculate how long it would take to recover from his many wounds and fractures. He felt the eggshell-like ocular cup pop behind what remained of his right eye. The bridge of his nose—was it broken? *Sure, why not? My entire face is broken,* he calmly concluded. Blood poured freely from his lips, eyes, and nose, yet Doyle did not lose his hold. For all the many things that he coldly calculated and considered as his body was being pulverized, he did not take the trouble to consider or debate the merit of letting his adversary go. More than an article of faith, almost a certainty embedded at the subconscious, perhaps the chromosomal level, Doyle knew without thinking that if he eased his grip on the glass dagger and stopped grinding it into the throat of this opponent, his own life would be forfeit in less time than it required mutter a 'Hail Mary.'

The rate of the pummeling began to slow, then subsided, and

finally stopped. Doyle tried to open his eyes. Through a haze of blood that had flowed over his face, he peered out in the wrong direction. He could not see what he was attempting to look at as he turned his head from side to side. His body had gone past the point of pain. He began to wretch as the Gray man collapsed against the bed rail. He forced himself up to a sitting position and started to heave up blood from the depths of his abdomen. Doyle had not noted any final gasp or exhalation of life from what now was a crumpled corpse that hung over him. In a forced action of self-control while every sense was either dazed or disconnected or screaming in pain, he checked for signs of life in a fumbling, groping, and poking examination. Satisfied, Doyle pushed his dead enemy off the rail and the fleshy sack plopped to the linoleum floor. Doyle reached over the rail to find a lever but was too tired and disoriented to figure out the simple workings of the bed. Instead, he gradually pulled himself forward to his knees and gingerly climbed down off the bed. He weaved across the floor as he approached what seemed to be a sink and a mirror, as best as he could discern through a crimson haze that almost entirely obscured his vision. He groped around the circumference of the sink and located a towel. Doyle reached forward, located a faucet, ran cold water upon the towel, and applied it to his throbbing eye. As he removed the bloodstained towel, he saw his reflection in the mirror.

"Awww, Christ, not again!"

His face was a now an unrecognizable mask of blood and rearranged facial features. His left eye had already begun to swell. Most alarming was the right eye that had now reopened but was aiming askew, no doubt inherited from the crashing blow that destroyed his orbital cup. James Parker Doyle was no longer forced to regard a faceless career bureaucrat in the mirror. He now looked upon a gargoyle.

Okay, what now?

Give me a minute.

You've had days to think this through.

We've both had days to think this through.

Same difference.

Yeah, and quite frankly, I didn't really expect to get this far.

Call Larry?

No. We don't know who at HQ has been compromised.

The guy in Vegas spooked you, didn't he?

That's what spooks do.

You're losing your touch.
He had devil eyes, for Krissake.
So, you're going balls-to-the-wall paranoid now?
Damnstraight.
Yeah, me too.

Doyle gingerly poked at the one remaining blood soaked bandage on his face. He carefully pulled it off and continued to wash his wounds. He found gauze and tape in the medicine cabinet behind the mirror and repatched the damage to the best of his ability. Doyle located his clothing in a nearby closet, cleaned and carefully folded in a drycleaner's box. He pulled out the shirt and found it to be free of any bloodstains and so painstakingly mended that he could barely see any telltale sign of the previous rips and punctures.

How did our Gray buddy do that?
Don't know, but from now on, I'm sending all my laundry to this town.

Doyle dressed as quickly as the layers of bandages and fusillade of stabbing pain would allow. He located his wallet in a small drawer together with his SEC-CEL as well as the burner cellphone he had obtained at the convenience store.

What good is this? His silent voice lectured him as he picked up the SEC-CEL. *You're not seriously considering taking this with you?*
Why not?
The phone has been compromised, you idiot. It probably will track you and most likely will be monitored for all transmissions.
The burner?
Same problem.

"What do I do?" Doyle asked aloud.

His internal advisor was not sympathetic. *Tag, you're it.*
Do you believe what Mister Goat Eyes said in the hotel room?
I don't believe anything anyone says, including you.
Goat Eyes knew too much.
We could have a tumor in ORCA.
But you haven't a clue who that might be.
There are probably a thousand clues, but you're in no condition to read them.
Am I trapped?
Yes, by your own over-thinking.
I know their capabilities.

276

You also know their weaknesses. You can elude them.

Doyle paused to reflect for a moment, then continued his silent colloquy. *Since when did ORCA become 'they' and 'them' instead of 'we' and 'us'?*

When 'they' and 'them' started trying to kill 'you' and 'me.'

I'm imagining things. It could have been the head injury from the explosion.

That's the one thing that knocked some sense into you.

Like having a dialogue with a ghost right now?

We're both ghosts right now.

Doyle looked back at the secured cellphone in his hand and then nodded gently as he made his decision. He detached the back of the phone and removed the battery. *So, you decided to punt?* remarked his relentlessly nagging self.

You never know when it could come in handy.

True.

Doyle approached the blood drenched corpse on the floor and began methodically searching through pockets. *Car key. Bingo! We have a way out of town.*

Assuming that we have a way out of this building.

Trust me. I'm on a roll.

How about a gun? Unless you want to keep killing with glass.

No, he doesn't have a gun. You must admit, glass works in a pinch. I'm living testament to that.

More like a last will and testament.

The Gray man's wallet contained thirty-seven dollars, all in new, crisp bills. Doyle then examined the other contents. Three driver's licenses. Three credit cards. A wide variety of federal credentials, no two items having the same last name: Grau, Siva, Grigio, Llwyd, Kelgbu.

This guy works for freekin' everybody. The CIA, NSA, DIA...

Or none of them. Most likely, these are bogus.

But pretty damn convincing.

I never said he was an amateur.

In a hidden pocket in the back of the wallet, Doyle found a slip of paper with a telephone number: (415) 557-4400.

That's a San Francisco area code.

How the hell do you know that?

Did you forget that we had to memorize those?

277

That was years ago.

At least we know where we are going now.

No, you don't. San Francisco is one hell of a large place. You don't have an address and you're not likely to get one if you can't use your cellphone to access the internet.

I'll take my chances.

I think those head injuries have taken their toll.

On both of us.

It could be a trap.

Anything could be a trap.

What do you calculate the odds to be?

Ninety-five percent chance that we'll be dead within twenty-four hours.

How about something a bit more optimistic?

There's a five percent chance that we may last as long as twenty-four hours and one minute before we're dead.

Well, that's more like it. What are we waiting for?

⌘

"Excuse me, we were told that you are the caretaker of the synagogue."

"The person who told you that must have been awfully mean-spirited, given the obvious fact that the caretaker clearly did not take enough care to avoid the destruction of this place."

"That's nobody's fault."

"Everything is somebody's fault. You just have to look hard enough or restrain yourself from trying to look elsewhere when the fault is staring you right in the eye."

"Is it staring us right in the eye now?" inquired Watt.

"Who are you?" the man asked. Watt offered his card to the man, who glanced at it and announced, "So, you are the ones whose job it is to look hard enough. In that case, go ahead and start looking."

"Are you the rabbi?"

"No, I think that we have already established that I am the failed caretaker."

"Can we speak with the rabbi?"

"There is no rabbi."

"How can you have a synagogue without a rabbi?"

"While we were constructing the synagogue, I tried to recruit a rabbi. No one was willing to move out here, particularly when they found out that there are no Jews in town, or within one hundred miles of this place. Every rabbi I contacted told me exactly the same thing before hanging up the phone."

"What was that?"

"They all called me *meshuggah.*"

"Sorry, but I didn't catch your name."

"That's because I didn't pitch it to you."

"I assume that it's not Mister Meshuggah."

The man uttered an amused grunt and announced, "I'm Kelman Bubble."

"Excuse me?"

"Bubble."

"Sorry."

"That's what my father said."

"Your father said about what?"

"What my father said when I asked him why our last name was Bubble."

Bill Watt decided to intervene. "We'd like to know something about the fire."

"Then you should have come here earlier while the fire was still raging. As it stands now, you're too late. The fire has come and gone."

"We're looking into the cause of the fire."

"The cause of the fire? You must have slept through high school physics. It's a thing called combustion. It has to do with a spark coming into contact with fuel. Wooden synagogues qualify as the latter."

"We think that this fire may be linked to the destruction of other houses of worship."

"You're suggesting that this fire was set on purpose."

"Yes."

"I suppose that a synagogue couldn't possibly burn down due to a routine mishap or natural causes."

"It's possible, but there is evidence to the contrary."

Their host shook his head in disagreement, "There are no swastikas, no decapitated pig head, no 'Dirty Jew' graffiti. This appears to be a simple mishap fire."

"Churches are burning across the country. What make you think

279

that is an isolated event?"

"I've been reading the news. There is no connection between this fire and any of those that have occurred throughout the South."

"And the North."

Kelman Bubble shrugged. "And the North."

"None of the fires seem to be connected, but that very fact suggests that they are."

"I see. There is no evidence of foul play, so naturally that means that there *was* foul play. That's genius. I don't know how I missed it."

"It's not that simple."

"Now you switch to a superior and patronizing attitude. You wouldn't happen to be a member of Congress, would you? Maybe a news anchor?"

"We can explain."

"Okay, Colombo, I'm listening."

"We've been following these fires for three weeks. My partner here was reporting on them for six weeks before that."

Gaude took the baton from Watt. "Every one of the fires was caused by an electrical event."

"The same electrical event?"

"No, but—"

"Then that doesn't prove anything. Maybe the churches in question had cheap appliances or bad wiring. There are incompetent electricians in every corner of the nation."

"You believe that the shoddy handiwork of a legion of inept electricians just happened to ignite churches from sea to shining sea all at the same time? Do you recall any other year that this happened? You don't see a pattern here?"

"No, and if this was being done intentionally, some group of crazies would be taking credit."

"There is a wide variety of crazies in this world, including those who prefer to skulk in the shadows."

"The ones that burn synagogues tend to be the publicity-seeking crazies. No one ever accused Nazis of being bashful wallflowers."

"You said that there isn't a Jewish community in the area?"

"Would one person constitute a community?"

"There's one Jewish member?"

"Nope."

"Oh," said Gaude, not quite understanding. "Then why did

someone build a synagogue?"

"It's a requirement of our charitable foundation."

"To build a synagogue in the middle of a barren desert?"

"No, to co-locate a synagogue with any charitable outreach center." Bubble gestured to the modern brick building standing beside the ruins of the synagogue. "Thankfully, the community rehabilitation center funded by our foundation was left untouched by the fire."

"So, this isn't some sort of Jewish mission?"

"Not exactly. Judaism, unlike Christianity and Islam, does not actively seek to evangelize people of other faiths—or no faith, for that matter. Converts are welcome but there is no tradition, history or culture of missionary work associated with Judaism—unless you include those Jewish missionaries of the first century who fanned out across the Mediterranean spreading the good news about a Galilean carpenter who was alleged to have been crucified and rose from the dead. On the other hand, charity is a mainstay of Jewish tradition. Aiding those in need is required by the Torah. Moses and the Prophets consistently taught the essential importance of charity."

"There are plenty of other deserts in this country. Why did you pick this one?"

"We discovered that it was the saddest place in the nation. We came to uplift, to restore hope."

"Why is it so sad?"

"Hard to say. Poverty is endemic in this part of the country. However, it goes deeper than that. It seems to be a case of bad luck all around. What could go wrong around here does go wrong around here. Berlin never gets a break. A few years ago, some wag dubbed the synagogue 'The Church of Saint Schlimazel.' That's rather irreverent, but there is an element of truth in that classically Hebrew humor."

"Have you made any progress in assisting the community?"

"You might say that. Since we established our relief effort and built the community center, the suicide rate in Berlin has dropped by half."

"That's excellent! What was the suicide rate before you arrived?"

"One hundred percent."

"One hundred percent? You mean that everyone killed themselves?"

"Sooner or later, yes."

"That's horrible."

"Yes, that is the primary reason that we came here to help."

"So, now only half of the residents commit suicide?"

"Yes, we are very proud of that fact. I mean that we are proud to have reduced the rate, not that half of the population continues to commit suicide. Obviously, that number is still tragically high."

"Perhaps the increase in population will help lift up the town."

"Unfortunately, that hasn't happened. You see, although the suicide rate has fallen significantly, the murder rate has skyrocketed."

"Murder rate?"

"Yes, it used to be negligible—"

"Let me guess, because everyone was committing suicide?"

"Exactly. No one had a chance to get murdered because they had already committed suicide. The suicides beat the murders to the punch."

"But now?"

"For the past three years, there have been a horrific string of homicides."

"What is the murder rate now?"

"It went from nearly zero to half the population."

"Half the population? And the other half commits suicide? So…that means—"

"That means Berlin still has a one hundred percent rate of untimely deaths. We are at a loss as to what we can do. You see, we are merely the latest in a long line of organizations that have sought to fix the problem. The Utah State Police have come in, Salt Lake sent in teams from the Criminal Intelligence Center, the legislature funded teams of psychologists and counselors, and there have been a slew of state and even federal programs to provide support and assistance over the years. Nothing seems to have helped. Eventually, the relief and charity workers started committing suicide too. The various agencies finally threw up their hands, surrendered, told those aid workers who were still among the living to pack up their bags and leave Berlin to its own devices."

"Why doesn't everyone else leave?"

"I just told you, everyone did leave."

"I mean the residents of Berlin. Why don't they leave?"

Bubble looked at Gaude in stunned silence. Finally, he responded, "Why?"

"To get away from here."

"Why would they want to get away from Berlin?"

Gaude could not disguise his dismay at this question. "To avoid dying."

"Everyone dies."

"Yes, but not in Berlin."

"Perhaps not, but they eventually die somewhere. If someone is willing to live in Berlin, shouldn't they be just as willing to die in Berlin?"

"They could live longer somewhere else."

"No one knows when or where they will die. It could be today in Berlin, Utah. It could be tomorrow anywhere else."

"Maybe there are better places to die."

"Can you name one?"

"Anywhere."

"Anywhere?"

"Yes."

"Would they go to die in Ghosts, North Dakota?"

Gaude was taken aback. "Ghosts?"

"Yes, have you ever heard of it?"

"Yes. How did you know about—"

"That's where our foundation is headquartered."

Gaude frowned, obviously perplexed. "But the population of Ghosts is Russian Orthodox."

"So, you really are familiar with Ghosts! I'm impressed. Very few people have heard of it, much less visited there."

"We were there last week." Gaude paused, trying to assemble his thoughts. "So, you're not Jewish?"

"No, I never claimed to be Jewish. Like you just said, everyone from Ghosts is Russian Orthodox, except me and the Commissar— that's our mayor, by the way."

"Yes, we met her."

"Small world."

"Getting smaller all the time." Gaude paused again. "You're not Russian Orthodox?"

"I was raised in the Church, but a few years ago, I decided to become an adherent of Falun Gong."

"That's Chinese, isn't it?"

"Yes, more or less."

"But you still work for a Russian Orthodox charity?"

"The money is American Orthodox dollars, so I'm not the first one to be implicated in a schism."

Gaude decided to not overthink this. "Why would a Russian Orthodox charity build a synagogue?"

"If you've been to Ghosts, then you certainly must know. We built the synagogue in honor of the departed. Our town charter states that any charitable outreach effort must be made in the name of the Jewish people."

"Oh." Gaude again pondered. "It seems a bit ironic that you built a synagogue in a town named Berlin."

"Yes, that wasn't lost on any of us. Actually, it isn't so much irony as poetic justice."

"I won't quibble with that."

"Oh, no," interjected Bill Watt with a transparently mocking tone, "my partner here would never quibble."

"Besides, there was a real silver lining being the only synagogue within a few hundred kilometers," observed Bubble.

"What is that?"

"We had a corner on the market for Sunday night bingo."

⌘

"Here's a quotable quote," she said. "*I believe in the theory of evolution because of the compelling evidence, daily confirmed, that men are descended from slime.*"

"That's a keeper!"

"I knew that once you met Reuben that you would become a fan."

"I suppose that he has some redeeming qualities."

"Unlike the driver of this car."

"You didn't choose me for any redeeming qualities."

"Ah, ha! See? Reuben is rubbing off on you. You're already appreciably more clever than when we started the trip." She turned a page in the notebook and began to read.

"Seldom can a person be summed up in but one word. Even more seldom can one word be truly descriptive of all that one person is. But in this rare and fantastic instance, the woman and the word had discovered one another and their common

284

destiny. For she and the word were one: petulant.
Consider the wondrous coincidence of the etymological
evolution of the word 'petulant' as it has come down from the
Indo-European, through a dozen Aryan and Germanic
tongues, joining with the Latin root to finally find its way in
the dictionary and then patiently wait four centuries as the
recessive genetic trait of pure petulance weaved through the
generations to finally manifest itself in her."

"Wow, Malachi was in a bad mood. Who was that girl? It wasn't you, was it?"

"You're becoming obsessed. Every time that Reuben mentions an unidentified *she*, you assume that he is writing about me."

"No, that isn't true. Unless, of course, it *is* true?"

"Wouldn't you like to know?" She then paused for an instantaneous reflection and added, "Why do you think it was me? Do you think I'm petulant?"

"Oh, no, I'm dead meat!" he said with a nervous laugh. "Maybe it's a good time for another one of his poems."

"You're trying to weasel out."

"Yes, I am. Have mercy on me."

"I don't think so."

"Have you forgotten that I'm driving the car right now? Any physical violence and we could wind up in a pretty terrible wreck."

"You are *temporarily* off the hook. Maybe I'll read *two* of Reuben's poems."

"It's a deal. I'll pay any price."

"You'll be paying a lot more." She turned a page in the notebook. "Hey, wait a minute! This is amazing! The perfect poem about your troublesome and petulant partner."

"You are my *partner* now?"

"You're already in the doghouse. No lip from you.

Truce

> *Seize ye my heart, tear out my chest,*
> *throw me in chains, sign my arrest,*
> *slice out my soul, rip off my limbs,*
> *burn me in bonfires, punish my sins.*

> *But Dear, sweet Dear, lose not your temper so.*

Boil me in oil, poke out my eyes,
mangle my body, give my flesh to the flies,
crush my thick skull (if it is in your power),
cut out my tongue, my organs devour.

But Dear, sweet Dear, lose not your temper so.

Flay me with whips, yank out my teeth,
feed me to sharks, chop off my feet,
carve me and slice me like a filet of cod
with so few remains I'm known only to God.

But Dear, sweet Dear, lose not your temper so."

"That is a perfect poem!" he announced with facetious enthusiasm. "I am now a devoted fan of Reuben Malachi."

"Meeting him a few nights ago didn't do the trick?"

"He should have showed me that poem. It would have won me over immediately."

"In that case, here's another one that you're bound to love. I remember this. I think I read it—or maybe Reuben wrote it—during my reincarnation phase."

"A reincarnation phase? I gotta hear about that one."

"On second thought, maybe it was my agrarian phase."

"What's an agrarian phase? Some type of vegan fad?"

"My phases are not fads, and no, it had nothing to with veganism. Besides, my vegan phase was a few years after that."

"A few years after what?"

"My agrarian phase."

"Oh, right…Where were you when you decided to become…an agrarian?"

"I was living in a farming commune in Wisconsin. It was about an hour's drive south of Eau Claire."

"Okay, so read me the inspired verse that you enjoyed in your bucolic paradise."

"You just used the word 'bucolic.' Do you realize that?"

"Well, maybe—"

"And you used it correctly."

"That's a surprise?"

"That transcends surprise. I am agog."

"I happen to know what agog means, too."

"Who the hell are you and what did you do with the man I've been riding with these past two weeks?"

"Go ahead and read your damn poem," he said, trying to suppress an irrepressible smile.

She turned back to the notebook and recited aloud.

"From time to time she has her moods,
And nothing helps to quell the fuss,
It must be something that I've done,
If only I knew what it was.

When she's hungry
When she's thirsty
When her closet's a mess
When the sun shines
When the rain falls
When tea spills on her dress

When she's rested
When she's sleepy
When she's broken a nail
When she's bored
When she's busy
When shoes aren't on sale

When she's cold
When she's fevered
When her legs need a shave
When she's quiet
When she's worried
When chocolate she'll crave

When she's walking
When she's sitting
When the power goes out
When she's losing
When she's gaining
When she's ever in doubt

When she's cooking
When she's eating
When she washes her hair
When she's reading
When she's writing
When she hasn't a prayer

When she's spending
When she's saving
When she crashes the car
When she's shouting
When she whispers
When she plays her guitar

When she's napping
When she's sleepless
When she's putting on rouge
When she's coming
When she's going
When she calls me a stooge

When she's working
When she's playing
When she needs a good cry
When she's nervous
When she's listless
When the day ends with 'y'

From time to time she has her moods,
I've learned by now to take in stride,
The causes which, I must conclude,
Will ever from clear reason hide."

"Actually, even though I know nothing about poetry—"

"The understatement of the century."

"I think that one is pretty good. Did this one get published, or have we made one of your collector's items finds?"

"It was published."

"You probably know the name—"

"*A Face in the Crowd.*"

"How do you remember this stuff?"

"I pay attention to the important things."

⌘

"Let's find someplace for lunch."

"Maybe we should look for it somewhere other than in Berlin," said Gaude.

"There isn't another town within eighty kilometers of here."

"Maybe it's time for a fast. I'm thinking that *El Niño* might be pushing the calendar ahead for an early Lent this year."

"Why aren't you keen on eating around here?"

"Given the suicide and murder rates, how do I know that they don't end their days in the local diner? Maybe someone will slip some cyanide into your chili."

"Actually, cyanide chili with pinto beans is surprisingly good."

"Where did they serve you cyanide chili?"

"My wife used to make it for me all the time."

"Who could blame her?" retorted Gaude. "I'll check for nearby eateries," he said, as he pulled out his cellphone.

"Or we can just ask a local resident," replied Watt as he spotted a man coming out of a doorway ahead of them. "Excuse me, sir, is there a diner in the town?"

The man looked up, slightly startled. "Sure, there are two, Osteria Bavaria and Horcher's Gasthaus. They're just a couple of blocks over to your left."

"Thank you."

"Are you visiting soon-to-be-departing relatives or are you here for a funeral?"

"Neither, we came here to examine the church fire—excuse me, synagogue fire—that happened yesterday."

The man nodded. "A tragedy. But then again, this is Berlin." He then extended his hand. "The name's Gundar Holyhosen. I'm chief municipal engineer and memorial program manager."

"Bill Watt."

"Dan Gaude."

"For a town this small, I'm surprised that they can afford to hire an engineer," remarked Watt.

"They can't. I work for free. That's okay because I'm not really an engineer. I majored in Turf and Golf Course Management at the University of Maryland."

"Are there any golf courses here in Berlin?"

"Nope. However, when I was a young boy growing up in this town, I had an inspiration to build a golf course."

"Most young boys want to be astronauts or firemen."

"True, but it occurred to me that golf might be the solution to the troubles of this town."

"How so?"

"I suspected that everyone here—including most of my family members—committed suicide out of an intense and inescapable sense of boredom. If there ever was a place designed for the hopelessly bored to revel in their boredom, that would be a golf course."

"There's no arguing with that," agreed Gaude.

"I went off to college and got my degree. When I returned, I had big plans to build a world-class resort. Even though we are surrounded by desert, it just so happens that in the plains to our west there is an aquifer just five meters below the surface that links into Lake Powell. I submitted a detailed proposal to the mayor for a three hundred and seventy acre spread with plenty of room for further expansion. I even had some investors lined up. The next day I dropped in at Town Hall to see what the mayor thought about it and found him swinging from the end of an extension cord."

"I guess he wasn't enthusiastic about the idea."

"That's what I thought when it happened. However, I was young at the time and have since accepted the fact that it was just the mayor's time to go."

"So, what do you do in the absence of any golf courses in the region?"

"I oversee the monuments."

"You mean monuments…like monuments in Monument Valley?"

"No, that area is managed by the Navaho Nation. I'm talking about the monuments raised in this town."

"Where are they?"

"In Monument Square. It's a short walk on the way to the diners. I'll take you there." Gundar Holyhosen guided his guests around the corner, up a narrow street and through a small passageway. Gaude hastened his pace as they walked through the short tunnel, alert to any whispers that might emanate from nowhere. They soon emerged onto a plaza measuring approximately one hundred meters on each side. In the space of cluttered profusion were items in stone, metal, and wood, some ungainly and awkward, others elegant and grand. Most, however, were peculiar and incomprehensible. Holyhosen approached what appeared to Gaude to be a polished aluminum sofa cushion mounted on a granite base. "This is the giant doughnut."

"Are doughnuts famous around here?"

"Other than this sculpture, not really."

"This doesn't have anything to do with Salvation Army Doughnut Day, does it?"

"Ummm…no, I'm pretty sure it doesn't."

"So, what motivated someone to create this? Are there some rules or guidelines?"

"There really are no particular rules. If someone wants to raise a monument, it's my job to approve, not disapprove. But then again, no one asks me. It just so happens, however, that this is one of the more sensible monuments here."

"Sensible?"

"Perhaps I should say relevant or appropriate. You see, in Germany, a jelly-filled doughnut is called a 'Berliner.' At least, that's what I've been told."

"I suppose that's plausible."

"Over to your left is a monument celebrating the invention of the toupee. Next to that is a statue depicting some kind of rodent, but we're not really sure of its significance. To the right is a small shrine containing one of Elvis Presley's baby teeth."

290

"It's a mixed bag," commented Gaude.

"Over here is the beer fountain."

"Is that actually beer coming out?"

"Yep. Today it's a pilsner, I believe."

"It isn't drinkable, is it?"

"Sure is, and it's cold. There's a refrigeration unit under the base of the fountain. I assume that it cost a fortune to build."

"How could a small town like this pay for it?"

"We don't pay for any of the monuments. They are all donations."

"Who are the donors?"

"We don't know. Like I said, it's supposed to be my job to approve and supervise the installation of monuments, but nobody asks, and truth be told, I don't really do much supervision. Contractors arrive, put up a monument, then they leave. We don't ask questions and the construction company employees aren't exactly chatty."

"What about this one?" Watt said gesturing back to the fountain, "Someone has to refill the beer every once in a while, I'd imagine."

"Every day, in fact. A small tanker truck drives up from Page, Arizona and changes out the beer—seven days a week."

"I assume that the beer is always German style."

"Yep. Saturdays is usually Schneider Weisse, my favorite." Holyhosen continued the impromptu tour by pointing out monuments honoring leisure suits, stuttering, Sony Beta-Max machines, kiwi fruit, bad breath, and static cling. He then arrived at the lifesize statue of a young woman. "Here is the monument to Eva Braun."

"Eva Braun? The Eva Braun who was Hitler's—"

"Yep, Hitler's lover and very briefly his wife."

"If you don't mind me saying so, that's a bit unusual."

"Sure, it's the world's only monument to Eva Braun. At least, we think it's the only one. Nobody actually went to the trouble of asking the authorities in Germany."

"What possessed anyone to create this?"

"This is Berlin, after all, so apparently someone thought it might be appropriate. We don't have any other monuments to historical figures, so it could be worse. Would you have preferred to see a statue of Herman Goering?"

"No, but—"

"There you go. Apparently, someone else agrees with you and decided that Eva Braun was the obvious choice."

Gaude read the inscription on the plinth below.

CERTAINLY NOT THE FIRST YOUNG WOMAN
TO FALL IN LOVE WITH THE WRONG OLD MAN

"This seems to be the only monument to a person," observed Watt looking across the square.

"Yes, that's true."

"There are no monuments to the dead? Given the high rates of suicides and murders in this place, I would have thought that there would be a large number of monuments for the deceased."

"No, there are no monuments, no memorials for the departed, unless we count Miss Eva right here. The cemetery here in Berlin doesn't even have headstones."

"That's remarkable."

"Yes."

"And odd."

"That all depends upon your perspective."

"The dead deserve a memorial."

"True, but the idea of a memorial might mean different things to different people. It's all in the definition, isn't it?" Gaude gave a sidelong glance to Watt who maintained a serene visage. "Here in Berlin, we believe that erecting headstones and statuary is not the right way to honor or remember those who have passed on," continued Holyhosen. "Even eulogies are meaningless, albeit kindly bestowed lies. An epitaph is a vacuous bromide. The truest accolade of a life well lived happens six months after they have put you in the ground or tossed your ashes in the wind. It happens at your place of work, or at a town hall meeting, or at your church board of advisors. The friends and neighbors you left behind are facing an intractable problem, an unforeseen crisis, or some other awkward quandary. One of the participants laments 'If only he were here! He would know what to do,' or 'What a pity she is no longer with us! She could have solved the problem, I'm sure.' That, and only that, is a tribute worth living for."

"I still believe that they should be remembered with a headstone."

"Here they are remembered with sorrow."

"Perhaps, but the departed were a blessing."

"Yes, but in this place, the living who wish to honor the dead curse them."

"Curse?"

"There is no greater blessing than being cursed—for having died. You were loved. You were needed. They still need you. They still love you. We miss you. We want you back."

Gaude looked over the assemblage of monuments and the one in the dead center of the square caught his eye. "What's that slab of concrete?"

"Oh, that. It's the one monument that this town did have a hand in putting into this square," answered Holyhosen as he began walking towards it, Watt and Gaude following suit. "When the Berlin Wall in Germany was being demolished, we arranged for a section of it to be shipped from Berlin to…well, Berlin."

"I suppose that was darkly appropriate," commented Watt.

The three arrived in front of the fragment of the Cold War concrete wall, recently augmented with verse painted in crimson. "Three weeks ago, that poem suddenly appeared," explained Holyhosen. "We're not sure if it constitutes vandalism of an historic object or a public improvement."

Berlin

Charred and twisted Madame,
Hostess to every whore,
Besotted by each freedom,
Dreading any more.

Too much life,
Too much death,
Such much dancing.

Bold and valiant sentinel,
Unyielding to the foe,
Strengthened by each injury,
Blind to its own woe.

Too much love,
Too much hate,
Such much dancing.

293

Grand and humbled Hochstadt
Fearless, but for fear,
Celebrating agonies,
Weeping in its beer.

Too much war,
Too much peace,
Such much dancing.

—*Reuben Malachi*

Gaude read the poem. "It seems to be rather gloomy."

"Yeah, it is. Most folks here really like it. In fact, there have been a disproportionate number of deaths right here in the short time since the poem appeared."

"You mean people commit suicide on this spot—right here?" asked Gaude, now taking a few steps back away from the wall fragment.

"Yes, give or take a meter or two."

"Wouldn't that make this poem a public nuisance?"

"The only person authorized to declare a public nuisance is the mayor."

"So, why doesn't he—"

"Or she," Gundar corrected.

"Right, or she. So, has the mayor issued the order?"

"We don't have a mayor."

"What happened?"

"I told you, the previous mayor kicked the bucket…in the most literal sense."

"You said that was years ago."

"Sure was."

"They still haven't replaced the mayor?"

"Nope."

"Why not?"

"Everyone else was too busy."

"Too busy doing what?"

"Too busy trying to snuff themselves out of existence."

"Is there anyone else in charge?"

"According to the town by-laws, in the absence of a mayor, the town council makes all executive decisions. Of course, the town council hasn't met in twenty years."

"Why not?"

"Every time a new council is elected, they all commit suicide."

"How do you get anything done?"

"We just wait it out. Problems either resolve themselves or simply go away because the people who care about those issues are no longer around."

"That's awfully fatalistic."

"Life is awfully fatalistic, even outside of Berlin."

"Do you have any idea why people here behave that way?"

"It could be the water, it could be the air, it could be the heat or the cold. All of those have been studied by medical experts and researchers and the results are always inconclusive. If you ask me, it has something to do with the spirits in the valley. I think that they haunt people about the other life. I think they show them the other life and that makes this one unbearable."

"What other life?"

"Your other life. Everyone's other life."

"You mean my private life?"

"No, the other life that you know you should have lived, and in a sense, actually do live in some other way, in some other place."

"This sounds like the kind of stuff you see in Hollywood movies—second chances and all that."

"Only in the vaguest way, and it doesn't involve an angel earning his wings. Have you ever thought, 'This isn't my life,' or even said it out loud to yourself?"

"I assume that everyone has at one time or another."

"Exactly. Doesn't the fact that it is a universal sentiment tell you something? This 'other' life of yours that must certainly be better than the one you now have. Do you have any idea of what it might be?"

"I dunno, something different...something..."

"Something more real? Something more authentic? More true? Something that resonates in your soul that is wholly distinct from the artificial mediocre misery you seem to be trapped in all these years? It is not merely the life you know you should have led, but rather the life that you know you are leading, and somehow you are isolated, separated from it. It is as if you stepped out of your house on a dreary winter's day in your bathrobe to toss a bag of garbage into the trash bin, only to have the wind slam the door behind you and lock you out. You desperately try to get back inside the house, but it is impossible. You try to look into the windows, but they are all fogged. You tap the windows and pound on the door, but no one hears you. There is Christmas music playing inside that drowns out your shouts and pounding. You put your ear to the glass and try to make out what is going on. You hear muffled voices. They are happy, enthusiastic, confident and content. Among those voices, you recognize…your own. You are in there living the real life while you are out here trapped in a fraudulent purgatory."

"So, I have two possible lives?"

"Oh, more than that. Dozens, scores, hundreds, perhaps thousands, but all of them are looking with the same regret, the same remorse, the same anguish as you in this life. We are all crowded together in a dismal theatre, watching the one real life performing on the stage, and we cannot help but applaud and hurl curses all at once at the life we missed."

"Everyone dreams of a better life, of fame and fortune."

"It doesn't need to be fame and fortune, honor and glory, or any of that. Perhaps it is the very opposite—peace and quiet and selfless service. It could be anything, but what it is not is what you are now living. It is just beyond your grasp. It floats in a murky aether of shadows beyond the curtain of your dreams. It's there, but as you reach for it, your fingertips barely make contact and it slips away. Eventually, you will stop trying to find it, to see it, or to hear it. You will surrender to this life and abandon the pursuit of the other. You shrug it off as a pipedream, a fantasy, a foolish pretention of youth. It fades, but it never completely goes away. As you lie on your deathbed with your family surrounding you, over the shoulders of your children you see it. You see the other life you could have lived, that you—the real you— actually did live. That life, however, is not yet over, as your ersatz existence seems to be. It is waiting for you, beckoning to you."

"You're talking about heaven."

"No, I'm talking about your one, true, authentic life, the one you need to live, the one you are living, but not at this here, not during this now, and not by this you."

"What if I have lived my true life all along? What if I am happy, content, and genuinely fulfilled in this life right here and right now?"

"Is that the case? Do you believe that?"

There was a moment of silence that translated into the

admission that it was not. "What if someone—anyone—else did have such a life? It must have happened."

"I suppose that's true. There have been saints. There have been heroes. There are those you read about in the history books. Not all of them, mind you, but certainly a few who lived their real lives among us."

"What about you? Do the spirits haunt you about your other life?"

"No, it seems that I am the lone holdout."

"Is there a reason for that?"

"Yeah, I'm already dead," Gundar said with a sly smile and a wink.

Gaude saw something in the sky over Gundar Holyhosen's shoulder. It appeared to be an aerobatic biplane that was beginning to expel a thick trail of smoke. At first, Gaude thought the airplane might be experiencing engine trouble, but with its first loop, he realized that the pilot was engaged in skywriting. He gestured above and asked, "Is this another Berlin tradition, or is it a special occasion?"

Holyhosen checked his Omega Perpetual wristwatch and muttered, "Right on time." He then looked back up at Gaude and smiled. "Yes, he's a standard fixture around here, although we have no idea who he is or where his plane takes off from. Most folks around here refer to him as the Red Baron."

"Because of the old-fashioned plane."

"That too."

The three watched the skywriter emit another stream of smoke to form the second letter. "He seems to know what he's doing," commented Gaude.

"He should. After all, the guy has been flying over Berlin for years," agreed Holyhosen as the third letter was being added.

"Assuming that it's the same pilot," said Gaude. "After all, there might have been pilots in the past who have been leaving messages, but all of them could have committed suicide."

"Good point," conceded Holyhosen.

The pilot finished the last letter and flew off to the west. The three men on the ground admired the billowy word floating overhead:

"Pink? What does it mean?" asked Gaude.

"I don't know," said Holyhosen with a shrug. "What does anything mean?" He then accompanied Watt and Gaude around the corner and down a side alley to another punctuation of space in the town. This one was occupied by two diners on opposing sides of the square and a gazebo-like food stand in the middle of the plaza featuring a sign identifying it as 'Schnitzel Shack.' The Osteria Bavaria appeared to be an oversized stainless-steel airstream trailer with crimson red awnings. Horcher's Gasthaus was an identical twin except that it featured indigo blue awnings. The schnitzel stand in the demilitarized zone featured a cheerful amber yellow roof. Holyhosen gestured forward. "There you go. It's your choice."

"Any recommendations?"

"Sure, I recommend that regardless of which diner you select, that you order food and drink. They both specialize in that."

"What about the food stand in the middle?"

"The Schnitzel Shack is out of business. Besides, it served bratwurst."

"No schnitzel?"

"Schnitzel is a large pork steak. It wasn't easy to sell from a stand."

"They could have put schnitzel on a stick," kidded Gaude.

"You're a quibbler, aren't you?" Holyhosen jibbed back good-naturedly.

"Do either of them specialize in chili?" asked Watt.

"Chili with an 'i' or chile with an 'e'?"

"We don't care."

"Good, because at the Bavarian they don't serve either kind."

"Then why did you—?"

"Horcher's it is!" announced Watt as he began to stride forward. Gaude followed his determined partner to the stainless-steel eatery. They arrived at an incongruous medieval style oak door which opened as soon as they reached for the wrought iron handle. A young blonde girl in a traditional dirndl greeted them with a curtsey and then wordlessly led them to a table. Music played from speakers embedded in the ceiling: 'Suicide is Painless,' the theme song from the movie M*A*S*H.

Gaude looked around the interior with muted amazement. The walls were clad in mahogany, the floors covered by Persian carpets, crystal chandeliers competed with ornate candelabras on the tables. The curtains were a heavy damask indigo, the chairs all upholstered in dark crimson velvet, and upon the amber-tinted linen tablecloths were set with what appeared to be expensive china and authentic silver service.

"This is a diner?" asked Gaude incredulously.

"Admittedly upscale," replied Watt matter-of-factly.

A portly man wearing a well-tailored tuxedo approached their table, handed over two menus, took a step back, clicked his heels in a faux Prussian style salute, and executed a deep bow. Gaude could see the reflection of his own face on the top of the man's perfectly round and brilliantly polished bald head.

"*Grüss Gott, mein Herren! Möchten Sie etwas zu trinken?*"

"*Danke Herr Ober. Ja, bitte. Mein freund hätte gerne eine...eine...*" Gaude struggled to recall the word in German. "*...eine* softdrink?"

"*Erfrischungsgetränk.*"

"*Genau!*"

"*Und für Sie?*"

"*Ein Bier, natürlich.*"

"*Hell oder dunkel?*"

"*Ich möchte die...*Hell...*vermeiden.*"

A flash of momentary confusion passed across the waiter's face until he processed the cross-lingual play on words indicating that Gaude wished to avoid both 'hell' and the same word for light-colored German beer. "Pretty good," the man responded in an unmistakable Oklahoma twang. "You actually speak German."

"A little."

"Probably more than me."

"I'm not so sure of that. I was stumped by 'softdrink.' I just couldn't dredge that one up from memory."

"You're right, that one is tricky. I memorized it just because we often have kids who visit for grandpa's funeral. They get a big kick out of the sound of *Erfrischungsgetränk*. Usually, I burn out once a word gets past a dozen letters."

"But you started the conversation in German."

"I know, but that's to lend atmosphere. I don't expect anyone to speak it back to me. After one or two phrases, our guests tell me that they don't speak German and I act like I am accommodating them. I can, however, play the part really well," the waiter said with a wink.

"Ja, eet verks effrehy time," he jested with a comically enthusiastic teutonic accent. "Well, that is, until you showed up," he said, reverting to his native Oklahoman version of English. "Now, the feller who I replaced, Ziggy, was fluent."

"What happened to Ziggy? I hope that he didn't commit suicide?"

"Worse, he turned traitor. He's now maître d' at the Bavarian across the square."

"What does the Bavarian have that Horcher's does not?"

"Ziggy, for one."

"We were told that the Bavarian doesn't serve chili."

"That's true. We do have that over them. Are you here for the chili?"

"Most definitely," answered Watt with enthusiasm.

"Rattlesnake or armadillo?"

"Pardon?"

"Would you like rattlesnake chili or armadillo chili?"

"They both sound like roadkill," scoffed Gaude.

The waiter responded with a blasé shrug of one shoulder. "Yeah, pretty much. What's your point?"

"Can I have both rattlesnake and armadillo in the same bowl of chili?" asked Watt, ignoring Gaude's critique of his lunch.

"Ah! Our *Strassenfleischchili Deluxe*! Good choice."

"I'll have a *Jägerschnitzel mit Spaetzle und Kraut*," requested Gaude, not bothering to look at the menu.

"I'm sorry, *Mein Herr*, but we don't serve *Jäegerschnitzel*."

"Perhaps *Zigeunerschnitzel*?"

"*Nein.*"

"What about *Wienerschnitzel*?"

"*Es tut mir leid*—I'm sorry. No schnitzels of any sort."

"That's odd. I would have thought that a German restaurant would always serve some kind of schnitzel."

"Yes, that would be expected, but many years ago, both the Bavarian and Horcher's signed a pact with the Schnitzel Shack that gave them exclusive rights to serve schnitzel in Berlin."

"You mean the Schnitzel Shack in the middle of the square?"

"The very same."

"But we were told that the Schnitzel Shack didn't serve schnitzel."

"Yes, that's true. Unfortunately, no one was aware of that fact when the agreement was signed."

"Isn't the Schnitzel Shack now out of business?"

"Yes, but that is because the owner committed—"

"Suicide," groaned Gaude.

"Yes, and his estate is still caught up in probate, so our lawyers have been unable to extricate us from those agreements."

"*Was empfehlen Sie?*" asked Gaude with a wry smile.

The waiter grinned back, "That much German I know. I assume that you are interested in a recommendation for something other than our road-kill chili?"

"Yes, definitely something else."

"Our *Nürnberger Bratwurst* is excellent, as is the *Rouladen.*"

"The bratwurst will do fine."

"Very good, *Mein Herren.* I will bring *ein Schwip-Schwap und dein dunkles Bier*—in just one moment—*sofort!*" The waiter again clicked his heels, made a quick bow, and then pivoted away briskly to the kitchen.

"What's a Slip Shot?" asked Watt as their waiter marched off.

"*Schwip-Schwap.* It's a mix of cola and orange soda."

"Excellent choice. I suppose that makes you my softdrink sommelier."

"In Germany the title is *Getränkemeister.*"

"Really?"

"I have no idea. I just made it up, but I wouldn't be surprised if that is really the correct term. Everybody in Germany is the *meister* of something or other. They'd probably call you *Herr Chilimeister* if given half a chance."

"*Herr Chilimeister.* I like the sound of that."

Gaude resumed his inspection of the luxurious interior of Horcher's, now noticing that the walls were decorated with a collection of watercolors depicting a variety of scenes in pre-war Vienna. He returned his attention back to his partner just as Watt was in the process of launching the paper covering of his drinking straw.

"No, Bill, please…" Gaude pleaded in vain.

The volley flew over to the next table and past the shoulder of a man eating a bowl of spargel soup. The startled man looked back and saw Watt waving cheerfully at him. He returned the pleasantry with an unadorned sneer of annoyance and contempt and then returned to his bowl of soup, but not before making the unmistakable gesture of circling his index finger to his temple.

"Don't you ever get tired of that?"

"Never."

"Well, I do."

"In that case, I recommend that you don't do it."

Gaude rolled his eyes and decided not to belabor the issue as he listened to the music coming down from above. He recognized it as 'California's Calling' by Ni'ihau Child.

You're wasting your time here
Gotta get to the coast
You'd better get started
Or soon you'll be toast

California's calling
You'd better answer today
Don't wait for an earthquake
To take it all away

The waiter returned with their drinks. As he departed, a straw envelope arrived from an entirely unexpected vector and floated across the table to hit Gaude in the chest. He looked over to the man at the table that Watt had attacked and saw nothing to indicate that the return fire originated from that quarter. Gaude then glanced around and saw an elderly woman approaching with a paper straw in hand. She had a sweet smile from what he could tell, given that her mouth seemed much too small for her face, as was the case for her diminutive button nose and tiny pinpoint eyes. It seemed to Gaude that ninety-nine percent of the woman's face was undistinguished wrinkled flesh and that her features were a mere comic strip illustration of a benevolent grandmother's visage. She wore a modest black dress reminiscent of a widow's gown from a bygone age and her head was framed in a white linen bonnet.

"I see that you are an aficionado of launching paper projectiles," she said to Watt in a surprisingly robust voice.

"Yes, I am a proud member of the International Association of Paper Straw Marksmen," announced Watt.

"Oh, really?" the woman responded with delight. "I was on the senior council of IAPSM back in the eighties. What chapter do you belong to?"

"Appalachian District of Virginia."

"That explains the high arc of your trajectory," she mused thoughtfully. Watt reached into his pocket and extracted one of his cards to hand to the woman. Gaude didn't bother to examine the transaction since he was sure it was handed facedown as always. As the woman read the card, Gaude had a sense that there was a twinkle in her tiny eyes. She looked back up and smiled. "I wish for you all of God's blessings on your travels, and on my behalf and my brethren, we will pray that the hidden, the obscure, the wearisome, and the tedious will be revealed to you."

"Thank you, I appreciate your prayers..." said Watt, "...and those of...your brethren?"

"Yes, the members of our congregation. We stand in constant solidarity to support in prayer those who are lost in confusion...or boredom."

"Boredom?"

"Yes, it can be a formidable obstacle to understanding. Discerning God's word in the midst of boredom is central to our faith. We are the Monotonites."

"Is that a type of Mennonite?"

"No, we're not an Anabaptist sect, although you might say that we have a somewhat common philosophy of living simply. Like the traditional 'plain folk,' we prefer simple dress and modest ways. All converts are expected to change their names unless it is already simple. My former name was Violetta Rasmussen. Now it's Jane Jones."

"Do you operate farms or make furniture?"

"No," she said with a laugh. "I spent a career as an arbitrage trader on Wall Street."

"So, Monotonites are rich plain folk."

"Now you're confusing us with the Amish," she joked. "Our most distinguishing characteristic is that we read the boring books of the Bible."

"The boring books?"

"Some of our adherents prefer to refer to them as the tedious texts. You know, Leviticus, Numbers, Chronicles, Nehemiah, Amos, and so on. In any case, they are the parts of the Bible that almost no one else reads, and if they try to do so, usually fall asleep."

"That has a detectable flavor of blasphemy."

"Honesty is not blasphemy. The truth shall set you free."

"Yes, but that quote is not from one of the boring books of the Bible."

"I'll give you that," conceded Jones. "Nevertheless, we study the boring books in order to better understand and appreciate God in full context."

"I'm not sure that I understand," said Gaude.

"It's all about appreciating the whole rather looking at the world…well, through a straw," Jones answered as she held her paper straw up to her pinpoint right eye. "There are millions of seemingly mundane and disparate items of data that coalesce into a life, but what might seem meaningless in isolation becomes essential in context."

"You find that context in extraneous passages in the Bible?"

"You assume that they are extraneous. In a strand of chromosomes there are tens of thousands of bits of genetic material that seem to have no particular or active purpose or function. Yet, if we were to remove them, that specific life form could not exist."

"You think that the Bible is designed the same way as a string of chromosomes?"

"They were both authored by the same God."

"I'll give you that," Watt offered as a reciprocal concession. "I've never heard of your Church before. How did it come to be established?"

"It was founded by a man named Mojo Bucephalus, whose conversion name is John Smith. It was he who famously asked when discussing the Bible: 'Why the boring parts?' He posed the question in his examination of why so much of God's word is plodding, repetitive, mundane, obscure, and contextually dense. Why does it take so much effort to read, understand, and appreciate some parts of the Bible? What is hidden there in places so few venture to seek?"

"All excellent rhetorical questions."

"Perhaps rhetorical, but also questions that can be answered. It is because God challenges us."

"He certainly challenges us to repent, have faith—"

"Yes," Jones interrupted, "and much more besides. He challenges us to think, to understand, and to act."

"Take up your cross and follow me," quoted Watt.

"Exactly," agreed Jones, "You shall drink from my cup."

"Then again," countered Watt, "my yoke is easy and my burden light."

"Yes, that's a mixed message, isn't it? Just another example of God throwing a curve ball when he wants to."

"Curve ball? What makes you think that God wishes to make things difficult for his children?"

"God makes it difficult because the way a disciple must learn, grow, develop, and master the necessary skills to achieve salvation is to apply effort. An apprentice must work diligently to acquire the skills of his trade. An athlete must commit to a strenuous regimen. A student must study assiduously to learn a subject. A student who does not apply herself, who does not study rigorously, who merely whines about the burdens of homework, is rarely the one who graduates with honors. You cannot achieve mastery of anything handed to you on a silver platter. Indeed, only one person in the Bible received something on a silver platter and she is presumably roasting in hell even as we speak."

"That's another reference to a non-boring story from the Bible."

"Admittedly, we sometimes dabble in the more exciting parts of the Old and New Testaments. It's a guilty pleasure."

Watt chuckled appreciatively. "What are you looking for while you are scouring through the less-than-entertaining passages of the good book?"

"That search is peculiar to each one of us—and always requires effort. Hence, God puts you in your best discomfort zone. Just as a student is expected to study to their full capacity and an athlete train to their very limit, so each of us are faced with an individual challenge."

"God leaves you in the dark?"

"Not exactly. God cleverly places hints before us, shadowy clues, amorphous innuendos, subtle suggestions, nuanced and nebulous signs and signals and a series of enigmatic oracles in our path, mixed in with messages so obvious as to render them as baffling and impenetrable as the mysteries. Thus is constructed the spiritual obstacle course known as life."

"It still sounds as if you believe that God is hiding the truth from us."

"No, not actually hiding. After all, the Bible texts are available for all to read. God is constantly calling to us, sending us signals, giving us his words. We are, however, amazingly adept and astonishingly clever in avoiding, evading, eluding, and ignoring those calls and signals."

"How do you know the difference between a signal from God and a mere coincidence?"

"Mere coincidences are also signals from God. We expect—or at least, we earnestly hope—that God will make a special effort to reach out and grab our attention, such as appearing to us in a burning bush, striking us blind as we travel the road to Damascus, or being swallowed whole by a great fish. We wait, we wait, we wait, but that never seems to happen. The truth is that God continually places burning bushes in our path, but all we see is smoldering shrubbery."

"What happens when you do recognize the burning bush?"

"That is but the beginning. God then steps back and says, 'Figure it out.' At that point, it's up to us."

"Why?"

"Because we are not invested until we devote the effort. We value what we work for. That is why we must carry the cross. That is why we must fight the good fight, finish the race."

"So, exerting effort is the way to salvation?"

"I'm not in a position to redefine the concept of the Protestant work ethic, but you're not going to get something out until you put something in."

"So, by working hard and through studious vocation, you hope to be saved?"

"In a sense."

"You believe that you can buy your way into heaven."

"You cannot buy your way to heaven, but you can work your way to faith." Jane Doe's left comic book eye folded into a wink and she returned to her table to resume her meal of *Sauerbraten mit Käsespätzle*. Within a minute, the waiter arrived with their orders.

"Interesting woman," commented Watt.

"Assuming that the word 'interesting' is synonymous with the term 'bat-shit crazy,' then I would agree with you," Gaude quipped.

"It's all in the definition, isn't it?" said Watt casually as he began digging into the steaming bowl of chili populated with chunks of freeway casualties. Gaude turned to his own lunch as the music overhead continued to play another Ni'ihau Child song.

> *Let the dead bury the dead,*
> *You've got a life to lead.*
> *Partake of your daily bread,*
> *Persistence is what you need.*

306

Let the bell toll for the dead,
Pay your respects all due.
But when all is done and said,
You've got to muscle through.

Gaude and Watt spent the remainder of their meal discussing the peculiar monuments of Berlin, Utah. Watt indicated that he fancied the tribute to bunny slippers while Gaude voiced his admiration for the shrine in honor of root canals. As they finished their meals, the waiter brought them a check as well as a folded napkin with the initials DG written in lipstick.

"What's this?"

"A woman told us to give this to you."

"What woman?"

"That woman," the waiter gestured towards an empty booth. "Oh, she's gone."

"Where did she go?"

"Through the front door is my guess."

"What did she look like?"

"Tall, short blonde hair, kind of artsy."

"Artsy?"

"Yeah. Definitely not a local."

Gaude unfolded the napkin.

"What is it?" asked Watt.

Daniel Gaude's face gradually transitioned from puzzlement to shock. His hands trembled and palsied as he looked from the note to Watt, trying to form words with an immobilized jaw and disconnected lips. "This...this...it's..."

"Calm down, Dan."

"It's from *her*." Gaude felt a bead of perspiration trickle from the ridge of his brow into his right eye. "I've seen that note before."

"When?"

"I'm not sure of when, or where, or even how. I just know."

"Déjà vu."

"No, something else."

"Have you figured out who she is?"

"She is *she*. I can't explain it. I feel as if I've known her all my life, as if I know everything about her, but when I try to concentrate on any detail, it disappears. I see her in my dreams, but when I awake, her face becomes..."

"Blurred?"

"Not exactly. More like generic *she*, sort of a bland approximation of the real *her*."

"Through a glass darkly," muttered Watt cryptically.

"The mere shell but lacking the true essence of the real woman that I know, but don't recognize."

"No one ever recognizes her."

"Apparently not. You didn't see her."

"Apparently, neither did you."

"Oh, but I've met her, all right," insisted Gaude tapping his temple, "just not in this life." Gaude then passed the note to Watt.

You won't find me in Chilchinbito
but go there anyway.

Beneath the script was the impression of crimson lips and a series of apparently random numbers.

"This doesn't look like the sort of invitation our dishonorable adversary would make." Watt handed the note back to Gaude.

"No, and there's no pretense that is from him. It's from *her*."

⌘

Kearn hovered in the doorway until the Director looked up from his computer terminal.

"Yes, Jeremy?"

"Are you busy, sir?"

"I was in the middle of editing an article for publication."

"Your article, sir?"

"No."

"May I speak with you, sir?"

"You are already doing so," responded the Director, patiently masking his impatience. The young man was motioned into the office and Kearn sat down in the chair furthest from the Director's desk.

"It's about Budapest."

The Director responded with the requisite frown of grave resignation. "Yes, Jeremy. Terrible. Absolutely terrible. I've been in meetings about it all morning."

"Yes, sir." Kearn paused, alternating his gaze between the

308

Director and the framed poster of Kandinsky's *Transverse Lines*.

"Out with it, Jeremy."

"I'm just wondering...could it have anything to do with the test we ran last week?"

"The test *you* conducted five days ago. Yes, we are considering it."

"...and?"

"...and...nothing, Jeremy. It's much too early to determine the whats, whys, and wherefores of this tragedy."

"I thought that the timing was—"

"Yes, very unfortunate."

Kearn paused again while deciding whether to ask the next question. "Sir, can you tell me why Budapest was selected for the test?"

"As opposed to any other location?"

"Yes sir."

The Director leveled a gaze at his subordinate that was devoid of any emotion that even the best poker player might reveal. "It seemed to be a convenient location, all things considered. Would you have any reason to believe that if a different site had been chosen for the test, the persons responsible for murdering our operatives wouldn't have done the same thing in London, or Rome, or Madrid, for that matter?"

"No."

"Neither do I."

Kearn shook his head despondently. "As I mentioned to you the other day, there were some unpleasant surprises."

"Leave that to me, Jeremy. Don't trouble yourself about it."

"Yes, sir. Anyway, before I turned in the device, just as a routine matter, I made a backup and loaded it onto our shared file."

"Really? Did you now?" asked the Director with a cocked eyebrow. "Who gave you the authorization to do that?"

"I thought you did, sir."

"Perhaps you have been thinking too much lately. Did you by any chance examine those downloads?"

"Yes, sir."

The Director raised his eyebrow again. "Really, Jeremy, that isn't your job."

"I was just trying to be thorough. The last message during the test indicated that an extraction had been accomplished."

"I see. So, what did your conscientious thoroughness dredge up for us?"

"The information didn't look like something taken from an adversary's database. In fact, it looked a lot like our own files."

"That comes as no surprise. You were conducting a test, after all."

"Sir?"

"Yes, the target location where you were directed to send a ping and pick up an Easter basket."

"A basket?"

"Yes, a package with a few test files—routine practice."

"Sir, I think that basket was a lot more than just a few test files. I found a number of referenced projects. Most of them were ours and Echelon VII Restricted. The one that really jumped out at me was Project Abaddon."

"Hmmm…that elusive, mysterious and semi-imaginary operation."

"Sir, from what I saw, it looked pretty real."

"I'll have some of our senior analysts pull those files for review. I think you may have read more into them than would be warranted under the circumstances."

"But, sir—"

The Director raised a commanding hand to stop Kearn in mid-sentence. "Jeremy, youthful enthusiasm can be a wonderful thing, to an extent. Let's not belabor the matter."

"Yessir, but…I suppose I need to mention that I reported this as a breach."

"You reported a breach?"

"Yessir, although I have no idea of where the leak may have occurred."

"You reported a breach without informing me first?"

Kearn sat in stunned silence. *Oh shit, I'm dead*, he thought. "I'm…I'm sorry sir."

"To whom did you send the breach report?"

"Mister Wylinski, sir."

"Alright, I'll handle it. From now on, everything passes through me. Understand?"

"Yessir."

"Now then, you are presupposing that the rupture was from one of our locations?"

"I'm not sure, but…how else?"

"We share Echelon VII information with NSA," said the Director.

"Oh."

"That's assuming that the information was that sensitive, which, quite frankly, I rather doubt." The Director now leaned forward at his desk. "Jeremy, I know that you are concerned that you may have made a mistake."

"Sir?"

"The test you conducted. I'm sure that you are worried that you may have made a mistake in the process and procedures to initiate the testing protocol."

"No, sir. I followed them exactly."

"You understand that we are required to look into the matter. One of the working theories is that the organization that sent the assassins into our Budapest office might have detected and traced your Comlink test signals."

"Sir, I didn't do anything."

"You conducted the test."

"Yes, but the box that was sent by the Air Force provided a self-executing program."

"Jeremy, weren't you the one who set up the communications parameters at the Budapest field office prior to initiating the test?"

"I gave the instructions."

"To whom?"

"The Chief…Mister Fremont."

"Are you saying that Wally Fremont mistakenly inputted instructions and coordinates?"

"No, there were no coordinates. The Air Force Program chose the target."

"I'm sorry Jeremy, but that's not possible."

"But…that's what happened!"

"You didn't mention this to me before."

"Sir, I'm sure that I did. Besides, we can check the device. That will confirm what I am saying is true."

"We've already done that, Jeremy. The box you returned to us says otherwise. The location of the testing target was entirely left up to the user interface."

"What location did it show?"

"Oddly enough, the box indicates that the user inputted coordinates but then issued a delete command that scrambled the record."

"I don't understand, sir."

"It says you keyed in a location and then covered your tracks."

"No, that's not true!"

"Jeremy, I'd like to believe you—"

"Sir, *please*. I'm telling the truth!"

"I'm sure you believe that you are, Jeremy, but there is nothing available to us to corroborate your version of the facts. Unfortunately, Wally Fremont, and everyone else in our Budapest office, is now dead."

"The terminals at Budapest. The hard drives will have a log of all commands and keystrokes."

"The Deep Comlink?"

"Yes, sir."

"The Comlink room was left in shambles and the drives and backups ripped out of the unit. We assume it was destroyed by the same assassins who cleared out our office."

"No."

"I understand that you sincerely want what you remember to be true, Jeremy. However, we will need to examine this more closely to arrive at any conclusions."

"Yes, sir. I understand," answered Kearn, not at all understanding. "Sir, perhaps we can get in contact with the Air Force. I intended to call their team in Research Triangle, but I got so caught up in—"

"I'm afraid that the Air Force Team you were dealing with has been disestablished."

"What?"

"Quite recently, in fact. Right after they sent you the device."

"Where are they?"

"The Air Force is not at liberty to say and I have no way of compelling them to tell us."

"Shit!"

"Jeremy, please calm down. I think the stress has confused you. I know that your head is probably swimming right now, but once the evidence is sorted out there is a good chance that none of this will appear as bleak as it seems now. Just to put your mind at ease, absolutely nothing happened to Nürnberg."

"Nuremberg, sir?"

"Yes, the target location where you were directed to send a ping and pick up the basket."

"No, sir. The program hit a site in Wisconsin. We extracted sensitive files. I told you that."

The Director now looked genuinely concerned. "Wisconsin? How is that possible?"

"But sir, I *told* you. The day I returned, I told you about the hit on the Wisconsin site. You said it was a domestic terrorist cell."

"A domestic terrorist cell." Kearn could not tell if the Director had echoed back a question or a statement.

"Yes, sir."

The Director now looked at Jeremy at disbelief. "You think that you engaged in a kinetic strike on a domestic target?"

"No, sir. It just happened. I told you, the Air Force program just…took off by itself."

"Jeremy, why on earth would I have sent you to Budapest to hit a target right here in the United States?"

"Sir, I don't know. I was just following your orders!"

The Director silently regarded the now nearly hysterical analyst. "Jeremy—"

"Sir, really—"

"Jeremy, this is the first I am hearing about this. You never mentioned anything about Wisconsin in your after-action report."

"Sir! You specifically ordered me not to include that information!"

"Jeremy, I think you've been under a lot of pressure lately." The Director paused and scowled down at his desktop for a few seconds, a time lapse that seemed to last for an hour from the terrified perspective of Jeremy Kearn. The Director looked back up with a sad and compassionate expression on his face. "I'm sorry, but I never said anything about a domestic terrorist cell, in Wisconsin or elsewhere."

"*What!* Sir…!"

The Director held up his hand, directing silence. "Jeremy, enough." The Director allowed himself another moment of reflection. He began to speak in a careful, measured, manner. "There is, however, something you should know. We have a contracted research site in Wisconsin. It is one of the most valuable and sensitive sites in our organization. In fact, it is the most sensitive site in our entire government, perhaps in the world. Last week, half the facility was destroyed by an explosion by what we thought was a major electrical disaster."

"Last week?"

"Yes. Five days ago, to be precise."

"The day I was in Budapest?"

"That appears to be the case. Alas, Babylon."

"Oh, *God...*" Kearn leaned forward in his chair, with the almost uncontrollable urge to assume the fetal position. "Sir, did you find anything that indicates...?"

"That this is the target that you hit? Not until this moment. However, given that you are now telling me about this strike on a Wisconsin location, we may need to refocus our investigation. We are still combing through the wreckage. We also must arrange for a number of funerals."

"*Funerals?*" Kearn felt the muscles in his abdomen begin to constrict and had to fight to control the spasms in his stomach. Although he was able to suppress the urge to retch, he could nonetheless taste gastric bile in his mouth. Kearn again involuntarily started to double up in his chair.

"Jeremy, I'm going to put you on administrative leave for the next few days. I believe it will give you a chance to clear your head."

The young analyst checked himself and slowly straightened up. He looked desperately at the Director. "Sir, you told me—"

Once again, the Director raised his hand, palm forward, to halt the young man's accusation. "Jeremy, go home. Get some sleep. You might also want to go down to the clinic. It's on the third floor, if you haven't found it already. I'll authorize them to prescribe you some sedatives."

Kearn started to open his mouth, but no sound came forth, and he could form no words in his head that would have come out as coherent speech. He stood up slowly and turned for the door. He finally was able to muster a phrase, but one that he was capable of whispering only to himself. "I'm a professional," he said. "I was doing my job."

⌘

"How much farther to…to…I'm sorry, what was that name again?" asked Watt.

"Chilchinbito."

"It sounds like fake Mexican food on the menu of a Chi-Chi's restaurant."

"Chi-Chi's?" asked Gaude.

"Maybe a bit before your time."

"We should be there in another forty minutes or so."

"How big is it?"

"I'm not sure. There were no measurements for it on the website."

"No, I mean what's the population?"

"There's a place called Chilchinbito with a population of about five hundred. However, we're being diverted to someplace outside of town."

"Less populated?"

"You could say that. The current census of where we are heading is ten jackrabbits and a lizard."

"I suppose we'll be in good company. Remind me why are we going there?"

"Because that is where we are being sent."

"How do you know that the location is outside of town?" asked an uncharacteristically skeptical Bill Watt. "The note merely indicated that we should go to Chilch….whatever."

"Did you notice the string of numerals at the bottom of the note?"

"Yes. That was the most complicated telephone number I have ever seen. Where does your mystery girlfriend live? Outer Mongolia?"

"Those are map coordinates. Latitude and longitude."

"How do you know that?"

"The Army expects Field Artillery officers to be able to read map grid coordinates. It's regarded as a useful skill when lobbing shells downrange during a battle."

"This could be a wild goose chase."

"You mean, in stark contrast to the wild goose chase we've been on since the first day I met you?"

"This is a completely different goose."

"How so?"

"I suspect that this goose is cooked," complained Watt. Gaude shrugged and continued driving. Watt persisted, "How much longer?"

"Take a look at my cellphone. The remaining distance should be right on the screen."

"Oh, no you don't. I won't be tricked that easily."

"Fine, then you'll just have to wait until I stop for gas," said Gaude as he turned on the radio that rendered up Ni'ihau Child's 'Desert Dilemma.'

> *Lost again in the desert*
> *That's happened many times*
> *Fleeing the mistakes of life*
> *Try to wipe away your crimes*
>
> *You found yourself in the desert*
> *But don't much like what you see*
> *No matter how far you run*
> *You never will be free*

Seven minutes later, Gaude pulled up to the lone gas pump at a Humble Oil station. While the tank was being filled, Gaude checked the map on his cellphone. "You'll need to drive," Gaude told Watt. "The directions on my navigator app put us on a pretty convoluted route."

"You could let your robot girlfriend dictate our way forward."

"Would you prefer that?"

"No."

They resumed their journey with Watt at the steering wheel. Gaude attempted to change the radio station, but the scan function returned him to the same frequency and the insistent song of 'Small Town' by John Mellencamp. He then consulted his navigation app.

"We're about twenty kilometers slightly to the northeast of Chilchinbito," Gaude announced. "We just crossed over from Navaho County to Apache County."

"Is that significant?"

"Nothing is significant."

"Everything is significant."

"At least we have plenty of landmarks."

"Assuming you want to triangulate where John Wayne had his shoot-out in *Stagecoach*," said Watt.

"What shoot-out?" asked Gaude.

"Never mind," responded Watt. After a pause, he asked, "Are we lost?"

"We have a navigation app."

"That doesn't mean that we aren't lost."

"The app tells us exactly where we are."

"But it doesn't tell *you* where you *should be*."

"At least it keeps me from being lost."

"Being lost is not necessarily a bad thing," said Watt. "There is the parable of the lost lamb in which the shepherd, having a flock of one hundred sheep, leaves the ninety-nine in the wilderness and goes after the one that was lost."

"Bad news for the remaining sheep. There are wolves out there."

"True, and being left alone by the shepherd certainly occasions a sense of abandonment and loneliness. Being left alone is often described as a dark night of the soul in which we feel deserted, ignored, isolated, unloved, and forgotten. However, rather than a sign of being snubbed or cast aside, God's leaving us in the dark as he goes out to find the one lost lamb is the surest proof of his confidence in us—his faith in us—I suppose."

"I'm not sure what you are getting at."

"For fifty years, Mother Teresa suffered from this spiritual darkness—even until the day of her death. This was perhaps the greatest saint in recent history and she nevertheless felt wholly abandoned by God. What does this tell us? That God was so certain of Mother Teresa's fidelity that he could leave her in the darkness and turn his attention to the other lost sheep that were not so reliable, dependable, and steadfast in their faith and obedience. God had Mother Teresa fly solo through the night because he trusted her. What greater compliment could one ever receive in this life or in the next? When the time comes to approach the throne of God, it will be the ones who were lost in the wilderness, yet still believed and persevered, who will be greeted with, 'Well done, my good and faithful servants.' Being lost in furtherance of God's plan is the greatest privilege that any human could ever achieve."

"Fine, in that case let's just celebrate that we are lost."

"Are we really lost?"

"No, the navigator app is working just fine."

"Where do we go now?"

"Right."

"Right where?"

"Right here."

"*Here* right here?"

"You already passed it," moaned Gaude.

"Why didn't you say so?"

"I did, when I said, 'right here.' Weren't you listening?"

"You needed to be more specific."

"What could be more specific than *right here*?" Gaude replied, clearly annoyed.

Watt brought the vehicle to a halt and then put the transmission into reverse. "Okay, say when."

"Turn right here." Watt complied and then followed a series of zigzags as the dirt road began to narrow down to a dirt trail and thence to a dirt path. "According to my navigation app, we're almost there," announced Gaude.

"How much farther?"

"A little more than a hundred meters northeast."

"I think that the trail ends here."

"In that case, I guess we will need to walk."

They exited the car and proceeded on a slope as the path meandered down in a serpentine pattern. After a few minutes of following the arid slalom course, they passed a cluster of boulders. They circled left around the perimeter and arrived at a small mound of gravel and sand. Planted on top of it was a weathered wooden tombstone.

WW
DG
666 w

"*This* is what we came to see?"

"I'm not the one who insisted on driving down to this garden spot," said Watt.

Gaude responded with a *hrrumph* and scanned the horizon.

"He's getting cocky now," said Watt.

"I thought you said he was already getting cocky."

"Alright, let's just say he's still in fine form, cocky-wise."

"The initials," said Gaude.

"Yes, I noticed. WW and DG."

"William Watt and Daniel Gaude."

"Interesting."

"Interesting? It doesn't tell us anything other than someone likes to taunt us."

"Actually, it does," said Watt. "It tells us that our opponent is capable of making mistakes."

"How so?"

"My initials aren't WW. My given name is not William. When I was born, my parents decided to cut to the chase. They named me Bill."

"Good call. You are definitely a Bill, not so much a William."

"What do you think about 666w?"

"I won't bother to try a websearch for 666. The results would be too numerous and too predictable."

"What about the 'w' after the 666?"

"I dunno…wicked? weird? wretched? wacky?"

"You're stretching."

"Maybe it refers to another Watt. Perhaps one of your seven sons? Were any of them particularly wicked?"

"They were boys."

"Sound like prime suspects."

"Okay, all kidding aside…"

"All kidding aside, I'm out of ideas."

"How about *west*?"

"666 miles to the west? Could it be that simple?"

"Don't jump to conclusions. Finding that exact spot might not be all that easy. Can that cellphone tell you the location?"

"So now you are suddenly a believer?"

"I've always been a believer, but not in cellphones. At this point, however, he already knows our every move. We need to catch up with him and confront him."

"Alright, let me see…" Gaude tapped out a location query on his cellphone. "My locator indicates that this garden spot is at latitude 36.59759, plus or minus a stone's throw."

"And to the west of us?"

"If we travel west, exactly 666 miles…."

"You're assuming it's miles and not kilometers."

"This tombstone looks like it has been here for a while. I don't think it has been brought into the fold of the Great Conversion."

"If our adversary put it up for us, it couldn't be all that old."

"Fine, I'll calculate kilometers. Would you also like me to make an estimate in terms of cubits, furlongs, or leagues?"

"A cubit happens to be a very fine unit of measurement."

"I'll keep that in mind if I ever need to build an ark, although out here in the desert, I'm thinking that it's a rather remote possibility."

"That's the same flawed premise that got a lot of people drowned in the desert a long time ago."

"Let's stick to the matter at hand, shall we?"

"Okay, fine, what's the result?"

"Give me a minute," said Gaude as he continued tapping on the screen.

"Yes?"

"Okay, if the distance is measured in kilometers, it would put us at the corner of the Desert National Wildlife Range in Nevada."

"That doesn't sound particularly promising."

"But not necessarily any more obscure than where we are right now or more desolate than some of the more out-of-the-way towns that we've visited during the past three weeks."

"With an attitude like that, you'll be hearing from the Chambers of Commerce of a few of the towns we've visited, I'll wager."

"Wait a minute," mumbled Gaude as he continued to browse. "The Wildlife Range is surrounded by Nellis Air Force Base and the Nevada Nuclear Test Site."

"That sounds even less promising."

"That's not the least of it."

"How could it get worse...or better?"

"It's not far from Area 51."

"Seriously? The secret base where they hold space aliens captive?"

"Something like that."

"Maybe measuring in kilometers wasn't such a great idea."

"Or perhaps inspired."

"Not inspired by anything good. I should know."

"On the other hand," said Gaude, still working the screen, "traveling six hundred sixty-six miles west will put us in the

320

geographic center of Monterey, California."

    "Y'know, I think you just sold me on miles."

    "Are you sure you wouldn't prefer cubits?"

    "No, miles will do just fine."

The Advisors

"Miss Ho, thank you for seeing me on such short notice."

"I suppose that this couldn't wait until I get back from my trip to California."

"No ma'am. We've had an incident in—"

"Budapest."

"Yes." There was a long pause during which Grace Ho knew the agent was trying to assemble his thoughts. She could tell from his congealing facial features that he decided to forego any facade. "How did you know?" he finally asked.

"You've apparently forgotten that your organization has agreed to never question my sources or methods. I provide answers. When I cannot provide answers, I render up leads and clues. When I can do nothing else, I'm willing to proffer a guess. Regardless, I never explain how."

"Yes, but—" She held up a finger in warning and slowly shook her head. The agent realized he had stepped beyond the bounds. "Sorry, ma'am. Anything you can provide us would be greatly appreciated."

"Of course," she replied, returning her attention to the computer screen. After a few minutes of scanning documents, Grace pulled open the desk drawer and removed a *Sekishu-Banshi* paper notepad and a Waterman pen. She then started taking notes using Chinese characters. The agent waited patiently and impassively. After approximately fifteen minutes of what appeared to be meticulous attention to the documents and painstaking efforts to assemble several pages of apparently indecipherable notes, she put down the pen and again opened the desk drawer, this time removing what appeared to be a deck of cards. Grace then cleared the center of the desk as she moved the computer aside and placed the notepad to her right. She removed the deck from the package, shuffled the cards, and began muttering in a barely audible voice that could have been in any language. She then started to lay cards face down in a complex array having no discernible pattern or sense of symmetry.

After the last card was laid, Grace Ho sat in silence with her eyes closed. Two minutes passed before she opened her eyes and then reached out to flip a card in the middle of the table. "The Six of Wands," she announced solemnly.

The agent immediately recognized this as a tarot card but was unsure of what his organization's most valuable consultant was attempting to accomplish.

Grace reached out and flipped another. "The Queen of Cups," she stated calmly.

The agent decided that there must be some significance to the process and immediately determined that he needed to memorize each card in the order revealed by Miss Ho.

"The Magician," she announced with a pitch to her voice signaling some degree of consternation.

The agent made a mental note that this card was apparently a matter that needed to be thoroughly researched when he returned to the office.

"The Three of Swords."

"The Nine of Wands."

"The Hanged Man," she gulped, clearly revealing a sense of horror.

Hanged Man. Serious problem, thought the agent.

"The Five of Pentacles."

"The Four of Cups." Grace's hand hovered over this card for an extended time, started breathing in rapid shallow gulps, and finally emitted a gentle sigh.

Four of Cups. Stressful situation, was the annotation made in the agent's mind.

"The Tower." Grace's eyes widened appreciably at the appearance of the card. She started reaching for another, stopped, changed her mind, and then hovered a gently shaking hand over a card far to the left. After a seemingly endless hesitation, she reached down and flipped the card.

"Death!" she gasped, clearly stunned by the grave and dire message.

Holy shit, silently wailed the agent.

Grace suddenly turned her face to the agent, displaying a mask of unrepressed terror. "Get out! Get out *now*!" she screamed.

The agent stumbled backwards, barely recovered his balance, and then rushed out of the room. The heavy tread of his running through the hallway and the slammed front door reverberated through the house.

Grace Ho collapsed back into her chair as an explosion of

laughter erupted in her head.

Sis, you are too much!

That was the best!

You are a naughty bitch! exclaimed the voice of the sister who really was the naughty bitch.

"Alright, everybody, calm down," she said aloud, trying to control herself from joining the outbreak of hilarity.

You are such a card! quipped the cleverest one.

Oh God! Oh God! I can barely breathe!

Since when did you start breathing?

I don't know, but I can't now! the soundless voice wheezed between laughs.

Please! Please, do it again next week! We want to help!

"C'mon, girls, it wasn't that funny," she reprimanded her invisible siblings as a giggle uncontrollably escaped from her diaphragm.

Did you see the look on the guy's face? squealed one of the usually quiet and reticent sisters, at which a new burst of laughter ensued.

"Enough!" Grace scolded, making no impression on the dozens of voices still shrieking in delight.

Finally, Grace surrendered to the inevitable, leaned back in her chair, switched off the lamp sitting on the desk, and joined the chorus of merriment as she sat alone—and in the best of company—laughing in the dark.

Twenty-Two: Monterey

He is age three. His family lives in one of the small bedroom villages of Falls Church. His father is still alive and is driving the car. It's a Dodge, isn't it? No, maybe a Ford. He tries to remember. He knows that he has been in this dream before and it is the ritual of the memory to always debate the make of Dad's car. Maybe it is a Chevrolet. It is a two-tone—navy blue and cream. The tires are whitewalls. The steering wheel is gigantic.

Dad is driving to Seven Corners. It is a time before the invention of child seats, the enforcement of safety belt laws, and the restriction upon young children in the front of the automobile. He sits on the front seat and watches through the windshield at a huge flock of starlings—but, of course, all flocks of migrating birds are 'blackbirds' to him at this age. They fly in fantastic pulsing cartwheels across the sky ahead of them. It is early November and the air has a dry, metallic taste to it.

They are driving to a pizzeria. He knows that soon the car will be filled with the aroma of a pizza.

"Are you gentlemen looking for something in particular?"

"We're looking for anything that might identify the cause of the fire."

"That's already been determined."

"An electrical problem of some sort, I imagine?"

"Yes," came the surprised answer. "Has that already been announced on the news?"

"I doubt it." Watt extracted a card from his pocket and offered it, as always, face down.

The man accepted the card, held it to his nose, sniffed it, licked it, and then put it into his jacket upper pocket, slightly poking out as if a decorative handkerchief. "I am Gottlieb Eucalyptus," said the man, making a slight bow, "the Director of Sacred Music here at Pacific Shore Church of the Living Jesus."

"Do you know anything about the cause of this fire?"

"Apparently, the public address system overloaded."

"How could that happen?"

"Frankly, I don't know. There was no load. Our P.A. was switched off. Besides, while we had a nice system, it didn't draw a lot of juice. It's not as if we were putting on a Van Halen concert here."

"Par for the course," remarked Gaude to Watt.

"Excuse me?" asked Gottlieb.

"We've been following church fires across the country. Every one of them was caused by an electrical or electronic fault. We believe that someone is behind all of this."

"Behind all of what?"

"The church fires around the country are being set intentionally."

"I thought you just said that the other fires were all electrical mishaps, just like ours."

"Yes, they were."

"Ours was ruled an accident."

"So were nearly all of the others. Too many accidents begin to look like no accident."

"You're saying that someone snuck into all of these churches and messed with the fuse boxes, or something like that?"

"We're not sure. There isn't any evidence of break-ins."

"So, the perpetrators somehow managed to burn down churches by fooling with electrical systems outside the buildings?"

"Maybe."

"You don't know?"

"No, we don't."

"Well, that's certainly compelling evidence," remarked Gottlieb sarcastically.

"There is a chance that the arsonist might be doing this from a remote location. Perhaps through the internet or using some flaw in the electrical infrastructure."

"That would be quite a trick."

"We believe that our arsonist is quite tricky."

"That level of deviousness and malice is a heavy yoke upon a soul. I will pray for their repentance and conversion by the Holy Spirit."

"It will take more than prayer," said Gaude.

"There is no such thing as *more than* prayer. Prayer unlocks the greatest power in the universe."

"Yes, the power of God."

"Not just *any* power of God. I'm talking about *the* greatest power of God."

"I didn't know that God had different levels of power."

"Yes, he has many powers. He has the power of creation, the power of destruction, and the power of preservation. Of all of God's power, the most awesome is the power of mercy and salvation."

"I would have thought that creating galaxies requires a great deal of power."

"I'm sure that it did, but the Bible indicates that forming the stars was a cakewalk in comparison to redeeming human souls."

"I don't recall ever hearing that argument being made."

"Think about it. Would anyone suggest that God is a silly chatterbox who prattles on needlessly?"

"Not unless they are inclined to be struck by lightning," said Watt.

Gottlieb smiled and nodded. "Anyone who believes in an omniscient and omnipotent God must assume that everything he does is for a reason—and a very good reason at that. Thus, if he devotes more time, effort, and attention to salvation than he did to creation, it must be intentional and significant."

"I don't follow you," said Gaude.

"Would you agree that it is generally asserted that the word of God is found in the Holy Bible?"

"Yes, of course," concurred Watt.

"It is also widely held that each and every word of God in the Bible has power beyond our understanding and reckoning. Indeed, all the heavens and the earth, the sun, moon and stars, the whirling galaxies extending into infinite space were created by the words of God. Does that make sense?"

"So far," answered Gaude cautiously.

"As a simple illustration of this truly unimaginable power, consider the momentary wrath of God, which is but the tiniest portion of his essence, when it was unleashed on Sodom and Gomorrah. This resulted in demolishing both cities in an Old Testament version of thermonuclear holocaust. The one person who turned around and faced that small facet of God's glorious wrath was Lot's wife. She was instantly turned into a pillar of salt."

"Yes," agreed Watt, "that is a particularly dramatic example."

"Now, imagine the power of God when he devotes his full attention, all his focus, all his will, all his love, on one particular object. Imagine something so important to him that he sends his only begotten and beloved son to be tortured and die on a cross in order to obtain. This effort would make the destruction of Sodom and Gomorrah pale to insignificance."

"Yes, I suppose that argument could be made."

"In that case, consider that the words of God we encounter in scripture that are devoted to creating the earth, the stars, the galaxies, the heavens, all the known and unknown expanse of existence, can be found in just the first few pages of the Bible. Look closely and you will see that the creation of the world, including God forming man and woman in his own image, was accomplished through the first two chapters of the Book of Genesis. The fall of man is recounted immediately thereafter in a few paragraphs. In most editions of the Bible, all of this constitutes about two or three pages. There are usually about a thousand or so pages in most Protestant Bibles, perhaps fifteen hundred in Catholic Bibles. In those thousand or more pages following the story of creation, we find words coming directly from God the Father, we read the words spoken directly by Jesus who is God the Son, and we examine all the other words of the Bible inspired by God the Holy Spirit. In these thousand or more pages of scriptures, ninety-nine percent of God's words, all the words of Jesus, and the words elsewhere throughout the Bible inspired by the Holy Spirit, are all devoted to the redemption of humanity. Thus, it appears that the redemption of our souls requires more of God's words, more of his attention, more of his power than the very creation of the world, the mountains, the oceans, the sun and moon, and the countless stars in the sky. The redemption of souls is thus a thousand times a greater miracle than the creation of the entire universe."

"That seems like a stretch."

"You might think it implausible, until we begin to contemplate the apparent impossibility of transforming a corrupt human soul into the purity of perfection that would be required for it to be united to the absolute perfection of God. Such a transformation, such a cleansing, such a renewal, must be recognized as impossible. Yet we know that it happens, thanks to the assurance that what may be impossible for a man is yet possible with God."

"Jeremy, how are you?"

"I'm fine."

Wylinski, uncharacteristically, decided to be candid. "Jeremy, you don't look fine. Actually, you look like death warmed over."

"I've been put on administrative leave."

"I saw that on the daily blotter. However, you somehow managed to get into the building this morning. If you outwitted our security system, I'll have you arrested and then recommend you for a presidential citation for achieving the virtually impossible."

"I didn't leave the building yesterday. I spent the night in the supply room on the north side of the building."

"The Office of the Comptroller. Good choice. They all walk out the door at 4:00 p.m., no exceptions." Wylinski paused for a moment, frowned, and then asked, "How did you avoid the midnight 'ping' from the security system? If someone doesn't leave the building by midnight, the front desk receives a message."

"I know. However, I realized that unlike the entry procedure, exits are monitored merely by a remote scan of our ID cards when we walk out past the door sensors. I went into the travel database and found someone scheduled for a trip overseas—George Duffey, Oversight Manager of Delta Zone. I hovered around his office area until he stepped out and then dropped my ID into the pocket of his suit jacket."

"You took a risk that he might find your card."

"That wasn't as big of a risk as being tracked down by the security team. Besides, Duffey wears tailored suits, which means he's a little bit vain. I doubted that he ever reaches in to put anything in a jacket side pocket—it might cause a slight bulge."

"For someone who wasn't sent through Basic, that's impressive. You have the makings of a field operative."

Kearn glanced nervously over his shoulder and then closed the office door. "I need your help."

329

"Are you in trouble?"

"I think that all of us are in trouble."

Wylinski processed this in his coldly dispassionate cerebral cortex, concluding that there was a substantial probability that the young analyst had been put on administrative leave for reasons relating to mental instability. He decided against calling for security guards—at least, not just yet.

"How can I be of assistance?"

"You remember our discussion two weeks ago?"

"Yes, odd and errant signals. You went to NORAD?"

"First NORAD and then to Research Triangle. I found something very interesting being developed by the Air Force and was able to adopt the project as our own."

"Kudos. That's quite an accomplishment."

"Thanks, but there have been some complications."

"Complications?"

"Yes."

"Serious complications?"

"That's why I'm here. I sent you a breach notice two days ago."

"Yes," said Wylinski with a nod. "The Director said that he would handle it." Wylinski then frowned. "Out of idle curiosity, why are you coming to me? Don't you direct report to the Director?"

"I'm..."

"Yes?"

"...afraid."

"You're afraid of the Director?"

"Yes."

"Afraid of what the Director will say or afraid what he will do?"

"Yes, but most of all, just afraid."

"Who happens to be three doors down the hallway."

"I'm painfully aware of that."

"Tell me what's going on."

"The Director had me working on a project. It involved a lot of moving parts, but for the sake of simplicity, let's just say that I was assigned to find the proverbial 'next big thing' in order to maintain the relevance—and the cash flow—for ORCA."

"I'm listening."

"I did some digging and that's when I came to you about the report on anomalous signals. Based on the lead you provided, I found the Air Force program. To some extent, it was running out of control. The important thing is that it had nearly unlimited and unimaginable potential for cyberespionage. I was able to secure it for the Director."

"Yes, go on."

"Even though we had the new tool, we still needed something else to make a budget pitch to Congress. I was assigned to identify a looming threat, to create an emotional 'hook' as the Director called it. I did a deep dive to find something. I searched through the background and biographical information of each member of Congress. I also sifted through information in just about every database we maintain or borrow throughout the intelligence community. I retrieved a lot of information, some of which was rather strange. Most of the time I was merely led down a series of rabbit holes with nothing to show for it. Eventually, I found one thing that was particularly curious. I discovered hints about ORCA's oldest project. It's called Abaddon."

"Never heard of it."

"Neither had the Director, or at least, that's what he led me to believe."

"What is Abaddon?"

"Something that never existed, at least officially. I originally tracked it down to the source, if you can call it that, from murky references in a retired file. As best as I was able to piece together, Abaddon has been around since the first day this organization was stood up and has lasted—as far as I can tell—until this very day. This is a project that has been operating under almost everyone's radar. I have no idea who authorized Abaddon's mission, no clue as to any operatives assigned, and no hint as to its location. There is only one thing I have been able to figure out. Abaddon has been in secret communication with a stealthy group in Congress for decades on end."

"I always assumed that we were that stealthy group," said Wylinski, almost succeeding in making an authentic display of wit.

"I wish it was that simple, sir."

"Simple espionage is a contradiction in terms."

"Yessir. In any event, our clandestine partnership has been responsible for nearly every illegal assassination committed in the past seventy years."

"All assassinations are illegal."

"I'm talking about the assassinations that even we would not be willing to perform."

Wylinski pondered this silently. After a minute of reflection, he asked, "What, exactly, do you know about the contacts with Congress?"

"It's called the Select Subcommittee on Miscellaneous Matters, but it isn't really a subcommittee since it apparently doesn't report to any committee. It seems to be comprised by members of both Houses of Congress, but I can't find a single name of a Congressman or Senator associated with this group. As far as I can tell, the Select Subcommittee doesn't exist in any official or unofficial records anywhere on earth, except in a lonely file in Room Eleven."

"You were given access to the Catacombs?"

"No, I wasn't given access, but I managed to get in."

"That was not wise."

"So I have learned. The hard way."

"You say that this Select Subcommittee has been in communication with Abaddon...in communication with *us*?"

"Yes."

"For decades?"

"Yes."

Wylinski frowned. "After all these decades, with...what... dozens, scores of members of Congress who must have been involved, none of this has ever leaked out?"

"That does seem odd, but I think I have an answer for that. I've culled down the information to the sub-atomic level, so to speak. It appears that the entire committee is not involved in identifying targets. The one person who actually communicates with us is called the EILi."

"Like a girl's name?"

"No, an acronym. E-I-L-i."

"What does that stand for?"

"I have absolutely no idea. However, what I do know is that this is a member of the committee that it is not the chairman and that the person doesn't change very often."

"Someone who remains in Congress for a long time?"

"Yes, I believe so."

"Senators have much longer terms than members of the House of Representatives."

"Exactly. However, the EILi seems to have a turnover much, much longer than every six years."

"Senators get re-elected."

"True, but not always and not reliably. How would someone holding the EILi position—which is a deep, dark secret, remember—get reelected predictably, over and over again?"

"Because they come from a very predictable state?"

"That's my working theory."

"There's more than one very predictable state, you know."

"I'm painfully aware of that. I assumed that the Deep South would be the happy hunting grounds for long-term senators, but I soon discovered that they are spread across the entire nation. However, as I churned through the evidence, I saw subtle hints of an occasional—make that rare—change of the guard in assignment of an EILi. If I can finish that list, I might be able to compare that turnover to the election records of the past century."

"How are you going to get back into Room Eleven?"

"I don't know. I was hoping that you might be able to help me."

"Even if you did finish that list, your theory presupposes that the mystery senator from the mystery state is appointed as the mystery EILi of your mystery committee as soon as they enter the Senate. Wouldn't a secret committee be rather careful of who it brings into the fold? Perhaps they might need a few years to size up their potential new secret committee member?"

"That's true…"

"Besides, how do you know for sure that the EILi is a member of Congress? Couldn't it be a career staff member?"

Kearn paused silently to absorb this critique. "You're right, that could complicate matters. We might never be able to figure out who the players are in this thing."

"Do you think that Abaddon has anything to do with the murders of our field agents?"

"It all lines up. I constructed a timeline. Nearly every assassination correlates with dates communicated to Abaddon."

"How did the Director react to this information?"

"He seemed genuinely concerned, but as I was about to leave the office, he suddenly came up with the idea of testing the Air Force program. That's when he sent me to Budapest."

"Budapest?"

"Yessir."

"To conduct a test?"

"Yessir."

"What kind of test?"

"I'm not really sure. The Air Force sent me a package on orders from the Director. I had no idea what was in there. The program was self-executing. Instead of a routine test, it conducted an actual strike and data extraction. No one said that this would be a domestic target. I was following orders."

"We've all been following orders."

"When I returned from Budapest, I reported the hit to the Director. He told me not to worry, it was a terrorist cell."

"Analysts don't conduct kinetic operations against terrorist cells."

"Young, stupid, inexperienced analysts do, or at least, are led to believe that they do. Five days later, the Budapest office was wiped out."

"That sounds like an unfortunate coincidence."

"I prayed that is was."

"I understand your concern."

"There's more."

"I find that hard to believe."

"After my return from Budapest, but before the office was attacked, I continued to engage in a wide-spectrum search. Among the things that I happened to notice was a data sort you conducted through the agent personality files almost two weeks ago."

"Yes," answered Wylinski impassively.

"Did the Director tell you to give him this information?"

"Why do you ask?"

"Because of what was in the report. Do you remember?"

"I have only a vague recollection," lied Wylinski. "It was a simple request. I merely keyed the personnel records program to issue a report based upon the requested parameters. I didn't spend much time looking over the results."

"What were those parameters?"

"I'm not at liberty to say."

"I'll tell you. It was courage and integrity."

Wylinski's face remained a mask of impassive caution. "Your research skills are impressive, even by our standards."

"Do you know why you were asked to collect the information?"

"The Director indicated that he was interested in making some new assignments and promotions."

"Sounds reasonable, particularly from a new Director who wants to make his mark on the organization."

"Yes, I would say so."

"Then again, there might be another explanation, not so reasonable, but perhaps more true."

"Such as?"

"Perhaps to get rid of anyone who might have the guts to stand up to him."

"Why would that be a concern? What would...what *could* the Director possibly do that conceivably results in a palace coup?"

"Until yesterday, I would not have thought anything. Things have changed."

"How?"

"I'll explain in a minute. In the meantime, it has occurred to me that with the new crypto program that I snagged from the Air Force, the Director could be making some frightening moves. As God is my witness, I'm not exaggerating. He could do anything. I mean *anything*. Sooner or later this would make him a threat."

"A threat to who?"

"To the organization, to all of us, to the nation, to the world. Someone here would eventually figure it out and feel legally obligated to expose him or morally obligated to kill him." Kearn looked down at his hands, not having realized that they were clenched in fists on his lap. "Since you don't clearly recall the results of the report, I assume that you don't remember the names of the operatives who were indicated to be in the top percentile of those personality characteristics."

"No, but I could check if it is important."

"I already have the names. There are about twenty operatives, but at the very top of the list are James Doyle, Diane McCraw, Theodore O'Brian, Pedro Smith, and Jack VonHallegin."

Wylinski momentarily forgot to breathe. After an interminable moment, he whispered to himself, "They're all dead, except Doyle."

"I tried to track down Agent Doyle. He was supposed to be at the Waterways Experiment Station, but he seems to have disappeared."

Wylinski shook his head. "He has disappeared, but not from WES. Doyle went to one of our contracted research facilities to track down what appears to be a significant lead relating to some elusive signals. He was caught in an explosion. We're still investigating the cause. Doyle was recuperating in a clinic and that's when he disappeared. For the past three days he's been invisible. You can presume that he is dead—or as good as dead."

"The explosion…was it in Wisconsin?"

"Yes," responded Wylinski with uncharacteristic surprise. "We have a particularly sensitive project there."

"Is…Babylon the name of the facility?" asked Kearn cautiously.

"How did you know that?"

"When I was at Budapest conducting the test, the target facility turned out to be in Wisconsin. After the…attack…and extraction, the message screen indicated 'Zedekiah Avenged.' I had to look that up, but it didn't take too much time. The name Zedekiah is found in the Book of Kings of the Bible. He was the last ruler of Judah before the armies of Babylon laid siege to Jerusalem and conquered the city. Zedekiah was taken prisoner, his sons were executed in front of him, his eyes were gouged out, and then he was dragged in chains to the city of Babylon. When I met with the Director yesterday, he mentioned the destruction of the laboratory and then said something odd that I didn't really understand at the time."

"What was that?"

"Alas, Babylon."

"Hmmm…I see."

"The Director then turned on me and denied ever having said anything about a terrorist cell, informed me about the strike on the Wisconsin site, and insisted that I was the one who inputted the target coordinates. He put me in the crosshairs."

"I can see why you slept in a supply room last night."

"I didn't spend much time sleeping."

Wylinski took a deep breath. "You were right."

"Right about what?"

"When you first came into my office. You said that you were in trouble. You are."

"What should I do?"

Wylinski silently considered this as he looked out the window featuring a view of another drab federal office building. "Well," he finally responded, "at the very least you have the information about Abaddon and the extracted data from the Budapest test."

"No, not really. I downloaded all the documents on the shared drive. They disappeared between the time I visited the Director yesterday and returned to my desk. He erased everything: my research, all the data, and all the documents I've been collecting. He also locked me out from access to the after-action report that I submitted after returning from Budapest."

"What about the original package the Director gave you containing the Air Force program?"

"The drive came to me directly from the Air Force. When I returned to the States, I handed it over to the Director. No one else knows about it."

"The Air Force does."

"As I learned from the Director, the Air Force team has been disbanded. I tried all day yesterday to track down anyone associated with their project. Everyone has disappeared into thin air. The company in Research Triangle that partnered with the Air Force was absorbed into DataGhad just a few days ago. I tried reaching out to those folks in San Francisco but hit a brick wall. They deny any knowledge of the project."

"Given that it was highly classified, that is hardly a surprise."

"That doesn't make the brick wall any less daunting."

"You say that the Director sent you Budapest? He was the one who chose the location for the test?"

"Yes."

"Alright, that's something we can sink our teeth into. I don't remember authorizing the travel, so it must have come from the Director himself. Just give me a minute." Wylinski turned to his computer terminal and started tapping on the computer keys and manipulating the optical cursor. At intervals, he would pause and issue a gentle grunt of annoyance or frustration. Kearn's already knotted stomach now churned with increased anxiety. Finally, Wylinski stopped, sighed, and turned to the younger man. "There is absolutely no record of the Director, or anyone else, sending you to Budapest. In fact, there is no evidence of you leaving the United States in the past two weeks."

"*What?*"

"According to our records, you were on sick leave. You called in that you had a cold."

"What about flight manifests?"

"You're not on them."

"I took an Uber to the airport."

"I checked, also for taxis. No go."

"They scanned my passport."

"No records in either the United States or Hungarian border control databases."

"I used my credit card during the trip."

"No, you didn't. Not according to the records. In fact, there are daily charges to your card at local venues during the entire time."

"But...." Kearn's face went blank and then a look of revelation appeared on his visage. "Wait a minute. If there is no record connecting me to Budapest, then there is no way I can be framed."

Wylinski's perfect Ken Doll brow was now knotted for perhaps the first time in his life. "That's true, unless...."

"Unless what?"

"Unless...." Wylinski returned to his computer and began working it furiously. Wylinski then leaned forward, more closely scrutinizing the computer screen. "That's odd..."

"What?"

"Are you a big fan of Starbucks?"

"No more than anyone else."

"There are a number of purchases from a Starbucks on Massachusetts Avenue."

"Yeah, that's right outside our door."

"Massachusetts Avenue crosses the entire city. This was a Starbucks across town—Northwest—up at Embassy Row."

"Embassy Row?"

"Can you explain why you would go to the trouble of heading across town to get a cup of coffee, including the time you were supposedly nursing a cold in Falls Church?"

"Falls Church?"

"That's where you live, isn't it?"

"Yes."

"And my guess is that six days ago is when you were in Budapest?"

"Yes."

"But according to every record now existing on every database in the world, you were right here."

"No, that's not true."

"Hold on a minute," said Wylinski distractedly as he returned to the computer. He resumed his tapping on the keyboard and darted his eyes across the screen, clicking pull-down menus. He continued for three minutes, then sat back with a capitulating sigh. 'We have your cell tracker records from that time. It's not good."

"Why? What is it?"

"According to your movement data, you were visiting foreign embassies."

"That's *impossible*."

"Impossible? Have you forgotten what we do here?"

"What about cross-checks of other surveillance systems?" suggested Kearn.

"Good idea!" Wylinski resumed typing. In three minutes, he leaned back, crestfallen.

"What?"

"I tapped into the NSA yellow light system. They indicate that your calls for the past few weeks have been under surveillance."

"Why?"

"Suspicious activity consistent with an espionage profile. They tapped your personal cell. The records indicate that you made multiple calls to entities of interest in Naples…Santiago… Johannesburg…Tehran. There are also some calls to area code 608, but the actual contact information has been deleted. Strange, I've never seen that before."

"Is area code 608 in Wisconsin?"

Wylinski did a quick google. "Yes."

"Of course," moaned Kearn.

"The last call was two days ago…"

"To Budapest."

"Yes."

"Oh, sweet Jesus…"

"That was the day of the—"

"I know! Oh God…Oh God!"

"It also indicates that at the same time you made a number of calls to the personal cell of another employee of ORCA."

"Who?"

There was an extended pause. "Me." Wylinski looked shell shocked as he stared at the computer screen, then at the office wall, and then at the coffee mug on his otherwise immaculate desk. "The Director…" Wylinski's voice trailed off.

"Yes?"

"He…"

"Yes?"

Wylinski settled into silence and pondered this carefully. "We should go to…"

"Yes?"

Wylinski fell back into brooding silence. Kearn exercised as much self-control as he could muster simply waiting for his framed co-conspirator to process the information and arrive at his own conclusions. He finally looked up at the younger man and said, "We're screwed."

"More or less."

"More."

⌘

"I need to stop by an ATM to get some cash," said Bill Watt.

"It's comforting to know that you occasionally rely on technology instead of awaiting a miracle to take care of your daily needs."

"I fly on airplanes. Isn't that technological enough for you?"

"Maybe not. I've always taken the position that airplanes levitate into the sky using dark magic and fairy dust."

"I can't argue with you there," said Watt with a chuckle. "However, I still need to find an automatic teller."

"I'll find one for you," offered Gaude has he reached for his cellphone.

"Please, give me one moment of respite from that hand-held demon. I'll find a bank using the old-fashioned method."

"You won't find a copy of the yellow pages anywhere in this place."

"I was referring to eyesight."

"Oh." Gaude mused for a moment and said, "I assume that you recognize the irony of rejecting help from one item of newfangled electronics in an effort to locate another item of newfangled electronics. An ATM is just a money computer."

"I will seek forgiveness for my hypocrisy at a later time and date."

"Over there," pointed Gaude. "There's a bank."

"See? That wasn't so hard, now was it?"

Gaude pulled the Studebaker into the parking area in front of the ATM booth. Both men exited the car and approached the machine, currently being utilized by a tall, slender man wearing white linen trousers, suede saddle shoes, an amber colored sports jacket, a plaid bow tie, and a Panama hat. He appeared to be arguing with the computer screen. "I am a customer and a depositor in good standing. You have no right to treat me this way."

Gaude gave a sidelong glance to Watt who waited patiently for his turn, exhibiting no sign that anything was amiss or that he considered the other man's behavior anything out of the ordinary.

"Are you going to give me my money or not?" the man demanded.

The ATM remained mute.

"I don't think that my request is at all unreasonable. Perhaps you should call in the manager," the man insisted.

The ATM did not summon the branch manager, which the man in the Panama hat interpreted as a sign of surly intransigence.

"You realize that I could take my business elsewhere, don't you?"

The ATM failed to acknowledge this indisputable truth and its impenetrable recalcitrance further enraged the customer.

Gaude finally decided to intervene. "Excuse me, sir. Is the ATM giving you any trouble?"

The man turned to face Gaude. "Yes, thank you. Perhaps you could have a word with it. I have come to withdraw some money and the ATM refuses to cooperate."

"Did it fail to read your ATM card?"

"No, the card is working just fine."

"Did it reject your PIN number?"

"No, that's not the problem."

"Is there something wrong with your balance?"

"No, I'm very steady."

"I mean the balance of money in your account."

"I don't think so. There is plenty of money available. The ATM readily admits that."

"Are you trying to withdraw more than the daily limit?"

"I doubt it. All I want is thirty-seven dollars."

"What's the problem then?"

"The ATM refuses to issue me thirty-seven dollars. It keeps insisting that I take forty dollars. I don't want forty dollars. I want thirty-seven."

"Why don't you take forty and get change somewhere else?"

"Why should I be forced to capitulate to a soulless money box?"

"I suppose that you could wait until the bank lobby opens," offered Gaude.

"The bank doesn't open until Monday morning."

"Is this the weekend?" Gaude asked, turning to Watt.

"It's Saturday," answered the man in the Panama hat.

"Well, regardless of the day of the week, you can't argue with a machine."

"Who says that I can't? I've been arguing with this machine for quite some time."

"I'm sorry, but it's somewhat illogical to expect that an ATM is going to respond to your complaints."

"A certain degree of illogic is necessary in life. We humans could not survive without illogic."

"I'm not sure that makes sense," said Gaude.

"You're right, it doesn't make sense. That's the point!"

"What was the point again?" asked a confused Dan Gaude.

The man grunted an indignant *hrrumph* and then asked, "How many romantic relationships have you had in your life?"

"A few."

"Women, I presume?" asked the man, giving Gaude a disapproving once-over.

"Yes."

"Did you base that relationship on logic?"

"Not always."

"Do you even *know* how to have a logical relationship with a woman?"

"Don't ask me about women, I'm single," answered Gaude.

"Don't ask me about women, I'm married," added Watt.

"I just recommend that you avoid any arguments with an ATM, logical or illogical," explained Gaude. "It's an argument you're not likely to win."

"If you wish to discuss unwinnable arguments, I could go back to my comparisons regarding women, but I won't belabor the point. Are machines now placed above us in a hierarchy that forbids that we quarrel with our mechanical masters?"

"It's not that, so much as it isn't practical for a machine to provide you exact change."

"Perhaps not practical for the ATM, but it is very practical for me. Besides, vending machines give me change and they are simpletons in comparison with this thing."

"I suppose you can keep fighting if you are willing to devote your life to changing the entire setup of our technological society."

"As a matter of fact, that is exactly what I have devoted my life to do."

"Really?"

"Yes, I am an anti-mathematician. My name is Doctor Earnest Prabhu."

"PhD, I assume, and not a medical doctor?"

"Yes, although I'm quite willing to advise you to cut down on alcohol and red meat and to get more exercise."

"An anti-mathematician? Does that mean you are bad at math?"

"No, not exactly."

"Does that mean you deal exclusively with negative numbers?"

"No, mathematicians deal with negative numbers. Of course, they deal with every other sort of number as well."

"Such as?"

"Such as natural numbers, whole numbers, integers, rational and irrational numbers, complex, imaginary numbers, polynomials, and so forth and so on."

"What kind of numbers are left?"

"Non-numbers."

"I don't recall hearing about those."

"You've encountered them all your life." Prabhu bent down and picked up a smooth stone from the ground. "What is the value of this rock?"

"You mean how much is it worth?"

"I might."

"I'm not sure. Maybe less than a penny."

"That's not worth, that's merely a number. You've just assigned a mathematical value to the rock of one one-hundredth of a United States dollar. If we carefully and painfully trace back the absolute quantifiable value of a dollar, we will again come up with another number to designate the proportional relationship of the small rock in my hand to everything else that could conceivably be purchased with American currency."

"What do you mean by worth?"

"That which is most essential to the rock but cannot be quantified by numbers. I don't measure the height, length, depth, volume, or weight of a rock. I study its *ultimate* worth. Is it useful? Is it beautiful? Is it good? Will it lead to enlightenment? To holiness? What is its place in the universe? What is the rock's relationship to other rocks? What is its relationship to humanity? To you? To me? To God?"

"How do you measure worth? By the beauty of the rock? By its color?"

"No, color can be measured mathematically. The color of light is determined by a measurable and predictable wavelength. In any medium other than a vacuum, different colors of light will have distinguishable refractions, which means they have different measurable speeds. The beauty of the rock is the expression in its soul."

"Rocks don't have a soul."

"Who told you that?"

"I'm sure that I learned it in school."

"The nuns of Blessed Sacrament Catholic School aren't qualified to judge or to pass on their biased judgment to the easily-influenced children assigned to their charge."

Gaude reacted with slackjawed surprise. *Not again*, he thought. *How does everyone seem to know my life history? What the hell is going on?*

Prabhu continued, "Those nuns were tainted by mathematics. They taught you to count trinities, Ten Commandments, seven sacraments, a dozen apostles, and begin and end the day by counting on your rosary beads. They were infected by numbers and passed the contagion on to the next generation."

"Then how do you measure?" intervened Watt.

"That's the point, I don't measure. Some things must be valued without being measured, recognized without being counted, perceived without being enumerated. There are things that must be known without being understood. When you stand at the edge of the Grand Canyon to take in the majestic beauty of God's creation, do you count the strata of the layers of rock?"

"Someone does."

"Yes, those held captive by mathematics."

"How do you determine worth...or worthiness?"

"I contemplate worthiness, or beauty, or other important attributes, by how it makes us feel."

"Then what you study is arbitrary. Beauty is in the eye of the beholder. You're not studying the rock. You're studying the person who is admiring the rock."

"It's no more arbitrary than saying you weigh ninety kilos—"

"Eighty-three."

"As you say, eighty-three kilos. On the moon, you would weigh fourteen kilos. In deep space, you are virtually weightless."

"My mass is constant."

"That can change based upon your velocity."

"Ummm…yeah, maybe I slept through high school physics class."

"No, you were distracted by a pretty girl sitting to your left. Susan, wasn't it?"

"Hey, wait a minute—"

"But you never got over your sixth grade crush on Sally Osborne, did you?"

"Okay, that's enough! Who the hell are you?"

"I believe that I introduced myself."

"How the hell do you know so much about my personal life? Stuff from twenty years ago. That's just not possible."

"Creepy, isn't it? There is a perfectly logical explanation. In fact, I've been trying to explain it to you for the past few minutes. Mathematicians can employ statistical analysis to chase down probabilities, correct? Based upon known data, such as your gender, your age, your race, your ethnicity, apparent level of education and intelligence, together with visual cues such as your apparel and verbal cues from your vocabulary and speech patterns, a good mathematician might be able to draw deductions and conclusions that are reasonably accurate."

"True, but they arrive at conclusions that are basic generalities."

"Exactly! It is a collective cultural myth that mathematics is precise. In fact, it is just a dull instrument," said Prabhu. "A mathematician could probably determine what part of the country, what state, perhaps in what city you were raised, perhaps even where you were born. They certainly could boil down the facts and figures and arrive at reasonably accurate conclusions about your profession and religion. They might be able to tweeze out where you went to college, and who knows, maybe your favorite color, food, and television show."

"That's pretty impressive from my perspective."

"Then you need to develop a new perspective. Mathematics cannot tell whether you enjoy drinking a glass of orange juice more than taking a stroll in the woods wearing a pair of comfortable walking shoes, or if growing a moustache promotes more harmony in your soul than owning a complete set of crescent wrenches."

"Anti-mathematics can?"

"I'm working on it."

"That's a lame answer."

"Is a lame answer less noble than a facetious excuse?"

"I'm not sure."

"Then you have no right to judge. Besides, you conceded the accuracy of my deductions about the heartthrobs of your youth."

"Okay, fine, but you just identified my elementary school and the name of the girl who sat in the desk beside me during high school physics. An excellent magic trick."

"What is the reaction of a member of a stone age society when confronted with modern technology? Magic."

"Fine, but your pseudoscience seems to lack any anchor in solid—"

"In solid mathematics? I should hope not. That is the difference between a mathematician and an anti-mathematician. Mathematicians get bogged down with numbers, probabilities, statistics, and cold, hard facts. It takes an anti-mathematician to grapple with the feelings, the emotions, the shadowy nuances and the residue of mystical clues that form the connective web of existence. It is a more nebulous process, but it yields an infinitely more detailed, textured and refined result. It allows us to isolate and embrace the soul."

"You can't ignore numbers."

"Yes I can and so can you. In fact, I'm sure you have done so countless times…pun intended."

"Such as?"

"Have you ever been at a bar and counted your drinks in order to assess whether or not you are having a good time?"

"Of course not. Well…at least not since college."

"Why not?"

"Because numbers—"

"Because numbers don't matter. That's what you were about to say."

"Yes."

"You don't calculate the number of ounces of alcohol that you consume?"

"No, that would take the fun out of it."

"Assuming all the fun had not been already been taken out by having to order drinks by the milliliter instead of the ounce," Earnest Prabhu added.

"Good point," Gaude agreed.

"And fun was the reason you went to the bar that evening, yes?"

"Yes, I suppose that's true," conceded Gaude. "So, you are on a one-man crusade to deliver us from the mathematicians?"

"Using the term 'one-man crusade' is a symptom of your dependency on mathematics. You again counted, didn't you?"

"Why are you so opposed to mathematics and mathematicians? Haven't they done a lot of good in this world?"

"The mathematicians first took over our finances, dictating the way ledgers are filled, interest is calculated, and invoices are to be completed. Then came physics, the mathematics of the physical universe. Then they moved on to chemistry, with its measurements of ingredients, the atomic weights, the molarity formulas, and so forth. Later they were to take biology captive, reducing us all down to numerical gene sequences. Even anthropology and sociology have been taken prisoner by statistical analysis. They've also taken over the arts. Architecture from day one, obviously. There is also music, a captive of mathematics as far back as the late Middle Ages. As soon as the Renaissance began, art became infested with the mathematics of perspective and balance, and ever so gradually succumbed, starting at the end of the nineteenth century, with the digitalization of painting with Seurat's pointillism, moving to Picasso's cubism, and culminating with the most purified mathematical artistic expressions of Mondrian's geometrics, all laid out in nice primary color boxes."

"I guess that there were no anti-mathematicians to oppose them?"

"There was a ray of hope, as the quantum physicists discovered a sub-atomic world that did not dance to the tune played by the great mathematical fiddlers. However, they refused to see the obvious—that anti-mathematics, not mathematics—is the solution to resolving the riddles of the foundation of existence. Accordingly, those scientists have labored in vain for decades to express their microscopic world in macroscopic mathematics. What they refuse to admit, or even contemplate, is that behind the quantum veil, in the dark place at the

347

very bottom of existence, is not a mathematical formula, but rather a sentiment."

"That's all very interesting," lied Gaude. "What is your goal?"

"Goodness."

"Like the goodness of the rock?"

"Yes, and how it impacts your soul and joins it with the soul of the rock, or with the goodness of God."

"How can you segue from a rock to God?"

"Because God segued from a man to a rock. Just ask Saint Peter."

"Conflating God and rocks seems like a wobbly theology."

"Yes, wobbly theology but solid anti-mathematics."

"Anti-mathematics will somehow locate God for us?"

"We don't need to locate God. Why should we? He isn't hiding."

"I don't see him," argued Gaude.

"You fail to see him because he is so obvious, so ubiquitous, so overwhelmingly omnipresent and enveloping that we cannot distinguish him. If you shove your face in the ground, you are faced with the world, but such a minuscule part that you cannot see the entirety of the world around you. This is not merely failing to see the forest for the trees. We are so deeply embedded in the wood that we cannot even see the tree. A grain of sand buried below the surface of the beach cannot see, much less comprehend or appreciate, the crashing surf or the magnificence of the ocean stretching out to the horizon."

"So, you at least worship God?"

"At least? Yes, at least. Without that, there is no hope."

"No hope for what?"

"No hope for redemption, no hope for salvation, no hope for reunification. You become what you worship."

"You think that by worshiping God that it will make you a god...or God?"

"No, 'become' has various nuanced meanings. When you consume a sandwich, it becomes part of you. I seek oneness with God, joinder with God, absorption by God, to become a part of God."

"One insignificant little particle of God?"

"While it is true that humility is the greatest of all virtues, and thus being a little particle is a matter of no shame, the fact is that there is no insignificant particle of God. After all, he is...God."

"Is that your ultimate goal? To determine the meaning of your life? It seems to have circled you back to a rather predictable philosophic tradition."

"Hmmm...*circled* back. Nice try, sneaking some geometry into the conversation."

"You're against geometry too?" asked Gaude.

"Actually, geometry is my great ally. I called you on it because you have no idea how truly redeeming it is."

"I wasn't—"

"In any event," said Prabhu, "I said that I know the meaning *of life*. I never said that I know the meaning of *my life*. Those who know what they want are either deliriously happy or suicidal. I am neither."

"It sounds like you are just as lost as the rest of humanity."

"In a sense, yes, and in another sense, no. You don't need to know where you are to know where you are going, and don't need to know where you are going to know where you are. The blind can lead the blind and the lost can find the lost. They always have."

"But blind is still blind."

"It's not what you see, but how you see it, even if you don't see it at all. That is the basis of all art, all philosophy, all understanding, all wisdom, and all salvation."

"That sounds like gibberish. What you are saying is that you know nothing."

"No, that's what Socrates said. I, on the other hand, do know something."

"What is that?"

"God is absolute good."

"That's it?"

"Yes, it's a solid working premise."

"That would make the devil absolute evil."

"No, that's not possible."

"Why?"

"Because absolute is the definition of infinity. According to mathematicians, if God is infinitely good, and the devil is infinitely evil, then they would be equal. Since, by definition, the devil is diametrically opposed to God, that would cancel the workings of the universe and end all existence. Do you see the trap that mathematics creates?"

"Perhaps good has a greater worth than evil."

"Congratulations, that is exactly what I study."

"Doesn't everyone already know that?"

"Everybody, or almost everybody, *hopes* that. Many *believe* that. Not many *know* that and those that do have a great deal of trouble articulating it. Describing something as holier or better does not necessarily mean that it can be specifically and objectively demonstrated to be positioned higher on a measured scale, but we try to articulate it somehow. There are writings by saints and mystics that hover around the subject and evoke ultimate truths, but no one has been able to capture the essence of the matter in an authentically non-objectified but accurate manner. No one has ever assembled a structured system of reckoning these ultimate truths by eschewing measurements in order to establish a unified anti-mathematical catechism."

"Maybe no one should."

"You would prefer the tyranny of mathematics?"

"How about neither mathematics nor anti-mathematics?"

"That has been tried. It's called ignorance. It is very popular, even to this day."

"Maybe humans were not destined to quantify good and evil."

"Maybe humans were not destined to fly, but thanks to the invention of aircraft, we've been doing it for more than a century. On balance, hurtling through the skies seems to have worked out quite well for the world. It is my life's mission to offer humanity a ticket on a transcontinental flight of spirituality."

"Then, if you can't measure, how do you distinguish something that is better or worse?"

"Faith."

"You've merely moved from philosophy to religion."

"Assuming that the faith I am referencing has a nexus to a deity of some sort, true. But what if I have faith in…faith itself?"

"That sounds awfully circular."

"Existence is circular. Birth, growth, procreation, deterioration, death, decay, rebirth…"

"Geometry again."

"Yes!"

"That sounds like reincarnation."

"The cycle doesn't need to be physical. Reincarnation means coming back in the flesh. Faith is the most ethereal of all concepts and need not manifest in concrete form."

"A spiritual cycle? Can spirits change? Evolve?"

"Spirit is the only thing that can eternally evolve. Incarnate evolution eventually leads to extinction."

"There are millions of species on this planet that are not extinct."

"And millions more that have gone extinct. Other than the earthworm, the cockroach, and the dragonfly, everything disappears into the mists of history. All flesh dies. It may be by accident, injury, war, pestilence, starvation, old age, or change in the environment. Half of life on earth is destined to be dinner for the other half of life. If all else fails, the sun will eventually explode. The end is inevitable, except for the souls."

Gaude paused, mentally meandering through Prabhu's labyrinthine lecture. Finally, he scratched his head and asked, "What's the difference between an anti-mathematician and a philosopher?"

"All western philosophers descend from—and aspire to be—Aristotle, and thus embrace mathematics and mathematical logic. Even the nihilists embrace mathematics by denying its existence and then using mathematical constructs to deny the existence of everything else. Anti-mathematics does not oppose or deny mathematics. It simply disregards and disdains mathematics."

"What about eastern philosophers?"

"Do I look like an eastern philosopher?"

"Yes, as a matter of fact, you do."

"Fine, you have me on that one."

"How did you get started on this?"

"Mathematics betrayed me."

"Betrayed you?"

"Betrayed me, defeated me, limited me, confined me. One day, I simply realized that the path to freedom was to stop the measurements, stop the counting, for goodness sake!"

"I can imagine that your theories did not endear you to the traditional academic community."

"Yes, I've been a pariah for quite some time. I was on the faculty of Cal Tech for five years when I collaborated on an article in *Defense* Magazine. It was bad enough that I associated myself with a publication that was part of the evil military-industrial complex. However, what my peers found to be altogether unforgivable was that I suggested that the nuclear armaments race was not merely mathematically logical, but aesthetically pleasing."

351

"That's...different."

"Weird, or perhaps unhinged, is what you were thinking. My co-author warned me that I would be fired within a month. She was wrong. It took three days."

"You should have listened to her."

"I did. She told me, in the words of William Faulkner, that I should move to the mountains and get stoned. I did exactly that. It was years later that I found out that the correct quote was 'the man who moves a mountain begins by carrying away small stones.' By then it was too late. I had discovered in my high-altitude cannabis-induced epiphany that I was destined to be the world's original anti-mathematician."

"You are the first?"

"That would require utilizing the number one."

"Right...Are there any others now? Have you developed a following?"

"Anti-mathematicians aren't allowed to have disciples."

"Says who?"

"The Anti-Mathematician Council."

"Of which you are the world's only member."

"You might not catch on fast, but you are good at catching on slowly."

"Then how do you expect the concept of anti-mathematics to be embraced by anyone else?"

"They must encounter it the same way I did. Katie Moscowicz must tell them to move to the mountains and get stoned."

"*Katie Moscowicz?*"

"Yes, Doctor Katherine Moscowicz. She was a visiting professor from Stanford, my co-author of the article I mentioned. 'Delusions of Armageddon in Post-Democratic World.' Do you know her?"

"Yes...no...I'm not...the name is so familiar..."

"It's a small world."

"Getting smaller all the time."

"Until it eventually disappears."

"You're not one of those prophets of doom who predict the end of the world?"

"Not in the way you are thinking. Any schoolboy can tell you that five billion years from now the sun will have fused its hydrogen into helium leading to the formation of heavier elements and thereupon result in the expansion of the sun into a red giant. It will thereupon absorb the earth. The end."

"I was talking about something more immediate."

"You are thinking of the end of you."

"How about the end of this investigation?"

"Ahhh...the end of the quest. Well, the end of you, the end of the quest, it's really one in the same, isn't it?"

"I'll take your word for it. After all, you're the anti-mathematician."

"So, you really want to know how it all ends?"

"Not with a bang, but a whimper."

"Truer words were never said, but that isn't the truth you are seeking."

"Really? So, what am I seeking?"

"You already know. You need to look back to where it all began. *Cherchez la femme.*"

⌘

"The connection is terrible," Doyle griped, yet grateful to hear even the faintest smidgeon of her voice. "It's probably this miserable burner."

"Where are you?" she asked.

"I'm on my way to San Francisco in a stolen car."

"Very funny. I'm on a lake in Maine. It's a miracle that there is any reception out here at all."

"Maine?"

"I had to come up to Boston for...some personal business. If you're in San Francisco, maybe we can meet there on the way to Hawaii."

"I can barely hear you."

"I said Hawaii. It's a very romantic place for a wedding and honeymoon."

"What about the cast of thousands who you planned to invite to our wedding in Atlanta?"

"That doesn't seem very important now."

"You faded out there. It could also be at my end. I'm using a cheap disposable cellphone that I got at a Seven-Eleven. It's worthless."

"It's priceless," responded Katie. "Voice will do just fine and it's wonderful to hear yours."

"Katie, I want you to know two things."

"I need you to know one."

"Okay, we take turns."

"Who's first?" Katie asked.

"That's right, Who's on first."

Despite herself, Katie found herself giggling. "Now I get it."

"Katie, my news isn't good."

"Mine is worse."

"I love you."

"*That's bad news?*" she answered incredulously.

"Only because of the second thing. I'm pretty sure that I'm dying."

"Oh God, don't say that."

"I'm so sorry Katie. It's true. My job deals with a lot of dead people. I know what it looks like." Doyle paused and then asked, "What did you want to tell *me*?"

"That I love you."

"And that's *also* bad news?" Doyle responded with as much playfulness as he could manage to muster.

"It couldn't possibly be worse. Goodbye, James."

Katie pushed the red button on her cellphone screen to terminate the call. She stood leaning on the rail of the bridge, looking out to the horizon over Kezar Lake. *I should be crying now*, she thought. *I really should be crying.*

What is wrong with me? her internal voice asked.

You're dying of goddamn cancer, for Krissake, you silly, stupid bitch! came the stern admonition from herself.

The cellphone rang in her hand. She glanced down at the empty circle that would have contained Doyle's photograph or avatar if he had been so inclined to load such foolishness on any phone. The cell continued to ring. Katie turned her gaze back to the sunset horizon and thought to herself, *This is a beautiful view.*

Yes, it is. Too bad the baby can't see it yet.

Maybe he will someday.

He?

Little Mort. You must admit, it's a poetic choice of name, considering our prognosis.
It's too early to get a test to tell if it is a he or a she.
I don't need a test. I know.
Yeah, well, let's keep that our little secret.
The phone ceased chiming for a moment and then began anew as Doyle persisted in his attempts to contact her.

"Goodbye, James," she whispered as she closed the phone app and switched to her playlist. Katie tapped her thumb on the screen several times until she arrived at the desired selection. She hit the play button to start Niʻihau Child's 'You're Still With Me.'

> *I should be blue*
> *Thinkin' of you*
> *When you're not right here*
> *But deep in my heart*
> *You never depart*
> *I can count on you, dear*
>
> *Darlin' you're still with me*
> *Don't care if you cross the sea*
> *No matter where you might be*
> *Darlin' you're still with me*

Katie released the cellphone and allowed it to plummet from the bridge down to its own watery grave in the river below. "Don't worry," she said while looking down at the spot where the cell had plunged into the lake, "I'll be seeing you soon."

Gaude and Watt stood in the line that had formed in front of the street vendor's mobile restaurant. "Y'know, I still have the winnings from Las Vegas," said Gaude. "Maybe we could treat ourselves to a really good steak dinner."

"As long as the steak is in a bowl of chili."

"Of course."

The customer in front of Watt finished making his order. Watt stepped forward, "I'll have a chilidog and a Shasta Wild Raspberry."

Gaude followed. "Calamari and chips and a Fort Ord Wheat."

As soon as they received their orders, Watt and Gaude went in search of park bench. As they turned past a public water fountain, Gaude glanced over to his right and saw a semicircle of automobiles perched on their sides surrounding a monolith composed of creosote pilings. "Ah! I think that I know what this is. I was beginning to worry that we had arrived at the one place in America that did not have a Malachi poem monumentally displayed for his adoring public."

"That would definitely mean we had come to the end of the line," agreed Watt.

They approached the tarry wall featuring a shield of planished copper, still ruddy and untouched by any patina of verdigris.

Aquarium

Billowing upon a pacific breeze,
Latin sails steal into the view
Of the cheerful otter and languid seal
As both regard the other new.
For profit they have crossed the world
In search of gold for Mother Spain,
Rough men without, brave hearts within,
For daring exploits upon the main.

Billowing upon a pacific breeze,
The coal black plumes of engines spew
From sardine armadas, set out again
Heedless of the fate of crew.
More profit for the overlords,
Flesh and fin bow to industry.
Lean men without, cold hearts within,
Exploiting those who farm the sea.

Billowing upon a pacific breeze,
The realtors' flags rich buyers woo
Into chic condos lined ashore
That cannery workers never knew.
They profit from the building boom
And sell the sunsets for a fee,
Smooth men without, no heart within,
Cleverly exploit the scenery.

Billowing upon a pacific breeze,
The cumulus lolls past endless blue.
The scientists wet census take
To husband the aquatic zoo.
Nonprofit is the righteous call
By the bottlers of this tourist bay,
Tanned men without, torn hearts within,
Exploit the life of Monterey.

—Reuben Malachi

⌘

    Thomas Chapele had not slept much since the bombing of the Brookguild building. The most deadly and devastating terrorist attack on New York since the disaster of 11 September 2001 impacted the entire city and the nation as well. The fact that Brookguild was across the street from the offices of *American Review,* and that Chapele had nearly been knocked off his office chair at the time of the explosion, left him anxious and fidgety still, these two days later. Chapele attempted to force his body to rest as he lay on the bed listening to his cellphone playlist. The late afternoon rain made a random patter on the window, which at any other time might have lulled him to sleep. Now it merely served to annoy and weary him further.

    The door buzzer harshly announced an unwelcomed visitor. Chapele arose, grabbed his frowsy oversized cardigan with the big pockets, and put it on over his t-shirt as he walked the short hall to the front door. He looked through the peephole and saw a sallow face beneath a FedEx hat. *Since when did they let the FedEx man up on the thirty-seventh floor?* asked Chapele's interior voice. Chapele answered his own silent question with a roll of the eyes to convey his response of *I dunno.* He opened the door and received a large padded envelope. Chapele checked the sending address.

    "Reuben," he announced to his empty foyer.

    Chapele pulled his cellphone out of the sweater pocket and entered Reuben's number. It was unlikely that the call would be received, or that Reuben would pick up, but Chapele felt obliged to make the effort. To his surprise, Malachi answered on the fifth ring.

    "Reuben, I received an envelope from you."

357

"Already?" Malachi asked. "Yes, of course already," he answered his own question. "Did you appreciate it? I won't go so far as to inquire whether you actually enjoyed it."

"I haven't opened it yet."

"Then why did you call me?"

"To thank you."

"Chapele, you are, and will always be, hopelessly *bourgeois*. How do you know that I didn't send you my soiled underwear?"

"I'm rather hoping that you did. A collection of Reuben Malachi artifacts would not be complete without your threadbare boxer shorts."

"You have inspired me. I shall be sending you another envelope tomorrow."

"Speaking of inspiration, are you closing in on the snark?"

"Not at all. The hunt is abandoned."

"What are you doing now?"

"Drinking."

"Besides drinking?"

"Imbibing."

"Aren't you writing?"

"No."

"You should write."

"I'm not a writer."

Chapele was almost physically thrown off balance by this reply and stuttered, "You...you... you've written...Jeeze, Reuben, what the hell are you talking about? What have you been doing your whole life?"

"That was then. This is now. Now, I'm not a writer."

"When did this all happen? You were writing when I left."

"That was then. This is today."

"What happened?"

"Yesterday happened."

"What about tomorrow?"

"You should know better than that," said Malachi. "There is no tomorrow. I haven't seen it. Have you? It's an illusion, an imaginary thing. A chimera."

"Reuben, I know that the bombing was hard on all of us."

"How many of those writers did you ever get drunk with? Get in a fistfight with over a woman? Spend a weekend in a jail cell with?"

"From the stories I heard, two of them were at your party."

"One of them a son of a bitch. The other a borderline saint."

"And you are going to miss them both."

"Yes, I am going to miss them both, especially the son of a bitch."

Chapele was not in the mood to digress. "So, you're no longer a writer? What are you now?"

"I am a man."

"That's it?"

"Isn't that enough?"

"Look, Reuben, I'm working my *tuchas* off to make you one of the best-known writers in the world."

"You just said *tuchas* like a pro. Is it me, or New York rubbing off on you?"

"The article should be coming out today. I'll send you a copy as soon as I pick it up at the office. How do I get it out to you?"

"A very large carrier pigeon should do it, or perhaps a moderately sized seagull."

"Seriously."

"Alright, you can send it to my other address."

"The one you refuse to tell me?"

"Yes. Send it to Asphodel Meadows, Kezar Lake, Maine."

"No other address?"

"That *is* the address."

"It's in a meadow?"

"Actually, it's a small island."

"I thought you said that your other home wasn't an island."

"I lied."

"You have a thing about islands?"

"If you have a problem with that, take it up with John Donne."

"When will you be heading up there?"

"In a month or so. I'll be there until spring."

"You actually spend the winter in Maine?"

"Of course."

"Of course," Chapele agreed, realizing who he was speaking with.

They exchanged goodbyes and Chapele then began to open the padded cardboard mailer. He removed what appeared to be an old style 'LP' record album. These seemed to dip in and out of favor with the hipster and retro crowd every few years, and Chapele had purchased a turntable while in college when vinyl had last been in vogue. "So, you cut another record," he observed to the invisible Malachi in his living room. Chapele had discovered during his research prior to venturing to South Carolina that his Lowcountry host had made a previous recording entitled *Songs That Offend Just About Everyone,* an appropriate—perhaps inspired—name. It certainly offended Chapele, who considered himself adequately jaded and immune to almost any obscenity after having lived in New York for the past three years.

The cover of the new record featured a parody of a Norman Rockwell painting of a clean scrubbed clan of twentieth century Anglo American middle class stereotypes gathering around a holiday table feast. The main course, on a large platter in the center of the table, was a starved African child with a baseball stuffed into his mouth. The title above the illustration was *Red Meat for Christmas.*

Chapele played the record. The recordings could not rightly be characterized as songs. He decided that they would be more properly described as unhinged and disjointed rants of violence, hatred, disease, sexual dysfunction and self-loathing with background instrumentation that vaguely approximated to some form of music. After suffering through the third manifesto of malevolence, Chapele left the room to attend to routine chores. He had intended to turn off the screeching, but prurient curiosity stayed his hand. As he was washing dishes in his small kitchen, his mind began drifting from one unfocused thought to another. Chapele was suddenly pulled out of his reverie as the fifth track began to play an expertly produced and beautifully performed rendition of 'Run-Around Sue.' He immediately recognized Reuben Malachi as the lead singer. The song had amazing energy and Reuben's arrangement gave the old standard a depth that had never before been achieved. The song faded out and there was a silence of almost a minute on the record. Just as he was about to check the needle for a possible malfunction, the stereo speaker came to life.

"I hope you enjoyed that, you pathetic putz."

The remaining four recordings were more screaming drivel.

Chapele returned to the small galley kitchen and popped a pod of Colotenango Supreme into his coffee maker. As the dark fluid began to fill his mug, he felt the buzz of his cellphone in his sweater pocket. He received a text message from his senior editor:

> < just finished hardcopy run—heading out door
> even as we speak—as i text—online post will be up
> in 15 min—didn't expect the bomb you dropped >

360

Chapele texted back:

> < Thx sounds great…bomb? Not funny >

His editor texted back:

> < sorry my bad—forgot myself frantic day—
> anyway, good job, kojak >

Chapele replied:

> < Kojak? Don't get it >

The response arrived a few seconds later:

> < detective old rerun tv show when I was a kid—u
> know, the charleston blackmail dead judge story >

Chapele looked at the screen and re-read it. He felt the urge to shake the cellphone but knew this would not change the text he had just received. He went to his home computer and opened the internet. The screen, as always, defaulted to *American Review*. His story had not yet been posted. Chapele picked up his cell and texted:

> < Can u pull the article? >

The response came thirty seconds later:

> < y? >

Chapele:

> < Long story >

Editor:

> < not too long, 4500 words ok >

Chapele:

> < Not what i mean…can u pull it? I didn't write that >

Editor:

> < hey SAS i didn't write it >

Chapele:

> < Story was hacked stuff added...NOT GOOD >

Editor:

> < sorry chappie, magz are out the door—showtime! >

Chapele went back to his computer and checked the website. Nothing. He refreshed the screen. Nothing. He refreshed again. Again. Again. Again. Again. Again.

Finally, the story link appeared with his byline. It was larger and more prominently displayed than anything previously authored and attributed to him. *Of all the luck*, he thought. *Please God, don't let it be.*

Chapele clicked on the link and the article opened. *Reuben Malachi, Crackhead of American Verse.* He began scanning through the article. It had been edited somewhat, but it was the article he wrote. He then arrived at the top the third page.

"Oh, God! No!"

He tried to force himself to read slowly, but his obstinate eyes kept rushing forward, impaling themselves on the salacious truth. His silent innerself continued the litany of *Oh, God! Oh, God! Oh, God! Oh, God! Oh, God!*

He kept reading.

Oh, God! Please, no!

Chapele reached down into his sweater pocket to make a call to Malachi. His hand arrived at the phone, but as he started to pull it out of the pocket, he was halted by the other him who was just as horrified by the article. *No, you can't. There is no way that you can explain this.*

The external body of Chapele continued to read, shaking his head gently back and forth in order to negate the reality of the words on the screen. *Who wrote this? Who wrote this?*

I didn't write this! The response from himself was equally emphatic.

I don't know! I don't know! His eyes started darting to the top of the page to read again, as if to check that they had not been deceived the first time.

I can't just do nothing. I have to call him.

His otherself tried to maintain some sense of composure, some semblance of rational objectivity. *You can't tell him on the phone. You just can't.*

He tried to bargain. *Text?*
The rebuke was immediate. *Text? Are you freekin' crazy?*
He conceded the point. *Okay! Okay! I gotta go.* Chapele broke the stalemate and sent a message to his editor at *American Review*.

< Heading back to Beaufort SC...2 days at most...
don't freak, I'll meet the next deadline...promise >

⌘

Gaude looked up from the browser on his cellphone. "There are two fires."
"Really? Where are they?"
"The first is Truth or Consequences, New Mexico."
"That's got to be it."
"It definitely sounds like our arsonist's perverse sense of humor—if you can call it that."
"Okay, let's see about flights."
Gaude began tapping on the cellphone screen. "Truth or Consequences actually has a local airport, but I don't give great odds as to catching a flight there. It's a two-hour drive from El Paso and a little more than that if we drive from Albuquerque."
"Okay, no real difference. Pick the earliest flight you can find. A two-hour drive isn't that much and if we happen to luck out and catch a puddle-jumper to Truth or Consequences just as we arrive, so much the better."
"Sounds like a plan."
"Let's get going."
"Let me finish my beer."
"Fine. By the way, what was the other location?"
"Other location for what?"
"The other church fire."
"Oh, yeah. That was at Panama, Idaho."
"Panama?"
"Uh-huh."
"Earnest Prabhu—Doctor Prabhu—wore a Panama hat."
"Another hat clue? Like the fez back in Savannah?"
"At least we know it's a clue."
"No, we don't. This time it may be a ruse. This time we could

be imagining things."

"How many times have these clues actually mislead us?"

"A few times."

"No, a few times we misinterpreted the clues."

"So, you think that we're chasing an honest psychopath?"

"As honest as an arsonist can be, but the real point is that he wants us to follow him. He needs for us to stay engaged."

"Why?"

"Because he's doing this for us."

"What?"

"Yes, I'm here."

"No, you know what I mean. At least we don't have to travel all the way down to the Republic of Panama."

"Let's not cross anything off the list of possibilities quite yet," joked Watt.

"Panama...there's a song by Van Halen named 'Panama.' Gottlieb Eucalyptus mentioned Van Halen."

"What do we know about Van Halen?"

"I'm pretty sure he was from California."

"Who's the 'he' this time?"

"Eddie Van Halen."

"You mean that Van Halen is named after Van Halen?"

"Sometimes it works out that way."

"Maybe it's a reference to the entire band."

"They're probably all from California too."

"That doesn't help. Panama is in Idaho, not California."

"What would Van Halen have to do with burning churches?"

"Early in their career, they replaced lead singer David Lee Roth with Sammy Hagar."

"You're an expert on Van Halen?"

"I grew up on Van Halen and...Van Cliburn..."

"Van Cliburn?"

Gaude reacted with mild shock and gentle confusion. "I...I don't know. It just came out. I have no idea why I said that..."

Watt arched his eyebrows and made a comic frown, "Okay, maybe too many economy class flights. You were saying something about lead singers?"

"Right," Gaude continued, trying to compose himself. "Remember back in Memphis, Nebraska?"

"Yes and no. I remember Memphis, Nebraska. I don't remember Van Halen in Memphis, Nebraska."

"No, Hagar. Our suspect and principal quarry wanted to order a black wool Haggar suit."

"You remain the reigning champion of solving clues after-the-fact. What good does any of this do for us? What happened to Truth or Consequences?"

"It seems to me that Truth or Consequences is exactly what is going on. We have to choose between two possibilities—"

"You're right. We're being directed to both."

"Should we split up?"

"No, separating us is the oldest trick in the book."

"That's definitely saying something, considering how old the book is."

"Okay, we're going to have to make a choice."

"What do you think?"

Gaude massaged his temples in frustration. "I have absolutely no idea. I'm grasping at straws."

"And you criticize *me* for playing with them."

The Advisors

I know that you are listening in on me.

That is simply not true, gently protested Sister Mary Margaret. *I was in prayer.*

No doubt praying for me, the hopeless sinner.

We are all sinners, my dear, but none of us is hopeless as long as there is hope. We both know that.

I beg to differ. I revel in my hopelessness. I don't need your prayers.

Is that why you are reaching out?

I am not reaching out.

You merely do not realize that you are reaching out. Grace, I know that you are in trouble. You are moving into very dangerous territory.

I've spent my life there. It is very familiar territory.

This is different. They are watching you.

They've always been watching me.

It is a different 'they' this time.

I suppose the new 'they' are very scary, yes? Demons intent on imprisoning my soul, perhaps? Maybe it's the devil himself.

Please do not be facetious. The devil and his minions are very real.

You and your church created an illusory devil to scare people into the arms of a non-existent god.

God is also very real—more real than reality itself. You can occupy your hours denying God, but he will affirm you. You can spend your days hiding from God, but he will find you. You can waste your life fleeing from God, but he will catch you.

None of those days have arrived yet and thus far your god has failed to make an appearance. Seeing is believing and I don't believe in your invisible friend.

We walk by faith and not by sight.

Thanks, but I'm not going to trust the blind to lead me. I will never have that much faith.

It does not take much. A tiny mustard seed worth of faith will move a mountain. With God, all things are possible, and our faith in God gives us that immeasurable power.

Those are merely words.

Mere words created the universe. Fiat Lux: Let there be light.

Glib answers.

One person's glib answer is another's profound insight.

How do you tell that one person from the other?

One goes to heaven. The other does not.

Are you trying to frighten me?

No, most certainly not.

Good, because it won't work.

I am trying to call you to repentance, to redemption, to holiness.

That won't work either.

We are all called to holiness, even you. Pray to the Blessed Mother.

The blessed mother? I know that you're not talking about my mother.

The Virgin Mary is the mother of us all.

No one would confuse me with the Virgin Mary and no one is about to convert me into her.

More's the pity. Believe me, nothing would give me greater pleasure than to be able to say, 'Hail, Grace, full of Mary…'

Twenty-Three: Panama

While walking the dog it begins to snow. It had snowed the day before, and the day before that, but this morning the snow is different. The snow doesn't come down in flakes. Instead, it looks like tiny balls of styrofoam. He imagines that a distant styrofoam factory had exploded and sent debris flying in every direction as far as the horizon. The new snow looks different even while on the ground. It is a different color white that the other snow. Is this a strange, unique sort of snow? He imagines that he has made a brilliant scientific discovery—they would name the species of snow after him. Alright, he thought, so it's ridiculous. There must be hundreds of different types of snow. Didn't the Inuits of Greenland have a dozen separate words for snow, each describing a different type? He thought that he was used to southern snow, not the stuff here in Maine.

He looks to the...north? He isn't sure. He briefly loses his sense of direction, something that rarely happens to him. Perhaps to the east. The sky is gray. No, make that gunmetal blue. Same to the south. Cut across the sky in an almost perfectly straight diagonal line was a river of lighter blue sky. White clouds bordered one side of the skyriver, but not both. It continued to snow.

Gunmetal blue. He always liked that color. The color of angry power. The color of a storm to come. The color of his eyes.

An indicator light appeared on the dashboard accompanied by a chime. "What's that?" asked Watt.

"Low tire pressure warning," explained Gaude. "Don't worry, it takes a while for a tire to go flat." Two minutes later, the indicator chimed again. "On second thought, time to worry. The pressure is going down fast. It appears that we have a small puncture."

"Should we change the tire?"

"We could do that, unless we can find a service station first."

"What's the closest town?"

"There is no closest town."

"We must be next to something."

"That's debatable. According to the map, we're just west of the Duck Valley Indian Reservation," said Gaude, consulting his cellphone.

"So, does that have a town?"

"I don't actually see any towns on the reservation or anywhere near the reservation."

"Do any of those magic internet apps tell you if there is a lone gas station sitting in the lonely desert just where lonesome travelers might need it?"

"Yes, but I don't see anything."

"What about that?"

"What about what?"

"That!" Watt gestured ahead of them.

Gaude looked up from his cellphone and saw in the distance a sign for a Red Crown gasoline station. "It's not open," declared Gaude dismissively.

"It looks open," argued Watt as they drew closer. "There are a couple of cars in front."

"It can't be open."

"Why not?"

"Because it can't."

"You've brought quibbling to a new low level."

"Maybe it's a museum."

"Maybe it's a museum that changes tires," retorted Watt.

"Fine, have it your way. Besides, the parking lot is a convenient place for us to change the tire instead of the side of the road."

Upon entering the parking lot, the partners could see that the Red Crown was a fully functioning service station. Watt pulled the DeLorean up to the left service bay and then the two exited the car and entered the front office. Two customers were sitting in the waiting area, a wizened pensioner wearing a crimson ballcap and a younger man in an amber colored windbreaker. Music came from a century-old Marconi radio standing in the corner. It was playing 'Life in the Fast Lane' by the Eagles.

"Heyahdoin," greeted the man behind the counter.

"We have a flat tire. We were hoping you could repair it."

"We'll take a look," the man responded cheerfully.

Watt turned to Gaude. "I'm going next door for a snack."

"I'll pass. What happens if they don't have chili?"

The man at the counter overheard Gaude's question and offered to Watt, "You lookin' for chili? Order the jackrabbit stew. It's basically chili."

"Why don't they call it jackrabbit chili?" asked Gaude.

"Because the guy who owns the diner likes to call it jackrabbit stew."

Watt left the office in pursuit of the local misnomer chili while Gaude took a seat on a chrome and naugahyde chair next to the younger man who seemed to be slightly agitated and kept glancing over to the plateglass window that permitted the customers to watch the goings-on in the service bays. Gaude picked up a twelve-year-old copy of *Reader's Digest*. After a few minutes of reading, he glanced up from page thirty-six. His eyes met those of the elderly veteran wearing the ballcap featuring a unit crest from the 85th Battalion of the 203rd Field Artillery. The old man regarded him with a crooked smile. "Bet you think you're in the middle of goddamn nowhere, don'tcha?" asked the acerbic octogenarian.

"Seems to be."

"Well, son, you're wrong. This place is a hell of a lot lonelier than nowhere. Why're you here?"

"Passing through."

"Most folks are passin' through. You've already passed."

"Maybe I'll stay."

"The folks who stay here are the folks a'ready been here."

Gaude made a noncommittal and meaningless nod back to the ancient across the room and then turned his attention to the man behind the counter. "How long will it take to fix the tire?"

"Assuming it's just a plug, about twenty minutes. That is…" the man said with a devious grin, "…depending on the waiting list," as he gestured to the row of mostly empty seats in the room. "On the other hand, if the hole is too big, we're gonna need to replace the tire with a new one."

"How long will it take to put on a new tire?" asked Gaude.
"About twenty minutes."
"Depending on the waiting list."
"Yep," answered the man at the counter.

Gaude put down the magazine, rose from the chair, and stepped out of the side door onto an unpaved alleyway. He then took a desultory stroll to the narrow asphalt ribbon that qualified in those parts as a highway. He walked along the road looking out at the expansive bleakness. The air was cold and dry and left a metallic taste in his mouth. As he circled back, he saw neatly printed in chalk on the side of an abandoned videotape rental store:

He was a man with a future
She was a woman with a past

This had to be a clue. Gaude stared at the message but could not force a single thought or association. He was tired. The travel, the destruction, the desecration, and now the landscape sapped his strength and will. Gaude walked over to the rusted hulk of a 1938 Ford sedan and leaned against its giant fender. His head drooped and he nagged himself. *Think, think, think.* This merely exacerbated the mental block and he stared down at his shoes in weary dejection. Gaude finally surrendered to the brick wall of forgetfulness and walked back to the garage. The old man was still sitting in the waiting room. The younger customer was nowhere to be seen.

"Well, sir, looks like you're gonna need a whole new tire," announced the man behind the counter.
"How much is that going to cost?"
"A lot less than calling a taxi from Boise."
"Alright, go ahead and put on the new tire. You said that it would take twenty minutes."
"That's a fact."
"Fine, I'll wait."
"You sure will. We're gonna need to order the tire to get shipped here. We don't have none in stock that fits your car."
"You just said it would take twenty minutes!"
"That's right, twenty minutes to install the tire. It'll take considerably longer for the tire to arrive before we can start installing it."
"In that case, just use the spare tire."

"We did, for a fellah who just drove off two minutes ago. He asked me to thank you. Said it was a godsend."

"He stole my tire?"

"No, I sold it to him."

"You stole my tire?"

"I wouldn't say that."

"I would."

"Well, if you're accusing me of theft, that would make things mighty complicated. First, you would need to call the tribal police. They don't answer the phone very often, so you'll have to keep on trying—for a few days, at least. After that, it generally takes a few weeks for them to get around to questioning any witnesses."

"A few weeks?"

"Eventually, they'll come over and impound the car."

"Impound the car? Why? I'm not the one who's done anything wrong."

"Evidence. They can't let the evidence drive down the road and disappear."

"That's outrageous." Gaude pondered for a moment. "How can they impound a car with a flat tire?"

"I would have wondered about that too, but last year I saw first-hand how they do it. The deputy walks up to the car and takes a long look at the flat tire. He then gets into the car, turns on the ignition, and puts the car into drive."

"I don't understand."

"He runs the car on the rim. Beats the hell out of it, of course. Pretty much destroys the shock absorbers too. Want me to order a new rim and shocks for you while I'm at it?"

"No."

"Just tryin' to help."

⌘

Weston Chao was annoyed. "Mackey, who changed my calendar for this morning?"

Chao's executive assistant, Ian McCarthy, spread his hands in a gesture of helplessness. "I received a text from Eugene Mueller saying that he had something urgent to discuss and needed to meet with you immediately."

"What could NBQ want to talk about that could be described as urgent?" Chao had more than once held up the National Bank of Quebec for gentle ridicule as the scared little old lady of world finance and could not imagine what their diffident chief executive officer would need to discuss at such short notice.

"I'm clueless. He seemed rather insistent that he meet with you at exactly 7:50 a.m. and that the meeting be conducted in private. Would you like me to go back and ask for something more granular?"

Chao considered this for a moment and then decided that courtesy demanded that he accept the request without putting his fellow banker through the third degree. As the CEO of the world's largest financial institution, Citi-Morgan-Chase, he was not beholden to smaller banks like NBQ. After thirty years in the business, however, he had learned how important it was to accommodate potential allies and avoid snubbing potential enemies. "No, Mack, don't bother. I'll see him."

"I thought Mueller was a late riser."

"So most of us were led to believe. I can't imagine why he would need to see me on short notice, but I suppose that my curiosity will be sated in a half hour."

Chao resumed his review of the pre-market activity and then turned his attention to the DAX. *What the hell do those maniacs in Frankfurt think that they are doing?* he wondered. Siemens was up to something, but it did not make any sense. They had started toying with BASF, then Daimler, now Allianz Insurance. It had the appearance of a ham-handed manipulation of the market, but there was something more—although he hoped less—to all of it. *It can't be*, he thought, *not after the bloodbath of their bribery scandal.* No, the current CEO of Siemens, Wolf Larsen, was squeaky clean. Since the last time Siemens was caught red-handed and prosecuted by a half dozen countries, it had remained on the straight and narrow. He gently shook his head in dismay as he continued examining the data on the screen. He was sure that this was something else, but he just could not see.

McCarthy entered the office and broke Chao's financial reverie. "Mueller has entered the building."

"Let him come up on my lift." Chao, born in Hong Kong, still retained a few select 'British-isms,' as he called them, and referring to an elevator as a 'lift' was one of the most ingrained examples of the habit. Three minutes later, Eugene Mueller stepped out of the private elevator. He wore a Westmancott bespoke suit, Tom Ford dress shirt,

374

Brioni paisley tie, and Ferragamo shoes. Chao, who could easily buy and sell Mueller a dozen times over, had little patience for such ostentation. Chao owned a car in his garage that cost appreciably less than the clothes in Mueller's closet and was proud of that fact. Chao stood up from his chair and greeted his guest with an obligatory smile.

Mueller did not waste any time with niceties. "I was told to give you this envelope."

"What's in it?"

"I don't know."

"Then why should I open it?"

"I don't know that either."

"Then I would naturally ask, why are you here?"

"I'm discharging a debt."

Chao permitted himself to indulge in a slight scowl. He accepted the envelope and opened it. He pulled out a sheaf of photographs. He recognized them immediately, although he wished he had not. They were taken decades ago when he was young and reckless, but even with the passing of time, he knew the devastating effect they could have in the wrong hands—anyone's hands, that is, other than his own.

"Are you blackmailing me?"

"No, I told you, I have nothing to do with the contents of that envelope. I assume, however, that whatever you received was unpleasant, as I've already been on the receiving end of that kind of arrangement. Today, I'm merely a delivery boy."

"What do you expect me to do?"

"I have no idea. I'm only following orders. I have nothing to do with this. You must believe me. I'm sure that I was chosen because I could manage to get a meeting with you. Wes, I am so sorry, but I didn't have any choice."

"I understand," said Chao quietly, now returning the photographs to the envelope.

"I must go now. I was told to leave immediately at 7:55 a.m."

"You were told by whom? Gene, who is doing this?"

"I'm sorry, Wes. I'm so sorry. I don't really know and I really can't tell you anything. I must go now." Mueller turned to exit by the private elevator and pressed the call button for the door. The doors opened immediately, revealing another man wearing a gray overcoat and sunglasses who had been waiting to enter. The uninvited stranger walked out as Muller passed to step in. Mueller pushed the button for the ground floor and offered a helpless and remorseful glance at his banking colleague as the elevator doors closed upon him.

"Who are you?"

"Your tourguide."

"Tourguide?" the banker responded incredulously.

"Yes," the man said as he approached with a steady and unblinking gaze. "I'll be hosting you on a fun-filled permanent vacation to hell." As he continued to move forward towards Chao, the visitor reached into his jacket and extracted a Sig Sauer P226, leveling it to the other man's forehead as he finished crossing the room. "Sit down."

Chao immediately complied.

"Take out the photographs, one by one."

The banker would have considered this a strange request, but with a handgun pointed at his face, such musings did not come naturally. Chao did as he was ordered.

"Put the photographs back in the envelope."

Once again, Chao did as instructed and then placed the envelope on the desk.

"Stand up."

Finally, Chao felt compelled to engage the gunman. "*What* is this all about? Are you here for money?"

"Take two steps back."

Once again, his mind filled with a mixture of fear and exasperation, Chao obeyed the man with the gun. He glanced back, seeing that he was a few centimeters from the floor-to-ceiling plate glass window.

The intruder checked the Omega Perpetual watch on his left wrist and waited for the sweep of the second hand to complete a revolution. "Okay, let's get down to business," the intruder said casually as he holstered the handgun. He then began to turn around, as if to retrieve a chair. Chao started to regain his composure and began calculating how much it would cost to pay off what obviously was evolving into a hostage situation.

The man now suddenly spun around and delivered a vicious flying kick to Chao's chest. His body smashed against the shattering glass. The last thing Chao saw was his executioner looking down at him. He felt himself falling backwards.

Into darkness.

The assassin moved quickly to the north side of the office and approached a large framed copy of Kandinsky's *Point and Line to Plane*. He reached to the left side of the wall panel and found the small release mechanism recessed there. He pushed it down and swung the panel forward, revealing the emergency escape stairwell. He exited and closed the panel behind him. After descending three floors, he removed his sunglasses, took off the topcoat, folded it over his right arm, and then pushed open the door onto the hallway of floor forty-four. A few meters down the hallway, he arrived at an elevator. When the doors opened, he joined a half-dozen occupants in the ride as they cast down their eyes or stared into a non-existent distance listening to the music being pumped into the stainless-steel cab: 'Dirty Deeds Done Dirt Cheap' by AC/DC.

The rider standing next to him was an older man with a crewcut of white hair, wearing a rumpled brown tweed jacket and carrying a leather saddlebag. He surprised the professional hit-man—who as a professional was never surprised—by addressing him directly. "Going out for some fresh air? You look like you could use some."

As the doors opened onto the main floor lobby, it was apparent that some crisis had occurred from the shouts, screams, and sound of approaching sirens. The other passengers exited into the frantic pandemonium as the man with the saddlebag looked over his shoulder at the remaining occupant of the elevator car. As he departed, the older man offered a typical American farewell gesture of pointing his fingers as to mimic a handgun. With a serene smile, he said, "See you in hell."

The hitman pushed the button for the next floor below. A minute later, he was walking into the building's food court. He moved in a deliberate yet unhurried gait of professional restraint past the varied venues until arriving at Big Apple Hero. He casually swiveled behind the counter of the sandwich shop and pushed past the swinging double doors into the kitchen. He was immediately confronted by an employee wearing a dirty white cap and a dirtier apron. The interloper flashed the credentials of an Inspector of the New York City Health Department and demanded to see the refuse bin behind the building. The employee wordlessly pointed to the back of the kitchen and let the official pass. He entered a short stairwell up one flight that brought him to the street level exit at the rear of the building. He then casually crossed the street and began walking to the subway half a block away. He glanced up at a billboard on the building ahead of him.

There are many choices in life

Conversion isn't one of them

**The Great Conversion
Get ready for the inevitable**

The cellphone in his shirt pocket vibrated silently. He pulled it out and answered. "Yes?"

"Are his fingerprints on the envelope?" the caller asked.

"Yes, he was holding it when I came in. I also had him handle the individual photographs."

"Well done. We have another job for you."

The hitman was still feeling rattled by the encounter with the saddlebag man in the elevator, but this news helped to distract him from such annoyances. "It seems to be my lucky day."

"We need you here in D.C. to take care of some loose ends. Can you get here tonight?"

"Yes. Will I need someone to...*introduce*...me?"

"No, that won't be necessary this time."

"Fine. How many loose ends do I need to handle?"

"Two."

"Two? As I said, it is my lucky day."

"You can pick up your instructions in the box at Union Station."

"Accompanied by my fee?"

"With our compliments."

"A pleasure as always."

He pressed the button to terminate the call and began walking down the subway steps. *See you in hell*, he heard replayed in his mind, as he descended into the darkness of the underground station.

⌘

"Is the car ready?" asked Watt as he entered the service station waiting area.

"No, and it won't be ready for quite some time. It appears that we are stranded."

"Stranded?"

"In the middle of nowhere."

The old man on the opposite side of the room suddenly came back to life. "A whole lot lonelier than nowhere!" he exclaimed.

"What's the problem?" Watt asked Gaude as he sat down beside his partner.

"They don't have a tire in stock."

"Couldn't they use the—?"

"They sold our spare to someone else."

"That was certainly resourceful."

"Yes, it was."

"And charitable as well. Reminds me of Saint Martin of Tours. In his youth, he was a Roman soldier who encountered a beggar freezing on a lonely road. Martin drew his sword and cut his military cloak in half to share with the man. It is said that Jesus visited Martin that night in his sleep. When he awoke, Martin found that his cloak had been restored to its full size."

"In that case, I look forward to the miraculous restoration of our tire as God's recompense for our generous gift to the guy who drove off with our spare."

"That's the spirit!" agreed Watt enthusiastically, as he now got up and approached the man behind the counter. "My colleague tells me that we are in a predicament."

"Yep, you're up the creek in a place that ain't got no creeks," the man replied with a sly grin.

Watt reached into his pocket and removed a business card, which Gaude knew would be offered facedown. As he handed it over, Watt smiled and said, "I'm wondering if you might help us find a way to navigate through this crooked path." The man read the card carefully and then his face suddenly blanched. He left the room muttering to himself as Watt returned to the chrome and naugahyde chair and smiled with calm assurance at Dan Gaude.

"What's going on?"

"Yes, Watt is. Just wait."

"Wait for what?"

"Yes."

"You're doing it again."

"Here we go," said Watt as he gestured at the plate glass view into the service bay where the man from the counter was engaged in a heated argument with another employee. They suddenly stopped, slowly turned, and realized that their contretemps had been observed. The counter man now walked back towards the waiting area, entered the door, and approached Watt.

"It just so happens that you are in luck. We found a tire in the back of the garage that will fit your car."

"Excellent! Thank you!" exclaimed a beaming Bill Watt.

"We'll have you on your way in half an hour."

"Or perhaps twenty minutes," chimed in Gaude.

The man nodded sheepishly in capitulation. "Or perhaps twenty minutes." He then returned to the counter and pretended to busy himself with something.

Gaude leaned over to Watt and whispered, "Alright, it's time to teach me that card trick."

"You're not ready."

"Why not?"

"Because you still call it a card trick, that's why."

Twenty-one minutes later, Gaude was behind the steering wheel traveling north on the indifferently paved road. A sign appeared in the distance.

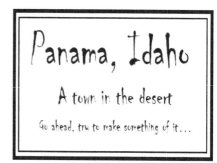

Panama, Idaho

A town in the desert

Go ahead, try to make something of it...

"This is the place."

"So it seems."

"The news reports weren't all that illuminating about the exact address of the fire."

"Good, we can ask someone. Perhaps a friendly townsperson," said Watt.

They drew closer to a cluster of buildings to the right. Gaude saw a sign on one of the buildings indicating that it was an animal clinic and noticed that a tall woman had just exited the front door. "There's your friendly townsperson."

"Yes, she does look friendly," replied Watt, ignoring Gaude's sardonic tone. Gaude pulled the car into a parking space as Watt rolled down his window and signaled to the woman. "Can you give us directions?"

"Sure," she said. "Turn around and go back the way you came and nobody will be the wiser that you accidentally stumbled into Panama, Idaho."

"Not quite as friendly as you were hoping, it appears," whispered Gaude.

Watt opened the car door and stepped out. "I was hoping to get some directions about how to travel into town, not out of it."

"Yeah, I know," said the woman, suddenly breaking out in a broad smile. "I was just pulling your leg. My television went out of whack two nights ago and I'm trying to make up for the lack of entertainment."

Gaude emerged from the driver's seat. "We're looking for the church that burned yesterday."

"Oh, the Bahá'í. Sure, I know them well. I attend their services occasionally. I'm not Bahá'í, but then again, I'm not particular."

"Why not?"

"I guess that I'm just a wandering Catholic."

"That almost sounds like a separate sect."

"It is."

"Does the Pope know?" asked Gaude with a playful grin.

"He should. I suspect that he's a wandering Catholic too."

"I'm afraid the nuns neglected to mention that when I went to school."

"You were probably too busy ogling Sally Osborne to pay attention to Sister Frances Angela."

"Wait a minute—" Gaude started to protest.

"But you were the shy one at that age, weren't you? It was the kid who sat in the desk behind her that caught her attention."

"What?"

"Of course, that was years before Sally ran off with a saxophone player."

"Hey, what the heck—?"

"Which is ironic, since she never had you pegged as a musician. You kept your piano lessons secret from your friends, didn't you?"

"Alright, that's enough of that!"

Watt cut off the conversation with a scolding look at Gaude as he offered the woman one of his cards. "I'm Bill Watt. My partner here is Dan Gaude."

"The name's Darling O'Dell. I'm the Doctor Doolittle in these parts, except for the fact that there are a substantial number of animals that need medical attention in the area, so that probably qualifies me to be called Doctor Dooalot."

"Pleased to meet you Doc," said Watt. "Not that God's furry creatures aren't fascinating, but we're a bit more interested in learning something about the Bahá'í."

"They are nice folks and very open-minded. In fact, when you get there, take a look at the statue in front of the temple—or at least, what remains of the temple. You might think it looks a lot like Saint Francis. That's because it *is* Saint Francis. I donated it a few years ago and they put it right in front of their place of worship."

"You're a big fan of Saint Francis?"

"Sure, why not? I'm a veterinarian."

"I suppose that now the Bahá'í church is also a fan of Saint Francis."

"Like I said, they're open-minded. They're not afraid of what they'll find in the search."

"The search?"

"To find something, you must be willing to look in new places and walk down untrod paths. There are those who search for a path to climb up the mountain, while there are others who search for a hole to hide. There are those who search for solutions while there are others who search for problems. There are those that search for truth, and others who search for an excuse. Everyone is searching."

"Well, I still haven't found what I'm looking for," said Gaude with a sly wink.

Darling O'Dell chuckled. "I suppose that Bono and his buddies in U2 forgot that most people don't know what they are searching for in the first place."

"What about the people who do know what they're searching for? That still doesn't guarantee that they will find it."

"True, but they're sure to find something, even if it is disappointment." O'Dell gave the pair an examining once-over and said, "From the looks of you, I'd say that you two are searchers."

"Hopefully, we'll be the ones who find something other than

disappointment."

"You can count on that," said O'Dell. "You'll get to your destination. Just stay on the path."

"Yes, but there are a lot of different paths," responded Gaude.

"Do you think that God cares which path you take to get to him?"

"I think...I don't really know."

"Remember the story of the prodigal son? How the young man who took his inheritance, turned his back on his family, and left home to squander it in a life of sinful indulgence?"

"Yes."

"When he came back home, destitute and humbled, his father saw him at a distance and his heart leapt for joy. He ran down the road to greet his son and embraced him warmly. Do you recall anything in the story that recounts how the father cross-examined the son about which routes he took to return back home?"

"No, that—"

"Didn't matter?"

"I suppose that it didn't."

"Even if everyone in the world were a member of the same religion, do you really believe that we would all be on the same path? We may belong to a community of faith, but the road to salvation is not followed single-file, no matter how much direction or encouragement we might get along the way. Christ told his followers that they would each have to carry a cross, not that they would join in carrying one cross together. Even if you follow the same road that others have traveled before, you will find on your particular journey that detour signs have been recently been posted, bridges suddenly closed, mountain passes blocked. We can worship together, but we arrive at the gates of heaven by ourselves. We climb up different paths together. We walk down the same path alone."

"I've heard that somewhere before."

"Probably while walking on a path."

"Something like that," Gaude agreed. "You make it sound very lonely."

"Not exactly. You will always encounter others during the search. There are friends, family, and pets, of course."

"Pets?"

"You don't think a veterinarian is going to leave out pets, do you?" she asked incredulously.

"No, I suppose not," Gaude agreed with a chuckle.

"God also gives us hints—travel tips, I suppose you could call them. Some people refer to them as miracles. They come in all shapes and sizes, large and small, animal, vegetable, and mineral. They show up at unexpected times and places. Take the poem, for instance…"

"The poem?"

"Yeah, the poem. When you first drove up, I assumed you had come to see it. The thing showed up out of nowhere a week ago and it's been the talk of the town. When you live in a desert town without much else to do, talking is what we do best. Lemme show you." O'Dell led them around the corner of the building to a whitewashed cinderblock wall with anodized metal letters.

En Medio Mundo

At the center of the world
Freight floats by tropic hills,
Amidst flutter of greenparakeets
And greenyankee dollar bills.

In a country of one city,
In a land of mixtos blood,
Two continents converge/divide
As lock waters purge and flood.

Clean, but for the dirt,
Rich, but for the poor,
Come to the ciudad of vice
For a virgin to adore.

Slow, but for the speed,
Sad, but for the joy,
Mañana, sir, I'll have it then,
Pero tengo nada hoy.

Atlantico y Pacifico
On a compass pushed askew.
A serpent bridge of jungle
Five hundred years still new.

A speeding schoolbus canvas,
Past mango trees in fruit,
The native crones sell molas bright
To tourists from Dubuque

Dry, but for the rain,
Safe, but for the crime,
A cut above, a cut below,
Where there's always, never, time.

Cheap, but for the price,
Cool, but for the heat,
An evening breeze is welcome
By the soldiers on the street.

Far too many troubles,
Why worry about them, then?
Vivo en linda Panamá
Y todo está bien.

—Reuben Malachi

"That's a Jim Dandy of a poem, isn't it?" asked O'Dell with a hint of civic pride.

"We've been seeing these all across the country."

"Poems about Panama?" asked O'Dell.

"No, poems about cities—all sorts of cities."

"Well, this one has got everybody talking. Like I said, it showed up last week out of nowhere."

"It must have come as a shock," observed Gaude.

"Miracles, by definition, tend to come as a shock. That's why we call them miracles instead of hum-drum occurrences," replied O'Dell.

"Do your neighbors consider this a miracle?"

"Some do, some don't. Some think it's a publicity stunt, others call it an eyesore. That's the usual reaction around here to just about everything that is new. Sooner or later the newcomer starts to sink in and become part of the landscape, part of our lives, part of our world. There's something about this town that attracts folks who you would think don't belong here, but now they do, and Panama wouldn't be the same without them. Take a walk around and you'll see for yourself."

"Our first stop needs to be the Bahá'í place of worship," said Watt.

"Yep, and that's as good of an example as I could come up with."

⌘

"Not another one!" he whined.

"Just for that, there will be two more."

"I suppose I should quit while I'm ahead."

"It seems that you are constantly re-learning that lesson, only to immediately forget it."

"Maybe those should be my famous last words. Put them on my tombstone."

"I have something entirely different selected for that purpose."

"I'm not sure if that is your typical banter or something darker."

"That presupposes my typical banter is not typically dark."

"My guess is that it depends upon which of your innumerable phases you are going through."

"Very good."

"I assume that we are not in one of your dark phases right now."

"No, there have been much, much darker ones. You didn't know me during my dying phase."

"Dying phase? I've never heard of that one before."

"That's because I've never mentioned it before."

"When did that begin?"

"Before I met you."

"And when did it end?"

"After I leave you."

"That certainly was informative," he said. "I'm glad we straightened that out."

She reopened the notebook and began to recite.

> *"The day was warm and gentle,*
> *The sky was bright and clear,*
> *The sun presided kindly*
> *Over the best day of the year.*
>
> *She slammed the door behind her,*
> *Displaying no remorse,*
> *Though no decree had issued,*
> *The verdict was divorce.*
>
> *It was not time for weeping,*
> *Too numb to feel the pain,*
> *I could not help but thinking:*
> *Shouldn't there be rain?"*

"That's a bit gloomy," he observed.

"Yes, it reminds me of my divorcing phase," she mused.

"You were married?" he asked, genuinely surprised.

"Let's see...was I actually married? Legally? I'm not sure."

"Let's just leave it at that."

She nodded in agreement as she turned a page. "Here's the last entry in Reuben's notebook."

"A bit of an anticlimax, after having met Reuben," he said.

"Look at you now! When would you have ever used the word 'anticlimax' before going on this trip?"

"Oh, yes, I stand corrected. A knuckle-dragger such as myself would never have been capable of intelligent conversation before being introduced to the hobnobbing clique of swells in the middle of

Reuben's swamp."

"You just said 'hobnobbing clique of swells,' in case you didn't notice. I rest my case."

"Okay, fine. Let's hear the finale."

She made a mock frown to indicate that she was not quite ready to forgive her partner's boorish behavior, but nevertheless turned her attention back to the notebook in order to read the last page.

> "*He finished the letter with a feeling of great self-satisfaction. Some might call it smugness. That ought to fix her, he thought. As close to a poisoned pen letter as Parker ink can supply. He imagined writing the letter in poison. Cyanide. Didn't that have a peculiar smell? He tried to remember. Vanilla? Vinegar? Something like that. At least he knew that hemlock smelled like parsnips, he was sure of that. Or was it radishes?*
>
> *He signed the letter, tempted to use his entire name, just as he might finish a business letter. 'Too melodramatic' he said to himself. 'Besides, you've slept with her for Krissake.' He signed the letter trying to make it look curt. How do you make a signature look curt? Use one letter? Too artistic. Anyway, unless it's a short memo, only sissies and CEO's use one letter for signatures. It occurred to him that he had many times before used only one letter—the first in his name. She had done it too, but it was always the last letter of her name. 'I'm losing my mind,' he said aloud. He was. For God's sake, just mail the damned thing, his advising inner voice scolded.*
>
> *He searched for an unsympathetic stamp. Nothing warm or cordial such as birds or flowers would do. Maybe a flag or a dead president. Not Kennedy, though. He was too engaging a personality. He needed someone dull. Besides, Kennedy was liberal and Irish. Eisenhower, maybe Coolidge.*
>
> *He couldn't find a stamp in the house, much less an appropriately unfriendly stamp. Two days later he mailed the letter having forgotten to ensure that the stamp was right. Now, he couldn't remember.*"

"I'm not sure whether it's because I met the guy, but his writing is starting to grow on me. I suspect that Reuben would say, like a fungus."

"That's almost exactly what he would say."

He was silent for an extended moment and then said, "Your friend Reuben asked me what I thought of Daniel Gaude."

"Did he? How odd."

"Yes, particularly since I've never met the man, nor have I really heard much mentioned about him."

"I mentioned him before."

"A few days ago."

"That qualifies as before."

"Were you keeping in touch with him?"

"Not really. His father forced him into the Army, more or less. I think he went off to war. Someone told me that he was writing for a newspaper now. I remember that he occasionally had articles published in *The Cyclops*."

"*The Cyclops*?"

"The name of our school newspaper."

"So, yet another of your literary chums. You always seem to gravitate to the writers."

"No, his heart was always in music. I'm not sure how he got stuck behind a typewriter."

"Typewriter?"

"Okay, word processor, although that doesn't conjure up much of a romantic image."

"Good. I'm not all that keen on you conjuring up romantic images of your old schoolmates."

"Schoolmates?"

"Okay, past relationships."

"Long past relationships."

"How long past?"

"Long enough."

"How did you break up?"

"It was a fight."

"Naturally."

"A really nasty, bitter fight."

"I know the feeling well."

"No, you don't. He swore that he would do whatever it takes to forget me."

"But you are unforgettable."

"Flatterer. It went deeper than that. He had written a few musical compositions in my honor. To forget me meant to forget that music."

"Harsh."

"Which goes to show what kind of lengths he was willing to go to when we broke up."

"What was the fight about?"

"Nosey, aren't you?"

"No…Okay, yes."

"The usual. There was another woman."

"I find that hard to believe. Who?"

"That's what I wanted to know. He denied everything, but I know that *she* was out there."

"Who was *she*?"

"I have no idea."

"How did you find out about her?"

"I didn't."

"What proof did you have of her existence?"

"None."

"Then how did you know that he wasn't telling the truth?"

"Even if he was telling the truth to me, he was lying to himself."

"This drive—this visit to Malachi's party—"

"Yes?"

"You're reliving your college road trip, aren't you?"

"No. You can never relive anything, you can merely memorialize it."

"Did you love him?"

"Who?"

"Gaude."

"Did I love Daniel Gaude?"

"Yes, did you love him?"

"Of course I did. I loved him, I slept with him. There were a dozen others as well. I loved them all. I slept with them all. Any additional questions you'd care to pose?"

There was an extended pause of uncomfortable silence. "No, Cheyenne. That pretty much covers it."

⌘

"Excuse me, gentlemen, do you need assistance?"

"That's a very polite way of asking us why we are trespassing on your property."

"Yes, and it's particularly effective on polite trespassers, which I hope that you both are."

Watt handed the man his card. "Forgive us our trespasses, as we forgive those who trespass against us."

The man chuckled in response, took a quick look at the card, and then extended his hand in greeting. "I'm Julius Huelva, Seneschal of the Censured Bahá'í House of Worship."

"Does that mean you are an official of the church?"

"I take care of things that need care taken."

"Does that include dealing with fire damage?"

"It does today."

"You have quite a job ahead of you then."

"Yes. I believe that would qualify as a B.G.O."

"Pardon?"

"A brilliant glimpse of the obvious."

"We were hoping to obtain a glimpse of the inside of the structure, brilliant or otherwise."

Huelva smiled and glanced down again at Watt's card. "I suppose that you can do a little rummaging around for what good that will do."

"Thank you. It appears that the central dome suffered extensive damage. Is it safe to walk through that area of the building?"

"I believe so, but I'll provide you some hard hats." Huelva glanced over at the house of worship and shook his head despondently. "It is a pity that so much of the dome has been destroyed. It was our pride and joy."

"From what remains, it appears to have been an unusual shape," observed Gaude.

"That's true. A dome is a common element of our temples, although it is not required. The shape of the dome can vary widely. One of my favorites—other than our House of Worship—is the temple in New Deli. The dome is in the shape of a stylized lotus flower. We took inspiration from that when we built this structure."

"Your dome was in the shape of a flower?"

"No, not at all. It was in the shape of a potato."

"A potato?"

"Yes, this is Idaho, after all. There has been some criticism of this, but the potato is one of God's great creations. It grows nearly everywhere on earth and sustains millions—billions, actually. Most Bahá'í Houses of Worship are white. Ours, however, is the color of the earth in tribute to the land that we farm and a celebration of the Idaho potatoes we produce. While other houses of worship may display intricate geometric tracery on the exterior and interior walls, we elected to base the decorative theme on the intertwining shoots and leaves of potato plants, interspersed with decorative tubers."

"But this is the desert," said Gaude. "I didn't think potatoes could grow out here."

"That's where you are mistaken. We are cultivating a new variety of drought-resistant potato. We started with blue potatoes—"

"Blue potatoes?"

"Yes. You've never heard of them?"

"Actually, I've eaten them," said Gaude.

"Wonderful!"

"Why are they blue?"

"That's a question better directed to God. There are several hundred types of potatoes. Blues are the most tolerant to a low-moisture environment."

"I see. How far along are you in growing a...desert spud...I suppose you might call them?"

"That's exactly what we call them! We have made great progress in developing a potato that not only survives in this harsh environment, but actually thrives and tastes delicious. Over the past few years, we've shared our terrific tubers with only a few isolated communities across the globe. About six weeks ago, we started marketing them more broadly and hope to further expand very soon. The Desert Blue Spud will be our gift to the world, particularly the arid regions of the earth."

"That sounds like a very noble undertaking."

"The potato is a humble thing, and by virtue of that, it is ennobled."

"I suppose that if you sell enough potatoes, you might be able to afford the restoration of your temple," said Gaude.

"It will be restored."

"Of course, with faith," agreed Watt.

"Yes, with faith," concurred Huelva, "and with the robust stock portfolio we have been nurturing almost as carefully as our potatoes."

"What's left of the temple is still quite beautiful," observed Watt.

"Very impressive," added Gaude.

"Like most Bahá'í Houses of Worship, ours has nine sides."

"Is that religiously significant?"

"We are taught by the First Guardian, Shoghi Effendi, that nine is the highest digit and thus symbolizes the comprehensive unity of Bahá'í Faith. Nine also has the numerical value of Baha in the Arabic alphabet, and Baha is the name of the Revealer of our Faith, Bahá'u'lláh."

"Is numerology part of the Bahá'í teachings?"

"Not exactly, although the mathematical design of the universe clearly evidences a divine plan, and to my way of thinking, nine is a truly magical number. Did you ever learn the trick of the number nine in the multiplication tables? No? As a young boy, I was terrible at simple arithmetic. My greatest torment was to be called up to the front of the classroom by Sister Mary O'Callaghan to recite the times tables."

"You went to Catholic school?"

"Yes, I was born in Boston. Parochial school could not be avoided."

"I know what you mean."

"My one consolation was that I was able to master the multiples of nine simply by using the fingers in my hands as place markers. If the question was one times nine, all I would need to do is bend down my first finger, leaving nine remaining: one times nine equals nine. If Sister commanded me to multiply nine by seven, I needed only to drop my seventh finger, leaving six fingers to the left—sixty—and three fingers to the right—three. Thus, sixty-three. Then, whatever the product of the multiplication, the individual integers will always add up to nine. No other number works like that. This is a clue left by the creator of mathematics—God himself—that nine has transcendent and mystical properties that can lead us closer to him."

"Interesting."

"Many say the nine also represents how our doors are always open to welcome the nine religions of the world."

"I thought there were a lot more than nine religions."

"Perhaps you are thinking about separate denominations and sects. We consider the great religions of the world to be Hinduism, Jainism, Judaism, Zoroastrianism, Buddhism, Christianity, Islam, Babism and the Bahá'í Faith."

"Babism?"

"It was the predecessor to Bahá'í Faith, much as the Anabaptists were to forerunners of the Mennonites and Amish. We have inherited much of the core beliefs and teachings of Babism."

"I'm not familiar with the teachings of Bahá'í Faith."

"The teachings of our faith centers on unity. Unity of God. Unity of religions. Unity of humanity. God is single and omnipotent. His creations—his children—reflect and yearn for that unity. Religion is key to that unity. Together we worship the one God. Together we evolve."

"Evolve?"

"Yes, evolve. Religion is an evolutionary process. It is a progression through the ages. God established evolution, whether that be biological or spiritual, so that we might progress towards him."

"An individual does not evolve. A species evolves."

"Very true, which is why we must be unified as one people—as a single species—if we are to progress towards true enlightenment and union with God."

"How do you achieve this progress?"

"You must progress into the spirit world and keep progressing."

"What is in the spirit world?"

"I don't know. I haven't gotten there yet."

"How do you know that it exists?"

"Have you ever been to Antarctica? If not, how do you know that it exists?"

"How is this progressive evolution achieved?"

"Manifestations such as Buddha, Jesus, and Mohammed give us dispensations, progressively more enlightened revelations relating to the essential qualities of God. With this knowledge, and with such enlightenment, we together progress and evolve."

"You seem very open to embracing other faiths."

"All religions are worthy. In the same way, all humans are equal, regardless of race, or sex, or nationality, or wealth. We are united in our faith. We are united in our humanity."

"Do you convert others?"

"This happens, but we gladly accept all as they are."

"You would describe yourselves as ecumenical?"

"Oh, yes. We embrace all religions. At least, all legitimate religions."

"Are there any that you don't recognize as legitimate?"

"We haven't quite made up our minds about the Methodists," Huelva said with a wink.

"What about atheists?"

"Atheists are an interesting question. They deny the existence of God and think that their own existence can be maintained without religion. They are misguided and sadly mistaken. Religion is like the ocean. You don't need to be in it to be dependent upon it. If the oceans suddenly dried up, all life on earth would die. Extinction would be universal, even in the most arid deserts. The dependency goes back to the very beginnings of life on earth. A billion years ago, amphibians left the water and ventured upon terra firma. Just the same, they have always come back to the water to feed, to hydrate, to procreate. We see that connection with all life, not merely newts and salamanders. Even to this day, the concentration of salt in our human blood matches the salinity of the seawater. That is the very model for the relationship of the human soul to religion. Your soul cannot avoid its attachment to religion any more than your body can escape its attachment to the bodies of water from which our distant ancestors emerged. An atheist claiming that there is no God is like the frog that claims that there is no pond—even though he must inevitably return to it in order to assure his survival."

"I doubt that many atheists would be pleased with being compared to a frog," said Gaude.

"We are all God's creatures, great and small," replied Huelva with an introspective smile. He now gestured toward the temple. "I am tempted to go on, but I understand that you have come to examine the fire damage. I will be pleased to escort you." Huelva led them into the grand entry of the House of Worship. In the antechamber, Gaude saw a large mosaic portrait of man with a small mustache, penetrating brown eyes, and wearing an unadorned crimson fez.

"Is he a patron saint?" asked Gaude.

"Not exactly," smiled Huelva with practiced patience. "We hold in special reverence the First and Last Guardian, Shoghi Effendi, grandson of Abdu'l-Bahá and son of Bahá'u'lláh. It is commonly accepted among Bahá'í that he and his wife, Rúhíyyih Khánum—who was a Canadian born of the name Mary Maxwell—had no children. Our community believes otherwise, based upon documents found in a secret archive in Tel Aviv, Missouri."

"Tel Aviv?" asked Gaude.

"Yes, the one in Missouri, mind you, not in Israel."

"We've been there."

"Yes, Israel is lovely, isn't it?"

"No, I mean that we've been to Tel Aviv, Missouri."

"Really? Small—"

"World...yes, it is."

"And getting smaller every day," added Watt.

"Anyway, as I was saying, the documents from the archive reveal the birth of a son to the Guardian. They also provide a prophesy that is the basis of our belief that there is a lineage of Secret Guardians whose eventual descendent, nine hundred years from now, will be the next great manifestation. This is not, however, a widely held belief among Bahá'í."

"Not widely held?"

"We are the only Bahá'í who maintain this belief," Huelva admitted sheepishly.

"Are you a separate sect?"

"We didn't consider ourselves such, at least not at first. However, it seems that we are considered a bit of a rogue community. That is why we are currently called the Censured Bahá'í House of Worship. At least we haven't been cast as heretics or covenant-breakers, not yet anyway."

"So, the Secret Guardian teachings caused the falling-out between you and the authorities?"

"There were a few other things as well. The unique design of our House of Worship, for one, and the fact that we built it without conferring with anyone, particularly the Bahá'í Council of Northwestern States and the Mother Temple of the West in Wilmette, Illinois."

"Is that a headquarters?"

"Not exactly, but then again, yes. It is where you will find the North American Council. They call the shots in this neck of the woods."

"Or desert."

"Yeah."

"So, you need to make nice with the powers-that-be?"

"Yes, but there are a few other items as well. Naturally, our doctrine of the Secret Guardian is probably the biggest sticking point. There are also some lesser irritants, I suppose you might call them. For instance, until three years ago, I was a member of the National Spiritual Assembly. I was asked to remove myself, and I suspect that this was due to the fact that I advocated for the selection of Latin as the auxiliary worldwide language of all peoples."

"Auxiliary language?"

"It is a goal of Bahá'í, in the furtherance of universal understanding and cooperation, to foster a language that all of humanity can speak."

"Latin isn't all that popular?"

"No, although I'm not sure why. It is a noble language, rich in literature and tradition, and was, until a century or two ago, regarded as a universal language of scholarship. I heard rumors that I was being accused of conspiring with the Vatican in order to conduct a hostile takeover of Bahá'í Faith."

"That doesn't sound all that tolerant or inclusive."

"No, it doesn't, does it? I suppose we all have our bad days. In any event, Bahá'í is tolerant enough not to jump to the conclusion that we have broken the covenants, so we have not been automatically excluded or excommunicated. We have, however, been called to task about our actions and beliefs by the Wilmette Bahá'í and have been summoned to provide an explanation before the Universal House of Justice."

"Is that in the Hague?"

"No, you are referring to the World Court of the United Nations. Bahá'í has a nine-member governing institution that provides guidance and rulings."

"Sounds like the Supreme Court."

"Oddly enough, the building in Haifa, Israel is in many ways similar to the Supreme Court in Washington, D.C."

"What happens when you have to go to court…I mean, before the House of Justice?"

"We will discuss many things, not least of which is why we took it upon ourselves to come to Panama and build this temple without consultation."

"They are angry that you built it without their permission?"

"Bahá'í are tolerant and seek peace and reconciliation, but they were rather annoyed at our choice of a potato dome, and even more so that we built the edifice here in Panama."

"They have something against this town?"

"Nothing personal, but it just so happens that one of the major Houses of Worship, the Mother Temple of Latin America, is located in Panama City, Panama. The regional and national councils feel that our building here was tantamount to a mockery of that Mother Temple, not to mention the confusion it has caused for some people because of the similarity of the names of the locations of each House of Worship."

"That *would* seem to be out of step with a religion that places such a premium on unity."

"Yes, we are painfully aware of the irony. However, our explanation will be that we did not come to Panama. Rather, Panama came to us."

"How is that?"

"This twelve thousand-acre tract of land was willed to us by Thaddeus Copperkettle," said Huelva, gesturing out at the expanse of desert.

"Interesting name."

"Interesting man. He was a physician, scientist, and inventor. He made a fortune in designing and manufacturing artificial limbs and later developed and perfected a cellular regeneration processes that is now leading to the growth of lost fingers, arms, and legs."

"Amazing."

"His final work revolved around regeneration that was aimed at fully reversing the aging process."

"Really?"

"Yes, it appears that he may have found the key to eternal life."

"Wouldn't that have been covered in the news?"

"It might have, but Doctor Copperkettle never published his breakthrough. At the end of his life, he destroyed all work on the program."

"Why?"

"He left a letter saying that God told him to do it."

"Blaming God, once again."

"No, this wasn't blaming God. This was giving him credit."

"How so?"

"In his farewell letter, Doctor Copperkettle explained that the first people mentioned in the Christian Bible are recorded as having lived for hundreds of years. Adam lived until the age of nine hundred thirty and his sons lived nearly as long. Methuselah lived nine hundred and sixty-nine years. However, these long lives did not necessarily lead to holiness. God gradually reduced the lifespan down to one hundred twenty years, but that didn't help things much. Eventually, God was fed up with sinful humanity and wiped nearly everyone off the face of the earth with a great flood. After that, and ever since, the span of years allotted to his children on earth has been much less. I believe the Book of Psalms pegs it between seventy and eighty years. According to Doctor Copperkettle, longer life gave the devil too much opportunity to lead humans astray."

"People haven't improved with shorter lives."

"Doctor Copperkettle didn't say that a shorter life will make people better. All he said is that less time here on earth means less time to sin. The longer that we sinful humans live, the more opportunities that we have to sin, and those opportunities are invariably seized upon. It reminds me of the quote from Martin Luther, who obviously recognized the proclivity of people to sin, at least in their waking moments. The more beer we drink, the more we sleep, and the more we sleep, the less we sin."

"Yes, that rings a bell," said Gaude, glancing over to his partner who was unsuccessfully attempting to restrain a smile.

"The problem with Luther's solution is that a sleeping drunk eventually wakes up and then goes right back to sinning. Doctor Copperkettle's point was that we are all sinful, always have sinned, and always will sin. The only way to lessen the number of sins is to lessen the time on earth that we have to sin."

"All the same, it seems extraordinary that Doctor Copperkettle would go to all the time and effort to develop a formula for eternal life and then destroy it."

"Yes, it does seem odd, doesn't it? There are those who believe that he destroyed the work simply to prevent it from falling into the wrong hands. There is some evidence that Doctor Copperkettle was afraid of a mysterious government agency that purportedly was spying on his work and eavesdropping on all of his communications."

"Was there any proof of that?"

"We cannot be sure. It is possible that the great Doctor

Copperkettle succumbed to a trace of delusional paranoia in his later years. On the other hand, there is no doubt that the government watches us, particularly if we do something interesting or unusual. After all, what would draw more interest from the government than a discovery of this nature?"

"Perhaps a new kind of bomb."

"Yes. Isn't it peculiar that governments are so interested in life and death, while all we really want them to do is take care of the matters that happen *between* life and death?"

"You mentioned that Doctor Copperkettle willed this land to the Bahá'í. When did he pass on?"

"Seven years ago. He died in Berlin, Utah. Doctor Copperkettle was a great admirer of Berlin. Have you ever heard of it?"

"Yes, as a matter of fact, we have."

"He donated half of his fortune to the town."

"Really? Was it to help fight the problem of suicides there?"

"Oh, no. It was to pay for the coffins. Doctor Copperkettle apparently thought that the people in Berlin were on to something. In fact, once he reached the age of seventy-five, he got into his car, drove down to Utah, and committed suicide."

"Sorry to hear that."

"No need for commiserations. Copperkettle rejected an eternal life on earth in preference for one elsewhere. He decided that it was his time."

"Wasn't God supposed to decide when it was his time?"

"Maybe he conferred with God. I wasn't privy to Doctor Copperkettle's discussions with the Almighty."

"I can't believe that God would condone taking of one's own life. Suicide is not the answer."

"Maybe it is, depending on the question."

James Parker Doyle turned the car from Market onto Larkin Street, passing by a police officer on the corner. He knew that it was long past the time he should have ditched the stolen car. *If only I could get to a secure terminal,* he thought.

That's not going to happen.

Okay, what's Plan B?
Crawl into a corner and die.
Not yet.
We're delaying the inevitable.
Death is always the inevitable.
Just so.

He slowly proceeded down to the first intersection. He had turned on the radio a few hours before not so much to be entertained as to help unfocus his mind from the pain. As he reached the corner, 'On the Run' by Ni'ihau Child began to play.

> *They know who you are*
> *They know where you're going*
> *They know where you hide*
> *Don't think about slowing*
>
> *They'll track you from dawn*
> *They'll pursue you 'til sunset*
> *They'll follow you all day*
> *No way you can stop yet*

To the left was the domed San Francisco City Hall. To the right, he saw the Main Library, a muscular nouveau-classical-quasi-modern-beaux-arts fortress of white granite. He glanced down Grove Street and saw a red banner indicating the library entrance.

That's it! I'll have to risk it.
What risk? At this point, there is really nothing to lose.
True.

He pulled into a small parking lot across from the library, adjacent to the Wells Fargo. He parked, rolled down the windows, and left the keys in the ignition as he slowly emerged from the car. The library entrance was about fifty meters away. He walked down the sidewalk. As he passed a gyro shop to his right, Doyle glanced up to see his reflection.

Not pretty.
Katie didn't pick me for my looks.
Yes, she did.
Shutup.

He crossed the street and passed through the library front doors. Doyle entered the austere polished granite five-story central atrium punctuated with ascending racks of lighted squares. It reminded him of tiered prison cells, or perhaps the cubicles for scrivening medieval monks.

Okay, where do I find the computer room?

There's an information desk right in front of you.

Doyle regarded the counter facing out to the atrium. *I can't chance it. I look like a wreck. They'll call the cops. I need to blend.*

Yes, you look like a wreck, but this is San Francisco. Trust me, you already blend. Besides, you don't have much choice.

Right.

Doyle approached the desk behind which stood a volunteer librarian.

Male. Young. Age twenty-four. European-Nordic-Scandinavian. Height, one point eight meter. Weight seventy-nine kilos. Light brown almost blonde hair—uncombed—greasy. Unkempt-scraggly beard. Small facial features. Minor scattered freckling. Small mole on forehead. Blue eyes. Tan t-shirt with silkscreen of Che Guevara. Functionally unemployed, but still sporadically attending art classes at City College of San Francisco. Identifies as pansexual but is a virgin— not by choice. Subsists wholly on pizza, corn chips, guacamole and Mountain Dew soda. Allergic to most brands of toothpaste. Older brother runs a meth lab in Zanzibar, Wyoming.

"Can I help you?" asked the young man at the counter.

Doyle silently stared ahead, observing the young man's eyes dart about nervously. After a seemingly interminable fifteen second pause, he mumbled, "Computers."

"You want to use one of our library computers?"

Doyle took a deep breath, looked slowly to the right and then left, returned his gaze to the front, and repeated, "Computers."

"Are you a member of the library?"

Doyle stared blankly at the young man, then rolled his left eye as he opened his mouth, shut it, then turned to what apparently was an invisible friend and whispered, "Computers."

"Do you have a library card?" the man at the desk asked patiently, his eyes continuing to dart nervously.

Doyle now turned his face up to the glass dome above the atrium as if lavishing the sunlight streaming down, then returned his attention to the volunteer librarian, and intoned, "Computers."

"You won't be able to use a computer without an account.

Would you like me to sign you up now?"

Doyle carefully examined his shoes for a moment, looked up and shook his head to convey his disinclination to accept the man's invitation to register for library membership. "Computers."

The young man tried to force a smile. "It's free, and it only takes a minute or two."

"Computers."

"Ummm…I'll sign you up right now. What is your name?"

"Computers."

A bead of sweat now dripped off the young man's mole and trickled down to be absorbed into his almost-blonde eyebrow. "Ah…ummm…you can find computers on the next floor," he said, gesturing above him.

Doyle maintained a vacuous stare into the distance as he emitted a stage whisper. "Computers." He then slowly swiveled to his left and departed.

Nice performance, Laurence Olivier.

I've always pictured myself as a Denzel Washington.

You apparently missed your true calling.

You waited 'til now to tell me?

Doyle took the stairs to the second floor and sat down at a computer terminal in the back corner of the room. He clicked on the small icon at the bottom of the screen bypassing the standard login page. He then typed 'cmd' in the search box which instantly summoned a prompt box. He began typing one command after another to bypass the library accounts login, sidestep the security system, disable the firewall, and elude the eager entreaties from DataGhad to enter its ever-expanding cyber realm. He strained his memory to recall the address that would gain him entry into the Department of Defense Top Secret darkweb, JWICS, the Joint Worldwide Intelligence Communications System.

Jaywicks? smirked his skeptical self with thinly veiled contempt. *How are you going to get past the security gate and gain access without your PIV card? Even if you still had the card, you don't have a chip reader here in a freekin' public library.*

I can sidestep the Personal Identity Verification card.

No, you can't.

Oh, yes I can, and I have to. Using my PIV would send up a flare.

Why not sneak in through Agora?

That would send up an even bigger flare. That's the first place they would be monitoring if they were trying to find me.

Right. What happens next, hotshot?

I'll come up from the basement.

There is no basement.

Watch me.

Do I have a choice?

Shutup. Doyle typed in an address and then engaged in an online tennis match to finesse his way into the site.

DSNET3? Seriously? That went the way of the dinosaurs. It was shut down years ago.

It still floats out there operating on the ARPANET skeleton.

How did you know that?

You told me.

Why do we have to pass through this abandoned cellar? Wait, don't tell me—it's unmonitored.

Let's just say that it is casually monitored.

Clever boy. Where next?

CRONOS.

CRONOS? The NATO system? Oh, I get it. The hall monitors in London will assume you are one of the clueless members. Who are you going to impersonate?

Montenegro.

Of course.

What good will CRONOS do?

That's how I can segue into JWICS.

I still think it's a mistake to stroll into Jaywicks, insisted his skeptical self. *You know that they'll see you coming.*

I'll play the same card I did in CRONOS. Nobody in Montenegro answers the phone, so by the time DoD finds out I'm an interloper, we'll be long gone.

Remind me never to play poker with you.

When have either of us ever played poker?

After a sort series of commands, Doyle entered JWICS.

Okay, but you're barely better off. What good will this do? We're not chasing down anyone in DoD, are we?

Shutup and watch. Doyle navigated through the site and then found a link to another portal.

Ahhh, a sidedoor into the National Reconnaissance Office. Jeeze Louise, now GWAN? You are really corkscrewing through the systems.

I assume that we are being tailed. We need to shake them.

Yeah, but this seems to be overkill. How good could they possibly be?

Let's assume that they are the best.

Other than us.

Maybe better than us. I need to punch above my weight. Doyle arrived at the Nongovernmental Entity Surveillance page and started scrolling over the potential accounts. *Okay, showtime. Let's choose a hacker net. Preferably one of the smaller ones.*

Needle in a haystack.

Shutup.

He continued scrolling. After three minutes of scanning the tables, Doyle saw a site that appeared to fit the bill and was currently active. The GWAN Intel synopsis read:

Network	Webmaster	AGE	NAT	LOC	EXP Level
	Templeton, Jerald C.				
Jägermeisters		23	USA	CAL	IV-A
	Alias/Handle 'Polycarp' 'Carp Man'			Palo Alto Stanford UNIV	
Address	Synopsis				
2025:cdba:1237: 1066:1215:1666: 1783:3737	Areas of Concentration: Conspiracy Theories. International Espionage. Ancient Extraterrestrials. Buddhist Philosophy. Pokémon. Heavy Metal. S2M2. Amish Pornography.				

Doyle entered the site and opened a chat box:

* Carp Man, you there? *

The response was almost immediate:

      * Always dude *

Doyle sent back:

* Looking for grayman *

Once again, there was a swift reply:

> * Too lite on the info—can't help you, boss *

Doyle followed up:

* He has goat eyes. Probably a contractor *

This time, the party at the other end of the communication took a full minute:

> * Goateyes—That's a bad dude *

* U know him? *

> * Know about him—that's enough. Freekin psycho. Part of some kind of teutonic cult, maybe political—dunno—they're wired in everywhere. Nasty German dudes totally into Schopenhauer, atheism, misogyny, twisted Buddhist beliefs, eugenics, weird concepts of eternal justice, you name it. No—on second thought, don't name it. *

* Nihilists? *

> * Maybe. It's all in the definition, isn't it? *

* Nazis? *

> * No. The Nazis at least loved their dogs and children *

* Know where I can find him? *

> * Don't look for him. Don't find him. Don't go there *

* Gotta go. No choice. Little help? *

> * Always got a choice. Your choice is a funeral, dogg *

* I'll take my chances. YOLO *

> * That one life of yours is about to end *

* Just the same—got a lead for me? *

> * He's here in CAL—Point Reyes. One hour north of SF—two west of Sacramento. In Vino Veritas *

* Coordinates?*

> * Damn, dude, you got a deathwish. You should go visit Berlin UT *

* Thanks for the travel tip *

> * Coordinates: 38.1295662-122.8925078. You owe me, MOFO. Make me a beneficiary on your life insurance—cause you are dead when you find Goateyes *

* Thx!!! You da man *

> * ??? You da man ??? How old are you, dude? *

Sunnavabitch! We did it.
Yeah, thanks for all the invaluable encouragement.
Do you think we'll be able to return the favor to our host in Las Vegas?
We'll see.
How did a guy sitting in his parent's basement, living off Cheetos and Red Bull, get a bead on some group of crazies that ORCA has never heard about?
I dunno. Maybe we're losing our touch.
Or maybe someone in the Sweatshop doesn't want us to know.
Something like that would be even scarier than the goat guy.
And to every bad there is a worse.

Doyle closed out and returned to the surface web. He then entered the map coordinates into the search bar. Within a few seconds, he was looking down from the aerial view at a forested area of the northern edge of the Point Reyes Peninsula. In the middle of his view was a cultivated rectangle with a large structure in the center.

In Vino Veritas. It's a vineyard.
Hold on…look right above it on the map.
For Krissake. Is this for real?
Yeah. That's what the map says, Hearts Desire Beach.
And you thought goat-eyes and our Gray friend had no sense of humor.

Doyle took another minute to clear out the computer cache and then downloaded a program from the web to wipe the hard drive.

The San Francisco Library will not be amused.

Life is unfair. Just ask John Kennedy.

Wait, before you bleach the drive, did you forget about the telephone number?

Telephone number?

The number in the Gray guy's wallet.

Jeeze Lousie. I need to get some sleep.

Tell me about it.

Doyle opened a basic search engine and conducted a reverse number query. The result appeared instantly.

Holy mother of—

Oh, screw me sideways!

Doyle stared at the screen in disbelief. Telephone number (415) 557-4400 was the front desk of the library, one floor beneath him.

They knew you would come here.

That's not possible.

To hell with possible. Stick to the facts.

They lured me here.

Same difference.

That means this is a trap.

Most likely. Let's get the hell out of Dodge.

Doyle initiated the 'Annihilator' disk erasure and reformatting program, stood up from the desk, walked down the steps to the lobby, exited the library, and retraced his steps up Grove Street, all the while carefully scanning his perimeter for a possible ambush. Unexpectedly, no one confronted or attacked him. On the other hand, as he passed the Wells Fargo, just as expected, the car was now gone.

Okay, good job ditching the car. Now, how are you going to get to Point Reyes?

No need to reinvent the wheel. I'll steal another car.

You don't have keys.

I'll manage.

Sure, MacGyver, you'll hotwire a car. That was something you were trained to do twenty years ago and have never tried again.

I haven't forgotten.

Fine, did it occur to you that cars now have electronic antitheft technology?

They've had that technology for twenty years.

Yeah, but now they are better. Did you learn how to bypass the new systems? It's not like doing an end run on a desktop computer.

I'll find an old car. It just might take a little longer.
You don't have the luxury of time.
Naysayer.
Find an Uber.
I'll be tracked if I use a cell.
Hail a taxi.
My card will be tracked.
There's a Wells Fargo right here.
I can't use an ATM without sending up a flare.
Stiff the driver.
Seriously?

Yes, seriously. You have no qualms about committing grand theft auto, but you balk at scamming a cabbie? What kind of freekin' spy are you, anyway?

I'm not sure if I can outrun a cabbie in my condition.

Okay, Einstein, in that case, how do you propose to confront the goatman from Las Vegas?

I haven't worked out that plan just yet.
Oh, great! I'm trapped in the head of a moron.
That makes two of us.

Doyle continued to walk as his mind began to wander despite his disapproving mental hall monitor's attempts to keep the psychic thoroughfare clear of any but essential traffic.

'May I call you some time?'
'Yes, do.' She paused, lost in thought, and then looked back to him. 'You have my number'
'No, I don't. I doubt that anyone does.'

The memory ended. James Parker Doyle shuffled painfully along the crowded sidewalks, clumsily swerving and veering past other pedestrians. Doyle bent over with pain, a rising fever, and an enveloping dizziness

'Why did you pick me?'
'You're the closest thing I know to a decent guy.'
'Well, thank you. I think.'

He paused briefly with a group of tourists at the intersection and then proceeded to cross. As a natural proclivity and an ingrained habit born of training, he continually surveyed his surroundings. Eight copedestrians. Three men, all in their twenties and thirties, two women, one middle aged, the other in her late twenties, three children, two boys, one girl. All dressed casually. He noted heights, weights, race, and hair colors. Except for one of the young children, all had earbuds, several nodded their heads in synch to their chosen tunes.

Without warning, he was sitting at a table in their restaurant in Budapest. Doyle slipped a five-thousand forint to the violinist to play 'Happy Birthday.'

> *'Everyone is looking at me.'*
> *'You're not self-conscious.'*
> *'I'll settle for modest.'*
> *'Are you really?'*
> *'No, but this just gives a room full of strangers free rein to stare instead of stealing sidelong glances.'*
> *'You prefer sidelong glances over being ogled?'*
> *'Yes. You alone have the exclusive license to ogle, gape and gawk at me.'*
> *'Which I do every waking moment.'*
> *'Actually, you also ogle in your sleep. It's one of your most endearing qualities.'*

Just as suddenly, he returned to the street. The traffic was moderately congested on the warm afternoon, as several convertibles and a few hardtops with windows rolled down shared their rap, country, pop, and R&B selections. Outdoor speakers at the café across the street played innocuous background music. He scanned the storefronts, including a clothier, a burger franchise, a pharmacy, and a frozen yogurt shop, all of which contributed their own tunes on outdoor speakers. Doyle looked over at a home electronics center featuring giant plasma screens behind the plate glass windows displaying the same television show featuring hopeful contestants singing before a panel of naturally unenthusiastic celebrity judges and an amphitheater filled with an artificially enthusiastic audience. A vintage open cockpit Coddington hot rod passed in front of him, and the eight-track tape player shared a familiar song: 'Fire and Rain' by James Taylor.

While he continued to scan the intersection, something in the latent analytical center of his brain made a connection. "The music..." he mumbled to himself, "it's everywhere."

Doyle responded to himself as if he was engaging in something other than a solitary conversation. "It's everywhere. It's anywhere. It's anywhere and everywhere…"

He tried to measure his breathing and calm down. He began talking to himself to maintain control of his mind. "Music. It's digital. It's *always* been digital, even from the beginning of civilization. Each note is an individual frequency. The chords are a combination of frequencies. All notes are based on mathematically determined vibrations and scales are mathematical progressions." Then his inner voice took over the monologue.

Mister X…Little Adolph…could have created these out of music…anytime. Jesus H. Christ, Mister X could have been Mozart…No, no…the 1930s…who was around then? The Nazis. Who could have done work like this? No, not Nicola Tesla?

Doyle then responded out loud, "I don't know…I don't know…" He hung his head, steadied his breathing, and tried to control his thoughts. Suddenly, he blurted out, "The music…everywhere…it's in…it's in our heads!"

A post-young, tall, athletic woman with blonde and blue hair, sporting particularly complex and exotic tattoos, walked by carrying a small 1960s era transistor radio. It played a Niʻihau Child tune.

> *You've just seen the light*
> *See how dark that it is?*
> *There's no means of escape*
> *If you're in the spy biz*
>
> *Yeah, we know who you are*
> *And what you have done*
> *It don't really matter*
> *We already have won*

Oh God, Doyle's interior voice moaned, *we're screwed.* He stood inert at the next street crossing. The pedestrian light cycled three times as Doyle leaned against a telephone pole, continuing to mutter to himself. Passers-by began to notice and then looked away quickly, inclined to neither confront nor assist. The light now indicated safe passage, and the latest group proceeded forward. Doyle remained in place and reached for the disposable cellphone in his pocket.

That won't get a call into the system.
Neither will the SEC-CEL. The system is down.

410

Do you know that for a fact?

I'm sure.

It's better to be right than to be sure.

Doyle made a shrug of surrendering resignation in response to his nagging self and pulled the secured cellphone out of his other coat pocket. With hands that never shook but now were shaking, Doyle fumbled with the cell as he removed the back of the case in order to insert the battery. Once the screen came to life, he executed the passcodes and opened the SEC-CEL operating system. It was back online.

They'll know exactly where we are. Do you think it's worth the risk?

What risk? I'm at the end of the line, he silently retorted.

Doyle quickly tapped out a text message. Once finished, he proceeded across the street. As he crossed, a soft and gentle voice spoke his name. As it was spoken, the blare and confusion of traffic, the chaotic mix of music, and the churn of city voices were muted. It was as if he had heard the voice in a quiet office...or in a church. James Parker Doyle turned around to see who spoke to him.

He saw.

*

Doug Bagsley's SEC-CEL began to vibrate on the desk. He had just finished responding to a series of emails that put him in a particularly vile mood. He was particularly irked by this morning's notice that secured cellphones would continue to remain out of order until further notice, as well as the distribution of new annoying travel policy restrictions recently issued by the new annoying Director of ORCA. Just as he began to reach for his phone, Jacobsen's screen on the desk beside him came to life and an even more annoying alarm signal began to emit from the tinny speakers of the workstation. Bagsley reflexively looked around for Jacobsen, almost immediately checking himself as his internal voice reminded him that his host had been absent all morning. The alarm continued its irritating blare, so Bagsley reached over and tapped the space bar on the keyboard, hoping to quell the querulous terminal. An alert box immediately opened on Jacobsen's screen. It indicated that the WATCHER ANGELS program had been initiated by an unauthorized user on the west coast.

"The *what* program? What the hell is Watcher Angels?" Bagsley griped to himself aloud.

The cell continued to vibrate. Under normal circumstances, Bagsley would have immediately tracked down Jacobsen to deal with the emergency alert message, as was required under well-established ORCA protocol, a protocol he had already violated by reading a message on someone else's computer screen. However, for reasons he was not inclined to analyze, he felt the need to answer the phone. *Headquarters just said that the phones aren't working yet,* he thought.

When was the last time that headquarters told you the truth? was the grouchy silent response.

Bagsley picked up the phone. It was a text message from James Parker Doyle.

< It is in the music. It is the music. All the music. Everywhere. >

⌘

"A ballet school? Here?" asked a skeptical Dan Gaude as he and Watt regarded the sign on the large barn-like building.

Relevé Ballet Academy

Guided by: Murakami

"Stranger things have happened."

"Name one."

"You woke up in a hospital room in Destinations, Maine and found me waiting for you."

"Okay, you win this round."

A voice spoke behind them, "Are you admiring the nondescript architecture of the building, or perhaps the advanced state of decay of the structure?"

Watt and Gaude turned to see a small gray-haired man dressed in denim, an open-collared work shirt, and a straw rancher's hat. Watt answered, "No, the sign caught our eye."

"Hmmm…I'm going to need to do something about that. It never occurred to me that anyone would actually come here and see the place up close."

"This is your business?"

"Yes, it is my business in every sense of the word, which means that it is none of your business."

"We apologize for intruding."

"Since you have already intruded, it is too late to dissuade you from visiting this town. I am curious enough to want to know what makes you so curious, so I shall constrain myself from shooing you away. I can tell that you aren't from the Bolshoi or ABT."

"ABT?"

"You really don't know ballet, do you? ABT is the American Ballet Theatre."

"No, we are from a different organization entirely," said Watt as he offered his card, extending it with two hands.

Their host examined it for a moment and then commented, "So you two are investigating something? I'm pretty sure it isn't my taxes, and my ex-wife already has anything that can be converted to ready cash." He looked at the card again, then looked back up at the two visitors, made a nodding gesture with his head, and said, "Well, then, come in." They entered through a warehouse-style steel door into a cavernous space. Mirrors and ballet barres lined the perimeter of the room. The floor was maple and the walls shiplap pine. Large arc lamps hung from the vaulted ceiling. To Gaude, the interior was little different from many of the churches he had visited over the past few weeks. The sole item of decoration was a framed lifesize black and white poster photograph of a *prima ballerina* during an on-stage performance. The man finally introduced himself. "I am Kohaku Murakami."

"I'm Bill Watt and this is my partner, Daniel Gaude. We're looking into church burnings across the country."

"You are here to look into the fire at the Bahá'í House of Worship."

"Yes."

"I used to go there for contemplation."

"I'm sorry that it burned down. Where will you go now?"

Murakami reacted with a look of candid disdain. "The same

413

place. Just because it burned down doesn't meant that it isn't still there. If you died, would it mean that you are gone?"

"Yes, wouldn't it?" replied Gaude, slightly surprised by the man's question.

"Strange that you would think that," answered Murakami cryptically.

"If you don't mind me saying, I find it remarkable that you can run a ballet school in…"

"In the middle of nowhere?"

"Yes."

"Actually, this isn't the middle of nowhere. This is thirty-seven kilometers southwest of nowhere."

"So I've been told. Why did you choose to live here?"

"Bigger is not better. More doesn't make merrier. Might doesn't make right. In solitude and loneliness, one finds no one else and thus is afforded the best opportunity to find one's own self. The world is a distraction, but there are a few places that are less so. Moving to Antarctica or the Farallon Islands was not really a practical alternative, so my best option was this empty desolate unknown nowhere."

"There are other empty spaces in the world and in this country."

"Silence."

"Science?"

"No, silence. Silence is the gateway to enlightenment."

"What does this place have to do with silence?"

"You didn't notice when you arrived? You need to pause in this frenetic search of yours. Don't stop to smell the roses—stop to hear the emptiness. This is where one can do just that. I visited the Negev Desert many years ago. I could not hear anything other than the inhalation and expiration of my breath and the pulse of blood that passed through the back of my skull from my jugulars. I found that same intensity of silence right here. In fact, Panama, Idaho has been officially certified as the quietest place in America."

"Who told you that?"

"Noah."

"Noah? Noah who?"

"Just Noah."

"The man who built the Ark?"

Murakami looked at them with withering disdain. "N-O-A-A, the National Oceanic and Atmospheric Administration."

"Oh."

"The silence provides me the ability to center myself in the universe, which in turn allows me to focus on my teaching."

"How many students do you have here?"

"One."

"Only one?"

"It's rather crowded with one, but it isn't possible to operate a school with less. I accept one disciple each year."

"Disciple?"

"When you spend a year devoted to bringing out the inner prima ballerina in a young woman, she is no longer your student, she is something more."

"I can't imagine one student qualifying this place as a school."

"I receive more than one thousand applications each year from hopeful young women and their anxious families who would beg to differ."

"That's impressive."

"I don't do it to impress anyone. I do it because I can help gifted artists who will one day impress people—an entire world of people—when they take their place on the stage. I assume that you noticed the photograph over here," said Murakami as he walked across the room to the image of a young woman in an old-world tutu that seemed to have come from a painting by Degas.

"Yes," confirmed Watt, "she is lovely."

"My most accomplished disciple—student, if you prefer— Diane McCraw. New York City Ballet. She redefined *Swan Lake* and her performance in the title role of *Giselle* at Paris is recognized as one of the three greatest performances of any ballerina anywhere, anytime, perhaps for all time. She, and the thirty-six other young women I have taught and mentored over the course of my career, are the reason I do this."

"How did you become involved in ballet?"

"It became involved in me."

"I don't get you."

"That comes as no surprise. You don't get me because you don't get ballet. Ballet is my vocation because of pain."

"Pain?"

"Pain. Ballet can be excruciatingly painful."

"Perhaps, but I don't understand the connection."

"Because you have not properly encountered pain. I was born with Trigeminal Neuralgia. There is an artery in my brain that compresses the trigeminal area. It results in chronic pain, mostly in my upper jaw, that is, to quote from the medical texts, 'akin to an electric shock, extreme, excruciating, and incapacitating.' Painkiller medications failed miserably and ultrasound therapy didn't take any edge off the agony."

"I'm sorry. It sounds terrible."

"It is terrible. That is where the beauty lies."

"I have never thought of pain as beautiful," said Gaude.

"You've never had children, have you? Never been in a delivery room while the woman you love is wracked by the pain of giving birth?"

"No."

"That explains it. Do you know what is the most beautiful thing that has ever occurred in this world?"

"I can't say."

"You've seen it innumerable times. In fact, given that you are crossing the country from church to church, perhaps you've seen it more often than most."

"Religious art?"

"Close. The crucifixion. You'll find it in just about every Catholic church and more than a few Anglican and Lutheran churches."

"But the crucifixion is a depiction of suffering and death. I'm not sure you can call it beautiful."

"There is nothing more beautiful than that beaten, tortured, and pierced body hanging lifeless on the cross. It is the sacrifice of sacrifices, ultimate pain giving birth to unlimited forgiveness and salvation. I have rarely stood before a crucifix without weeping in awe of its transcendent beauty." Murakami paused to reflect for a moment. "You said that you are in pursuit of someone or something."

"Yes."

"Do you intend to pursue them to the ends of the earth?"

"I'm not sure I can say that."

"Feel free to say that. This place qualifies as the end of the earth. That's why I came here. That's why you came here, whether you realize it or not." Murakami paused again, this time closing his eyes briefly and then reopening them. "You are here for a reason."

"We told you the reason."

"No, you told me what you believe is the reason. You think that you are searching for someone, but you are not."

"Why would you say that?"

"Because you are in Panama, Idaho. It is one of the places on earth that it can truly be said that there is nothing here. Accordingly, you are not here to see anything. You are not here to find anything. You are here to because something has eluded you in all the other places in the world in which there is something to see."

"That doesn't make much sense."

"Have you been applying logic to find what you have been looking for?"

"As best we can."

"And how has that worked out thus far?"

"We might be making progress."

"And you might be running in circles."

"That has occurred to me."

"Chasing the devil, aren't you?"

"In a manner of speaking."

"That's a fool's errand. You don't need to chase the devil. It is God who you need to track down. The devil is anywhere you are, but God is everywhere you can't be." Murakami shook his head gently in apparent vexation. "You're not searching for something. You're searching for something to search for."

"There's a difference?"

"Fundamentally. When someone searches for a rare work of art, they are ultimately searching for the artist. When someone wants to acquire a first-edition book, their purpose is to find the author. When someone searches for the meaning of life, the quest is to meet the creator."

"We're not searching for any of that."

"What do you think you are searching for?"

"An arsonist."

"What will you do if you catch this person?"

"Bring him to justice."

"No, the evil you are chasing is merely a reflection of all that you accuse in yourself. You cannot bring this person to justice. You are instead seeking to present yourself before a trial."

"You think that what we are doing is futile?"

"No, what you are doing is very important, but what you *think* that you are doing is misguided. You are doing the right thing for the wrong reason."

"What is the right reason?"

"You need to accept the right reason when it is offered to you."

"How do you suggest that we do that?"

"You stand in a shadow of one who blocks the light of truth. As long as you pursue this, the shadow will fall upon you. If you turn and flee, you will be pursued, and again the shadow will be upon you."

"What can anyone do?"

"Stand firm in one place. Eventually the sun reaches its zenith and all shadows will disappear. In the glaring light all secrets are illuminated, all lies uncovered, all truth revealed."

Watt and Gaude thanked Murakami for his time and took their leave. As they exited the building and walked down the street, they encountered two men standing in front of an Osco Drug Store behind a folding card table upon which was piled a stack of books. The man on the left was short, stocky, balding, and had a complexion of milk white punctuated by random patches of ruddy scarlet. The man on the right, was tall, thin, wore his hair in a tangled profusion of dreadlocks, and had skin the color of antique walnut interspersed with patches of sandy beige. On a corner of the table was perched a vintage cassette tape player that shared a Niʻihau Child song named 'Bay Town.'

There are those scenic hills
And charming fishing fleets
The views may give you thrills
As you walk on twisting streets

There's so much more to see
But not what tourists seek
When you find it you'll agree
It isn't cool or chique

Did you not read the news?
Perhaps you missed the sign
You should have seen the clues
You're at the end of the line

Watt and Gaude paused to look at the books on the table.

"Hello, new in town?" asked the taller of the two.

"Yes, how did you know?"

"Because you're new in town," said the short man. "We notice things like that."

"I'm Gary," said the tall man.

"And I'm Gary," added the short man.

"We're the Garys," they announced in unison, nodding cheerfully.

"You spell your names differently, don't you?" asked Gaude.

"No, not at all."

"There's only one way to spell Gary."

"That's right, so far as I know."

"Any other spelling would be an imposter Gary."

"Such as a Garry with two r's?" asked Gaude.

"That's not Gary."

"No definitely not. Gary with one r, that's the real thing."

"Yep, the genuine article."

"Speaking of the genuine article, how would you like to buy a nice book?" asked the first Gary.

"They're bootlegged," said the second Gary in a conspiratorial stage whisper. "Don't ask how we got them."

"But we did get them," boasted the first Gary.

"We sure did," agreed the other, "and it wasn't easy."

"These books are somehow hard to come by?" asked Gaude in a mixture of confusion and curiosity.

"Oh yes, they were supposed to be published, but fate intervened, and they disappeared."

"Then we intervened."

"So to speak."

Gaude picked up a copy of the book from the table. The cover was black matte with the title written in simple white font.

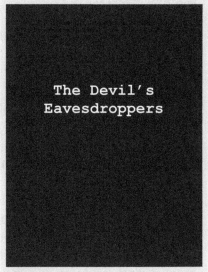

"We're fundraising to erect a monument in Berlin, Utah," explained the tall Gary.

"Berlin?" asked Gaude.

"Utah," confirmed the short Gary.

"We were there two days ago," responded Gaude in mild amazement.

"Small world."

"Getting smaller…" Gaude stopped in mid-sentence, restraining himself from indulging in his seemingly autonomic response.

"What kind of monument are you trying to fund?" asked Watt.

"We have it right here…well, half of it right here."

"That's right. We're raising money to pay for the base to put it on."

"It's called a plinth," corrected Gary Primus.

"Really? A plinth?" asked Gary Secundus.

"Yes, a plinth."

"How about that! Learn something new every day. Why didn't you tell me that before?"

"Tell you what?"

"That it's called a plinth."

"I assumed that you knew that a plinth was a plinth. That's the name of it."

"You could have told me about plinths."

"I didn't think a plinth was important," shrugged off Gary.

"You think it's important *now*," replied Gary in an annoyed and accusatory tone. "After all, we're going to the trouble of raising money for it."

"I suppose it's more important that it was yesterday," blithely responded Gary.

"Definitions are always important," insisted Gary.

"You're right," conceded Gary. "It's all in the definition."

"Are either of you from Kenai, Alaska?" asked Gaude.

"Kenai?"

"Alaska?"

Gary and Gary looked at one another and then simultaneously conducted a reciprocal head-to-toe inspection. "Nope!" they announced in unison as soon as they finished, satisfied than neither displayed any telltale signs of having made an excursion to America's last frosty frontier.

"You don't know anyone named Barbirah or Barbyra, do you?"

"Can't say that I do," answered tall Gary.

"That's coming up as a total blank," responded short Gary.

Gaude stepped forward to examine the portion of the proposed monument that was on display. It was an antique reliquary of finely wrought silver and lead crystal panes. It reminded Gaude of one he had seen as a schoolboy on a fieldtrip conducted by the nuns to the cathedral of the Catholic diocese. He remembered that it housed the desiccated left ear of Saint Gangulphus and that this relic had both horrified and fascinated him as a boy. He did not, however, dwell on the fact that this same sentiment of horror and fascination was to later characterize his view of Catholicism as a whole, and eventually evolved into ironic bemusement of all things religious. Inside the reliquary he saw an amber-colored silk cushion and upon it a mummified deep crimson human heart.

"Is that a…?"

"Yes, it's a heart," replied Gary.

"Whose?"

"It's Doctor Copperkettle's."

"Didn't he die in Berlin, Utah?"

"He sure did, which is why we need to get that heart right back to him," said Gary. "You don't think we were collecting money to build a monument for frivolous reasons, do you?"

Gaude looked more closely and saw below the desiccated organ a small slip of parchment with a message inscribed with calligraphic care in indigo ink.

I just had to leave it there

Watt and Gaude's faces mirrored each other's shocked expression.

"I left my heart in—" began Watt.

"San Francisco," finished Gaude.

The Advisors

There were two letters in the file, both written on the same day, New Year's Eve, thirty-seven years apart. Sister Mary Margaret wasn't sure how her predecessor had come to put them in the same file, but from the first time she read the missives, she instinctively understood why they belonged together. She could not ascribe with certainty that this knowledge was bestowed by the Holy Spirit, but it was nonetheless true. As she had done countless times for reasons that were beyond her ken, she opened the first and read it by candlelight in the dead of night.

I thought that I was getting over her, but the dreams keep coming. I dread the dreams just as I desperately long for them.

The holiday season brings her back so vividly that I can taste her kisses. On Christmas Eve morning I found one of her letters that I thought that I had lost. I made the mistake of reading it.

These past three weeks I have been recalling all the special things about her:

> *She loved to give and receive presents. It was very important to her that the gift was just right. It had to suit the person and she would go to great pains either to get just the right gift or else to carefully rationalize why the gift suited the recipient even if it really did not.*

> *When she was especially pleased, she would sometimes emit a little squeal. It is difficult to describe—she would begin to say 'aah,' as in, 'aah, that's nice,' but with a pitch and intensity that would make me catch my breath.*

> *She used my last name. I liked it that way. There was a certain sexual power there.*

> *She drank champagne. God, how she loved champagne.*

> *She would make a face of mock stubbornness by half closing her eyes, pursing her lips, and making a sound that was a hybrid of a growl and a hum. Then she would stop, smile, and her eyes would sparkle.*

I miss her so.
I wonder who she was.
I wonder who she is.

Sister Mary Margaret then opened the companion letter.

He is there, somewhere, I know he is.

Remember how Cinderella sings 'Some Day My Prince Will Come'? Maybe it was Snow White? It doesn't really matter. Of course, I know he is not a prince. He isn't perfect. It doesn't matter. He's mine. I know it. I feel it. Actually, it's more than I feel it—but it's hard to say any other way. Maybe I can try. It's not that I know because I think it or I feel it, I know because I am it. The certainty of it is me. It's in my heart, in my soul, it's in every cell of my body. No, no, no, no! It's more than that. The space that my body occupies here on earth is completely filled with the casual confident certainty of him. His existence. His love for me. My love for him. We are a figment of each other's imagination. We are a figment of each other's love.

Where is he? He's not here, but I can feel him. I can feel his gentle breath on the back of my neck as I lay sleeping. He's real, more real than anything I have ever seen, touched, felt, heard, or tasted. Why isn't he right here, right now? But he is here, I just can't hold him. Please God—please, please, please, please God—let me hold him, not just in my dreams, but hold him right here and now. Let me hear his voice. Let me see his smile. Let me be with him.

I feel so empty. I am so empty. I'm not even me. Fill me with him and then finally I will be me. Let me be him and let him be me.

I can't wait forever.

No, I will wait forever. I have no other choice. There is no choice. It's only him. It is him only.

Who is he? I don't know. And yet, I really do know, don't I?

He is him.

Twenty-Four: San Francisco

He knows that she is leaving on a flight that evening and takes a chance that she will be at the airport terminal restaurant where they first met. He walks though the entryway and sees that relying on his instincts has again paid off. She is sitting at the bar in the same place he remembers from years past. As he wends his way towards the bar, she pretends not to have seen him when he first walked through the door. She sees that he is in his dress blues and, as usual, wears them with a casual disregard that she knows was the result of careful calculation. His hair is cut short, well within regulation, but she knows that his shoes will not be quite freshly polished, his blouse will be unbuttoned and that he has eschewed the rows of ribbons sported by other officers. As he approaches her, she realizes that they are both constructing a tableau.

'Enchanté,' he says as he takes her hand in both of his and grandly kisses it in a European and theatrical gesture. 'What a delight to see you again.'

She smiles with practiced grace and tilts her head as would an advertising model. 'How did you know I was here?'

'How could you be anyplace else?'

'So, you have found me.'

'In the flesh,' he whispers as his eyes make a leisurely survey of that very same flesh to her great amusement and satisfaction.

'Are you aware that I am about to become delightfully single?' she asks.

'Are you aware that I've always been delightfully single?'

She smiles graciously while retaining composure despite an almost overwhelming desire to laugh and scream and throw him to the floor and tear off his clothes in the midst of the crowd. 'I'd love to say that I'd forgotten how wonderfully charming you are, but actually, I've never forgotten. I think about it continually.'

'Which is the reason why I continue to be charming,' he replies. 'If it was not for your constant vigilance of thinking of my charm, I wouldn't trouble myself at all.'

She leans forward and whispers into his ear, 'That's bullshit.'

He smiles and then returns a whisper into her ear, 'Charm is quite high in polyunsaturated bullshit.'

Her laugh always caused him excruciating pleasure. 'Tell me, have you always been so charming?'

'Yes, in a profoundly insufferable sort of way,' he agrees.

'I'm not suffering.'

'Wait until you get to know me better.'

'I'm tired of waiting.'

'I wonder if you'll ever get tired of me.'

'That's a chance worth taking,' she says. 'There is a lot of honesty in a failed relationship.'

'Are you looking for an honest man?'

'Yes, particularly since I'm not an honest woman.'

'I honestly don't care.'

"Bill…"

"I know, another dream."

"No, a memory. I think that I have run out of dreams."

The aircraft spiraled tightly over the airport, reminding Gaude of a carnival ride. It then plunged down, righting itself only moments before the plane made contact with the tarmac. The passenger to their right mumbled, "God, how I hate ex-Army chopper pilots."

As they exited the gate, Gaude mused, "We seem to be running out of country."

"Come again?"

"We've been chasing these fires from one coast to the other. We've even been up to Alaska. Where do we go from here?"

"Maybe Hawaii."

"Over my dead body."

"You have something against Hawaii?"

"No, but I'm not flying six hours just to find another burned church and an obscure clue that leads me to Midway Island or Guam. We've come to the Pacific. I think we need to stop here."

Watt and Gaude threaded through the clusters of fellow travelers enroute to carousel three. Once they secured their bags, Watt nodded toward the transportation sign in front of them. "What shall it be? Rental or taxi?"

"I'm not keen on driving through San Francisco."

"Neither am I, so a taxi it is."

"You don't think…?"

"You never know." Just as the two exited through the revolving door, the anticipated Yellow Checker cab, operated by the hoped-for cabbie wearing an indigo turban, pulled up in front of them. Gaude and Watt eagerly jumped into the back seat.

"Sinbad, my friend! How did we know that you would be here to greet us?"

"How indeed? Perhaps because you prayed?"

"I don't think that I did."

"But you are not sure that you did not."

"I'm glad to see you no matter what made you materialize. We need your help."

"Lean on me."

"Do you know where we are going?"

"Truly. My dispatcher has given me the address of your burned church."

"How do you know that it's *our* burned church?"

"You are now becoming particular about your burned churches?"

"*Touché*," Gaude acknowledged with a chuckle. "Sinbad, I've given up trying to figure out how you magically appear in different cities, but I'm still confounded by how you can arrange for different dispatchers across an entire continent."

"Is it too difficult to believe?"

"Yes, it is."

"That is because you are trying to believe or not trying to believe. Instead, you should stop trying and just believe. If it is, then so it is."

"Okay, fine, you can keep your secret on how you skip from dispatcher to dispatcher."

"Who said that I use different dispatchers?"

Gaude and Watt exchanged a look, finally broken by Bill Watt whispering, "We've got to stop staring at each other every time we're flabbergasted by Sinbad."

Gaude responded to Sinbad, "Once again, you win."

"If God would tell me that I win as much as you say it, truly, I would go out and buy a lottery ticket."

"By the way, Sinbad, when we were in Las Vegas, someone coined a new nickname for you."

"Yes?"

"Aladdin."

"That is the nickname of my cousin Kuwarjeet who lives in Detroit."

"Does he drive a taxi?"

"He is an ophthalmologist."

"Well, if we're ever in Detroit—"

"Yes, I know, you will keep an eye out for him."

"Sinbad, I think that you've been in America too long."

"That is what all the cousins in Amritsar say."

"How far is it to the church?"

"Today traffic is not so light, but not so heavy. It will take as long as *The Rite of Spring,* I believe."

"Stravinsky," replied Gaude absent-mindedly.

"Yes, it is a ballet by Stravinsky. This is a favorite of mine," said Sinbad as he inserted a disk into the sound system of his cab. "I am optimistic that you will enjoy this also."

"Perhaps this music can cheer us up."

"I do not think that this will give us cheer, but it is music that is wonderful to hear at a time of destruction, for this is the sound of creation."

"Creation?"

"Yes, this was the music God played as he formed the earth. Stravinsky said that he wrote this to be a ballet of Russian girls performing folk dances, but he cheated. He listened in on God creating the universe."

> *A cautious, gentle opening of a bassoon.*
> *Soft, mysterious, gradually awakening.*

"I welcome God's soundtrack. I wish that I could call upon God's judgment," said Watt.

"I am quite certain that this is not necessary. God doubtless has issued his judgment. God is truly angered by these outrages."

"The wrath of God?" asked Gaude.

"Yes, and we shall all see this wrath someday. In the meantime, God is contented to grieve," said Sinbad gravely as he turned off Airport Access Road and began the merge onto Bayshore Expressway.

The accompanying instruments wander in,
slowly joining, intermittently advancing.

"You believe that God can be sad?"

"Truly. God is both angered and saddened by the desecration of holy places. As a Christian, do you not believe in a grieving God? Do you think he was happy when he saw your Jesus dying in agony on the cross? He is also capable of regret. I remember that in your Bible Book of Genesis it says that God regretted creating mankind and sent a flood."

"Can God cry?"

"Can you cry?"

"Of course."

"Surely you do not say that you can do something that God cannot do? Who would claim an ability beyond that of the creator and ruler of the universe? Is there anything you can do that God is incapable of doing?"

The machine-like progress of the strings competes with staccato
of the woodwinds and intermittent shouts of brass.

"Yes, sin. God doesn't sin."

"Then once again, you limit his capabilities, making him finite."

"But God, by definition, is without sin."

"You define God without sin, as do I. But neither you nor I can say that God is incapable of sin. He simply chooses not to sin. God is— and must be, if we consider him God—the being having every conceivable power. That means that there is nothing, absolutely nothing, not within the power and capacity of God. All that was, is, and will be constitute the handiwork of God."

"But not evil."

Chirping and tweeting flutes are pushed aside
by the intermittent yet progressive cacophony of horns,
then percussion, creating a rising tide of excitement punctuated
by brief silences and then the gentle voice of a clarinet.

"You are making God small—quite small, in fact, since there is so much evil in the world. God created a spiritual being, Lucifer, who had the capacity to do evil," continued Sinbad. "He creates humans, each of us with the capacity to do evil."

"That's our free will."

"Is it not also true that God created free will? Surely, he created it when he designed the intellect of humans and bestowed upon us all sentience. It is certain that God could have created all life without free will, much as he created plants and primitive animals. He did not do this, did he? That is because he is not plagued with the doubt that we lesser beings suffer. He is confident in his completeness, in his infinite power, knowledge, and wisdom. Truly, God has his most powerful hand on the throttle of evil by giving life to entities capable, and sometimes eager, to commit evil. God's hands are not clean, but they do not need to be. Indeed, they should not be. If the hands of God's were incapable of being dirty, then he would be a lesser God, which means not God at all."

The music continues to build.
The workings of nature, desperate and energetic, furious,
afraid, yet determined and relentless, twist and merge.

Bill Watt raised an eyebrow and asked, "How do you come to the conclusion that a God with clean hands is somehow lesser for it?"

"Because truly, God must encompass all of existence. Everything, absolutely everything, without an exception, is created, maintained, and destroyed by God. If there were exceptions, he would be an unexceptional God," declared Sinbad authoritatively as he merged onto Eisenhower Highway.

"Something about that reeks of paradox, but I can't put my finger on it," said Gaude.

"God is truly the master of all paradox. He proved that well when he first created man and woman."

"So, God is responsible for evil?"

"Responsible? No, he made us responsible for our own decisions."

"If we are responsible, then God cannot control us."

"I am afraid that you are mistaken. Who could deny that God can control us? He has a choice, just as we do. He chooses not to control us. He could just as easily choose to do the opposite. He makes a choice between those powers he will exercise. Thus, there is no limitation."

"Except the limitation which he imposes upon himself."

"My friend, that is not a limitation. It is not that God passed a law that he himself is incapable of violating. He simply decides what he wishes to decide. If you walk into the kitchen and see a cookie jar, what prevents you from taking one? They are your cookies, are they not? You are free to take one—or all of them for that matter—and no one will stop you. You do not to take a cookie because you are not hungry now. Perhaps you are in the mood for a sandwich."

"Just as long as the sandwich is *jhatka*," quipped Gaude.

"Agreed," said Sinbad with a smile. "Perhaps also you started to diet or maybe you are fasting. Making a choice is not a limitation, it is a decision that you can make and unmake at will."

The strings relentlessly throb and crawl forward.
A crash, the strings scream desperately then race forward
heedlessly as in terror only to be chided
by the punctuating flutes and clarinets.
Bangs of percussion, throbbing, rushing, tearing and then—silence.

"But there are innumerable decisions that I am unable to make, and plenty that I make have consequences that cannot be escaped."

"Because you are not God. Imagine a being who can make decisions about everything in the galaxy with the same ease that you can make about taking a cookie from the cookie jar. If God so chooses, he could make the cookie jar wink out of existence or create a million companion cookie jars to sit beside it. Once you put a limit on God, you deny his divinity."

"God did create rules. Rules of science, psychics, mathematics."

Cautious strains depict the mystic circle of young women
gradually working up to a pounding of the tympani.
A thrumming march—the cadences ordered by the strings,
the horns and trumpets join into acclaim.

"Are you saying that God is penned in by those rules?" asked Sinbad. "He made the rules. He can change them, he can break them, he can destroy or eliminate them. Surely, you know this. I do not think that your nuns would allow you to sleep through your Bible school, my friend. Tell me how the standard and accepted rules of the universe explain the parting of the Red Sea? The earth stopping on its axis? A man raised from the dead? Miracles are things that confound scientists and ignore the so-called rules of the universe. God made those rules and he can unmake them. He is all, and capable of all that can be imagined, and everything that cannot be imagined, for God's imagination is infinite, which means that his imagination is… unimaginable."

Now a measured dance, step-by-step, interrupted
by an energetic outburst,
but then retreating back into regulated steps
until peace descends.

"You make God impossible to understand."

"As they say here in America: 'Bingo!' I say that, of course, in all due reverence to the very sacred institution of bingo," Sinbad added with a coy smile. "You have said it. Now, stop saying anything. You arrived at the right place, the right answer. You cannot understand God. I cannot understand God. No one other than God will understand God. Truly, no one will ever know what God knows. Even your savior Jesus, who you believe is God's own son, says that there is knowledge reserved to God that even he does not know." Sinbad now took the exit to Seventh Street.

The insistent demanding strings, the brass arguing,
the pulse returns, a few disputing voices attempt vainly
to compete with the inexorable downpull of the stings,
forward, always forward, to meet their fate.

"But you are presuming to lecture me on God as if you *do* understand his mind."

"Oh, no! Please, not at all! It is only that I have an appreciation of my own ignorance of God. I know that God is impossible to understand. I spend countless waking hours contemplating my profound ignorance of God. In doing so, I gain a better appreciation of my shortcomings, my weakness, and my frailties. The more I understand my insignificance, the more I can appreciate God's significance. Even so, I can never understand the overwhelming majesty of God. And yet it is also true—in a way that I can never understand—that I am his creation and child. This is true of us all, is it not? We inherit the glory of God. I do not presume, but rather hope to discern some small aspect of the Almighty. I think about God constantly, not to understand him, but to better share with my fellow children of God how unfathomable he is. The devil whispers into people's ears and fools them into believing that they can understand God, and once they so understand him, they can be like him. Truly, we must stop thinking about *what* God is and simply accept *who* God is." At the corner of Seventh and Market, Sinbad turned left.

Sometimes leaping ahead, circling around,
surging, the horns register their objections,
cautioning the determined headstrong strings.

"And who is God?"

"You know the truth already, my friend. God is you. God is me. God is all of us. God surrounds and encompasses us. God gave us life, and when he considers it the proper time, he will usher us into death. Live as if you are in God and he is in you, because that—and only that—is the one truth we can be assured."

The entire orchestra engages in the melee of the argument
as the sacrificial dance throws itself heedlessly ahead,
giving its all, its last, as the music comes to a conclusion
and the chosen one perishes into immortality.

Sinbad turned right at Hyde and came to a stop just as the orchestra arrived at its last notes. "I will leave you here and pick you up later. Perhaps in two hours. If you are pleased to do it, you may ride the train downtown and I will find you at the waterfront terminal."

"Another errand with a cousin?"

"Yes. My cousin, Talib, needs my help to move a piano."

"You also have a cousin in San Francisco?"

"Yes, does not everyone?"

Chapele left the police station after having signed his statement. The autopsy would be conducted later that day and the body released to family the next morning. He checked his cellphone and opened an incoming text message. It was from the attorney he had met three hours before.

< Mr. Chapele, Please meet me at Reuben Malachi's cabin on the Coosaw River this afternoon. 3:00 pm. Thank you. >

Oh, God no! thought Chapele. *Not back there! Is this guy crazy?*

He's Reuben's lawyer, his own silent voice said in reply. *Birds of a feather.*

I have to go all the way back there in a lousy jon boat?

You could rent something bigger.

I don't know how to handle something bigger.

Sucks to be you.

Thanks so much.

Make sure to check the tides this time.

After stopping for lunch at Cooter's Sandwich Shop, Chapele walked to the marina. One hour later, he was cautiously navigating the small olive drab green aluminum boat through a narrow path of water between banks of tall marshgrass, towards Malachi's now-familiar cabin. As luck would have it, flow tide had commenced and he was able to reach the dock without having to debark and slog through the muddy ooze that constituted the so-called land of the marshlands. A new Boston Whaler was already tied up.

Why didn't this guy offer me a ride instead of making me come out all this way by myself in a lousy jon boat?

He's a lawyer.

He's a shithead.

Same thing.

Chapele put a quick hitch on an open cleat and climbed onto the dock. He walked to the cabin, entered the door and announced himself. He saw the lawyer standing out on the back deck in the exact spot Chapele had seen Reuben Malachi three weeks before. The attorney's clothing adhered to the unofficial yet rigorously obeyed dress code of the South Carolina Bar during the months falling between March and October: A navy blue blazer, khaki trousers, a pale blue cotton oxford shirt and yellow tie. As an attorney from Beaufort, he exercised the privilege of exchanging the usual brown wingtips or penny loafers for a pair of Sperry Topsiders.

"Mister Chapele," the attorney said, stepping forward. "Thank you for coming out to meet me."

They exchanged a perfunctory handshake. "I assume that this meeting couldn't be conducted in your office?" Chapele asked.

"I'm following orders," the lawyer responded.

"That was the same answer given by the guards at…" Chapele stopped himself and shook his head. "Never mind."

The lawyer shrugged and made a motion with his hand towards the front door that Chapele had just entered. He then walked past Chapele to the door, turned around, and took an envelope from the interior pocket of his jacket. Chapele accepted it and saw that it was covered with the unmistakable handlettering of Reuben Malachi. The letters were elaborate, almost gothic, and precise. The envelope was addressed to *Homo Sapiens Inhabiting the Planet Yentz*. "It appears to be the last thing he wrote."

"Are you sure?"

"They found it on him."

"I was the first person here and I didn't see it."

"That, at least, speaks to your integrity. You obviously didn't search the pockets of a corpse. It was in his jacket."

Chapele paused before opening the envelope. He noticed that the seal had already been broken. "You read it?"

"It's my job. There was a substantial chance that it might have been a document that impacted his will—we refer to that as a codicil."

"It wasn't addressed to you."

"It could have been addressed to the tooth fairy for all I care. I am Reuben Malachi's attorney, regardless of whether he is alive or dead. Besides, I am a member of *Homo Sapiens*, although I haven't a clue where the Planet *Yentz* might be."

"*Yentz* is Yiddish for 'screwed,' I believe."

"A perverse sense of humor is not an infallible indicator of sanity."

Chapele decided to move on with the subject. "Was it a will...or codicil?"

"No. Just as well. For a will to be valid, the testator...the person writing the will...must have been of a sound and disposing mind."

"Reuben wasn't?"

"At the time he executed his will last year, he was undeniably sane, although he certainly had his quirks."

"And at the time of his death?"

"Not at all relevant, since his will was already signed, sealed, witnessed, and delivered, and this letter makes no attempt to change his bequests. Read the letter. Call me if you have any questions." The lawyer handed Chapele a card and walked towards the door. He hesitated near one of Reuben's sculptures and pretended to admire it, then exited. Chapele walked back into the greatroom and sat in the old overstuffed chair near the picture window, Reuben's favorite chair. He heard the rev of a boat engine signaling the lawyer's departure. Chapele looked out the window overlooking the seemingly endless marsh. He then opened the letter and began to read.

To Everyone, to Anyone, to No-One in Particular:
No, only to Thomas Chapele.
Hand this to him at the front door of my cabin.
That is where we met and that is where we will bid adieu.

My Dear Chappie,

The authorities will doubtless discover my body, perhaps several weeks putrefied, with a bullet hole in my head, dried blood and brains spattered on the wall, and a pistol dropped on the floor beside a copy of American Review featuring your exposé. By the power of shrewd deduction, they shall arrive at the conclusion that I must have died due to an allergic reaction to the local shellfish. Do me a favor, my friend, and let them on to our little secret. I blew out my brains with a gun.

I must admit that I struggled with the decision to end my life in this way. After all, I dread to be depicted a copycat suicide. The kindly disposed might connect this to Hemingway. The less friendly would refer to Hunter Thompson.

You are, no doubt, wracked with guilt. You need some comforting words from me. If you expect any such consolation in this letter, then you are an even bigger fool than I ever imagined, and my vivid imagination, albeit not universally praised, could never be categorically denied. However, fret not, my friend. No delicate snowflake am I. Despite the unpleasantness of your investigative revelations, I was not plunged into such guilt or despair that I felt it necessary to end the heartache of a thousand natural shocks with a bare bodkin. Nay, I will be using a Smith & Wesson revolver. It is about time I make my exit, stage left, and your screed was as convenient an excuse as any that I'd likely encounter for many a year. In our last conversation, you mentioned that you were working your tuchas off to make me famous. I decided that you needed a little help, so I went out with a bang, not a whimper.

If you are inclined to wallow in self-pity, please yourself. Feel free to interview my so-called uncle, who, I have little doubt, arranged to have your magazine delivered by the same mysterious courier employed to deposit his malevolent letters at my front door.

To further your career in the literary world, assuming that you do not decide to segue to investigative journalism, I am giving you exclusive rights to the following little poem that I wrote on the very day I slipped this mortal coil.

WILLY SONG

Willy is as Willy was
And Willy'll always do,
But anything that Willy feels
Is all the same to you.

Fuzzy breath and Willy deep,
No holds barred, that's true,
But circles mended
When life is ended
Is all the same to you.

So ring a bell, clasp a hand,
Pay any debt that's due,
But flesh, remember,
Is legal tender,
And is all the same to you.

The last words above his initial were hand-printed in simple, childish, block letters:

I FORGIVE YOU ALL.
WHO IS COMING TO FORGIVE ME?

Beneath was a post-script:

Tell the undertaker to bury me next to Disraeli.

Katie has fled to the desert west of Eden and the Beast pursues.
Help her if you can and watch over El Niño.

—R

Chapele stood up and looked over Reuben's worktable which was uncharacteristically organized and clutter-free. Neat piles of manuscripts were arranged in rows, with notes on top of each stack providing instructions for either publication, archiving, or destruction. In the middle of the table, a small placard of cardstock folded as a tent bore the inscription:

The living quite often lead very messy lives,
but once deceased,
they have the opportunity
of being the very model of orderliness.

Chapele scanned the contents of the table and noticed that one of the piles of paper was much taller than the rest. He reached for the note on top.

Chappie,

My last major effort. You were here at Macondo (I will defer to my dear Katie's preference as to the name of my realm) as I put down the finishing touches, so be sure to regale the family with anecdotes about your stay here when your grandchildren are assigned to read this book in eleventh grade English class. This tome is as bad as my best and as good as my worst, which says nothing of whether it will be a commercial success. Given that my need for money is not nearly as dire as when I was breathing, I really don't give a rat's derrière. This book is to be published one year from the day of my death. Obviously, Ripley will not be engaged for this work, and assuming their lawyers have not brought all my postmortem publishing efforts to a standstill through liens and litigation, I recommend offering this to whatever might be left of—and whoever might be left at— Brookguild.

Chapele picked up the large manuscript and glanced down at the title page. He walked back to the overstuffed flamestitch armchair and sat down. As he did so, his eye drifted over the portraits covering the walls. He was suddenly struck with the sense that the faces—*the face*—of the woman in every portrait had changed. They were still sad and weary, but now each visage was beset with a look of enlightened confusion and hopeful despair. The faces displayed a whiff of the religious, but the eyes betrayed that she had been dragged through the stench of the secular. Chapele shook his head in gentle resignation and then turned his attention back to the book. As he did so, he saw a gray cat slink into the room.

"Where the hell did you come from?" Chapele asked out loud. The cat responded with a look of suspicion and disdain that matched that of the man. Both the cat and the man shrugged, and Chapele then opened to the first page of the book's prologue.

> *America had seduced him. Only six weeks earlier he had casually sported a well-laid veneer of expatriate sophistication. This, at least, was the image that his mind's eye portrayed...*

⌘

"The remains of this building don't look much like a church."

"You've developed an eye for examining post-catastrophic houses of worship."

"I suppose I need to update my resume to include that skillset."

As Watt and Gaude approached the carbonized remains of the former church, they saw just beyond the yellow tape barricade a team of young men and women placing a variety of blooms into a complex wire armature that resembled a small New England chapel. A cargo delivery van pulled up alongside the new project. Emblazed on the side of the van was a hand-lettered sign.

> ## Heavenly Bouquets
> Flower Shop Extraordinaire
> Specialists in Funeral Arrangements

The driver exited the vehicle and opened the back doors, revealing a delivery of every imaginable flower, from roses to tulips, from orchids to azaleas, from marigolds to hydrangeas, and from lotus to lilacs to lilies. The driver began giving instructions to the group, clearly evidencing his role as leader of the floral construction enterprise. Watt and Gaude stepped forward.

"If you don't mind me saying, you seem to be in charge," said Watt.

"If it comes to flowers, that would be an accurate observation," the driver replied. "I am Umar Wahib. I own the flower shop."

Watt handed Wahib the ubiquitous business card. "I am Bill Watt and my partner is Dan Gaude."

"You are here for more than merely satisfying your curiosity, I see," said Wahib as he finished examining the card. He looked back up and then reexamined both visitors. "Pardon my candor, but you look more like a bookkeeper," he said to Watt. "And you..." addressing Gaude, "...I'd wager would be a quantum physicist."

"A what?"

"My roommate at Berkley majored in physics. I know one when I see one."

"How about if you humor an erstwhile bookkeeper and an out-of-work physicist and point us in the direction of someone we can talk to about the church burning?"

"Besides the fire department?"

"Yes, perhaps someone who might be a caretaker of the church?"

"You are in luck. That would be me."

"You are the pastor?" asked Gaude.

"There is no pastor of our community except Jesus, the good shepherd."

"Who makes decisions in the absence of Jesus?"

"Jesus is never absent. He promised to be with us always, even to the end of the age."

Bill Watt joined in. "Agreed. Perhaps we could discuss this with a disciple?"

"In that case, I am at your service."

"You are a member of the congregation?"

"Yes, but we prefer to use the term 'community' instead."

"Is there a difference?"

"Yes."

"What is that?"

"The difference is that we use the term 'community' to describe ourselves because we wish to be called a community. The other groups use the term 'congregation' to describe themselves because they wish to be called a congregation. We are called the Community Tabernacle of the Faithful Church of Patmos."

"That works for me," conceded Bill Watt. "Can you tell us something about the fire?"

"It was hot, it was bright, and it took away our church."

"Yes, I suppose that pretty much sums it up. Do you know the cause?"

"We were told the cause, although it is difficult to understand it. We had a landline in our church connected to an old rotary telephone. It was rarely used, but it was difficult to part with. You see, an article of our faith is that nothing should be discarded as useless. God made humans for a purpose. We humans, in turn, make objects for a purpose. So long as the purpose of the object is pleasing in God's eyes, it is incumbent upon us to respect that object until it no longer is capable of functioning for the purpose it was created."

"What if there is no apparent purpose?"

"Then it is our duty to seek out that purpose."

"Did you ever discern the purpose of the rotary phone?"

"Other than the obvious fact that it still continued to function as a telephone? Yes, it seemed to many of us that it as a charming conversation piece, at the risk of making a play on words."

"How could a telephone start a fire?"

"No one knows. Telephones operate on twelve volts. That's not enough to create a respectable spark, much less set off a flame. The firefighters, however, traced back the source of the outbreak to the phone. That is all we know."

"The fire happened last night?"

"Technically speaking, today, at about three in the morning."

"Did you or anyone else in your community see anything strange or suspicious that night or perhaps a day or two before?"

"We are in San Francisco. In this city, there is only the strange and suspicious."

"Anything abnormally normal, then? Anything that sticks out?"

"Like I said, this is San Francisco."

Gaude joined in. "Speaking of out of the ordinary, from what I can tell of what's left of this structure, it doesn't look like it was much like a traditional church."

"The tabernacle was converted from a Western Sizzlin'

Steakhouse."

"Oh."

"You don't approve?"

"No, it's not that, it's just…"

"Odd?"

"Perhaps."

"The process of conversion is inherently odd. A billion years ago, God took the bubbling pools of toxic chemicals that he had originally created and converted them into the formula of life. Microbes were transformed into moss and worms. In turn, those simple creatures were converted into more complex creatures. Finally, all of this conversion culminated with the creation of sentient beings with a mind and a soul. Consider the miserable sinner who is converted and redeemed. That pathetic failure is now a child of God. Converting a derelict steakhouse into a place of worship is absolutely unremarkable in comparison."

"That's a strained analogy."

"You think so? Haven't you heard the teachings from the Bible that the human body is a temple of God? It's not a strained analogy in the least."

"To each their own."

"Perhaps, but I'm sure you know that we are not unique. From coast to coast, America is strewn with storefront churches. Admittedly, not many of them befall the ironic fate of having previously been referred to as 'Sizzlin' and then later succumb to a fire."

"I hope no one has been tempted to make jokes—"

"Too late. There are already postings on the web."

"I'm sorry to hear that."

"Bearing the whips and scorns of time is the inheritance of humanity."

Gaude gestured to the project being undertaken by the half dozen young people at the site. "The flowers are beautiful, but I'm not sure of the purpose. What are you doing here?"

"We are replacing the tabernacle."

"With a chapel of flowers?"

"Its design is based on the chapel where I attended services as a young boy in Maine. That place also recently burned to the ground."

"That wouldn't happen to have been a chapel in Destinations, Maine?"

Wahib was visibly surprised. "Yes, exactly! Have you ever been there?"

"A few weeks ago, on the day after it burned down."

"A strange coincidence."

"There are no…" Gaude hesitated and then resumed, "Yes, you're right, a very strange coincidence."

"It is beautiful, no?" asked Wahib, gesturing to the flowerful work in progress.

"It's beautiful, yes, but it seems rather impermanent."

"So was the chapel in Maine that it commemorates. So was the original tabernacle right here that it replaces. Both buildings burned down and are no more. Is the fact they are now gone a good reason to suggest that it should never have been built?"

"I'm not saying that, but the building lasted longer than you can expect a chapel of flowers to exist. How long will these flowers live?"

"They will last as long as they last. A building will stand as long as it stands. A person will live as long as he lives. It is all relative, but those things that pass away quickly are no less important, no less significant, no less worthy."

"The flowers could all die tomorrow."

"So could you. So could I. So what if something good is short-lived? Jesus died as a young man. What if something bad endures for a long time? Stalin died of old age. The important thing is that while it exists in that moment it is beautiful, fills us with joy, and brings us closer to the Almighty. What more could you ask of a church?"

"Nothing," Bill Watt agreed. "Nothing at all."

"Do you mind if we search through the remains?" asked Gaude.

"The city inspectors have already combed through the wreckage. I doubt that you'll find anything new."

"Perhaps we'll find something old."

"Be my guest."

Watt and Gaude sifted through the charred waste as Wahib returned to supervise the construction of the floral chapel. Twenty minutes later, the partners returned.

"Nothing to show for your troubles?" asked Wahib.

"What about this?"

"What about what?"

"A bottle of wine," replied Gaude, showing the ash-covered bottle to their host.

"A half-empty wine bottle by the look of it," said Wahib dismissively.

"Yes, but apparently untouched by the flames."

"A bit surprising," conceded Wahib, "but hardly qualifying as a miracle."

"Does your church—your community—use sacramental wine during its worship services?"

"Yes, but we don't leave half-empty bottles lying around."

"Do you know why this is here?"

"For one, we're surrounded by California wine country."

"I suppose…"

"And for another, this place is not exactly Presidio Heights. There must be at least a hundred thousand discarded bottles within a few square blocks of here."

"So, I guess you wouldn't consider this unusual?"

"I'd be amazed if an old bottle *wasn't* left here. Although…"

"Yes?"

"Bottles are usually empty. That wine must be corked or very cheap." Wahib extended his hand in a gesture to request the bottle from Gaude. The bottle was surrendered and their host examined the label. His eyebrows elevated in surprise. Wahib blinked his eyes repeatedly as if to regain focus and his hands began to shake slightly as he continued to stare in stunned silence. He looked back up to the two visitors. "Don't…" his voice squeaked. Wahib cleared his throat and tried again. "Don't mistake me for a connoisseur or a wine snob, but this is the stuff of legend."

"What do you mean?"

"This is the most exclusive, the most sought-after, the most—"

"Are you sure?"

"I know enough to be dangerous. Both of my brothers are oenologists in Napa Valley."

"Oenologists?"

"Part wine scientist, part winemaker. I suppose you might call them the wine version of a beer brewer or a whiskey distiller, but on a more elevated status. My brothers call themselves grape engineers. I've picked up a few things from them." Wahib then pulled out the cork and cautiously sniffed the contents. He whispered something to himself that Gaude could not quite hear.

"Is there anything significant about this wine?"

"Please, give me a moment," Wahib gently reprimanded as he continued to make short gentle sniffs from the bottle. He finally lowered the bottle, slightly shook his head in amazement and muttered to himself, "How in the blue blazes did it survive a fire?" Wahib returned his attention to Gaude, "You were asking…?"

"Could you tell us what is so special about this wine?"

"Other than the fact that this bottle has a retail price roughly equivalent of a month's rent? I'm talking about rent here in San Francisco, by the way, and of a fairly large apartment. I remember my brothers taking about this vintage. James Suckling gives it a ninety-nine-point-nine. The *Wine Spectator* offered an apology that they could not give it a higher score than one hundred. They say this is what was poured into the Holy Grail at the Last Supper. There are stories that Hugh Johnson came back from the dead three years ago to bid on a bottle at auction. I have no idea where this wine has been, who has touched it, or whether it has been poisoned by some malicious homicidal maniac. Even so, I have an almost overwhelming urge to take a drink of this right now."

"I wonder how it was left here."

"It must be stolen."

"Maybe it was accidentally donated to a charity. Y'know, like when a Picasso is found in an attic and given to Goodwill."

"Given away by mistake?" asked Wahib indignantly. "A Picasso? Maybe. This wine? Never!"

"It's a California wine?"

"It is *the* California wine. In fact, it is more than that. The French, in their own pretentious and possessive way, declared it a universal legacy of the original Bordeaux root stock."

"Where is the winery located?"

"That's somewhat shrouded in mystery. Rumor has it that the vineyard is owned by a secret society—something like the Freemasons but far more shadowy. Twelve bottles are released each year to the public for auction. It's believed that all the rest are shipped to Russian oligarchs and Middle-Eastern royalty, and perhaps a bottle or two reserved for the Pope. The label alone is probably worth more than one hundred dollars."

"Where is this secret vineyard?"

Wahib looked at Gaude with disdain. "If I knew where it was—"

"It wouldn't be secret. Right. Sorry, I must have taken stupid

445

pills this morning."

"If you washed down those stupid pills with this wine, it would truly have been a memorable event."

"Is it likely that anyone in the wine business could tell us where to find the vineyard?"

"As I said, my brothers qualify as bonafide experts. I recall them talking about how this was a better kept secret than the identity of the spy agency that listens to our cellphone calls and reads our emails. Most experts would assume that the grapes are from Napa or Sonoma, but my brothers have a theory that wine this unique and extraordinary must come from a unique geography and an extraordinary microclimate. That widens the aperture considerably."

"Hmmm…that doesn't give us much to work with."

"Or perhaps too much to work with. They did mention there is a strong possibility that these grapes grew near the ocean."

"How do they know that?"

"You're asking the wrong guy. Like I told you, I know enough to be dangerous, nothing more."

"I suppose you would prefer to keep this bottle?" Gaude asked Wahib.

"That is a very safe assumption. Getting this bottle from me falls into the 'over my dead body' category."

"May I take a photograph of the label?"

"Of course," agreed Wahib, as he tenderly cradled the bottle at an angle while Gaude took out his cellphone to capture the image.

"I suppose that we'd better be going," suggested Watt.

"Is that a bus station over there?" asked Gaude, pointing to a small glass and steel structure across the street.

Wahib nodded. "Sort of. You've come to the end of the line."

"Say again?" asked Gaude, startled.

"The streetcar." Wahib gestured across the street. "Our church is located at the last streetcar station on Market Street. After the most recent earthquake destroyed the metro subway, there was a debate whether to replace it with a reproduction cable car or a monorail system. The arguments, meetings, and street protests went on and on. This is San Francisco, after all. Finally, it was announced that a decision was made to rebuild the subway. That led to even more acrimonious arguments, meetings, and street protests. Then, one day without any fanfare, construction crews showed up and started repairing tracks and transmission lines. It turns out that someone—we will never know who—decided that the city would simply extend the existing streetcar system, which is a perfectly reasonable solution. Of course, if that common sense had been proposed in the first place and submitted for public debate we would still be mired in protests, demonstrations and lawsuits."

"It sounds like you're not too keen on grassroots democracy."

Wahib shrugged. "The opposite has its drawbacks as well. You see, the non-democratically imposed restoration project stopped right here at the edge of the Tenderloin when the funding disappeared. No one is sure who stole the money, but no one was particularly surprised. One hundred years ago, there was a cable car that went from the waterfront all the way up to Castro and then to Twenty-Sixth Street. Now, the line is a mere shadow of its former self. So much for progress. Anyway, no further construction appears to be forthcoming, so for the time being, this is the end of the line."

"I see."

"You can ride it down to the terminal if you wish."

"Yes, thank you."

"You're in luck. This is the last Friday of the month. Streetcar Four is running today. It's a vintage beauty. You're sure to enjoy the ride." Wahib carefully switched the bottle into the crook of his left arm and then extended his right hand for a farewell handshake.

Watt and Gaude took the open streetcar along the uncharacteristically flat and level Market Street of the quintessentially hilly San Francisco. A raw, cold wind coming off the bay and funneling down Market Street lashed at them, stinging Gaude's cheeks. "It's cold. Don't tell me that we had another sudden shift in the seasons."

"The one constant is change," replied Watt.

"*El Niño* again?"

"No, not that. This is San Francisco. It's business—or perhaps I should say weather—as usual."

Watt and Gaude stepped off Tram Number Four near the Steuart Street intersection and walked along the variegated pedestrian throughway flanked by an honor guard of towering palms. Gaude saw a large open plaza before them leading to the Ferry Terminal Tower. The passing foot traffic consisted of an unremarkable mix of locals and tourists, with the singular exception of a very tall woman, wearing what appeared to be a circus ringmaster's costume, leading a hippopotamus

447

on a rope. None of the other pedestrians paid any notice to the incongruous couple. As the woman crossed Gaude's path, she turned her head towards him, smiled and winked. Gaude stopped and stared in a stunned stasis as she continued to walk past, heading south. *That smile that was her smile,* he realized, *that wink that was her wink.* He knew without being able to identify the specific *her* of the perfect recall of his imperfect memory.

"Anything wrong?" asked Bill Watt after a sustained pause.

"Are you kidding?" responded Gaude in disbelief. "Didn't you see her?"

"See who?"

"Her!" insisted Gaude, gesturing to the left.

"I see a number of hers…shes…women…in that direction," said Watt patiently as he scanned the crowd.

Gaude began to gesture again but checked himself as he realized that the woman and her rotund companion had disappeared from sight. "She's gone…"

"So it would seem."

"Again."

"Pardon?"

"Never mind."

Watt reacted with his characteristic good-natured shrug and resumed walking forward. Gaude then followed, and as they approached the terminal, Gaude saw a larger-than-life bronze statue of Harry Bridges perched on a granite plinth. The adored and abhorred labor leader was dressed in a wrinkled topcoat and fedora, one arm akimbo, and the other holding a cigarette. The alloy Harry made a skeptical glare to his right, seemingly directed at another monument ten meters away.

"Well, there it is," said Gaude, as he pointed to the slab inscribed with verse. "I assumed that sooner or later we'd come across another poem."

"That's the one thing you've consistently predicted before-the-fact," said Watt. "We need to cultivate that power of prognostication to focus upon targeted churches."

"Prognostication? Don't you mean prophesy?"

"Let's not get ahead of ourselves," cautioned Watt with a grin.

City on the Bay

She exudes charm and beauty
'neath a filthy petticoat,
A suave and cultured debutante
Who will dance with any beau.

In the face of disappointment
She decrees redecorate
And flies into a nervous fit,
More laws to procreate.

Smarmy with self-confidence
And chauvinistic pride,
She marches more for kiss-and-tell
Than for any martyr died.

Casual and comfortable
Beautiful and calm,
Everything is open-air
And tres chic, nes pas?

Openness and opulence,
Grandeur on the cheap,
Refinement and intelligence,
Just don't scratch too deep.

To foundations shaken
For those living in the street,
A feast for all who network here
But can't afford to eat.

On the bulliest of pulpits
She cries freedom to oppress
And none dare oppose the dame
On the highway to regress.

Browse not the map for Eden,
This was the paradise,
And fittingly the community
Was evicted for a price.

She had a chance to save herself,
But mortgaged off her soul.
Who, say who, will blame the earth
When it swallows this place whole?

—Reuben Malachi

Gaude turned to Watt. "I'm surprised that the city allowed this to stand. It's not exactly a ringing endorsement of the place."

"The history of San Francisco is a series of pendulum swings from self-adulation, to self-delusion, to self-loathing. The residents are drawn to revulsion and repulsed by success and then turn upon themselves in an agonizing cycle of dissatisfying reincarnation."

"That doesn't sound very pleasant."

"It's an acquired taste."

"Like chili with Rice-A-Roni?"

"Dan, you don't really think that they eat Rice-A-Roni in San Francisco?"

"Have you ever tied to order it?"

"Hmmm…come to think of it, you might be on to something,"

Watt replied with a wry grin. His face suddenly dropped as he looked above Gaude's head. "What's that?" he asked, clearly distressed by the sight.

"What's what?" responded Gaude as he spun around. He then saw the black plume of smoke rising to the south. "It could be anything," said Gaude, trying to reassure his partner.

"Anything includes a church."

"We've been at this too long. I think that we're getting jumpy."

"Perhaps, but let's check it out just to be sure," said Watt. Gaude pulled out his cellphone and began a search. "I meant, check it out by going over and looking."

"That might be too far away," said Gaude. "Besides, I use the tools at my disposal." After thirty seconds of consulting his phone, Gaude looked back up. "Nothing yet."

"Can you get the news on that thing?"

"What do you think that I've been doing for the past three weeks?"

"I don't mean cellphone news or internet news. I mean real news—radio news."

"Yes, but let me check tweets, they're faster." Gaude scrolled the screen of his cell. "Here it is," Gaude declared, and then paused as he read. "Okay, it's a church. Thyatira Taborite." Gaude grimaced as he culled through his memory. "What is a Taborite?"

"They are a predecessor sect to the Moravians," explained Watt.

"Moravians?"

"Do you think we have time to give you a history lesson?" asked Watt. "How do we contact Sinbad?"

"I'm not sure. We've never needed to call him before. He always seems to show up at the right time."

"Should we get another taxi?"

"I suppose so. Where can we get one?" asked Gaude as he scanned down the street. He then noticed another cloud of dark smoke. "No, that's a coincidence," he said. "It can't be another one. It can't be…"

"Why do I suspect that 'it can't be' means 'it might be'?"

Gaude ignored Watt's comment. "Here's a twitter just sent out a few seconds ago. Another one. Smyrna Sabbatarians."

"One to the south, one to the west."

"If you're trying to eke out yet another clue, I'd say you are a day late and a dollar short."

"We don't know that yet."

"I'll order us up an Uber ride."

"Sinbad would not approve."

"Sinbad isn't here."

Watt gestured over Gaude's shoulder. "As a matter of fact, he is here."

Gaude turned and saw the taxi pulling up behind him. He headed for the back left side door as Watt walked over to the right. "My dispatcher contacted me about the church fires and I drove here as fast as I could," explained Sinbad, as Watt and Gaude entered the cab.

"We're not sure which one we should go to first, Thyatira or Smyrna?"

"It was my belief that there is also another house of worship that is burning. It is Pergamum Presbyterian Church."

"Pergamum? There's a third church?"

"It would appear that this is true."

"Which one is closest?"

"I believe that the Church of Smyrna is in the Richmond District, which you can see over to the west. It is not too far away. The Church of Thyatira is in Potero Hill, which is equally not far distant but in the opposite direction, as you can see from the smoke rising in the south. Pergamum is on Holloway Avenue. That is on the border of Twin Peaks and Ingleside. It is not so close."

"Hang on...hang on..." said Gaude distractedly, tapping and swiping on this cellphone screen. "There's another. Ephesus Evangelical."

"The Ephesus Church is on Chestnut Street. That is in the area known as the Marina."

"Is that far away?"

"As you can see," said Sinbad as he gestured towards a new smoke plume, "it is near at hand."

"I'm starting to get confused as to which church is where."

"They are all burning churches," calmly observed Sinbad, "and are equally in peril. Does it matter which is which or which is where?"

"Let's go to the closest first," suggested Watt.

"I'm getting more twitters," interrupted Gaude.

"About Ephesus?"

"Yes, and all the others, including a new one, Sardis

Swedenborgian Chapel."

"This is New York all over again," moaned Watt.

"It is altogether worse, my friends," responded Sinbad, checking a message on his own cellphone. "My dispatcher informs me that there is another fire, Philadelphia Pentecostal Church."

"Philadelphia? You mean as in Pennsylvania?"

"No, Philadelphia as in Hunter's point, here in San Francisco."

"Laodicea," announced Gaude as he read from his cellphone screen.

"What?"

"Laodicea Lutheran Church. It was just reported on Twitter."

"Sunset District," replied Sinbad without hesitation.

"How many churches is that?"

"Seven."

"Sinbad, how do you know San Francisco so well?" asked Watt.

"I have a medallion," said Sinbad as he gestured to a small yellow license plate on the dash of his cab, "and I am a member in good standing with my brothers of the Bay Area United Taxicab Workers."

"Which church is closest now?"

"The most close of all the burning churches is Ephesus," answered Sinbad.

"Let's go."

The ten-minute drive was accompanied by the mix of ominous strains and heroic interludes of *Finlandia* by Jean Sibelius, coming to a triumphant finale just as they arrived at their destination which was cordoned off, surrounded by a profusion of flashing lights and being inundated by a downpour from a dozen hoses.

Gaude's cellphone buzzed. It was a snapchat. Underneath the cartoon ghost was the name:

HEROSTRATUS

Gaude pressed the screen and saw a watercolor of a burning church and a message below.

> < This is just the beginning. They all will burn.
> From sea to shining sea unless you stop me.
> But you must find me first >

Gaude shook his head and silently brooded for a moment. Watt watched carefully but did not interrupt as his partner contemplated their next move. Finally, Gaude nodded to himself and looked up to the front seat. "Sinbad, take us to the highest point in the city."

"Dan, we just got here," implored Watt, gesturing to the church in flames.

"It doesn't matter. We need to go. Now."

"Mount Davidson is in the middle of San Francisco," said Sinbad, pointing out over the city. "From it you can see in every direction. Do you see it over there? At the top is a large cross."

"That's where we need to go."

"I shall take you where you wish, but I assure you that there is no burning church for you to see on the top of that very high hill."

"I don't want to see a burning church. I need to see them all."

Sinbad nodded his assent casually, as if Gaude's request made perfect sense. He immediately made a u-turn on Chestnut Street and began threading through the city to their destination due south. Sinbad turned on his sound system and Gaude immediately recognized the music as the second movement of the *Firebird Suite*. "Darkly appropriate," muttered Gaude, before he realized that he could come up with no explanation why he was able to identify the music so precisely.

Twenty minutes later, they arrived at the crest of the hill and could see the signs of fires spread across the city.

"The fires…they're in a circle, almost evenly spaced."

"Except one. The church we visited."

"Patmos?"

"Yes. The other churches seem to be surrounding it—and us."

"Which of them should we go to first?"

"None of them."

"This is a disaster," declared Watt.

"No, this is a distraction," announced Gaude.

"I think that seven burning churches constitutes a bit more than a mere distraction."

"A major distraction is a distraction all the same," said Gaude dismissively. He looked over the vista, turning slowly to survey the various plumes of smoke surrounding them. After a full minute of gazing into the distance, he announced, "It's that vineyard from the bottle of wine we found. That's where we need to go."

"How do you know that?"

"I just know it."

"How?"

"I just do. You have to trust me."

"You mean that you're asking me to take a leap of faith."

"Yes, that is exactly what I mean."

Watt nodded in agreement. "Works for me."

⌘

These were frugal times. The city budget had been severely curtailed and the coroner would often forgo a required autopsy when the cause of death was obvious or even arguably so. He looked over the body of the man who had arrived this morning, imbued with the pungent scent of refrigerated manflesh. Although the sense of smell was the most devoted of memory's handmaidens, the coroner had long since ceased to associate the aroma of chilled corpses with the bad, with the good, with anything.

The coroner was not much given to sympathy, which would have been an impossible handicap in his position. Nevertheless, the cause of death on the receiving form nettled him: *death by streetcar*. The man had been struck down by the vintage model, Streetcar Number Four. It was the second streetcar fatality this month caused by vintage models. The antiquated streetcars had pleased the nostalgic while the more cynical and realistic complained that it was merely a gimmick to prop up San Francisco's declining tourist trade. The papers made little of the dangers faced by residents and visitors unfamiliar with the vehicles and the confusingly arcane traffic signals. The coroner had himself, when a young boy growing up in Nürnberg, narrowly escaped being crushed by a streetcar. He was practicing *fussball* with Dieter Hackl. He chased the ball, oblivious to the oncoming streetcar. Just as he reached for the ball, he sensed a moment of quiet, stillness. Was his name being called? He suddenly lunged aside, not sure why, as the streetcar, now furiously ringing its bell and engaging squealing brakes, passed by him. Even now, so many, many years later, the old coroner recalled that mixture of surprise, awe, confusion and a strange sort of calm that he had felt then. How had he avoided the streetcar? He hadn't seen it coming, had not looked up, and did not hear it until after it had passed him. *Strange, memory*. He gently shook his head with a European idiosyncrasy that he had never outgrown, despite having lived in America for all but the first twelve years of his life. He opened a manila file folder and made some notations on the processing checklist for the cadaver. There was no time for daydreaming. Nevertheless, in the quiet of his mind, he had been thinking of Streetcar Number Four by its German name. *Strassenbahn Vier.* He softly muttered the German word for four—*vier*—pronounced identically as a word in English: *fear.*

The coroner knew the city lawyers would ask for an autopsy in the hope that they could argue that the victim died of heart failure before being crushed by a public transit vehicle. This time, he would not need to argue with them. Almost as soon as the man's name was registered, the Feds were on the line and issued explicit instructions not to tamper with the remains. Despite the harsh warnings, he had made a cursory examination of the body. *Those other wounds, older wounds. Mine Gott,* he thought, *what has this man been through?* The coroner ambled over to his small and cluttered office and busied himself with assembling the proper paperwork and filling in the blocks on the forms that would transfer the body from the custody of the State of California to the United States of America. He has been warned that agents were coming over to pick up the body 'immediately.' *That means in about three hours,* he reckoned to himself, but decided to finish the documentation before his coffee break. He had reckoned wrong. Just as he had placed his signature on the last of the piece of paper, two men dressed in gray wool suits entered his office.

Gott im Himmel, schon jetzt?

"We have come to pick up Agent Schwartz."

There was a disembodied quality to that voice. It would have given the coroner the creeps if he was not so used to listening to the same ghoulish voice possessed by the medical examiner. *They must be related. What a horrible thought—an entire family of them.*

"Agent Schwartz? That's not the name on the driver's license and credit cards that were found on the body."

"Agent Schwartz," was the indifferent and passionless response.

"That is that his name? Really?" asked the skeptical coroner.

"Yes," was the laconic reply.

The coroner shrugged and then picked up an old-style clipboard from the counter. "First you must sign these two forms, here…here…and here." The agent who had spoken pulled a ballpoint pen from inside his suit jacket and complied with the instructions. "I will need to make photocopies of these papers," instructed the coroner.

455

"In the meantime, you must please wait in my office. My assistant will prepare the body for shipment."

"There will be no preparation of the body." There was neither annoyance nor anxiety in the voice. The man could have been reading the words, without any previous practice, off a teleprompter.

"We will be putting him in a body bag. Does that violate your federal regulations?"

"No."

"Good." The word came out sounding almost like 'goot.' Even decades after living in California, he had not completely escaped the accent of his youth. The coroner returned several minutes later to find his assistant zipping a black vinyl chrysalis around the body to be released to the visiting agents. He handed copies of the required paperwork to one of the agents and then helped place the bagged body on a gurney. The assistant rolled the corpse out of the lab, down the hall to the disposition room, where the bagged body would be deposited into a more substantial container for final shipment. The two Gray agents followed the assistant, paying no attention and saying nothing further to the coroner. The coroner watched the short procession disappear down the hallway as he stood in the doorway of the lab. He then returned to his work and began the processing of the next corpse that had arrived that night. The receiving forms indicated that this was a John Doe, an unidentified body found floating in the San Francisco Bay. He opened door seven of the morgue refrigerator and pulled out the shelf.

It was Agent Schwartz.

The coroner reflexively turned toward the exit door in order to dash out and inform the federal agents of the mistake. Then, just as suddenly, he paused. For reasons he did not wholly comprehend, and for which he had no desire to better understand, he returned to the body and gazed down at the battered face. "Your name is not Schwartz, is it?" he asked the chilled corpse. "No, of course not. That will be our little secret. You prefer to be here, don't you? We will take care of everything, *mine freund*."

The coroner pushed the shelf back in to the refrigerator and closed the small stainless-steel door. He again silently shook his head, this time in self-admonishment. He had never spoken to the dead before, at least not aloud. Perhaps it was time to take a vacation or maybe even retire. He imagined spending a few weeks, or perhaps the remainder of his life, in his family's ancestral home in the beech forest of the *Geistwald.* He could see in his mind's eye the ancient stone and hewn beam cabin surrounded by yet more ancient towering trees. He remembered the smell of the musty, damp, and almost perpetually dark home. "*Ja, ja, ja…*" he muttered to himself, "*Vielleicht später.*" Maybe later. There would be time. There would always be time. Even if it was after his time. Even if it was someone else's time.

⌘

Watt looked out from the car across a seemingly infinite vista of vineyards. "Why are we heading north without a clue?"

"Why did we cross the entire country without a clue?" retorted Gaude.

"We had plenty of clues."

"Most of which we didn't understand."

"It seems now we don't even have that."

"We might be better off because of it."

"How do you propose to find him?"

"I'm not sure, but at least we'll be closer than if we simply sat on our hands in San Francisco."

"So, we're just going to circle aimlessly around the California wine country until we miraculously happen upon the right place?" asked Watt.

"I thought you were fond of miracles."

"Do not put the Lord thy God to the test."

"I should have known that you'd have a biblical comeback."

"Maybe there were clues at each of those churches. Maybe the churches weren't a diversion. Maybe *this* is a diversion."

"Not this time."

"What makes you think that he's anywhere within one hundred kilometers of San Francisco?"

"Seven burning churches, not to mention the church that burned down last night."

"Most of the churches we've seen these past few weeks were burned down through means that could conceivably have been arranged through some remote technology."

"Like my evil cellphone?"

"Yes, its brethren are prime suspects."

Sinbad inserted a new disk into the sound system of the cab and within a few seconds the vehicle was filled with the strains of violins, violas, cellos, and then the woodwinds. The music was deliberate, with a constrained energy that gave the impression that the listener was being guided along a well-charted route, only to be suddenly detoured and delayed and rerouted. Gaude was sure that he had never heard of this work, but he was just as sure that he somehow knew it. As the music progressed, he anticipated every phrase as if he was wandering through a shadowy labyrinth of orchestral *déjà vu*. His hand twitched, wanting to signal upstroke and downstroke to the surrounding crowd of invisible musicians. He asked Sinbad about the piece that was playing.

"It is called the *Sojourner Symphony*. It is beautiful, yes? Being a sojourner myself, it speaks deeply to my soul. It is my new favorite."

"I thought you were a fan of Stravinsky."

"Truly, but this has a special meaning to me in many ways. Does it not speak to you?"

"I'm not sure. It's strangely familiar."

"Perhaps, instead, you speak to it," said Sinbad with a knowing nod.

Gaude listened for a few minutes, finding himself merging into the score. "It's muscular, yet fluid," he observed, "candid, but at the same time guardedly sentimental."

"It depicts a reader of a book of poetry," responded Sinbad. "It relates the thoughts and emotions he experiences as he moves through the book and journeys through the poems which themselves are verses depicting travel. They say that the composer and the poet he is honoring were close friends years ago."

"Interesting. The architecture of the piece is unique, almost as it was packaged in separate and progressively smaller boxes and revealed one by one, like opening a Russian doll."

"It has been compared to *Pictures at an Exhibition* by Mussorgsky, but with the introspective soul of Chopin, the wistfulness of Schubert, yet sometimes punctuated with the wit and gentle humor of Haydn," observed Sinbad.

"That's quite an accolade."

"Yes, the greatest of all swan songs."

"Pardon?"

"Sadly, it was his last symphony."

"Whose?"

"The composer's. He was recently killed in an accident most tragic. He had just returned from Europe and was driving a rented car from the airport. A news van pulled into his lane without warning. When he swerved his car to avoid it, he was hit head-on by a fire truck."

"He didn't have a chance," murmured Gaude.

"Yes, he had a chance. Truly, we all have a chance, in whatever life we find ourselves," stated Sinbad confidently.

Gaude looked out the window of the cab at the rolling landscape. There was something about the vista that triggered an associated memory, but it was nevertheless unfamiliar, as if the memory had been borrowed from an entirely different person. The scenery seemed to depict an image or pattern. It was an illustration containing a meaning. It was a message, but he could not quite decipher its vocabulary and syntax. He sat transfixed and removed for twenty minutes until suddenly jolted back into the interior of the taxi. Gaude involuntarily blurted out, "He's here! He's nearby!"

"How can you be sure?" asked Watt.

"I don't know why, but I'm sure. Something tells me that he could not resist confronting his pursuers this time. Call it intuition, a hunch, a gut feeling. Feel free to ascribe it to the Holy Spirit, if you prefer."

"As a matter of fact, the Holy Spirit would be my first choice."

Gaude went to his cellphone and started searching for any communications traffic that might direct them to a burning church in the immediate vicinity. After three minutes of searching, he looked back up, clearly annoyed. "Nothing."

"Technically speaking, that's good news," offered Watt.

"Bill, we need to find that vineyard. We need to find this guy. Time may be running out."

"There's no need to panic."

"This isn't panic, this is simply recognizing that this could escalate into something than is much more than a string of tragedies. When we were in New York, you said that there was something that might be able to track...*him*. I think that this is the time to use it."

"It's dangerous, Dan."

"Will it help us find him?"

"I think so, which is one of the reasons that I think it is dangerous."

"What is the other reason?"

"This…tool…for want of a better term, is not supposed to be used by…visitors, such as us. By meddling with it, we might set off a series of events that could have some serious consequences."

"We've crossed the entire country trying to catch up to him. Why the hesitation?"

"It requires your cell phone."

"See? I told you it was useful resource."

"A dangerous one and never so dangerous as right now."

"And never so urgent as right now. We need to do this, Bill."

Bill Watt bowed his head in resignation. "You'll need to go to the web and enter this URL." Watt pulled out a pen and notepad and began writing several seemingly random numbers and letters.

"You know what a URL is?" was the mixed question and snide comment returned by Gaude.

"I have acquired a smidgeon of knowledge over the years," responded Watt tartly.

"This seems like gibberish."

"That's what they say about the Book of Revelation."

"I don't see the connection."

"No one does, which is why they can't get into this website." As Gaude put the last few numbers into his cell, Watt briefly hung his head and uttered a brief plea, "Father forgive us, for we know not what we do." The cellphone screen went black, then began to gradually transition to a brilliant glowing crimson red, then amber yellow, settling into a deep indigo blue. Finally, the screen filled with silver-hued letters.

ἐγρήγοροι

"Greek? What does that mean?" asked Gaude.

"We don't have time for that."

A map of the region emerged from the haze of the screen. "This looks like a typical locator app. Not such a big deal," said Gaude dismissively.

"Just wait, it may surprise you."

A small dialog box appeared in the upper right corner of the screen.

Search For:
Location/Address
Monument/Landmark
Organization
Individual
Flora
Fauna
Document

Gaude impulsively said aloud, "We need to find a person."

The box highlighted 'Individual' and then morphed into a new box.

"Okay, it's voice activated. That's good, but certainly not revolutionary."

"It was in my day."

"Internal combustion engines were revolutionary in your day," Gaude chided.

"Who should we be looking for?"

"Simon Todd."

Again, the screen responded to Gaude's voice.

"Nearest Simon Todd."

Search For:
Location/Address
Organization
Individual: *State Full Name*
  - *List of all Simon Todd*
  - *Nearest Simon Todd to this location*
Document
Item

The dialogue box disappeared from the screen and a crosshair bullseye replaced it, hovering over the map. The view elevated above San Francisco and then slowly moved north. Gradually, the map began to zoom down. It segued from satellite view, then bird's eye view, and finally, as the images of trees, streets, buildings, and vehicles became larger and defined, to street level view. Gaude had the sense that he had been looking through the eyes of a descending angel. "I admit that the clarity and definition is extraordinary, but I've seen other apps that pretty much do the same thing. In fact, maybe better. At least, those other apps told me where I was on the map."

"Just wait a moment."

Gaude continued to watch and now realized that the image was moving through the scenery without any directional prompt. Then, suddenly, an automobile came around the corner and passed across his view. "This is in real time?" asked Gaude incredulously. "How it that possible?"

"You tell me."

"Magic. No, wait, drones. This works with on-demand drones? How many of them are there? How would they be powered? How could they be maintained? That must cost a fortune!"

"No doubt."

"Who can afford that?" asked Gaude. He then decided to answer his own question. "The government."

"Maybe."

"Then again, we're a stone's throw from Silicon Valley. If anyone other than the Pentagon or CIA would be motivated to create this, it would be a technology billionaire living hereabouts."

"Does it matter?"

"I'm not sure. Is this is some kind of spy technology?"

"If it is, that would be a very good reason not to use this," insisted Watt.

"If there is a fleet of drones out there, it must have resulted in some publicity or news stories."

"You won't find any mention of them in the web or even in newspapers."

"Why not?" asked Gaude.

"It's just possible that these drones are microscopic."

"Seriously?"

"Serious as—"

"I know, the Book of Doom and Gloom."

"There is no such book in the Bible."

"That describes nearly all the books in the Bible."

Watt delivered an annoyed *hrrumph* as he looked out the car window.

"How did you find this and who gave you access?" asked Gaude.

"I'm not at liberty to say, but perhaps now you can understand my reluctance to use this technology." The view on the screen turned by its own volition as if deliberately searching for someone. Gaude suddenly realized that was exactly what was happening. He then caught a glimpse of a lone figure's back as it darted between some vegetation.

"I think that's him."

"Are you sure?"

"No. Apparently this computer program of yours believes it has the right person, but I still can't tell where we are in relation to him.

What good is this?"

"Ask it," instructed Watt.

"Ask what?"

"It."

"It?"

"The computer, cell, app wizard thingy."

"Ask it what?"

"Ask it to tell us where we are."

Gaude's face briefly wrinkled with skepticism. "Okay, fine. Show us our location." Immediately, a pulsing blue ball appeared on the screen. "Sonnavagun!" muttered Gaude. "So that's us? We're only about twenty kilometers away from the target." Gaude leaned forward and held up the cellphone for Sinbad, who glanced furtively at the screen while still driving on the winding road. "Can you get us there?"

"Most certainly."

"Does this feature a voice—?"

"That will not be necessary," interrupted Sinbad. "I have seen the destination. I know where you will be going."

"You knew about this place before?"

"Truly."

"Why didn't you tell us?"

"We all know about this place, my friend. I just did not realize that it was your time to go."

Gaude sat in silence, having a sense that he was being conveyed to a final reckoning. He then returned his attention back to the cellphone screen. For the next ten minutes, he kept checking the progress of their car and the location of the targeted Simon Todd. As Gaude looked back up, Sinbad began to slow the taxi to a stop at a bend in the road. They were in a small vale with vineyards surrounding them on all four points of the compass.

"I must drop you off here," announced Sinbad.

"But we haven't gotten to where we are going."

"Oh yes, but you have. I cannot go with you down this road. I cannot share this part of the journey with you."

"Why not?"

"It is not my time. We climb up different paths together. We walk down the same path alone. Do not be concerned, we will meet again."

"When?"

"When we meet again," said Sinbad serenely.

"This is a strange place."

"Which makes you a stranger in a strange land."

"I can't argue with that."

"But you must pass through here to get to your destination."

"How do you know that?"

"I have always known this, as have you."

Gaude heard the strains of the symphony and knew that it was nearing the end. The strings, wistfully sad and resignedly mournful, cried of lost love, a squandered life, and a journey coming to an end. The orchestra gradually withered into quietude and then quiet. After a moment of silence long enough to expend a regretful sigh, a solitary piccolo began to play a bittersweet farewell, slowly fading into a dark and empty world and succumbing to a final and eternal sleep. Gaude looked up at the rear-view mirror and saw the sad and encouraging eyes of Sinbad.

Gaude's cellphone buzzed in his pocket. He removed it to find a text.

< You have come to the end of the line >

Gaude and Watt exited the taxi and Sinbad immediately departed towards the west.

"Where to now?" asked Watt.

"That depends upon whatever your mysterious internet app tells us," answered Gaude has he examined the cellphone screen.

"I'd rather not know."

Gaude gestured to the left. "I suppose we need to continue down this road."

"As we always do."

Gaude and Watt followed the road for a few minutes before approaching an imposing gate. Attached to the left sidepost was a hand-painted sign that announced the name of the estate upon which they were about to trespass.

Abaddon Vineyards

The gate was unlocked. As Gaude and Watt entered, the sun proceeded to set with surprising haste, as if eager to escape its celestial obligations of the day. The remains of the western sky were fading swaths of fresh-drawn blood and angry tangerine caught between layers of desultory purple and gray, gradually dimming to a placid cobalt and thence to a serene black. Almost as an actor cued to enter from stage left, the unnaturally magnified full moon, glowing a gentle crimson, began to rise and cast stark shadows behind the disciplined ranks and files of grapevines.

"Where is he?" asked Watt.

"Here on this property," said Gaude, checking his cellphone screen. "He's within three hundred meters of us, moving fast, from right to left."

"Which direction?"

"Due east. It appears that he's traveling parallel to the street." The satellite view image of the map on the cellphone labeled the route 'Babylon Road.' Gaude shook his head gently. "That name…I've seen that name before."

"Should we split up and surround him?" asked Watt.

"We can't do a lot of surrounding with only two of us."

"We need to catch up with him somehow."

"We can head him off at the trail."

"You sound like an old John Wayne movie."

"Right now, I'd settle for Gabby Hayes."

"I doubt that I can keep pace with you. Go ahead and I'll try to catch up later."

Gaude started to run ahead. After one hundred meters, he stopped and looked back, but he could barely discern the path behind him. His partner was nowhere to be seen. "Bill, where are you?" he called. Gaude thought that his voice betrayed the fear that had begun to crawl up from below his stomach and press into the hollow cavity of his chest. "Bill?" he called out weakly.

A snowflake fell, then another. Within a few minutes, thousands of flakes were falling, all illuminated by the brilliant full moon. A gentle breeze wandered across the open expanse, causing the snow to twist and spin in vortices disproportionate to the strength of the wind. Gaude moved forward cautiously. No snow touched his face or fell on his clothes. It simply danced and swirled around him. The night breeze remained warm, far too warm for any snowfall. "*El Niño*," Gaude

465

whispered to himself.

To his left he heard a shuffling sound and gentle panting. Behind him, he was certain that there was a whimper. *Dogs*, he thought. Then, his interior voice immediately responded with a correction. *No, wolves.* There was no logical reason to believe that he was being followed by a pack of wolves in a California vineyard on a freak snowy summer's night, but he knew it was happening. Gaude began to increase his pace, but marginally, so as not to alert the suspicions of the pack that was tracking him to…to where? *Where the hell am I going?* He began to silently curse Bill Watt for losing him in the darkness. "Bill," he whispered so cautiously that as soon as it passed from his lips, he was sure that the only creatures with sharp enough ears to hear the plea were the wolves he hoped to evade. *Stupid, very stupid,* he chastised himself. He was now exerting as much effort to restrain himself from breaking into a blind dash as he was to force his legs forward against the immobilizing fear that made them leaden. *Walk more quickly*, he coached himself, *but not too quickly*, he cautioned, *just quickly enough*. He felt the breeze grow cooler before realizing that the sensation was a result of his clothes being soaked with perspiration. *Breathe slowly*, he told himself. *Walk calmly, think calmly, just calm down*, he silently counseled. He heard the muffled padding of several feet—paws—to his right. The moon provided ample illumination, but the rows of vines obscured his view. In the distance, he heard a canine yip.

Gaude saw a large wooden building, unadorned by decoration, unpunctuated by windows. It was an indeterminate shade of charcoal gray, barely distinguishing itself from the surrounding and enveloping grayness of the moonlight nightsky. He approached massive double doors, more reminiscent of the entrance of a gothic cathedral than a typical barn. As he arrived at the entry, he heard a soft, raspy, whispering voice singing.

> *Were you there when they crucified my Lord?*
> *Were you there when they crucified my Lord?*
> *Oh, sometimes it causes me to tremble, tremble, tremble.*
> *Were you there when they crucified my Lord?*

Gaude looked for handles on the doors but could locate none. Impulsively, he gave a push to the door on the right. It swung open effortlessly to reveal a vast space lined on both the left and right with floor-to-ceiling racks of wooden wine barrels. An oblong overhead gallery ran along the interior perimeter of the building, giving access to the barrels stacked at the higher levels. At the end of the building, centered in the isle before him, was a single barrel of colossal proportions standing upright. It seemed to be more like a giant vertical swimming pool than a container for wine. Arc lamps suspended from the ceiling cast theatrical shadows throughout the expanse. Gaude stepped in cautiously. He now heard the singing voice more clearly.

Were you there when they nailed him to the tree?
Were you there when they nailed him to the tree?
Oh, sometimes it causes me to tremble, tremble, tremble.
Were you there when they nailed him to the tree?

As he began to walk into the building, he noticed an incongruous but familiar smell. The scent of beeswax and starched linen of the old Catholic church of his boyhood was unmistakable, and yet it had to be a mistake. He was once again an altar boy, carrying a cruet of wine—he could smell a faint whiff of the sweet red wine as well.

Gaude was ten meters into the building when the arc lights suddenly went out. He instantly turned back to the entrance, but the door was closing—an oblong of moonlight quickly narrowing and then disappearing. Gaude stood still in the darkness, forcing himself to formulate a mental map of the interior he had seen for less than one minute. He made a tentative step forward and then to the right, then another, hand extended, expecting to make contact with the wall of wooden casks. Instead, his hand encountered a two-by-four. He ran his hand over it and realized it was the roughhewn balustrade for the stairs he had seen leading up to the overhead gallery.

Gaude cautiously took a step, then another. A dozen or so steps later Gaude arrived at a landing. He heard a light tread on the wooden steps behind him. One, two, three, four, then silence. He waited, but nothing happened. Perhaps this was a trick calculated to intimidate. Gaude groped out in the darkness and his hand encountered a wooden slat door. He reached for the handle, hesitating momentarily. The whispery voice could be heard more clearly, now seeming to come from somewhere below him.

Were you there when they laid him in the tomb?
Were you there when they laid him in the tomb?
Oh, sometimes it causes me to tremble, tremble, tremble.
Were you there when they laid him in the tomb?

Gaude tried the door handle and found it unlocked. As the door swung open, he saw that the room was dimly illuminated by an antique lantern sitting on an equally vintage rolltop desk. He assumed that this must be the winery office, seemingly trapped in the temporal amber of a century before. Gaude entered and was startled to discover a man behind the door, sitting silently in a rocking chair.

"Jesus Christ!" blurted Gaude.

The man in the chair laughed appreciatively. "No, I'm afraid that would be a case of mistaken identity. All the more curious, as I am confident that I have little or nothing in common with a first century carpenter from Galilee."

"Who are you?"

"We've met before, in a space even more poorly lit that this."

"You're Simon Todd."

"In the flesh."

"I came because of your message."

"What message? I didn't send you any message."

"Then why are you here?"

"I was told to come here."

"Who told you to do that?"

"Someone I work for."

"You'll need to do better than that."

"I wish that I could right now, but there are a dozen federal laws that prohibit me from disclosing anything about my employer. I've taken a substantial risk in coming here, even under orders."

"I don't understand."

"Neither do I, but you are a special case, so I suppose some rule-bending is forgivable."

"You're making no sense."

"You say that because you've allowed Bill Watt to drag you across the continent and spin your head with his unintentional deceits. I know that he sincerely believes the codswallop that he is peddling to you, but that doesn't make it true."

"How do you expect me to trust you? You said that you would burn them all down, sea to shining sea."

"Burn what down?"

"Presumably, churches."

"It seems that you received a message from—"

"From whom?"

"From the person we both seem to be chasing and perhaps are being chased by."

"You're lying. You are the one behind all of this."

"Not that again? Please, Dan, I can only imagine the sanctimonious swill that Bill Watt is pouring into your head. For once and for all, I am not the party responsible for the burning of those churches. I am not your enemy."

"But you're here."

"Hopefully, not on a similar wild goose chase that you seem to have been lured into."

"My goose chase involves trying thwart evil."

"As does mine."

"Why?"

"It would be easy to say that it is my job. It would be just as easy to say that I wish to protect and preserve the interests of my…friends."

"Then say something that isn't easy."

"You are in danger. We are willing to help."

"Who is 'we,' if you don't mind me asking?"

"I'll get to that in a minute or two. First, you must understand that in many ways, our interests, beliefs, and philosophies are aligned."

"I'm not sure that I'm convinced about that, but in any case, tell me about the person you and I are both chasing."

"For now, suffice it to say that the elusive firebrand was a rogue member of our organization who mangled the meaning and intent of our beliefs. We are dedicated to the elimination of ignorance and superstition, but thorough logical persuasion. He has taken a more violent and militant approach, which is something we cannot support or even tolerate."

"And just who is this arsonist?"

"*What* is the arsonist would be a better question."

"I'll take an answer to either."

"A relic, a throwback, an anachronism. At the same time, something new, frightening, and unfathomable. We are dealing with someone as deserving of extinction as the stupidity that he brutally attacks."

"You say that you represent an entire organization, but you can't cope with the actions of one man?"

"Oh no, he is not acting alone. Unfortunately, he has assembled a league of followers. We call them the Shades."

"Yes, I believe I met one of them."

"They are dangerous."

"I figured that out all on my own. You are somehow different?"

"Fundamentally different and our different paths offer a fundamental choice."

"What choice is that?"

"One that you have been making your entire life. I'm asking you to stay the course. There are three paths you could take. I offer the one that you have always had the wisdom and insight to take, until recently, that is. This is the path of reason, justice, peace and truth. There is the second path that leads to ignorance, hate and destruction. That path has been cutting a fiery swath across this continent, as you have personally witnessed. The third path is in some ways more dangerous than that taken by our church-burning fanatic. Bill Watt leads you on a path of beguiling but duplicitous sanctity, of holy hypocrisy. He invites you to worship an invisible god that supposedly loves us. That same god loves us so much that he tolerates wars, sends plagues, dispenses natural disasters, creates cripples, leaves widows and orphans to fend for themselves, overlooks every conceivable form of criminal activity, tolerates racial strife, and permits economic inequality and social injustice. That god is the god who permits our church-burner to destroy with impunity."

"That doesn't make sense."

"Neither does worshiping an invisible figment of society's collective delusion."

"So, you're an atheist."

"It's not as simple as that. Society has deluded itself into believing that a powerful being is a supreme being and that such a being is necessarily good. It believes that *a god* is *The God*."

"What do you mean by that?"

"The so-called god is worshiped as an all-powerful, all-knowing, ever-present being who is described as the very essence of love."

"That's right."

"That's wrong. A loving paternal god, who page after page in the Bible demonstrates hatred of own children? That same god adopts the descendants of Abraham as his chosen people, but what of his other creations? For example, what about the Philistines? You certainly remember the story of brave little David defeating the ogre-like Goliath. It does not take a biblical scholar to figure out that there was no love lost between the god of Israel and the Philistines. In addition, look to see what that god said of the Hittites, Midianites, Moabites, Girgashites, Ammonites, Amorites, Amalekites, Canaanites, Edomites, Perizzites, Hivites, and Jebusites. He hated them all and encouraged his chosen Israelites to destroy them, sometimes down to the last woman and child. Do you really believe these other peoples were more sinful than the tribes of Israel? Do you really believe that they were irredeemable? How many times did Israel turn its back on their god, yet he forgave them? Where do we see the same degree of tolerance, mercy, and forgiveness for the other peoples of Mesopotamia? What kind of loving, generous, rational and unbiased god demonstrates such unwarranted favoritism?"

"My elementary school catechism is a bit rusty, but I recall that Abraham passed a rather brutal test in order to get into God's good graces."

"Which was squandered time after time by his progeny. Beyond that, there is plenty of other evidence of that god's vicious nature, found in the very pages of the book we ascribe to his authorship. To say that the Israelite god is a homophobe of the first order would be an understatement of the first order. The Bible unconditionally and unequivocally condemns the gay population and prescribes the penalty of death. Death, in fact, seems to be that god's favorite remedy for anything he doesn't like. Have an affair? Stone the adulterer to death. Someone worships a golden calf? Stone them. How about if some kids get together to play on a Ouija board? Stone them. Have an argument with your parents? You must be stoned. Utter a mild curse that invokes that god's ever-so-special name? He has decreed that you deserve to die—once again—by stoning. Engage in labor during the Sabbath? Look in the Book of Numbers and you'll find that the god of Israel personally instructed Moses to put a man to death for gathering a little bit of firewood for his family on the supposed day of rest. The list goes on and on. My personal favorite is in the ninth chapter of Exodus. Anyone who has the temerity to approach Mount Sinai? That's right, stone them!"

471

"I think that you are exaggerating more than a little."

"Everything I have just said came straight from the Bible."

"Which can be misinterpreted."

"Oh yes, quite so, but not by me. Give the so-called good book a good read anytime you like. What you will find is a very bad book, with a story of men and women bedeviled by pain, misery, want, despair, deceit, and treachery. Have you ever wondered why one of the most consistent unifying facets of humankind has been the existence of some form of religion in every culture, in every land, in every age? Do you know why? There is no human society without some kind of religion because there is no human society without some kind of tragedy. Increase the pain and suffering and you increase the faith and worship. That's why the violent, ignorant, and impoverished middle ages are called 'The Age of Faith' and the modern era of prosperity, enlightenment, and science is an age of atheism."

"And you ascribe all this pain and tragedy to a loveless God?"

"That depends upon your choice of a god."

"When you ambushed us in Rome, in that dark elevator, you said that God was a fantasy—that he did not exist."

"No, I said that it was childlike to believe in an invisible friend. The god you refer to is an invisible enemy."

"So says you."

"So says me and so says the Christian Bible."

"If God were such an enemy, then where does good come from?"

"From god, of course. The god who is actually on our side."

"I'm not following you."

"Have you ever *actually* read the Bible?"

"Portions of it," Gaude responded sheepishly.

"Did any of those portions include the first few chapters of the Book of Genesis?"

"As a matter of fact, I have read those parts."

"No doubt in compliance with some new year's resolution to redeem yourself. Let me guess, you tanked out as soon as you got to the Book of Leviticus."

"Something like that," admitted Gaude.

"Or perhaps you didn't even finish Exodus."

"Is there a point you are trying to make, other than upbraiding me for my backsliding ways?"

"Sorry," said Todd with a seemingly genuine gentle smile. "Rendering judgment is precisely what I did not intend." He paused for a moment and then continued. "You may recall that there are two stories of the creation of humankind, separate and distinct."

"Yes, the stories in Genesis are inconsistent. There are plenty of contradictions in other books as well. The editors of the Bible were a bit sloppy."

"No, not inconsistent—they are entirely different. In the first chapter of Genesis—indeed, it is the first chapter in the entire Bible—god says simply and directly, 'Let us make man in our image and after our own likeness.' That was it. That was all. There was nothing more need be said or done. With those simple and powerful words, man and woman were created. In the other story of creation, god creates man out of clay and then blows the breath of life into the man's nostrils. Later, god engages in the apparently ridiculous charade of offering each of the animals of the world as a potential mate for his human creation. After that abysmal failure, god put Adam into a deep sleep, removed a rib, and built a woman around it. Seriously, can you imagine two more different versions of the same story?"

"The nuns taught us that these stories were not incompatible."

"I'm sure that they did. However, I'd wager that you can't remember how they explained the compatibility, can you?"

"No, admittedly, I've forgotten that."

"Because you never actually learned it. That is due in no small part because your devoted nuns never actually taught it. They simply ordered you to accept a nonsensical proposition. Given that this was just one of thousands of nonsensical propositions taught in Catholic schools, it really was not all that difficult to swallow one more preposterous lie."

"So, what is the truth, according to you?"

"According to me? No, there is no truth according to me. The truth—regardless of what I might say or not say—is still the truth. You need but listen to it to realize that it is the unspoiled and authentic word—not of god, mind you—but of truth itself."

"It sounds to me like you are making your own pitch that I should have faith, but faith in your teachings, rather than those of Christianity."

"Listen, and you won't need faith, merely intelligence and reason. The truth is that both versions of creation happened. As related in the first chapter of Genesis, god created man and woman in his divine image. As related in the second chapter of Genesis, another god created man of dirt and genetically engineered a woman out of a sample of the man's ribcage."

"*Another* God? *Another* couple? That's ridiculous!"

"Is it really?"

"Yes, there was one couple, Adam and Eve."

"Really? Would it surprise you to discover that neither the name Adam nor Eve receives any mention in the first chapter of Genesis? It was the mud-man of the second chapter of Genesis who was named Adam and the rib-woman was later named Eve."

"What were the names in the first chapter?"

"The text is silent, but there are innumerable references in ancient writing dating to the same time as the Bible that provide us the identities of the other couple: Samael and Lilith."

"Never heard of them."

"Not surprisingly. Even if you had, chances are that what you would encounter are distortions and outright lies. Some suggest Lilith was Adam's first wife—"

"How is that possible?"

"It isn't," Todd answered dismissively. "Other stories attempt to confuse Samael with an evil archangel."

"What makes you think that there were two different couples in the Garden of Eden?"

"I didn't say that Samael and Lilith were in the Garden of Eden, but that isn't important. We know that there was another man and woman who preceded Adam and Eve because the Bible itself gives us proof of the fact."

"Such as?"

"You may recall that Cain murdered his brother, Abel, who at that time was the only other offspring of Adam and Eve. Yet Cain, upon receiving a sentence of banishment by god, cries out in fear that he may be killed by another person for his crime. What other person? If Cain was the sole remaining offspring of the first parents in the world, there shouldn't have been anyone else to fear. He later went to settle in the land of Nod and there found a wife. Let's assume this was a human wife and not one of the animal suitors previously rejected by Cain's father. Where did this woman come from? The Bible also relates that Cain founded a city. I don't care how prolific Cain and his mystery wife might have been, and even if he lived for hundreds of years as apparently was common in the first book of the Bible, the best Cain could have done was to have fathered a small town."

"Maybe there is some confusion due to the various translations of the Bible."

"For more than sixteen hundred years, western civilization has assigned its most celebrated scholars the task of translating the Bible from every available source. I think we can safely conclude that as many linguistic bugs that could be worked out of the Bible have been worked out of the Bible. To the extent that there still seems to be inexplicable nonsense in the Bible, that is not due to the vagaries of translation, but many of the inherent lies in the book itself."

"And yet you quote it."

"As you would find in any court of law in the world, the most damning evidence is the word of the accused himself. If the Bible is the word of god, I have the right to submit it as People's Exhibit Number One, lies and all."

"So, the creation story has a hole in it. That's not...wholly convincing...at the risk of tossing out a pun."

"The two chapters are also different regarding the fall of humanity. The first chapter does not mention this at all."

"Just because it isn't mentioned in that one chapter doesn't mean that it didn't happen."

"In most situations, that would be a reasonable observation. You do remember the story of the temptation by the serpent?"

"Of course. Eve ate the apple and then gave it to Adam."

"Actually, the Bible never identified the fruit as an apple, but I'm not here to quibble."

"I agree," said Gaude, "Quibbling should be categorized as an unforgivable sin. I don't suppose that quibblers were condemned to death by stoning in the Bible?"

Todd laughed. "Maybe in one of the more modern translations."

"So, what is significant about Eve and the...unnamed fruit?"

"The crucial distinction between the two different creation stories is that in the first chapter, one god clearly and unconditionally grants to man and woman every tree that has seed-bearing fruit as their food. There are no exceptions, there is no off-limits tree of knowledge, there is no forbidden fruit."

"What are you saying?"

"What I have already said and what is plainly stated in the Bible itself. There were two gods, there were two creations, there were two originally created couples of man and woman. Since the beginning of human history, these have been in competition. The first couple—Samael and Lilith—was loved, nurtured, and grew up in a world of reason guided by a tolerant and beneficent deity. The second couple—Adam and Eve—led a tortured existence under the thumb of a jealous and wrathful god."

"I suppose that you're going to tell me that the God of Abraham, the same God worshiped by Christians—"

"Let's not leave out Islam."

"If you also want to tangle with Islam, that's your choice."

"Just so."

"You're saying that the mean-spirited and angry God is the one we worship?"

"The one that Bill Watt worships. I'm hoping that you are not fully committed to that fallacy."

"And you have the kind and generous god, I suppose?"

"Yes, but over the course of millennia, he has been slandered and libeled with a very different name."

"I suspected as much," said Gaude. "I also suspect that this more benevolent god of yours isn't all that welcome in heaven."

"Our god does not live in a distant and inaccessible celestial palace cooked up in some weary monk's imagination."

"I suppose that you are going to try to convince me that this god's underworld is somehow preferable to heaven?"

"Underworld? No, that's yet another myth. I gave you a hint as to the dwelling place of our god when we first met in Rome."

"Sorry, I don't recall you providing that address."

"Yes, I did. I identified the location quite precisely, in fact. I told you to look in the mirror to find your god."

Gaude made no attempt to mask his bewilderment. "You're now saying that there is no God?"

"No, I'm saying that the god who accepts us just as we are resides in our hearts. Unlike the scolding bitter biblical god who dwells in some distant heavenly kingdom, our humanistic and humanitarian god dwells here on earth amidst the humanity he cherishes. He is among us, he is in us, and we in him."

"In that case, I should be all powerful."

476

Todd chuckled. "Maybe you are. All the more reason I'm seeking to recruit you."

"What makes you think that I would believe that your supposed god represents good and the God that billions worship embodies evil?"

"Bill really has been getting to you, hasn't he? His world is so simplistic, isn't it? Everything is a matter of black and white, positive and negative, good and evil. Don't you see how mindless, how childish, that is? Now, I don't for a moment deny that there is good and evil in the world, but they are not separately packaged or mutually exclusive. We see it all around us. The relationship and the conflict between the two is complex and nuanced and so deeply embedded in our society that it is sometimes difficult to make out the heroes from the villains. Consider, for instance, those who spell the word 'doughnut' properly and others who spell it as 'D-O-N-U-T.' The horror…the horror…"

Gaude could not contain his laugh. "That is a compelling case."

"In a more serious vein, however, you must see that the choice between good and evil is not the real struggle. I described Bill Watt's god as wrathful, stern, cranky, and unreasonably biased. I never characterized him as evil. Good and evil is not what actually rends us apart. The great conflict in this life is not between good and evil but between good and good. We have one god's standard of good as opposed to another god's standard of good and one person's version of good as opposed on another person's version of good. My good versus your good. Our good versus their good. It has been this way throughout human history."

"Are you selling yourself as a historian or a philosopher?"

"How about a rational man? You lived in Germany for a while, didn't you?"

"Yes."

"Do you know what the motto of the German Army was in the First World War? It was *Gott Mit Uns:* God is with us. That was the same god to whom their enemies, the French, the English, the Russians and the Americans, earnestly prayed for the defeat of the so-called ruthless Huns. For more than one thousand years, the western Christian world has been locked in a conflict—sometimes waxing, sometimes waning—with Islam, both sides convinced that they are righteous, virtuous, god's chosen children. The glorious crusades of the tenth century were, in the eyes of a Muslim, a shameful and unprovoked attack by bloodthirsty Christians. Islam's celebrated conquest of the Byzantine empire was, in the eyes of a Christian, a terrible and mournful loss to the fanatical Muslims."

"Just because there are situations in which we can stand in another's shoes doesn't necessarily mean that there is no such thing as objective evil."

"You're right," Todd agreed. "Enslaving another human being, torturing or murdering for any reason, wars of aggression and genocide are innately evil and objectively immoral. There are also other, darker, things no human should ever lower themselves to be become, such as..."

"Yes?"

"A Red Socks fan."

Gaude again succumbed to Todd's humor and responded with an appreciate chuckle.

"I couldn't resist," Todd offered as a feigned apology. "All the same, it is not a denial of the existence of evil to observe the sad but uncontestable truth about human nature that when confronting someone with a different viewpoint, who has different interests, or who is simply *different*, the first reaction is to condemn them as evil."

"Perhaps you're right. I suppose that humans have been doing that since the beginning of time."

"Even before the beginning of time and even before the beginning of humanity. Have you ever wondered why the other god—the so-called devil—is depicted as a fallen angel? Why not as pure evil from the very beginning of his existence? We all know that, by definition, an angel is good. One day, this deity, or this angel, if you prefer, realized that *his* good was somehow different and superior to the good of other gods or other angels. He was a freethinker, he was...disruptive. That caused the great rift. We use the word 'demons' to describe the half of the heavenly host that was cast out because they defined good differently than those who defeated them."

"Now it sounds like you *are* conflating good and evil."

"Why? Because the example has a religious context? Fine, let's take a look at religion. Take the Reformation movement of the sixteenth century, for instance. Do you seriously maintain that Martin Luther, John Calvin, and Huldrych Zwingli were all evil men? Do you think that they were morally and spiritually inferior to Popes who fathered scores of children out of wedlock, ruthlessly squeezed money from the poor, sold indulgences without scruple, both accepted and handed out bribes on a routine basis, arranged for murders, toppled governments, started wars, and committed a host of other sins and crimes perhaps known only to the god they ostensibly served? The Protestant reformers had a legitimate difference of opinion, not to mention a legitimate list of grievances, with the established Church. Do you really believe that that these men deserved to be condemned by the Catholic Church as evil heretics?"

"You're trying to convince me that the apparent dispute between you and Bill Watt is merely a matter of opinion?"

"Yes, but the difference is that I recognize this for what it is—the exercise of free will and rational judgment—while Bill and his ilk ascribe this as a titanic spiritual battle between his chosen god and my supposed devils. Let's take Bill Watt, your tour guide these past few weeks, as a prime example of the breed who follow the god of wrath and anger. I've known him for quite some time. I might tease and disparage him a bit, but I know that he is sincere in his beliefs, doggedly misguided as they might be. I respect the fact that he chooses another path, although I do my best to enlighten those who are being led down that same path to a very dead end. In fact, my moral compunction to save misguided souls from the folly of believing in calculated lies and inadvertent fairy tales is every bit as sincere as Bill Watt's conviction to delude them. I do not characterize Bill as evil. Foolish, perhaps. Simpleminded, maybe. Naïve, definitely. I do not, and never have, attached the label of 'evil' on Bill Watt simply because he defines 'good' as obedience to cruel and intolerable rules established by a cruel and intolerant god. On the other hand, Bill has no intention or inclination to return the courtesy in acknowledging that my beliefs, and my vision of good, is anything other than wicked, sinful, and immoral. He does not accuse me of being mistaken or misguided. That, at least, would be fair game. No, instead he declares that I am evil, that I am in league with the so-called devil."

"What makes the label of 'evil' so much worse than foolish or misguided?"

"An excellent question. Because a foolish or misguided individual is still someone who can be taught, who can be dissuaded, who can be reformed. Evil, on the other hand, must be combatted and destroyed. Once you have declared someone to be evil, you have closed the door on them. There is no conversation, no communication, no offer to find common ground. Bill and his cronies have shut me out, and by doing so, have closed themselves off from the truth."

"What is it, specifically, that you claim to be the truth?"

"I tried to explain it to you in a darkened elevator shaft."

"That was creepy."

"It was a metaphorical lesson, an illustration of the darkness in which Bill Watt and his ilk want you to dwell. It was an unusual experience, but a memorable one, I hope."

"If memorable experiences include bad dreams, then I suppose that qualifies."

"I cannot imagine that is it any more frightening than to succumb to the misguided philosophy that we walk by faith and not by sight. I apologize for any lingering psychic trauma, although from what I know about you, I believe you will recover in time."

"What do you know about me?"

"A great deal. Please don't be paranoid. In this day and age, privacy is on the wane, if not outright extinct. Beyond that, any association worth its salt needs to exercise due diligence when recruiting. Membership in the higher echelons of our organization is by invitation only."

"What are the lower echelons?"

"Agents provocateur and internet trolls, Neo-Nazis and Social Justice Warriors, doomsday cults and doomsday preppers. Find someone who is dissatisfied with society in general or their life in particular and you are looking at a member of each of our opposing legions."

"Who has the allegiance of the Neo-Nazis?"

"You will discover that in due time."

"And the higher echelons?"

"You will discover that in due course."

"Just who is recruiting me and what am I being recruited for?"

"Both legitimate questions. As to the first, we are an organization, a society, a fellowship, if you will, dedicated to the rebuilding of civilization according to the teachings of a more enlightened god, a god who truly loves all of his children."

"Civilization hasn't fallen, at least not yet."

"But it is in the process of falling apart and the eventual colossal crash is inevitable. Our role is to speed up that process so that the rebuilding can take place as soon as possible."

"Speed up the process?"

"Our formal designation is Bureau of Counter-Historical Corrections. But we usually are referred to by friend and foe as the Disruption Guild."

"Disruption Guild?"

"DG for short, if you prefer."

"The same initials as my name?" asked Gaude.

"Yes, I consider that a lucky coincidence."

"There are no coincidences."

"As you say."

"What sort of 'speeding up' does your agency—your Guild—actually do?"

"A great number of things on both the micro and macroscopic scale."

"Something tells me that those things are not pretty."

"All life evolves out of conflict, so naturally there will be casualties, sometimes unfortunate ones. Our work may seem to be unsavory at times, but sacrifice, whether it be on an altar, a battlefield, or the city streets, will always entail a certain amount of bloodshed."

"But not burning churches?" Gaude replied archly.

"We are not back to that again, are we?"

Gaude shook his head dismissively. "Whatever your name, that doesn't sound like a legitimate agency of the government."

"In a sense, we may be the one and only legitimate organization in the government. We aim to reinfuse a scientific and intellectual renaissance into a world that is teetering on the brink of a new dark age by ushering in that dark age immediately. The former collapse of our ancient western civilization handed us a world beset by violence, lawlessness, and religious bigotry for an entire millennium. Think of it, a thousand years of ignorance, poverty, injustice, and despair! We hope to avoid that fate by expediting the process."

"Expediting? How? Why?"

"In the same way that early medical intervention can save the life of a patient, we are intervening early in the historical cycle to save the viability of civilization. We are sowing seeds of disruption that will topple the current world order. However, unlike what happened in medieval Europe, this fall into a new dark age will brief and far less painful, destructive, and inhumane."

"That's insane!"

"As insane as removing a diseased organ or amputating a gangrenous limb in order to save a life?"

"That's not the same thing."

"You're right, it isn't. What we are doing is far greater and far more noble than saving a single life. We are saving the lives, and the destinies, of all future generations of humanity. We are freeing the world from a pathetic reliance on the unrequited love of a being that has been undeservingly elevated to the status of an all-powerful, all-knowing, benevolent parent."

"So, you are trying to make me believe that religion is to blame for the ills of society?"

"A religion that accepts the rational teachings of a benevolent god who generously bestows the gifts of logic, reason, and science in order to nurture and elevate his children? No, the curses of the modern world cannot be attributed to those faiths. On the other hand, religions that seek to worship the angry, petulant, cranky god? Yes, they constructed the box of Pandora and then opened its lid."

"Let me guess: Christianity is at fault for the fall of the Roman Empire?"

"Let's consider that example. The Roman Empire was strong, vigorous, energetic, creative and triumphant during its thousand years of paganism, and equally successful during the three centuries that it persecuted the newly emerging Christian religion. Not that I advocate or applaud such persecutions—they were definitely brutal and uncalled for. However, the cold hard fact remains that once Christianity was embraced by the Romans, their brilliant civilization soon crumbled. The Emperor Constantine issued the Edict of Milan in the year 313, granting religious toleration to the Christians. In the year 380, Emperor Theodosius I issued the Edict of Thessalonica making Christianity the state religion. In less than one hundred years after Christianity triumphed in Rome, there was no Rome. In less than two lifespans, Christianity toppled a civilization that had successfully ruled from the Baltic to the Sahara spreading law, science, industry, art, and literature. That's quite an accomplishment for any religion, if you wish to use the term accomplishment when referring to wanton destruction."

"Islam could also be accused of some serious destruction."

"You'll get no argument from me on that. I selected Christianity as the immediate and convenient example of how institutionalized superstition is a threat to civilization. It is by no means the only danger."

"But both Islam and Christianity launched even greater civilizations."

"Are you so sure?"

"Yes, I am sure."

"It's better to be right than to be sure."

"We are the inheritors of science, technology, medicine, literature and art that would never have been possible without the influence of Christianity and Islam. We have reached heights that the Romans could never have attained."

"And plumbed depths that the Romans would have never descended."

"The Romans were cruel. They crucified thousands—and Calvary is only one example."

"The inheritors of your civilization systematically murdered millions—and Auschwitz is only one example."

"Those weren't Christians."

"*Au contraire*. Nearly every one of them were born into, raised and educated into your Christian world. Hitler was no less a product of Christendom than Pope John Paul."

"Hitler rejected Christianity, just as you do."

"That's where you are seriously mistaken. Hitler was poisoned by Christian prejudices. Where do you think he inherited his anti-Semitism? His Aryan worldview has been depicted as a return to German paganism—that's rubbish. Scratch the surface of Nazi ideology ever so lightly and you will find Christian philosophies and myths abounding."

"Hitler sought to copy much of what was your beloved Roman Empire."

"Do you know what Hitler was referencing when he declared the birth of the Third Reich? The First Reich was the Holy Roman Empire, a construct of the Catholic Church. The Second Reich was the empire formed by Chancellor Bismarck in the nineteenth century—an unapologetically Germanic Christian empire. No, the evil madman at the head of the Nazi party was merely emulating the evil madmen who had preceded him throughout the history of Christendom: Cesare Borgia, Torquemada, Vlad the Impaler."

"What does any of this have to do with me?"

"Yes, the cosmic question: 'Why me?' That is the nub of the matter, isn't it?"

483

"Yes, and I haven't a clue what the answer might be. I'm no theologian."

"Good, that would doubtless be a handicap. On the other hand, you have some other special talents that would greatly benefit our cause."

"What special talents?"

"Several, but one for which we have a pressing need. Effective communications are key to the viability of any complex organization, and you have a particular genius that we wish to employ. I was hoping that in time this would start coming back to you."

"Communications? You mean my experience as a newspaper reporter?"

Todd shook his head and laughed. "No, not as a newspaper reporter. I hope that the somewhat overwrought eulogy we wrote for you in the *Capital Guardian* did not go to your head."

"You…" gasped Gaude, now genuinely at a loss for words. He tried to regain his composure. "Then what? What skill do I have that is so important to you?"

"I don't wish to rush things. That has a way of backfiring. It is best for the memory to return in its own good time. Tell me, do you know the notes in E Flat Major?"

Despite the shock of the incongruous question, Gaude suddenly *knew*. He reflexively blurted out, "E-flat, G, B-flat."

"Good. You are coming back. What else do you remember?"

"Remember what?" asked Gaude, feeling slightly dazed and disoriented.

"Scarlatti's Sonata in G Minor."

"The Cat Fugue," Gaude again answered without hesitation, but without understanding how he knew the answer.

"Well done."

"What the—?" exclaimed Gaude.

"Tell me about the 'collapse section' of the second movement in Ives' *4th Symphony*."

Once again, Gaude somehow knew this. "The orchestra divides into two, one plays in a slow 3/2 meter, the other in 4/4. They're synchronized at first, but 4/4 accelerates on top of the other, collapses, waits for the 3/2 to catch up, and then the orchestra resynchronizes."

"Excellent!"

"What did I just say?" asked Gaude, perplexed.

"In what key was the *Sojourner Symphony* composed?"

"The *Sojourner Symphony*?" Gaude responded in surprise.

"You remember it?"

"I was listening to it in a taxicab on the way here."

"What is the key?" Todd repeated.

"How should I know?"

"But you do know it, don't you?"

"Yes…no…" Gaude hesitated, his mind groping for a memory, walking down a dimly lit corridor in a cerebral archive he did not wish to visit.

"You know." It was more of a demand than an inquiry.

"D Major."

"Brilliant! What about *Melancholia Serenade*?"

"What about *Melancholia Serenade*?"

"The key, Gaude! Tell me the key!"

Gaude was flummoxed, and yet, somehow he knew: "G Minor."

"Excellent!"

"How…how did that happen?" asked Gaude, disoriented by his own inexplicable answer.

"What is the time signature at the beginning of *Sojourner*'s third movement?"

"You've got to be kidding."

"Tell me! The third movement!"

"The…the…" Gaude stuttered. Suddenly, it came to him. "The same as second and fourth," Gaude blurted out. "Every movement begins with 4/4 and then transitions to an introductory march…2/4 time. The pattern repeats at the sub-movements before moving to 3/4 in order to…in order to…" Gaude trailed off, confused and mystified by his own words.

"Sub-movements? There is no such thing as a sub-movement!"

"I made them up…"

"You mean that you just lied?"

"No, I made them…I wrote them…there were four movements….each with six sub-movements…I…I…was…invoking Alan Hovhaness…his *Saint Vartan Symphony*…but that had twenty, mine had twenty-four…it needed to be twenty-four…"

"Wonderful!" shouted Todd triumphantly.

"I…what?" Gaude asked himself, unsure of how or why he was able to answer Todd's questions.

"You did!" affirmed Todd.

"I don't know what you are talking about or what I'm talking about, for that matter. How did I know?" asked Gaude, perplexed by the inexplicable information he had just spoken but did not fully understand.

"The better question is to ask who you really are," Todd answered.

"I don't know what you are talking about."

"How old were you when you graduated from college?"

"Twenty-two."

"How long were you in the Army?"

"Five…almost six years."

"What about your stint with the *Capital Guardian*?"

"About another six years."

"That adds up to twelve years."

"What's your point?"

"You are thirty-seven years old. What happened to the other three years?"

"I…I…I'm not sure…" fumbled Gaude. "I don't know…"

"You will soon, and when you do—"

Todd was interrupted by a scratching sound at the door. He made a quizzical look, shrugged, stood up from his chair, and then walked over to open it. A Chihuahua suddenly appeared and fearlessly launched an attack on the cuff of his right trouser leg. Another diminutive combatant joined him, then another. Within less than thirty seconds, a half dozen Chihuahuas were wildly nipping at Todd's trousers. He repeatedly kicked them way, but the dogs stubbornly returned to continue the miniature canine assault.

Todd turned back to Gaude with a look of exasperated annoyance as if to consult with him as to the best method to eradicate the little yipping pack of hostility. Gaude saw a shadow appear in the doorway just as Todd also sensed a presence behind him. He swung around to face a young woman, her face grossly disfigured with rage. She reached into her jumper pocket, withdrew a carving knife, and plunged it into the gut of Simon Todd. He screamed in pain, clutched his wound with his right hand, and teetered backwards against the doorjamb. She lunged at him again and Todd now grabbed the woman's arm with his free hand and slammed it repeatedly against the wall. The knife broke free and clattered down the steps. Gaude recognized the woman. It was Lyla Singleton, who he had last seen mourning the loss of her choir loft in Georgia.

Todd gave Singleton a forceful shove backwards and she began tumbling down the steps. He then stumbled forward out of the doorway and fell against the wooden balustrade of the landing area overlooking the expanse of the warehouse. He slowly turned around and faced Gaude who was now in the doorway. Todd took his hand off the wound and looked at his bloody palm in confused amazement. "She stabbed me."

"How deep is it? How wide?"

Todd slumped back against the railing and returned a feeble smile. "Not so deep as a well, nor so wide as a church door, but 'tis enough, 'twill serve." He started to sink to the floor of the landing as Gaude turned to rush back into the office in search of something that might serve as a makeshift bandage. He then heard the scream of a female voice behind him and upon turning around saw that Lyla Singleton had come back up the steps to resume her attack. Todd delivered a vicious kick and then launched himself on to her, grabbing her neck with slippery blood coated hands, desperately trying to get enough of a grip to strangle his assailant. They now rolled down several steps, locked in an embrace of hate. Gaude followed, clambered down the steps and grabbed Todd by the shoulders, attempting to shake loose his grip on the woman. He received a fierce jab to the ribs from Todd's elbow, which forced Gaude to stagger back against the wooden railing along the stairs. He heard the sixteen-penny nails holding the two-by-four railing start to give as the barrier began to sag. Gaude tried to maintain his balance on the unsteady platform and fell back against the opposite wall. Todd continued to strangle Lyla Singleton, who made no attempt to struggle, but instead glared at her enemy with unseeing eyes of unrestrained loathing. *Jump!* commanded a voice that Gaude didn't recognize and yet was intimately familiar. *Jump!* it said again. Gaude shoved himself along the wall into a crouching position and then launched himself against Todd.

They fell together against the railing, which now gave way. Todd released his grip on Singleton and she rolled down the steps with no more resistance than she had demonstrated during her strangulation. Gaude instinctively grabbed the two-by-four rail as he felt himself launch into freefall. The end of the rail was attached to the top of the staircase by a steel bracket. This too began to fail. He looked over his shoulder to see Todd hanging on the edge of the gigantic wood barrel, now appearing even more like a swimming pool full of blood-red water. As his face barely cleared the edge, Todd looked at Gaude, and grimacing to maintain his grip, shouted out, "Don't take the amber door!"

The steel bracket that had secured the railing now gave way with a sickening squeal and Gaude swung down in a giant arc onto the concrete floor. His head and shoulders smacked the surface and a flood of agony overwhelmed him. Gaude was engulfed in dizziness and darkness. *Concentrate!* the voice told him, *Concentrate, Brother Dan, you gotta stay 'wake. You gotta be ready.* Gaude pounded his fist against the floor and bit the inside of his cheek to stay awake and remain focused. Another voice came to him, this one feminine, unknown yet familiar.

Come find me Dan, I'm waiting for you.

Gaude yearned to pass out in order to escape the agony coursing through his head and down his spine. *Stay ready.* He again heard the first disembodied voice, *Stay ready.* Who was saying this? Why was he saying this?

A new voice joined in. A deep baritone. *You know not the time nor the day.* He knew this voice…he knew…he remembered…and then the memory suddenly vanished.

What the hell is going on here? Gaude tried to make sense of it all.

The answer came from the original voice. *Stay on the narrow path, Brother Dan. Stay ready.* It made no sense at all.

"What do I do now?" Gaude whispered, addressing the invisible advisor.

Whatever you can do now, responded the voice.

"That's not much."

Not much is more than nuthin' at all.

In his unreal state of semiconsciousness he heard his own inner voice ask, *What the hell are you talking about?*

The answer came back, and this time he recognized it as the voice of Gareth Eubanks. *It's all in the definition, son. It's all in the definition.*

Gaude pushed himself up from the floor and drunkenly stumbled to his feet. Above him towered the seven-meter tall wooden vat of wine. There was pounding. He realized that the pounding came from inside the vat, rather than from inside his aching, throbbing head.

He looked around for a moment and suddenly made the connection. Todd had fallen into the vat of red wine.

Watt appeared from behind him. "You don't look good."

Gaude brought his hands up to his thumping cranium and tried to press the pain back into a manageable package. "Thanks. You are such a comfort." He was beginning to feel nauseous and fought the urge to heave. "Where is she?"

"Who?"

"Lyla...Lyla Singleton."

"She's here?"

Gaude was in too much pain to press the matter. "Todd is in there," he said, gesturing at the gigantic wooden barrel. Watt nodded in acknowledgement and started up the ladder permanently attached to the side of the vat. Gaude, unsteadily, mounted the first ladder rung and then followed. As Watt reached the top, he moved to the side to allow Gaude to squeeze in beside him. "Don't they make platforms on the top of these things?"

Gaude was in no condition to tolerate a diatribe about the poor design of this wine vat. He looked down to see Simon Todd thrashing in a pool of *Sangre de Christo*. He submerged and then bobbed up again.

"Tread water!" Watt shouted.

Todd went under, then struggled back, letting loose a furious curse as he bobbed, choking and splashing. "CAN'T SWIM!"

Gaude and Watt extended their hands down to the struggling man. He reached up, spastically slapping the blood-red liquid, his fingertips several times almost touching the outstretched hands of assistance. Todd submerged again.

Gaude took a further step on a ladder rung and prepared to jump in. Watt reached forward and with a firm restraining grip, pulled him back down. "No, Dan."

"But..."

"No."

A moment later, they heard furious banging from the depths of the vat. This soon slowed and then there was stillness. Gaude looked at Watt for an explanation. Watt understood the silent inquiry, and with an expression that was as simple as it was complex, Gaude received his answer.

"Some things just are, Dan. This is out of our hands. Let it be."

⌘

      Senator Emilio Casagrande leaned back in his leather armchair as he examined the dossier of the new Director of the Office of Research for Clandestine Activities. The man was an absolute contradiction of everything Casagrande had come to know and expect in the espionage community. The Director had served in a variety of government posts that spanned across nearly four decades. On the one hand, no one could describe the man's rise through the ranks as meteoric. There were a series of minor postings and then a gradual ascent through the ranks—slow and steady. The man's career path reflected judicious, patient, and skillfully calculated movement up the ladder. At a time when many of this man's peers might be submitting their retirement paperwork, it seemed that he had just hit his stride. This, Casagrande rationalized, might be a good thing, as he had become weary of political wunderkind and hoped that a seasoned professional might provide a needed change. As for the Director's personal life, it was clean as the proverbial whistle. Single, never married, no children, no embarrassing complications with members of any sex or gender, no inexplicable debts, no peculiar habits, no addictions, no awkward affiliations with any groups on either end of the political spectrum, no loose ends. There was a brief mention of a much younger sibling, who apparently led a somewhat more reckless and colorful lifestyle, but all indications were that the two had never actually met. Of course, like all members of the clandestine community, there were blanks and ambiguities in his record, particularly relating to his childhood, schooling, and selected stretches of time that were doubtless associated with sensitive missions, unaccounted for and unaccountable to the press, the people, and the body politic. The left side of the dossier—that which was reserved for sensitive matters such as scandals, addictions, or questionable associations or dalliances—was almost empty. There was only one letter, addressed directly to the president, written three years before by an obviously delusional crank accusing Todd of being a veritable antichrist. An FBI special agent had been assigned to follow up on the dubious allegations, but reported that before an interview could be arranged, the man had driven across the country and committed suicide in a small town named Berlin, Utah.

      While Todd's career trajectory might have reflected cautious restraint, everything Casagrande saw in the file about the new

Director's work product suggested a man who was both unorthodox and brilliant. His proposals, plans and programs were always pushing the envelope and often were located far outside of the proverbial box. This was not the behavior of a typical career public servant. How this carefully calculating yet unorthodox man has survived and advanced through the layers of the bureaucracy was a puzzle. He was, Casagrande pondered, a safe man with dangerous ideas, and yet, in the nether world where they existed, a necessary man. The kind of man who could get you ahead.

Or get you in trouble, he thought.

Or get you dead, added his silent inner voice.

Casagrande continued to flip through the file, peering into a world that always warranted closer examination that was neither welcomed by the subterranean community that was being watched nor enjoyed by the people's representatives who conducted the oversight. Once again, he descended into the infernal reaches of espionage and felt the gnawing discomfort of a late-night driver forced to halt at an intersection stoplight in the midst of a dark and decaying inner city, anxiously awaiting the green signal to effect an escape. Yet he knew that it was just this type of activity that had motivated him to come to Washington. Emilio Casagrande never spent a sleepless night pondering questions about the meaning of life or the purpose of his existence. He knew exactly why he was here. God and the people of New Mexico had sent him to the nation's capital to stop evil from preying upon the good.

Casagrande had been elected and reelected, each time by a landslide, on that most commonly touted—but rarely effective—platform of 'integrity.' Rarer still, Senator Casagrande had fulfilled his promises to the electorate. He had served for eight years in the House of Representatives and was currently in his fifth term as a United States Senator, yet in all those years not a whiff of scandal had ever emanated from his office. The reason for this was a simple as it was remarkable: Emilio Casagrande was an honest man. "Leave me out of the spy cesspool," he had told Howard Danville, Senate Majority Leader. He had said those words almost twenty years ago. *Had it really been that long?* he mused.

Casagrande recalled how he 'got into this mess' as he referred to his unofficial appointment as chairman of the equally unofficial and wholly unrecognized Select Subcommittee on Miscellaneous Matters.

491

It was during his first term as a Senator, in the month of May of his third year, he remembered. As Casagrande was walking out of the Senate Restaurant after lunch, Howard Danville came up from behind and with a characteristic—almost a signature—gesture, took Casagrande by the left upper arm. Danville began talking about the committee as if the topic had been broached many times in the past and it was merely the details that need to be ironed out. "What are you talking about, Howie?" Casagrande remembered the disorientation. Casagrande always felt more comfortable turning his head to the right while conducting an ambulatory conversation. He was not sure whether this was a personal quirk, a feature of being right-handed, or something to do with those things one saw on educational television about right or left brained people. He made it a point to watch Howard Danville 'working' many of the other Senators and came to the conclusion that right-handed Senators were approached from the left, left-handed Senators were approached from the right, and very often from behind. This did not cause Casagrande to distrust the Majority Leader, but rather to grant the man the wary respect one owes to a master hunter who is armed with a keen-edged weapon, chasing a well-known quarry.

Danville convinced, or perhaps coerced, Casagrande to chair the subcommittee. As a first-term Senator, an offer of a chairmanship was difficult to refuse, even if the job could never be added to a resume and even if the work was unpalatable. "Howie," he had protested, "I've never heard of that committee."

"Neither has ninety-five percent of the Senate or one-hundred percent of the press."

"What good is a chairmanship of a stealth committee?"

Danville stopped, turned to Casagrande, firmly clasped his colleague by the shoulders, and leveled deceptively sad brown eyes upon his colleague. The Majority Leader stared silently. Casagrande's initial sense of unease was gradually replaced with an emotion that was even more foreign to him: shame. He accepted the appointment.

During the next two decades, Casagrande's opinion of the spy business as a cesspool had changed very little. He did not, however, allow this to be a license for despair. If there was an opportunity to make even the smallest repair in the shredded ethical fabric of clandestine operations, he would toil mightily to do so. Over the years, he had earned a reputation among his colleagues as the one man to go to for the answer to the inevitable and unavoidable question: 'what should I do?' He was not a mere rock of integrity. A visit to his office for ethics advice was known around the Capitol as 'a visit to the mountain.' It was a reputation for which any other member of the Senate would have traded a million votes, and a reputation that fueled the rumors, often encouraged and abetted by his fiercely devoted staff, of his run for the presidency in next year's election.

The Senator picked up the proposal package submitted by the new Director of ORCA and glanced over it for the third time that day. It carried a classified restriction that officially did not exist. Casagrande and the members of the subcommittee joked that these items were designated as 'Kill Yourself Before Opening.' Jerome Delatour, the junior member of the committee referred to such files as 'Gouge Out Your Eyes Before Reading.' Casagrande smiled to himself as he thought of this and then returned to pondering the scope and details of the proposal. *Brilliant,* he thought again. *Brilliant and dangerous.*

The desk intercom buzzed. His secretary announced that the new Director had arrived. "Yes, please show him in." The secretary ushered the new Director into the senatorial inner sanctum.

"Thank you, Delores. Oh, by the way, please go home. I apologize for keeping you here so late."

Despite having already examined a recent portrait photograph in the Director's dossier, Casagrande still found the appearance of the man to be somewhat of a shock. People in this profession tended to look either like IBM salesmen—usually the folks who had come up via the military or the FBI—or baggy, wrinkled, herringbone tweed, sport-jacketed academics. This career public servant was wearing a bespoke charcoal gray suit, a Brioni necktie, and rather expensive Italian shoes. In addition, the Director appeared to be at least two decades younger than the age indicated in the file. On the other hand, the man's haircut was a haphazard affair. Had Casagrande not already familiarized himself with his visitor's lengthy civil service record, he would have ventured to guess that the Director had spent his entire youth as a guitar player in a Seattle coffeehouse. Then, there were those eyes: blue, penetrating, unblinking. *This guy is a mixed bag*, Casagrande thought. *The most stable, conservative, and reliable weirdo I've ever met.* The Senator made a mental shrug. Politics required a certain amount of tolerance for eccentrics and the politics of the classified world required tolerance for the outright abnormal. *Besides*, Casagrande mused, *unpredictability is a force multiplier. We need someone who can't be outflanked*. The Senator rose and moved to the front corner of his desk. The men shook hands.

"I've read your proposals," said Casagrande, "They're mighty ambitious. Are you trying to save the world for us?"

The Director's left eyebrow arched. With the shadow of a smile, he responded, "Save the world? Heaven forbid."

The Senator returned to his chair. "Then maybe it's to save your job." Casagrande found it useful to be blunt with civil servants. In their world of doublespeak, not unlike the obfuscated world of Congress, a straightforward and unvarnished question or statement could throw the bureaucrat off balance and sometimes extract candid conversation.

The Director was unflappable. "My job is to get information that no one else can find."

"I've heard that before."

"From tarot card readers and telephone psychics. I'm not a screwball. You wouldn't have agreed to meet with me if I was." The new Director settled himself casually into the guest chair opposite the Senator's desk.

The Senator was impressed. The Director possessed an air of casual confidence that reflected authentic competence. It was refreshing to meet someone who spoke his mind instead of attempting to curry favor. In a world where lobbyists, bureaucrats, and the chairborne military brass behaved more like scheming palace eunuchs than public servants, the new Director was a welcome anomaly. The Director also knew how to push the right buttons. Casagrande had nothing but contempt for some of the arcane programs that DoD had experimented with in previous decades. He had labored mightily to terminate funding for Pentagon projects that employed remote viewers, telepaths, spoon benders and an assortment of circus acts as a substitute for serious intelligence gathering activities. "So now that the CIA has stepped on it again for the umpteenth time this year, you are here to tell me that your Sweatshop is where we must place our trust."

The Director had no intention of rising to the bait. The CIA had, indeed, been afflicted by problems recently. Another highly placed mole had been discovered, the leak of a proposed plan to steal a prototype nuclear warhead from Russia had been exposed, and a failed coup attempt in Angola was pinned on the agency. All of this paled to insignificance, however, in comparison to what was perhaps the greatest disaster in CIA's history. About four months ago, the *Capital*

Guardian broke the story that a team of scientists had been employed by the agency to develop a virtually undetectable 'Nazi Virus' that interfered with the hormonal balance in the amygdala and hippocampus of the brain, resulting in memory loss, general anxiety, xenophobia, mass hysteria, and a proclivity to be swayed by bombastic oratory. The *Guardian* had uncovered an informant who disclosed that the CIA planned to release the virus upon the American public shortly before the next presidential election in an effort to ensure that any challenger would be soundly defeated by the current resident at 1600 Pennsylvania Avenue. The Director of the CIA was summarily dismissed, a special prosecutor appointed to prepare criminal charges, and legislation was promptly drafted to dismantle the agency. Although conventional and unconventional wisdom both concluded that the CIA would eventually survive and weather this storm, the near future for his covert world colleagues at Langley was not bright. Dunning the competition would serve no purpose. "We've had our own problems recently," admitted the Director. "We lost an entire overseas operation a few days ago and a number of field operatives across the globe during the past few weeks."

"How?"

"Assassination. We've suffered a rupture in the security seal and believe we have been harboring a tumor."

"Tumor?"

"Infiltrator."

"A tumor! You boys have your own lingo, don't you? First moles, now tumors. It gives me the hives to try to keep track of all this slang. CIA talks one way, NSA another, every DoD spook shop has their own jargon. Heck, can't you folks agree on just one of your little secret spy terms?"

The Director could tell that the Senator was speaking without rancor and was both changing the subject as well as feeling him out. The Director knew that the Senator had previously served as a Lieutenant Commander in the Navy Reserve. Casagrande was checking the cut of his jib. "We discovered that one of our senior headquarters personnel, Peter Wylinski, was conspiring with a new employee to betray agency secrets to a recently emerging threat, unofficially labeled as the 'Shades.' Among other things, it appears that they were culling through our most sensitive files in order to identify the top-performing ORCA field agents. Those agents became the targets of the assassinations I just mentioned. Our people are sorting through the mess even as we speak."

"Do you have Wylinski in custody?"

"He's dead. It appears that the junior agent, Jeremy Kearn, stabbed Wylinski, but Wylinski survived long enough to break Kearn's neck. That means in addition to the inherent tragedy of the deaths, that we also suffer the misfortune of being unable to interrogate the principle actors. We're still trying to sort this out, but from the evidence we've gathered so far, it appears that there have been some devastating compromises. First and foremost was an attack on our contractor's facility in Wisconsin. We lost several people and irreplaceable IT infrastructure. I've been forced to scuttle Project Navaho and might need to keep cutting deeper to preserve what little is left under our partnership with Babylon."

"So, you need to do some serious housecleaning and reorganizing. Perhaps while you are at it, you can publish an updated dictionary of spy talk so that the rest of us can understand what you are jabbering about."

The Director smiled pleasantly. "Certainly. How about the spy term, 'additional funding'?"

Casagrande chuckled softly but immediately sobered. "Perhaps you've been too busy with your spy business to pay attention to the latest news? In case you haven't noticed, churches across the country are still being torched, there have been four major high school shootings during the past month, and three days ago one of the largest publishing houses in the world was bombed in New York—while hosting a conference of prominent authors, no less."

"The Brookguild explosion is still being investigated. This morning we received word from the forensics team that the source might not have been a bomb."

"From the photos of the wreckage, it sure as hell looked like a bomb."

"In this case, it may have been an electrical overload in the central data processing and storage facility on the thirty-seventh floor."

"Computers explode like that?"

"Apparently, these did."

Casagrande made a noncommittal shrug. "Meanwhile, a Wall Street CEO jumps to his death yesterday morning, the stock market is now in freefall, and from all indications it will continue to plummet down into an economic sewer. Tax revenues are guaranteed to shrink this year and for who-knows-how-many years into the future. If that wasn't crazy enough, this morning we started getting frantic telephone calls from back in New Mexico about thirty-seven Jehovah's Witnesses from Alaska who appeared out of nowhere at Los Alamos Trinity Test Site, claiming to have been abducted back in 1975 by space aliens called...Elouise?"

"Elohim," corrected the Director. "We are familiar with that cult. We have them under observation."

"Crazier and crazier by the minute," lamented the Senator.

"It does appear that things are getting grim. The proverbial end of western civilization."

"Perhaps not so proverbial. There are predictions of a nationwide catastrophic collapse, not only from the pundits of the press, but joined by voices in this building as well."

"Yes, and your committee's unwritten charter—for want of a better term—gives you some rather extraordinary authority to deal with national emergencies, including domestic terrorism and economic meltdowns. What's more to the point, this market crash was triggered by a tragic event that just might have been averted if ORCA had the tools that I'm asking you to purchase for me."

"I didn't see anything in your proposal that indicates you would be in the market for crystal balls."

"I don't claim to have telepathic powers, but if you examine the files, you will see that I actually sent up a flare. I've been in my current position for not much more than two months, which I realize means nothing to the committee. Nevertheless, in the summary of my pre-selection interview, and the first memo I sent to your office, I outlined my concerns. Take a look and make up your own mind if I was not spot-on."

"What pre-selection interview?"

"There is a process."

"None that we've ever seen. I was under the impression that your organization worked for my committee, but ORCA is the only agency that doesn't give us an opportunity to review and assess the placement of a political appointee."

"I'm not a political appointee."

"What are you then?"

"A patriot."

"One with a murky past."

"It's a prerequisite for the job."

"Being a patriot or being murky?"

"Take your pick."

"Maybe I'll choose clairvoyant."

"Fund my program and I'll start reading the tea leaves."

"So, you're saying that these problems preceded your arrival and that you were sandbagged before you had a chance to get a solid footing."

"In a sense. Perhaps not unlike President George Bush—the younger—having Nine-Eleven foisted upon him thanks to security shortfalls that had existed in this country for decades."

"I thought your organization wasn't all that fond of Bush One or Two."

"I'm beginning to empathize with their predicaments."

"I didn't think that empathy was an essential skillset at the Sweatshop."

"Neither did I."

"I recommend that we don't empathize our way into a two-decades-long quagmire on the other side of the world."

"I'll do my best to be more domestic while not becoming domesticated."

"So, what makes your proposal so special that you can look around the corner and peek at the shadowy future?"

"You are familiar enough with big data to know that with the right instreams of information, and a processor of adequate power, we can make predictions with reasonable accuracy, at least in the short term. That would include drilling down to specific events, such as the death of Weston Chao."

"You can predict an individual suicide?"

"This wasn't just any suicide. This was the CEO of Citi-Morgan-Chase who jumped out of his office window on the forty-seventh floor. Against all possible odds, he landed on the Federal Reserve Governor who chairs the Committee on Bank Supervision. There are always telltale signs of an impending suicide, and with someone like Mister Chao, there is a vast quantity of data that streams above, below, through, and out of him on a daily basis. He, and hundreds of key individuals like him, would have been on the short list for observation. In Mister Chao's case, his suicide appears to have been motivated by blackmail, which happens to be one of the situations that is most amenable to being detected by our new technology. We would have spotted this."

"Would that short list you just mentioned include members of Congress?"

The Director leaned forward in his chair. "Senator, honestly, do you think that you are currently immune from prying? If anyone in this Administration, or any Administration in the past or future, tells you that we don't peek, they are outright lying to you. But you already know that. I don't have to lie. I'll tell you straight right now, I already know just about everything, and with this technology, I'll probably know everything. However, without this program, the proverbial *they* will know just about everything and unless I get there first, *they* will know *absolutely* everything."

"What's to stop *them* from acquiring this after you do?"

"One of the most compelling reasons to implement this program immediately is that we will be able to monitor everything in the cybersphere, regardless of how much effort our adversaries make to cloak their communications. Once detected, as you can see from Appendix D to the report, we will have offensive capabilities."

"I saw that. Frankly, I don't understand it, but I saw it."

"To be equally frank, I *do* understand it and it scares me. However, it scares me more to contemplate a world in which we don't have it and our enemies do. Say the word and I'll accompany you to our inner sanctum for a controlled demonstration. You won't like it, but you'll understand why we must have it."

"Sounds like the situation this country faced when developing the atomic bomb."

"Yes, even its creators were frightened."

"Given that you've just intimated that your agency has a dossier on me, it probably told you that I wrote my PhD thesis on Robert Oppenheimer."

"Yes."

"When Oppenheimer saw the first explosion of the atomic bomb at Trinity Site, his thoughts turned to a passage in *Bhagavad Gita*."

The Director recited softly, "Now I am become Death, the destroyer of worlds."

"Yes." Casagrande sat a moment in silence, locking his dark

brown dark eyes with the nearly transparent blue of the Director's.

The Director knew that he had passed the test. More important, however, was to clinch the deal on the current proposal that was pending before the subcommittee. The program needed to receive the Senator's support, and with it, the approval of a skeptical colleagues. "We've made phenomenal advances in the art of decryption. Unfortunately, the same is true of both our honorable and dishonorable adversaries."

"There's some poetry I haven't heard in a while."

"I wish it was as poetic as it sounds. The reality is far more prosaic. The problem is that once we've intercepted and decrypted a signal, we forward the communication to headquarters. Our opponents then intercept us and decrypt *that* message. You see, reading another gentleman's mail is not so appalling as being caught reading another gentleman's mail. Once they are on to us, they can track down our field operatives, change their plans, or both. Our interception program becomes not merely worthless, it actually becomes a liability."

"I thought one-time pad encryption was impossible to decipher."

"We all thought that. We were wrong. Times change quickly. Technology changes faster."

"You can hand-carry the messages."

"From operations spread across the globe? Every day? Our people are assigned to covert operations in hostile theaters. Constant travel to the United States is not exactly the best way to keep a low profile. Besides, even if it weren't prohibitively expensive, the delay is unacceptable and the risk of loss or interception would be even higher than we now face."

"It sounds to me that you merely need to plug some leaks. What have you done to upgrade your current systems?"

"I'm not asking for money to add a few bells and whistles to our current technology. We make incremental changes and whoever is trying to pry into our business merely needs to keep pace. My proposal is the great leap forward."

"The Chinese Communist Party used that slogan in the nineteen-sixties. It was a flop then."

"For the past decade, they have been the only surviving communist government in the world and their economy is poised to eclipse ours this year. They obviously did not flop too badly."

"They've been saying that about the Chinese economy since I was a junior Senator."

"There was that little matter of the crash of the Hang Seng and Shanghai exchanges which caused the Chinese Great Depression. Let's face it, they've roared back in the past few years and there's no stopping them. We are going to be forced to take greater risks and display more courage to compete in this brave new world."

Casagrande had to admit that this new director could hold his own. His predecessor would have reached the sniveling stage by now. "Okay, then, time for the bottom line."

"The proposed budget breakdown is in the last appendix of the proposal. I'm sure that you've examined it. The bottom line is the top line. I need to close shop in Vicksburg and build an entirely new center. There isn't any fluff in this program. Senator, I need it all."

Casagrande did not have a particularly expressive face. He was an adroit poker player, as his colleagues had discovered both socially and professionally. Nevertheless, the Director could read the ever so subtle alteration in the pitch of the Senator's eyebrows to correctly interpret that this was an incredulous prospect. "You just opened that center down in Mississippi. Now you want to close it? We've already stretched the Ghost Ledger to the breaking point, and now this?"

"We just lost an entire office. Without this new program, I'll lose more offices and more people." The Director leaned forward and with earnest gravity locked eyes with the statesman. "Senator, when I say I'll lose people, that means in plain English that they'll be hunted, tortured, and brutally murdered. I have photographs of the slayings in Budapest. Would you care to see them?" Without waiting for an answer, he reached into a leather haversack and deftly extracted a manila folder. He then pulled out a sheaf of photographs, casually tossing them on the Senator's desk. Casagrande waved aside the photos without looking at them. The Senator was not squeamish, but he had simply seen enough photographs of assassinations over the years to need no further education on the subject. "These were good people," the Director continued. "All of them had families. Two of them were mothers of young children."

"I'm painfully aware of the human cost," said the Senator.

"And the human cost has an associated dollar cost. We will be closing the Budapest operation and consolidating it with a number of other offices at a new European central operations center."

"Yes, I saw that bill also—a few million more added to the tab, it would seem. Just where will you be setting up shop?"

"Nürnberg."

"Nuremberg, Germany?"

"The same."

"You pronounce it like a native."

"There is a family history."

"Wasn't that the city where Hitler planned to rule his Aryan empire?"

"The place has a tragic past."

"I'm more concerned with our tragic future."

"That's why I am here to ask for funding. Agents are being picked off around the world. In the past month, we've lost mission chiefs in Naples, Johannesburg, Teheran and Santiago. We also lost an agent yesterday on the West Coast. It was made to look like an accident, but he just happened to be the returning Budapest Chief of Operations. Whoever tracked him down has capabilities as good or better than we have. Actually, much better." The Director paused, dropped his voice almost to a whisper, and again leaned forward, as if he was imparting a secret that required enhanced secrecy in a room currently occupied by only the two men. "We just discovered that someone has been surreptitiously engaging our Shanghai Program for more than three weeks—"

"Shanghai? China?"

"No, Project Shanghai. We provided a preliminary brief to your office two weeks ago. The false-front cellphone environment."

"Right. You mean the fake cell system was actually used on a foreign agent?"

"We're not sure about the identity of the target."

"I'm starting to get uneasy about all of this."

"As well you should. Just an hour ago we had a compromise on the west coast of a particularly valuable and sensitive system called *EGREGORE.*"

"E-Gregory? Like the actor, Gregory Peck?"

"No, it comes from a Greek term, ἐγρήγοροι, which is a reference of watcher angels and hive-mind entities."

"That's a bit esoteric, not to mention…weird."

"I've often suspected that the names of our programs are the result of overworked programmers who suffer from cabin fever."

"I don't recall being brought aboard on this one."

"This was developed during the tenure of my predecessor. If you haven't been provided the white paper, I'll see that it's sent to you immediately. With the compromise of that system, we are being forced to fly in the blind. We are in some deep…" the Director trailed off, leaving it to the Senator to finish the sentence.

"Buffalo chips," the Senator offered.

The Director nodded. "Fresh ones."

"Looks to me like your organization is going to hell in a handbasket."

"My diagnosis exactly."

"Why should I be your rock and salvation?"

"We are the eyes and ears of Congress. Would you prefer to dismantle us and rely exclusively on the executive agencies?" There was a pause of silence as the two men regarded one another. The Director broke the impasse. "I'm sure there are people who come in here to try to bluff you. This is no bluff. Help me get this program approved and funded or help me dismantle my organization. I can't allow our people to be slaughtered like cattle." The Director looked straight into Casagrande's eyes. "I'm not making threats. This isn't poker. I'm not blowing smoke. We are dealing with the lives of real people, good people, whose fate absolutely depends upon what we decide here today. They are out there without a net."

The Senator paused while he took this all in. He did not have the sense that the visitor was pressing him for a hasty decision and believed that the Director would have patiently sat across the desk for twelve hours if that were how long it took for Casagrande to ponder the issues. He had already come to a number of conclusions from reading the report. He watched the Director. The man sat patiently. The expression on his face was dogged determination mixed with mannerly deference. *A professional*, the Senator thought, *a real professional*. He exuded a sort of courage and uncompromising courtesy that Casagrande had imagined was lost to the world since the nineteenth century. After the silent passage of a seemingly interminable minute, the Senator rose from his chair and walked around the elaborately carved walnut desk. "Alright, let's walk over to Carla Stevenson's office. I told her that we'd have a chat about this tonight."

"It seems that your committee burns the midnight oil."

"You and your folks aren't the only ones lurking in the dark."

"Hmmm…I'm not sure we can handle so much competition," said the Director with an engaging grin.

"I'll do what I can to give you a leg up on whatever competition might come your way."

"Thank you, Senator." The Director's tone was at once deferential and yet dignified, self-confident. Casagrande had the strange feeling that he had somehow been manipulated by this new Director. The Senator was never one to bask in self-adulation, and yet he could not resist the feeling that he had just performed some grand and heroic act on behalf of the Republic. Casagrande now knew that this man was not simply a pro, but also a player. Strange, the dossier on the Director indicated very little that could shed light on his political acumen. He had never held office, never worked on the hill, never been involved in any level of politics, and although he had been a career civil servant for four decades, he had only recently risen to executive leadership level in the past few years. "Senator?" The query broke onto Casagrande's reverie. "I'm afraid that I haven't received the SIIC on Senator Stevenson."

Casagrande knew the importance of obeying security measures within the Congress in general and the subcommittee in particular. The Special Item Investigation Clearance, or 'sick' as it was pronounced in the subcommittee, was the means to ensure that there would be no leaks of the very deep, and very dark, secrets shared by the intelligence community with the legislative branch. A new SIIC was required for each member whenever a significant operation or technological breakthrough was to be introduced to the committee. Despite the necessity of the procedure, it could nevertheless be a damned nuisance, especially when it caused delays on particularly important projects. Casagrande frowned. "Well, where is it?"

"I believe it has been held up by your EILi."

Casagrande's frown transitioned to a grimace. "Hagar," he said as steadily as possible, despite wishing to groan and curse. Paul Hagar, the Executive Intelligence Liaison, was a member of his own party, but this was cold consolation for all the problems he was forced to endure due to the man's rabid politics. Congressman Hagar had been in office—and in the subcommittee—seemingly forever. For reasons that Casagrande could not fathom, Hagar had declined to take more significant leadership roles despite his seniority, preferring instead to perform the thankless scutwork of coordinating clearances with the covert agencies littered across the Executive Branch. Despite Hagar's obvious competence and unquestioned devotion to duty, he was nevertheless an intractable partisan. Even something as routine and necessary as a SIIC would be delayed if it was needed by, as Hagar called them, 'the disloyal opposition.'

"I'm afraid that without Congressman Hagar's cooperation this matter may not get out of the gate."

"And without Carla Stephenson's support, the project is dead on arrival. As the ranking House Minority member, she is my right hand. In this subcommittee, everything is a team effort. We don't just mouth the word bipartisan, we live it."

"Would that be true of everyone on the committee?" asked the Director pointedly.

Casagrande experienced an involuntary internal grimace. *God help me, this spy is actually spying on us.*

That's his job.

Perhaps he's doing it too well.

We should just be thankful that he's on our side, the Senator's silent counselor concluded.

"We'll get the support," Casagrande replied.

"Yes sir, these proposals don't have a prayer without that."

"And are you a praying man?"

"Is it a job requirement?"

The Senator chuckled. "When was the last time you tried to get money out of this Congress?"

"We both know that I don't need Congress. I just need your committee."

"Perhaps so, but don't discount prayer. After all, *it coudd'n hoit.*"

The Director laughed. "Let's see Senator Stevenson's reaction before we get out the rosary beads."

Casagrande smiled appreciatively. "Fine. We'll stop by Hagar's office on the way to get that 'sick' issued right now." They started for the door of the Senator's office but Casagrande stopped short. "There's just one thing about your satellite transmission proposal. A number of the scrambled bandwidth transmissions will be virtually undetectable by any monitoring station—either foreign or domestic."

"Senator, that is the whole idea."

"Yes, and it's brilliant. Absolute invisibility. Artificially intelligent communication signals that are encrypted, stealth, disassembled, enmeshed in self-destruct strings of subatomic viruses and then randomly spattered across the background of the electro-magnetic spectrum driven by quantum computers that are straight out of the pages of a science fiction novel."

"Other than the observation that this is science fiction, that is a rather good synopsis of the project."

"How did you crack the code, so to speak, on quantum computing? It's my understanding that most other efforts keep hitting brick walls."

"Yes, and subatomic brick walls can be rather daunting. To be candid, it wasn't easy. The reason we arrived at the finish line first can be ascribed to a combination of maniacal focus and an element of dumb luck."

"What kind of dumb luck?"

"The kind of luck that avoids the bad luck of our colleagues and rivals. You can add to the list of recent security disasters the rather untimely and suspicious deaths of a large segment of the quantum computing scientists and engineers in this country. IBM, Google, Honeywell, Microsoft, HP, MIT and Sanford have all lost their best people. Two days ago, the body of Darius Gambrell of Oregon Tech was found washed up on the banks of the Willamette River. This morning, I just received a report that Sven Berglund at the University of Chicago was gunned down in front of his house and that Doctor Mort Moscowicz of Georgia Tech fell down a flight of stairs at the Ted Turner facility. The same death toll can be seen at universities around the country as well as at NSA and DoD. We've been monitoring the phenomenon worldwide and losses of physicists have been reported in Japan, China, Russia, Abu Dhabi, Australia and the UK. As for ORCA, it just so happens that our transition to Vicksburg during the past year, and the development of the technology you see in the proposal, required our teams of technicians and researchers to be cloistered like Circumcellion monks in a variety of secured locations. As a result, they haven't been…well… dropping like flies."

"I see," said Casagrande, nodding thoughtfully. "Since we are being candid, let me point out something that is, quite candidly, a little bit troubling."

"Of course, Senator."

"According to your proposal, no one other than members of

your organization will have access to equipment that can transmit or receive these communications. This makes your outfit wholly unsupervised. There won't be anyone monitoring you. Even more than that, it's conceivable that your operation would actually be able to exercise control over the global communication system."

"You don't trust us?"

Casagrande frowned. "Do I have to lecture you about trust in this so-called profession of yours?"

"*Touché*. However, any monitoring will destroy the integrity and security of the system. Sometimes, Senator, you just have to make that leap of faith."

"Maybe so, but with a system like this, a dangerous man could literally rule the world. I don't want a pact with the devil."

"Don't worry, Senator, I won't seize your immortal soul until well after the next election."

Emilio Casagrande chuckled. "I've been in Congress for thirty-seven years, most of those years right here in the Senate. I assure you, I forfeited my soul several elections ago." It was now the visitor's turn to snicker. "By the way," the Senator added, "this new location you mention in the proposal...the Farallon Islands?"

"West of San Francisco. Forty kilometers off the coast."

"Never heard of them."

"Desolate. Dismal. Dreary. Deserted. Sort of like the Capitol building in August, but colder and with more seagulls."

Casagrande laughed out loud. It wasn't often that people in the profession of spying had a healthy sense of humor. Despite the natural intelligence of many of members of the unnatural intelligence community, they were seldom witty. "Be sure to give it an appropriately unpleasant name," he quipped back.

"Actually, I've been toying with 'Project Halcyon' as the assigned designation."

"Halcyon? Doesn't that mean happy times of yesteryear?"

"Yes, but the original derivation of the word comes from a mythical bird said by ancient writers to breed in a nest floating at sea during the winter solstice, charming the wind and waves into calm."

"I'm sure your lonely operatives assigned to that garden spot will appreciate the irony." Casagrande nodded to himself introspectively. "I suppose that setting up a lonely monastery in the Pacific will ensure the security of the operation."

"Hermits make excellent analysts," agreed the Director with a crooked grin. "The location has another significant advantage. We will be laying a secure undersea cable to connect us with DG in San Francisco."

"DG?"

"DataGhad. As you can see in the proposal, we will be teaming with them."

"I thought that ORCA prided itself on its self-sufficiency," the Senator needled with a good-natured grin. "Except when it comes to funding from my office, of course."

"Pride goeth before the fall," responded the Director, not missing a beat. "Our nodes and server farms spread across the rural landscape are overtaxed and sadly out of date. Yesterday, for example, our connection with servers in Ghosts, Wyoming winked out for more than eight hours. Given DG's reliability, their access to nearly all social media on the planet, their strength in developing algorithms, and their willingness to help leverage our expenses, they are a natural fit. If it weren't for our lash-up with DG, my request for a cash infusion would be twice as large."

"It sounds as if you will be rearranging the chess board," observed the Senator.

"Yes. In fact, we will also be closing our interrogation cells at Guantanamo Bay, Greenbrier, and Mount Weather, and consolidate all those operations at Banshee Mountain."

"Banshee Mountain?"

"In Tennessee."

"Somehow, that rings a bell."

"There is a distillery there. It happens to make a very fine bourbon of which I'm particularly fond."

The Senator nodded thoughtfully and then took a few steps over to the credenza on the north wall. He lifted the top revealing a minibar. "Speaking of which, would you care for a quick shot before we walk down the hall?"

"Don't mind if I do."

"Sorry, I don't have your favorite bourbon. Any other preference?" asked the Senator as he reached for a dark green bottle.

"Would you happen to have *Jägermeister* in your private stash?"

Casagrande's usual poker face gave way to an unmasked look

of pleasant surprise as he brought up his hand already holding the very same liquor requested by his guest. "What a coincidence! You're also a fan?"

The Director nodded, accompanied by a sly grin as he bestowed a friendly pat on the Senator's shoulder, deftly planting a nanotransmitter—smaller than a mustard seed—into the fabric of the man's jacket, identical to the one he had affixed to the bottom of the Senator's desktop just five minutes before.

The Senator lined up two shotglasses and prepared to pour. "Sorry, it's not chilled."

"I prefer it that way," said the Director. "Cooling it down takes the edge off."

"Some people are not at all fond of this liquor. They complain that it tastes like medicine."

"They are entitled to their opinion under the First Amendment. My job is to protect the rights and freedoms of all of our citizens, even the sissies."

Casagrande chuckled. "Yes, it is still a free country."

"But not cheap."

"No, not cheap."

As the Senator poured the drinks, the Director offered, "You should try it with a chaser of *Frankenwein*."

"*Frankenwein*?"

"A German white wine from the area around Nürnberg."

"Hmmm…Nuremberg again. When we stop by Paul Hagar's office, I might order up a SIIC on you just to make sure you aren't bent on world domination," the Senator joked.

The Director laughed and responded with a playful wink. "The world has little to worry about from the likes of a politically agnostic spy like me. I have trouble enough getting through the op-ed pages of the *Capital Guardian* in the morning, much less trying to rule over the partisan morass of both the democratic and despotic governments on this planet."

"Mister Todd," said the Senator as he handed a glass of the dark brown liquid to the Director, "I think this is the beginning of a beautiful friendship."

⌘

They stood on a street devoid of traffic. It was damp and fog had settled in for the night.

"Something is wrong with my cellphone," griped Gaude in evident annoyance as he tapped ineffectually on the screen.

"It took you this long to figure it out? I've been telling you that since we first met."

"No, I mean that it is malfunctioning. The screen says that there is no carrier service."

"Consider it a blessing."

"A blessing for you. More like a curse for me. I need to contact my cellphone company. I suppose that I need to find another cellphone to contact them."

"Sorry, Dan, I can't help you with that," answered Watt sincerely. His eyes then darted over Gaude's shoulder and he pointed at an object across the street. "There's a payphone right there."

Gaude spun around. "Hmmm…I haven't seen one of those since…since that one payphone in downtown D.C. Looks like we have a case of *deus ex machina.*"

"You should know by now that he isn't a machine."

"I'm sure that there are some machines out there that would beg to differ," said Gaude with a slight smirk has he began to cross the street. Upon arriving at the booth, he found that the telephone appeared to be in working order. Like the one he had encountered at the beginning of their journey, it was a veritable antique and accepted only coins. He dug into his pockets but found that he had no change. Watt, who had followed him across the street, offered him three quarters. Gaude deposited the money, dialed directory assistance, was shunted to an automated service, and after a few minutes of repeatedly requesting the computer to place him in contact with an actual human being, was finally connected with a customer assistance representative of his wireless provider.

"Good day, this is Annabelle. May I help you?"

"My cellphone indicates that there is no service carrier."

"Yes, and how can we help you?"

"You are my service carrier."

"Your account is still current?"

"I thought so."

510

"Let me check for you. Your name, please?"

"Daniel Gaude."

"G-A-W-D-A-Y?"

"G-A-U-D-E."

"Thank you, just one moment." There was a pause on the other side of the line. Gaude could hear the faint clicking of a keyboard. "Your address?"

"37 Dupont Circle, Washington, D.C., Apartment 12-D."

"Mister Gaude, do you have your account number with you?"

"No, sorry, I don't."

"For security purposes, could you please give me your password?"

"It's…it's…" Gaude paused, struggling to recall, but come up blank. "I'm sorry, I don't remember it."

"I'm sorry, sir, I can't access the account without verifying your password."

"Yes, I understand. I'm sorry…" Gaude was stopped short as a word suddenly occurred to him. Although he was unsure why, and had no recollection of its significance, he blurted it out. "Maestro."

There was a momentary pause and then the representative at the other end of the line responded, "Thank you, Mister Gaude. I'm checking your account right now." Gaude waited while further keyboard clatter ensued. Thirty seconds later, the voice re-engaged. "I'm sorry, Mister Gaude, but your account was closed approximately three weeks ago."

"Closed? Three weeks ago? That's not possible. I've been using my cellphone for the past few weeks. It was working until about an hour ago."

"Sir, the account record shows that we terminated service."

"But I've been using it."

"Just one moment, please." Again, Gaude waited, this time for about three minutes. The representative finally returned to the line, and in a well-rehearsed tone of commercial service sympathy, explained, "I'm very sorry, Mister Gaude, but I've checked the call and service records associated with your account. There has been no activity on your phone since we cut off service twenty-three days ago. Are you sure that you have been using your phone rather than someone else's?"

"Yes, I'm sure, I…" Gaude looked at Watt who was regarding him with a gentle smile of blended consolation and compassion. Gaude suddenly understood without comprehending. He then thanked the service representative for her assistance and ended the call.

"The cellphone service was terminated."

"Yes."

"It was terminated from day one."

"Yes."

"You knew that all along."

"Yes."

"But the cellphone *was* working."

"Was it?" asked Watt.

"I thought it was," answered Gaude, now uncertain.

"Things aren't what they seem to be. Things aren't what we thought they were."

"It was functioning. I'm sure of it."

"It was functioning, but not in the way you thought it was."

"It was functioning but not functional."

"Exactly."

"It all depends on the definition."

"Yes, it does," agreed Watt. "Let's go," he said, as he made a motion with his head to go back across the street.

"Where?"

"Right there," Watt responded, indicating what appeared to be an emergency room entrance to a hospital.

"We are making a full circle, aren't we?"

"How full the circle becomes will entirely depend on you." They crossed the street and entered through large automatic sliding glass doors. They soon found themselves in a brightly lit corridor filled with medical personnel moving purposefully. Gaude accidentally brushed past a young doctor, stocky, black hair, blue eyes, and thick eyebrows. "Sorry," they said in unison as each continued on their own path. Gaude heard music coming from the nurses' station. He recognized it as Ni'ihau Child's 'Going Home.'

The road has been long
As you followed the song
You'll be going home

Keep right on the course
Til you locate the source
You'll be going home

There's a journey ahead
But at least now instead
You'll be going home

Watt led Gaude to the end of the hallway, and it occurred to him that no one in the hospital had stopped them, challenged them, or asked for any identification. They paused by an open window overlooking the city. Gaude took in the view of the waterfront nightscape. Curiously, he was unable to recognize any landmark that identified the iconic downtown. It was as if the night scene of San Francisco had been replaced with a generic metropolis, an undistinguished all-purpose urban mélange. To their right was a closed door. Watt gestured towards it. "It's your turn now."

"Where am I going?"

"That is an existential question."

"Perhaps it is. Can you give me an existential answer?"

"To your destination."

"What is that?"

"Don't you know?"

"Obviously not. If I knew my destination…" Gaude trailed off, his eyes focusing past the horizon in thought.

"Yes?"

"Destination…Destinations, Maine is where we started this trip."

"That's right."

"It might be where others end the journey."

"Astute observation."

"But it's not…"

"Not what?"

"I'm not sure. It's not where I'm going this time, is it?"

"Every mortal has a destination. You will find yours."

"I feel almost as lost as on the first day we met."

"There's no shame in that. You still have a long way to go from here."

"And where is here?"

"Better question. It's where you must travel through before you get to where you are supposed to be."

"That sounds like another way of describing life."

"And death."

"There's a difference?"

"Not really."

"So, I just have to…?"

"Carry on, drive forward, and finish the race."

"Keep the faith."

"You're catching on. You'll do fine."

"You leave me precious little choice."

"Not true. You've made your choice, or I should say, you are making it. I've just been keeping you company as you work your way towards it."

"And now?"

"You'll see. You're a sojourner and there's still a journey ahead of you."

"How much farther?"

"I don't know. No one knows."

"But now I go alone."

"Do you?"

"We climb up different paths together. We walk down the same path alone."

"Perhaps someday," replied Watt, shaking his head, "but not yet." Watt handed a small envelope to Gaude. "Here, these are for you."

"Your business cards?"

"No, *your* calling cards."

"Finally, I get to see what is on the other side." Gaude accepted the proffered envelope, removed a small rectangle of cardstock, and turned it over.

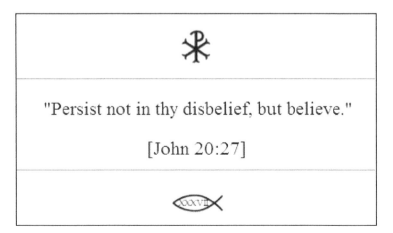

"Persist not in thy disbelief, but believe."

[John 20:27]

"What is this?"

"I've already told you."

"There's nothing on this card that qualifies as identification."

"Some people seem to think so. It's all in the definition, isn't it?"

"What good will this do?"

"What good do you *want* it to do?"

"This is what you've been handing out to everyone?"

"Yes, it seems to work, doesn't it?"

"Okay, Bill, I guess I've gone down the road with you this far. What have I got to lose at this point?"

"Other than your immortal soul?"

"Right, other than that."

"It's entirely up to you."

A warm breeze from the open window caressed Gaude's face. He reacted with gentle surprise and turned to is partner—his friend—Bill Watt. "It's spring? Already?"

"*El Niño.*"

"Of course, *El Niño.*"

"Haven't you ever wondered what that name means?"

Gaude shrugged and gave Watt a wan smile. "I've been associating it with Spanish for 'bad weather' for so long that I hadn't given it much thought," he offered lamely. "It means a child, a little boy."

"No, not *a* child. It is *the* child. It is *your* child. It is *every* child. Just as a priest during Mass stands *in persona Christi*, so does every child dwell in, and exhibit out, the element of divinity that is the patrimony of an immortal human soul. Every newborn boy is a recapitulation of our Savior. Each is called to be *him*. Every arriving baby girl is a reiteration of our Blessed Mother. All are called to be *her*. We never stop being children of God and our Heavenly Father never ceases to beckon us as his beloved *him* and his cherished *her*. In each waking moment, we seek the *him* and *her* who are ourselves and our immortal destiny."

Gaude sucked on a tooth for a moment. "I think that all of this is over my head."

"Don't worry about it, that's par for the course."

"Does it get easier?"

"Well, I've been at it quite a while and…" Watt paused and then broke into a chuckle. "No, no, it doesn't get any easier at all."

"Why didn't you tell me the truth?"

"I always told you the truth. I think you are asking why I didn't lay it all out for you. Would you have wanted me to do that?"

Gaude looked out over an imaginary horizon. "Maybe not. I suppose that we are always closest to the truth when we are the least aware of it."

Watt's eyes locked onto Gaude's. He gave a slight nod that said nothing but revealed much. He then motioned with his head to direct Gaude's attention to the door. "There will be someone else beyond that door."

"Something tells me that there will always be someone else behind the door."

"You're catching on. Keep in mind that they help you find your way just as much as you will help them find their own."

"Thanks, I'll try to remember that. So, are you heading through another door?"

"Of course."

"Who are you planning to befriend now?"

"A poet."

"Hmmm...that's a change of pace. Anyone I know?"

"In a manner of speaking, yes."

"So, it's back to Destinations, Maine?"

"No, this will be a different path." Bill Watt paused and the two erstwhile partners regarded each other silently. There was no uneasiness or restlessness in the pause. Watt then reached into his pocket and withdrew a small pewter lapel pin. Gaude recognized it from the hotel room in Las Vegas. Watt leaned forward and affixed the stag's head badge to Gaude's sports jacket.

Gaude grinned. "What, not a white chrysanthemum?"

Watt shook his head with a faint smile. "That was my story, this is yours."

"Bill, at the winery, I heard voices in the dark."

"You're not the first to hear them."

"I think I'm starting to remember who they were."

"Which will help you figure out who you are."

"And what then? My other life? The real one?"

"Something like that, but it's more complicated than you can possibly imagine."

"And simpler that I can possibly believe."

"You're learning faster than I ever did. At this rate, you'll beat me to the finish."

"Is it a race?"

"It is, but only with yourself."

Gaude took a step into the doorway, hesitated, and then turned back. "There is just one thing that I haven't been able to figure out."

"I hope that I can help you."

"Why do you always eat chili?"

Watt's face assumed a cast of careful reflection. He pursed his lips, cautiously weighed the question and his answer, looked down at his battered suede shoes, and after a few moments of calmly pondering the matter, said, "I like chili."

Gaude nodded, satisfied by the answer. He shook Watt's hand and then turned and stepped into a small private hospital room. On the opposite wall were three other doors: crimson, amber, indigo. There was a bed to his left with a man lying in it, asleep. Gaude gently closed the door behind him and walked to the bed occupied by a sleeping man. He found the patient's medical chart on a stand beside the medcomp apparatus. In the remarks column of the admittance control sheet he read:

```
         Struck by a streetcar.
    Appointment with Cairo tonight.
```

Gaude waited by the bed until the patient awoke. "Good evening. Ready to get going?"

"Who are you?"

"A friend."

"We've never met."

"That doesn't make me any less of a friend."

"Not in my book."

Gaude reached over to open the nightstand drawer. "You need to start reading different books," he responded.

"You're speaking in riddles."

"I know...union rules."

"Excuse me?"

"Excuse me," Gaude smiled apologetically. "My name is Dan."

"Dan what?"

Gaude hesitated, tempted by the opportunity to institutionalize the running joke. He then silently chuckled to, and at, himself. "I'm Dan Gaude," he answered. "It's good to meet you. Any interest in getting out of here?"

"Wouldn't mind that a bit. Are you from my...organization?"

Before he could deny any affiliation, Gaude heard himself replying in a matter-of-fact tone, "I'm your new navigator. We'll conduct the debriefing when we're at a secure shelter." Gaude was surprised that these words came out of his mouth but decided that the unexpected was now part of his job description.

"Navigator...somehow that term is familiar, but I can't..."

"Can't remember?"

"No, I can't, not entirely. There are broken bits and pieces that I recall, but so much is missing."

"What do you remember?"

"Someone named Dayton. I think that I also had a friend named Larry. Something tells me he's behind this, but it's so hazy."

"Anything else?"

"There is...*her*."

Gaude paused before responding and then asked, "Do you know who she is?"

"No...yes...no..."

"I understand. Don't worry, you'll find her...eventually."

"How do you know?"

"Let's just call it an article of faith."

The man nodded and then eased himself out of the hospital bed and walked to the closet where he found unfamiliar, but adequately fitting clothes. "Where are my things?"

"Things?"

"Sorry, forgot. I'll wait for the...ummm... debriefing," he said, straining to capture fleeting and foggy memories just beyond the grasp of recollection. He started dressing while Gaude quietly hummed the Rolling Stones' tune 'Satisfaction.' In less than a minute, the man was fully dressed. "Let's go. I'm sure I've been in that bed too long." He then hesitated, scanned the room and then went to the bedside stand and opened the top drawer. "Where's my cellphone?"

"I have no idea. Don't worry, I've recently discovered that it doesn't necessarily provide all life's answers."

"I'd be satisfied with just a few answers."

"So would I," said Gaude with a reassuring smile. "All in good time—for both of us."

The man frowned in thought for a moment. "Why did it take me so long?"

"You weren't that old, actually."

"No, I didn't mean that. I mean here. How long have I been here?"

"A day."

"One day? It hasn't been years?"

"Yes, it's been that too."

Gaude's new partner considered this as he studied the floor tile for a few moments. "Yes, but it was all over before it began, wasn't it?"

Gaude nodded. "Go through the door."

"Where are we going?"

"That's something that needs to be figured out. I received instructions but not an explanation. I suspect that we will be paying a visit to someone I recently met in D.C. or maybe a friend of his. He has a different way of…seeing things."

"That makes sense," the man agreed. "I've been to D.C. before…recently, I think." He frowned and shook his head, hoping to dislodge the murk from mind. He then turned and faced the three colorful doors and asked, "Do we know which door is the right one?"

"Yes, but that doesn't mean that we always choose it."

"What happens when we walk through?"

"I'm not sure. I've been a newspaper reporter for the past few weeks. Something tells me that might change."

"Interesting cover."

"More than you can imagine."

James Parker Doyle paused a moment in thought, stepped forward and opened a door. He hesitated before walking through. "Which way?" he asked.

"Straight ahead," replied Daniel Gaude.

The Advisors

There was the usual tap on the door.

"Come in, please."

She did not recognize him. He was new. *This is not a good sign,* she thought.

"Good afternoon, I am Agent Dahlgren."

He's lying.

"I've been sent to close out some business," he continued.

That, at least, is the truth...in its own way. She forced a smile that was indistinguishable from authentic. "You must be here to collect the Sorenson file."

"Yes."

She hadn't really harbored any doubts, but even if she had, all such would now have been dispelled. There was no Sorenson file. She knew if she offered to leave the room in order to get the nonexistent file, she would not make it to the door. "I assume that you have also come to pick up the refund?"

"Yes."

He has no idea about any refund. Let's see if we can sweeten the pot. She smiled again, successfully blending in a gentle hint of charming embarrassment. "Oh, I'm so sorry, but I've already converted the cashier's cheque to cash. Do your rules allow you to carry so much money?"

"I'm sure there will be no problem."

He's hooked. "Fine, I have it right here." She made sure that her movements were neither hurried nor overly nonchalant as she walked over to the bookcase. She removed the hefty volume of *Strong's Concordance* and reached into the dark void. "Here we go!" she announced cheerfully.

She turned back to the visitor who immediately realized his error. Without hesitation, she squeezed off three rounds of nine-millimeter from a Kimber Micro. The bullets hit the real agent with the phony name squarely in the chest. He fell back against the wall and began to reach for his service pistol. Another round from her handgun entered his forehead, the bullet making contact three centimeters from dead center of a now dead brain. The agent collapsed onto the floor.

She approached the corpse, the pistol still trained on him. When she was within one meter, she let off another round into the top of his skull. Blood and brains splattered on her perfectly tailored designer dress. *No matter, I've already worn it twice.* Satisfied, she bent down and carefully felt for a cellphone in his outside left jacket pocket, where she knew it would be and where, indeed, it was.

You can't hack an ORCA cell, the most skeptical of the sisters warned.

Perhaps not the SEC-CEL function, conceded Grace, *but this cat can be skinned.* She then took out his wallet that, as expected, was in his interior right jacket pocket. *He's a stupid man. Let's see just how stupid.* She opened the wallet and found the man's driver's license. The year of birth was listed as 1984. She switched the cell interface from official to personal and entered '1984' as the four-digit passcode into the cellphone. The screen immediately opened to the applications. *Yes, very stupid.*

There won't be anything useful on the private side.

The secured network has been down most of this week, Grace explained. *Let me play a hunch.* She began tapping the screen and soon discovered that the dead man, while he was still among the living, had committed the unforgivable sin and regulatory infraction of transferring the telephone numbers of his work supervisors into the 'favorites' bar of the personal function.

How did you know that? asked the sister with the slight lisp.

I assumed that he had called the Sweatshop during the past few days while the secured system was down. He wasn't just stupid, he was also lazy.

She looked at the list of names. She saw one that stirred a memory. She had seen it in a document two years ago. *That's him.*

Grace Ho was now moving down the hallway to her bedroom. She pushed the autodial. The connection was immediate. "Yes," announced the baritone voice.

He was waiting for this call. It's him, all right. She could not resist a smile. "Hello my dear. I have some very sad news for you."

"Who is this?"

Oh my God. Have they gotten so bush league that they respond like that? asked the testy one.

It's just as well our little arrangement is over, observed the most dispassionate member of the group.

The smile disappeared from her face. Grace Ho had precious

little tolerance for dealing with anyone who wasn't a real professional. "Why don't you make a wild guess, darling?" she asked as she entered her large walk-in closet.

There was a moment of silence at the other end. *Do they hire only low-grade morons at the Sweatshop nowadays?* the slightly bitchy and highly judgmental one asked the other incorporeal cerebral siblings listening in on the call.

So it would seem, responded one of the serene personalities.

Grace pushed the speaker function, put the cell on her dresser, and with the confidence and economy of action of a woman who had in earlier years traversed the catwalk in Milan, she kicked off her shoes and slipped out of her dress, as she started reaching for another tasteful and expensive alternative.

"Miss Ho, perhaps there has been a misunderstanding."

She picked up the phone and disengaged the speaker as she stepped into a new set of heels. "Can you venture to guess who might have caused this little misunderstanding?"

"I sincerely apologize if one of our agents may have misinterpreted his instructions."

"I would have loved to have been there when he received those instructions. I'm sure there were some rather tricky interpretations involved. It's all in the definition, isn't it?"

"Miss Ho—"

"Pity that he didn't listen carefully. That sort of thing usually leads to tragic results," she sighed as she walked over to a Louis XVI style armoire. She opened the right door of the large piece of furniture where she kept her traveling handbag containing cash, credit cards, and her passports. "Will you be calling his widow with the sad news?"

There was another moment of silence on the other end. "I'm sure we can work something out, Miss Ho. Would you like to meet?"

"Why yes, that would be delightful," she agreed while exiting into the main hallway and heading to the back of the house.

"Where do you suggest?" the voice asked, successfully sounding to the untrained ear to be maintaining composure, while painfully aware that Grace Ho's ear was more than highly trained.

"I have a wonderful place in mind," she responded breezily, as she took a keyless fob off the hook near the door leading to the garage.

"Where is that?"

"In hell," Grace replied sweetly as she entered the spacious garage and then terminated the call. She looked across a file of polished performance vehicles and made a nod to bid them farewell. She then walked past the white Peugeot 310 DG Racing Edition, the red BMW M8, the black Maserati GranTurismo, to the last car in the line: an Omega Generation, six hundred sixty-six horsepower, bespoke Ford Mustang she had purchased the week before. "My little horseman," she whispered to the pale gray automobile as she opened the driver's door. Grace Ho sat down in the driver's seat, pushed the button to the right of the sun visor to open the garage door, and reversed the vehicle out onto the driveway. She put the car in drive, leaving the garage door open as a convenience to the operative who she knew would be arriving in fifteen minutes to clean up the remains of the fallen colleague.

You realize that they can track you. They can hunt you down, said the cynical one in her usual cranky way.

But they won't, answered the level-headed and optimistic voice.

That's right, they won't, agreed the family chorus.

"We can discuss this when we get to Dulles," she informed her ethereal sisters.

Why not now? several voices peevishly demanded.

"I need to clear my head."

We're in your head.

"Exactly."

Grace exited her neighborhood for the last time and turned right at the intersection of Babylon Road and Prince William Parkway. "Playlist three," she told the onboard computer. It complied immediately. 'Parting Shot' by Ni'ihau Child filled the car's interior:

> *Into the darkness go*
> *They'll never find us there*
> *Where hidden secrets go*
> *We'll dissolve and disappear*

> *Into the night we'll fly*
> *We will be safe real soon*
> *We need not say goodbye*
> *Just sing a parting tune*

> *So long for now dear friend*
> *We will come back some day*
> *When you see us again*
> *There will be hell to pay*

Arrival

The medcomp alarm brought an emergency response team to the bed in less than ninety seconds. The team worked diligently, but after fifteen minutes of effort, the monitors registered no heartbeat and no cerebral activity. The team leader had already been briefed that there were to be no extraordinary measures at this bed. The patient's living will directed the attending physician to honor his wishes for a 'death with dignity,' as the document described it. After seven attempts at electro fibrillation, the doctor called a halt to their efforts.

The patient had been brought into the Saint Damien Hospital the day before, having apparently collapsed while exiting onto his apartment's back deck. It had been an unusually brutal winter—snow flurries had actually been reported in Wahiawa last month. Everyone said that it was one of those things caused by *El Niño*, or perhaps the deepwater currents recently welling up from the Farallon Islands. No one could remember which was which and either was usually shrugged off as just another consequence of global climate change. There had been an electrical outage in Mililani. A neighbor stopped by with a kerosene space heater and found the man unconscious and unresponsive. The parameds who brought in the patient had remarked that at his age he probably would have died from hypothermia if they had arrived even a mere ten minutes later. He never awoke.

The physician team leader was thirty-seven years old. Much younger than the man in the bed, but allowing for the difference in their ages, still quite similar in appearance. Slightly above average height, stocky, and thick black eyebrows a bit too bushy and close to each other. His eyes were steel gray blue and focused intensely upon everything in the world he chanced to look upon. Eyes of energy, and fury, and passion, and life. The eyes of the man in the bed were closed, but the young doctor knew what they would look like if he raised the lids. This was the one thing about death that continued to concern him, to frighten him. The pain he could understand and seek to ameliorate.

The last breath, even the death rattle, was fathomable and natural to him. Those did not distress him. No, it was the eyes. The dilated eyes of the dead looked at him, through him, beyond him to some distant truth, to a greater truth, to *the* truth. How did the light disappear from the eyes only to be replaced by something deeper, more mysterious, yet more honest, candid, uncontrived? He sensed that those eyes contained a life more profound than when the body had been animated. How do you diagnose the departure of a soul as it bids you goodbye with an unwavering stare, preparing to transit to another realm of reality— perhaps far more real than this world? The medical school doctors and their medical school texts gave glib answers for this appurtenance of death. He did not believe these explanations and suspected that his teachers were as mystified, and as frightened, as he.

The doctor directed the lead nurse to disengage the deceased patient from the multiple tethering wires of the medcomp system. Before he turned to leave the room, he glanced up above the headboard. Most of the other rooms in the hospital featured a crucifix above a patient's bed. This room alone had a portrait of the Blessed Mother. As a lifelong Catholic, he had seen innumerable depictions of Mary, the mother of Jesus, but never one like this. She looked out from her picture frame with a subtle shade of a smile. It was a sad, compassionate, weary, and sympathetic countenance of loss and redemption that said much but explained very little.

The doctor returned to the emergency reaction team office with the others. As team leader, it was his responsibility to complete the death certificate. He sat down at his workstation and entered the necessary information into the datafields as the radio on the counter played an oldie.

> *You are out there on the edge*
> *Where there isn't any net*
> *You have charted a new course*
> *But you don't dare make a bet*

The software was somewhat slow, cranky, and uncooperative this evening, and the doctor struggled to complete the form. He assumed it was due to the recent migration to the new DataGhad system upgrade. After a few more minutes of digital toil, he finished with a sigh of relief mixed with exasperation and reviewed the information on the screen.

Name: Daniel Hunter Gaude
Address: 37 Leina-a-ka-'uhane Lane, Capital Heights, HI
Age: 73
Sex: M
Place of Birth: Destinations, Maine
Occupation: Retired—Travel Agent
Identifying Marks:
    Appendectomy Scar
    Missing Toe, LFT Foot
    Tattoo, Sacred Heart of Jesus, RT Upper Arm
Cause of Death: Cardiac Arrest
Period of Hospitalization: 24 Hours

By pressing a few keys and entering predetermined codes from the drop-down menus, a certificate attesting to death of the patient slipped out of a laser printer. One last step, however, was not relegated to the machine. The State of Hawaii required an ink signature on all birth and death certificates, a rule generally attributed to the national contretemps over the birth certificate of the forty-fourth President of the United States.

Just be careful now, there's fire, fire, fire...
You don't know it yet, but you're chasin' a great liar

The doctor looked over the certificate held in his very strong and capable hands and reached into his pocket for his pen, only to find it missing.

Not again, his interior voice griped. *Maybe you should carry it on a string around your neck like a librarian.*

He barked back to himself, *Oh, shut up!* and reached beneath the desk for a worn leather postman's haversack he had carried since his college days, given to him by that peculiar, erratic, and passionate girl he dated in a peculiar, erratic, and passionate relationship over the course of a peculiar, erratic, and passionate three years. She had disappeared from his life some time ago and this was the one physical manifestation of her existence that he had left. A bag with a metal disk engraved with two letters: DG, her taunting reference to the *distinguished graduate* bound for medical school who she predicted would drift away and forget about her. She was right only about the drifting—but he had not forgotten and he never would. The doctor found his Parker pen in the bag, returned his attention to the matter at hand, and signed the death certificate of Daniel Gaude.

Kandinsky, M.D.

A cat jumped onto his lap. It was the senior nurse's pet, tolerated by the hospital administrators, adored by all the department staff, and detested by him. The feline was a uniform charcoal gray and the color of its antagonistic eyes matched the fur. Those eyes of malice and disdain locked with the young doctor's for an instant. The cat then leapt back onto the floor, satisfied that it had successfully annoyed the nemesis physician.

A technician walked into the room holding a mug of Colotenango Supreme. "They need you on the third floor."

"Urgent?"

"It would be good for you to go up as soon as you can. It's a medivac from Ni'ihau."

"Another DIPG?"

"Yeah. Maui Memorial punted to us again."

"How old?"

"Late-twenties, maybe early thirties, I'd say. I didn't check her chart. She's not doing well."

"Her speech?"

"Slurred, and her English isn't great, but we can understand her. She has some trouble swallowing, of course."

"I'll be there in a minute."

"She's also delusional."

"Delusional? DIPG is cancer of the brain stem. It doesn't impact rational thought."

"I'm not the doctor, but I can tell you that she's raving about some boogie man who is lurking around the island. She says it's a giant Gray *haole* with the eyes of a goat who is trying to snatch babies."

"A Gray Anglo with goat's eyes?" the doctor asked incredulously.

"No, not Anglo—not White—just Gray."

The doctor paused for a moment and then shrugged. "The islanders live in an ancient culture. I suppose that they are entitled to their ancient myths."

"Sure," agreed the technician, "to each their own. *E hele kāua.*"

"You do know that means 'let's party,' don't you?"

"Oh."
Another tune started to play on the radio.

Death, you are vain,
And vainly you assail.
I feel no pain,
You will forever fail.

Death, frightening Death,
We make a solemn vow.
Death, beautiful Death,
I'm ready for you now.

The doctor's interior voice muttered, *Hey, that's a Ni'ihau Child song. Strange coincidence.*
There are no coincidences.
There are only coincidences.
The doctor distractedly shook his head and then began to gather up the documents spread across his desk.
"Will this take much more time?" asked the tech assistant.
"Just let me finish up here with the paperwork on Room 37."
The technician took a sip from his mug. "That guy never came out of the coma, did he?"
"No."
"Y'know, I've always wondered if the terminals ever dream. D'you think he dreamed?"
"No," responded the young doctor picking up the death certificate and placing it in a file folder. "I don't believe he did."

Death, frightening Death,
We make a solemn vow.
Death, beautiful Death,
I'm ready for you now.